HINDU TEMPLES: WHAT HAPPENED TO THEM

The Islamic Evidence

HINDU TEMPLES
WHAT HAPPENED TO THEM

VOLUME II
The Islamic Evidence
(Second Enlarged Edition)

SITA RAM GOEL

VOICE OF INDIA
NEW DELHI

First published: 1991
Second Enlarged Edition: 1993
First Reprint: 2000
Twelfth Reprint 2025

ISBN 978-81-85990-94-1

Published by Voice of India, 2/18, Ansari Road, New Delhi – 110 002.
Printed at Replika Press Pvt. Ltd

PREFACE

A court order in 1986 threw open for Hindu worship the gates of the temple-turned-mosque at the Rāmajanmabhūmi at Ayodhya. Hindus were overjoyed, and started looking forward to the coming up of a grand Rāma Mandir at the sacred site. But they were counting without the stalwarts of Secularism in the Nehruvian establishment. It was not long before a hysterical cry was heard—"Secularism in danger!"

The Marxist–Muslim combine launched a two-pronged campaign. On the one hand, they proclaimed that Muslims had destroyed no Hindu temples except those few which were stinking with hoarded wealth or had become centres of local rebellions, and that Islam as a religion was never involved in iconoclasm. On the other hand, they accused the Hindus of destroying any number of Buddhist, Jain and Animist shrines in the pre-Islamic days.

As a student of India's history, ancient as well as medieval, I could see quite clearly that they were playing the Goebbelsian game of the Big Lie. But they could not be countered because they had come to dominate the academia and control the mass media during the heyday of the Nehru dynasty. Most of the prestigious press was owned by Hindu moneybags. But they had placed their papers in the hands of the most brazen-faced Hindu-baiters.

The most unkindest cut of all, however, came from the Vishva Hindu Parishad and the Bharatiya Janata Party. They were doing nothing towards debunking Secularist lies about Hinduism vis-a-vis Buddhism and Jainism. But they were trumpeting from the house-tops that Islam did not permit the destruction of other people's places of worship, and that *namāz* offered in a mosque built on the site of a temple was not acceptable to Allāh! They were laying the blame for the destruction of the Rām Mandir not on Islam as an ideology of terror but on Bābur as a foreign invader!

The only ray of light in this encircling gloom was Arun Shourie, the veteran journalist and the chief editor of the *Indian Express* at that time. On February 5, 1989, he frontpaged an article, *Hideaway Communalism*, showing that while the Urdu version of a book by Maulana Hakim Sayid Abdul Hai of the Nadwatul-Ulama at Lucknow had admitted that seven famous mosques had been built on the sites of Hindu temples, the English translation published by the Maulana's son, Abul Hasan Ali Nadwi (Ali Mian) had eschewed the "controversial evidence". He also published in the *Indian Express* three articles written by me on the subject of Islamic iconoclasm. This was a very courageous defiance of the ban imposed by Islam and administered by Secularism, namely, that crimes committed by Islam cannot even be whispered in private, not to speak of being proclaimed in public.

Finally, VOICE OF INDIA published in April, 1991 Volume I of a projected series—*Hindu Temples: What Happened to Them.* It was a collection of relevant articles by Arun Shourie, Harsh Narain, Jay Dubashi, Ram Swarup, and myself. An important part of the volume was a list of 2000 Muslim monuments built on the sites and/or with the materials of Hindu temples. This list became famous all over the country as soon as it came out.

Meanwhile, the evidence I had collected regarding Islamic iconoclasm could already cover several, and much bigger volumes. VOICE OF INDIA published in May, 1991 Volume II of the series. It was devoted exclusively to Islamic evidence, historical as well theological. It was received very well, particularly by the world of scholarship. Only the prestigious newspapers and periodicals in this country ignored it completely; they did not even acknowledge it in their "Books Received" column. But an extensive review written by the Belgian scholar, Koenraad Elst, was published by VOICE OF INDIA in 1992 under the title *Negationism in India: Concealing the Record of Islam.*

This second edition of Volume II is a thoroughly revised and somewhat enlarged version of the first edition. Its main merit is that the lengthy chapters in the earlier edition have been divided into smaller ones, and placed under several well-defined sections. A new Appendix on the meaning of the word "Hindu" has been added. And the Appendix which carries the Questionnaire For the Marxist Professors, has been considerably expanded by inclusion of correspondence between myself and Professor Romila Thapar, the doyen of Marxist historians.

I take this opportunity to point out that the subject of this volume is not so much the destruction of Hindu temples as the character of Islam—an imperialist ideology of terrorism and genocide masquerading as a religion, in fact, as the only true religion. It is high time for Hindus to see Islam not with its own eyes but from the viewpoint of the great spiritual vision which is their inheritance.

New Delhi
25 March 1993

SITA RAM GOEL

CONTENTS

SECTION I

THE TIP OF AN ICEBERG

CHAPTER ONE

THE DISPUTE AT SIDHPUR

The Fourth Annual Report of the Minorities' Commission submitted to the President of India through the Ministry of Home Affairs on April 19, 1983, carries an account of a dispute over the Jāmi' Masjid at Sidhpur in the Mehsana District of Gujarat. The account raises some significant questions about certain aspects of Islam as a religion and the character of Muslim rule in medieval India. We have to go to primary source materials in order to find satisfactory answers to these questions.

Sidhpur is a Taluka town, sixty-four miles north of Ahmadabad. It is situated on the left bank of the river Saraswati, fifteen miles upstream of Aṇhilwāḍ Pāṭan, the old capital of Gujarat before Ahmadabad was founded in the first quarter of the fifteenth century. "In a part of the town," says the Commission's Report, "is located what is known as Rudramahalaya complex. This complex was built by Siddhraj Jayasimha in the 12th century.... This temple seems to have been destroyed partly by Ulugh Khan in AD 1297–98 and partly by Ahmedshah in AD 1415. Some of the cubicles and a number of pillars on the Western side of the temple it would appear were later converted into a mosque."[1]

At the dawn of independence in 1947, Sidhpur was in the territory of Baroda, the princely state ruled by the Maratha house of the Gāekwāḍs. "The princely state of Baroda," proceeds the Report, "had treated the complex consisting of the mosque and the remnants of the temple as a monument of historical importance. Subsequently, by virtue of an agreement between the Trustees and the Archaeological Survey of India on 31st March, 1954, the mosque was declared as a national monument and its maintenance and protection were taken over by the Archaeological Survey of India. One of the terms of this agreement was that the mosque would continue to be used by the Muslims for offering prayers."[2]

The Trustees of the Jāmi' Masjid, however, became dissatisfied with the Archaeological Survey which, they complained, was not doing its duty towards maintenance of the mosque. "Subsequently," continues the Report, "a dispute arose between the Trustees of the mosque and

---

[1]*Fourth Annual Report of the Minorities' Commission* for the Period 1.1.1980 to 31.3.1981, New Delhi, 1983, p. 130.

[2]Ibid., pp. 130–131.

the officials of the Archaeological Department with regard to the maintenance of the mosque as according to the Trustees, necessary repairs to the mosque were not being carried out by the Archaeological Department and the mosque was in danger of falling down. These disputes led to some litigation in the High Court which, however, ended in a compromise. An undertaking was given by the Archaeological Department in terms of the compromise that they would carry out the necessary repairs to the mosque. It is alleged that the undertaking was not given effect to and this resulted in further litigation which again ended in a compromise. Under the fresh compromise terms, the Archaeological Department again gave an undertakiing to carry out the repairs of the mosque and also to lay out a garden in the courtyard of the mosque. Unfortunately, this compromise again did not bring about a final settlement between the Trustees of the mosque and the Archaeological Department. According to the Muslims, the Archaeological Survey of India, instead of carrying out repairs to the mosque, started digging operations which exposed the relics of the temples and also the rich sculptural carvings on the two wings of the mosque. These exposures appear to have attracted the attention of the Hindus and they demanded that not only should these ancient temple relics be preserved but that the mosque should also no longer be used by the Muslims for offering prayers or they may also be allowed to worship the Siva Linga discovered during the excavations within the premises of the mosque."[3]

The Minorities' Commission came into the picture on October 4, 1979 when it received a letter from the Trustees of the mosque, "conveying the apprehensions of the Muslims of Sidhpur that the Hindus were trying to usurp the Jama Masjid."[4] The letter from the Trustees reported : "On the 6th September, 1979, one Yogeshwar Dutt had illegally led a huge crowd into the mosque and instigated them to usurp it. He again entered the mosque on 2nd October, 1979 and demanded that Namaz in the Jama Masjid should be stopped and also incited the Hindus to demolish the mosque."[5] The Commission referred the matter to the Director General of the Archaeological Survey of India and called for a report.

But before the Commission could receive a reply from the Survey, "Begum Ayesha Sheikh, MLA, of the Gujarat Assembly wrote to the Chairman, Minorities' Commission about the threats to which the local

---

[3]Ibid., p. 131.
[4]Ibid., p. 129.
[5]Ibid., p. 133.

Muslims were being continually subjected by the majority community and especially the Jan Sangh and the RSS elements for their use of the Jama Masjid and that this had created a serious communal tension in the town."[6] The Commission wrote to the Government of Gujarat on December 7, 1979 and asked for a factual report. "On 16th January, 1980," says the Commission's Report, "Government of Gujarat denied any RSS hand in the demand of the local Hindus for conversion of the Jama Masjid at Sidhpur into a temple as alleged. The State Government further reported that the dispute between the Muslims and the Hindus about the use of the Jama Masjid had been going on for quite some time past and that the local police and State Government were aware of the situation. They also assured the Commission that there was no possibility of any communal trouble at Sidhpur."[7]

A Hindu–Muslim riot, however, broke out at Sidhpur on March 14, 1980 and took some toll of limbs and property. "The critical stage," records the Commission, "was reached on 14th March, 1980, when a group of Hindus led by a local Sadhu started Bhajans at the Rudramahalaya. At about 10.00 A.M. a group of boys started closing shops and people started coming towards the Rudramahalaya. Everything was peaceful till the Muslims started assembling for their Namaz around 1.00 P.M. By 1.15 P.M. both Bhajans and Namaz were going on simultaneously. According to reports, some Muslims from the houses adjoining the Rudramahalaya started throwing stones on the Hindus. The Hindus retaliated. By this time about 800 to 900 Hindus and about 300 to 400 Muslims had collected. The police, anticipating trouble, was on the spot along with the Taluka Magistrate. They burst teargas shells to disperse the crowd. The Muslims who had to pass through Hindu localities before reaching their houses, were stoned by the Hindus from housetops and lanes. Six shops were forced open and looted. Two of them belonged to the Hindus. The jeep of the Mamalatdar was also burnt and the Mamalatdar himself also sustained some minor injuries due to the stone throwing. In all 72 persons sustained injuries during the incident on the 14th March, 1980. The situation was brought under control by 2.15 P.M. Curfew was immediately imposed and the situation at Sidhpur remained peaceful for some time barring some minor incidents."[8]

---

[6]Ibid., pp. 131–34. It may be noted that no Jana Sangh existed at that time, the party having merged itself in the Janata Party in May, 1977.

[7]Ibid., p. 134.

[8]Ibid., p. 132.

Begum Ayesha Sheikh again wrote to the Commission on March 28, 1980, reporting the communal trouble that had broken out on March 14. "She also mentioned that the State Government had been deliberately trying to play down the gravity of the incident and, therefore, any report submitted by the State Government would not be fair and impartial. She, therefore, requested that instead of asking for a report from the State Government the Minorities' Commission itself should undertake an on-the-spot inquiry into the incidents."[9]

But before the Commisssion could decide what to do, another round of Hindu–Muslim riots took place at Sidhpur on April 8, 1980. "However again on the 8th April, 1980," records the Commission, "at about 11.45 A.M. one Muslim was assaulted by three Hindus as a result of which two Hindus were stabbed by the Muslims. Incidents of assault took place thereafter in different parts of the town. Curfew was imposed on the 8th April, 1980, and 42 persons were arrested."[10] On April 14, "nine important Muslim representatives including one Member of Parliament met the Chairman and handed over a memorandum on the dispute and requested the Commission to visit Sidhpur."[11]

The Commission, however, could not visit Sidhpur without prior consultation with the Government of Gujarat. By that time the State had been placed under Governor's rule. It had neither an elected Assembly nor a popular Ministry. Shri K.T. Satarawala, Adviser to the Governor of Gujarat, came to New Delhi on May 1, 1980 and met the Chairman of the Commission. After a discussion on the prevailing communal situation at Sidhpur, it was agreed that the Adviser would send to the Chairman "a detailed note on the communal incidents which took place during March and April 1980."[12] The Adviser's "Note on Rudramahalaya and Jama Masjid" was duly sent to the Chairman on May 16, 1980. It was accompanied by "a map of the area and some photographs."[13]

The Note starts by giving a slightly different version of the status of the Jāmi' Masjid under the Baroda State and the frequency of Muslim prayers in the Masjid. "The erstwhile Baroda State," says the Note, "took under protection in 1936–37 the Toranas and other architectural remains of the Rudramahalaya *excluding the Masjid portion.* After the merger of the State, the Rudramahalaya and other State protected

---

[9]Ibid., p. 134.
[10]Ibid., p. 132.
[11]Ibid., p. 134.
[12]Ibid.
[13]Ibid., p. 140.

monuments were declared as Monuments of National Importance under the 1951 Act. Subsequently, the Jami Masjid being originally a part of the Rudramahalaya was also declared a monument of National Importance. However, as it was a monument in religious use, an agreement under the Ancient Monuments and Sites and Remains Act was entered into between the Trustees and the Archaeological Survey of India on behalf of the President of India on the 31st March, 1954. At that time, the monument was used *for Friday prayers only* and that too by a small number of persons."[14]

Next, the Note provides the background before the dispute arose between the Survey and the Trustees. "In 1959," proceeds the Note, "the then Superintending Archaeologist recommended that the modern buildings covering the view of the Rudramahalaya and Jami Masjid should be removed for improving the environs and to throw open the grand edifice to view. The Superintending Archaeologist recommended the removal of the intermediate wall also as it was a modern accretion. The proposals were accepted and the acquisition of buildings was undertaken."[15]

It took the Survey ten long years to acquire the modern buildings. "After compensation was paid," continues the Note, "the buildings were handed over to the Survey in 1969. The Joint Director General (later Director General) inspected the site on 3.6.69 and after discussion with the Collector, Mehsana, and the Trustees of the Masjid, drew up an Inspection Note in which he instructed that (i) the demolition of buildings should be done in one sweep (ii) the compound wall of the Masjid may be retained with necessary modifications to include the acquired area and (iii) the architectural remains that may be found in the clearance operations should be preserved as they are likely to throw light on the plan of the Rudramahalaya and (iv) a garden should be laid out in the acquired area."[16]

For various reasons, the Survey could start operations at Sidhpur only after ten more years had elapsed. "As the Trustees were pressing for pulling down the acquired houses, the Superintending Archaeologist, Baroda, inspected the site early in May, 1979 and decided to implement the decision of the Joint Director General of Archaeology by pulling down the acquired houses."[17] The operations were started on May 29, 1980. "As the northern wall was very shabby and in a dilapi-

[14]Ibid., p. 141. Emphasis added.
[15]Ibid., pp. 141-42.
[16]Ibid., p. 142.
[17]Ibid.

dated condition, it had to be repaired after pulling down. The digging of the acquired area was necessary for the preparation of a garden. He discussed the operation with the Trustees but before any step to pull down the compound wall was taken, the Trustees filed a Writ Petition in the High Court on 12th June, 1979 and an injunction asking the Archaeological Survey of India to maintain *status quo* in the Masjid area was issued."[18]

The Note gives greater details about the litigation and the compromises that followed. The Writ Petition No. 1662 of 1979 *versus* Union of India was filed by six Trustees of the Jāmi' Masjid. They prayed for "(a) an order or direction permanently restraining the correspondent, his servants and agents from demolishing the surrounding buildings situated on the southern side of the land bearing survey No. 37 of Sidhpur town in Mehsana district in which the ancient Mosque named Jumma Masjid is situated, without constructing a protecting wall surrounding the said Masjid; (b) to issue an order or direction directing the respondent to erect or allow the petitioners to erect a compound wall surrounding the said survey No. 37 of the town of Sidhpur in Mehsana district; (c) issue an injunction restraining the respondent, his servants or agents from demolishing the walls of the buildings on the southern side and northern side of survey No. 37 which have yet not been demolished by him."[19]

The Survey decided to contest the Writ Petition. "Shri B.L. Nagarch, Superintending Archaeologist, Western Circle, Baroda, filed an affidavit in reply in the Gujarat High Court in July, 1979 wherein he stated that the purpose of demolishing the modern buildings situated around the Jumma Masjid and Rudramahalaya acquired by the Government of India was to arrest further damage caused by the modern accretions and natural causes such as rain and growth of vegetation, that it is the responsibility of the Department to preserve the Masjid and the Rudramahal and they have not interfered with the established religious usage of a portion near the Jumma Masjid and that the Department has taken clearance work necessary for undertaking structural repairs to the roof and back wall which is out of plumb and has some cavities. He further stated that the structures being demolished were not within the Jumma Masjid but outside the monument, that the acquisition was solely with a view to undertaking the repairs to the monument and improve the surroundings by laying a garden. He further stated that the

[18]Ibid.
[19]Ibid., pp. 149-50.

Department would only demolish the modern wall and not any ancient structure."[20]

The Honourable Judge suggested a compromise as he felt that the Archaeological Survey was only trying to improve the monument and its surroundings. "A 'Compromise' was then arrived at according to which the compound walls were to be repaired and a garden was to be laid out in the courtyard of the Masjid. Its back wall was also to be repaired."[21] The Trustees withdrew their Writ Petition on July 30, 1979.

The 'Compromise', however, did not work. "While digging for examining the foundation of shrines and the back wall of the Masjid, important temple remains were found on the west and the north. According to para 3 of 'Compromise' when garden operations (digging) were started in the open courtyard temple remains were found there also." The Trustees started "hindering further work." The Superintending Archaeologist appealed to the Collector of the District. The Collector called a meeting at Mehsana on November 30, 1979. "The Trustees were also present in the meeting. It was agreed that further digging should be stopped and that measures to preserve the temple remains such as the provision of a canopy over it could be thought of. It was pointed out that area within the courtyard for the garden was not used for prayers as could be made out from the debris etc., that were lying there."[22]

This agreement also did not work. "Shri A.S. Quereshi, Advocate for the Trustees, issued a notice dated the 6th Feb. 1980 to the Superintendent, Archaeological Department asking the Department to build the compound walls as per the compromise and *cover up the temple remains*. The Supdt. Archaeological Deptt. explained in person the importance of the discoveries made and the need for revision of the compromise in the interest of preserving the precious cultural heritage of the country. As Shri Quereshi wanted to visit the site along with Supdt. Archaeological Deptt. he went to Sidhpur on the 8th March, 1980. At first, he agreed to the preservation but later he insisted on closing the trenches in his very presence that day. The Supdt. Archaeological Department ordered closure of the trenches and construction of compound wall and both the works were started in his presence."[23]

The Hindus of Sidhpur objected to the covering of the temple remains that had been uncovered. Tension mounted in the town as re-

[20]Ibid., p. 150.
[21]Ibid., p. 143.
[22]Ibid.
[23]Ibid., Emphasis added.

ports spread that the Survey was filling up the trenches. "Upto the 14th March, 1980, a major part of the complex was covered and the northern compound wall was constructed over some length but then the trouble started and the labourers refused to work."[24] On March 15, 1980, the Puratatva Sanskrutik Abhyas and Sansodhan Mandal, an organisation formed by some Hindus of Sidhpur in January, 1980, filed a Civil Application No. 644 of 1980 against the Union of India and Mr. S.R. Rao, Superintending Archaeologist. "Their prayer is mainly that the excavated area in the courtyard of the Masjid should not be filled up and that *status quo* should be maintained in the excavated area."[25] The High Court granted a stay and the Archaeological Survey could not proceed further with the construction of the compound wall.

Yet another attempt at a compromise was made after the riot on March 14 had been controlled. "Soon after the incident," says the Commission's Report, "a series of meetings were held by the District Magistrate with the representatives of the Muslims and Hindus to work out an amicable solution. An agreement was reached between the representatives of the two communities to the effect that the Muslims would forgo their right of prayer at the Jama Masjid on the following conditions: (a) a suitable plot of land situated near the railway station is allotted to them for the construction of an alternative Masjid; (b) pending the construction of the Masjid by the Muslims on this plot of land, they should be allowed to offer their Namaz at the Jama Masjid; and (c) the Jama Masjid should be maintained as a national monument by the Archaeological Department and should not be open for any other use."[26]

But this compromise made by the Muslims of Sidhpur was rejected by some Muslim organisations at the State level. "However, on the instigation of some of the Muslim organisations," proceeds the Report, "the local Muslim leaders, who had earlier agreed in the presence of the Distt. Magistrate to the above terms of settlement conveyed their decision to wait until a decision was taken on the terms of settlement at the State level. At the same time, some of the Muslim organisations stepped up their demand for allowing the Muslims to use the Jama Masjid for Namaz."[27]

The Note from the Government of Gujarat gives some more details in this context. "On the 26th March, 1980, Her Excellency the Governor visited Sidhpur. She met both Hindus and Muslims and advised

[24]Ibid., p. 144.
[25]Ibid., p. 151.
[26]Ibid., pp. 132-33.
[27]Ibid., p. 133.

them that they should select five persons and then sit together and find out an amicable solution. Since both the parties wanted some Government representative to remain present during the discussion, the Collector was instructed to help them. The same afternoon i.e. on the 26th March, both the parties met and the above proposal was put up by the Muslims and discussed at length. It was decided that they should effect this agreement before the High Court the next day. Next day, they left for Ahmedabad but on the intervention of certain organisations such as the All India Muslim League, Jamat-e-Islami, Gujarat Avkaf and Trust Federation, they decided to wait till a decision at the Gujarat level was taken."[28]

Finally, eight Muslim leaders joined together to file a further Writ in the Gujarat High Court on April 5, 1980. The Note gives their names and designations[29] as follows:-

1. Shri Gulzarsha Ahmedshah Hakim, Managing Trustee of Jumma Masjid, Sidhpur.
2. Haji Hussainbhai Habibur Mansuri, Trustee Jumma Masjid Trust, Sidhpur.
3. Haji Ibrahim Haji Issak Quoreshi, Vice-President, Jamiet-ul-Ulema-e-Hind, Branch Sidhpur.
4. Imtiskhan Mahabubkhan Pathan, Secretary, Jamiet-ul-Ulema-e-Hind, Sidhpur Branch.
5. Maulvi Dawoodbhai Haji Suleman, President, Jamiet-ul-Ulma-e-Hind, Mehsana Distt. Branch—Resident—Patan.
6. Maulvi Mohammed Ussian Fateh Mohammed, President, Uttar Gujarat Masjid Bachao Samiti, Village Bhagal, Taluka Palanpur.
7. Abbas Tajmohammed, Vice-President of Uttar Gujarat Masjid Bachao Samiti, Village Bhagal, Tal—Palanpur.
8. Dr. Rehmatulla Ahmedullah Hakim, President, Gujarat Muslim Vakf and Trust Federation, Ahmedabad.

"Their prayers," according to the Note, "are: (a) Jumma Masjid should be declared Masjid open for offering Namaz; (b) To fill up the excavation at the floor of the 'Kibla' (Western) wall and in the courtyard of the Masjid before 1.5.80; (c) To put a compound wall where it existed before and it should be of stone and high enough to prevent outside interference; (d) To cover the entire courtyard with stone slab flooring and to rebuild muazams quarter with stone slab; (e) To give permission to the Trustees to have electric points in adequate

[28]Ibid., p. 146.
[29]Ibid., pp. 151-52.

number."[30]

The Muslim Organisations, according to the Note, adopted some other methods also for pressing their demands. "Some of the organisations appear to have taken the decision that telegrams should be sent to Government requesting to allow Muslims to use the Jumma Masjid for Namaz and accordingly, a large number of telegrams have been received by Government from the Muslims of Gujarat and Bombay."[31] Again: "The Muslims appear to have also decided to send printed letters to Government requesting that any compromise or any writings regarding conversion of Jumma Masjid at Sidhpur into a protected monument will not be binding on them. Accordingly, more than 2400 printed letters have been received by Government."[32]

Having "considered the totality of the situation in the light of the representation/memorandum received from the Muslims of Sidhpur and the report sent by the Adviser to the Governor," the Commission decided to visit Sidhpur for an "on-the-spot study of the dispute."[33] But the visit had to be postponed due to various reasons. "The Commission was finally able to visit Sidhpur on 2nd November, 1980, when it inspected the site of the Jama Masjid and also held discussions with representatives of the Muslims and Hindus at Sidhpur and the State Govt. officials."[34] The list of persons who "appeared before the Commission in connection with the dispute," names 15 Muslims, 7 Officials and 5 Hindus.[35]

As a result of the discussion the Commission suggested an 8-point formula for settlement: "(1) The Rudramahalaya complex including the mosque would be retained as a national monument. (2) The Mosque would be maintained in its original shape. The sanctity of the mosque would be ensured by the A.S.I. and the State Government. Also the sanctity of the newly exposed temple on either side of the mosque would be maintained. (3) The excavations on the western side of the mosque as well as those in the courtyard on the eastern side of the mosque will be filled up. Ancient relics found in the present excavations would be removed before the filling up. The existing Western Qibla wall of the mosque proper would be restored to its original condition and strengthened. The outer wall which was covering the two

[30]Ibid., p. 152.
[31]Ibid., p. 146.
[32]Ibid., p. 147.
[33]Ibid., pp. 134-35.
[34]Ibid., pp. 135.
[35]Ibid., pp. 139.

towers on either side containing sculptures would not be rebuilt. (4) No worship in any form would be offered by any community within the precincts of the Rudramahalaya Complex. (5) The A.S.I. would not make any further excavations within the mosque area formerly enclosed by the compound wall. (6) No gathering for any religious purpose would be permitted within the Rudramahalaya complex. (7) The enforcement of these items would be guaranteed by the State Government and the Central Government. (8) The State Government would provide at nominal cost an alternative site for the construction of a new mosque at the Government Dharmashala near the clock tower after removing all existing cabins and evicting the occupants of the Dharmashala."[36]

The formula was hailed by the then Home Minister and Chief Secretary of the Government of Gujarat. They assured the Commission that "they would be able to bring about a solution of the dispute to the satisfaction of both the communities on the basis of the above-mentioned terms."[37] But it did not lead to a final settlement. The Commission records at the end of its Report on this dispute: "Five months have elapsed since the Commission visited Sidhpur and settled most of the differences between the two communities over the use of the Jama Masjid and the Rudramahalaya complex. The Home Minister and the representatives of the State Government had extended the assurance to the Commission that they would be able to bring about a satisfactory solution to the above dispute on the basis of the terms of settlement suggested by the Commission within a reasonable span of time. However, no final settlement seems to have been reached yet."[38]

The story as related in the Commission's report combined with the Note from the Government of Gujarat tells us a few things about the behaviour patterns of the different parties involved in the dispute—the Trustees of the Jāmi' Masjid, the Archaeological Survey of India and the Government of Gujarat. It also gives us a glimpse of the quality and character of leadership thrown up by the two communities in the dispute over a place of worship. But what interests us primarily in the present study is the "temple remains" exposed by the Archaeological Survey of India in and around the Jāmi' Masjid. These "temple remains" point towards a far more momentous story which has yet to be told.

---

[36]Ibid., pp. 136-37.
[37]Ibid., p. 137.
[38]Ibid., p. 138.

II

A picture of the "temple remains" exposed in the Jāmi' Masjid area at Sidhpur has to be pieced together from five sources which we have arranged according to the extent of details given. First, we have the Note from the Government of Gujarat. Secondly, we have the reply received by the Minorities' Commission from the Archaeological Survey of India. Thirdly, we have the Annual Reports of the Archaeological Survey of India for 1979–80 and 1980–81. Fourthly, we have a description in the Minorities' Commission's Report of what its members saw during their visit to Sidhpur on November 2, 1980. Lastly, we have an article by B.L. Nagarch included in a commemoration volume brought out by a private publishing house in 1987. Shri Nagarch was one of the Superintending Archaeologists at Sidhpur at the time the "temple remains" were sighted.

The Note from the Government of Gujarat

The main purpose of the Note was to narrate the incidents which took place at Sidhpur during March and April, 1980. It refers to "temple remains" only when the narration touches them while describing the dispute between the Trustees of the Jāmi' Masjid and the Archaeological Survey. The narration mentions "temple remains" several time in different contexts. But we are left wondering whether they are architectural or sculptural or both.

The Archaeological Survey of India

The Minorities' Commission had called for a report from the Director General of the Archaeological Survey of India immediately after it received on October 4, 1979 a letter from the Trustees of the Jāmi' Masjid stating that the Hindus of Sidhpur were trying to usurp the Masjid. The date on which the Commission wrote to the Survey is not given in the Commission's Report, nor the date on which it received a reply from the Survey. All we have is one para incorporated in the Commission's Report. It says, "The matter was taken up with the Archaeological Survey of India which reported that ruins of Rudra Mahalaya Complex and Jama Masjid at Sidhapur, though forming one Complex were being protected individually under the Ancient Monuments and Archaeological Sites and Remains (Declaration of Places of National Importance) and were being preserved on the lines they were originally protected. The dispute arose out of demolition of the surrounding buildings, while constructing a protective wall around the

Masjid, which exposed some Hindu idols within the precincts of the mosque."[39]

The Annual Report of Archaeological Survey of India for 1979–80 published in 1983 has three entries on what was discovered at Sidhpur. The first entry is in Chapter IV which deals with "Other Important Discoveries", State by State. We find the following entry under Gujarat:

> 7. SCULPTURES, SIDHPUR, DISTRICT MEHSANA—Shri P.K. Trivedi of the Western Circle of the Survey, discovered sculptures of Hindu and Jaina pantheons, assignable variously from the tenth to eighteenth century AD and an inscribed brass image of Vishnu dated Samvat 1485 (AD 1429).[40]

Next, it has the following two entries in Chapter IX dealing with "Preservation of Monuments" in different Circles of the Survey:

> 288. JAMI-MASJID, SIDHPUR, DISTRICT MEHSANA—The dilapidated western wall of the mosque is being repaired. While carrying out demolition and clearance of wooden structures from the acquired area the remains of some earlier structures have been found. The work is in progress.
>
> 289. RUDRAMAHALAYA, SIDHPUR, DISTRICT MEHSANA — The clearance of debris after demolition of the modern buildings from the acquired area yielded number of loose sculptures, including remains of an earlier temple.[41]

The publication has sixty-four plates carrying one hundred and thirty photographs. No photograph of what was found at Sidhpur has been included.

The Annual Report for 1980–81 also published in 1983 has one entry in Chapter IV dealing with "Other Important Discoveries." It says:

> 13. MEDIEVAL SCULPTURES, SIDHPUR, DISTRICT MEHSANA—B.L. Nagarch, P.K. Trivedi and H. Michael of the Western Circle of the Survey noticed sculptures of seated Uma–Mahesvara, a royal worshipping couple, a head of Siva (pl. XXXVI A) and a fragment of *Salabhanjika* recovered from the Jami Mosque. All these are assignable to *circa* twelfth century AD.[42]

---

[39]Ibid., p. 9.
[40]*Indian Archaeology 1979-80—A Review*, p. 99.
[41]Ibid., p. 148.
[42]*Indian Archaeology 1980-81—A Review*, p. 90.

The publication has fifty-eight plates carrying one hundred and forty photographs. Only one photograph, A on plate XXXVI, shows the "Head of Siva" found at Sidhpur.

Report of the Minorities' Commission

The Report has recorded in eight paras what its members saw with their own eyes while visiting the site at Sidhpur. Out of them, six paras — 1, 2, 3, 5, 6, and 8 — relate to "temple remains". They are as follows:

1. A portion of the courtyard of the mosque in the east was dug upto a depth of 10 ft. In a portion of this pit a stone Nandi (bull) was embedded in the earth. We also saw several pieces of temple architecture which had been dug up and kept in the pit.
2. The open site to the North of the mosque was also found similarly dug up and several temple relics were lying exposed in these pits.
3. There were two cubicles, one at the Northern and the other one at the Southern side of the mosque. In the Northern cubicle, there was a Siva Linga embedded in the earth and an idol carving embedded in the wall while in the Southern cubicle there was only an idol carving in the wall but no Siva Linga.
5. The Northern and Southern wings of the mosque which had hitherto been covered up were now lying exposed obviously as a result of removal of the covering material on these two wings disclosing rich temple carvings.
6. The foundation of the Northern wing was also lying exposed and it also revealed rich temple carvings.
8. A portion of the ground on the Western side of the mosque was also found dug up and this was found to contain some temple relics as well as the stone slabs which had been removed from the outer wall of the mosque.[43]

It may be mentioned that by the time the Commission came to Sidhpur, a major part of the excavations had been covered up. The Note from the Government of Gujarat states that, "upto the 14th March, 1980, a major part of the complex was covered and the northern compound wall was constructed over some length..."[44]

Article by B.L. Nagarch

B.L. Nagarch is a trained archaeologist familiar with the technical

---

[43]*Fourth Annual Report*, pp. 135–36.
[44]Ibid., p. 144.

language used for describing details of Hindu temples. He also knows how to identify and describe various sculptures and decorative designs. As the major part of his article is devoted to "temple remains", we have to cite him at some length and under several sections.

1. The Buried Temples

"For carrying out repairs to the bulged western wall of the masjid and overhanging foundation of the south-western shrine, it was necessary to examine the foundation by excavating. Ornamental plinth of a pre-Solanki temple (Period-I) was found in the course of excavation for underpinning overhanging foundation of south-western shrine. This plinth (*jagatī*) consists of a *bhiṭṭa*, *kapota* decorated with *kuḍūs*, *karṇikā*, *tamāla-paṭṭikā* (frieze decorated with *tamālapatras*), plain *khura*, *kumbha* decorated with half diamond designs and plain *kalaśa* (Pl. I). The dislodged courses of the western wall of the masjid below the ground level were also revealed during the course of examination of its foundation by excavation. A Jar *in situ* was also exposed over the plinth of this pre-Solanki temple.

"The debris near the entrance of masjid was removed. The hidden plinth of north-western shrine was exposed as a result of excavation for examining its foundation. During the course of examination of the foundation of this north-western shrine, the plinth of another pre-Solanki temple was found (Pl. II). The stone flooring of the plinth showed the use of clamps and dowels for binding the stones together. The mouldings of this plinth show from bottom upwards *bhiṭṭa*, *kapota* decorated with *kuḍūs*, *antarapatra*, *karṇikā*, *antarapatra*, *tamāla-paṭṭikā* carved with *tamāla-patras*, *khura*, *kumbha* decorated with half diamond designs, *kalaśa* and *kapota* decorated with *kuḍūs*.

"Another exquisitely carved temple attached to the aforesaid pre-Solanki temple (I) was laid bare in the north-west corner outside the mosque while excavating for gardening (Pl. III). The plinth of this temple shows from bottom upwards *bhiṭṭa*, *kapota* decorated with *kuḍūs*, *antarapatra*, *karṇikā*, *antarapatra*, *tamāla-paṭṭikā* carved with *tamāla-patras*, *narathara* and diamonds in panels. Only the plinth of the *maṇḍapa* of this temple has survived. The sanctum of this temple is missing. The door-sill of the sanctum door-way is fortunately *in situ*. The *mandāraka* carved with spiral lotus scroll is flanked on either side by a bold *kīrtimukha*. A panel on the right of the *kīrtimukha* on the right depicts worship of Gaṇeśa (Plate-IV). Four-armed Gaṇeśa is seated in a niche. He is flanked on the right by a standing male and on the left by a standing female attendant. The niche is flanked on the right by a standing female standing in *tribhaṅga* and carrying *kaṭi* and *kalaśa* and on the left by two female attendants, each standing in *tribhaṅga* and carrying *kaṭi* and upraised in praise of god (*praśansā mudrā*). Gaṇeśa carries chopped off *paraśu*, *padma* and *modaka-pātra*. He wears a *karaṇḍamukuṭa*, *hāra* and *sarpayajñopavīta*.

"A panel on the left of the *kīrtimukha* on the left shows niche containing an image of a four-armed Kubera seated in *lalitāsana* with his consort. He is flanked on the right by a female *chaurī*-bearer standing in *tribhaṅga* and holding a *chaurī* by her right hand. The niche is flanked on the right by two female attandants, each standing in *tribhaṅga* and on the left by a male attendant standing in *tribhaṅga*. Kubera and his consort wear each a *karaṇḍamukuṭa*. Kubera holds a purse. His belly has been chopped off.

"A beautifully carved panel shows a fighting scene (Period-IA) with warriors holding swords in their hands, a horse rider and an elephant (Pl. V). Another panel on *narathara* depicts a fighting scene with three warriors holding swords, a galloping horse and a running camel.

"Other noteworthy (Pl. VI) among the scenes carved on the *narathara* is a hunting scene wherein a man holding a bow and arrow is seen shooting an arrow at the band of seven deers. (Pl. VII).

"A small shrine of Indrāṇī opposite the aforesaid temple IA (pre-Solanki), was also laid bare during excavation for gardening after demolishing modern buildings (Pl. VIII). This shrine is composed of two ornamented pilasters and is surmounted by a *chhadya* carved with lotus petals. Each of the pilasters shows from bottom upwards *kumbhikā*, decorated with half-diamond design, plain *kalaśa*, shaft showing square, octagonal and circular sections carved with a human figure, *kūrtimukha* with pearls coming out, *bharaṇī* consisting of *karṇīkā* and *padma* surmounted by vase and foliage motif. The human figure on the right pilaster is a female standing in *tribhaṅga* and carrying *kaṭi* and *praśansā mudrā*. Above this is carved the name of the sculptor वोडदेव (Voḍa deva) in Devanāgarī characters. The human figure on the left pilaster is a dancing male. Above this is carved the name of the sculptor as 'ददा' (Dadā).

"Four-armed Indrāṇī is seated in *lalitāsana* and carries *varadāksha*, *modakapātra*, lotus-stalk and *kamaṇḍalu*. She wears *karaṇḍamukuṭa*, *vaikakshayaka*, *hāra*, *keyūras*, *valayas*, *nūpuras* and a *sārī* fastened by a *mekhalā*. The mount elephant is carved below. On the pedestal is inscribed the name of the sculptor in Devanāgarī characters (Pl. IX).

"The mouldings of the plinth of north-western shrine with friezes of sculptures carved on a number of them, were exposed in course of removal of debris and digging for gardening. They show from bottom upwards *bhiṭṭa*, *bhiṭṭa*, plain *jāḍaṁba*, *antarapatra*, *karṇikā*, *antarapatra*, *grāsapaṭṭi*, *gajathara*, *narathara*, *khura*, *kumbha*, decorated with friezes of sculptures and bejewelled *kalaśa* (Pl. X). Carvings on the plinth and parapet of the *sabhāmaṇḍapa* of north-west shrine were also revealed during clearance of debris. The full view of the *sabhāmaṇḍapa* of north-west shrine was exposed after removing the rubble-and-mud compound wall (Pl. XI). The plinth of temple II which served as base for north-west shrine was also revealed (Pl. XII).

"The open area in front of the prayer hall of the masjid with shabby pavement where shrubs and trees were growing and debris had accumulated and which was not used for prayer, was excavated for laying out a garden. While excavating for garden in the eastern part of open courtyard in front of the prayer hall, the sculpture of an elephant and remains of a temple were found. The ornamented plinth of this temple shows from bottom upwards *jāḍaṁba* decorated with bold lotus-scroll, *karṇikā*, *kapota* decorated with *kuḍūs* and *grasapaṭṭi* (Pl. XIII). The plinth shows that the temple above it was *pañcharatha* in plan. An underground passage below the plinth of this temple (Period-II) also came to light. Well polished stones have been used for the construction of this underground passage. Besides the sculptures of the elephant mentioned above, a human figure and lotus designs were also found by the side of the beautifully carved plinth of the temple. This temple found during excavation for gardening operation is perhaps of the time of Mūlarāja (Period-II)."[45]

2. Smothered Sculptures

"When the bulged portion of the western wall of the masjid was being dismantled, it was brought to light that this wall was a double wall. When the outer wall was dismantled the debris including sculptural and architectural fragments filled in between the inner and outer wall came out. There was a difference of one metre between the inner and outer wall and all this space was filled with debris. It could now be seen that the inner wall was built out of the *vedikā* pilasters and other ruins of Rudramahālaya. When the outer wall was removed, a number

[45]'Recent Archaeological Discoveries from Rudramahālaya and Jāmi Masjid, Sidhpur', *Kusumañjali: Shri Śivarāmamūrti Commemoration Volume*, Delhi, 1987, Vol. II, pp. 396-97.

of hidden sculptures of the south-west and north-west shrine, which were previously hidden due to wall, were also exposed to view (Pl. XIV). Noteworthy among the sculptures of the south-western shrine are:

1. A standing *apsaras.*
2. A standing ascetic.
3. Four-armed Varuṇa standing in *tribhaṅga.*
4. Four-armed Vāyu standing in *tribhaṅga.*
5. A standing ascetic.
6. A standing naked ascetic.
7. Two-armed dancing female-deity holding a sword and a chopped head.
8. Two-armed female-deity holding *aṅkuśa* and *kapāla.*
9. A standing ascetic.
10. A standing female with her right hand upraised and left hand in *kaṭi.*
11. A niche-shrine on the northern *bhadra* (central projection) containing an image of eight-armed Chāmuṇḍā standing in *tribhaṅga.*

"Noteworthy among the sculptures of the north-western shrine are:

1. A chopped niche.

2,3. A standing bearded ascetic holding a dagger in his right hand.

4. Four-armed standing Nirriti with a serpent canopy above his head.
5. Four-armed standing Yama with his head and hands chopped off.
6. A standing ascetic holding a *kamaṇḍalu* in his left hand.
7. A standing ascetic wearing a *kaupīna*. His right hand is upraised.
8. Two-armed dancing female-deity. A dancing dwarf male attendant is seen on her right.
9. Two-armed standing female-deity.
10. A standing ascetic. His right hand is upraised and he holds a knife by his left hand.
11. Two-armed dancing female-deity.
12. A niche-shrine on the southern *bhadra* containing an image of sixteen-armed Śiva with his right foot upraised and placed on a lotus. A warrior with a sword is shown below the lotus. Śiva holds *sarpa, khaṭvāṅga* and *kheṭaka* in his surviving hands. He is multi-headed."[46]

[46]Ibid., pp. 397-98.

3. Inside the Qibla Wall of the Masjid

"While the bulged and out of plumb western wall of the Jami Mosque was being dismantled the following sculptures and architectural members embedded inside the wall came to light:-

1. An elephant rider.
2. A beautiful head of Śiva.
3. A dancing *gaṇa*.
4. A bust of a four-armed bearded male-deity.
5. A bearded male drummer.
6. Fragments of an elephant.
7. Three busts of *Śālabhañjikā* bracket figures.
8. An image of four-armed dancing Śiva (Naṭarāja).
9. Fragments of an *āmalaka*.
10. Fragments of *chandrikā*.
11. Fragments of *Saṁvarṇā* roof of the *maṇḍapa*.
12. Fragments of *śhikhara* decorated with *chaitya-gavākshas*.
13. Fragments of *vedikā*, *kakshāsana* and *rājāsana*.

"Among the sculptures recovered from the western wall of the mosque noteworthy is a head of Śiva wearing elaborately carved *jaṭāmukuṭa*. The expression of his face with half open eyes, gracefully carved nose and prominent chin is serene (Pl. XVI). It measures 40 × 25 × 25 cms."[47]

4. Converted Shrines

"During the course of dismantling of the western wall of the mosque, two of the three shrines which were converted into mosque, were also exposed to view. The debris filled inside them was removed. The shrine on the southern side has inside it a circular *yonipaṭṭa* fixed into its floor. The *śivalinga* above this *yonipaṭṭa* is missing. The rear wall of this shrine has niches composed of three pilasters and each surmounted by a small pediment of *chaitya* arches. One of the niches contains seated *Umā-Maheśvara* on the mount bull and the other contains a donor couple (probably King Siddharāja Jaisingh and his queen). The bearded male (Siddharāja Jaisingh) is shown standing with folded hands in an attitude of supplication. His queen is standing on his left. On the south-western corner is a small water cistern for storage of water (Plate-XVI).

"The ceiling of the shrine is elaborately carved. The architrave of the ceiling is carved with *padmalatā* and cut-triangles. The ceiling is

[47]Ibid., pp. 398-99.

carved with a *kīrtimukha* at each corner. This domical ceiling has four concentric courses of lotuses. The centre of the dome is carved with a full-blown lotus. It has an elaborately carved door-way. The ceiling of the *antarāla* is carved with fine full blown lotuses. The shrine measures 2.08 × 2.15 × 3.07 mtrs.

"The northern shrine measures 2.19 × 2.02 × 2.95 mtrs. internally.

"The architrave of the ceiling is elaborately carved with lotus scroll and cut-triangles. Each of the corners of the ceiling is carved with a *kīrtimukha*. The domical ceiling consists of three courses of lotus courses of concentric circles. At the centre of the domical ceiling is carved a full blown lotus. There is a *chandraśilā* in front of the shrine.

"The shrine has an elaborately carved doorway which has been badly damaged. The ceiling of the *antarāla* is carved with five full blown lotuses.

"The northern shrine has inside its sanctum a Śivaliṅga installed on a *yonipaṭṭa*. The rear wall of the sanctum is carved with two niches, one of which contains a donor, a royal couple (probably Siddharāja Jaisingh with his wife). A female is seen holding a parasol above the head of the bearded king the head of whose wife has been chopped off. The pilasters of this niche are highly ornamented. The other niche contains an image of a queen standing in *tribhaṅga*. Her both hands and head have been chopped off. She is flanked on either side by two female attendants standing in *tribhaṅga*. (Pl. XVIII). Both of these sculptures are of white marble. The other images which are at present kept in the sanctum are:

1. Bust of a dancing *apsaras*, her male attendant holding a parasol above her head is depicted on her left. Her right breast has been chopped off. It measures 45 × 17 × 12 cms.
2. Śiva Naṭarāja inside a niche with a *makara toraṇa*. The niche is flanked on either side by a standing male attendant. It measures 48 × 58 × 25 cms.
3. A stone slab carved with a niche composed of two circular pilasters and surmounted by a small pediment of *chaitya*-arches. The niche is carved with an elaborate door from which a woman is seen coming out and catching hold of a child in her right hand. Her head has been chopped off. The niche is flanked on either side by a dwarf male attendant. It is made of white sand-stone and measures 70 × 60 × 42 cms.
4. Four-armed dancing Naṭarāja inside a niche, carrying indistinct *paraśu*, *khaṭvāṅga* and *kapāla*. It is made of white sand-stone and measures 40 × 55 × 8 cms.

5. Head of a deity wearing *karaṇḍamukuṭa*. It is made of white sand-stone and measures 20 × 15 × 15 cms.
6. A dancing male. It measures 35 × 27 × 7 cms. Made of white sand-stone.
7. Head of Yama wearing *karaṇḍmukuṭa*. He has long moustaches, protruding teeth, bulging eyes, and is bearded. It measures 27 × 15 × 7 cms.
8. Bust of a bearded male drummer measuring 20 × 19 × 20 cms.
9. Head of an *apsaras* measuring 20 × 20 × 20 cms.
10. Bust of a dancing *apsaras*. It measures 40 × 15 × 20 cms.
11. A dancing male inside a small niche. At the left end of this slab is carved a beautiful head of an *apsaras* whose hair are very elaborately arranged. It is made of white sand-stone and meas-ures 40 × 40 × 25 cms.
12. A stone slab carved with a dancing male. On his right is carved a bearded male drummer whose head has been partly chopped off. It is made of white sand-stone and measures 32 × 35 × 12 cms.
13. A bearded male dancing. Both his legs have been chopped off. He has moustaches. It measures 52 × 35 × 20 cms. It is made of white sand-stone. He wears earlobes."[48]

The article by B.L. Nagarch is accompanied by eighteen plates of photographs and a plan of the Rudramahālaya complex. The photographs show the "temple remains", sculptural and architectural, discovered in and around the Jāmi' Masjid. The plan shows three unexcavated zones where it is most likely that many more "temple remains" are lying buried, waiting to be exposed some day by the excavator's spade.

[48]Ibid., pp. 399-400.

CHAPTER TWO

THE STORY OF RUDRAMAHĀLAYA

In order to understand fully the meaning of what was exposed at Sidhpur and the strife it caused, we have to know what the Rudramahālaya was, how it came to be built at Sidhpur and how a Jāmi' Masjid was raised on its site and from its debris. The Report of the Minorities' Commission provides some historical background. So does the Note from the Government of Gujarat. But the information is meagre and leaves a lot to be told. Both of them were dealing with a "communal problem" and were not expected to give a detailed history of Sidhpur, the Rudramahālaya and the Jāmi' Masjid.

Sidhpur

The Note from the Government of Gujarat gives no information about the historical or religious importance of Sidhpur. The Report of the Minorities' Commission says that "Sidhpur is a historical town" and that "it was ruled successively by Hindu Rajas and Muslim Sultans."[1] There is no reference to the religious importance of Sidhpur as a place of Hindu pilgrimage. The article by B.L. Nagarch brings out that point when it says that "as the obsequial offerings to the paternal ancestors must be made at Gaya, so corresponding offerings to the maternal ancestors have to be performed at Sidhpur." Nagarch tells us also that "the ancient name of Sidhpur appears to have been Śrīsthala or Śrīsthalaka" and that "the name of Sidhapur was given to this place in honour of Siddharāja Jayasiṁha who completed the Temple of Rudra-Mahādeva in the twelfth century here."[2]

The Purāṇas regard Śrīsthala as the most sacred spot in the Sārasvata-maṇḍala of Gujarat. The *Bhāgvata Purāṇa* associates it with Kardama *rishi*, who had his hermitage here, and also with Kapila *muni*, who was born in this place on the bank of the sacred Sarasvati river. It was also known as Vindusara.[3] It is said that Aṇahillapāṭaka or Aṇahillapaṭṭaṇa, the capital of medieval Gujarat before Ahmadabad came up in the first quarter of the fifteenth century, was founded where it was because of its nearness to Śrīsthala.

---

[1]*The Fourth Annual Report*, p. 130.

[2]B.L. Nagarch, op cit., p. 395.

[3]Nundo Lal Day, The Geographical Dictionary of Ancient and Medieval India, third edition, New Delhi, 1971, p. 38.

Pl. 1. Part of the plan of pre-Solanki Temple (Period I).

Pl. 2. Full height of the beautifully moulded plinth of a pre-Solanki Temple (Period I) in the North-West Corner.

Pl. 3. Exquisitely carved Temple (Period IA) attached to the pre-Solanki Temple (Period I) laid bare in the North-West Corner outside the Masjid while excavating for gardening.

Pl. 4. A panel depicting worship of Gaṇeśa by a royal(?) couple.

Pl. 5. A beautifully carved panel depicting fighting scene (Period IA). For the first time this pre-Solanki school of art is brought to light.

Pl. 6. A fighting scene (Period IA).

Pl. 7. A hunting scene (Period IA).

Pl. 8. A view of the Indrānī Shrine.

Pl. 9. Goddess Indrāṇī with elephant as her vāhana. Names of sculptures are carved on the pilasters etc.

Pl. 10. Friezes of sculptures of the North-West Shrine Temple (Period III) after removal of debris and digging for gardening.

Pl. 11. Details of carving on the plinth and parapet of the Sabhāmaṇḍapa of the North- West Shrine (Period III).

Pl. 12. View of North-West Shrine (Period III) and plinth of Temple (Period II) which served as a base for Temple (Period III).

Pl. 13. Details of carving of Temple (Period II)

Pl. 14. General view of the sculptures from south side of the Temple after removing the debris

Pl. 15. Close-up view of the Lord Śiva's head which was found in the back wall of the Jāmi' Masjid.

Pl. 16. Interior view of the Northern Shrine.

Aṇahillapaṭṭaṇa, now known as Patan, was built in AD 745 by Vanarāja, the founder of the Chāvoṭkaṭa or Chāpā or Chāvdā dynasty. It reached its greatest glory, however, in the reign of Jayasiṁha (AD 1094–1143), the most illustrious ruler of the Chaulukya or Solāṅkī dynasty of Gujarat. Jayasiṁha was very much devoted to Śrīsthala and visited it often in order to keep the company of sages and saints living at this place. There is a popular legend that Jayasiṁha defeated and captured Barbara, a demon who was molesting the holy men at Śrīsthala. Barbara, we are told, became his obedient servant and performed many superhuman deeds for him. That is how Jayasiṁha earned the sobriquet of Siddharāja. He built at Śrīsthala a temple dedicated to Rudra Mahākāla which became known as Rudramahālaya or simply Rudramāla. Because of its close association with Siddharāja, Śrīsthala became known as Siddhapura which name was corrupted to Sidhpur in course of time.

The spiritual fame of Sidhpur, however, proved to be its misfortune when Gujarat passed under a long spell of Muslim rule towards the close of the thirteenth century. Thereafter it attracted the attention of every Islamic iconoclast. Its temples were reduced to ruins and its holy men were either killed or scared away. Its spiritual importance had become greatly reduced when Muṅhata Naiṇasī, the famous historian of Rajasthan, visited it in Samvat 1717 (AD 1660). Naiṇasī was at that time the Dīwān of Mahārāja Jaswant Singh of Jodhpur who had been appointed the Governor of Gujarat by Aurangzeb in AD 1658. He has left for us a brief description, historical and topographical, of Sidhpur as he saw it. "Sidhpur," writes Naiṇasī "is a pleasant city. It was founded by Sidharāo after his own name. He invited from the East one thousand Udīchya Brāhmaṇas who were well-versed in the Vedas and gave them seven hundred villages around Sidhpur...He had built a big temple named Rudramāla. That was razed to the ground by Sultān Alāuddīn. Even so, several temples survive today. Beyond the city, towards the east, there is the river Sarasvatī. A temple dedicated to Mādhava had been built on its bank. A *ghāṭa* [flight of steps leading to the river] has also been constructed. The temple was destroyed by the Mughals but the *ghāṭa* can still be seen...A Turk has built his bungalow on the *ghāṭa*."[4]

Sidhpur was liberated from the Muslim stranglehold by the Marathas in the first quarter of the eighteenth century. By the first quarter of

---

[4]*Muṅhatā Naiṇasīrī Khyāta*, Jodhpur, 1984, Vol. 1, pp. 261-62. The passage quoted has been translated from the original in Māravāṛi language.

the nineteenth, the Marathas lost to the British and in the settlement that followed Sidhpur was included in the princely state of Baroda along with Patan. The Marathas made no attempt to revive Sidhpur as a centre of Hindu pilgrimage. Nor did they try to restore Patan as the seat of a Hindu government. Neither the spiritual nor the political capital of Gujarat at one time has retained anything of a great past except wistful memories.

Rudramahālaya

The Note from the Government of Gujarat says that the Rudramahālaya was "built by Siddharaja Jayasimha in the 12th century" and that "it had eleven shrines dedicated to *Akadasa Rudras*."[5] The Report of the Minorities' Commission repeats this description with the elucidation that "in the centre of this complex was situated the temple and in and around the courtyard were 11 other shrines dedicated to the Rudras..."[6] Both of them say that the temple was profusely sculptured and ornamented. But none of them mentions what has survived of the central temple or the surrounding shrines.

B.L. Nagarch gives greater details in his aforementioned article. He writes:

"In about AD 944 Mūlarāja had founded the Rudra Mahālaya, but as he had to remain busy in invasions and other engagements he could not complete it. This temple fell into ruins during the following centuries. Siddharāja Jayasiṁha took up the work of reconstruction of this temple on a scale greater than that originally conceived and could not finish the work till his death in AD 1143.

"Rudramahālaya is the grandest and the most imposing conception of a temple dedicated to Śiva. Only a few fragments of the mighty shrine now survive, namely, four pillars in the north and five in the eastern side, porches of the three storeyed *maḍapa*. Four pillars in the back of it, a *toraṇa* and a cell at the back remain *in situ* after being dismantled in the 13th century AD. With its adjacent shrines, possibly eleven, part of which was converted into Jami mosque later in the Mughal period, it must have formed part of a grand conception dedicated to Ekādaśa Rudras.

"Originally it covered an area of 100 × 66 mtrs. The central building itself occupies an area of about 50 × 33 mtrs. The mighty pillars of

[5]*The Fourth Annual Report*, p. 141.
[6]Ibid., p. 130.

this temple are the tallest so far known in Gujarat."[7]

It is difficult to visualize what the Rudramahālaya looked like when it stood intact and in all its majesty. No other edifice of a similar conception has survived. We have only some legendary accounts, one of which is from Naiṇasī who tells us how the Rudramahālaya was conceived and constructed. We give below a summary of what he has written at length.

Sidharāo, says Naiṇasī, saw the Earth in a dream, appearing in the form of a damsel and demanding that she be decorated with a choice ornament. The king consulted the learned men who could divine dreams and they told him that the ornament for the Earth could mean only a magnificent temple. So the king invited architects from every land and they presented to him models of what they could conceive to be the best. But no model satisfied Sidharāo and he became despondent. At that time there were two notorious thieves in his kingdom, Khāprā and Kālā. As they started gambling on the Dīvālī day, Khāprā wagered that he would give Koḍidhaja, the renowned steed of Sidharāo, if he lost the game. He lost and promised to the winner that he would procure the steed by the time of the next Dīvālī day. He wormed himself into the confidence of Sidharāo, first as a sweeper in the royal stable and then as a syce of Koḍidhaja. The king who visited the stable everyday was very much pleased with Khāprā's services and spent some time talking to him. One day the king confided to Khāprā his (the king's) disappointment in the matter of a suitable temple. Soon after, the thief ran away with the horse and stopped for rest only when he reached the valley of Mount Abu. All of a sudden he saw the earth split and a temple came out. Gods and Goddesses staged a play in the temple as Khāprā watched sitting in a window of the divine edifice. He was reminded of Sidharāo's despondence and thought that this was the temple which would meet the king's expectations. He found out from the Gods that the same miracle would be enacted again on the night of the day after next and rushed back to Pāṭaṇa where he gave a graphic account to the king. The king came to the same spot and saw the temple which fully satisfied him. The Gods told him how to find the master architect who would build a similar temple for him. It took sixteen years to be completed, even though thousands of artisans were employed.[8]

[7]B.L. Nagarch, op.cit., p. 395.
[8]Muṅhatā Naiṇasī, op.cit., pp. 258-61.

Naiṇasī has included in his chapter on the Rudramāla a poem written in its praise by Lalla Bhaṭṭa.[9] The first two stanzas which describe the architecture and sculptures of the temple are as follows:

Fourteen storeys rise above the earth and seven thousand pillars,
In row after row, while eighteen hundred statues studded with emeralds adorn it.
It is endowed with thirty thousand flagstaffs with stems carved and leaves of gold.
Seven thousand sculptured elephants and horses stand in attendance on Rudra.
Seeing it all, Gods and men get struck with wonder and are greatly charmed,
Jayasiṁha has built a temple which excites the envy of emperors.
The sculptured elephants and lions trumpet and roar, all around, again and again,
The golden *kalaśas* glitter on the *maṇḍapa* upheld by numerous pillars.
The statues sing and dance and roll their eyes,
So that even the Gods jump with joy and blow their conches.
The ecstatic dance of Gods is watched by Gods and men who crowd around,
That is why the Bull,[10] O Sidha! O King of Kings! is feeling frightened.

A modern expert on medieval Hindu architecture has speculated about the Rudramahālaya on the basis of what has survived. "The Solāṅkī tradition maintains," writes Dr. S.K. Saraswati, "a rich and prolific output in the twelfth century AD which saw two eminent royal patrons of building art in Siddharāja Jayasiṁha and Kumārapāla. With the former is associated the completion of an imposing conception, the Rudra Mālā or Rudra Mahālaya, at Siddhapur (Gujarāt). Unfortunately it is now completely in ruins but a picture of its former splendour seems to have survived in a Gujarātī ballad which speaks of the temple as covered with gold, adorned with sixteen hundred columns, veiled by carved screens and pierced lattices, festooned with pearls, inlaid with gems over the doorways and glistening with rubies and diamonds. Much of this is, no doubt, exaggeration full of rhetoric; but the impressive character of the conception is evidenced by the scanty, though co-

---

[9]Ibid., pp. 262-63.

[10]The reference to the Bull who according to Hindu mythology supports the Earth on his horns.

lossal, remains. They consist of groups of columns of the pillared *maṇḍapa*, which seems to have been in more than one storey, and had three enterance porticos on three sides. The surviving foundations suggest that the conception with the usual appurtenances occupied a space nearly 300 feet by 230 feet. In front there stood a *kīrti-toraṇa* of which one column still remains. From the dimensions the Rudra Mālā seems to have been one of the largest architectural conceptions in this area. The rich character of its design is fully evident in the few fragments that remain."[11]

The Jāmi' Masjid

The Note from the Government of Gujarat says that "the temple was destroyed and three shrines in the eastern flank of the temple were converted into a mosque but there is no evidence as to the date of conversion."[12] The Report of the Minorities' Commission gives more details about the destruction and conversion of the temple. "This temple," says the Report, "seems to have been destroyed partly by Ulugh Khan in AD 1297–98 and partly by Ahmadshah in AD 1415. Some of the cubicles and a number of pillars on the Western side of the temple, it would appear were later converted into a mosque. The prayer hall of the mosque so converted has three domes. In the Western (Qaba) wall of the mosque Mimbar and Mehrabs were provided by using the doors of the shrines which were then filled with debris. The exact date of conversion of this part of Rudramahalaya complex is not known. However, according to inscriptions at the entrance it appears that the mosque known as Jama Masjid, was constructed during the reign of Aurangzeb in 1645."[13]

B.L. Nagarch, on the other hand, writes that "the inscription fixed in the modern entrance gate to the mosque mentions the construction of shops by Ali Askari in Adil Ganj and there is no reference to the mosque."[14] Moreover, Aurangzeb was not the ruling Mughal monarch in 1645, having ascended the throne thirteen years later in 1658. The "temple remains" discovered inside the mosque also go to show that at least that part of the structure was built not long after the Rudramahālaya was demolished. The Minorities' Commission, it seems, has relied

[11]R.C. Majumdar (ed.), *The History and Culture of the Indian People*, Vol. V, *The Struggle For Empire*, Third Edition, Bombay, 1976, pp. 595–96.
[12]*The Fourth Annual Report*, p. 141.
[13]Ibid., p. 130.
[14]B.L. Nagarch, op. cit. p. 395.

upon some local tradition about Aurangzeb having built the mosque. Aurangzeb did live in Gujarat in 1645 when he was appointed Governor of that province by Shāh Jahān. He also destroyed Hindu temples in Gujarat as is evident from his *firmān* dated November 20, 1665 which says that "In Ahmedabad and other parganas of Gujarat in the days before my accession (many) temples were destroyed by my order."[15] It seems that somewhere along the line several stories have got mixed up and Aurangzeb has been credited with a pious deed he did not perform at Sidhpur, not at least in respect of the Jāmi‘ Masjid built on the site and from the debris of the Rudramahālaya. What might have happened is that some major repairs to the Jāmi‘ Masjid were carried out while he was the Governor of Gujarat and at his behest. The subject needs examination with reference to records, if any.

Nor do we find a specific mention of Sidhpur or the Rudramahālaya in the available accounts of Ulugh Khān's invasion of Gujarat. The Minorities' Commission has made a mistake in giving the date of the invasion as AD 1297–98. The correct date is 1299.

There is, however, no doubt that Ahmad Shāh I (AD 1411– 43), the Sultān of Gujarat, destroyed the Rudramahālaya and raised a mosque on the site. "Soon after his return to Ahmadabad," writes S.A.I. Tirmizi, "Ahmad marched to Sidhpur, which was one of the most ancient pilgrim centres in north Gujarat. It was studded with beautiful temples, some of which were laid low."[16] A.K. Majumdar is more specific. "Ahmad Shāh like his grandfather," he says, "was a bigot and seized every opportunity to demolish Hindu temples. In 1414, he appointed one Tāj-ul-Mulk to destroy all temples and to establish Muslim authority throughout Gujarat. According to Firishta, the task was 'executed with such diligence that the names of Mawass and Girass (i.e. Hindu *zamindārs*) were hereafter unheard of in the whole kingdom.' Next year Ahmad attacked the celebrated city of Sidhpur in north Gujarat where he broke the images in the famous Rudramahālaya temple and converted it into a mosque."[17]

A poetic account of what Ahmad Shāh did at Sidhpur is available in *Mirāt-i-Sikandarī*, the history of Gujarat, written by Sikandar ibn-i-Muhammad alias Manjhū ibn-i-Akbar in the first quarter of the sixteenth century. "He marched on Saiyidpur,"[18] writes the historian, "on

[15]Quoted by Jadunath Sarkar, *History of Aurangzeb*, Vol. III, Calcutta, 1972 Impression, p.285.

[16]Mohammad Habib (ed.), *A Comprehensive History of India*, Vol. V, *The Delhi Sultanat*, First Reprint, New Delhi, 1982, p.853.

[17]R.C. Majumdar (ed.), op. cit., Vol. VI, *The Delhi Sultanate*, Bombay, 1960, p.158.

[18]The Islamic name of Sidhpur, unless it is a mispronunciation on the part of the historian. As we shall see in this study, Muslim rulers had Islamicized practically every important place–name in India.

Jamād-ul-Awwal in AH 818 (July/August, AD 1415) in order to destroy the temples which housed idols of gold and silver.

Verse

He marched under divine inspiration,
For the destruction of temples at Saiyidpur,
Which was a home of the infidels,
And the native place of accursed fire-worshippers.[19]
There they dwelt, day and night,
The thread-wearing idolaters.[20]
It had always remained a place for idols and idol-worshippers,
It had received no injury whatsoever from any quarter.
It was a populous place, well-known in the world,
This native place of the accursed infidels.
Its foundations were laid firmly in stone,
It was decorated with designs as if drawn from high heaven.
It had doors made of sandal and *ūd*.[21]
It was studded with rings of gold,
Its floors were laid with marble,
Which shone like mirrors.
Ūd was burnt in it like fuel,
Candles of camphor in large numbers were lighted in it.
It had arches in every corner,
And every arch had golden chandeliers hanging in it.
There were idols of silver set up inside,
Which put to shame the idols of China and Khotān.
Such was this famous ancient temple,
It was famous all over the world.
By the effort of Ahmad, it was freed from the idols,
The hearts of idol-worshippers were shattered with grief.
He got mosques constructed, and *mimbars* placed in them,
From where the Law of Muhammad came into force.
In place of idols, idol-makers and idol-worshippers,
Imāms and callers to prayers and *khatībs* were appointed.
Ahmad's good grace rendered such help,
That an idol-house became an abode of Allāh.

---

[19]Applied to Zoroastrians of Iran to start with, the term 'fire-worshippers' was later on used for idol-worshippers in India.
[20]The Brāhmaṇas wearing the sacred thread.
[21]A kind of costly wood.

"When the Sultān was free from Saiyidpur, he marched on Dhār in AH 819 (AD 1416–17)."[22]

Siddharāja Jayasiṁha

The destruction of Hindu temples and their conversion into mosques was, as we shall see, a normal occupation for most of the Muslim rulers in medieval India. What adds a touch of pathos to the destruction and conversion of the Rudramahālaya is that its builder, Siddharāja Jayasiṁha, had become known to the Muslims as a protector of their places of worship in Gujarat. Many other Hindu rulers provided the same protection to their Muslim subjects, as is evident from the presence of Muslim populations and religious establishments in all leading towns of western, south-western and northern India long before these towns were sacked and occupied by Islamic invaders. K.A. Nizami has devoted a long essay to this subject and named Lahore, Benares, Bahraich, Ajmer, Badaun, Kanauj, Bilgram, Gopamau and Koil (Aligarh), etc., in this context.[23] Other sources point to Muslim presence in the towns of Bengal, Bihar, Rajasthan, Gujarat and Maharashtra. The doings of Siddharāja Jayasiṁha have, however, found place in a Muslim history, *Jami'u-l Hikāyāt*, written by Muhammad 'Ufī who lived at Delhi in the reign of Shamsu'd-Dīn Iltutmish (AD 1210–36). The writer was a great collector of anecdotes regarding persons, places and events. He wrote:

"Muhammad 'Ufī, the compiler of this work, observes that he never heard a story to be compared with this. He had once been to Kambāyat (Cambay), a city situated on the sea-shore, in which, a number of Sunnīs, who were religious, faithful, and charitable lived. In this city, which belonged to the chiefs of Guzerāt and Nahrwāla,[24] was a body of Fire-worshippers[25] as well as the congregation of Musulmāns. In the reign of a king named Jai Singh, there was a mosque and a minaret from which the summons to prayers were cried. The Fire-worship-

[22]Translated from the Hindi rendering in S.A.A. Rizvi's *Uttara Taimūra Kālīna Bhārata*, Aligarh, 1959, Vol. II, pp. 268-69. Strangely enough, this poem has been omitted from the English translation by Fazlullah Lutfullah Faridi published from Dharampur and recently reprinted (Gurgaon, 1990). The English translation says, "In AH 818 (AD 1416), the Sultān attacked Sidhpur and broke the idols and images in the big temple at that place and turned the temple into a mosque" (p. 14).

[23]Mohammad Habib, op. cit., pp. 137-42.

[24]The Muslim pronunciation of Aṇahilwāḍa.

[25]"The word in the original is *Mugh* which has been generally accepted to indicate the Zoroastrians or fire-worshippers, but Prof. S.H. Hodiwala, *Studies in Indo-Muslim History* (Bombay, 1939) pp. 172-73, thinks it may refer to Jains" (*Epigraphia Indica—Arabic and Persian Supplement*, 1961, p. 5n).

pers instigated the infidels to attack the Musulmāns and the minaret was destroyed, the mosque burnt, and eight Musulmāns were killed.

"A certain Muhammadan, a Khatīb, or reader of the Khuṭba by name Khatīb 'Ali, escaped and fled to Nahrwāla. None of the courtiers of the Rāī paid any atttention to him, or rendered him any assistance, each one being desirous to screen those of his own persuasion. At last, having learnt that the Rāī was going out to hunt, Khatīb 'Ali sat down behind a tree in the forest and awaited the Rāī's coming. When the Rāī had reached the spot, Khatīb 'Ali stood up, and implored him to stop the elephant and listen to his complaint. He then placed in his hand a *kaīsda*, which he had composed in Hindi verse, stating the whole case. The Rāī having heard the case placed Khatīb 'Ali under charge of a servant, ordering him to take the greatest care of him, and produce him in court when required to do so. The Rāī then returned, and having called his minister, made over temporary charge of the Government to him, stating that he intended to seclude himself for three days from public business in his harem, during which seclusion he desired to be left unmolested. That night, Rāī Jai Singh, having mounted a dromedary started from Nahrwāla for Kambāyat and accomplished the distance, forty parasangs, in one night and one day. Having disguised himself by putting on a tradesman's dress, he entered the city, and stayed a short time in different places in the market place, making inquiries as to the truth of Khatīb 'Ali's complaint. He then learnt that the Muhammadans were oppressed and slain without any grounds for such tyranny. Having thus learnt the truth of the case, he filled a vessel with sea-water and returned to Nahrwāla, which he entered on the third night from his departure. The next day he held his court, and summonning all complainants he directed the Khatīb to relate his grievance. When he had stated his case, a body of the infidels wanted to intimidate him and falsify his statements. On this the Rāī ordered his water-carrier to give the water pot to them that they may drink from it. The Rāī then told them that he had felt unable to put implicit confidence in any one because a difference of religion was involved in the case; he had himself therefore gone to Kambāyat, and having made personal enquires as to the truth, had learnt that the Muhammadans were victims of tryanny and oppression. He said that it was his duty to see that all his subjects were afforded such protection as would enable them to live in peace. He then gave orders that two leading men from each class of Infidels, Brahmans, Fire-worshippers and others should be punished. He then gave a lac of Balotras[26] to enable them to build their mosque and minarets. He also granted to Khatīb four articles of dress. These are preserved to this day, but are exposed to view on high festival days. The mosque and minaret were standing until a few days ago."[27]

---

[26]Unit of a silver currency at that time.

[27]Elliot and Dowson, *History of India as told by its own Historians*, Vol. II, pp. 162-64. 'Ufī expresses surprise at the Hindu King's behaviour because such behaviour was inconveivable for a Muslim. According to the Islamic norm, a king is expected to destroy rather than restore other people's places of worship.

CHAPTER THREE

MUSLIM RESPONSE TO HINDU PROTECTION

The protection provided by Siddharāja Jayasiṁha to Muslims and their placces of worship was continued by his successors in Gujarat. The population of Muslims as well as their places of worship continued to multiply in several cities of Gujarat as is borne out by numerous inscriptions, particularly from Khambat, Junagadh and Prabhas Patan, dated before Gujarat passed under Muslim rule in the aftermath of Ulugh Khān's invasion in AD 1299.

"These records," observes Z.A. Desai, the learned Muslim epigraphist, "make an interesting study primarily because they were set up in Gujarat at a time when it had still resisted Muslim authority. That the Muslims inhabited quite a few cities, especially in the coastal line of Gujarat, quite long before its final subjugation by them, is an established fact. The accounts of Arab travellers like Mas'ūdī, Istakharī, Ibn Hauqal and others, who visited Gujarat during the ninth and tenth centuries of the Christian era, amply testify to the settlements of Muslims in various towns and cities. The inscriptions studied below also tend to corroborate the fact that the Muslims had continued to inhabit Gujarat until it became a part of the Muslim empire of Delhi. Moreover, they furnish rare data for an appraisal of the condition of Muslims under non-Muslim rulers of Gujarat. On one hand, they indicate the extent of permeation of Islamic influence in Gujarat at a time when it was still ruled by its own Rajput princes and show that Muslims had long penetrated into different parts of Gujarat where they lived as merchants, traders, sea-men, missionaries, etc.; these settlements were not only on the coastal regions but also in the interior as is indicated by some of these records. On the other hand, these epigraphs form a concrete and ever-living proof of the tolerance and consideration shown *vis-a-vis* their Muslim subjects by Hindu kings who were no doubt profited by the trade and commerce carried on by these foreign settlers."[1]

It seems, however, that these "merchants, traders, sea-men and missionaries" were not satisfied with the situation obtaining under Hindu rule. They kept looking forward to the day when the *Dār al-*

[1] 'Arabic Inscriptions of the Rajput period from Gujarat', *Epigraphia Indica—Arabic and Persian Supplement*, 1961, pp. 1–2. It is, of course, his personal view that Hindu tolerance towards Muslims was inspired in part by profits derived from foreign trade.

Harb (land of the infidels against which Muslims are obliged to wage war) that was Gujarat would become *Dār al-Islām* (land of the faithful). The evidence of how these Muslim settlers worked as sapppers and miners of Islamic invasions of Gujarat remains to be collected from Muslim annals. Here we are citing an inscription from Prabhas Patan, the city which was famous for its temple of Somanatha.

The inscription is dated AD 1264 and records the construction of a mosque at Prabhas Patan by a Muslim ship-owner. The stone slab containing its Arabic version is now fixed in the Qazi's Mosque at Prabhas Patan and is not *in situ*. The Sanskrit version which, it seems, was removed at some time and is now in a wall of the Harasiddha Mata temple in the nearby town of Veraval, has been summarised as follows by Z.A. Desai:

"Ship-owner Nūru'd-Dīn Pīrūz, son of ship-owner Khwāja Abū Ibrāhīm, a native of Hormuz,[2] had come for business to the town of god Somnath during the reign of Arjunadeva, the Vāghelā king of Gujarat (c. AD 1261–74) when Amīr Ruknu'd-Dīn was the ruling chief of Hormuz; Pīrūz purchased a piece of land situated in the Śikottari Mahāyānpāl outside the town of Somnath in the presence of the leading men like Thakkur Śri Palugideva, Rānak Śri Someśvaradeva, Thakkur Śri Rāmdeva, Thakkur Śri Bhimsiha and others and in the presence of all (Muslim) congregations, from Rājakula Śri Chhādā, son of Rājakula Śri Nānasiha; Pīrūz, who by his alliance with the great man Rājakula Śri Chhādā, had become his associate in meritorious work, caused a mosque to be constructed on that piece of land; for its maintenance, i.e., for the expenses of oil for lamp, water, preceptor, crier to prayers and a monthly reader (of the *Qur'ān*) and also for the payment of expenses of the particular religious festivals according to the custom of sailors, as well as for the annual white-washing and repairs of rents and defects in the building, the said Pīrūz bequeathed three sources of income: firstly, a *palladika* (particulars regarding whose location and the owner are-given in detail); secondly, a *dānapala* belonging to one oil-mill; and thirdly, two shops in front of the mosque, purchased from Kilhanadeva, Lunasiha, Āśādhar and others; Pīrūz also laid down that after meeting the expenses as indicated above, the surplus income should be sent to the holy cities of Mecca and Medina; as regards the management, he desired that the various classes of Muslims such as the communities of sailors, ship-owners, the clergy (?), the artisans (?), etc., should look

[2]A principality in the Persian Gulf.

after the source of income and properly maintain the mosque."[3]

The English translation of the first seven lines of the Arabic text as given by Z.A. Desai, is as follows:

1. Allāh the Exalted may assign this (reward) to one who builds a house in the path of Allāh.... [This auspicious mosque was built].
2. on the twenty-seventh of the month of Ramaḍān, year [sixty-two].
3. and six hundred from migration of the Prophet (23rd July AD 1264), in the reign of the just Sultān and [the generous king].
4. Abu'l-Fakhr (lit., father of pride), Ruknu'd-Dunyā wa'd-Dīn (lit., pillar of State and Religion), Mu'izzu'l-Islām wa'l-Muslimīn (lit. source of glory for Islām and the Muslims), shadow of Allāh in [the lands],
5. one who is victorious against the enemies, (divinely) supported prince, Abi'n-Nusrat (lit., father of victory), Mahmūd, son of Ahmad, may Allāh perpetuate his....
6. and may his affair and prestige be high, in the city of Somnāt (i.e. Somnath), may God make it one of the cities of Islām ad [banish?].
7. infidelity and idols...[4]

Z.A. Desai has noted some differences between the Arabic and the Sanskrit versions. "For example," he writes, "the Arabic inscription does not give all the details regarding the sources of income, the procedure for its expenditure, management, etc., which are mentioned at some length in the Sanskrit record. Also, the Arabic version mentions only the leader of prayer (*imām*), caller to prayers (*mu'addhin*) and the cities of Mecca and Medina among the beneficiaries...Likewise, no mention is made of the provision for the celebration of religious festivals as stated in the Sanskrit record. Further, in the extant portion of the Arabic record, we do not find mention of the then Vāghelā king of Gujarat, Arjunadeva...On the other hand, the Arabic version gives some more information regarding the status and position of Pīrūz (Fīrūz) and his father Abū Ibrāhīm. For example, Fīrūz is called therein 'the great and respected chief (*sadr*), prince among sea-men, and king of kings and merchants.' He is further eulogised as the 'Sun of Islām and Muslims, patron of kings and monarchs, shelter of the great and the elite, pride of the age', etc. Likewise, his father, Abū Ibrāhīm, son of Muhammad al-'Irāqī, is also mentioned with such lofty titles as 'the great

[3]*Epigraphia Indica—Arabic and Persian Supplement,* 1961, pp. 11-12.
[4]Ibid., p. 14.

chief of fortunate position, protector of Islām and the Muslims, patron of kings and monarchs, prince among great men of the time, master of generosity and magnanimity', etc. Needless to say, all these titles are absent in the Sanskrit version."[5]

One wonders, however, why the learned epigraphist has overlooked the most glaring difference in the two versions and tried to cover it up by stating that "in the extant portion of the the Arabic record, we do not find mention of the then Vāghelā king of Gujarat." The record is complete for all practical purposes except for a few gaps which the epigraphist has filled up creditably with the help of his long experience in reading and reconstructing such inscriptions. It is difficult to imagine that the name of Arjunadeva, the then Vāghelā king of Gujarat, could have occurred in any of these gaps even if the king was stripped of all his appellations. Moreover, the name of a Hindu king could have found no place in the scheme followed in the inscription.

The scheme followed in the inscription is similar to that which we find in thousands of such inscriptions set up on mosques and other Muslim monuments all over India, before and after AD 1264. The name of the ruling Muslim monarch with his appellations finds a prominent place in most of these inscriptions. And that is exactly what we find in the present instance. The only difference is that there being no Muslim monarch at that time in Gujarat and Gujarat being a Hindu kingdom independent of the Delhi Sultanate, the builder of the mosque chose the king of Hormuz for showing his solidarity with *Dār al-Islām.*

That in itself was objectionable enough for a subject of the Hindu king of Gujarat or a resident alien doing business in Gujarat. The mosque was erected at Prabhas Patan which was situated in the kingdom of Gujarat and not at a place in the kingdom of Hormuz. But the builder went much farther as, after extolling the king of Hormuz as "the source of glory for Islām and the Muslims," he prayed fervently that "may his affair and prestige be high in the city of Somnāt, may Allāh make it one of the cities of Islām, and [banịsh?] infidelity and idols" from it. In other words, he was praying for and looking forward to another Islamic invasion of Gujarat.

Comparing the Sanskrit and Arabic versions of this inscription, the conclusion is unavoidable that the Muslim merchant from Hormuz had eschewed carefully from the Sanskrit version what he had included confidently in the Arabic text. He must have been sure in his mind that no Hindu from Prabhas Patan or elsewhere was likely to compare the

[5]Ibid., p. 12.

two texts and that even if a Hindu noticed the difference between the two he was not likely to understand its meaning and purport. At the same time, he was sharing with his co-religionists in Gujarat a pious aspiration enjoined on all believers by the tenets of Islam.

There was a similar Muslim settlement at Aṇhilwāḍ Pātan, the capital of Gujarat under the Chaulukya and the Vāghelā dynasties of Hindu kings. An inscription dated AD 1282 fixed in the wall of a mosque in this place, records the death of a Muslim merchant in the reign of the Vāghelā king Sāraṅgadeva (AD 1274–96). "Within our present state of knowledge," writes Z.A. Desai, "this is the only record at Pātan which is dated in the pre-Muslim period of Gujarat, furnishing evidence of the settlement, or at least presence, of Muslims in the very capital of the Rajput rulers."[6] But as he himself admits "Muslim remains also have not survived the ravages of time"[7] in this town. It is quite likely that an inscription similar to that at Prabhas Patan existed at Aṇhilwāḍ Pātan also.

Cambay or Khambat, the famous port of Gujarat, abounds in Muslim inscriptions from the time when Gujarat was a Hindu kingdom. An inscription dated AD 1218 in the reign of the Chaulukya king Bhīmadeva II (AD 1178–1242), records the construction of a Jāmi' Masjid and says in the very first sentence that no one else would be invoked with Allāh.[8] Another inscription dated AD 1232 in the reign of the same Hindu king records the death of a Muslim and declares, again in the first sentence, that "Surely, the true religion with Allāh is Islām."[9] A third inscription dated 1284 in the reign of the Vāghelā king Sāraṇgadeva (AD 1274–96), records the death of another Muslim and says that "whoever disbelieves in the communications of Allāh—then, surely Allāh is quick in reckoning."[10]

An inscription dated AD 1286–87 records the construction of a mosque at Junagadh in the reign of Sāraṅgadeva. The record invests the name of the builder, Abu'l Qāsim, with high-sounding titles. "The titles," observes Z.A. Desai, "may be taken to suggest that Abu'l Qāsim, probably an influential merchant conducting business in that part, was associated in some way with the liaison work between the state and its Muslim population. The record also indicates that there was a considerable number of Muslim population residing at Junagadh,

---

[6]Ibid., p. 16.
[7]Ibid., p. 15.
[8]Ibid., p. 6.
[9]Ibid., p. 8.
[10]Ibid., p. 17.

which necessitated the building of a prayer house and that some of the Saurashtra ports used to clear the traffic of Haj pilgrims from Gujarat and possibly from outside too."[11]

Settlements of Arab and other merchants from West Asia were nothing new for Gujarat. These merchants had established colonies all along the West Coast of India and even farther afield, long before the prophet of Islam was born. The ports of Gujarat being the most prosperous had exercised a particular attraction for them. They also travelled in the interior of Gujarat in search of merchandise fit for the markets in Africa, West Asia and Europe. Mecca itself was an entrepot for trade between India and the Far East on the one hand and the Roman Empire on the other. At the same time, Indian merchants including those from Gujarat had established their colonies in most of the coastal towns along the Persian Gulf, the Red Sea and the Mediterranean. Neither religion nor politics had ever divided the two merchant fraternities.

All this, however, changed radically after Arabia was conquered by the sword of Islam and every Arab was forced to become a Muslim on pain of death or permanent exile from his homeland. The Indian colonies along the Persian Gulf, the Red Sea and the Mediterranean were attacked by Islamic legionaries, both from land and sea. Indian merchants, except a few who opted for the new faith, were killed or hounded out from every place which came under Islamic occupation. Meanwhile, Arab merchants added a new item to their merchandise—they became salesmen of Islam as well. Arab settlements in India had not suffered the slightest discomfort or dislocation following from the stormy events in Arabia and the march of Islamic hordes towards the frontiers of India. Many more people to the west and north of India passed under the yoke of Islam in the next few decades. Merchants from all these places had also to embrace Islam and make a common cause with the Arab merchants. A new fraternity known as the *ummah* or *millat* of Islam emerged all along the West Coast of India as also at many places in the interior.

Only a state and a population that did not know or understand the tenets of Islam and the obligations which those tenets imposed upon every Muslim, could permit these seditious settlements in its leading cities and ports. There is little doubt that each one of these settlements served as an intelligence network for Islamic invaders. The missionaries of Islam who took care of the flock might have hoodwinked the

[11]Ibid., p. 18.

Hindus around them with their pieties. But the faithful understood the message of these missionaries and readily served as advance guards of the armies of Islam hovering on the borders of Gujarat.

II

It cannot be said that at the time these inscriptions were set up at Aṇhilwāḍ Pāṭan, Prabhas Patan, Khambat, Junagadh and other places, the Hindus of Gujarat had had no taste of what Islam had in store for them, their women, their children, their cities, their temples, their idols, their priests, and their properties. The invasion of Ulugh Khān that was to subjugate Gujarat to a long spell of Muslim rule, was the eighth in a series which started within a few years after the Prophet's death at Medina in AD 632. Five Islamic invasions had been mounted on Gujarat before Siddharāja Jayasiṁha ascended the throne of that kingdom in AD 1094 — first in AD 636 on Broach by sea; second in AD 732–35 by land; third and fourth in AD 756 and 776 by sea; and fifth by Mahmūd of Ghazni in AD 1026. Two others had materialised by the time the Muslim ship-owner set up his inscription in AD 1264 on a mosque at Prabhas Patan. The sixth invasion was by Muhammad Ghūrī in AD 1178, and the seventh was by Qutbu'd-Dīn Aibak in AD 1197. The only conclusion that can be drawn from the evidence is that either the Hindus of Gujarat had a very short memory or that they did not understand at all the inspiration at the back of these invasions. The temple of Somnath which stood, after the invasion of Mahmūd of Ghazni in AD 1026, as a grim reminder of the character of Islam, had also failed to teach them any worthwhile lesson. Nor did they visualize that the Muslim settlements in their midst could play a role other than that of carrying on trade and commerce.

The foreign merchants turned Muslims had continued to do business and amass wealth as in the earlier days. But the leadership in the Muslim settlements had now passed into the hands of the missionaries of Islam known as Sufis, Walīs, Dirvishes and by several other high-sounding names. The sole occupation of these missionaries was to see the frontiers of *Dār al-Islām* extend towards Gujarat. All Muslims in Gujarat were now expected to serve as the eyes and ears of the Caliphate which had started on a career of imperialist aggression in all directions. Gujarat had had a taste of this aggression earlier than any other part of India. As the armies of Islam marched towards the land frontiers of India in Makran and Seistan, Indian ports on the West Coast became targets for the newly created Islamic navy.

Legends about Mahmūd of Ghazni

Mahmūd of Ghazni had led twelve to seventeen expeditions to India, according to different accounts. He destroyed many temples and smashed or burnt numerous idols wherever he was victorious over Hindu resistance. But what made him into a myth was his expedition to Somnath. "The destruction of the temple of Somnāth," observes Muhammad Nāzim, "was looked upon as the crowning glory of Islam over idolatry, and Sultān Mahmūd as the champion of the Faith, received the applause of all the Muslim world. Poets vied with each other in extolling the real or supposed virtues of the idol-breaker and the prose writers of later generations paid their tribute of praise to him by making him the hero of numerous ingenious stories."[12]

One such story was told by Shykh Farīdu'd-Dīn Aṭṭār, the renowned "mystic poet" in his *Manṭiqu't-Ṭair* (Conference of Birds). "In this story," writes Muhmmad Nāzim, "the Sultān is made to show his preference for the title of idol-breaker to that of idol-seller." While rejecting the offer of the Brāhmaṇas to ransom the idol of Somnath with its weight in gold, Mahmūd is supposed to have said, "I am afraid that on the Day of Judgment when all the idolaters are brought into the presence of Allāh, He would say, 'Bring Ādhar and Mahmūd together: one was idol-maker, the other idol-seller'." Ādhar or Ezra, the uncle of Abraham, according to the Qur'ān, made his living by carving idols. "The Sultān," according to Aṭṭār, "then ordered a fire to be lighted round it. The idol burst and 20 *manns* of precious stones poured out from its inside. The Sulṭān said, 'This (fire) is what Lāt[13] (by which name Aṭṭār calls Somanāth) deserves; and that (the precious stones) is my guerdon from my God."[14]

Another story is told in the *Futūhu's-Salāṭīn*. "It is stated," summarises Muhammad Nāzim, "that shortly after the birth of Mahmūd, the astrologers of India divined that a prince had been born at Ghazna who would demolish the temple of Somanāth. They therefore persuaded Rājā Jaipāl to send an embassy to Mahmūd while he was still a boy, offering to pay him a large sum of money if he promised to return the idol to the Hindūs whenever he captured it. When Mahmūd captured Somanāth the Brahmins reminded him of his promise and demanded the idol in compliance with it. Mahmūd did not like either to return the

[12]Muhammad, Nāzim, *The Life and Times of Sultān Mahmūd of Ghazna*, second edition, 1971, p. 219.

[13]Al-Lāt was a Goddess of the pre-Islamic Arabs. Prophet Muhammad had got her idols destroyed. She was seen by Islamic iconoclasts in many Hindu idols.

[14]Muhammad Nāzim, op. cit., p. 221.

idol or to break his promise. He therefore ordered the idol to be reduced to lime by burning and when, on the following day, the Brahmins repeated their demand, he ordered them, to be served with betel-leaves which had been smeared with the lime of the idol. When the Brahmins had finished the chewing of the betel-leaves they again repeated their demand, on which the Sultān told them that they had the idol in their mouths."[15] As we would see at a later stage in this study, this story inspired some other Sultāns to do actually what Mahmūd was supposed to have done in the imagination of a story-teller.

Finally, we have a story which presents the Muslims as a persecuted community in the Hindu kingdom of Gujarat and Mahmūd's invasion as a punitive expedition. The Rājā of Gujarat, we are told, used to sacrifice a Muslim everyday "in front of the idol of Somnāth." So Prophet Muhammad appeared in a dream to Hājjī Muhammad of Mecca and told him to go to the rescue of the Prophet's beloved people in Gujarat. The Hindu Rājā tried to kill the Hājjī but did not succeed. "The Hājjī," the story goes on, "now invited Sultān Mahmūd of Ghazna to come with his army and stop this iniquity." The Sultān came, reduced the idol of Somnath to powder which he fed to Rājā Kunwar Rāy in betel-leaves. The deputy he appointed at Somanātha before his return to Ghazni "demolished the temple and set fire to it."[16]

The story, of course, seeks psychological compensation for an unprovoked aggression against a king and a people who had been kind to the Muslims settled in Gujarat. We hear similar stories about many other places which were invaded by the armies of Islam and which had provided protection to Muslim settlements, particularly the Sufis. But at the same time, it betrays the secret that the Muslim community in Gujarat had invited Mahmūd to invade the kingdom and destroy the temple of Somnath. Professor Mohammad Habib was telling this truth when he wrote that "the far-flung campaigns of Sultan Mahmud would have been impossible without an accurate knowledge of trade routes and local resources, which was probably obtained from Muslim merchants."[17]

Sidhpur, like many other famous Hindu cities, is a small town today. But it reminds us of the days when it was the most important place

---

[15]Ibid., pp. 221-22.

[16]Ibid., pp. 222-24. The story is based on a ballad written by some Muslim in Gujarati language in AH 1216 (AD 1800). The ballad was summarised by Major J.W. Watson in *Indian Antiquary*, Vol. VIII (June, 1879), pp. 153-61.

[17]Quoted by Ram Gopal Misra in his *Indian Resistance to Early Muslim Invaders upto AD 1206*, Meerut City, 1983, p. 101.

of Hindu pilgrimage in North Gujarat.

The Rudramahālaya, like many other magnificent Hindu temples, is a heap of ruins at present. But it reminds us of a past when it was one of the most magnificent temples ever built in India.

The Jāmi' Masjid, like many other historical mosques, stands as a dilapidated structure now. But it reminds us of a regime under which it symbolised the might of Islam.

The destruction of the Rudramahālaya at Sidhpur in Gujarat was not an isolated event; it was only a link in the long chain which stretches from the middle of the seventh century, when the first Islamic invaders stepped on the soil of India, to the closing years of the eighteenth century when Tīpū Sultān led his expedition into Malabar. The vast land which is spread from Transoxiana, Khurasan and Seistan in the West to Assam in the East, and from Sinkiang in the North to Tamil Nadu in the South, is literally littered with the ruins of temples belonging to all Hindu sects— Bauddha, Jaina, Śaiva, Śākta Vaishṇava, and the rest.

The Jāmi' Masjid at Sidhpur is not the only mosque built on the site and from the debris of a demolished Hindu temple. There are innumerable mosques all over India, Pakistan, Bangladesh, Afghanistan and the neighbouring lands towards the north-west which have, embedded in their masonry, some epigraphical or sculptural or architectural evidence that they were places of Hindu worship in the past. Quite a few of these mosques have failed to withstand the ravages of time and are in ruins at present. But quite a few are still in use by the worshippers of Allāh.

Conclusion

The story of Gujarat was repeated all over India in wave after wave of Islamic invasions from the middle of the seventh century onwards. Hindus fought the invaders at every step and defeated them quite often. But they failed to study and understand the theology of Islam, and the aspirations of Muslims living in their midst. The invaders continued to forge ahead for several centuries. The situation is the same today. Afghanistan, North-West Frontier Province, Punjab, Sindh, and East Bengal have been lost. No one can say how things will turn out in Kashmir. Muslims inside India continue to create street riots on an ascending scale. But the Hindus have refused to learn, either from history or from contemporary experience.

SECTION II

SUPPRESSIO VERI SUGGESTIO FALSI

CHAPTER FOUR

THE MARXIST HISTORIANS

What was uncovered at Sidhpur only to be covered up again was verily *the tip of an iceberg* which remains submerged in hundreds of histories written by Muslim historians, in Hindu literary sources which are slowly coming to light, in the accounts of foreign travellers who visited India and the neighbouring lands during medieval and modern times, and above all in the reports of the archaeological surveys carried out in all those countries which had been for long the cradles of Hindu culture. No systematic effort has yet been made by scholars to see the iceberg emerge from the dark depths and tell its own story in a simple and straight-forward manner. Rare is the historian or archaeologist who has related this vandalism to the theology of Islam based on the Qur'ān and the Sunnah of the Prophet. On the contrary, the subject has been politicised by the votaries of 'Secularism' who become hysterical by the very mention of the untold story. Politicians in power have made and are making frantic efforts to suppress every tip of the iceberg which chances to surface in spite of the conspiracy to keep it out of sight.

Some of these politicians are masquerading as academicians and selling far-fetched and fantastic apologies for the havoc caused by Islamic iconoclasm. The following story illustrates what happens whenever the subject comes into the open and invites attention.

One day in August, 1986, *The Times of India* printed on its front page the photographs of two stones carrying defaced carvings of some Hindu deities. There was a short statement beneath the photographs that the stones had been found by the Archaeological Survey of India in course of repairs to the Qutb Mīnār at Delhi. The stones, according to the Survey, had been built into a wall with the carved faces turned inwards. But the daily had dropped this part of the news.

Some correspondence cropped up in the letters-to-the-editor column of the newspaper. The majority of writers congratulated the editor for breaking a conspiracy of silence regarding publication of a certain type of historical facts in the mass media. A few writers regretted that a news item like that should have been published in a prestigious daily in an atmosphere of growing communal tension. None of the writers raised the question or speculated as to how those stones happened to be there. None of them drew any inference from the fact that the Qutb Mīnār stands near the Quwwat al-Islām Masjid which, according to an inscription on its eastern gate, was built from the materials of twenty-seven Hindu temples.

The correspondence would have closed after a few days but for another photograph which was front-paged by *The Times of India* dated September 15, 1986. It depicted the Īdgāh built by Aurangzeb on the site of the Keśavadeva temple at Mathura and gave the news that a committee had been formed by some leading citizens for the liberation of what is known to be Śrī Krishṇa's place of birth. A few more letters for and against the photograph and the news item were published in the newspaper. None of them was well-informed. None of them threw any light on what was the Keśavadeva temple and why and when Aurangzeb converted it into a mosque.

But even these meagre and ill-informed comments were too much for a dozen professors from Delhi. They wrote a long letter of protest which was published in *The Times of India* on October 2, 1986. The letter is being reproduced in full because it reveals the line laid down by a well-entrenched clique which has come to control all institutions concerned with the researching, writing and teaching of history in this country. They said:

"Sir-We have noted with growing concern a recent tendency in *The Times of India* to give a communal twist to news items and even to editorial comments. An example of this is a report from Mathura dated 15 September and entitled, 'Krishna's Birthplace after Aurangzeb.' It evoked considerable correspondence some of which, as could be expected, was markedly communal in tone.

"Your readers should know that historical analysis and interpretations involve more than a mere listing of dates with an eye to pious sentiments. The Dera Keshava Rai temple was built by Raja Bir Singh Deo Bundela during Jahangir's reign. This large temple soon became extremely popular and acquired considerable wealth. Aurangzeb had this temple destroyed, took the wealth as booty and built an Idgah on the site. His actions might have been politically motivated as well, for at the time when the temple was destroyed he faced problems with the Bundelas as well as Jat rebellions in the Mathura region. It should be remembered that many Hindu temples were untouched during Aurangzeb's reign and even some new ones built. Indeed, what is really required is an investigation into the theory that both the Dera Keshava Rai temple and the Idgah were built on the site of a Buddhist monastery which appears to have been destroyed.

"Your news report also gives credence to the suggestion that this site was the birthplace of Krishna. This is extraordinary to say the least, when even the historicity of the personality is in question. It creates the kind of confusion such as has been created, probably deliberately, over the question of the birthplace of Rama in the matter of the Rama-janam-bhumi. A Persian text of the mid-nineteenth century states that the Babari mosque was adjacent to the Sita-ka-rasoi-ghar and was known as the Rasoi-Sita mosque and adjoined the area associated with the birthplace of Rama. It would be worth enquiring whether there is reliable historical evidence of a period prior to the nineteenth century for this association of a precise location for the birthplace of Rama. Furthermore such disputes as there were between Hindus and Muslims in this area upto the nineteenth century were not over the Babari mosque but the totally different site of Hanuman-baithak.

"It cannot be denied that acts of intolerance have been committed in India by followers of all religions. But these acts have to be understood in their context. It is a debasement of history to distort these events for present day communal propaganda.

"The statement in your news report that the site at Mathura is to be 'liberated' and handed over to the 'rightful owners' as the birthplace of Krishna raises the question of the limits to the logic of restoration of religious sites (and this includes the demand for the restoration to worshippers of disused mosques now under the care of the Archaeological Survey of India). How far back do we go? Can we push this to the restoration of Buddhist and Jaina monuments destroyed by Hindus? Or of pre-Hindu animist shrines?"

The letter was signed by Romila Thapar, Muzaffar Alam, Bipan Chandra, R. Champaka Lakshmi, S. Bhattacharya, H. Mukhia, Suvira Jaiswal, S. Ratnagar, M.K. Palat, Satish Saberwal, S. Gopal and Mridula Mukherjee. Most of them are minor fries who merely lent their names to the protest letter. But four of them, namely, Romila Thapar, Bipan Chandra, H. Mukhia and S. Gopal are well-known as Marxist historians. It is for future scholarship to judge the worth of their work in the field of historical research. What is relevant to our present purpose is that the prestige which they have come to enjoy in our times, succeeded in suppressing what might have been an informative and interesting debate in *The Times of India.*

Quite a few readers of *The Times of India* including several professors of equal rank wrote letters challenging the facts as well as the logic of the Marxist professors. But none of these letters was published in the letters-to-the-editor column of the newspaper. After a fortinght, the daily published some non-descript letters from its lay readers and announced that the "controversy has been closed". It was a curious statement, to say the least. The controversy had only started with the publication of the long letter from the Marxist professors, accusing *The Times of India* of spreading "communalism" and making a number of sweeping statements. The other side was waiting for its rejoinders to appear in print. *The Times of India* would have been only fair to itself and its readers to let the other side have its say. But it developed cold feet. Perhaps it was not prepared to get branded as "communalist" for the sake of "a few facts from the dead past." Perhaps it was in a hurry to retrieve its reputation which had been "compromised" by the publication of the "controversial photographs." Whatever the reason or calculation, the Marxist professors walked away with victory in a match which the other side was not permitted to contest, leaving an impression on the readers of the newspaper that the Marxist case was unassailable.

It would, therefore, be worthwhile to examine the Marxist case and find out if it has any worth. Incidentally, the Marxist historians have equipped the Muslim historians as well with what is now considered to be a fool-proof apologetics vis-a-vis the destruction of Hindu temples during Muslim rule in India. An examination of the Marxist case in this context, therefore, constitutes an examination of the Muslim case as well.

We are leaving aside the Marxist accusation of "communalism" against *The Times of India*. Marxist of all hues have a strong nose for smelling communalism in the faintest expression of Indian nationalism which they have fought with great vigour and vigilance ever since they appeared on the Indian scene in the twenties of this century. Their writings and doings during nearly seven decades testisfy to the type of patriotism they preach and practise.

We are also overlooking the ex-cathedra tone which characterises their pronouncements regarding interpretation of history. The tone comes quite easily to those who have enjoyed power and prestige for long and, therefore, begun to believe that they have a monopoly over truth and wisdom. We shall confine our examination to what they have stated as facts and what they claim to be the correct interpretations of those facts.

The Keśavadeva Tradition at Mathura

It is true that the temple of Keśavadeva which was destroyed and replaced with an Īdgāh by Aurangzeb, was built by Bir Singh Deva Bundela in the reign of Jahāngīr. But he had not built it on a site of his own choosing. An age-old tradition[1] had continued to identify the Kaṭrā mound (on which Aurangzeb's Īdgāh stands at present) with the spot where Kaṁsa had imprisoned the parents of Śrī Krishṇa, and where the latter was born. The same tradition had also remembered with anguish that an earlier Keśavadeva temple which stood on this spot had been destroyed by an earlier Islamic iconoclast.

Romila Thapar has herself testified to this tradition about Keśavadeva. Referring to descriptions of the Mathura region by Greek historians, she writes, "The identification of Sourasenoi, Methora and Iobares/Jomanes do not present any problem. But the identification of Cleisobora or Carisobora or the other variants suggested such as Carysobores remain uncertain.... The reading of Cleisobora as Kṛṣṇpura has not yielded any firm identification. A possible connection could be suggested with Keshavadeva on the basis of this being an alternative name for Kṛṣṇa and there being archaeological evidence of a settlement at the site of Keshavadeva during the Mauryan period."[2]

Dr. V.S. Agrawala is well-known for his study of the sculptures and inscriptions found on the ancient sites of Mathura and around. He was Curator of the museum at Mathura as well as that at Lucknow. He makes the following observations:

1. "Mathurā on the Yamunā is famous as the birthplace of Kṛishṇa. It was the seat of the Bhāgvata religion from about second century BC to fifth century AD...[3]
2. "Brāhmanical shrines of Mathurā began to be built quite early as shown by the discovery of an epigraph, viz. the Morā Well-Inscription as well as other records like the lintel of the time of Śoḍāsa. It was in the reign of Chandragupta Vikramāditya that a magnificent temple of Vishṇu was built at the site of Kaṭrā Keśavadeva...[4]
3. "The rich store of Brāhmanical images in Mathurā Museum is specially noteworthy. The formulation of these images was a

---

[1]The Varāha Purāṇa says, न केशव समो देवः न मथुरा समो द्विजः (There is no God like Keśava and no Brāhmaṇas like those of Mathurā).

[2]Romila Thapar, 'The Early History of Mathurā, upto and including the Mauryan period' in *Mathurā: The Cultural Heritage*, edited by Doris Meth Sriniwasan, New Delhi, 1989, p. 15. It is her habit to speak with two tongues — one when she is in the midst of scholars who know the facts, and another when she functions as a professional Hindu-baiter.

[3]V.S. Agarawala, *Masterpieces of Mathura Sculpture*, Varanasi, 1965, p. 1.

[4]Ibid., p. 2.

> natural result of the strong Bhāgavata movement of which Mathurā had been the radiating centre from about the first century BC.... The chronological priority in the making of Brāhmanical images to that of the Buddha should be taken as a settled fact on the basis of an image of Balarāma from Jānsuṭī village. It is definitely in the style of the Śuṅga period. Patañjali also writing in the same age informs us of the existence of shrines dedicated of Rāma and Keśava i.e., Balarāma and Kṛishṇa..."[5]

An inscription of Svāmī Mahākṣatrapa Śoḍāsa recovered by Pandit Radha Krishna in 1913 testifies that a temple dedicated to Vāsudeva existed at Mathura in the first century BC. "From an examination of the stone," writes Professor H. Luders, "Mr. Ram Prasad Chanda came to the conclusion, which undoubtedly is correct, that the epigraph was originally incised on a square pillar which was afterwards cut lengthwise through the inscribed side into two halves and turned into door jambs."[6] Scholars have differed regarding the location of the temple mentioned in the epigraph. The latest to study and interpret the inscriptions of Śoḍāsa is Professor R.C. Sharma. "Luders thought," he writes, "that it belonged to the Bhāgvata shrine of Morā about 12 kms to the west of Mathurā. But V.S. Agrawala opined that it must have originated from the site of Kaṭrā, the famous Bhāgvata spot. We shall see that the conjecture of Agrawala carries weight...The upper part of the inscription is corroded and five lines cannot be made out properly. The remaining part is better preserved and it can be translated as: 'At the great temple of Lord Vāsudeva, a gateway and a railing was erected by Vasu son of Kauśiki Pākṣakā. May Lord Vāsudeva be pleased and promote the welfare of Svāmī Mahākṣatrapa Śoḍāsa.' This is the earliest archaeological evidence to prove the tradition of the building of Kṛṣṇa's shrine."[7] It is possible that some more inscriptions may surface in future and take the tradition of Krishṇa-worship at Mathura still farther in the past.

Another inscription found at the same site points to the same tradition prevailing in the seventh and eighth centuries AD. "A fragment of an inscribed stone slab," writes Dr. D.C. Sircar, "was discovered in 1954 at Katra Keshavdev within Mathurā city, headquarters of the District of that name in Uttar Pradesh. It was presented by the Shri Krishna Janmabhumi Trust, Mathurā, to the local Archaeological Museum."

---

[5]Ibid., p. 11.

[6]*Epigraphia Indica*, Vol. XXIV (1937-38), New Delhi, Reprint, 1982, p. 208.

[7]R.C. Sharma, 'New Inscriptions from Mathurā' in *Mathurā: The Cultural Heritage*, op. cit., p. 309.

After describing the size of the slab and the style of writing that has survived on it, he continues, "The characters resemble those of such inscriptions of the seventh and eighth centuries belonging to the Western parts of Northern India as the Banskhera plate of Harsh (AD 606–47), the Kundesvar inscription (VS 718 = AD 661) of Aprajita, the Jhalarpatan inscription (VS 746 = AD 689) of Durgagaṇa, the Kudarkot inscription of about the second half of the seventh century, the Nagar inscription (VS 741 = AD 684) of Dhanika, and the Kanaswa inscription (VS 795 = AD 738) of Śivagaṇa."[8] The inscription was composed "in adoration of a god whose epithets *kāl-āñjana-rajah-puñja-dyuti*, *(ma)hāvarāha-rūpa* and *jaṅgama* have only been preserved". It leaves "no doubt that the reference is to the god Vishṇu since the expression *mahāvarāha-rūpa* certainty speaks of the Boar incarnation of the deity."[9] The hero of the *praśasti* is a king named Diṇḍrāja of the Maurya dynasty. "It therefore seems," concludes Dr. Sircar, "that the king performed the deed in question in the chain of many other pious works and at the cost of a large sum of money. The purpose seems to have been to put garlands around the head of a deity whose name seems to read *Śauri* (i.e. Vishṇu; cf. the Vaishnavite adoration in verse 1)."[10]

That Bir Singh Dev Bundela's choice of the site was not arbitrary is proved by another inscription discovered by Dr. A. Fuhrer in 1889 "from the excavations made by railway contractors at the Keśava mound."[11] It is a long *praśasti* in Sanskrit stating that "Jajja, who long carried the burden of the *varga* together with the committee of trustees (*gosṭhījana*) built a large temple of Vishṇu brilliantly white and touching the clouds."[12] The colophon in prose informs us that the *praśasti* was composed by "two 'wise' men, Pāla and Kuladdhara (?)" and "incised by the mason Somala in Saṁvat 1207 on the full moon day of Kārttika, duing the reign of his glorious majesty, the supreme king of kings, Vijayapāla." The king cannot be identified with certainty. But Saṁvat 1207 corresponds to AD 1149–51. "This king," concludes the epigraphist, "certainly was the ruler of Mathurā at this period, and Jajja was one of his vassals. This much is absolutely certain, and the inscription also settles the date of at least one of the temples buried under the Keśava mound."[13]

---

[8]*Epigraphia Indica*, Vol. XXXII (1957–58), New Delhi, Reprint, 1987, p. 206.
[9]Ibid., p. 208.
[10]Ibid., pp. 208–09.
[11]*Epigraphia Indica*, Vol. I (1892), New Delhi, Reprint, 1983, p. 287.
[12]Ibid., p. 288.
[13]Ibid., p. 289.

Why Aurangzeb Destroyed the Temple

There is no substance in the Marxist statement that the temple was destroyed because it had "acquired considerable wealth" which attracted Aurangzeb's greed for booty or that the destruction of the temple was "politically motivated as well, for at the time when the temple was destroyed he faced problems with the Bundela as well as the Jat rebellions in the Mathura region." We have only to refer to contemporary records to see how these explanations are wide of the mark.

The temple of Keśavadeva was destroyed in January, 1670. This was done in obedience to an imperial *firmān* proclaimed by Aurangzeb on April 9, 1669. On that date, according to *Ma'sīr-i-Ālamgīrī*, "The Emperor ordered the governors of all provinces to demolish the schools and temples of the infidels and strongly put down their teaching and religious practices."[14] Jadunath Sarkar has cited several sources regarding the subsequent destruction of temples which went on all over the country, and right up to January 1705, two years before Aurangzeb died.[15]

None of the instances cited by him make any reference whatsoever to booty or the political problem of rebellion. The sole motive that stands out in every case is religious zeal. Our Marxist professors will find it very hard, if not impossible, to discover economic and/or political motives for all these instances of temple destruction. The alibis that they have invented in defence of Aurangzeb's destruction of the Keśavadeva temple are, therefore, only plausible, if not downright fraudulent. It is difficult to believe that the learned professors did not know of Auranzgeb's *firmān* dated April 9, 1669 and the large-scale destruction of Hindu temples that followed. If they did not, one wonders what sort of professors they are, and by what right they pronounce pontifically on this subject.

Putting the Cart Before the Horse

The veneer of plausiblility also comes off when we look into the chronology of Hindu rebellions in the Mathura region. We find no evidence that Aurangzeb was faced with any Hindu rebellion in that region when he destroyed the Keśavadeva temple. There was no Bundela uprising in 1670 when the Keśavadeva temple was destroyed. The first Bundela rebellion led by Jujhar Singh had been put down by December, 1635 in the reign of Shāh Jahān when that Rajput prince was killed

[14]Quoted by Jadunath Sarkar, op. cit., p. 186.
[15]Ibid., pp. 186–89.

and the ladies of his house-hold were forced into the Mughal harem. The second Bundela rebellion had ended with the suicide of Champat Rai in October, 1661. The third Bundela rebellion was still in the future. Champat Rai's son, Chhatrasal, had joined the imperial army sent against Shivaji in 1671 when Shivaji drew his attention to what was being done to the Hindus by Aurangzeb. It may also be pointed out that our professors stretch the Mathura region too far when they include Bundelkhand in it.

The professors have put the cart before the horse by holding the Jat rebellion in the Mathura region responsible for the destruction of the Keśavadeva temple. The Jats had risen in revolt under the leadership of Gokla (Gokul) *after* and not *before* Aurangzeb issued his *firmān* of April, 1969 ordering destruction of Hindu temples everywhere. This highly provocative *firmān* had come as a climax to several other happenings in the Mathura region. The Hindus of this region had been victims of Muslim high-handedness for a long time, particularly in respect of their women. Murshid Qulī Khān, the *faujdār* of Mathura who died in 1638, was notorious for seizing "all their most beautiful women" and forcing them into his harem. "On the birthday of Krishna," narrates *Ma'sīr-ul-Umara*, "a vast gathering of Hindu men and women takes place at Govardhan on the Jumna opposite Mathura. The Khan, painting his forehead and wearing *dhoti* like a Hindu, used to walk up and down in the crowd. Whenever he saw a woman whose beauty filled even the moon with envy, he snatched her away like a wolf pouncing upon a flock, and placing her in the boat which his men kept ready on the bank, he sped to Agra. The Hindu [for shame] never divulged what had happened to his daughter."[16]

Another notorious *faujdār* of Mathura was Abdu'n Nabī Khān. He plundered the people unscrupulously and amassed great wealth. But his worst offence was the pulling down of the foremost Hindu temple in the heart of Mathura and building a Jāmi' Masjid on its site. This he did in AD 1660–61. Soon after, in 1665, Aurangzeb imposed a pilgrim tax on the Hindus. In 1668, he prohibited celebration of all Hindu festivals, particularly Holi and Diwali. The Jats who rightly regarded themselves as the defenders of Hindu honour were no longer in a mood to take it lying.

It is true that the capture and murder of Gokul with fiendish cruelty

[16]Quoted by Ibid., pp. 193–94, The Jat rebellion is dealt with in detail by Girish Chandra Dwivedi in his book, *The Jats: Their Role in the Mughal Empire*, New Delhi, 1979.

and the forcible conversion of his family members to Islam, coincided with the destruction of the Keśavadeva temple. But there is no reason to suppose that the temple would have been spared if there was no Jat rebellion. There were no rebellions in the vicinity of many other temples which were destroyed at that time or at a later stage. The temples were destroyed in obedience to the imperial *firmān* and for no other reason.

The Logic of the Argument

The real worth of the defence of Aurangzeb put up by the professors becomes evident if we lead their argument for economic and political motives to its logical conclusion. The Keśavadeva temple was not the only place of worship which was wealthy. Many mosques and dargāhs and other places of Muslim worship were bursting with riches in Aurangzeb's time. But he is not known to have sought booty in any one of them. There were several rebellions led by Muslims against the rule of Aurangzeb. Some of these rebellions had their centres in places of Muslim worship. Yet Aurangzeb is not known to have destroyed any one of these places before or after suppressing the rebellions. So, even if we accept the economic and political motives for the destruction of Hindu temples, an irreducible minimum of the religious motive remains. That alone can explain the erection of an Īdgāh on the site of the Keśavadeva temple and taking away the idols to Agra for being trodden under foot by the faithful.

The Argument about Historicity

Now we can take up the last point by raising which the professors seem to clinch their case in defence of Aurangzeb. They question the historicity of Śrī Krishṇa and dismiss him as a mythological character who can have no place of birth. The implication is that Hindus are getting unduly excited by associating the Keśavadeva temple with the birth-place of Śrī Krishṇa and should cool down after discovering that the temple was built by a Rajput protege of Jahāngīr, at a non-descript place and on a much later date. This is a strange argument, to say the least. It means that the sanctity of a religious place declines in proportion to its dissociation from a historical personality. One wonders if the professors would extend the logic to Muslim *ziārats* and *qadam-sharīfs* which are associated with characters who cannot be traced in any history. Some of these *ziārats* have been built on the sites and from the debris of Hindu temples according to unimpeachable archaeological evidence. The *qadam-sharīfs* are without a doubt the Buddha's feet carved in the early phases of Buddhism and worshipped in subsequent ages by the Buddhists as well as the Hindus. The Ka'ba at Mecca was taken over by Muhammad because, according to him, it was built by Abraham in the first instance and occupied by the polytheists at a later stage. Should the Muslims take the desecration or demolition of the Ka'ba less seriously if they are told that Abraham has never figured in human history? There is no evidence that he did.

Of course, Śrī Krishṇa is a historical character which the professors can find out for themselves by reading Bankim Chandra, Śrī Aurobindo and many other savants who have, unlike them, studied the subject. But that is not the point. The Śrī Krishṇa for whom the Hindus really care is a far greater figure than the Śrī Krishṇa of history. What they really worship is the Śrī Krishṇa of mythology. There are many temples and places of pilgrimage all over India associated with this mythological Śrī Krishṇa. So are the various *śaktipīṭhas* associated with the limbs of Pārvatī scattered by Śiva during the course of his anguish over her death. So are the various *jyotirliṅgas* and most other places of Hindu pilgrimage. In fact, a majority of the renowned places of Hindu worship and pilgrimage have only mythology in support of their sanctity. Are the professors telling the Hindus that the desecration or destruction of these places should cause no heart-burn to them because the characters associated with these places are drawn from mythology, and that an iconoclast is badly needed in every case for blowing up the myth?

The Birth-Place of Śrī Rāma

Having cleared the "confusion" over the birth-place of Śrī Krishṇa, the professors proceed to clear a similar "confusion" regarding the birth-place of Śrī Rāma. We are ignoring their insinuation that the second "confusion" has been created "probably deliberately". The insinuation has its source in political polemics and not in academic propriety to which professors are expected to adhere. We are also ignoring the implication that Śrī Rāma being another mythological character is not entitled to a place of birth because, mercifully, the professors concede that a place called *Rāma-janmabhūmi* did exist at Ayodhya, and that it did not occupy the site of a Buddhist monastery demolished by the devotees of Śrī Rāma. We shall only examine the point they have raised, namely, that the mosque known as the Babari Masjid does not stand on the site of the *Rāma-janmabhūmi*.

The professors have referred us to a "Persian text of the mid-nineteenth century" which "states that the Babari mosque was adjacent to the Sita-ka-rasoi-ghar and was known as Rasoi-Sita mosque and adjoined the area associated with the birthplace of Rama". What they mean in plain language is that the real Babari Masjid, also known as Rasoi-Sita Masjid, has disappeared or been demolished by the Hindus at some stage, and that there is no substance in the current Hindu claim that the mosque known as the Babari Masjid at present stands on the site of a temple built on the *Rāma-janmabhūmi.*

This contention could have been examined satisfactorily if the professors had named the Persian text and told us whether, according to it, the Rasoi-Sita Masjid stood on the right or left of the Sita-ka-rasoi-ghar. We can, therefore, thank the professors only for admitting that the Muslims did raise a mosque on a spot which, we may be permitted to infer, was also sacred for the Hindus. But, at the same time, we cannot help wondering why the professors are at pains to pin-point the exact spot where Śrī Rāma was born instead of conceding that the temple built in his memory must have occupied a large area. Maps of the area in which the mosque now known as the Babari Masjid stands, show clearly that the site of the Sita-ka-rasoi-ghar is adjacent to the mosque. Is it not possible that what is now known as the Babari Masjid was also known as Rasoi-Sita Masjid in the mid-nineteenth century? Moreover, the mosque in dispute has been named as the Babari Masjid by the Muslims and not by the Hindus.

Thus the Persian text dragged in by the professors creates complications rather than clear the "confusion" which, according to the professors, exists in the Hindu mind. On the face of it, it looks like a deliberate attempt to side-track the issues involved. The suspicion gets strengthened when the professors go on to suggest that prior to the nineteenth century the dispute was not over the *Rāma-janmabhūmi* but over "the totally different site of Hanuman-baithak." No doubt the suggestion admits, although inadvertently, that there was a Hanuman temple at Ayodhya which also the Muslims had converted into a mosque. But we are trying to straighten the record regarding a mosque standing on the site of the *Rāma-janmabhūmi* temple.[17]

Finally, their thesis is that "acts of intolerance have been committed in India by followers of all religions." Having found it difficult to

[17]The Hindu case is presented in two publications of Voice of India — *Ram Janmabhoomi Vs. Babri Masjid.* by Koenraad Elst (1990) and *History Versus Casuistry: Evidence of the Ramajanmabhoomi Mandir presented by the Vishva Hindu Parishad to the Government of India in December-January 1990–91* (1991)

hide the atrocities committed by Islam in India, they have invented stories of Buddhist, Jain and Animist temples destroyed by the Hindus. We shall examine these stories in some detail at a later stage in this study. Here it should suffice to say that in their effort to whitewash Islam they have ended by blackening Hinduism. The exercise is devoid of all academic scruples and is no more than a neurotic exhibition of their deep-seated anti-Hindus animus.[18]

The Appropriate Context

What is most amazing about our Marxist professors, however, is that while they are never tired of preaching that facts of history should be placed in their proper context, they have studiously managed to miss the only context which explains simply and satisfactorily the destruction of Hindu temples by Islamic invaders. Our reference here is to the theology of Islam systematised on the basis of the Qu'rān and the Sunnah of the Prophet. This theology lays down loud and clear that it is a pious act for Muslims to destroy the temples of the infidels and smash their idols. Conversion of infidel temples into mosques wherever practicable, is a part of the same doctrine. We have presented this theology at some length in Section IV.

Destruction of idols and conversion of infidel places of worship into mosques became obligatory on Muslim conquerors and kings whenever they got the opportunity. The plunder which the iconoclasts obtained from infidel places of worship was not the main motive; that was only an additional bounty which Allāh had promised to bestow on them for performing pious deeds and earning religious merit. Those who want to know the relevant prescriptions of Islam should read the orthodox biographies of the Prophet, the orthodox collections of Hadīth, and the authentic commentaries by recognised imāms rather than swallow old wive's tales told by Marxist professors.

This is the simple and straightforward explanation why Muslim invaders of India destroyed Hindu temples on a large scale and converted many of them into mosques. The economic and political motives, invented by the Marxists, are not only far-fetched but also do not explain the destruction and/or conversion of numerous temples which contained no riches, and where no conspiracy could be conceived.

The Muslim apologists who have been in a hurry to borrow the Marxist explanation do not know what they are doing. The explanation

[18]See Appendix 4 for the Marxist proposition of placing Hinduism on the same level as Islam.

converts Islam into a convenient cover for brigandage and the greatest Muslim heroes into mere bandits. In the mouth of those Muslims who know what their religion prescribes vis-a-vis infidel places of worship, this apologetics is dishonest as well. They should have the honesty to admit the tenets of the religion to which they subscribe. It is a different matter whether those tenets can be defended on any spiritual or moral grounds. That is a subject on which Islam will have to do some introspection and hold a dialogue with Hinduism some day.

Finally, the professors want us to remember that "many Hindu temples were untouched during Aurangzeb's reign, and even some new ones were built". The underlying assumption is that Aurangzeb's writ ran in every nook and corner of India, all through his reign. But the assumption is unwarranted. There is plenty of evidence in Persian histories themselves that there were regions in which Hindu resistance to Aurangzeb's terror was too strong to be overcome even by repeated expeditions. It is no credit to Aurangzeb that the Hindus in those regions were able to save their old temples and also build some new ones. The Hindus all over north India were up in arms against the Muslim rule during Aurangzeb's long absence in the South. If they built some new temples, it was in spite of Aurangzeb. The subject needs a detailed scrutiny on the basis of concrete cases located in space and time. It must, however, be pointed out that the professors bid goodbye to all sense of proportion when they gloat on the few temples that survived or were newly built while they forget the large number of temples that were destroyed. They also forget that, in the present context, exceptions only prove the rule.

CHAPTER FIVE

SPREADING THE BIG LIE

According to the Marxist professors "what is really required is an investigation into the theory that both the Dera Keshav Rai temple and the Idgah were built on the site of a Buddhist monastery which appears to have been destroyed." Thank God, they have suggested it only as a theory; elsewhere in their writings they have not been that cautious. In fact, they have gone out of their way in spreading the Big Lie that the Hindus destroyed many Buddhist and Jain temples and monasteries in the pre-Islamic past. They have never been able to cite more than half-a-dozen instances of dubious veracity. But that has sufficed for providing a vociferous plank in the "progressive" party line. "If the descendants of Godse," writes the executive editor of a prestigious Marxist monthly, "think that every medieval mosque has been built after demolishing some temple, why should we stop at the medieval period? After all, Hindu kings had also got *a large number* of Jain and Buddhist temples destroyed. The Krishṇa temple at Mathurā rose on the ruins of a Buddhist monastery. There are hundreds of such places (that is, Hindu temples built on the ruins of Buddhist and Jain places of worship) in Karnataka, Rajasthān, Bihār and Uttar Pradesh."[1] The author of the article did not think it necessary to quote some instances. The proposition, he thought, was self-evident. Herr Goebbles, too, never felt the need of producing any evidence in support of his pronouncements.

It is unfortunate that some Buddhist and Jain scholars have swallowed this lie without checking the quality and quantity of the evidence offered. Some of these "scholars" are known for their "progressive" inclinations. But there are others who have become victims of a high-powered propaganda. The happiest people, however, have been the Christian missionaries and the apologists of Islam. Does it not, they say, blow up the bloody myth that Hinduism has a hoary tradition of religious tolerance and that all religions coexisted peacefully in this country before the advent of Islam and Christianity? We shall examine this canard exhaustively at a later stage in this study. For the present we are confining ourselves to the "evidence" offered in the context of the Keśavadeva temple. We reproduce below the relevant reports of the Archaeological Survey of India.

---

[1]Gautama Navalakhā, 'Bhakti Sāhitya kā Durupayoga', *Haṁsa*, Hindi monthly, New Delhi, June 1987, p. 21. Emphasis added.

"In 1853," writes Dr. J. Ph. Vogel, "regular explorations were started by General Cunningham on the Kaṭrā and continued in 1862. They yielded numerous sculptural remains; most important among them is an inscribed standing Buddha image (height 3'6") now in the Lucknow Museum. From the inscription it appears that this image was presented to the Yaśā-Vihāra in the Gupta year 230 (AD 549–50)...[2]

"The last archaeological explorations at Mathura were carried out by Dr. Fuhrer between the year 1887 and 1896. His chief work was the excavation of the Kaṅkālī Tīlā in the three seasons of 1888–91. He explored also the Kaṭrā site. Unfortunately, no account of his researches is available, except the meagre information contained in his Museum Reports for those years...The plates of which only a few are reproductions of photographs and the rest drawings, illustrate the sculptures acquired in the course of Dr. Fuhrer's excavations but do not throw much light on the explorations themselves...[3]

"He [Cunningham] proposes to identify Kesopura, the quarter in which the Kaṭrā is situated, with 'the Klisobora or Kaisobora of Arrian and the Calisobora of Pliny.' It is, however, evident that the Mohalla Kesopura was named after the shrine of Keso or Kesab (Skt. Keśava) Dev. This temple stood, as we noticed above, on the ruins of a Buddhist monastery which still existed in the middle of the sixth century. It is, therefore, highly improbable that the name Kesopura goes back to the days of Arrian.[4]

"All we can say from past explorations is the following: The Kaṭrā must have been the site of a Buddhist monastery named the Yaśā-Vihāra which was still extant in the middle of the sixth century. It would seem that in the immediate vicinity there existed a *stūpa* to which the Bhūtesar railing pillars belong. Dr. Fuhrer mentions indeed in one of his reports that, in digging at the back of Aurangzeb's mosque, he struck the procession path of a *stūpa* bearing a dedicatory inscription."[5]

Dr. Vogel returned to the theme in 1911–12. He wrote:

"The Keshab-Dev temple, of which the foundation can still clearly be traced stood again on earlier remains of Buddhist origin. This became at once apparent from General Cunningham's explorations on this site in the years 1853 and 1862, which opened the era of archaeological research at Mathurā. Among his finds was a standing Buddha image (4'

---

[2]Archaeological Survey of India, *Annual Report 1906-07*, p. 137.
[3]Ibid., p. 139.
[4]Ibid., p. 140.
[5]Ibid., pp. 140-41.

3.5"), now in the Lucknow Museum, bearing an inscription, which is dated in the Gupta year 230 (AD 549–50) and records that the image was dedicated by the Buddhist nun Jayabhaṭṭā at the Yaśā-Vihāra.

"Several Buddhist sculptures, mostly of the Kushāṇa period have since been discovered in the Kaṭrā mound. So that there can be little doubt, that it marks the site of an important monastic establishment. It was particularly 'one' find which seemed to call for further investigation. Dr. Fuhrer while describing his last exploration of the year 1896 on the Kaṭrā, says the following, 'About 50 paces to the north of this plinth [of the Keśavadeva Temple] I dug a trail trench, 80 feet long, 20 feet broad and 25 feet deep, in the hope of exposing the foundations and some of the sculptures of this Keśava temple. However, none of the hoped for Brahmanical sculptures and inscriptions were discovered, but only fragments belonging to an ancient *stūpa*. At a depth of 20 feet I came across a portion of the circular procession-path leading round this *stūpa*. On the pavement, composed of large red sandstone slabs, a short dedicatory inscription was discovered, according to which this *stūpa*, was repaired in samvat 76 by the Kushana King Vasushaka; unfortunately, I was unable to continue the work and lay bare the whole procession-path, as the walls of the brick structure, adjoining the Masjid are built right across the middle of this *stūpa*.'

"Unfortunately, the inscription referred to by Dr. Fuhrer was never published, nor were estampages of it known to exist. Since the discovery of the inscribed sacrificial post (*yūpa*) of Isāpur had established the fact that between Kanishka and Huvishka there reigned a ruler of the name of Vāsishka, it became specially important to verify the particulars given by Dr. Fuhrer in the above quoted note.

"The endeavours made by Pandit Radha Krishna to recover Dr. Fuhrer's inscription were not crowned with success. It is true, however, that on the spot indicated the remains of a brick *stūpa* honeycombed by the depredations of contractors came to light. This monument, however, cannot be assigned a date earlier than about the sixth century of our era. Of the circular procession path of red stone slabs mentioned in Dr. Fuhrer's report, no trace was found, but at a much higher level there was a straight causeway of stone referable to about the 12th or 13th century AD. Evidently it has nothing whatsoever to do with the *stūpa*. The causeway in question, which is 48' long, 4' 6" wide, runs straight from north to south and is constructed of large sandstone slabs roughly dressed and apparently obtained from different quarries. The size of these stones shows considerable variations, one measuring 6' 6" by 1'6" by 9" and another 4' 7" by 1' 7" by 9". The causeway consists of a double layer of these slabs laid three by three, the whole being very irregular. The slabs were bound with iron clamps, some of which still remain. Five of the stones are marked with a trident (*triśūl*).

"In course of excavation numerous sculptural fragments came to light mostly of a late date and apparently decorative remains of the Kesab Deb temple destroyed by Aurangzeb. Among earlier finds I wish only to mention a broken fourfold Jaina image (*pratimā sarvato bhadrikā*) with a fragmentary inscription in Brāhmī of the Kushan period."[6]

A perusal of these reports yields the following facts and conclusions:

1. General Cunningham's surmise about a Buddhist monastery being buried in the Kaṭrā mound was no more than a mere speculation. The speculation was based on the discovery of a loose sculpture and not on the laying bare of any foundations or other remains of a monastery. Can the subsequent discovery of a Jain sculpture at the same site be relied upon to say that a Jain monastery also lies buried there? It has to be noted that in Mathura many Brahmanical sculptures and architectural fragments have been found on sites such as the Jamālpur and Kaṅkālī mounds which are definitely known as Buddhist and Jain sites on the basis of foundations of monasteries etc., discovered there. No one has ever speculated that the Buddhist and Jain monuments at these sites were built on the ruins of Brahmanical temples.[7]
2. Dr. Vogel rejected General Cunningham's identification of the Kaṭrā site with Kesopura on the basis of the latter's speculation that a Buddhist monastery was buried under the Keśavadeva

---

[6]Ibid., *Annual Report* 1911-12, pp. 132-33.

[7]How much mistaken General Cunningham could be in his speculations sometimes is shown by Dr. R.C. Sharma who has been a Curator of the Museum at Mathura. "Sir Alexander Cunningham," he writes, "during his first exploration in 1853 found some pillars of a Buddhist railing at the site of Kaṭra Keshavadev renowned as birthplace of Lord Kṛṣṇa. Later he recovered a gateway from the same spot and a standing Buddha figure from a well recording the name of the monastery as *Yasā Vihāra*. He remarks, 'I made the first discovery of Buddhist remains at the temple of Kesau Ray in January 1853, when, after a long search I found a broken pillar of a Buddhist railing sculptured with the figure of Māyā Devī standing under the *Śāla* tree'. Cunningham was mistaken when he identified the lady on railing as Māyā Devī. Since it was the first discovery he thought the representation conveyed some special event. Now we know that the lady under tree was a common representation on the rail posts of Kuṣāṇa period and it does not specifically represent Māyā Devī" (R.C. Sharma, *Buddhist Art of Mathurā*, Delhi, 1984, p. 51).

temple. This was tantamount to proving what he had already assumed. With equal logic, he could have rejected General Cunningham's speculation about a Buddhist monastery and confirmed his identification of the Kaṭrā site with Kesopura. It seems that a pro-Buddhist and anti-Brahmanical bias, which was as dominant in his days as it is in our own, was responsible for his arbitrary choice from two equally plausible speculations on the part of the same explorer, namely, General Cunningham.

3. That a *stūpa* existed in the vicinity of the Keśavadeva temple is clear from the findings of Dr. Fuhrer as well as Pandit Radha Krishna. But Dr. Fuhrer's discovery of a circular procession path belonging to the *stūpa* and passing under the Kaṭrā mound was not confirmed by the digging undertaken by Pandit Radha Krishna. It seems that the large sandstone slabs which Dr. Fuhrer construed as belonging to the procession path of the *stūpa* belonged in fact to the causeway which was uncovered by Pandit Radha Krishna and which had nothing whatsoever to do with the *stūpa*. Obviously, Dr. Fuhrer was misled into another speculation because of his reliance on the earlier speculation by General Cunningham.
4. Dr. Fuhrer had surmised that the *stūpa* was repaired in the reign of Vāsishka, that is, in the first decade of the second century AD. This he had done on the basis of an inscription he claimed to have read on a slab in what he thought to be the circular procession path of the *stūpa*. He is not known to have copied the inscription, nor has it ever been published. Pandit Radha Krishna who excavated in 1911–12 with the specific purpose of discovering that inscription failed not only to find it but also the circular procession path. What is more, the *stūpa* which was the same as that seen by Dr. Fuhrer could not be assigned to a date earlier than the sixth century AD, that is, four centuries after the reign of Vāsishka!

That is the picture which emerges from the explorations and excavations undertaken at the Kaṭrā site by General Cunningham in 1853 and 1862, Dr. Fuhrer in 1896, and Pandit Radha Krishna in 1911–12. There is no positive evidence about the existence of a Buddhist edifice in the Kaṭrā mound. All that can be said is that a Buddhist *stūpa* was built in the vicinity of the site some time in the sixth century.

No trace of a Buddhist monastery or any other Buddhist monument was found in the extensive exploration and excavation undertaken by the Archaeological Survey of India at the Kaṭrā site during 1954–55, 1973–74, 1974–75, 1975–76 and 1976–77. None of the archaeologists who undertook the diggings has subscribed to the theory propounded earlier by General Cunningham, Dr. Fuhrer and Dr. Vogel and now by the Marxist professors. "Thirty eight sculptures," wrote R.C. Sharma in 1984, "saw their way to the Mathurā Museum in July 1954 when Sri K.D. Vajpeyi (later Professor) was the Curator. They were unearthed as a result of levelling and digging of the Kaṭrā site for renovating the birthplace of Lord Kṛṣṇa and were made over to the Museum by the Janmabhūmi Trust. Some other objects which were casually picked up by others from Kaṭrā site were also acquired. The finds include terracottas from Mauryan to Gupta periods, a few brick panels with creeper designs and several Brāhmanical objects ranging from Gupta to early Medieval age. The number of fragments of Viṣṇu figures is quite considerable and this suggests that a big Vaiṣṇava or Bhāgvata complex once stood on the site."[8]

The controversy should stand closed with what Professor Heinrich Luders, the great expert on Mathura, has to say on the subject. "Considering the well-known untrustworthiness of Dr. Fuhrer's reports," he writes, "there can be no doubt that the Vasuṣka inscription is only a product of his imagination."[9] Steven Rosen has accused Dr. Vogel of "attempted forgery" in editing the Morā Well inscription discovered by Cunningham in 1882. "Many early archaeologists in India," he writes, 'were Christian — and they made no bones about their motivation."[10] He adds, "Dr. Vogel in attempting to distort the Morā Well inscription was right in the line with many of his predecessors in the world of Indology and archaeology."[11]

II

It is welcome that the professors are prepared for an investigation for finding whether the Kaṭrā mound hides the remains of a Buddhist monastery under the remains of the Keśavadeva temple. Only a thorough excavation of the site on which the Īdgāh stands can settle the question. But it must be pointed out that the excavation may not stop at the Buddhist monastery if it is uncovered at all. If it is true, as they say, that Hindus and Buddhists were at daggers drawn in the pre-Islamic

[8]RC. Sharma, op. cit., pp. 83–84.

[9]Heinrich Luders, *Mathura Inscriptions*, Goettingen, 1961, p. 30.

[10]Steven Rosen, *Archaeology and the Vaishnava Traditions: The Pre-Christian Roots of Krishna Worship*, Calcutta, 1989, pp. 25–26.

[11]Ibid., p. 28.

period, they should be prepared for the possibility that the Buddhist monastery itself was built on the ruins of an earlier Hindu temple. After all, the most ancient and prolific Indian literature associates Mathura with the birth and youth of Śrī Krishṇa, while the Buddhist associations with Mathura do not go beyond Greek and Kushāṇa times. We have already quoted Romila Thapar regarding the Keśavadeva tradition going back to the Mauryan period. It is quite plausible on the hypothesis of the professors that some Greek or Kushāṇa patron of Buddhism destroyed a Hindu temple which stood at Śrī Krishṇa's place of birth before he raised a Buddhist monastery on the site. Of course, we do not subscribe to this story of Hindu–Buddhist conflict. There is no evidence that the Hindus ever destroyed a Buddhist place of worship or vice versa. We are only proposing a test for the Marxist hypothesis.

It is intriguing indeed that whenever archaeological evidence points towards a mosque as standing on the site of a Hindu temple, our Marxist professors start seeing a Buddhist monastery buried underneath. They also invent some Śaiva king as destroying Buddhist and Jain shrines whenever the large-scale destruction of Hindu temples by Islamic invaders is mentioned. They never mention the destruction of big Buddhist and Jain complexes which dotted the length and breadth of India, Khurasan, and Sinkiang on the eve of the Islamic invasion, as testified by Hüen Tsang. We should very much like to know from them as to who destroyed the Buddhist and Jain temples and monasteries at Bukhara, Samarqand, Khotan, Balkh, Bamian, Kabul, Ghazni, Qandhar, Begram, Jalalabad, Peshawar, Charsadda, Ohind, Taxila, Multan, Mirpurkhas, Nagar-Parkar, Sialkot, Srinagar, Jalandhar, Jagadhari, Sugh, Tobra, Agroha, Delhi, Mathura, Hastinapur, Kanauj, Sravasti, Ayodhya, Varanasi, Sarnath, Nalanda, Vikramasila, Vaishali, Rajgir, Odantapuri, Bharhut, Champa, Paharpur, Jagaddal, Jajnagar, Nagarjunikonda, Amravati, Kanchi, Dwarasamudra, Devagiri, Bharuch, Valabhi, Girnar, Khambhat, Patan, Jalor, Chandravati, Bhinmal, Didwana, Nagaur, Osian, Ajmer, Bairat, Gwalior, Chanderi, Mandu, Dhar, etc., to mention only the more prominent ones. The count of smaller Buddhist and Jain temples destroyed by the swordsmen of Islam runs into hundreds of thousands. There is no dearth of mosques and other Muslim monuments which have buried in their masonry any number of architectural and sculptural pieces from Buddhist and Jain monuments.

It is not so long ago that Western scholars, even Christian missionaries, used to credit the Hindus at least with one virtue, namely, religious tolerance. Hindus had received universal acclaim for providing refuge and religious freedom to the Jews, the Christians, and the Parsis who had run away from persecutions at the hands of Christian and Islamic rulers in West Asia and Iran. It was also conceded that though Brahmanical, Buddhist and Jain sects and subsects had had heated discussions among themselves and used even strong language for their adversaries, the occasions when they exchanged physical blows were few and far between. The recent spurt of accusations that Hindus also were bigots and vandals like Christians and Muslims, seems to be an after-thought. Apologists who find it impossible to whitewash Christianity and Islam, are out to redress the balance by blackening Hinduism. Till recently, the Marxists were well-known for compiling inventories of capitalist sins in order to hide away the crimes committed in Communist countries.

The professors see some retributive justice in the destruction of the Keśavadeva temple by Aurangzeb because they believe that the temple was built on the ruins of a Buddhist monastery destroyed by the Hindus in the pre-Islamic past. It does not speak very highly of whatever moral sense the professors may possess that they should justify or explain away the wrong done by someone during one period in terms of another wrong done by someone else at some distant date. The whole argument is tantamount to saying that the murder of A by B is justified or should be explained away because the great-great-great grandfather of A had murdered C!

But after all is said about the Marxist professors, we must admit the merit of their last point, namely, “the question of limits to the logic of restoration of religious sites.” Our plea is that the question can be answered satisfactorily only when we are prepared to face facts and a sense to proportion is restored. That is exactly what this study intends to do.

SECTION III

FROM THE HORSE'S MOUTH

CHAPTER SIX

THE EPIGRAPHIC EVIDENCE

Commenting on the history of Central Asia, Heinrich Zimmer writes: "During the sixth and early seventh centuries AD the whole tract was controlled by Turkish rulers, but in the course of the seventh, with increasing strength of the T'ang Emperors, China gained control. Finally, however, under the onslaught of Islam, from the eighth century to the tenth, both Buddhist and Manichaean as well as the Nestorian Christian culture and monuments of the region were destroyed."[1]

Coming to North India, he continues: "In the north very little survives of the ancient edifices that were there prior to the Muslim conquest: only a few mutilated religious sites remain[2].... It is clear from Indian literature that both temples and images must have existed in the second century BC and perhaps earlier. Very little architectural evidence remains, however, antedating the epoch of the Gupta dynasty (c. AD 320–650), for it was precisely in the Ganges Valley, the central and chief area of the Gupta empire, that the Muslim empire flourished a millennium later and most of the monuments above ground were destroyed by the sectarian zeal of Islam. The oldest stone ruins that have been found represent not the beginnings of a style, but fully developed forms."[3]

He is specific about the destruction of Buddhism in India. "Since the earliest important body of Indian art surviving to us," he says, "stems from the century of Aśoka, it is pre-dominantly Buddhist. During subsequent periods, however, Buddhist and Hindu (Brahmanical) themes alternate in rich profusion. The two traditions flourished side by side, even sharing colleges and monasteries, for nearly two millenniums, until about the height of the Muslim conquest (c. AD 1200), Buddhism disappeared from the land of its birth."[4]

By now there are hundreds of publications which provide detailed studies of the architecture and sculpture of many Hindu monuments from all over India. But only a few of them, mostly written by foreigners, state clearly that what have been studied are heaps of ruins dug out by archaeologists from under tell-tale mounds. Hindu writers, by and

---

[1]Heinrich Zimmer, *Art of Indian Asia*, Princeton, Paperback Edition, 1983, Vol. I, p. 201.

[2]Ibid., p. 246.

[3]Ibid., p. 270.

[4]Ibid., p. 5n.

large, leave the impression as if they have studied monuments which stand intact and in all their original majesty. It is only when we come to the plates that the truth dawns upon us. What we find there staring us in the face are mostly ruins with architectural fragments and mutilated sculptures lying scattered on the surface or brought up from underneath.

The travels of Buddhist pilgrims from China and the pre-Islamic epigraphic records on stones and copper plates tell us how many temples and monasteries stood at what place and at what time. Histories written by medieval Muslim historians inform us as to who made these monuments disappear and when. The two sources, taken together, present a total picture which historians have so far studied in separate parts.

Hindus are famous (or notorious) for their poor sense of history as Christians, Muslims and the modern Westerners understand it. Hindus of medieval India were no exception. They have left no record of what happened to their places of worship and pilgrimage at the hands of Islamic iconoclasm. We do come across descriptions of the Muslim behaviour pattern in the Hindu literature from that period. An invariable ingredient of that pattern is the destruction of temples and the desecration of idols. Accounts relating to destruction of particular temples at particular dates and places are very rare. That sort of detailed evidence comes almost entirely from medieval Muslim sources, literary and epigraphic. Archaeological explorations and excavations in modern times have only confirmed and supplemented that evidence.

Times have changed and so also some moral standards of mankind. Religious tolerance is a value which is cherished today universally by the dominant intellectual elite of the world. Muslim theologians, scholars and politicians in present-day India, therefore, want us to believe that Islam stands for religious tolerance and that there was never a time when it interfered by means of force with the religious beliefs or practices of other people. They resent any reference whatsoever to the destruction of Hindu temples by Muslim invaders and rulers in medieval India. Leftist professors and politicians who subscribe to what they describe as Secularism, dismiss this significant chapter in medieval India's history as a canard spread by "Hindu communalists". As most of these worthies happen to be Hindus by accident of birth, they add considerable weight to Muslim assertions.

There was, however, a time not so long ago when Muslim theologians prescribed and Muslim swordsmen practised destruction of Hindu temples[5] on a large scale. Hundreds of Muslim historians have credited their heroes with what they rightly regarded as a pious performance according to the principal tenets of Islam. Most of these histories, written in India as well as elsewhere in the Islamic world, have been printed and translated in one or more of the modern languages. They are on the shelves of public and private libraries all over the world. Then there are inscriptions in Arabic and Persian which proclaim the destruction of Hindu temples or their conversion into mosques with considerable pride. These, too, have been deciphered, translated and published by archaeological surveys covering India, Central Asia, Eastern Iran, Afghanistan, Pakistan and Bangladesh. They leave us in no doubt about one of the favourite pastimes of pious Muslim princes in all these countries which constituted at one time the vast cradle of Hindu culture.

In this and the following chapter we shall present evidence of temple destruction from Islamic sources which we have been able to reach within limits of our resources. Many sources have remained untapped. It is hoped that future scholars will fill the gaps in what is a very important subject in the domain of religious studies. Destroying places of worship of the conquered people has been an important aspect of Christianity and Islam. But religious studies in the West have so far neglected this aspect because of their Christian bias. Religious studies in India have failed to take it up partly because we follow the Western patterns of research but mostly because we subscribe to a mistaken notion of Secularism. Secularism arose in the modern West as a revolt against the closed theology of Christianity which had acquired a stranglehold on the State; in India, unfortunately, 'Secularism' has become the biggest single protector of closed theologies promoted by Christianity and Islam.

There will be frequent references to Muslim kings and dynasties in this narrative. Appendix 1 can be consulted for placing every reference in its proper historical context. At a later stage in this study we shall follow the trail of Islamic invasions as they advanced towards different parts of the Hindu homeland and worked havoc all along their path. That will facilitate an understanding of the evidence from modern archaeological explorations and excavations which we shall present subsequently.

---

[5]The word "Hindu" has been used throughout this book to denote all schools of *Sanātana Dharma* — Brahmanical, Buddhist, and Jain. See Appendix 3 for how the words "Hindu" and "Hinduism" have been made to mean what they never meant.

There are many Muslim monuments all over India which provide unmistakable evidence that materials from demolished Hindu temples have been used in their construction. Most of them carry inscriptions in Arabic or Persian stating when they were built and by whom. Some of these inscriptions, installed in mosques, proclaim that the mosques occupy the sites of Hindu temples which were destroyed. Others say that temple materials were used in the construction of the mosques. Similar inscriptions on stone slabs lying loose or not *in situ* have been discovered in many places; it is difficult to determine as to on what mosques or other Muslim monuments they were installed. It is a safe bet that many more inscriptions which refer to destruction of Hindu temples and construction of mosques etc., remain undiscovered or undeciphered or unpublished. Epigraphists in secular India do not seem to be keen or scrupulous in searching and publishing evidence which compromises the picture of this country as a "haven of communal amity and peace before the advent of the British."

We give below some instances of inscriptions discovered and copied quite some time ago but not published so far:

1. An Arabic inscription was discovered in the Jāmi' Masjid at Srikakulam in Andhra Pradesh in 1953–54. It says that the idol was broken and the mosque constructed by Sher Muhammad Khān Ghāzī in AH 1051 (AD 1641–42). Another inscription in the same place says that this Sher Muhammad Khān was given the title of Fīrūz Jang by Sultān Abdullāh Qutb Shāh of Golconda in AH 1055 (AD 1645–46).[6] The inscription has not been published so far.
2. A Persian inscription on the entrance gateway of a mosque at Nuh in the Gurgaon District of Haryana states that the founda-tion of this mosque was laid by Bahādur Khān Nāhar in the reign of Muhammad Shāh, son of Fīrūz Shāh (Tughlaq), from the materials of a Hindu temple in village Sainthali where Hindus used to assemble in large numbers every year. The *qāzī* of Nauganwa made a representation to Bahādur Khān Nāhar who destroyed the temple and completed the mosque in AH 803 (AD 1400).[7] This inscription has yet to be published though it was discovered in 1963–64.
3. Another Persian inscription discovered in the Jāmi' Masjid at Ritpur in the Amraoti District of Maharashtra proclaims that the

[6]*Annual Report of Indian Epigraphy* 1953-54, C-70 and C-71.
[7]Ibid., 1963–64, D-286.

mosque which was originally built by Aurangzeb on the site of a Hindu temple, having become desolate through passage of time, was reconstructed in AH 1295 (AD 1878) with the help of contributions raised by the local Muslims.[8] This inscription discovered in 1964–65 has not been published so far.

4. An inscription discovered in 1978–79 on the facade of the Jāmi' Masjid in Mahalla Sunhat at Balasore in Orissa states that in AH 1079 (AD 1668–69) a mob of Muslim mendicants (*faqīrs*) led by Tālib stormed and set fire to the temple of Śrī Chaṇḍī which was being resorted to by the Hindus. Five years later, the local *faujdār* built the mosque on the same site.[9] This inscription, too, remains unpublished.
5. An inscription in the Jāmi' Masjid at Tadpatri in Andhra Pradesh records that the mosque was constructed on the site of a temple by Maḥmūd for offering prayers to Allāh. The inscription dated AH 1107 (AD 1695) was discovered in 1980–81.[10] It is not yet published. We do not know anything about Maḥmūd who performed this pious deed in the reign of Aurangzeb.

Similar inscriptions are known to exist in some mosques which are still in use. But they cannot be copied because they have been covered with plaster. Years ago, Dr. Bloch had seen an inscription in the *Patthar-kī-Masjid* at Patna, the capital of Bihar, stating that the materials for the mosque were obtained from a Hindu temple at Majhauli (now in the Gorakhpur District of Uttar Pradesh).[11] The temple was demolished in AH 1036 (AD 1626) by Prince Parwiz, a son of the Mughal emperor Jahāngīr. "I made the car stop," writes Syed Hasan Askari, "and took my friends to the upper part of the historic *Patthar-ki-Masjid*. One of my American friends was an Arabist, but there was nothing for him to read, for the demoralised custodians had the inscription plastered with cement, considering that it contained provocative references."[12] Some friends of this author who visited the Jāmi' Masjid at Sambhal in the Moradabad District of Uttar Pradesh had the same experience when they expressed a desire to have a look at the inscriptions. This mosque was built in AD 1526 by an officer of Bābur on the site and from the materials of the local Hari Mandir.

---

[8]Ibid., 1964–65, D-123. The date is significant. As late as AD 1878, Muslims in Maharashtra took pride in proclaiming that a Jāmi' Masjid occupied the site of a demolished Hindu temple.

[9]Ibid., 1978–79, C-56.

[10]Ibid., 1980–81, C-14.

[11]Archaeological Survey of India, *Annual Report* 1906–07, p. 196.

[12]Qeyamuddin Ahmad (ed.), *Patna through the Ages*, New Delhi, 1988, p. 64.

It may also be mentioned that similar inscriptions which have been published by the archaeological surveys in countries outside the present-day precincts of India have remained beyond our reach because of the paucity of our means.

The inscriptions that we present below have been deciphered for the most part by learned Muslim epigraphists and placed in their proper historical context. The Archaeological Survey of India has published their fascimilies in its learned journals. They are being presented in a chronological order with reference to the dates they carry and not in the order in which they were discovered or published.

1. Delhi

This inscription can be seen over the inner eastern gateway of the Quwwat al-Islām Masjid near the Qutb Mīnār. It is *in situ*. Its language is Persian. It states:

"This fort was conquered and this Jāmi' Masjid built in the months of the year 587 by the Amīr, the great, the glorious commander of the Army, Qutb-ud-daula wad-dīn, the Amīr-ul-umarā Aibeg, the slave of the Sultān, may God strengthen his helpers! The materials (?) of 27 idol temples, on each of which 2,000,000 Deliwāl had been spent were used in the (construction of) this mosque. God the Great and Glorious may have mercy on that slave, every one who is in favour of the good (?) builder prays for this faith."[13]

The Amīr mentioned in the inscription was Qutbu'd-Dīn Aibak, a slave of Shihabu'd-Dīn or Muizzu'd-Dīn Muhammad bin Sām popularly known as Muhammad Ghūrī. Aibak died at Lahore in 1210. He had crowned himself at the same place in 1206 and is counted as the first sultān of the Slave or Mamlūk Dynasty.

The date AH 587 mentioned in the inscription presents a problem. It corresponds to AD 1191 while it is indisputable according to all sources that Delhi came under Muslim occupation for the first time in 1192, after the second battle of Tarain. Moreover, Delhi like Ajmer, was left at that time in the hands of a Hindu prince who was to rule as a tributary of the Ghurid empire. Soon after, Delhi was besieged by a Hindu army under the leadership of Jhat Rai, a Chauhan general. Qutbu'd-Dīn Aibak whom Muhammad Ghūrī had left in charge of his Indian conquests had to rush back from Meerut which he had captured in the meanwhile. He was able to reoccupy Delhi and drive away the Hindu prince only in 1193. It is difficult to say whether the destruction of the

[13] *Epigraphia Indo-Moslemica*, 1911-12, p. 13.

Hindu temples and construction of the mosque mentioned in the inscription took place during the first occupation in 1192 or the second occupation in 1193. It is surmised that it could not have happened while Delhi was in charge of a Hindu prince, though it is not a very strong argument; the Hindu prince must have been a helpless witness of what the conquerors did. The only thing that is certain is that the mosque could not have been built in 1191 when Delhi was still in the hands of an unconquered Hindu king.

The epigraphist has tried to solve the puzzle. "This inscription," he writes, "exhibits the titles which he had assumed in 602 when he received his manumission from the ruler of Ghaznī. Before that date, as long as his master was alive, there was nothing to prevent him from inscribing his own name on any building he liked, but he could have done so only if he included the name of his overlord in the record. Now in our inscription Shihabuddīn's name is not mentioned, nor does Qutbuddīn appear in it as anything higher than the Amīr-ul-Umarā. This leads us to the conclusion that the inscription was put up after Qutbuddīn's death by order of some ruler, who wished Qutbuddīn's memory to be preserved as the conqueror of Delhi, but who had no interest in having it stated that Shihabuddīn was his sovereign at that time. Had Qutbuddīn's descendants ruled at Delhi, they might have preferred to assign to him the titles he assumed as an independent ruler; but his successors were not of his lineage.... How long after Qutbuddīn's death it was put up, it is difficult to say. But a *terminus ante quem* is furnished by Ibn Battūtā who read it when at Delhi during the reign of Muhammad Tughlaq Shāh."[14] It is surmised that the inscription was installed in the reign of Shamsu'd-Dīn Iltutmish (AD 1210–1236) and the date on it was somehow bungled.

There is thus no doubt that the inscription is very old. Ibn Battūta had reached Delhi in AD 1334 and seen the mosque immediately after his arrival. "On the site of this mosque," he writes, "there was a *budkhāna*, that is an idol-house. After the conquest of Delhi it was turned into a mosque."[15] He also makes a mistake about the date of the conquest which he says was given to him by the Sadr-i-Jahān, chief justice of Hind and Sind. But he confirms that "I read that date in an inscription on the arch of the great congregational mosque there."[16]

---

[14]Ibid., p. 14.

[15]*The Rehalā of Ibn Battūta*, translated into English by Mahdi Hussain, Baroda, 1976, p. 27.

[16]Ibid., p. 32.

2. Vijapur

This town is the headquarters of a Taluka in the Mehsana District of Gujarat. The Manṣūrī Masjid in the town has been "entirely reconstructed in the past decade or so, but the inscribed tablet from the old mosque has been retained and fixed above the central *miḥrāb*."[17] The Persian inscription reads as follows:

"The Blessed and Exalted Allāh says, 'And verily, mosques are for Allāh only; hence invoke not anyone else with Allāh.' This edifice was (originally) built by the infidels. After the advent (lit. time) of Islām, it was converted into (lit. became) a mosque. Sermon was (delivered here) for sixty-seven years. Due to the sedition of the infidels, it was again destroyed. When during the reign of the Sultān of the time, Aḥmad, the affairs of each *Iqtā* attained magnificence, Bahādur, the Sarkhail, once again carried out repairs. Through the generosity of Divine munificence, it became like new."[18]

The inscription does not mention the date when the Hindu temple was destroyed and a mosque built on its site, nor the date when the mosque was repaired after the restoration of Muslim authority. "The reconstruction," comments the epigraphist, "must have obviously taken place at a time when Sultān Aḥmad Shāh had established his unquestioned sway over that region, that is to say, in about 1428. Again, it is not easy to determine when the Hindu building was first used as a mosque. It is reasonable to think that after the conquest of Gujarāt, and the consolidation of Muslim rule in the province, by 'Alāu'd-Dīn Khaljī, the building might have been used as a place of Muslim worship and it was used as such till the time when, about three quarters of a century later, sometime towards the end of the fourteenth century synchronising with the defiance of central authority by the Gujarāt governor Malik Mufarrīh, the mosque was desecrated or destroyed."[19]

The reference to sermon being delivered in the mosque indicates that it was a Jāmi' Masjid. The Hindu temple, too, it means must have been a major temple. Muslim iconoclasts generally used the sites of the most important Hindu temples for raising Jāmi' Masjids.

3. Chittaurgarh

At present this place is the headquarters of a District of the same name in Rajasthan. But in medieval times it had become famous on

---

[17]*Epigraphia Indica—Arabic and Persian Supplement*, 1974, p. 10.
[18]Ibid., p. 11.
[19]Ibid., p. 12.

account of its very strong fort with which was associated the glory of Mewar. It was occupied by Muslims for the first time in AD 1303 after a seize of eight months by 'Alāu'd-Dīn Khaljī (AD 1296–1310), the second sultān of the Khaljī dynasty of Delhi.

At a distance of about one mile outside the Delhi Gate of the fort there is a tomb known as that of Ghaibī Pīr. Opposite to the tomb is a Muslim graveyard in which there is a small one-wall mosque. The prayer niche of the mosque carries a Persian inscription of which only a small portion has survived. The learned epigraphist has read it as follows after restoring some words by conjecture: "He constructed the congregational mosque. There was temple lying in ruins.'[20]

The inscription is not *in situ* as it belongs to a Jāmi' Masjid which this small mosque is not. The epigraphist thinks that the tablet bearing the inscription seems to be a fragment of another tablet fixed in the west wall of the tomb of Ghaibī Pīr. The second tablet bears another inscription which mentions the name Bu'l Muzaffar, the second Sikandar, that is, 'Alāu'd-Dīn Khaljī, and the year AD 1310.[21] "If this guess is correct," the epigraphist concludes, "it would mean that 'Alāu'd-Dīn had ordered the construction in Chitor, of a congregational mosque, which was completed on the day of Sacrifice, the 10th of Dhi'l-Hijja of the year AH 709 (11 May AD 1310). Needless to say, no trace remains of any old mosque in Chitor today."[22]

There is another conclusion drawn by the epigraphist after his conjectural restoration of the first inscription. "It is also interesting to note," he writes, "provided of course I am not wrong in my conjectural reading of the second hemistich, that the said Jāmi' mosque was constructed at the site of a temple which was then lying in ruins.. This is particularly important as showing that, not always as is generally supposed, the Hindu buildings were pulled down to provide materials for mosques and other similar monuments."[23] We find it difficult to agree. The conjectural reading, "lying in ruins," is not the only possible reading. It can as well be read as "made into ruins", which is the standard expression used in many other inscriptions.

4. Manvi

It is the headquarters of a Taluka of the same name in the Raichur District of Karnataka. A mosque in this place has a Persian inscription

[20]*Epigraphia Indica—Arabic and Persian Supplement*, 1959-60, p. 73.
[21]Ibid., p. 72.
[22]Ibid., p. 73.
[23]Ibid., p. 72.

fixed above its door. It reads as follows:

"He (Allāh) is Omniscient. Praise be to Allāh that by the decree of the Nourisher, a mosque has been converted out of a temple as a sign of religion, in the reign of the world-conquering emperor, the king who is asylum of the Faith and possessor of the crown, whose kingdom is young (i.e. flourishing), viz. Fīrūz Shāh Bahmanī, who is the cause of exuberant spring in the garden of religion, Abu'l-Fath the king who conquered (lit. on horseback). After the victory of the emperor, the chief of chiefs, Safdar (lit. the valiant commander) of the age, received (the charge of) the fort. The builder of this noble place of prayer is Muhammad Zaḥīr Aqchī, the pivot of the Faith. He constructed in the year eight hundred and nine from the Migration of the Chosen (prophet Muhammad) this Ka'ba like memento."[24]

The year AH 809 corresponds to AD 1406–07. Fīrūz Shāh Bahmanī (AD 1397–1422) was the eighth ruler of this independent Muslim dynasty established by 'Alāu'd-Dīn Bahmanī in AD 1347. The capital of Fīrūz Shāh was at Gulbarga. It was shifted to Bidar by his son, Ahmad Shāh Bahmanī, some time about AD 1425.

5. Dhar

This is a famous town in the Malwa region of Madhya Pradesh, and head-quarters of a district of the same name. It was the capital of the renowned Bhoja Parmāra who ruled between AD 1000 and 1055. It has a mausoleum known to be that of Shykh 'Abdullāh Shāh Changāl, now in ruins. The doorway of the entrance to the mausoleum has a long inscription in Persian which, after singing fulsome praises of the Shykh, says:

"This centre became Muhammadan first by him (and) all the banners of religion were spread.... This lion-man came from the centre of religion to this old temple with a large force. He broke the images of the false deities, and turned the idol temple into a mosque. When Rāi Bhoj saw this, through wisdom he embraced Islām with the family of his brave warriors. This quarter became illuminated by the light of the Muhammadan law, and the customs of the infidels became obsolete and abolished. Now this tomb since those days has become the famous pilgrimage-place of the world. Graves from their oldness became levelled (to the ground), (and) there remained no mound on any grave. There was [no place] also for the retirement, wherein the distressed *dervish*

[24]*Epigraphia Indica — Arabic and Persian Supplement,* 1962, p. 58.

could take rest.... The Khaljī king Maḥmūd Shāh who is such that by his justice the world has become adorned like paradise; he built afresh this old structure, and this house with its enclosure again became new.... From the *hijra* it was 859 (AD 1455) that its (the building's) date was written anew..."[25]

The inscription was put up by Maḥmūd Shāh Khaljī of Malwa, who overthrew the independent Ghurī dynasty of that province in AD 1436 and ruled as the founder of the independent Khaljī dynasty of Malwa till 1469. Nothing is known about 'Abdullāh Shāh Changāl except that he hailed from Medina and was one of the earliest crusaders of Islam in Malwa. G. Yazdani who has published and translated this inscription speculates that "Abdullāh belonged to the army of Maḥmūd of Ghaznī who fought with Rājā Bhoja" and though he "might have converted only a few Hindus to Islām, after a period of four hundred years, can easily have been believed to have converted Rājā Bhoja with all his family and others to Islām."[26] It is, however, more probable, as some other scholars have surmised, that the Hindu king was Bhoja II who ascended the throne at Dhar in AD 1283 and during whose reign Jalālu'd-Dīn Khaljī (AD 1290–1296) of Delhi is known to have invaded Malwa. In that case Abdullāh Shāh Changāl seems to have been a Muslim missionary who accompanied the army of Islam from Delhi, destroyed a Hindu temple, built a mosque in its place, and forced the Hindu king to profess the faith of the victor.

6. Malan

This is now a small village in the Palanpur Taluka of the Banaskantha District of Gujarat. But in the reign of Maḥmūd Shāh I, also known as Maḥmūd Begḍhā (AD 1458–1511), of Gujarat, it was the seat of a Thana and had a Fort. That is why the place has a Jami' Masjid. A Persian inscription, fixed on the central *mihràb* of the mosque, reads as follows:

"I seek refuge in Allāh from (the mischief of) the accursed Satan (and begin) in the name of Allāh, the Beneficent, the Merciful. Praise be to Allāh! Allāh the Blessed and Exalted says, 'And verily the mosques are for Allāh only; hence, invoke not anyone else with Allāh.'[27] (The prophet), on him be peace, says 'He who builds a mosque in the world, the Exalted Allāh builds for him a palace in Paradise.' In

[21]*Epigraphia Indo-Moslemica,* 1909–10, pp. 4–5.
[26]Ibid., p. 1.
[27]Qur'ān, 72.18.

the auspicious time of the government and peaceful time of Maḥmūd Shāh, son of Muhammad Shāh, the sultān, the Jami', mosque was constructed on the hill of the fort of Mālūn (or Mālwan) by Khān-i-A'zam Ulugh Khān, may Allāh prolong his life for justice, generosity and benevolence, at the request of the thānadār Kabīr, (son of Diyā), the building was constructed by a servant of Ulugh Khān (who is) magnanimous, just, generous, brave (and who) suppressed the wretched infidels. He eradicated the idol-houses and mine of infidelity, along with the idols in the enemy's country with the blow of the sword, and made ready this abode with different kinds of stone, marble and *marim* (?). He made its walls and doors out of the stone of the idols; the back of every stone became the place for prostration of the believers... the date was Thursday, fifth of the month of Rajab of the year eight hundred and sixty at the time (5th April, AD 1462)."[28]

At the end of the inscription, we find a verse from the Qur'ān (73.20). It says, "And whatever of good you send on beforehand for yourselves, you will find it with Allāh—that is the best and greatest in reward. And ask forgiveness of Allāh. Surely, Allāh is Forgiving, Merciful."

Khān-i-A'zam Ulugh Khān was the title conferred upon 'Alāu'd-Dīn Suhrāb, the Governor of Sultanpur, by Qutbu'd-Dīn Ahmad Shāh or Ahmad Shāh II (AD 1451–1458) of Gujarat. He "is last heard of as being sent to fetch Prince Fath Khān to be crowned as Maḥmūd Shāh I in AH 862 or 863,"[29] that is, AD 1457 or 1458.

7. Amod

It is the headquarters of a Taluka of the same name in the Bharuch District of Gujarat. Above the central *mihrāb* of its Jāmi' Masjid there is a Persian inscription providing particulars of its construction. It reads as follows:

"Allāh and His grace. When divine favour was bestowed on Khalīl Shāh, he constructed the Jāmi' Masjid for the decoration of Islām; he ruined the idol-house and temple of the polytheists, (and) completed the Masjid and pulpit in its place. Without doubt, his building was accepted by Allāh. *What a pleasing edifice* became the calculation of its year."[30]

The italicised portion of the last line is a chronogram which yields the year AH 911 corresponding to AD 1505–06. Khalīl Shāh was the

---

[28]*Epigraphia Indica—Arabic and Persian Supplement*, 1963, pp. 28–29.
[29]Ibid., p. 27.
[30]*Epigraphia Indo-Moslemica*, 1933–34, p. 36.

third son of Sultān Mahmūd Begḍhā of Gujarat. At the time he constructed the Jāmi‘ Masjid at Amod, he was the Governor of Baroda. He succeeded Begḍhā in AD 1511 as Muzaffar Shāh II and ruled till 1526.

8. Narwar

It is a town in the Shivpuri District of Madhya Pradesh. Inside its fort there is a Muslim place of pilgrimage known as the shrine of Shāh Madār. An inscription from this shrine was removed to the Archaeological Museum at Gwalior. Written partly in Arabic and partly in Persian, it reads:

"Dilāwar Khān, the chief among the king's viceroys, caused this mosque to be built which is like a place of shelter for the favourites. Infidelity has been subdued, and Islām has triumphed because of him. The idols have bowed (to him) and the temples have been laid waste on account of him. The temples have been razed to the ground along with their foundations, and mosques and worship houses are flowing with riches."[31]

The mosque to which the inscription refers was built in AH 960 (AD 1552) when Islām Shāh, the second king of the Sūr dynasty founded by Sher Shāh in 1538, was the reigning sultān. He was the son of Sher Shāh and ruled from AD 1545 to 1554. The inscription was composed by Sayyid Ahmad and written by Nazīr Shattārī. Both of them belonged to the Shattārī sect of Sufism. An outstanding Sufi of this sect, Shykh Muhammad Ghaus, had settled down at Gwalior before the invasion of Bābur and helped the latter to seize the fort of Gwalior in AD 1527. His services have been recognized by Bābur in his memoirs.[32] The Shykh's shrine inside the fort is reported to have replaced a Hindu temple. He had received great favours from Bābur (AD 1526–1530) and Humāyūn (AD 1530–1538 and 1555–1556). Akbar (AD 1556–1605) "revered the Shykh (Muhammad Ghaus) and afterwards became his disciple."[33] Shāh Madār belonged to the same Sufi sect.

9. Jaunpur

It is the headquarters of a District of the same name in Uttar Pradesh. Its Hammām-Darwāza Masjid has three inscriptions which are complimentary to each other. The first inscription which is over the

---

[31]*Indian Antiquary*, June 1927, pp. 101–04.

[32]*Bābur-Nāma*, translated into English by A.S. Beveridge, New Delhi Reprint, 1979, Vol. II, pp. 539–40.

[33]Majumdar, R.C. (ed.), op. cit., Vol. VII, *The Mughal Empire*, Bombay, 1974, p. 106.

central *mihrab* of the mosque says that it was built in the reign of "Abu'l-Muzaffar Jalālu'd-Dīn Muhammad Akbar Bādshāh Ghāzi (AD 1556–1605)." The second inscription is built into the wall above the right *mihrāb*. It reads as follows:

"Thanks that by the guidance of the Everlasting and Living (Allāh), this house of infidelity became the niche of prayer (i.e. mosque). As a reward for that, the generous Lord, constructed an abode for its builder in paradise: The Pen of Reason wrote (the words): *the mosque of Nawwāb Muhsin Khān* for the date of its construction."[34]

The italicised words in the last line form a chronogram and yield the year AH 975 (AD 1567–68), which is the same as in the third inscription fixed above the right *mihrāb* of the mosque. The builder of the mosque was Nawwāb Muhsin Khān. Muhammad Fasīhu'd-Dīn writes in *The Sharqi Monuments of Jaunpur* (Allahabad, 1922) that the materials of the mosque were "taken from those of the temple of Lachman Das, Diwan of Khan-i-Zaman Ali Quli Khan.... Akbar made over all the property of the Diwan to Nawab Mohsin Khan."[35]

"It is surprising," writes the learned epigraphists, W.H. Siddiqi and Z.A. Desai, "that practically nothing is known about Nawwāb Muhsin Khān, the builder of this mosque and several other edifices, from contemporary or later records. The title Nawwāb prefixed to his name clearly suggests that he was a man of high status in the reign, probably holding *jāgīr* or a high post in the *sarkār* of Jaunpur, which was included in Akbar's time in the *sūba* of Allāhābād."[36] Abu'l Fazl mentions a Muhsin Khān in *Akbar Nāma* in the annals of the year 1571. He was a brother of the "celebrated Shihābu'd-Dīn Ahmad Khān" who belonged to "a Sayyid family of Nishāpur in Iran." This Muhsin Khān is probably the same as the Muhsin Khān who, according to Abu'l Fazl again, "in AH 982 participated in the Bengal expedition led by Khān-i-Khānān Munīm Khān."[37]

10. Ghoda

It is now a village in the Khed Taluka of Poona District in Maharashtra. The old Jāmi' Masjid of this place is known for two Persian inscriptions on two of its pillars. Joined together, the inscriptions read as follows:

[34]*Epigraphia Indica—Arabic and Persian Supplement,* 1969, p. 69.
[35]Quoted in Ibid., footnote 2.
[36]Ibid., p. 70.
[37]Ibid., p. 71.

"Oh Allāh! Oh Muhammad! O 'Alī! Mīr Muhammad Zamān made up his mind, he opened the door of prosperity on himself with his own hand. He demolished thirty-three idol-temples (and) by divine grace, laid the foundation of a building in this abode of perdition. That the mosques are Allāh's, therefore call not upon any one with Allāh (Qur'ān LXXII, 18). He opened the arms of magnanimity with goodness and scattered gold, (and) laid the foundation of a mosque like the palace of paradise. I went in contemplation and sought its date from Wisdom. Wisdom was astonished and said, he *built this blessed building*."[38]

The chronogram contained in the italicised words yields the year AH 994 (AD 1586). The Poona region at that time was in the Nizām Shāhī kingdom of Ahmadnagar. The ruler was Murtazā Nizām Shāh I (1565–1588) during whose reign the kingdom reached its greatest territorial extent. The epigraphists do not tell us anything about Mīr Muhammad Zamān, the builder of the mosque. But one thing is clear from the mention of Imām 'Alī in the inscription, namely, that Mīr Muhammad Zamān was a Shi'ah.

11. Poonamalle

This is a town in the Sriperumbudur Taluka of Chingleput District in Tamil Nadu. It has a mosque which has two inscriptions, one in Persian and the other in Telugu. The Persian inscription states that the mosque was built in AH 1063 (AD 1653) in the reign of Sultān 'Abdullāh Qutb Shāh (AD 1626–1672) of the Qutb Shāhī dynasty of Golconda when Mīr Jumlā was the governor of the Carnatic province. The builder was Rustam ibn Zul-Fiqār of Istarabad in Iran. "In the margin of the tablet," writes the epigraphist, G. Yazdani, "two Persian couplets are carved, the letters of which have been abraded by the effect of weather. The following words, however, can be deciphered: 'Destroyed the house of idols... and built a mosque, demolished... infidels... built.' "[39]

The Telugu version, engraved below the Persian inscription, mentions Rustam, the builder , as "*Havaludārū* of the fort at Pūnamalli" and Mīr Jumla as "Hajarati Navābu-Sāhebulugāru, the agent of Hajarati Ālampanna Sultānu Abdullā Kutupu Śahārājugāru, the lord of Golconda throne." The mosque, it says, is "to last as long as the Moon and Sun," and "those that cause obstruction (to it) will incur the sin of killing cow at Kāśi [Varanasi]." The epigraphist adds, "The superstructure of the mosque is built of brick and mortar, the base being of stone,

[38]*Epigraphia Indo-Moslemica,* 1933–34, p. 24.
[39]*Epigraphia Indo-Moslemica,* 1937–38, p. 53, footnote 2.

which may have originally formed part of a Hindu temple."[40]

Mīr Jumla whose name was Muhammad Sayyid was "an adventurer from Ardistān in Persia." He rose in the service of the Sultān of Golconda as whose general he invaded the Carnatic and became Governor of the conquered territories. "By plundering Hindu temples," writes J.N. Chaudhuri, "and searching out hidden treasures, Mīr Jumla accumulated a vast fortune, and according to Thevnot, he had twenty maunds of diamonds in his possession. His *jāgīr* in Carnatic was like a kingdom.... He was almost an independent ruler and absented himself from the court of Golconda. Alarmed at the growing power of the *Wazir*, the Sultān attempted to bring him under his control but Mīr Jumla entered into intrigues with Bijāpur and Persia."[41] Later on, he deserted his first employer and entered the service of the Mughals under Aurangzeb. He destroyed many Hindu temples while operating as a Mughal general in Kuch Bihar.

12. Udayagiri

It is the headquarters of a Taluka of the same name in the Nellore District of Andhra Pradesh. It is famous for its fort which was held by the Vijayanagara kings before it fell to the Qutb Shāhī rulers of Golconda. The big mosque on the Udayagiri Hill has a Persian inscription which reads as follows:

"Ghāzī 'Alī, lord of the age, victor in war... with the help and support of the victorious king, pivot (*Kutb*) of the world, king (*Shāh*) of the throne of the Dakhan, from one end to the other, he (Ghāzī 'Alī) burnt away the sweepings of idolatry... with the fire of his sword (he) burnt in one moment the idol of the idol-worshippers; he killed all, that breaker-through (annihilator) of the army; when he captured the fort of Udayagiri, the world became full of Jessamine; (he) began to construct the mosque and the date was, '*Founder of the mosque—(Ghāzī) 'Alī the iconoclast*'." [42]

The chronogram yields the year AD 1642–43. Ghāzī 'Alī was presumably a general of Abdullāh Qutb Shāh (AD 1626–1672) of Golconda. Nothing more is known about him.

The small mosque on the same Hill carries another Persian inscription which reads as follows:

---

[40]Ibid., pp. 53–54.

[41]Majumdar, R.C. (ed.), op. cit., Vol. VII, *The Mughal Empire*, pp. 475–76.

[42]Allen Butterworth and V. Venugopaul Chetty, *Copper-plate and Stone Inscriptions of South India*, Delhi Reprint, 1989, pp. 385–86.

"During the days of Abdulla Kutb Shāh, the pride of kings, Husain Khān secured the blessings of God in that he constructed a new mosque and embellished it. May God accept it for the purpose of prayers. A thousand and sixty and ten and one elapsed from Hijra (AD 1660–61). He destroyed a temple and constructed the House of God."[43]

Husain also was most probably another general of the same Sultān of Golconda. Histories of the reign or period do not supply information about his status or role.

13. Bodhan

It is the headquarters of a Taluka of the same name in the Nizamabad District of Andhra Pradesh. "The place," writes G. Yazdani, "is strewn with sculptures of Jaina and Brahmanical professions of faith.... Contemporary history does not mention Bodhan; but the array of antiquities and the discovery of both Hindu and Muslim inscriptions in recent times establish the fact that the town possessed considerable religious and strategic importance in early days."[44]

The town has a mosque known as Deval Masjid. It carries two inscriptions which state that it was built in the reign of Muhammad Tughlaq (AD 1325–1351). "The Deval Masjid," comments G. Yazdani, "as its name signifies, was originally a Hindu temple, and converted into a mosque by Muhammad Tughlaq at the time of his conquest of the Deccan. The plan of the building is star-shaped; it has undergone little alteration at the hands of Moslems excepting the removal of the shrine-chamber and the setting up of a pulpit. The original arrangement of the pillars remains undisturbed and the figures of *tirthankaras* may be noticed on some of them to this day."[45] The date of the conversion of this temple into a mosque is not mentioned in the inscriptions. The building of the temple is assigned by experts to 9–10th century AD.

The eastern part of the same town has a small mosque known as the Ālamgīrī Masjid. One of the two inscriptions on this mosque reads as under:

"In obedience to the commandment of the Almighty God, the Lord of both the worlds; and in love of... the exalted Prophet: During the reign of Shāhjahān, the king of the seven climes, the viceregent of God (lit. Truth), the master of the necks of people... the benevolent and generous Prince Aurangzeb, whose existence is a blessing of the Merci-

---

[43]Ibid., pp. 381–82.
[44]*Epigraphia Indo-Moslemica,* 1919–1920, p. 16.
[45]Ibid.

ful God on people: He built a house for worship with (all) the qualities of heaven: after the site has been previously occupied by the temple of infidels...."[46]

The chronogram, "*Most blessed House*", given at the end of the inscription yields the year AH 1065 (AD 1655) "which tallies with the period of Aurangzeb's governorship of the Deccan, shortly before his marching upon Delhi against his imperial father."[47]

14. Mathura

The Jāmi' Masjid in the heart of this Hindu city has a Persian inscription which reads as follows:

"In the reign of Shāh 'Ālamgīr Muhīu'ddin Walmillah, the king of the world, Aurangzeb, who is adorned with justice, the lustre of Islām shone forth to the glory of God; for 'Abd-un-Nabi Khān built this beautiful mosque. This second 'Holy Temple' caused the idols to bow down in worship. You will see the true meaning of the text, 'Truth came and error vanished.'[48] Whilst I search for a *tārikh*, a voice came from blissful Truth ordering me to say 'Abd-un-Nabi Khān is the builder of this beautiful mosque.' May this Jāma Masjid of majestic structure shine forth for ever like the hearts of the pious! Its roof is high like aspirations of love; its court-yard is wide like the arena of thought."[49]

The chronogram which contains the name of the builder, 'Abdu'n-Nabī Khān, yields the year AH 1070 corresponding to AD 1660–1661. 'Abdu'n-Nabī Khān had risen high in the service of Shāh Jahān. He fought on the side of Dārā Shukoh in the decisive Battle of Samugadh in 1658. After the defeat and flight of Dārā Shukoh, he joined service under Aurangzeb who appointed him *faujdār* in various places. "Abdun Nabi Khan," says *Mā'sīr-i-'Ālamgīrī*, "after removal from his post in Fathpur Jhunjhnu, was created a 2-*hazari* and appointed faujdar of Mathurā."[50] Jadunath Sarkar adds, "Aurangzeb chose him as faujdar of Mathurā probably because he, being 'a religious man' (as the Court history calls him), was expected to enter heartily into the Emperor's policy of 'rooting out idolatry.' Soon after joining this post Abdun Nabi

[46]Ibid., p. 18.

[47]Ibid., p. 17.

[48]Qur'ān, 17.83. This *āyat* was recited first by Muhammad when he destroyed the idols of Pagan Arabs in the Ka'ba at Mecca.

[49]The inscription has been reproduced and translated into English by F.S. Growse in his *Mathura: A District Memoir*, third edition (1883) reprinted from Ahmadabad in 1978, pp. 150–51.

[50]*Māā'sir-i-'Ālamgiri*, translated into English by Sir Jadunath Sarkar, Calcutta, 1947, pp. 47–48.

built a Jama' Masjid in the heart of the city of Mathurā (1661–1662) on the ruins of a Hindu temple. Later, in 1669, he forcibly removed the carved stone railing presented by Dara Shukoh to Keshav Rai's temple. When in 1669, the Jat peasantry rose under the leadership of Gokla, the zamindar of Tilpat, Abdun Nabi marched out to attack them in the village of Bashara, but was shot dead during the encounter (about 10th May)."[51]

15. Gwalior

There is a small mosque on the right hand side of the Gaṇeśa Gate in the fort at Gwalior, headquarters of a District in Madhya Pradesh. It has a Persian inscription which reads as follows:

In the reign of the great Prince Ālamgīr,
Like the full shining moon,
The enlightener of the world,
Praise be to God that this happy place,
Was by Motamid Khān completed as an alms.
It was the idol temple of the vile Gwālī,
He made it a mosque, like a mansion of paradise.
The Khān of enlightened heart,
Nay light itself from head to foot,
Displayed the divine light, like that of mid-day,
He closed the idol temple:
Exclamations rose from earth to heaven,
When the light put far away the abode of darkness,
Hatif said "light be blessed."[52]

"Gwālī" mentioned in the inscription refers to the famous Siddha Gawālīpā after whom Gwalior is supposed to have been named. Whatever be the truth of the legend, a temple dedicated to Gawālīpā did exist at the site now occupied by the mosque. A small temple dedicated to the Siddha exists even now in the vicinity of the mosque. It seems to have been built after the fort was freed from Muslim occupation.

Mu'tmad Khān who destroyed the original temple and built the mosque on its site was the Governor of Gwalior under Aurangzeb. The chronogram in the inscription gives AH 1075 (AD 1664) as the date when the mosque was completed.

---

[51]Jadunath Sarkar, op. cit., Vol. III, pp. 194–95.

[52]Archaeological Survey of India, *Four Reporis Made During the Years 1862–63–64–65* by Alexander Cunningham, Varanasi Reprint, 1972, p. 335.

16. Akot

It is the headquarters of a Taluka of the same name in the Akola District of Maharashtra. The central *mihrāb* of its Jāmi' Masjid carries a Persian inscription which reads as follows:

"In the name of Allāh, the Beneficent, the Merciful. There is no god except Allāh. Muhammad is His Prophet, verily. In the just reign of 'Ālamgīr, the king who is the asylum of Faith (and) whose universal generosity makes the sea and mine shame-stricken, one of his devoted servants, Muhammad Ashraf of good faith, saw a place where there was a temple. Like Khalīl (Prophet Abraham), he broke the temple at the command of God, and arranged for the construction of a very steadfast mosque. Year (AH) one thousand and seventy-eight" (AH 1078 = AD 1667).[53]

Nothing is known from history about Muhammad Ashraf who constructed this Jāmi' Masjid, though it can be surmised that he was some official of the Mughal empire under Aurangzeb (AD 1658–1707).

17. Bidar

It is the headquarters of a District of the same name in the State of Karnataka. It was the capital of the Bahmanī Empire from AD 1422 to 1569 when it became the seat of the Barīd Shāhī kingdom, one of the five Muslim states which arose on the eclipse of the Bahmanī dynasty. There is a small mosque on the slope of a mountain, some two miles to the south-east of Bidar. It has an inscription in Persian which says:

"God there is none but He and we worship not anyone except Him. (He) built a mosque in place of the temple, and wrote over its door the (*Qur'ānic*) verse—'Verily, We conquered.'[54] When the exalted mind of the Khedive, the refuge of Religion, supported by Divine Grace, Abu'z-Zafar Muḥi-ud-dīn Muhammad Aurangzeb Bahādur 'Ālamgīr, the victorious, was inclined to, and occupied in, destroying the base of infidelity and darkness and to strengthen the foundation of Islamic religion, the humblest servant Mukhtār Khān al-Husaini as-Sabzwārī, the governor of the province of Zafarābād, demolished the temple and built a mosque and laid out a garden which by the Grace of the Omniscient God were completed on the 25th of Rabi'-ul-Awwal in the 14th year of the auspicious reign (AH 1082) corresponding with the date contained in this hemistich—*By the Grace of God this temple became a mosque...*"[55]

[53]*Epigraphia Indica—Arabic and Persian Supplement*, 1963, p. 54.
[54]Qur'ān, 48.1
[55]*Epigraphia Indo-Moslemica,* 1927–28, p. 33.

The corresponding year of the Christian era was 1670. Aurangzeb was the Mughal emperor from AD 1658–1707. Mukhtār Khān was his local officer. It may be noticed that Bidar is described as Zafarābād in this inscription. This is only one instance of many attempts to Islamicise the names of Indian cities, towns and even villages. Many of these Islamic place-names have become current so that the original names have to be excavated from ancient records. Others did not stick and are found only in Muslim histories.

18. Siruguppa

This is now a small town in the Bellary Taluka of the Bellary District of Karnataka. The name means "pile of wealth" which is justified by its location in a rich wet land as compared to the dry land around it. Its Lād Khān's Masjid has a Persian inscription regarding the construction of the mosque. "The present building of the mosque," writes G. Yazdani, "is of modest dimensions and does not seem to be very old, but it is not unlikely that it stands upon the site of an older mosque."[56] The inscription reads as follows:

"In Eternity when the Founder of the Fort of 'blue firmament' opened the gates of grace and benevolence and mercy into the face of mankind, since then a ball of 'religion' and 'state', justice and benevolence, was thrown in the pologround and arena of the world. Each of the rulers, monarchs and sovereigns came (into this world) in turn, and manifested majesty according to his 'star'; (each) gallopped the horse of ambition, but could not bear away the ball, hence (each) threw down the ball of his head on the *chaughān* of 'prostration'. Now when the turn of Mas'ūd Khān came, he bore away the ball with the *chaughān* of courage. Know him of pure faith and belief, and of mature fortune and glory; his justice has been praised by Naushīirwān and his generosity (applauded) by Hātim. The court of his (kingly) grace is (resplendent) like the Moon; but in the battle-field his awe destroys heads, his wrath and grace in respect of infidelity and faith add darkness and light (to each). Destroyed temples and idols and built mosques and *Mihrabs*, levelled the mountains in several places and raised walls touching the sky..."[57]

The inscription goes on to credit Mas'ūd Khān with the construction of a gate at Adoni and another at Sirkopa (Siruguppa) in the year AH 1086, corresponding to AD 1674. "Mas'ūd Khān's name," comments

[56]*Epigraphia Indo-Moslemica*, 1921–22, p. 8.
[57]Ibid., pp. 11–12.

G. Yazdani, "is given by Khāfī Khān in connection with the conquest of the fortress of Ādoni by the Mughal army under Firoz Jang in AH 1098–99 (AD 1687–88). Mas'ūd Khān defended the fort gallantly on behalf of the Bijapur king, but being unsuccessful in repulsing the Imperial troops, he ultimately made over to them the key of the Fortress and asked for the safety of his life."[58] His bragging about his own prowess was of no avail when he was faced with superior military might.

19. Cuddapah

It is the headquarters of a District of the same name in the State of Andhra Pradesh. "*Kadapa* means a 'gate' in Telegu and the name is said to be derived from the fact that Cuddapah town is the gate to the holy places at Tirupati."[59] The District was a part of the Chola Empire of Tanjore from the eleventh to the thirteenth century. In the fourteenth century it became a part of the Vijayanagara Empire. The Qutb Shāhī Sultāns of Golconda seized it after the defeat of Vijayanagara in 1565 and renamed it Neknāmābād. It passed under Mughal rule in 1688.

A mosque in Cuddapah town carries an inscription which reads as follows:

"In the name of God, the most Merciful and Compassionate. Praise be to God, the Lord of all worlds, and blessing and peace be upon Muhammad, the apostle of God, and upon all his descendants and companions. O God, help Islām and the Muslims by preserving the kingdom of Abu'z-Zafar Muhīu'd-Dīn Muhammad Aurangzeb Bahādur 'Ālamgīr, the victorious king. Blessed be the ruler of the world, the refuge of the universe; whose name effaces the existence of sin. Since the time of Tīmur who conquered the kingdom of Romans, there has been no ruler just like the present king (Aurangzeb). The bow which he has stretched by his powerful arms, is such that the echo of its twing has reached the (distant) seas. By the sword, which the powerful king has wielded, panic has sprung (even) in the ocean. Although the king of the time is not a prophet, yet there is no doubt in his being a friend of God. He built the mosque and broke the idols (at a time) when 1103 years had passed from the flight (of the Prophet)."[60]

The year AH 1103 corresponds to AD 1692. The first two lines of the inscription are in Arabic and eight hemistiches that follow are in Persian. Aurangzeb needs no introduction.

---

[58]Ibid., p. 10.

[59]*Imperial Gazetteer of India, Provincial Series, Madras*, New Delhi Reprint, 1985, Vol. I, p. 370.

[60]*Epigraphia Indo-Moslemica*, 1937–38, p. 55.

20. Surat

It is a large town and the headquarters of a District of the same name in the State of Gujarat. A prosperous port on the West Coast of India since ancient times, it passed under Muslim rule at the end of the 13th century. As a gateway to Mecca, it became *Bandar Mubārak*, the blessed port.

The walls of a stepped well known as Gopī Talāo have two Persian inscriptions. The first one in which several lines are lost reads as follows: "...The dust of whose feet is the crown of all. Farrukh Siyar the king, by the fame of whose justice, the creation and the world are in the cradle of repose. The sky of beneficence, Haidar Qulī Khān during whose reign tyranny has become extinct...By the grace of God he completed it...He laid waste several idol temples, in order to make this strong building firm..."[61]

The second inscription is intact and reads as follows: "[During] the period of the second 'Ālamgīr, king of the faith, Farrukh Siyar, whose sword became the guardian of the realm of Islām. The hand of his justice struck a blow on the head of Naushīrwān (i.e., surpassed him in justice), the country and the nation everywhere secured tranquility by his justice. Mīr 'Ālam, sincere friend of Haidar Qulī Khān, a reservoir of water constructed in Sūrat, which became life-giving to the high and the low. *Salsabīl* (a fountain of Paradise) of the *Ka'ba of heart, this reservoir of the water of life.* The inspirer communicated this chronogram and showed eloquence. As its bricks were taken from an idol temple, one rose and said, *Mīr 'Ālam became the founder of this reservoir by revelation 1130.*"[62]

The chronogram also yields AH 1130 which corresponds to AD 1718. Haidar Qulī Khān mentioned in the two inscriptions was the Mughal officer in charge of Surat in the reign of the Mughal emperor Farrukh Siyyar (AD 1713–1719) who got Bandā Bairagī tortured and killed and who himself died a dog's death at the hands of the Sayyid Brothers. We have a locality in old Delhi which is known as Havelī Haidar Qulī.

21. Cumbum

It is the headquarters of a Taluka of the same name in the Kurnool District of Andhra Pradesh. The central *mihrāb* of its Gachīnālā Masjid carries a Persian inscription which reads as follows:

[61] *Epigraphia Indo-Moslemica*, 1933–34, p. 42.
[62] Ibid., p. 41.

"He is Allāh, may He be glorified, the Most Exalted. During the august rule of the emperor, king of the world, Muhammad Shāh, there was a well-established idol-house in Kuhmum which was strengthened and fortified by a small fortress. The Khān of lofty dignity (and) of high position, the source of generosity and mine of beneficence, the Khan who is the master of (high) position, (namely), Muhammad Sālih, who prospers in the rectitude of the affairs of Faith, son of Hājī Muhammad Kāzim was the ruler of Kuhmum. He is one of the select grandees of the city of Tabrīz which place is celebrated for producing great persons. (He) razed to the ground the edifice of the idol-house, and also broke the idols in a manly fashion. (He) constructed on the site a suitable mosque, towering above the buildings of all. The Angel of the Unseen communicated the date of its construction in the words: *A mosque pleasant in appearance, well founded, and elegant.* The year of the migration of the Prophet, may peace (of God) be upon him, was forty-two, one hundred and one thousand. Year AH 1142."[63]

The chronogram also yields AH 1142 which corresponds to AD 1729–30. Muhammad Sālih was the Governor and *Nāzim* of Cumbum in that year under the Mughal emperor, Muhammad Shāh (AD 1719–48).

Conclusions

Three conclusions can be safely drawn from a study of these 21 inscriptions. Firstly, the destruction of Hindu temples continued throughout the Muslim rule, from the date of its first establishment at Delhi in AD 1192 to its downfall with the death of the Mughal emperor Muhammad Shāh in 1748. Secondly, the destruction took place all over India and was undertaken by rulers belonging to all Muslim dynasties, imperial as well as provincial. Thirdly, the destruction had no economic or political motive as has been proposed by Marxist scholars and Muslim apologists; it was inspired by religious zeal and regarded as a pious performance by Muslim kings and commanders, all of whom took considerable pride in it and sought blessing from Allāh and the Prophet. The iconoclasts, it may be added, have been idolised all along as paragons of faith, virtue, justice and generosity. These conclusions become clearer still when we come to evidence from Islamic literary sources.

---

[63]*Epigraphia Indica—Arabic and Persian Supplement*, 1959, pp. 65–66.

Chapter Seven

THE LITERARY EVIDENCE

Islamic literary sources provide far more extensive evidence of temple destruction by the Muslim invaders of India in medieval times. They also cover a larger area, from Sinkiang and Transoxiana in the North to Tamil Nadu in the South, and from the Seistan province of present-day Iran in the West to Assam in the East. As we wade through this evidence, we can visualise how this vast area, which was for long the cradle of Hindu culture, came to be literally littered with the ruins of temples and monasteries belonging to all schools of Sanātana Dharma—Bauddha, Jaina, Śaiva, Śākta, Vaishṇava and the rest. Archaeological explorations and excavations in modern times have proved unmistakably that most of the mosques, *mazārs*, *ziārats* and *dargāhs* which were built in this area in medieval times, stood on the sites of and were made from the materials of deliberately demolished Hindu monuments.

Hundreds of medieval Muslim historians who flourished in India and elsewhere in the world of Islam, have written detailed accounts of what their heroes did in various parts of the extensive Hindu homeland as they were invaded one after another. We have had access only to a few of these histories on account of our limitations in terms of language and resources. Most of the histories pertaining to what are known as provincial Muslim dynasties, have remained beyond our reach. One thing, however, becomes quite clear from the evidence we have been able to compile, namely, that almost all Muslim rulers destroyed or desecrated Hindu temples whenever and wherever they could. Archaeological evidence from various Muslim monuments, particularly mosques and *dargāhs*, not only confirms the literary evidence but also adds the names of some Muslim rulers whom Muslim historians have failed to credit with this pious performance.

We are citing the literary evidence also in a chronological order, that is, with reference to the time at which a particular work was written and not with reference to the period with which it deals. Appendix 1 provides the names and dates of dynasties and kings described in these histories in the context of India. Most of these histories start with the creation of Adam and Eve or the rise of the Prophet of Islam, and come down to the time when the authors lived. Glorification of Islam, as its armies invaded various countries and laid them waste with slaughter and rapine, is their common theme. The writers have exhausted their imagination in describing the holocaust that was caused everywhere and in coining names for those whom they look down upon as infidels and idolaters.[1]

The apologists of Islam are likely to point out that quite often the instances of iconoclasm have been copied by succeeding historians from the writings of their predecessors and that this repetition should be kept in mind while assessing the extent of temple destruction. There is no substance in this argument. Firstly, there are many instances of temple destruction which are not reported in the histories but which archaeological evidence proves. Secondly, what is relevant in this context is that the historians regard some instances as significant enough to bear repetition. It is obvious that no account of some reigns was considered complete unless the concerned ruler was credited with the destruction of Hindu temples. Had it not been an important pious performance from the point of view of Islam, it is inconceivable that historians who wrote in times when the dust of war had settled down, would have cared to mention it. The repetitions are valuable from another point of view as well. In quite a few cases, succeeding historians add details which are not found in the preceding accounts. It is immaterial whether the details were missed by the earlier historians or are the products of the succeeding historians' imagination. What matters is that the historians thought them fit for the glorification of Islam.

(1)
Futūhu'l-Buldān

The author, Ahmad bin Yahya bin Jābir, is known as al-Bilādhurī. He lived at the court of Khalīfa Al-Mutawakkal (AD 847–861) and died in AD 893. His history is one of the earliest and major Arab chronicles. It gives an account of Arab conquests in Syria, Mesopotamia, Egypt, Iran, Armenia, Transoxiana, Africa, Spain and Sindh. The account is brought down to Khalīfa Mu'tasim's reign in AD 842. We have had no access to a translation of the full text in a language we know, and have depended on extracts.

[1]The language which is uniformly used by Muslim writers in describing the slaughter of people, destruction of cities and towns, and enslavement of the conquered men, women and children, has to be read in the original Arabic or Persian in order to realize that the writers themselves must have been bloodthirsty thugs masquerading as theologians, poets and historians. Amir Khusrū and Ziāu-'d-Dīn Baranī, the two distinguished disciples of Nizāmu 'd-Dīn Auliyā', excel them all in this respect. The Urdu translations retain some of the flavour which is lost in translations in other languages. Urdu is truly an Islamic language.

Ibn Samūrah (AD 653)

His full name was 'Abd ar-Rahmān bin Samūrah bin Habīb bin 'Abd ash-Shams. He was appointed governor of Seistan after the first Arab invasion of that province in AD 650 was defeated and dispersed. Ibn Samūrah reached the capital of Seistan in AD 653.

Seistan (Iran)

"On reaching Dāwar, he surrounded the enemy in the mountain of Zūr, where there was a famous Hindu temple."[2]

"...Their idol of Zūr was of gold, and its eyes were two rubies. The zealous Musalmāns cut off its hands and plucked out its eyes, and then remarked to the Marzabān how powerless was his idol to do either good or evil..."[3]

Qutaibah bin Muslim al-Bāhilī (AD 705–715)

He was a general of Al-Hajjāj bin Yūsuf Saqafī, the notorious Governor of Iraq under Caliph Al-Walīd I (AD 705–715). He was made Governor of Khurasan in AD 705 and is renowned in the history of Islam as the conqueror of Central Asia right upto Kashghar.

Samarqand (Farghana)

"Other authorities say that Kutaibah granted peace for 700,000 dirhams and entertainment for the Moslems for three days. The terms of surrender included also the houses of the idols and the fire temples. The idols were thrown out, plundered of their ornaments and burned, although the Persians used to say that among them was an idol with which whoever trifled would perish. But when Kutaibah set fire to it with his own hand, many of them accepted Islām."[4]

Muhammad bin Qāsim (AD 712–715)

He was the nephew as well as son-in-law of Al-Hajjāj, who sent him to Sindh after more than a dozen invasions of that province had been defeated by the Hindus.

Debal (Sindh)

"...The town was thus taken by assault, and the carnage endured for

---

[2]Cited by Abdur Rahman, *The Last Two Dynasties of the Shāhīs*, Delhi Reprint, 1988, pp. 55–56.

[3]Elliot and Dowson, op. cit., Vol. II, pp. 413–14.

[4]*Kitab Futuh Al-Buldan of al-Biladhuri*, translated into English by F.C. Murgotte, Columbia University, New York, 1924, p. 707.

three days. The governor of the town, appointed by Dāhir, fled and the priests of the temple were massacred. Muhammad marked a place for the Musalmans to dwell in, built a mosque, and left four thousand Musalmans to garrison the place...

"...'Ambissa son of Ishāk Az Zabbī, the governor of Sindh, in the Khilafat of Mu'tasim billah knocked down the upper part of the minaret of the temple and converted it into a prison. At the same time he began to repair the ruined town with the stones of the minaret..."[5]

Multan (Punjab)

"...He then crossed the Biyās, and went towards Multān.... Muhammad destroyed the water-course; upon which the inhabitants, oppressed with thirst, surrendered at discretion. He massacred the men capable of bearing arms, but the children were taken captive, as well as the ministers of the temple, to the number of six thousand. The Muslamāns found there much gold in a chamber ten cubits long by eight broad, and there was an aperture above, through which the gold was poured into the chamber..."[6]

Hashām bin 'Amrū al-Taghlabī

He was appointed Governor of Sindh by Khalīfa Al-Mansūr (AD 754–775) of the Abbāsid dynasty. He led many raids towards different parts of India, both by land and sea.

Kandahar (Maharashtra)

"He then went to Kandahār in boats and conquered it. He destroyed the *Budd* there, and built in its place a mosque."[7]

(2)
Tārīkh-i-Tabarī

The author, Abu Ja'far Muhammad bin Jarīr at-Tabarī, is considered to be the foremost historian of Islam. His *Tārīkh* is regarded as *Umdatu'l-Kutab*, mother of histories. He was born at Amil in Tabaris-

---

[5]Elliot and Dowson, op. cit., Vol. I, pp. 120–21.

[6]Ibid., pp. 122–23.

[7]Ibid., p. 127. "*Budd*" in Islamic parlance means an idol. The word is derived from "*Buddha*" whose idols were known as *Budd* or *But* in Iran long before the Muslims conquered that land. The Muslims borrowed the word and extended it to mean all idols. The Iranian text of *Bundahism* translated by H.W. Bailey says that "The demon *But* is that which they worship in India and in his image a spirit is resident which is worshipped as *Bodasf*" (*Indian Studies*, Volume in Honour of Edward James Rapson, edited by J. Bloch et al., London, 1931, Delhi Reprint, 1988, p. 279). *Bodasf* is Persian for *Bodhisattva*.

tan in the year AD 839. He was educated at Baghdad and lived in Basra and Kufa as well. He travelled to Egypt and Damascus in order to perfect his knowledge of Traditions. He spent the last days of his life in Baghdad where he died in AD 922. We have had no access to his work in a translation we could follow. The citations below are only summaries made by modern historians.

Qutaibah bin Muslim al-Bāhilī (AD 705–715)

Beykund (Khurasan)

"The ultimate capture of Beykund (in AD 706) rewarded him with an incalculable booty; even more than had hitherto fallen into the hands of the Mahommedans by the conquest of the entire province of Khorassaun; and the unfortunate merchants of the town, having been absent on a trading excursion while their country was assailed by the enemy, and finding their habitations desolate on their return contributed further to enrich the invaders, by the ransom which they paid for the recovery of their wives and children. The ornaments alone, of which these women had been plundered, being melted down, produced, in gold, one hundred and fifty thousand meskals; of a dram and a half each. Among the articles of the booty, is also described an image of gold, of fifty thousand meskals, of which the eyes were two pearls, the exquisite beauty and magnitude of which excited the surprise and admiration of Kateibah. They were transmitted by him, with a fifth of the spoil to Hejauje, together with a request that he might be permitted to distribute, to the troops, the arms which had been found in the place in great profusion."[8]

Samarqand (Farghana)

"A breach was, however, at last effected in the walls of the city in AD 712 by the warlike machines of Kateibah; and some of the most daring of its defenders having fallen by the skill of his archers, the besieged demanded a cessation of arms to the following day, when they promised to capitulate. The request was acceded to by Kateibah; and a treaty was the next day accordingly concluded between him and the prince of Samarkand, by which the latter engaged for the annual payment of ten millions of dirhems, and a supply of three thousand slaves; of whom it was particularly stipulated, that none should either be in a state of infancy, or ineffective from old age and debility. He further

[8]Major David Price, *Mahommedan History*, London, 1811, New Delhi Reprint, 1984, Vol. I, pp. 467–68.

contracted that the ministers of his religion should be expelled from their temples and their idols destroyed and burnt; that Kateibah should be allowed to establish a mosque in the place of the principal temple, in which, to discharge the duties of his faith... To all this, Ghurek, with whatever reluctance, was compelled to subscribe, and he proceeded accordingly to prepare for the reception of Kateibah; who at the period agreed upon, entered Samarkand with a retinue of four hundred persons, selected from his own relatives, and the principal commanders of his army. He was met by Ghurek, with a respect bordering on adoration, and conducted to the gate of the principal temple, which he immediately entered; and after performing two rekkauts of the ritual of his faith, directed the images of pagan worship to be brought before him, for the purpose of being committed to the flames. From this some of the Turks or Tartars of Samarkand, endeavouring to dissuade him, by a declaration, that among the images, there was one, which if any person ventured to consume, that person should certainly perish; Kateibah informed them, that he should not shrink from the experiment, and accordingly set fire to the whole collection with his own hands; it was soon consumed to ashes, and fifty thousand meskals of gold and silver, collected from the nails which has been used in the workmanship of the images."[9]

Yā'qūb bin Laith (AD 870–871)

He was a highway robber who succeeded in seizing Khurasan from the Tāhirid governors of the Abbāsid Caliphate. He founded the short-lived Saffārid dynasty.

Balkh and Kabul (*Afghanistan*)

"He first took Bāmiān, which he probably reached by way of Herāt, and then marched on Balkh where he ruined (the temple) Naushād. On his way back from Balkh he attacked Kābul....[10]

"Starting from Panjhīr, the place he is known to have visited, he must have passed through the capital city of the Hindu Śāhīs to rob the sacred temple—the reputed place of coronation of the Śāhī rulers—of its sculptural wealth....[11]

"The exact details of the spoil collected from the Kābul valley are lacking. The *Tārīkh [-i-Sīstān]* records 50 idols of gold and silver and

---

[9]Ibid., pp. 474–75.
[10]Abdur Rahman, op. cit., p. 102.
[11]Ibid., pp. 103–04.

Mas'udī mentions elephants. The wonder excited in Baghdād by elephants and pagan idols forwarded to the Caliph by Ya'qūb also speaks for their high value.

"The best of our authorities put the date of this event in 257 (870–71). Tabarī is more precise and says that the idols sent by Ya'qūb reached Baghdād in Rabī' al-Ākhar, 257 (Feb.–March, 871). Thus the date of the actual invasion may be placed at the end of AD 870."[12]

(3)
Tārīkhu'l-Hind

The author, Abū Rīhan Muhammad bin Ahmad al-Bīrūnī al-Khwārizmī, was born in about AD 970–71. He was an astronomer, geometrician, historian and logician. He was sent to Ghazni in an embassy from the Sultān of Khwārizm. On invitation from Sultān Mahmūd of Ghazni (AD 997–1030), he entered his service, travelled to India and spent forty years in the country, chiefly in the Punjab. He learnt Sanskrit and translated some works from that language into Arabic. His history treats of the literature and learning of the Hindus at the commencement of the eleventh century.

Jalam ibn Shaiban (Ninth century AD)
Multan (*Punjab*)

The Sun Temple at Multan has been described by early Arab geographers like Sulaimān, Mas'udī, Istakhrī and Ibn Hauqal who travelled in India during the ninth and tenth centuries of the Christian era. The Arab invaders did not destroy it because besides being a rich source of revenue, it provided protection against Hindu counter-attack. "Mūltan," wrote Mas'ūdī, "is one of the strongest frontier places of the Musalmāns ....In it is the idol also known by the name of Mūltān.[13] The inhabitants of Sind and India perform pilgrimages to it from the most distant places; they carry money, precious stones, aloe wood and all sorts of perfumes there to fulfil their vows. The greatest part of the revenue of the king of Mūltān is derived from the rich presents brought to the idol.... When the unbelievers[14] march against Mūltān and the faithful[15] do not feel themselves strong enough to oppose them, they threaten to break their idol, and their enemies immediately withdraw."[16]

[12]Ibid., p. 104.

[13]The ancient name of Multan was Mūlasthāna and the Sun God was probably named accordingly.

[14]Hindus under the leadership of the Gurjara-Pratihāra rulers of Kanauj.

[15]The Muslim occupants of Multan.

[16]Elliot and Dowson, op. cit., Vol. I, p. 23.

Al-Bīrūnī records: "A famous idol of theirs was that of Multan, dedicated to the sun, and therefore called *Aditya*. It was of wood and covered with red Cordovan leather; in its two eyes were two red rubies. It is said to have been made in the last *Kritayuga*.... When Muhammad Ibn Alkasim Ibn Almunabih conquered Multan, he inquired how the town had become so very flourishing and so many treasures had there been accumulated, and then he found out that this idol was the cause, for there came pilgrims from all sides to visit it. Therefore he thought it best to have the idol where it was, but he hung a piece of cow's flesh on its neck by way of mockery. On the same place a mosque was built. When the Karmatians[17] occupied Multan, Jalam Ibn Shaiban, the usurper, broke the idol into pieces and killed its priests...."[18]

Sultān Mahmūd of Ghazni (AD 997–1030)

Thanesar (Haryana)

"The city of Taneshar is highly venerated by Hindus. The idol of that place is called *Cakrasvamin*, i.e. the owner of the *cakra*, a weapon which we have already described. It is of bronze, and is nearly the size of a man. It is now lying in the hippodrome in Ghazna, together with the Lord of Somanath, which is a representation of the *penis* of Mahadeva, called *Linga*."[19]

Somnath (Gujarat)

"The *linga* he raised was the stone of Somnath, for *soma* means the moon and *natha* means *master*, so that the whole word means *master of the moon*. The image was destroyed by the Prince Mahmud, may God be merciful to him!—AH 416. He ordered the upper part to be broken and the remainder to be transported to his residence, Ghaznin, with all its coverings and trappings of gold, jewels, and embroidered garments. Part of it has been thrown into the hippodrome of the town, together with the *Cakrasvamin*, an idol of bronze, that had been brought from Taneshar. Another part of the idol from Somanath lies before the door of the mosque of Ghaznin, on which people rub their feet to clean them from dirt and wet."[20]

---

[17]A Shī'ah Muslim sect.

[18]E.C. Sachau (tr.), *Alberuni's India*, New Delhi Reprint, 1983, p. 116.

[19]Ibid., p. 117.

[20]Ibid., pp. 102-03.

(4)
Kitābu'l-Yamīnī

The author of this history in Arabic was Abū Nasr Muhammad ibn Muhammad al Jabbāru'l-'Utbī. The family from Utba had held important offices under the Sāmānīs of Bukhara. 'Utbi himself became Secretary to Sultān Mahmūd of Ghazni (AD 997–1030). His work comprises the whole of the reign of Subuktigīn and that of Sultān Mahmūd down to the year AD 1020. He lived a few years longer. Persian translations of this history are known as *Tarjuma-i-Yamīnī* or *Tārīkh-i-Yamīnī*.

Amīr Subuktigīn of Ghazni (AD 977–997)

Lamghan (*Afghanistan*)

"The Amīr marched out towards Lamghān, which is a city celebrated for its great strength and abounding wealth. He conquered it and set fire to the places in its vicinity which were inhabited by infidels, and demolishing idol temples, he established Islām in them. He marched and captured other cities and killed the polluted wretches, destroying the idolaters and gratifying the Musalmāns."[21]

Sultān Mahmūd of Ghazni (AD 997–1030)

Narain (*Rajasthan*)

"The Sultān again resolved on an expedition to Hind, and marched towards Nārāīn, urging his horses and moving over ground, hard and soft, until he came to the middle of Hind, where he reduced chiefs, who, up to that time obeyed no master, overturned their idols, put to the sword the vagabonds[22] of that country, and with delay and circumspection proceeded to accomplish his design..."[23]

Nardin (*Punjab*)

"After the Sultān had purified Hind from idolatry, and raised mosques therein, he determined to invade the capital of Hind to punish those who kept idols and would not acknowledge the unity of God....He marched with a large army in the year AH 404 (AD 1013) during a dark night...[24]

"A stone was found there in the temple of the great Budda on which an inscription was written purporting that the temple had been founded fifty thousand years ago. The Sultān was surprised at the igno-

---

[21]Elliot and Dowson, op. cit., Vol. II, p. 22.
[22]This is one of the names by which Muslims means Hindus.
[23]Elliot and Dowson, op. cit., Vol. II, p. 36.
[24]Ibid., p. 37.

rance of these people, because those who believe in the true faith represent that only seven thousand years have elapsed since the creation of the world, and the signs of resurrection are even now approaching. The Sultān asked his wise men the meaning of this inscription and they all concurred in saying that it was false, and no faith was to be put in the evidence of a stone."[25]

Thanesar (*Haryana*)

"The chief of Tānesar was... obstinate in his infidelity and denial of God. So the Sultān marched against him with his valiant warriors, for the purpose of planting the standards of Islām and extirpating idolatry...[26]

"The blood of the infidels flowed so copiously, that the stream was discoloured, not withstanding its purity, and people were unable to drink it...The victory was gained by God's grace, who has established Islām for ever as the best of religions, notwithstanding that idolaters revolt against it...Praise be to God, the protector of the world, for the honour he bestows upon Islām and Musulmāns."[27]

Mathura (*Uttar Pradesh*)

"The Sultān then departed from the environs of the city, in which was a temple of the Hindūs. The name of this place was Maharatul Hind.... On both sides of the city there were a thousand houses, to which idol temples were attached, all strengthened from top to bottom by rivets of iron, and all made of masonry work...[28]

"In the middle of the city there was a temple larger and firmer than the rest, which can neither be described nor painted. The Sultān thus wrote respecting it:—'If any should wish to construct a building equal to this, he would not be able to do it without expending an hundred thousand, thousand red dīnārs, and it would occupy two hundred years even though the most experienced and able workmen were employed'.... The Sultān gave orders that all the temples should be burnt with naptha and fire, and levelled with the ground."[29]

---

[25]Ibid., p. 39. According to Firishta the temple in which the inscription was found was destroyed.

[26]Ibid., p. 40.

[27]Ibid., p. 40–41.

[28]Ibid., p. 44.

[29]Ibid., pp. 44–45. The conspicuous temple referred to in this passage was most probably that of Keśavadeva, predecessor of those destroyed by latter-day Islamic iconoclasts, the latest by Aurangzeb.

Kanauj (*Uttar Pradesh*)

"In Kanauj there were nearly ten thousand temples, which the idolaters falsely and absurdly represented to have been founded by their ancestors two or three hundred thousand years ago....Many of the inhabitants of the place fled and were scattered abroad like so many wretched widows and orphans, from the fear which oppressed them, in consequence of witnessing the fate of their deaf and dumb idols. Many of them thus effected their escape, and those who did not fly were put to death."[30]

(5)
Dīwān-i-Salmān

The author, Khwājah Mas'ūd bin Sa'd bin Salmān, was a poet. He wrote poems in praise of the Ghaznavid Sultāns — Mas'ūd, Ibrāhīm and Bahrām Shāh. He died sometime between AD 1126 and 1131.

Sultān Abu'l Muzaffar Ibrāhīm (AD 1059–1099)

"As power and the strength of a lion was bestowed upon Ibrāhīm by the Almighty, he made over to him the well-populated country of Hindustān and gave him 40,000 valiant horsemen to take the country, in which there were more than 1000 *rāīs*.... Its length extends from Lahore to the Euphrates, and its breadth from Kashmīr to the borders of Sīstān.... The army of the king destroyed at one time a thousand temples of idols, which had each been built for more than a thousand years. How can I describe the victories of the king..."[31]

Jalandhar (*Punjab*)

"The narrative of thy battles eclipses the stories of Rustam and Isfandiyār. Thou didst bring an army in one night from Dhangān to Jālandhar.... Thou didst direct but one assault and by that alone brought destruction upon the country. By the morning meal not one soldier, not one *Brāhman*, remained unkilled or uncaptured. Their heads were severed by the carriers of swords. Their houses were levelled with the ground with flaming fire....Thou hast secured victory to the country and to religion, for amongst the Hindus this achievement will be remembered till the day of resurrection."[32]

[30]Ibid., p. 46.
[31]Ibid., Vol. IV, pp. 518-19.
[32]Ibid., pp. 520–21.

Malwa (Madhya Pradesh)

"Thou didst depart with a thousand joyful anticipations on a holy expedition, and didst return having achieved a thousand victories...On this journey the army destroyed a thousand idol-temples and thy elephants trampled over more than a hundred strongholds. Thou didst march thy arm to Ujjain; Mālwā trembled and fled from thee.... On the way to Kālinjār thy pomp obscured the light of day. The lip of infidelity became dry through fear of thee, the eye of plural-worship became blind..."[33]

(6)
Chach-Nāmah

This Persian history was translated from Arabic by Muhammad 'Alī bin Hamīd bin Abū Bakr Kūfī in the time of Nāsiru'd-Dīn Qabācha, a slave of Muhammad Ghurī, who contested the throne of Delhi with Shamsu'd-Dīn Iltutmish (AD 1210–1236). The translator who lived at Uccha had gone to Alor and Bhakkar in search of accounts of the Arab conquest. He met a Maulāna who had inherited a history written in Arabic by one of his ancestors. The translation in Persian followed because Kūfī found that the Hijājī Arabic of the original was little understood by people in those days while the work was "a mine of wisdom." The Arabic original has been lost. The author remains unknown.

Muhammad bin Qāsim (AD 712–715)

Nirun (Sindh)

"Muhammad built at Nīrūn a mosque on the site of the temple of Budh, and ordered prayers to be proclaimed in the Muhammadan fashion and appointed an Imām."[34]

Siwistan and Sisam (Sindh)

Muhammad bin Qāsim wrote to al-Hajjāj, the governor of Iraq: "The forts of Siwistān and Sīsam have been already taken. The nephew of Dāhir, his warriors, and principal officers have been despatched, and infidels converted to Islām or destroyed. Instead of idol temples, mosques and other places of worship have been built, pulpits have been erected, the Khutba is read, the call to prayers is raised so that devotions are performed at the stated hours. The takbīr and praise to the

[33]Ibid., p. 524.
[34]Ibid., Vol. I, p. 158.

Almighty God are offered every morning and evening."[35]

Alor (*Sindh*)

"Muhammad Kāsim then entered and all the town people came to the temple of Nobhār, and prostrated themselves before an idol. Muhammad Kāsim enquired: 'Whose house is this, in which all the people high and low are respectfully kneeling and bowing down.' They replied: 'This is an idol-house called Nobhār.' Then, by Muhammad Kāsim's order, the temple was opened. Entering it with his officers he saw an equestrian statue. The body of the idol was made of marble or alabaster, and it had on its arms golden bracelets, set with jewels and rubies. Muhammad Kāsim stretched his hand and took off a bracelet from one of the idol's arms. Then he asked the keeper of the Budh temple Nobhār: 'Is this your idol?' 'Yes,' he replied, 'but it had two bracelets on, and one is missing.' 'Well' said Muhammad Kāsim, 'cannot your god know who has taken away his bracelet ?' The keeper bent his head down. Muhammad Kāsim laughed and returned the bracelet to him, and he fixed it again on the idol's arm."[36]

Multan (*Punjab*)

"Then all the great and principal inhabitants of the city assembled together, and silver to the weight of sixty thousand dirams was distributed and every horseman got a share of four hundred dirams weight. After this, Muhammad Kāsim said that some plan should be devised for realizing the money to be sent to the Khalīfa. He was pondering over this, when suddenly a Brahman came and said, 'Heathenism is now at an end, the temples are thrown down, the world has received the light of Islām, and mosques are built instead of idol temples. I have heard from the elders of Multān that in ancient times there was a chief in this city whose name was Jībawīn, and who was a descendent of the Rāī of Kashmīr. He was a Brahman and a monk, he strictly followed his religion, and always occupied his time in worshipping idols. When his treasures exceeded all limits and computation, he made a reservoir on the eastern side of Multān, which was hundred yards square. In the middle of it he built a temple fifty yards square, and he made a chamber in which he concealed forty copper jars each of which was filled with African gold dust. A treasure of three hundred and thirty *mans* of gold

[35]Ibid., p. 164.

[36]*The Chachnamah*, translated into English by Mirza Kalichbeg Fredunbeg, Delhi Reprint, 1979, pp. 179–80.

was buried there. Over it there is an idol made of red gold, and trees are planted round the reservoir.' It is related by historians, on the authority of 'Ali bin Muhammad who had heard it from Abū Muhammad Hinduī'[37] that Muhammad Kāsim arose and with his counsellors, guards and attendants, went to the temple. He saw there an idol made of gold, and its two eye were bright red rubies.

"....Muhammad Kāsim ordered the idol to be taken up. Two hundred and thirty *mans* of gold were obtained, and forty jars filled with gold dust...This gold and the image were brought to the treasury together with the gems and pearls and treasures which were obtained from the plunder of Multān."[38]

Jānakī's Evidence

Jānakī was one of the daughters of King Dāhir of Sindh. She was captured along with her sister and sent to the Khalīfa at Baghdad. When the Khalīfa invited Jānakī to share his bed, she lied to him that she had already been violated by Muhammad bin Qāsim. Her sister supported her statement. The Khalīfa ordered that Muhammad be sewed up in raw hide and sent to his court. Muhammad was already dead when the chest containing him arrived in Baghdad. Jānakī accused the Khalīfa of having killed one of his great generals without making proper enquiry. She said:

"The king has committed a very grievous mistake, for he ought not, on account of two slave girls, to have destroyed a person who had taken captive a hundred thousand modest women like us...and who instead of temples had erected mosques, pulpits and minarets...."[39]

(7)
Jāmiu'l-Hikāyāt

The author of this collection of stories was Maulāna Nūru'd-Dīn Muhammad 'Ufī. He was born in or near the city of Bukhara in Transoxiana. He came to India and lived in Delhi for some time in the reign of Shamsuīd-Dīn Iltutmish (AD 1210–1236). He travelled to several other places in India.

---

[37]This man was most probably the Brahmana who led Muhammad bin Qāsim to the temple treasure. He had accepted Islam simply because its arms were victorious.

[38]Elliot and Dowson, op. cit., Vol. I, pp. 205–06.

[39]Ibid., p. 21.

'Amrū bin Laith (AD 879–900)

Sakawand (Afghanistan)

"It is related that Amrū Lais conferred the governorship of Zābulistān on Fardaghān and sent him there at the head of four thousand horse. There was a large Hindu place of worship in that country, which was called Sakāwand, and people used to come on pilgrimage from the most remote parts of Hindustān to the idols of that place. When Fardaghān arrived in Zābulistān he led his army against it, took the temple, broke the idols in pieces and overthrew the idolaters...."[40]

(8)
Tāju'l-Ma'sīr

The author, Sadru'd-Dīn Muhammad Hasan Nizāmī, was born at Nishapur in Khurasan. He had to leave his ancestral place because of the Mongol invasion. He came to India and started writing his history in AD 1205. The history opens with the year 1191 and comes down to AD 1217.

Sultān Muhammad Ghūrī (AD 1175–1206)

Ajmer (Rajasthan)

"He destroyed the pillars and foundations of the idol temples and built in their stead mosques and colleges, and the precepts of Islām, and the customs of the law were divulged and established...."[41]

Kuhram and Samana (Punjab)

"The Government of the fort of Kohrām and of Sāmāna were made over by the Sultān to Kutbu-d dīn.... He purged by his sword the land of Hind from the filth of infidelity and vice, and freed it from the thorn of God-plurality, and the impurity of idol-worship, and by his royal vigour and intrepidity, left not one temple standing...."[42]

Meerut (Uttar Pradesh)

"Kutbu-d dīn marched from Kohrām 'and when he arrived at Mirāt —which is one of the celebrated forts of the country of Hind, for the strength of its foundations and superstructure, and its ditch, which was as broad as the ocean and fathomless—an army joined him, sent by the dependent chiefs of the country'. The fort was captured, and a Kotwal

---

[40]Ibid., Vol. II, p. 172.
[41]Ibid., p. 215.
[42]Ibid., pp. 216–17.

appointed to take up his station in the fort, and all the idol temples were converted into mosques."[43]

Delhi

"He then marched and encamped under the fort of Delhi.... The city and its vicinity were freed from idols and idols-worship, and in the sanctuaries of the images of the Gods, mosques were raised by the worshippers of one God."[44]

"Kutbu-d dīn built the Jāmi' Masjid at Delhi, and adorned it with stones and gold obtained from the temples which had been demolished by elephants, and covered it with inscriptions in Toghra, containing the divine commands."[45]

Varanasi (Uttar Pradesh)

"From that place [Asni] the royal army proceeded towards Benares 'which is the centre of the country of Hind' and here they destroyed nearly one thousand temples, and raised mosques on their foundations; and the knowledge of the law became promulgated, and the foundations of religion were established..."[46]

Aligarh (Uttar Pradesh)

"There was a certain tribe in the neighbourhood of Kol which had...occasioned much trouble....'Three bastions were raised as high as heaven with their heads, and their carcases became the food of beasts of prey. That tract was freed from idols and idol-worship and the foundations of infidelity were destroyed'...."[47]

Bayana (Rajasthan)

"When Kutbu-d dīn heard of the Sultān's march from Ghazna, he was much rejoiced and advanced as far as Hānsī to meet him.... In the year AH 592 (AD 1196), they marched towards Thangar, and the centre of idolatry and perdition became the abode of glory and splendour..."[48]

Kalinjar (Uttar Pradesh)

"In the year AH 599 (AD 1202), Kutbu-d dīn proceeded to the in-

[43]Ibid., p. 219.
[44]Ibid., p. 223.
[45]Ibid., p. 222.
[46]Ibid., p. 219.
[47]Ibid., p. 224. Kol was the old name of Aligarh.
[48]Ibid., p. 226. Thangar or Tahangarh is the name of the Fort near Bayana.

vestment of Kālinjar, on which expedition he was accompanied by the Sāhib-Kirān, Shamsu-d dīn Altamsh.... The temples were converted into mosques and abodes of goodness, and the ejaculations of bead-counters and voices of summoners to prayer ascended to high heaven, and the very name of idolatry was annihilated..."[49]

Sultān Shamsu'd-Dīn Iltutmish (AD 1210–1236)

Delhi

"The Sultān then returned [from Jalor] to Delhi... and after his arrival 'not a vestige or name remained of idol temples which had raised their heads on high; and the light of faith shone out from the darkness of infidelity...and the moon of religion and the state became resplendent from the heaven of prosperity and glory."[50]

(9)

Kāmilu't-Tawārīkh

Also known as *Tārīkh-i-Kāmil*, it was written by Shykh 'Abu'l Hasan 'Alī ibn 'Abu'l Karam Muhammad ibn Muhammad ibn 'Abdul Karīm ibn 'Abdul Wāhid as-Shaibānī, commonly known as Ibn Asīr. He was born in AD 1160 in the Jazīrat ibn 'Umar, an island on the Tigris above Mosul. The book embraces the history of the world from the earliest period to the year AD 1230. It enjoys a very high reputation.

Khalīfa Al-Mahdī (AD 775–785)

Barada (*Gujarat*)

"In the year 159 (AD 776) Al Mahdī sent an army by sea under 'Abdul Malik bin Shahābu'l Musamma'ī to India...They proceeded on their way and at length disembarked at Barada. When they reached the place they laid siege to it...The town was reduced to extremities, and God prevailed over it in the same year. The people were forbidden to worship the *Budd*, which the Muhammadans burned."[51]

Sultān Mahmūd of Ghazni (AD 997–1030)

Unidentified Places (*Rajasthan and Gujarat*)

"So he prayed to the Almighty for aid, and left Ghaznī on the 10th of Sha'bān AH 414... with 30,000 horse besides volunteers, and took the road to Multān. After he had crossed the desert, he perceived on one

[49]Ibid., p. 231.
[50]Ibid., pp. 238–39.
[51]Ibid., p. 246.

side a fort full of people, in which there were wells. People came down to conciliate him, but he invested the place, and God gave him victory.... So he brought the place under the sway of Islām, killed the inhabitants, and broke in pieces their images....[52]

"The chief of Anhilwāra called Bhīm, fled hastily... Yamīnu-d daula again started for Somnāt, and on his march he came to several forts in which were many images serving as chamberlains or heralds of Somnāt, and accordingly he (Mahmūd) called them Shaitān. He killed the people who were in these places, destroyed the fortifications, broke in pieces the idols and continued his march to Somnāt...."[53]

Somnath (*Gujarat*)

"This temple of Somnāt was built upon fifty-six pillars of teak wood covered with lead. The idol itself was in a chamber... Yamīnu'd daula seized it, part of it he burnt, and part of it he carried away with him to Ghaznī, where he made it a step at the entrance of the Jāmi'-masjid...."[54]

(10)
Tārīkh-i-Jahān-Kushā

The author, 'Alāu'd-Dīn Malik ibn Bahāu'd-Dīn Muhammad Juwainī, was a native of Juwain in Khurasan near Nishapur. His father who died in AD 1253 was one of the principal revenue officers under the Mongol ruler of Persia. 'Alau'd-Dīn followed in his father's office. He was with Halākū during the Mongol campaign against the Ismāi'lians and was later on appointed the governor of Baghdad. He fell from grace and was imprisoned at Hamadan. He was, however, exonerated and restored to his office which he retained till his death in AH 681 (AD 1282). His history comes down to the year AD 1255.

Sultān Jalālu'd-Dīn Mankbarnī (AD 1222–1231)

Debal (*Sindh*)

"The Sultān then went towards Dewal and Darbela and Jaisī.... The Sultān raised a Jāmi' Masjid at Dewal, on the spot where an idol temple stood."[55]

[52]Ibid., p. 469.
[53]Ibid., pp. 469-70.
[54]Ibid., p. 471.
[55]Ibid., p. 398.

(11)
Tabqāt-i-Nāsirī

The author, Maulāna 'Abū 'Umr 'Usmān Minhāju'd-Dīn bin Sirāju'd-Dīn al-Juzjānī, was born in AD 1193. In 1227 he arrived in Uccha where he was placed in charge of Madrasa-i-Fīrūzī. He presented himself to Sultān Shamsu'd-Dīn Iltutmish when the latter came to Uccha in 1228. The same year he accompanied Iltutmish to Delhi and joined the expedition to Gwalior, which city was placed in his charge. He returned to Delhi in 1238 and took charge of Madrasa-i-Nāsiriya. His fortune brightened after Nāsiru'd-Dīn became the Sultān in 1246; he was appointed *Qāzi-i-mamālik* in 1251. His history starts with Adam and comes down to the year 1260.

Sultān Mahmūd of Ghazni (AD 997–1030)

Somnath (Gujarat)

"When Sultān Mahmūd ascended the throne of sovereignty, his illustrious deeds became manifest unto all mankind within the pale of Islām when he converted so many thousands of idol temples into masjids.... He led an army to Nahrwālah of Gujarāt, and brought away Manāt, the idol, from Somnāth, and had it broken into four parts, one of which was cast before the entrance of the great Masjid at Ghaznīn, the second before the gateway of the Sultānīs palace, and the third and fourth were sent to Makkah and Madīnah respectively."[56]

The translator comments in a footnote: "Among the different coins struck in Mahmūd's reign one bore the following inscription: 'The right hand of the empire, Mahmūd Sultān, son of Nāsir-ud-Dīn Subuk-Tigīn, Breaker of Idols.' This coin appears to have been struck at Lāhor, in the seventh year of his reign."[57]

Sultān Shamsu'd-Dīn Iltutmish (AD 1210–1236)

Vidisha (Madhya Pradesh)

"After he returned to the capital in the year AH 632 (AD 1234) the Sultān led the hosts of Islām toward Mālwah, and took the fortress and town of Bhīlsān, and demolished the idol-temple which took three hundred years in building and which, in altitude, was about one hundred ells."[58]

---

[56]*Tabqāt-i-Nāsirī*, translated into English by Major H.G. Reverty, New Delhi Reprint, 1970, Vol. I, pp. 81–82.

[57]Ibid., p. 88, footnote 2.

[58]Ibid., pp. 621–22.

Ujjain (*Madhya Pradesh*)

"From thence he advanced to Ujjain-Nagarī and destroyed the idol-temple of Mahākāl Dīw. The effigy of Bikramjīt who was sovereign of Ujjain-Nagarī, and from whose reign to the present time one thousand, three hundred, and sixteen years have elapsed, and from whose reign they date the Hindūī era, together with other effigies besides his, which were formed of molten brass, together with the stone (idol) of Mahākāl were carried away to Delhī, the capital."[59]

Among his "Victories and Conquests" is counted the "bringing away of the idol of Mahākāl, which they have planted before the gateway of the *Jāmi' Masjid* at the capital city of Delhī in order that all true believers might tread upon it."[60]

(12)
Āsāru'l-Bilād

The author, Zakarīya bin Muhammad, was born in the town of Kazwin in Iran and became known as al-Kazwīnī. His work is a compilation from the writings of travellers like Istakhrī and Ibn Hauqal. It was written between AD 1263 and 1275.

Sultān Muhmūd of Ghazni (AD 997–1030)

Somnath (*Gujarat*)

"SOMNĀT—A celebrated city of India, is situated on the shores of the sea, and washed by its waves. Among the wonders of that place was the temple in which was placed the idol called Somnāt.... When the Sultān Yamīnu-d Daula Mahmūd bin Subuktigīn went to wage religious war against India, he made great efforts to capture and destroy Somnāt, in the hope that Hindus would become Muhammadans. He arrived there in the middle of Zīl K'ada AH 416 (December AD 1025). The Indians made a desperate resistance...The number of slain exceeded 50,000..."[61]

Muhammad bin Qāsim (AD 712–715)

Multan (*Punjab*)

"Muhammad Kāsim, ascertaining that large offerings were made to the idol, and wishing to add to his resources by those means, left it uninjured, but in order to show his horror of Indian superstition, he

[59]Ibid., pp. 622–23.
[60]Ibid., p. 628.
[61]Elliot and Dowson, op. cit., Vol. I, pp. 97–98.

attached a piece of cow's flesh to its neck, by which he was able to gratify his avarice and malignity at the same time."[62]

(13)
Nizāmu't-Tawārīkh

The author, 'Abū Sa'īd 'Abdullah bin 'Abū'l Hasan 'Alī Baizāwī, was born at Baiza, a town near Shiraz in Iran. He became a Qāzī, first at Shiraz and then at Tabriz, where he died in AD 1286. His history starts from the earliest period and comes down to the Mongol invasions.

Sultān Mahmūd of Ghazni (AD 997–1030)

"Nāsiru-d dīn [Subuktigīn] died in the year AH 387 (AD 997) and the command of his troops descended to Mahmūd by inheritance, and by confirmation of Nūh, son of Mansūr.... He demolished the Hindū temples and gave prevalence to the Muhammadan faith...."[63]

(14)
Miftāhu'l-Futūh

The author, Amīr Khusrū, was born at Delhi in 1253. His father occupied high positions in the reigns of Sultān Shamsu'd-Dīn Iltutmish (AD 1210–1236) and his successors. His mother was the daughter of another dignitary under Sultān Ghiyāsu'd-Dīn Balban (AD 1266–1286). He himself became a companion of Balban's son, Prince Muhammad, and stayed at Multan till the prince was killed in a battle with the Mongols. Reputed to be the dearest disciple of Shykh Nizāmu'd-Dīn Auliyā', he became the lick-spittle of whoever came out victorious in the contest for the throne at Delhi. He became a court poet of Balban's successor, Sultān Kaiqubād (AD 1288–1290) and wrote his *Qirānu's-S'ādaīn* in the Sultān's praise in AD 1289. Next, he joined Sultān Jalālu'd-Dīn Khaljī (AD 1290–1296) as a court poet after the latter murdered Kaiqubād. He wrote in 1291 the *Miftāhu'l-Futūh* which describes Jalālu'd-Dīn's victories.

Sultān Jalālu'd-Dīn Khaljī (AD 1290–1296)

Jhain (Rajasthan)

"The Sultān reached Jhāin in the afternoon of the third day and stayed in the palace of the Rāya.... He greatly enjoyed his stay for some

[62]Ibid., p. 470.
[63]Ibid., Vol. II, p. 252.

time. Coming out, he took a round of the gardens and temples. The idols he saw amazed him.... Next day he got those idols of gold smashed with stones. The pillars of wood were burnt down by his order.... A cry rose from the temples as if a second Mahmūd had taken birth. Two idols were made of brass, one of which weighed nearly a thousand *mans*. He got both of them broken, and the pieces were distributed among his people so that they may throw them at the door of the Masjid on their return [to Delhi]..."[64]

Another version of the same text is available in the translation by Elliot edited by Dowson:

"Three days after this, the king entered Jhāin at midday and occupied the private apartment of the *rāi*.... He then visited the temples, which were ornamented with elaborate work in gold and silver. Next day he went again to the temples, and ordered their destruction, as well as of the fort, and set fire to the palace, and 'thus made hell of paradise'....While the soldiers sought every opportunity of plundering, the Shāh was engaged in burning the temples, and destroying the idols. There were two bronze idols of Brahma each of which weighed more than a thousand *mans*. These were broken into pieces and the fragments distributed amongst the officers, with orders to throw them down at the gates of the *Masjid* on their return."[65]

Sultan 'Alāu'd-Dīn Khaljī (AD 1296–1316)

Vidisha (Madhya Pradesh)

"When he advanced from the capital of Karra, the Hindūs, in alarm, descended into the earth like ants. He departed towards the garden of Behār to dye that soil with blood as red as tulip. He cleared the road to Ujjain of vile wretches, and created consternation in Bhīlsān. When he effected his conquests in that country, he drew out of the river the idols which had been concealed in it."[66]

Devagiri (Maharashtra)

"But see the mercy with which he regarded the broken-hearted, for, after seizing the *rāī*, he set him free again. He destroyed the temples of the idolaters, and erected pulpits and arches for mosques."[67]

---

[64]Translated from the Hindi version by S.A.A. Rizvi included in *Khalji Kālīna Bhārata*, Aligarh, 1955, pp. 153–54.

[65]Elliot and Dowson, op. cit., Vol. III, p. 542.

[66]Ibid., p. 543.

[67]Ibid.

(15)
Khazāinu'l-Futūh

This work is also by Amīr Khusrū who wrote it in praise of 'Alāu'd-Dīn Khaljī when the latter became the Sultān after murdering his uncle and father-in-law, Sultān Jalālu'd-Dīn Khaljī. Khusrū was among the foremost notables who welcomed 'Alāu'd-Dīn when the latter reached Delhi with the head of the late king held aloft on the point of a spear. He completed this history in AD 1311. It is famous for its flowery language and figures of speech.

Sultān 'Alāu'd-Dīn Khaljī (AD 1296–1316)

Delhi

"He started his building programme with the Jāmi' Hazrat mosque.... Thereafter he decided to build a second *mīnār* opposite to the lofty *mīnār* of the Jāmi' Masjid, which *mīnār* is unparalleled in the world....[68] He ordered the circumference of the new *mīnār* to be double that of the old one. People were sent out in all directions in search of stones. Some of them broke the hills into pieces. Some others proved sharper than steel in breaking the temples of the infidels. Wherever these temples were bent in prayers, they were made to do prostration."[69]

Somnath (*Gujarat*)

"On Wednesday, the 20th of Jamādī-ul Awwal in AH 698 (23 February, 1299), the Sultān sent an order to the manager of the armed forces for despatching the army of Islām to Gujarāt so that the temple of Somnāt on its shore could be destroyed. Ulugh Khān was put in charge of the expedition. When the royal army reached that province, it won a victory after great slaughter. Thereafter the Khān-i-'Āzam went with his army to the sea-shore and besieged Somnāt which was a place of worship for the Hindūs. The army of Islām broke the idols and the biggest idol was sent to the court of the Sultān."[70]

Professor Mohammed Habib's translation provides a fuller version. It reads: "So the temple of Somnath was made to bow towards the Holy Mecca; and as the temple lowered its head and jumped into the sea, you may say that the building first said its prayers and then had a bath...It seemed as if the tongue of the Imperial sword explained the meaning of

---

[68]The reference is to the tower known as Qutb Minār at present.

[69]Translated from the Hindi version by S.A.A. Rizvi included in *Khaljī Kālīna Bhārata*, Aligarh, 1955, pp. 156–57. The last sentence means that the temples were first made to topple and then levelled with the ground.

[70]Ibid., p. 159.

the text: 'So he (Abraham) broke them (the idols) into pieces except the chief of them, that haply they may return to it.' Such a pagan country, the Mecca of the infidels, now became the Medina of Islam. The followers of Abraham now acted as guides in place of the Brahman leaders. The robust-hearted true believers rigorously broke all idols and temples wherever they found them. Owing to the war, '*takbir*,' and '*shahadat*' was heard on every side; even the idols by their breaking affirmed the existence of God. In this ancient land of infidelity the call to prayers rose so high that it was heard in Baghdad and Madain (Ctesiphon) while the 'Ala' proclamation (*Khutba*) resounded in the dome of Abraham and over the water of Zamzam..... The sword of Islam purified the land as the Sun purifies the earth."[71]

Jhain (*Rajasthan*)

"On Tuesday, the 3rd of Ziqād in AH 700 (10 July, 1301), the strong fort [of Ranthambhor] was conquered. Jhāin which was the abode of the infidels, became a new city for Musalmāns. The temple of Bāhirdev was the first to be destroyed. Subsequently, all other abodes of idolatry were destroyed. Many strong temples which would have remained unshaken even by the trumpet blown on the Day of Judgment, were levelled with the ground when swept by the wind of Islām."[72]

Warangal (*Andhra Pradesh*)

"When the blessed canopy had been fixed about a mile from the gate of Arangal, the tents around the fort were pitched together so closely that the head of a needle could not go between them...Orders were issued that every man should erect behind his own tent a *kathgar*, that is wooden defence. The trees were cut with axes and felled, notwithstanding their groans; and the Hindus, who worship trees, could not at that time come to the rescue of their idols, so that every cursed tree which was in that capital of idolatry was cut down to the roots....[73]

"During the attack, the catapults were busily plied on both sides.... 'Praise be to God for his exaltation of the religion of Muhammad. It is not to be doubted that stones are worshipped by Gabrs,[74] but as the

[71]Quoted by Jagdish Narayan Sarkar, *The Art of War in Medieval India*, New Delhi, 1964, pp. 286–87.

[72]S.A.A Rizvi, op. cit., p. 160. Bahirdev seems to be Bhairavadeva.

[73]Elliot and Dowson, op. cit., Vol. III, p. 81.

[74]"Gabr" was a term which the Muslims used for the Zoroastrians to start with. Later on, the term was sometimes extended to mean the Hindus as well.

stones did no service to them, they only bore to heaven the futility of that worship, and at the same time prostrated their devotees upon earth'...."[75]

Deccan and South India

"The tongue of the sword of the Khalīfa of the time, which is the tongue of the flame of Islām, has imparted light to the entire darkness of Hindustān by the illumination of its guidance...and on the right hand and on the left hand the army has conquered from sea to sea, and several capitals of the gods of the Hindūs in which Satanism had prevailed since the time of the Jinns, have been demolished. All these impurities of infidelity have been cleansed by the Sultān's destruction of idol temples, beginning with his first expedition against Deogīr, so that the flames of the light of the law illumine all these unholy countries, and places for the criers to prayers are exalted on high, and prayers are read in mosques. God be praised!"[76]

Chidambaram (*Tamil Nadu*)

"After returning to Bīrdhūl, he again pursued the Rājā to Kandūr.... The Rāī again escaped him, and he ordered a general massacre at Kandūr. It was then ascertained that he had fled to Jālkota.... There the Malik closely pursued him, but he had again escaped to the jungles, which the Malik found himself unable to penetrate, and he therefore returned to Kandūr.... Here he heard that in Brahmastpūrī there was a golden idol, round which many elephants were stabled. The Malik started on a night expedition against this place, and in the morning seized no less then two hundred and fifty elephants. He then determined on razing the beautiful temple to the ground —'you might say that it was the Paradise of Shaddād which, after being lost, those hellites had found, and that it was the golden Lanka of Rām,'—'the roof was covered with rubies and emeralds',—'in short, it was the holy place of the Hindūs, which the Malik dug up from its foundations with the greatest care... and heads of the Brahmans and idolaters danced from their necks and fell to the ground at their feet,' and blood flowed in torrents. 'The stone idol called Ling Mahādeo which had been a long time established at that place and on which the women of the infidels rubbed their vaginas for [sexual] satisfaction, these, up to this time, the kick of the horse of Islām had not attempted to break.' The Musalmāns

[75]Ibid., pp. 82–83.
[76]Ibid., p. 85.

destroyed all the lings, 'and Deo Narain fell down, and the other gods who had fixed their seats there raised their feet, and jumped so high, that at one leap they reached the fort of Lanka, and in that affright the lings themselves would have fled had they had any legs to stand on.' Much gold and valuable jewels fell into the hands of the Musalmāns, who returned to the royal canopy, after executing their holy project, on the 13th of Zī-l Ka'da, AH 710 (April 1311 AD). They destroyed all the temples at Bīrdhūl, and placed the plunder in the public treasury."[77]

Madura (Tamil Nadu)

"After five days, the royal canopy moved from Bīrdhūl on Thursday, the 17th of Zī-l Ka'da, and arrived at Kham, and five days afterwards they arrived at the city of Mathra (Madura), the dwelling place of the brother of the Rāī Sundar Pāndyā. They found the city empty, for the Rāī had fled with the Rānīs, but had left two or three elephants in the temple of Jagnār (Jagganāth). The elephants were captured and the temple burnt."[78]

(16)
Dawal Rānī-Khizr Khānī

Amīr Khusrū wrote this epic in AD 1315. It is popularly known as '*Āshīqa*, love-story. Its main theme is love between Dawal Rānī, the captured daughter of the last Hindu King of Gujarat, and Khizr Khān, the eldest son of 'Alāu'd-Dīn Khaljī. It also describes Muslim history in India upto the reign of 'Alāu'd-Dīn Khalji, including Malik Kāfūr's expedition to South India in AD 1310.

Sultān 'Alāu'd-Dīn Khaljī (AD 1296–1316)

Pattan (Tamil Nadu)

"There was another *rāī* in those parts, whose rule extended over sea and land, a Brahmin named Pandyā Gurū. He had many cities in his possession, and his capital was Fatan, where there was a temple with an idol in it laden with jewels... The *rāī*, when the army of the Sultān arrived at Fatan, fled away, and what can an army do without its leader? The Musalmāns in his service sought protection from the king's army, and they were made happy with the kind of reception they met. 500

---

[77]Ibid., pp. 90–91. The Hindi translation by S.A.A. Rizvi says that temples at Birdhul touched the sky with their topes, and reached the nether world in their foundations, but they were dug up (*Khaljī Kālīna Bhārata*, p. 169).

[78]Ibid., p. 91.

elephants were taken. They then struck the idol with an iron hatchet, and opened its head. Although it was the very *Kibla* of the accursed *gabrs*, it kissed the earth and filled the holy treasury."[79]

(17)
Nuh Siphir

It is the fourth historical *mathnavī* which Amīr Khusrū wrote when he was 67 years old. It celebrates the reign of Sultān Mubārak Shāh Khaljī. It consists of nine (*nuh*) *siphirs* (parts). In *Siphir* III, he says that the Hindus "worship...stones, beasts, plants and the sun, but they recognize that these things are creations of God and adore them simply because their forefathers did so."[80]

Sultān Mubārak Shāh Khaljī (AD 1316–1320)

Warrangal (Andhra Pradesh)

"They pursued the enemy to the gates and set everything on fire. They burnt down all those gardens and groves. That paradise of idol-worshippers became like hell. The fire-worshippers of *Bud* were in alarm and flocked round their idols..."[81]

(18)
Siyaru'l-Auliyā'

It was written by Sayyid Muhammad bin Mubārak bin Muhammad 'Alwī Kirmānī known as Amīr or Mīr Khwurd. He was the grandson of an Iranian merchant who traded between Kirman in Iran and Lahore, and who became a disciple of Shykh Farīdu'd-Dīn Ganj-i-Shakar, the Sufi luminary of Ajodhan near Multan. His father was also a disciple of the same Sufi. The family travelled to Delhi after Shykh Farīd's death and became devoted to Shykh Nizāmu'd-Dīn Auliyā'. Mīr Khwurd was forced to migrate to Daulatabad by Sultān Muhammad bin Tughlaq but allowed to return to Delhi after some time. It was then that he wrote this detailed biography of the Auliyā' and his disciples.

---

[79]Ibid., pp. 550–51. Other histories identify this place as Birdhul, the Pāṇḍya capital. Capitals and seaports were often called *pattana* in ancient India. This was not the only instance of Muslims employed by Hindu rulers deserting to Islamic invaders. Muslims have always placed their loyalty to Islam above loyalty to the employer whose salt they have eaten, sometimes for many years.

[80]Mohammad Wahid Mirza, *The Life and Works of Amir Khusrau* (1935), Delhi Reprint, 1974, pp. 183–84.

[81]Elliot and Dowson, op. cit., Vol. III, p. 559.

Shykh Mu'īn al-Dīn Chistī of Ajmer (d. AD 1236)

Ajmer (Rajasthan)

"The other miracle is that before his arrival the whole of Hindustan was submerged by unbelief and idol-worship. Every haughty man in Hind pronounced himself to be Almighty God and considered himself as the partner of God. All the people of India used to prostrate themselves before stones, idols, trees, animals, cows and cow-dung. Because of the darkness of unbelief over this land their hearts were locked and hardened.

"All India was ignorant of orders of religion and law. All were ignorant of Allāh and His Prophet. None had seen the Ka'ba. None had heard of the Greatness of Allāh.

"Because of his coming, the Sun of real believers, the helper of religion, Mu'īn al-dīn, the darkness of unbelief in this land was illumined by the light of Islam.

"Because of his Sword, instead of idols and temples in the land of unbelief now there are mosques, *mihrāb* and *mimbar*. In the land where there were the sayings of the idol-worshippers, there is the sound of 'Allāhu Akbar'.

"The descendants of those who were converted to Islam in this land will live until the Day of Judgement; so too will those who bring others into the fold of Islam by the sword of Islam. Until the Day of Judgement these converts will be in the debt of Shaykh al-Islām Mu'īn al-dīn Hasan Sijzī and these people will be drawing closer to Almighty Allāh because of the auspicious devotion of Mu'īn al-dīn."[82]

(19)
Tārīkh-i-Wassāf

The author, 'Abdu'llāh ibn Fazlu'llāh of Shiraz, is known by his literary name which was Wassāf, the panegyrist. The history he wrote is titled *Tazjiyatu'l Amsār Wa Tajriyatu'l Āsār*. But it is popularly known as *Tārīkh-i-Wassāf*. The first four volumes of the work were published in AD 1300. Later on, the author added a fifth volume, bringing the history down to AD 1328. The work was dedicated to Sultān Uljāītū, the Mongol ruler of Iran.

[82]Cited in P.M. Currie, *The Shrine and Cult of Mu'in al-Dīn Chishtī of Ajmer*, OUP, 1989, p. 30.

Sultān 'Alāu'd-Dīn Khaljī (AD 1296–1316)

Somnath (Gujarat)

"...In short, the Muhammadan army brought the country to utter ruin, and destroyed the lives of the inhabitants, and plundered the cities, and captured their offspring, so that many temples were deserted and the idols were broken and trodden under foot, the largest of which was one called Somnāt, fixed upon stone, polished like a mirror of charming shape and admirable workmanship...Its head was adorned with a crown set with gold and rubies and pearls and other precious stones...and a necklace of large shining pearls, like the belt of Orion, depended from the shoulder towards the side of the body.

"The Muhammadan soldiers plundered all these jewels and rapidly set themselves to demolish the idol. The surviving infidels were deeply affected with grief, and they engaged 'to pay a thousand pieces of gold' as ransom for the idol, but they were indignantly rejected, and the idol was destroyed, and 'its limbs, which were anointed with ambergris and perfumed, were cut off. The fragments were conveyed to Delhi, and the entrance of the Jāmi' Masjid was paved with them, that people might remember and talk of this brilliant victory.' Praise be to God, the Lord of the worlds. Amen !"[83]

(20)
Tārīkh-i-Guzīda

The author, Hamdu'llāh bin 'Abū Bakr bin Hamd bin Nasr Mustaufī of Kazwin in Iran, composed this work in AD 1329. He was secretary to Ghiyāsu'd-Dīn as well as his father Rashīdu'd-Dīn, the ministers of Sultān Uljāītū. His work contains matter not found elsewhere.

Sultān Mahmūd of Ghazni (AD 997–1030)

Nagarkot Kangra (Himachal Pradesh)

"...He now attacked the fort of Bhīm, where was a temple of the Hindus. He was victorious, and obtained much wealth, including about a hundred idols of gold and silver. One of the golden images, which weighed a million *mishkāls*, the Sultān appropriated to the decoration of the Mosque of Ghaznī, so that the ornaments of the doors were of gold instead of iron."[84]

---

[83]Elliot and Dowson, op. cit., Vol. III, pp. 43–44.
[84]Ibid., p. 65.

(21)
Masālik'ul Absār fi Mamālik'ul Amsār

The author, Shihābu'd-Dīn 'Abu'l Abbās Ahmad bin Yahya bin Fazlu'llāh al-'Umrī, was born in AD 1301. He was educated at Damascus and Cairo. He is considered to be a great scholar of his time and author of many books. He occupied high positions in Syria and Egypt. This book of his is a large collection of history, geography and biographies. He himself never visited India about which he based his account on sources available to him. He died at Damascus in AD 1348.

Sultān Muhammad bin Tughlaq (AD 1325–1351)

"The Sultān is not slack in *jihād*. He never lets go of his spear or bridle in pursuing *jihād* by land and sea routes. This is his main occupation which engages his eyes and ears. He has spent vast sums for the establishment of the faith and the spread of Islām in these lands, as a result of which the light of Islām has reached the inhabitants and the flash of the true faith brightened among them. Fire temples[85] have been destroyed and the images and idols of Budd have been broken, and the lands have been freed from those who were not included in the *dāru'l Islām*, that is, those who had refused to become *zimmīs*. Islām has been spread by him in the far east and has reached the point of sunrise. In the words of 'Abū Nasr al-Āinī, he has carried the flags of the followers of Islām where they had never reached before and where no chapter or verse (of the Qur'ān) had ever been recited. Thereafter he got mosques and places of worship erected, and music replaced by call to prayers (*azān*), and the incantations of fire-worshippers stopped by recitations of the Qur'ān. He directed the people of Islām towards the citadels of the infidels and, by the grace of Allāh, made them (the believers) inheritors of wealth and land and that country which they (the believers) had never trodden upon...[86]

"The Sultān who is ruling at present has achieved that which had not been achieved so far by any king. He has achieved victory, supremacy, conquest of countries, destruction of the forts of the infidels, and exposure of magicians. He has destroyed idols by which the people of Hindustān were deceived in vain...."[87]

---

[85]Hindu temples were often called 'fire temples' by Muslim writers as Hindus were often described as 'fire-worshippers' or 'gabrs'. The appellations were transferred from the Zoroastrian temples and the Zoroastrian people.

[86]Translated from the Hindi version by S.A.A. Rizvi included in *Tughlaq Kālīna Bhārata*, Aligarh, 1956, Vol. 1, p. 325.

[87]Ibid., p. 327. The saints, sages, scholars and Brahmin priests of the Hindus were regarded as "magicians" by the theologians of Islam.

(22)

Futūhu's-Salātīn

The author whose full name is not known is famous by his surname of Isāmī. His forefathers had served the Sultāns of Delhi since the days of Shamsu'd-Dīn Iltutmish (AD 1210–1236). He was born in AD 1311–12 and lived at Daulatabad (Devagiri) till 1351 when he finished this work at the age of forty. It covers the period from Mahmūd of Ghazni (AD 997–1030) to Muhammad bin Tughlaq (AD 1325–1351).

Sultān 'Alāu'd-Dīn Khaljī (AD 1296–1316)

Devagiri (Maharashtra)

"Malik Nāib [Kāfūr] reached there expeditiously and occupied the fort....He built mosques in places occupied by temples."[88]

(23)

Rehalā of Ibn Battūta

The full name of this book is *Tuhfātu'n-nuzzār fi Gharāibu'l-amsār wa Ajāibu'l-afsār*. The author was Shykh 'Abū 'Abdu'llāh Muhammad ibn 'Abdu'llāh ibn Muhammad ibn Ibrāhīm al-Lawātī at-Tanjī al-Ma'ruf be Ibn Battūta. He belonged to an Arab family which was settled in Spain since AD 1312. His grandfather and father enjoyed the reputation of scholars and theologians. He himself was a great scholar who travelled extensively and over many lands. He came to India in 1325 and visited many places—east, west, north and south—till he left in 1346. India during this period was ruled by Muhammad bin Tughlaq with whom Ibn Battūta came in close contact. He was very fond of sampling Hindu girls from different parts of India. They were presented to him by the Sultān and other Muslim big-wigs during his sojourn in various places. He also married Muslim women wherever he stayed, and divorced them before his departure. He finished his book in 1355 after reaching Fez in Morocco where his family lived after migration from Spain.

Lahari Bandar (Sindh)

"One day I rode in company with 'Alā-ul-mulk and arrived at a plain called Tarna at a distance of seven miles from the city. There I saw innumerable stone images and animals, many of which had under-

---

[88]Translated from the Hindi version by S.A.A Rizvi included in *Khalji Kālīna Bhārata*, Aligarh, 1955, p. 206

gone a change, the original shape being obliterated.[89] Some were reduced to a head, others to a foot and so on. Some of the stones were shaped like grain, wheat, peas, beans and lentils. And there were traces of a house which contained a chamber built of hewn stone, the whole of which looked like one solid mass. Upon it was a statue in the form of a man, the only difference being that its head was long, its mouth was towards a side of its face and its hands at its back like a captive's. There were pools of water from which an extremely bad smell came. Some of the walls bore Hindī inscriptions. 'Alā-ul-mulk told me that the historians assume that on this site there was a big city, most of the inhabitants of which were notorious. They were changed into stone. The petrified human form on the platform in the house mentioned above was that of their king. The house still goes by the name of 'the king's house'. It is presumed that the Hindī inscriptions, which some of the walls bear, give the history of the destruction of the inhabitants of this city. The destruction took place about a thousand years ago..."[90]

Delhi

"Near the eastern gate of the mosque lie two very big idols of copper connected together by stones. Every one who comes in and goes out of the mosque treads over them. On the site of this mosque was a *bud khānā* that is an idol-house. After the conquest of Delhi it was turned into a mosque..."[91]

Maldive Islands

"Reliable men among the inhabitants of the islands, like the jurist (*faqīh*) and teacher (*mu'allim*) 'Alī, the judge 'Abdullāh—and others besides them—told me that the inhabitants of these islands were infidels....Subsequently a westerner named Abul Barakāt the Berbar who knew the great Qur'ān came to them....He stayed amongst them and God opened the heart of the king to Islām and he accepted it before the end of the month; and his wives, children and courtiers followed suit...They broke to pieces the idols and razed the idol-house to the ground. On this the islanders embraced Islām and sent missionaries to the rest of the islands, the inhabitants of which also became Muslims.

---

[89]The figures were defaced. That is how Islamic iconoclasts spent some of their fury against "false gods".

[90]The Rehalā of Ibn Battūta translated into English by Mahdi Hussain, Baroda, 1967, p. 10. It shows how local legends grew about a whole city destroyed by Muslim invaders during one of their invasions of Sindh. This was most probably the site of Debal.

[91]Ibid., p. 27.

The westerner stood in high regard with them, and they accepted his cult which was that of Imām Mālik. May God be pleased with him! And on account of him they honour the westerners up to this time. He built a mosque which is known after his name..."[92]

(24)
Tārīkh-i-Fīrūz Shāhī

The author, Ziau'd-Dīn Baranī was born in AH 684 (AD 1285–86) at Baran, now known as Bulandshahar, in Uttar Pradesh. His ancestors, paternal as well as maternal, had occupied important positions in the reigns of Sultān Ghiyāsu'd-Dīn Balban (AD 1266–1286) and the Khaljīs. His uncle was a confidant of 'Alāu'd-Dīn Khaljī (AD 1296–1316). Baranī became a friend of Amīr Khusrū and a disciple of Nizāmu'd-Dīn Auliyā', the renowned Chishtī saint of Delhi. His prosperity continued in the reign of Sultān Ghiyāsu'd-Dīn Tughlaq (AD 1320–1325) and he became a favourite of Sultān Muhammad bin Tughlaq (AD 1325–1351). But he fell from favour with the rise of Sultān Fīrūz Tughlaq (AD 1351–1388) and was imprisoned for five months for some offence. He completed this history in AD 1357. It covers a period of 82 years, from AD 1265 onwards. He wrote several other books among which *Fatwa-i-Jahāndārī* is famous for its tenets regarding how an Islamic state should be run. Baranī's ideal ruler was Sultān Mahmūd of Ghazni. He exhorted Muslim rulers to follow Mahmūd's example in their treatment of Hindus, for whom he often uses very foul language.

Sultān Jalālu'd-Dīn Khaljī (AD 1290–1296)

Jhain (*Rajasthan*)

"In the year AH 689 (AD 1290), the Sultān led an army to Rantambhor.... He took ...Jhāin, destroyed the idol temples, and broke and burned the idols..."[93]

Vidisha (*Madhya Pradesh*)

" 'Alāu'd-dīn at this time held the territory of Karra, and with the permission of the Sultān he marched to Bhailsān (Bhīlsa). He captured some bronze idols which the Hindus worshipped and sent them on carts with a variety of rich booty as presents to the Sultān. The idols were

[92]Ibid., pp. 203–04. The "westerner" was a Muslim missionary from North Africa which is known as *Maghrib* (the West) among the Arabs. See Thor Heyerdahl, *The Maldive Mystery*, Bethesda (Maryland, USA), 1986, for the large number of Hindu temples destroyed. Many mosques stand on their sites now.

[93]Elliot and Dowson, Vol. III, p. 46.

laid before the Badāūn gate for true believers to tread upon..."[94]

Sultān 'Alāu'd-Dīn Khaljī (AD 1296–1316)

Somnath (Gujarat)

"At the beginning of the third year of the reign, Ulugh Khān and Nusrat Khān, with their *amīrs* and generals, and a large army marched against Gujarāt... All Gujarāt became a prey to the invaders, and the idol, which after the victory of Sultān Mahmūd and his destruction of (the idol) of Manāt, the Brahmans had set up under the name of Somanāt, for the worship of the Hindus, was carried to Delhi where it was laid for the people to tread upon..."[95]

Ma'bar (Tamil Nadu)

"....Malik Nāīb Kāfūr marched on to Ma'bar, which he also took. He destroyed the golden idol temple (*but-khānah i-zarīn*) of Ma'bar, and the golden idols which for ages had been worshipped by the Hindus of that country. The fragments of the golden temple, and of the broken idols of gold and gilt became the rich spoil of the army...."[96]

(25)
Tārīkh-i-Fīrūz Shāhī

The author, Shams Sirāj Afīf or Shamsu'd-Dīn bin Sirāju'd-Dīn, became a courtier of Sultān Fīrūz Shāh Tughlaq and undertook to complete the aforementioned history of Baranī who had stopped at the sixth year of Fīrūz Shāh's reign.

Sultān Fīrūz Shāh Tughlaq (AD 1351–1388)

Puri (Orissa)

"The Sultān left Banārasī with the intention of pursuing the Rāī of Jājnagar, who had fled to an island in the river...News was then brought that in the *jangal* were seven elephants, and one old she-elephant, which was very fierce. The Sultān resolved upon endeavouring to capture these elephants before continuing the pursuit of the Rāī...[97]

---

[94]Ibid., p. 148. The last line according to S.A.A. Rizvi should be translated as "so that people may be educated" (*Khaljī Kālīna Bhārata*, p. 29), and as "for the fun of the people" according to Dr. Mu'īn-ul-Haq (Urdu translation of Baranī, Lahore, 1983, p. 335).

[95]Ibid., p. 163. Dr. Mu'īn-ul-Haq translate it as "for the fun of the people," (Ibid., p. 377), but S.A.A. Rizvi agrees with Elliot's translation.

[96]Ibid., p. 204.

[97]Ibid., p. 313. Banārasī is the name of Cuttack which was known as Kataka-Vārāṇasī to the Hindus of medieval India.

"After the hunt was over, the Sultān directed his attention to the Rāī of Jājnagar, and entering the palace where he dwelt he found many fine buildings. It is reported that inside the Rāī's fort, there was a stone idol which the infidels called Jagannāth, and to which they paid their devotions. Sultān Fīroz, in emulation of Mahmūd Subuktigīn, having rooted up the idol, carried it away to Delhi where he placed it in an ignominious position..."[98]

Nagarkot Kangra (Himachal Pradesh)

"The idol, Jwālāmukhī, much worshipped by the infidels, was situated on the road to Nagarkot...Some of the infidels have reported that Sultān Fīroz went specially to see this idol and held a golden umbrella over it. But the author was informed by his respected father, who was in the Sultān's retinue, that the infidels slandered the Sultān, who was a religious, God-fearing man, who, during the whole forty years of his reign, paid strict obedience to the law, and that such an action was impossible. The fact is, that when he went to see the idol, all the *rāīs*, *rānas* and *zamīndārs* who accompanied him were summoned into his presence, when he addressed them, saying, 'O fools and weak-minded, how can ye pray to and worship this stone, for our holy law tells us that those who oppose the decrees of our religion, will go to hell?' The Sultān held the idol in the deepest detestation, but the infidels, in the blindness of their delusion, have made this false statement against him. Other infidels have said that Sultān Muhammad Shāh bin Tughlik Shāh held an umbrella over the same idol, but this is also a lie; and good Muhammadans should pay no heed to such statements. These two Sultāns were sovereigns especially chosen by the Almighty from among the faithful, and in the whole course of their reigns, wherever they took an idol temple they broke and destroyed it; how, then, can such assertions be true? The infidels must certainly have lied!"[99]

Delhi

"A report was brought to the Sultān that there was in Delhi an old Brahman (*zunār dār*) who persisted in publicly performing the worship of idols in his house; and that people of the city, both Musulmāns and Hindus, used to resort to his house to worship the idol. The Brahman had constructed a wooden tablet (*muhrak*), which was covered within

[98]Ibid., p. 314.

[99]Ibid., p. 318. Hindus had to spread such "lies" in order to save their temples from demolition and their idols from desecration by succeeding sultāns and swordsmen of Islam.

and without with paintings of demons and other objects...An order was accordingly given that the Brahman, with his tablet, should be brought into the presence of the Sultān at Fīrozābād. The judges and doctors and elders and lawyers were summoned, and the case of the Brahman was submitted for their opinion. Their reply was that the provisions of the Law were clear: the Brahman must either become a Musulmān or be burned. The true faith was declared to the Brahman, and the right course pointed out, but he refused to accept it. Orders were given for raising a pile of faggots before the door of the *darbār*. The Brahman was tied hand and foot and cast into it; the tablet was thrown on top and the pile was lighted. The writer of this book was present at the *darbār* and witnessed the execution. The tablet of the Brahman was lighted in two places, at his head and at his feet; the wood was dry, and the fire first reached his feet, and drew from him a cry, but the flames quickly enveloped his head and consumed him. Behold the Sultānīs strict adherence to law and rectitude, how he would not deviate in the least from its decrees !"[100]

(26)
Inshā-i-Māhrū

The author, Āīnu'd-Dīn Abdullāh bin Māhrū, was a high official in the court of Sultān Fīrūz Shāh Tughlaq. *Inshā-i-Māhrū* is a collection of 133 letters related to various events.

Sultān Fīrūz Shāh Tughlaq (AD 1351–1388)

Jajnagar (*Orissa*)

"The victorious standards set out from Jaunpur for the destruction of idols, slaughter of the enemies of Islām and hunt for elephants near Padamtalāv...The Sultān saw Jājnagar which had been praised by all travellers...[101]

"The troops which had been appointed for the destruction of places around Jājnagar, ended the conceit of the infidels by means of the sword and the spear. Wherever there were temples and idols in that area, they were trampled under the hoofs of the horses of Musalmāns...[102]

"After obtaining victory and sailing on the sea and destroying the

---

[100]Ibid., p. 365. *Zunār or Zunnār* is the Muslim term for the sacred thread worn by the Brāhmaṇas who were accordingly called *Zunār-dārs*.

[101]Translated from the Hindi version by S.A.A. Rizvi included in *Tughlaq Kālīna Bhārata*, Aligarh, 1957, Vol. II, p. 380.

[102]Ibid., p. 381.

temple of Jagannāth and slaughtering the idolaters, the victorious standards started towards Delhi..."[103]

(27)
Futūhāt-i-Fīrūz Shāhī

This small history was written by Sultān Fīrūz Shāh Tughlaq (AD 1351–1388) himself. The writer of *Tabqāt-i-Akbarī*, Nizām'ud-Dīn Ahmad, a 16th century historian, says that the Sultān had got the eight chapters of his work inscribed on eight slabs of stone which were fixed on eight sides of the octagonal dome of a building near the Jāmi' Masjid at Fīrūzābād.

Prayers for Temple-destroyers of the Past

"The next matter which by God's help I accomplished, was the repetition of names and titles of former sovereigns which had been omitted from the prayers of Sabbaths and Feasts. The names of those sovereigns of Islām, under whose happy fortune and favour infidel countries had been conquered, whose banners had waved over many a land, under whom *idol-temples had been demolished*, and mosques and pulpits built and exalted, the fragrant creed had been extended, and the people of Islām had waxen strong and warlike, the names of these men had fallen into neglect and oblivion. So I decreed that according to established custom their names and titles should be rehearsed in the *khutba* and aspirations offered for the remission of their sins."[104]

Delhi and Environs

"The Hindus and idol-worshippers had agreed to pay the money for toleration (*zar-i zimmiya*) and had consented to the poll-tax (*jizya*) in return for which they and their families enjoyed security. These people now erected new idol-temples in the city and the environs in opposition to the Law of the Prophet which declares that such temples are not to be tolerated. Under divine guidance I destroyed these edifices and I killed those leaders of infidelity who seduced others into error, and the lower orders I subjected to stripes and chastisement, until this abuse was entirely abolished. The following is an instance:- In the vil-

---

[103]Ibid., p. 382.

[104]Elliot and Dowson, op. cit., Vol. III, pp. 376–77. This translation does not mention "idol-temples had been demolished." This qualification of the "former sovereigns", however, is mentioned in the Hindi translation by S.A.A. Rizvi included in *Tughlaq Kālīna Bhārata*, Aligarh, 1957, Vol. II, p. 328.

lage of Malūh[105] there is a tank which they call *kund* (tank). Here they had built idol-temples and on certain days the Hindus were accustomed to proceed thither on horseback, and wearing arms. Their women and children also went out in palankins and carts. There they assembled in thousands and performed idol-worship...When intelligence of this came to my ears my religious feelings prompted me at once to put a stop to this scandal and offence to the religion of Islām. On the day of the assembly I went there in person and I ordered that the leaders of these people and the promoters of this abomination should be put to death. I forbade the infliction of any severe punishments on Hindus in general, but I destroyed their idol-temples, and instead thereof raised mosques. I founded two flourishing towns (*kasba*), one called Tughlikpūr, the other Sālārpūr. Where infidels and idolaters worshipped idols, Musulmāns now, by God's mercy, perform their devotions to the true God. Praises of God and the summons to prayer are now heard there, and that place which was formerly the home of infidels has become the habitation of the faithful, who there repeat their creed and offer up their praises to God.

"Information was brought to me that some Hindus had erected a new idol temple in the village of Sālihpūr, and were performing worship to their idols. I sent some persons there to destroy the idol temple, and put a stop to their pernicious incitements to error."[106]

Gohana (*Haryana*)

"Some Hindūs had erected a new idol-temple in the village of Kohāna, and the idolaters used to assemble there and perform their idolatrous rites. These people were seized and brought before me. I ordered that the perverse conduct of the leaders of this wickedness should be publicly proclaimed, and that they should be put to death before the gate of the palace. I also ordered that the infidel books, the idols, and the vessels used in their worship, which had been taken with them, should all be publicly burnt. The others were restrained by threats and punishments, as a warning to all men, that no *zimmī* could follow such wicked practices in a Musulmān country."[107]

---

[105]It was probably Malzā or Malchā where, according to Shams Sīrāj, Sultān Fīrūz had built a dam. This place is near the Kalka Temple in the area of Okhla (S.A.A. Rizvi, *Tughlaq Kālīna Bhārata*, Vol. II, p. 333, footnote 1).

[106]Elliot and Dowson, op. cit., Vol. III, pp. 380–81. The apologists of Islam tell us that *zimmīs* are guaranteed freedom of worship once they agree to pay *jijyah*. Here we have a most pious sultān saying and acting otherwise.

[107]Ibid., p. 381.

(28)

Sīrat-Fīrūz Shāhī

It is a text either written or dictated by Sultān Fīrūz Shāh Tughlaq himself. According to this book, the objects of his expedition to Jajnagar were: "extirpating Rai Gajpat, massacring the unbelievers, demolishing their temples, hunting elephants, and getting a glimpse of their enchanting country." 'Ain-ul-Mulk also says, "The object of the expedition was to break the idols, to shed the blood of the enemies of Islām (and) to hunt elephants."[108]

Sultān Fīrūz Shāh Tughlaq (AD 1351–1388)

Puri (Orissa)

"Allāh, who is the only true God and has no other emanation, endowed the king of Islām with the strength to destroy this ancient shrine on the eastern sea-coast and to plunge it into the sea, and after its destruction, he ordered the nose of the image of Jagannāth to be perforated and disgraced it by casting it down on the ground. They dug out other idols, which were worshipped by the polytheists in the kingdom of Jājnagar, and overthrew them as they did the image of Jagannāth, for being laid in front of the mosques along the path of the Sunnis and way of the *musallis* (the multitude who offer prayers) and stretched them in front of the portals of every mosque, so that the body and sides of the images may be trampled at the time of ascent and descent, entrance and exit, by the shoes on the feet of the Muslims."[109]

(29)

Tārīkh-i-Mubārak Shāhī

The author, Yahya bin Ahmad bin Abdu'llāh Sirhindī, lived in the reign of Sultān Muizu'd-Dīn Abu'l Fath Mubārak Shāh (AD 1421–1434) of the Sayyid dynasty which ruled at Delhi from AD 1414 to 1451. This history starts from the time of Muhammad Ghūrī (AD 1175–1206) and closes with the year AD 1434.

Sultān Shamsu'd-Dīn Iltutmish (AD 1210–1236)

Vidisha and Ujjain (Madhya Pradesh)

"In AH 631 he invaded Mālwah, and after suppressing the rebels of that place, he destroyed that idol-temple which had existed there for the

---

[108]Quoted in R.C. Majumdar (ed.), op. cit., Vol. VI, *The Delhi Sultanate*, Bombay, 1960, p. 94.

[109]Quoted in Ibid., pp. 105–06.

past three hundred years.

"Next he turned towards Ujjain and conquered it, and after demolishing the idol-temple of Mahākāl, he uprooted the statue of Bikramājīt together with all other statues and images which were placed on pedestals, and brought them to the capital where they were laid before the Jāmi' Masjid for being trodden under foot by the people."[110]

Sultān 'Alāu'd-Dīn Khaljī (AD 1296–1316)

Somnath (*Gujarat*)

"Ulugh Khān invaded Gujarāt. He sacked the whole country....He pursued the Rāī upto Somnāth. He destroyed the temple of Somnāth which was the principal place of worship for the Hindūs and great Rāīs since ancient times. He constructed a mosque on the site and returned to Delhi..."[111]

(30)
Tārīkh-i-Muhammadī

The author, Muhammad Bihāmad Khānī was the son of the governor of Irich in Bundelkhand. He was a soldier who participated in several wars. At last he became the disciple of a Sufi, Yūsuf Buddha, of Irich and spent the rest of his life in religious pursuits. His history covers a long period—from Prophet Muhammad to AD 1438–39.

Sultān Ghiyāsu'd-Dīn Tughlaq Shāh II (AD 1388–89)

Kalpi (*Uttar Pradesh*)

"In the meanwhile Delhi received news of the defeat of the armies of Islām which were with Malikzādā Mahmūd bin Fīrūz Khān...This Malikzādā reached the bank of the Yamunā via Shāhpur and renamed Kālpī, which was the abode and centre of the infidels and the wicked, as Muhammadābād, after the name of Prophet Muhammad. He got mosques erected for the worship of Allāh in places occupied by temples, and made that city his capital."[112]

---

[110]Translated from the Urdu version by Dr. Āftāb Asghar, second edition, Lahore, 1982.

[111]Translated from the Hindi version by S.A.A Rizvi included in *Khalji Kālīna Bhārata*, Aligarh, 1955, p. 223.

[112]Translated from the Hindi version by S.A.A Rizvi included in *Tughlaq Kālīna Bhārata*, Aligarh, 1957, Vol. II, pp. 228–29.

Sultān Nasīru'd-Dīn Mahmūd Shāh Tughlaq (AD 1389–1412)

Kalpi (Uttar Pradesh)

"Historians have recorded that in the auspicious year AH 792 (AD 1389–90) Sultān Nasīru'd-Dīn got founded a city named Muhammadābād, after the name of Prophet Muhammad, at a place known as Kālpī which was a home of the accursed infidels, and he got mosques raised in place of temples for the worship of Allāh. He got palaces, tombs and schools constructed, and ended the wicked ways of the infidels, and promoted the Shariat of Prophet Muhammad..."[113]

Khandaut (Uttar Pradesh)

"He laid waste Khaṇdaut which was the home of infidels and, having made it an abode of Islām, founded Mahmūdābād after his own name. He got a splendid palace and fort constructed there and established all the customs of Islām in that city and place."[114]

Prayag and Kara (Uttar Pradesh)

"The Sultān moved with the armies of Islām towards Prayāg and Arail with the aim of destroying the infidels, and he laid waste both those places. The vast crowd which had collected at Prayāg for worshipping false gods was made captive. The inhabitants of Karā were freed from the mischief of rebels on account of this aid from the king and the name of this king of Islām became famous by this reason."[115]

(31)
Jawamiu'l Kilām

The book contains the *malfūzāt* of Khwājah Sayyid Muhammad bin Yūsuf al-Husainī Bandā Nawāz Gisū Darāz (AD 1321–1422), one of the leading disciples of Shykh Nasiru'd-Dīn Mahmūd Chirāgh-i-Dihlī. He settled down at Gulbarga, the capital of the Bahmanī Empire in the Deccan, and became the mentor of Sultān Ahmad Shāh Bahmanī (AD 1422–1436).

Shykh Jalālu'd-Dīn Tabrizī (AH 533–623)

Pandua (Bengal)

"An anecdote relating to Shaikh Jalaluīd-Dinīs stay in Deva Mahal

[113]Translated from the Hindi version by S.A.A Rizvi included in *Uttara Taimūr Kālīna Bhārata*, Aligarh, 1959, Vol. II, p. 27.

[114]Ibid., pp. 27–28.

[115]Ibid., p. 29.

reads like other stock-in-trade stories and fairytales. It was related by such an authority as Gisu Daraz. According to him Shaikh Jalalu'd-Din stayed at Pandua in the house of a flower vendor. On the day of his arrival, he found each of the house members crying. On enquiry he was told there was a demon in the temple who daily ate a young man. It was the king's duty to provide the demon with his daily food. On that day it was the turn of the young son in the family. The Shaikh requested them to send him in place of their son but they refused to accept the offer for fear of the king. The Shaikh, then followed the young man to the temple and killed the demon with a single blow from his staff. When the king accompanied by his retinue reached the temple to worship the demon they were amazed to find the demon killed and an old man dressed in black with his head covered with a blanket. The Shaikh invited them to see the fate with their god. The sight of their vanquished idol prompted them to accept Islam."[116]

(32)
Habību's-Siyar

The author, Ghiyāsu'd-Dīn Muhammad bin Humāmu'd-Dīn, is known as Khondmīr. He was the son of Mīrkhond, the author of the famous Persian history, *Rauzatu's-Safa*. Born at Herat in AD 1475 he reached Agra in 1528–29 when he was introduced to Bābur. He accompanied Bābur in his expedition to Bengal and Humāyūn in his expedition to Gujarat where he died in 1534–35. His *Khulāstu'l-Akhbār* is a history of Asia brought down to AD 1471. The *Habību's-Siyar* which he started writing in 1521 starts with the birth of the Prophet and comes down to AD 1534–35.

Sultān Mahmūd of Ghazni (AD 997–1030)

Somnath (Gujarat)

"He several times waged war against the infidels of Hindustān, and he brought under his subjection a large portion of their country, until, having made himself master of Somnāt, he destroyed all idol temples of that country...[117]

"...Sultān Mahmūd, having entered into the idol temple, beheld an excessively long and broad room, in so much that fifty-six pillars had

---

[116]Summarised by S.A.A. Rizvi in *History of Sufism in India*, New Delhi, 1978, Vol. I, pp. 201–202, footnote 4. Tabrizī is most probably the hero of *Sekasubhodaya*, a Sanskrit work ascribed to Halāyudha Miśra, discovered at Gaur in Bengal and edited with an English translation by Sukumar Sen, Calcutta, 1963.

[117]Elliot and Dowson, op. cit., Vol. IV, p. 166.

been made to support the roof. Somnāt was an idol cut out of stone, whose height was five yards, of which three yards were visible, and two yards were concealed in the ground. Yamīnu-d daula having broken that idol with his own hand, ordered that they should pack up pieces of the stone, take them to Ghaznīn, and throw them on the threshold of the Jāmaī Masjid...."[118]

Mathura (*Uttar Pradesh*)

"From that place the Sultān proceeded to a certain city, which was accounted holy by the people of the country. In that city the men of Ghaznīn saw so many strange and wonderful things, that to tell them or to write a description of them is not easy... In short, the Sultān Mahmūd having possessed himself of the booty, burned their idol temples and proceeded towards Kanauj."[119]

Kanauj (*Uttar Pradesh*)

"...The Ghaznivids found in these forts and their dependencies 10,000 idol temples, and they ascertained the vicious belief of the Hindus to be, that since the erection of these buildings no less than three or four hundred thousand years had elapsed. Sultān Mahmūd during this expedition achieved many other conquests after he left Kanauj, and sent to hell many of the infidels with blows of the well tempered sword. Such a number of slaves were assembled in that great camp, that the price of a single one did not exceed ten *dirhams*."[120]

(33)
Bābur-Nāma

It is an autobiography written in the form of a diary by Zahīru'd-Dīn Muhammad Bābur, founder of the Mughal dynasty in India, who proclaimed himself a Pādshāh after his victory in the First Battle of Panipat (AD 1526), and a Ghāzī (killer of *kāfirs*) after the defeat of Rāṇā Sāṅgā in the Battle of Khanwa (AD 1528). While presenting himself as an indefatigable warrior and drug-addict he does not hide the cruelties he committed on the defeated people, particularly his fondness for building towers of the heads of those he captured as prisoners of war or killed in battle. He is very liberal in citing appropriate verses

[118]Ibid., pp. 182–83.
[119]Ibid., pp. 178–79.
[120]Ibid., pp. 179–80. The number of temples mentioned in this passage means the number of temples destroyed.

from the Qur'ān on the eve of his battle with Rāṇā Sāṅgā. In order to ensure his victory, he makes a covenant with Allāh by breaking the vessels containing wine as also the cups for drinking it, swearing at the same time that "he would break the idols of the idol-worshippers in a similar manner."[121] In the *Fath-Nāma* (prayer for victory) composed for him by Shykh Zain, Allah is described as "destroyer of idols from their foundations."[122] The language he uses for his Hindu adversaries is typically Islamic.

Zahīru'd-Dīn Muhammad Bābur Pādshāh Ghāzī (AD 1526–1530)

Chanderi (Madhya Pradesh)

"In AH 934 (AD 1528), I attacked Chanderī and, by the grace of Allāh, captured it in a few hours...We got the infidels slaughtered and the place which had been a *dāru'l-harb* for years, was made into a *dāru'l-Islām*."[123]

Gwalior (Madhya Pradesh)

"Next day, at the time of the noon prayer, we went out for seeing those places in Gwālior which we had not yet seen...Going out of the Hāthīpole Gate of the fort, we arrived at a place called Urwā...

"Solid rocks surround Urwā on three sides..On these sides people have carved statues in stone. They are in all sizes, small and big. A very big statue, which is on the southern side, is perhaps 20 yards high. These statues are altogether naked and even their private parts are not covered...

"Urwā is not a bad place. It is an enclosed space. Its biggest blemish is its statues. I ordered that they should be destroyed."[124]

(34)
Siyaru'l-'Ārifīn

The author, Hamīd bin Fazlullāh is also known as Dervish Jamālī Kamboh Dihlawī. He was a Sufi of the Suhrawardiyya sect who died in AD 1536 while accompanying the Mughal Emperor Humāyun in the latter's expedition to Gujarat. His son, Shykh Gadāī was with the

[121]Translated from the Hindi version by S.A.A. Rizvi included in *Mughal Kālīna Bhārata: Bābur*, Aligarh, 1960, p. 233.

[122]Ibid., p. 237.

[123]Ibid., p. 167. Professor Sri Ram Sharma cites from *Tārīkh-i-Bāburī* that "His Sadr, Shaikh Zain, demolished many Hindu temples at Chanderī when he occupied it" (*Religious Policy of the Mughal Emperors*, p. 9).

[124]Ibid., p. 277. It seems that for some reason, the statues could not be destroyed, though they were mutilated. All of them are Jain statues.

Mughal army in the Second Battle of Panipat (AD 1556) and advised Akbar to kill the Hindu king, Hīmū, with his own hand. On Akbar's refusal, according to Badāunī, Shykh Gadāī helped Bairam Khān in doing the same deed. *Siyaru'l-'Ārifīn*, completed between AD 1530 and 1536, is an account of the Chishtī and Suhrawardī Sufis of the period.

Shykh Jalālu'd-Dīn Tabrizī (AH 533–623)

He was the second most outstanding disciple of Shykh Shihabu'd-Dīn Suhrawardī (AD 1145–1235), founder of the Suhrawardiyya *silsilā* of Sufism. Having lived in Multan, Delhi and Badaun, he finally settled down in Lakhanauti, also known as Gaur, in Bengal.

Devatala (Bengal)

"Shaikh Jalalu'd-Din had many disciples in Bengal. He first lived at Lakhnauti, constructed a *khanqah* and attached a *langar* to it. He also bought some gardens and land to be attached to the monastery. He moved to Devatalla (Deva Mahal) near Pandua in northern Bengal. There a *kafir* (either a Hindu or a Buddhist) had erected a large temple and a well. The Shaikh demolished the temple and constructed a *takiya* (*khanqah*) and converted a large number of *kafirs*... Devatalla came to be known as Tabrizabad and attracted a large number of pilgrims."[125]

Shykh 'Abū Bakr Tūsī Haidarī (Thirteenth Century AD)

He was a qalandar (anchorite) of the Haidarī sect founded by a Turk named Haidar, who lived in Sawa in Kuhistan. His disciples migrated into India when the Mongols sacked their homeland.

Delhi

"The most prominent Indian Haidari was Shaikh Abu Bakr Tusi Haidari, who settled in Delhi in the mid-thirteenth century. There he demolished a temple on a site on the banks of the Jamna where he built a *khanqah* and organized *sama* gathering. Shaikh Nizamu'd-Din Auliya' was a frequent visitor of Abu Bakr as was Shaikh Jamalu'd-Din of Hansi when he was in Delhi. The latter gave Shaikh Abu Bakr the title Baz-i Safid (White Falcon) symbolizing his rare mystical achievements."[126]

---

[125]Summarised by S.A.A. Rizvi in his, *A History of Sufism in India*, Vol. I, New Delhi, 1978, pp. 201–02.

[126]Summarised by Ibid., p. 307.

(35)
Tārīkh-i-Shāhī

The author, Ahmad Yādgār, was an old servant of the Sūr sultāns. He started writing this history on order from Da'ūd Shāh bin Sulaimān Shāh. It is also known as *Tārīkh-i-Afāghana* and *Tārīkh-i-Salātīn-i-Afāghana*. It deals with the history of the Lodīs down to AD 1554. He completed it in AH 1001–02 (AD 1592–93). He calls the Hindu kings "rascally infidels", "black-faced foes", "evil-doers", "dark-faced men", etc. He extols the plunder and depopulation of entire regions by Bahlūl Lodī (AD 1451–1489). He reports how Bābur presented to his sons, Humāyūn and Kāmrān, two daughters of the Rājā of Chanderi.

Sultān Sikandar Lodī (AD 1489–1517)

Kurukshetra (Haryana)

"One day he ordered that 'an expedition be sent to Thaneswar, (the tanks at) Kurkaksetra should be filled up with earth, and the land measured and allotted to pious people for their maintenance,'...He was such a great partisan of Islām in the days of his youth...."[127]

Nagarkot Kangra (Himachal Pradesh)

"Sultān Sikandar led a very pious life...Islām was regarded very highly in his reign. The infidels could not muster the courage to worship idols or bathe in the (sacred) streams. During his holy reign, idols were hidden underground. The stone (idol) of Nagarkot, which had misled the (whole) world, was brought and handed over to butchers so that they might weigh meat with it."[128]

Sultān Ibrāhīm Lodī (AD 1517–1526)

Gwalior (Madhya Pradesh)

"It so happened that Rājā Mān, the ruler of Gwālior who had been warring with the Sultāns for years, went to hell. His son, Bikarmājīt, became his successor. The Sultān captured the fort after a hard fight. There was a quadruped, made of copper, at the door of the fort. It used to speak. It was brought from there and placed in the fort at Agra. It remained there till the reign of Akbar Bādshāh. It was melted and a cannon was made out of it at the order of the Bādshāh."[129]

---

[127]Translated from the Hindi version of S.A.A. Rizvi included in *Uttara Taimūr Kālīna Bhārata*, Aligarh, 1955, Vol. I, p. 322.

[128]Ibid., p. 331.

[129]Ibid., p. 343.

(36)
Tārīkh-i-Sher Shāhī

The author, Abbās Sarwānī, was connected with the family of Sher Shāh Sūr by marriage. He wrote this work by order of Akbar, the Mughal emperor, and named it *Tuhfāt-i-Akbar Shāhī*. But it became known as *Tārīkh-i-Sher Shāhī* because of its main theme. He wrote it probably soon after AD 1579.

Sher Shāh Sūr (AD 1538–1545)

"...The nobles and chiefs said, 'It seems expedient that the victorious standards should move towards the Dekhin'....Sher Shāh replied : 'What you have said is most right and proper, but it has come into my mind that since the time of Sultān Ibrāhīm, the infidel *zamīndārs* have rendered the country of Islām full of unbelievers, and having thrown down masjids and buildings of the believers, placed idol-shrines in them, and they are in possession of the country of Delhī and Mālwā. Until I have cleansed the country from the existing contamination of the unbelievers, I will not go into any other country'...."[130]

(37)
Wāqi'āt-i-Mushtāqī

The author, Shykh Rizqu'llāh Mushtāqī, was born in AD 1492 and died in 1581. He heard accounts of the past from the learned men of his times and compiled them in a book. He was a great story-teller who revelled in "marvels". He was known for his study of Sufi doctrines and spiritual exercises.

Sultān Sikandar Lodī (AD 1489–1517)

Nagarkot Kangra (*Himachal Pradesh*)

"Khawās Khān, who was the predecessor of Mīān Bhūa, having been ordered by the Sultān to march towards Nagarkot, in order to bring the hill country under subjection, succeeded in conquering it, and having sacked the infidels' temple of Debi Shankar, brought away the stone which they worshipped, together with a copper umbrella, which was placed over it, and on which a date was engraved in Hindu characters, representing it to be two thousand years old. When the stone was sent to the King, it was given over to the butchers to make weights out of it for the purpose of weighing their meat. From the copper of the umbrella, several pots were made, in which water might be warmed,

[130]Elliot and Dowson, op. cit., Vol. IV, pp. 403–04.

and which were placed in the *masjids* and the King's own palace, so that everyone might wash his hands, feet and face in them and perform his purifications before prayers..."[131]

Mathura (*Uttar Pradesh*)

"He got the temples of the infidels destroyed. No trace of infidelity was left at the place in Mathurā where the infidels used to take bath. He got caravansarais constructed so that people could stay there, and also the shops of various professionals such as the butchers, *bāwarchīs*, *nānbāīs* and sweetmeatsellers. If a Hindu went there for bathing even by mistake, he was made to lose his limbs and punished severely. No Hindu could get shaved at that place. No barber would go near a Hindu, whatever be the payment offered."[132]

Sultān Ghiyāsu'd-Dīn Khaljī of Malwa (AD 1469–1500)

Jodhpur (*Rajasthan*)

"Once upon a time a temple had been constructed in Jodhpur. The Sultān sent the Qāzī of Mandū with orders that he should get the temple demolished. He had said to him, 'If they do not demolish the temple on instructions from you, you stay there and let me know.' When the Qāzī arrived there, the infidels refused to obey the order of the Sultān and said, 'Has Ghiyāsu'd-Dīn freed himself from lechery so that he has turned his attention to this side?' The Qāzī informed the king accordingly. He climbed on his mount in Mandū and reached Jodhpur in a single night. He punished the infidels and laid waste the temple..."[133]

(38)
Tārīkh-i-Alfī

It was composed in AD 1585 by Mullā Ahmad Thaṭāwī and Āsaf Khān. It covers a period of one thousand years from the death of the Prophet.

Sultān Mahmūd of Ghazni (AD 997–1030)

Somnath (*Gujarat*)

"Mahmūd, as soon as his eyes fell on this idol, lifted up his battle-

---

[131]Ibid., p. 544.

[132]Translated from the Hindi version by S.A.A. Rizvi included in *Uttara Taimūr-Kālīna Bhārata*, Aligarh, 1958, Vol. I, p. 102.

[133]Ibid., Vol. II, p. 138. Ghiyāsu'd-Dīn had collected 16,000 women in his harem and was notorious for his lewdness. Piety in Islam has no relation with personal character. Lechers can serve the faith as well as the recluse.

axe with much anger, and struck it with such force that the idol broke into pieces. The fragments of it were ordered to be taken to Ghaznīn, and were cast down at the threshold of the Jāmi' Masjid where they are lying to this day...."[134]

(39)
Burhān-i-Ma'sir

The author, Sayyid 'Alī bin 'Azīzu'llāh Tabātabā Hasanī, served Muhammad Qutb Shāh (AD 1580–1627) of Golconda at first and then Sultān Burhān Nizām Shāh (AD 1591–1595) of Ahmadnagar. He wrote this history in AD 1592. It deals with the Bahmanī Sultāns of Gulbarga (AD 1347–1422) and Bidar (AD 1422–1538) and the Nizām Shāhī Sultāns of Ahmadnagar upto AD 1596.

Sultān 'Alāu'd-Dīn Hasan Bahman Shāh (AD 1347–1358)
Dankuri (Karnataka)

"The Sultān sent Khwāja-i-Jahān to Gulbargā, Sikandar Khān to Bīdar, Qīr Khān to Kūtar, Safdar Khān to Sakar which is called Sāgar, and Husain Garshāsp to Kotgīr. He appointed other chiefs to invade the kingdom of the infidels. 'Aitmādul Mulk and Mubārak Khān led raids upon the river Tāwī and laid waste the Hindu Kingdom. After having invaded the province of Dankurī and cutting off the head of Manāt,[135] they attacked Janjwāl..."[136]

(40)
Tabqāt-i-Akbarī

The author, Khwājah Nizāmu'd-Dīn Ahmad bin Muhammad Muqīm al-Harbī, was a Bakshī in the reign of Akbar, the Mughal emperor (AD 1556–1605). He worte this history in AD 1592–93 and added to it, later on, events upto 1593–94. He died next year. The history starts with the times of the Ghaznivid Sultāns. The work was initially known as *Tabqāt-i-Akbar Shāhī* but became known as simply *Tabqāt-i-Akbarī*. It is also known as *Tārīkh-i-Nizāmī*. It is the first Muslim history which confines itself to India and excludes matter relating to other countries.

---

[134]Elliot and Dowson, op. cit., Vol. II, p. 471.

[135]The reference is to some Hindu Goddess. Islamic iconoclasts often named Hindu Goddesses after those of Arabia whose idols the prophet of Islam had destroyed.

[136]Translated from the Hindi version of S.A.A. Rizvi included in *Tughlaq Kālīna Bhārata*, Aligarh, 1956, Vol. I, p. 370.

Amīr Subuktigīn (AD 977–997)

"After this with kingly energy and determination, he girded up his loins for a war of religion, and invaded Hindustān, and carried away many prisoners of war and other plunder; and in every country, which he conquered, he founded mosques, and he endeavoured to ruin and desolate the territories of Rājā Jaipāl who, at that time, was the ruler of Hindustān."[137]

Sultān Mahmūd of Ghazni (AD 997–1030)

Thanesar (Haryana)

"The Sultān now received information that there was a city in Hindustān called Thānessar, and there was a great temple there in which there was an idol called Jagarsom, whom the people of Hindustān worshipped. He collected a large force with the object of carrying on a religious war, and in the year AH 402 marched towards Thānessar. The son of Jaipāl having received intelligence of this, sent an envoy and represented through him, that if the Sultān would relinquish this enterprise, he would send fifty elephants as tribute. The Sultān paid no heed to this offer, and when he reached Thānessar he found the city empty. The soldiers ravaged and plundered whatever they could lay hands upon, broke the idols and carried Jagarsom to Ghaznīn. The Sultān ordered that the idol should the placed in front of the place of prayer, so that people would trample upon it."[138]

Mathura (Uttar Pradesh)

"From that place [Mahāwan] the Sultān advanced to Mathurah, which is a large city containing many temples...and the Sultān completely destroyed the city and burnt the temples...There was one golden idol which was broken up under the orders of the Sultān..."[139]

Somnath (Gujarat)

"Then in accordance with his custom, he advanced with his army towards Hindustān with the object of the conquest of Somnāth...there were many golden idols in the temple in the city, and the largest of these idols was called Manāt...

"...When he reached Somnāth, the inhabitants shut the gate on his face. After much fighting and great struggles the fort was taken, and

---

[137]The *Tabqāt-i-Akbari* translated by B. De, Calcutta, 1973, Vol. I, p. 3.
[138]Ibid., p. 7.
[139]Ibid., p. 11.

vast multitudes were killed and taken prisoners. The temples were pulled down, and destroyed from their very foundations. The gold idol Somnāth was broken into pieces, and one piece was sent to Ghaznīn, and was placed at the gate of the Jāmi' Masjid; and for years it remained there."[140]

Sultān 'Abū-Sa'īd Mas'ūd of Ghazni (AD 1030–1042)

Sonipat (Haryana)

"...He marched with his army to the fort of Sonipat, and the commandant of that fort, Daniāl Har by name, becoming aware of his approach, fled...the army of Islam, having captured that fort, pulled down all the temples and obtained an enormous quantity of booty."[141]

Ikhtiyāru'd-Dīn Muhammad Bakhtiyār Khaljī (AD 1202–1206)

Bengal

"In short, Muhammad Bakhtiyar assumed the canopy, and had prayers read, and coin struck in his own name and founded mosques and Khānkahs and colleges, in place of the temples of the heathens."[142]

Sultān Shamsu'd-Dīn Iltutmish (AD 1210–1236)

Ujjain (Madhya Pradesh)

"...In the year AH 631, he invaded the country of Mālwah and conquered the fort of Bhīlsā. He also took the city of Ujjain, and had the temple of Mahākāl.... completely demolished, destroying it from its foundations; and he carried away the effigy of Bikramājīt...and certain other statues which were fashioned in molten brass, and placed them in the ground in front of the Jāmi' Masjid, so that they might he trampled upon by the people."[143]

Sultān Jalālu'd-Dīn Khaljī (AD 1290–1296)

Vidisha (Madhya Pradesh)

"About the same time Malik Alāu'd-Dīn, the nephew of the Sultān, begged that he might have permission to march aganist Bhīlsah and pillage those tracts. He received the neccessary orders, and went and ravaged the country and brought much booty for the Sultān's service. He also brought two brass idols which had been the object of the wor-

[140]Ibid., p. 16.
[141]Ibid., p. 22.
[142]Ibid., p. 51.
[143]Ibid., pp. 68–69.

ship of the Hindus of these parts; and cast them down in front of the Badāūn Gate to be trampled upon by the people..."[144]

Sultān 'Alāu'd-Dīn Khaljī (AD 1296–1316)

Somnath (*Gujarat*)

"In the third year after the accession, the Sultān sent Ulugh Khān and Nasrat Khān, with large armies to invade Gujarāt. They ravaged and plundered Nahrwālah, and all the cities of the province...Ulugh Khān and Nasrat Khān also brought the idol, which the Brāhmans of Somnāth had set up, and were worshipping, in place of the one which Sultān Mahmūd had broken to pieces, to Delhi, and placed it where the people would trample upon it..."[145]

M'abar (*Tamil Nadu*)

"Again in the year AH 716 Sultān Alāuddīn sent Malik Nāib towards Dhor Samundar (Dvar Samudra) and M'abar...they then advanced with their troops to M'abar, and conquered it also, and having demolished the temples there, and broken the golden and jewelled idols, sent the gold into the treasury..."[146]

Sultān Fīrūz Shāh Tughlaq (AD 1351–1388)

"Sultān Fīrūz Shāh composed a book also in which he compiled an account of his reign and which he named *Futuhāt-i-Fīrūz Shāhī*...[147]

"He writes in its second chapter... 'Muslim and infidel women used to visit sepulchres and temples, which led to many evils. I stopped it. I got mosques built in place of temples'..."[148]

Sultān Sikandar Lodī (AD 1489–1517)

Mandrail (*Madhya Pradesh*)

"After the rainy season was over, he marched in Ramzān AH 910 (AD February–March, 1505) for the conquest of the fort of Mundṛāil. He stayed for a month near Dholpur and sent out armies with orders that they should lay waste the environs of Gwālior and Mundṛāil. Thereafter he himself laid siege to the fort of Mundṛāil. Those inside the fort surrendered the fort to him after signing a treaty. The Sultān got

---

[144]Ibid., p. 144.
[145]Ibid., p. 157.
[146]Ibid., p. 184.
[147]Translated from the Hindi version by S.A.A. Rizvi included in *Tughlaq Kālīna Bhārata*, Aligarh, 1957, Vol. II, p. 349.
[148]Ibid., p. 350.

the temples demolished and mosques erected in their stead..."[149]

Udit Nagar (*Madhya Pradesh*)

"After the rainy season was over, he led an expedition towards the fort of Udit Nagar in AH 912 (AD 1506–07)...[150]

"...Although those inside the fort tried their utmost to seek a pardon, but he did not listen to them, and the fort was breached at many points and conquered...The Sultān thanked Allāh in the wake of his victory...He got the temples demolished and mosques constructed in their stead..."[151]

Narwar (*Madhya Pradesh*)

"After the rainy season was over, he made up his mind to take possession of the fort of Narwar which was in the domain of Mālwā. He ordered Jalāl Khān Lodī, the governor of Kālpī, to go there and besiege the fort... The Sultān himself reached Narwar after some time... He kept the fort under siege for an year... The soldiers went out to war everyday and got killed...

"Thereafter the inhabitants of the fort were in plight due to scarcity of water and dearness of grains, and they asked for forgiveness. They went out with their wealth and property. The Sultān laid waste the temples and raised mosques. Men of learning and students were made to reside there and given scholarships and grants. He stayed for six months under the walls of the fort."[152]

Mathura (*Uttar Pradesh*)

"He was a stout partisan of Islām and made great endeavours on this score. He got all temples of the infidels demolished, and did not allow even a trace of them to remain. In Mathurā, where the infidels used to get together for bathing, he got constructed caravansarais, markets, mosques and *madrasas*, and appointed there officers with instructions that they should allow no one to bathe; if any Hindū desired to get his beard or head shaved in the city of Mathurā, no barber was prepared to cut his hair."[153]

---

[149]Translated from the Hindi version by S.A.A. Rizvi included in *Uttara Taimūr Kālīna Bhārata*, Aligarh, 1958, Vol. I, p. 210.

[150]Ibid., p. 220.

[151]Ibid., p. 221.

[152]Ibid., p. 222.

[153]Ibid., p. 227.

Sultān Ibrāhīm Lodī (AD 1517–1526)

Gwalior (Madhya Pradesh)

"At the same time the Sultān thought that though 'Sultān Sikandar had led several expeditions for conquering the fort of Gwālior and the country attached to it but met with no success.' Consequently he sent 'Āzam Humāyūn, the governor of Karā, with 300,000 horsemen and 300 elephants for the conquest of Gwālior...After some time the royal army laid a mine, filled it with gunpowder, and set fire to it. He entered the fort and took possession of it after the wall of the fort was breached. He saw there a bull made of brass, which the Hindūs had worshipped for years. In keeping with a royal order, the bull was brought to Delhī and placed at the Baghdād Gate. It was still there till the reign of Akbar. The writer of this history saw it himself."[154]

Sultān Mahmūd bin Ibrāhīm Sharqī (AD 1440–1457)

Orissa

"After some time he proceeded to Orissa with the intention of *jihād*. He attacked places in the neighbourhood of that province and laid them waste, and destroyed the temples after demolishing them..."[155]

Sultān Mahmūd Khaljī of Malwa (AD 1436–1469)

Chittaurgarh (Rajasthan)

"After he had crossed the river Bhīm, he started laying waste the country and capturing its people by sending expeditions towards Chittor everyday. He started constructing mosques after demolishing temples. He stayed 2-3 days at every halt."[156]

Kumbhalgadh (Rajasthan)

"When he halted near Kumbhalmīr which was a very big fort of that province, and well-known for its strength all over Hindustān, Devā the Vakīl of the Governor of Kumbhā took shelter in the fort and started fighting. It so happened that a magnificent temple had been erected in front of that fort and surrounded by ramparts on all sides. That temple had been filled with weapons of war and other stores. Sultān Mahmūd planned to storm the ramparts and captured it [the

---

[154]Ibid., pp. 236–37. The bull was most probably a Nandī standing outside a temple of Śiva.

[155]Translated from the Hindi version by S.A.A. Rizvi included in *Uttar Taimūr Kālīna Bhārata*, Aligarh 1959, Vol. II, p. 9.

[156]Ibid., p. 74.

temple] in a week. A large number of Rajpūts were made prisoners and slaughtered. About the edifices of the temple, he ordered that they should be stocked with wood and fired, and water and vinegar was sprinkled on the walls. That magnificent mansion which it had taken many years to raise, was destroyed in a few moments. He got the idols broken and they were handed over to the butchers for being used as weights while selling meat. The biggest idol which had the form of a ram was reduced to powder which was put in betel-leaves to be given to the Rajpūts so that they could eat their god."[157]

Mandalgadh (*Rajasthan*)

"He started for the conquest of Manḍalgaḍh on 26 Muharram, AH 861 (AD 24 December, 1456) after making full prepration... Reaching there the Sultān issued orders that 'trees should be uprooted, houses demolished and no trace should be left of human habitation'...A great victory was achieved on 1 Zilhijjā, AH 861 (AD 20 October, 1457). Sultān Mahmūd offered thanks to Allāh in all humility. Next day, he entered the fort. He got the temples demolished and their materials used in the construction of a Jāmi' Masjid. He appointed there a *qāzī*, a *muftī*, a *muhtasib*, a *khatīb and* a *mu'zzin* and established order in that place..."[158]

Kelwara and Delwara (*Rajasthan*)

"Sultān Mahmūd started again in AH 863 (AD 1458–59) for punishing the Rajpūts. When he halted at Āhāḍ, Prince Ghiyāsu'd-Dīn and Fidan Khān were sent towards Kīlwārā and Dīlwārā in order to lay waste those lands. They destroyed those lands and attacked the environs of Kumbhalmīr.

"When they came to the presence of the Sultān and praised the fort of Kumbhalmīr, the Sultān started for Kumbhalmīr next day and went ahead destroying temples on the way. When he halted near that fort, he mounted his horse and went up a hill which was to the east of the fort in order to survey the city. He said, 'It is not possible to capture this fort without a siege lasting for several years'..."[159]

Sultān Muzaffar Shāh I of Gujarat (AD 1392–1410)

Idar (*Gujarat*)

"In AH 796 (AD 1393–94), it was reported that Sultān Muhammad

[157]Ibid., p. 75.
[157]Ibid., p. 85.
[158]Ibid., p. 86.

bin Fīrūz Shāh had died at Delhī and that the affairs of the kingdom were in disorder so that a majority of *zamīndārs* were in revolt, particularly the Rājā of Īdar. Zafar Khān collected a large army and mountain-like elephants and proceeded to Īdar in order to punish the Rājā...The Rājā of Īdar had no time to prepare a defence and shut himself in the fort. The armies of Zafar Khān occupied the Kingdom of Īdar and started plundering and destroying it. They levelled with the ground whatever temple they found...The Rājā of Īdar showed extreme humility and pleaded for forgiveness through his representatives. Zafar Khān took a tribute according to his own desire and made up his mind to attack Somnāt...[160]

"In AH 803 (AD 1399–1400) 'Āzam Humāyūn paid one year's wages (in advance) to his army and after making great preparations, he attacked the fort of Īdar with a view to conquer it. After the armies of the Sultān had besieged the fort from all sides and the battle continued non-stop for several days the Rājā of Īdar evacuated the fort one night and ran away towards Bījānagar. In the morning Zafar Khān entered the fort and, after expressing his gratefulness to Allāh, and destroying the temples, he appointed officers in the fort..."[161]

Somnath (*Gujarat*)

"In AH 797 (AD 1394–95)...he proceeded for the destruction of the temple of Somnāt. On the way he made Rajpūts food for his sword and demolished whatever temple he saw at any place. When he arrived at Somnāt, he got the temple burnt and the idol of Somnāt broken. He made a slaughter of the infidels and laid waste the city. He got a Jāmi' Masjid raised there and appointed officers of the Shari'h..."[162]

"In AH 804 (AD 1401–02) reports were received by Zafar Khān that the infidels and Hindūs of Somnāt had again started making efforts for promoting the ways of their religion. 'Āzam Humāyūn started for that place and sent an army in advance. When the residents of Somnāt learnt this, they advanced along the sea-shore and offered battle. 'Āzam Humāyūn reached that place speedily and he slaughtered that group. Those who survived took shelter in the fort of the port at Dīp (Diu). After some time, he conquered that place as well, slaughtered that group also and got their leaders trampled under the feet of elephants.

[160]Ibid., pp. 177–78. Zafar Khān crowned himself as Muzaffar Shāhs a few years later, and founded the independent kingdom of Gujarat.
[161]Ibid., p. 180.
[162]Ibid., p. 178.

He got the temples demolished and a Jāmi' Masjid constructed. Having appointed a *qāzī*, *muftī* and other guardians of Shari'h...he returned to the capital at Paṭan."[163]

Sultān Ahmad Shāh I of Gujarat (AD 1411–1443)

Champaner (Gujarat)

"Sultān Ahmad... encamped near Chāmpāner on 7 Rabī-us-Sāni, AH 822 (AD 3 May, 1419). He destroyed temples wherever he found them and returned to Ahmadābād."[164]

Mewar (Rajasthan)

"In Rajab AH 836 (AD February–March, 1433) Sultān Ahmad mounted an expedition for the conquest of Mewāṛ and Nāgaur. When he reached the town of Nāgaur, he sent out armies for the destruction of towns and villages and levelled with the ground whatever temple was found at whichever place...Having laid waste the land of Kīlwārā, the Sultān entered the land of Dīlwārā, and he ruined the lofty palaces of Rāṇā Mokal and destroyed the temples and idols..."[165]

Sultān Qutbu'd-Dīn Ahmad Shāh II of Gujarat (AD 1451–1458)

Kumbhalgadh (Rajasthan)

"...Sultān Qutbu'd-Dīn felt insulted and he attacked the fort of Kumbhalmīr in AH 860 (AD 1455–56)... When he reached near Sirohī, the Rājā of that place offered battle but was defeated.

"From that place the Sultān entered the kingdom of Rāṇā Kumbhā and he sent armies in all directions for invading the country and destroying the temples..."[166]

Sultān Mahmūd Begḍhā of Gujarat (AD 1458–1511)

Junagadh (Gujarat)

"In AH 871 (AD 1466–67) he started for the conquest of Karnāl [Girnār] which is now known as Jūnāgaḍh. It is said that this country had been in the possession of the predecessors of Rāi Mandalīk for the past two thousand years...Sultān Mahmūd relied on the help of Allāh and proceeded there; on the way he laid waste the land of Soraṭh...From that place the Sultān went towards the temple of those people. Many

[163]Ibid., p. 180.
[164]Ibid., p. 192.
[165]Ibid., pp. 201–02.
[166]Ibid., pp. 206–07.

Rajpūts who were known as Parwhān, decided to lay down their lives, and started fighting with swords and spears in (defence) of the temple... Sultān Mahmūd postponed the conquest of the fort to the next year... and returned to Ahmadābād."[167]

Dwarka (*Gujarat*)

"After some time the Sultān started contemplating the conquest of the port of Jagat which is a place of worship for the Brahmaṇas... With this resolve he started for the port of Jagat on 16 Zil-Hajjā, AH 877 (AD 14 July, 1473). He reached Jagat with great difficulty due to the narrowness of the road and the presence of forests... He destroyed the temple of Jagat..."[168]

Sultān Muzaffar Shāh II of Gujarat (AD 1511–1526)

Idar (*Gujarat*)

"Sultān Muzaffar...started for Īdar. When he arrived in the town of Mahrāsā, he sent armies for destroying Īdar. The Rājā of Īdar evacuated the fort and took refuge in the mountain of Bījānagar. The Sultān, when he reached Īdar, found there ten Rajpūts ready to lay down their lives. He heaped barbarities on them and killed them. He did not leave even a trace of palaces, temples, gardens and trees..."[169]

Sultān Sikandar Butshikan of Kashmir (AD 1389–1413)

Kashmir

"On account of his extensive charities, scholars from Irāq, Khorāsān and Mawāraun-Nahar started presenting themselves in his court and Islām was spread. He held in great regard Sayyid Muhammad who was a very great scholar of the time, and strived to destroy the idols and temples of the infidels. He got demolished the famous temple of Mahādeva at Bahrāre. The temple was dug out from its foundations and the hole (that remained) reached the water level. Another temple at Jagdar was also demolished... Rājā Alamādat had got a big temple constructed at Sinpur. He had come to know from astrologers that after 11 hundred years a king by the name of Sikandar would get the temple destroyed and the idol of Utārid, which was in it, broken. He got this [forecast] inscribed on a copper plate which was kept in a box and buried under the temple. The inscription came up when the temple was

---

[167]Ibid., p. 214.
[168]Ibid., pp. 218–19.
[169]Ibid., pp. 233–34.

destroyed [by Sikandar]...[170]

"...The value of currency had come down, because Sultān Sikandar had got idols of gold, silver and copper broken and turned into coins..."[171]

Sultān Fath Shāh of Kashmir (AD 1489–1499 and 1505–1516)

Kashmir

"Fath Shāh ascended the throne in AH 894 (AD 1488–89)...In those days Mīr Shams, a disciple of Shāh Qāsim Anwar, reached Kashmir and people became his devotees. All endowments, *imlāk*, places of worship and temples were entrusted to his disciples. His Sūfīs used to destroy temples and no one could stop them..."[172]

Jalālu'd-Dīn Muhammad Akbar Pādshāh Ghāzī (AD 1556–1605)

Nagarkot Kangra (Himachal Pradesh)

"On the 1st Rajab 990 [AD 1582] he (Husain Qulī Khān) encamped by a field of maize near Nagarkoṭ. The fortress (*hissār*) of Bhīm, which is an idol temple of Mahāmāī, and in which none but her servants dwelt, was taken by the valour of the assailants at the first assault. A party of Rajpūts, who had resolved to die, fought most desperately till they were all cut down. A number of Brāhmans who for many years had served the temple, never gave one thought to flight, and were killed. Nearly 200 black cows belonging to Hindūs had, during the struggle, crowded together for shelter in the temple. Some savage Turks, while the arrows and bullets were falling like rain, killed those cows. They then took off their boots and filled them with the blood and cast it upon the roof and walls of the temple."[173]

(41)
Muntakhābu't-Tawārīkh

The author, Mullā 'Abdul Qādir Badāunī son of Mulūk Shāh, was born at Badaun in AD 1540 or 1542. He was a learned man who was introduced to the court of Akbar by Shykh Mubārak, father of Abu'l Fazl and Faizī, two of the favourite courtiers of that king. He was employed by Akbar for translating Sanskrit classics into Persian, a work which he hated. He was a pious Muslim who acquired great aver-

---

[170]Ibid., p. 515. The discovery of an inscription seems to be true, but the reading is obviously wishful and fictitious.

[171]Ibid., p. 517.

[172]Ibid., p. 527.

[173]Elliot and Dowson, op. cit., Vol. V, p. 358.

sion for Akbar due to the latter's liberal policies vis-a-vis the Hindus. His history, which is known as *Tārīkh-i-Badāunī* also, is the general history of India from the time of the Ghaznivids to the fortieth year of Akbar's reign.

Sultān Muhmūd of Ghazni (AD 997–1030)

Somnath (Gujarat)

"...'Asjadi composed the following *qaṣīda* in honour of this expedition:

When the King of kings marched to Somnāt,
He made his own deeds the standard of miracles...[174]

"Once more he led his army against Somnāt, which is a large city on the coast of the ocean, a place of worship of the Brahmans who worship a large idol. There are many golden idols there. Although certain historians have called this idol Manāt, and say that it is the identical idol which Arab idolaters brought to the coast of Hindustān in the time of the Lord of the Missive (may the blessings and peace of God be upon him), this story has no foundation because the Brahmans of India firmly believe that this idol has been in that place since the time of Kishan, that is to say four thousand years and a fraction...The reason for this mistake must surely be the resemblance in name, and nothing else...The fort was taken and Mahmūd broke the idol in fragments and sent it to Ghaznīn, where it was placed at the door of the Jāma' Masjid and trodden under foot."[175]

Thanesar (Haryana)

"In the year AH 402 (AD 1011) he set out for Thānesar and Jaipāl, the son of the former Jaipāl, offered him a present of fifty elephants and much treasure. The Sultān, however, was not to be deterred from his purpose; so he refused to accept his present, and seeing Thānesar empty he sacked it and destroyed its idol temples, and took away to Ghaznīn, the idol known as Chakarsum on account of which the Hindūs had been ruined; and having placed it in his court, caused it to be trampled under foot by the people..."[176]

Mathura (Uttar Pradesh)

"...From thence he went to Mathra which is a place of worship of

[174] *Muntakhābu't-Tawārīkh*, translated into English by George S.A. Ranking, Patna Reprint, 1973, Vol. 1, p. 17.
[175] Ibid., pp. 27–28.
[176] Ibid., pp. 21–22.

the infidels, and the birthplace of Kishan, the son of Basudev, whom the Hindūs worship as a divinity — where there are idol temples without number, and took it without any contest and razed it to the ground. Great wealth and booty fell into the hands of the Muslims, among the rest they broke up by the orders of the Sultān, a golden idol..."[177]

Ikhtiyāru'd-Dīn Muhammad Bakhtiyār Khaljī (AD 1202–1206)
Navadvipa (Bengal)

"...In the second year after this arrangement Muhammad Bakhtyār brought an army from Behār towards Lakhnautī and arrived at the town of Nūdiyā, with a small force; Nūdiyā is now in ruins. Rāi Lakhmia (Lakhminīa) the governor of that town...fled thence to Kāmrān, and property and booty beyond computation fell into the hands of the Muslims, and Muhammad Bakhtyār having destroyed the places of worship and idol temples of the infidels founded Mosques and Monasteries and schools and caused a metropolis to be built called by his own name, which now has the name of Gaur.

There where was heard before
The clamour and uproar of the heathen,
Now there is heard resounding
The shout of 'Allāho Akbar'."[178]

Sultān Shamsu'd-Dīn Iltutmish (AD 1210–1236)
Ujjain (Madhya Pradesh)

"...And in the year AH 631 (AD 1233) having made an incursion in the direction of the province of Mālwah and taken Bhīlsā and also captured the city of Ujain, and having destroyed the idol-temple of Ujain which had been built six hundred years previously, and was called Mahākāl, he levelled it to its foundations, and threw down the image of Rāi Vikramājīt from whom the Hindūs reckon their era... and brought certain other images of cast molten brass and placed them on the ground in front of the door of the mosque of old Dihlī and ordered the people to trample them under foot..."[179]

Sultān Jalālu'd-Dīn Khaljī (AD 1290–1296)
Ranthambhor (Rajasthan)

"...and in the same year the Sultān for the second time marched

[177]Ibid., p. 24.
[178]Ibid., pp. 82–83.
[179]Ibid., p. 95.

against Rantambhor, and destroyed the country round it, and overthrew the idols and idol-temples, but returned without attempting to reduce the fort..."[180]

Sultān 'Alāu'd-Dīn Khaljī (AD 1296–1316)
Patan and Somnath (Gujarat)

"And in the year AH 698 (AD 1298) he appointed Ulugh Khān to the command of a powerful army, to proceed into the country of Gujarat...Ulugh Khān carried off an idol from Nahrwāla...and took it to Dihlī where he caused it to be trampled under foot by the populace; then he pursued Rāi Karan as far as Somnāt, and a second time laid waste the idol temple of Somnāt, and building a mosque there retraced his steps."[181]

Sultān Sikandar Lodī (AD 1489–1517)
Mandrail (Madhya Pradesh)

"...At the time of his return he restored the fort of Dholpur also to Bināyik Deo, and having spent the rainy season in Āgra after the rising of the Canopus in the year AH 910 (AD 1504), marched to reduce the fortress of Mandrāyal, which he took without fighting from the Rājah of of Mandrāyal, who sued for peace; he also destroyed all the idol-temples and churches of the place..."[182]

Udit Nagar (Madhya Pradesh)

"And in the year AH 912 (AD 1506), after the rising of the Canopus, he marched against the fortress of Ūntgaṛh and laid siege to it, and many of his men joyfully embraced martyrdom, after that he took the fort and gave the infidels as food to the sword...He then cast down the idol-temples, and built there lofty mosques."[183]

Sultān Ibrāhīm Lodī (AD 1517–1526)
Gwalior (Madhya Pradesh)

"...The fortress of Bādalgarh, which lies below the fortress of Gwāliār, a very lofty structure, was taken from Rāi Mān Singh and fell into the hands of the Muslims, and a brazen animal which was worshipped by the Hindūs also fell into their hands, and was sent by them

[180]Ibid., pp. 235–36.
[181]Ibid., pp. 255–56.
[182]Ibid., p. 420.
[183]Ibid., p. 422.

to Āgra, whence it was sent by Sultān Ibrāhīm to Dihlī, and was put over the city gate. The image was removed to Fathpūr in the year AH 992 (AD 1584), ten years before the composition of this history, where it was seen by the author of this work. It was converted into gongs, and bells, and implements of all kinds."[184]

Jalālu'd-Dīn Muhammad Akbar Pādshāh Ghāzi (AD 1556–1605)

Siwalik (*Uttar Pradesh*)

"In this year on the dismissal of Husain Khān the Emperor gave the *pargana* of Lak'hnou as *jāgīr* to Mahdī Qāsim Khān...Husain Khān was exceedingly indignant with Mahdī Qāsim Khān on account of this...After a time he left her in helplessness, and the daughter of Mahdī Qāsim Bēg at Khairābād with her brothers, and set off from Lak'hnou with the intention of carrying on a religious war, and of breaking the idols and destroying the idol-temples. He had heard that the bricks of these were of silver and gold, and conceiving a desire for this and all the other abundant and unlimited treasures, of which he had heard a lying report, he set out by way of Oudh to the Siwālik mountains..."[185]

Nagarkot Kangra (*Himachal Pradesh*)

"...The temple of Nagarkot, which is outside the city, was taken at the very outset... On this occasion many mountaineers became food for the flashing sword. And that golden umbrella, which was erected on the top of the cupola of the temple, they riddled with arrows...And black cows, to the number of 200, to which they pay boundless respect, and actually worship, and present to the temple, which they look upon as an asylum, and let loose there, were killed by the Musulmāns. And, while arrows and bullets were continually falling like drops of rain, through their zeal and excessive hatred of idolatry they filled their shoes full of blood and threw it on the doors and walls of the temple...the army of Husain Qulī Khān was suffering great hardships. For these reasons he concluded a treaty with them...and having put all things straight he built the cupola of a lofty mosque over the gateway of Rājāh Jai Chand."[186]

Sultān Sulaimān Karrānī of Bengal (AD 1563–1573)

Puri (*Orissa*)

"In this year also Sulaiman Kirrānī, ruler of Bengal, who gave

[184]Ibid., pp. 432–33.
[185]Ibid., Vol. II, pp. 128–29.
[186]Ibid., pp. 165–66.

himself the title of *Hazrati Ā'la*, and had conquered the city of Katak-u-Banāras, that mine of heathenism, and having made the stronghold of Jagannāth into the home of Islām, held sway from Kāmru to Orissa, attained the mercy of God..."[187]

(42)

Shash Fath-i-Kāṅgrā

The author is unknown. It is supposed to have been written in the reign of Jahāngīr.

Nūru'd-Dīn Muhammad Jahāngīr Pādshāh Ghāzī (AD 1605–1628)

Nagarkot Kangra (*Himachal Pradesh*)

"The Emperor by the divine guidance, had always in view to extirpate all the rebels in his dominions, to destroy all infidels root and branch, and to raze all Pagan temples level to the ground. Endowed with a heavenly power, he devoted all his exertions to the promulgation of the Muhammadan religion; and through the aid of the Almighty God, and by the strength of his sword, he used all his endeavours to enlarge his dominions and promote the religion of Muhammad..."[188]

(43)

Tārīkh-i-Da'ūdī

The author, 'Abdu'llāh, says nothing about himself and does not give even his full name. As he mentions the name of Jahāngīr, it can be assumed that he wrote it at some time after AD 1605. He starts with the reign of Sultān Bahlūl Lodī (AD 1451–1489) and ends with the reign of Da'ūd Shāh who was beheaded in AD 1575 by the order of Bairam Khān.

Sultān Sikandar Lodī (AD 1489–1517)

Kurukshetra (*Haryana*)

"It is also related of this prince, that before his accession, when a crowd of Hindūs had assembled in immense numbers at Kurkhet, he wished to go to Thānesar for the purpose of putting them all to death..."[189]

Mathura (*Uttar Pradesh*)

"He was so zealous a Musalmān that he utterly destroyed divers

[187]Ibid., pp. 166–67.
[188]Elliot and Dowson, op. cit., Vol. VI, p. 528.
[189]Ibid., Vol. IV, p. 439.

places of worship of the infidels, and left not a vestige remaining of them. He entirely ruined the shrines of Mathurā, the mine of heathenism, and turned other principal Hindu places of worship into caravansarais and colleges. Their stone images were given to the butchers to serve them as meat-weight, and all the Hindus in Mathurā were strictly prohibited from shaving their heads and beards, and performing their ablutions...."[190]

Dholpur (*Madhya Pradesh*)

"In that year the Sultān sent Khawās Khān to take possession of the fort of Dhūlpūr. The Rājā of that place advanced to give battle, and daily fighting took place. The instant His Majesty heard of the firm countenance shown by the *rāī* of Dhūlpūr in opposing the royal army, he went there in person; but on his arrival near Dhūlpūr, the *rāī* made up his mind to fly without fighting...He (Sikandar) offered up suitable thanksgivings for his success, and the royal troops spoiled and plundered in all directions, rooting up all the trees of the gardens which shaded Dhūlpūr to the distance of seven *kos*. Sultān Sikandar stayed there during one month, erected a mosque on the site of an idol-temple, and then set off towards Āgra..."[191]

Gwalior (*Madhya Pradesh*)

"...Sultān Sikandar passed the rainy season of that year at Āgra. After the rising of the star Canopus, he assembled an army, and set forth to take possession of Gwālior and territories belonging to it. In a short space of time he took most of the Gwālior district, and after building mosques in the places of idol-temples returned towards Āgra..."[192]

Narwar (*Madhya Pradesh*)

"Sultān Sikandar, after the lapse of two years, in AH 913 (AD 1507) wrote a *farmān* to Jalāl Khān, the governor of Kālpī, directing him to take possession of the fort of Narwar... Jalāl Khān Lodī, by the Sultān's command, besieged Narwar, where Sultān Sikandar also joined him with great expedition. The siege of the fort was protracted for one year...Men were slain on both sides. After the time above mentioned, the defenders of the place were compelled, by the want of water and scarcity of grain, to ask for mercy, and they were allowed to go forth

[190]Ibid., p. 447.
[191]Ibid., p. 465.
[192]Ibid., p. 466.

with their property; but the Sultān destroyed their idol-temples, and erected mosques on their sites. He then appointed stipends and pensions for the learned and the pious who dwelt at Narwar, and gave them dwellings there. He remained six months encamped below the fort."[193]

Sher Shāh Sūr (AD 1538–1545)

Jodhpur (Rajasthan)

"His attack on Māldev, Rājā of Jodhpur, (was due) partly to his religious bigotry and a desire to convert the temples of the Hindus into mosques."[194]

(44)
Zafaru'l-Wālih Bi Muzaffar Wa Ālīhi

The author, 'Abdu'llāh Muhammad bin 'Umar al-Maqqī al-Asafī Ulugh-Khānī, is popular as Hājjiu'd-Dabīr. He arrived in India with his father in AD 1555. After 1573 he started living in Ahmadabad where Akbar had put his father in charge of many endowments, the income from which was sent to Mecca and Medina. After the death of his father he entered the service of another Amīr, and finally went to Khandesh in 1595. He finished his history in 1605 but took some more years to revise it. The English translation we have is pretty bad.

Sultān Shamsu'd-Dīn Iltutmish (AD 1210–1236)

Vidisha (Madhya Pradesh)

"...In 631 (1233), Shamsuddīn marched to Mālwā and conquered the city of Bailsan and its fort and demolished its famous temple. The historians have narrated that its citizens built the temple by digging its foundation and raising its walls one hundred cubits from the ground in 300 years. All the images are fixed with lead. The temple is called Gawājit (?) (Vikramajit) Sultan of Ujjain Nagari. The history of the temple is a proof of what is said about its construction and demolition, that is, eleven hundred years. People of Hind are ignorant of history."[195]

Sultān Jalālu'd-Dīn Khaljī (AD 1290–1296)

Jhain (Rajasthan)

"He marched from it to Ranthanbhor. He first encamped at Jhāyan

[193]Ibid., pp. 466–67.

[194]Cited by Sri Ram Sharma, op. cit., p. 11.

[195]*Zafaru'l Wālih Bi Muzaffar Wa Ālihi*, translated into English by M.F. Lokhandwala, Baroda, 1970 and 1974, Vol. II, p. 575.

and conquered it. He demolished temples and broke idols. He killed, captured and pillaged..."[196]

Vidisha (*Madhya Pradesh*)

"He permitted 'Alāuddīn for a religious war in Bhilastān. Jalāluddīn had marched to Mandu. 'Alāuddīn influenced his uncle by the booty of the religious war. It was immense. It contained a Nandi idol carved in yellow metal and equal in weight to an animal. Jalāluddīn ordered it to be placed at the entrance to the Gate of Delhi famous as Badāun Gate. He was pleased with 'Alāuddīn and put the 'Diwan-ul-'Ard' under his charge and added Oudh to Kara..."[197]

Sultān 'Alāu'd-Dīn Khaljī (AD 1296–1316)

Devagiri (*Maharashtra*)

"...He routed Rāmdev everywhere except the fort. The fort contained temples of gold and silver and images of the same metals. Besides, there were jewels of different varieties. He ordered them to be destroyed and collected its gold. Ruler of the fort was surprised at this action and his mind got confused. He sent an envoy for conclusion of peace on condition of sparing the temples from destruction which was agreed to..."[198]

Somnath (*Gujarat*)

"...Maḥmud demolished Somnath in the year 416 (1122)... and carried its relics to Ghazni. After his death, unbelief returned to Naharwāla as its residents took an idol and buried it on a side. There was publicity of return of Somnāth. They took it out from its burial place. It was exhibited and fixed at a place where it was. Malek Ulugh Khān took it along with all the spoils to Delhi. They made it the threshold at its gate. This victory took place on Wednesday, 20th Jamādi I, 698 (1299)...[199]

"It was kept by a Brahmin after being mutilated by Maḥamud. It was Lamnat. They named it Somnāth. They worshipped it out of misguidance from ancient times. They carried it to Delhi. It was placed at the entrance of the gate..."[200]

[196]Ibid., p. 626.
[197]Ibid., pp. 627–28.
[198]Ibid., Vol. I, p. 138.
[199]Ibid., Vol. II, pp. 646–47.
[200]Ibid., p. 650.

Ma'bar (Tamil Nadu)

"...In 710 (1310) Kāfur conquered the region of Ma'bar (Malabar) and Dahur Samand. Both these regions belonged to Bir Rāi. He marched further to Sarandip (Ceylon) and Kāfur broke the famous idol of Rām Ling Mahādev. It was wonderful that the swordsmen deserted the temple. The Brahmins assembled to fight with him at the time of his breaking the idol till they collected all broken parts and got displeased with swordsmen. Kāfur marched further to Sirā and demolished the temple of Jagannāth...[201]

"...Kāfur always gained one victory after another until he dominated over Jagannāth and consigned it to fire. He returned from it on 5th Zilhajj of the year 710 (1310) and arrived at Delhi on 4th Jamādi II of the year 711 (1311). It was a day worth witnessing. No one had undertaken such campaigns before him and there would be none after him. A good omen was drawn from his arrival with that booty for his sultān and for general Muslim public. They believed that all these victories were facilitated by the blessings of Qutb-uz-Zamān, Qiblat-ul-Asfiyā Mawlānā Shaikh Nizāmuddīn Awliyā and Qutb-uz-Zamān, Madār ul-Jamkin Mawalāna Shaikh Nasiruddin and similarly the two Qutbs of people of the world and faith Mawlānā Shaikh Ruknuddin and Mawlānā Shaikh 'Alāuddīn, may God benefit us through them. During their life time, whatever they desired from their Lord, became the sunna (rule and regulation of the Prophet, may peace and benediction of God be on him). Every member of the house of the 'Alāiya Sultān was a disciple and spiritual follower of Mawalānā Shaikh Nizāmuddin Awliya includding the wazirs and amirs and persons of rank. His blessings were upon them all..."[202]

Sultān Mahmūd Begḍhā of Gujarat (AD 1485–1511)

Junagadh (Gujarat)

"In AH 871 (AD 1466–67) the Sultān led an expedition to Karnāl [Girnār]...He spread the story that he was out for hunting. Thereafter he suddenly attacked and his army also arrived. He took possession of those treasuries which were beyond estimation. Many people living in those valleys lost their lives. They had a famous idol there. When Mahmūd decided to break it, many members of the Barāwān clan gathered round it. All of them were slaughtered and the idol was

---

[201]Ibid., Vol. I, p. 139. Malabar is wrongly indicated by the translator.

[202]Ibid., Vol. II, p. 676. This is a revealing report. The Sufis were not only instigators but also beneficiaries of *jihād* and iconoclasm.

broken..."[203]

Dwarka (*Gujarat*)

"In the same year of AH 877 (AD 1472–73) the Sultān made up his mind to destroy Jagat...Jagat is a very famous abode of infidelity and idolatry. Its idol is regarded as higher than all other idols in India and it is because of this idol that the place is called Dwārkā. It is a very big nest of Brāhmaṇas too. The idolaters come here from far off places and the great hardships they undergo in order to reach here is regarded by them as earnest worship...There is a fort nearby known as Bait...[204]

"...The Sultān mounted (his horse) in the morning. The people of Jagat also got this information. They shut themselves in the fort along with Rāi Bhīm. After a few days the Sultān entered Jagat and got its idols broken. He got its canopies pulled down and established the way of Islām there."[205]

(45)
Zubdatu't-Tawārīkh

The author, Shaykh Nūru'l-Haqq al-Mashriqī al-Dihlivī al-Bukhārī, was the son of 'Abdul Haqq who wrote *Tārīkh-i Haqqī* in AD 1596–97. Nūru'l-Haqq's history is an enlarged edition of his father's work. The history commences with the reign of Qutbu'd-Dīn Aibak and ends with the close of Akbar's reign in AD 1605.

Sultān Sikandar Lodī (AD 1489–1517)

"In his time Hindū temples were razed to the ground, and neither name nor vestige of them was allowed to remain..."[206]

Jalālu'd-Dīn Muhammad Akbar Pādshāh Ghāzī (AD 1556–1605)

Mewar (*Rajasthan*)

"When Mewar was invaded [AD 1600] many temples were demolished by the invading Mughal army [led by Prince Salīm]."[207]

---

[203]Translated from the Hindi version by S.A.A. Rizvi included in *Uttara Taimūr Kālīna Bhārata*, Aligarh, 1959, Vol. II, p. 413.

[204]Ibid., p. 417.

[205]Ibid., p. 418.

[206]Elliot and Dowson, op. cit., Vol. VI, p. 187.

[207]*Tārīkh-i-Haqqi* (of which *Zubdatu't-Tawārīkh* is an extension) cited by Sri Ram Sharma, op. cit., p. 62.

(46)
Tārīkh-i-Firishta

The author, Muhammad Qāsim Hindū Shāh Firishta, was born in Astrabad on the Caspian Sea and came to Bijapur in AD 1589. He lived under the patronage of Sultān Ibrāhīm 'Ādil Shāh II of Bijapur where he died in 1611. He claims to have consulted most of the earlier histories in writing his *Gulshan-i-Ibrāhīmī* which became known as *Tārīkh-i-Firishta*. He completed it in 1609. It contains sections on the independent sultanates of the Deccan, Gujarat, Malwa, Khandesh, Bengal, Multan, Sindh and Kashmir besides narrating the history of the kings of Ghazni, Lahore, Delhi and Agra. This is the most widely read Persian history at present.

Amīr Subuktigīn of Ghazni (AD 977–997)

NWFP and Punjab

"Even during the fifteen years of Alptigin's reign Subuktigin is represented by Firishta in an untranslated passage to have made frequent attacks upon India, and even to have penetrated as far as Sodra on the Chinab, where he demolished idols in celebration of Mahmud's birth, which, as it occurred on the date of the prophet's birth, Subuktigin was anxious that it should be illustrated by an event similar to the destruction of idols in the palace of the Persian king by an earthquake, on the day of the prophet's birth."[208]

Sultān Mahmūd of Ghazni (AD 997–1030)

Nagarkot Kangra (Himachal Pradesh)

"The king, in his zeal to propagate the faith, now marched against the Hindoos of Nagrakote, breaking down their idols and razing their temples. The fort, at that time denominated the Fort of Bheem, was closely invested by the Mahomedans, who had first laid waste the country around it with fire and sword."[209]

Thanesar (Haryana)

"In the year AH 402 (AD 1011), Mahmood resolved on the conquest of Tahnesur, in the kingdom of Hindoostan. It had reached the ears of the king that Tahnesur was held in the same veneration by idolaters, as

---

[208]Elliot and Dowson, op. cit., Vol. II, pp. 435–36.

[209]*Tārīkh-i-Firishta*, translated by John Briggs under the title *History of the Rise of the Mahomedan Power in India*, first published in 1829, New Delhi Reprint 1981. Vol. I, pp. 27–28.

Mecca by the faithful; that they had there set up a number of idols, the principal of which they called Jugsom, pretending that it had existed ever since the creation. Mahmood having reached Punjab, required, according to the subsisting treaty with Anundpal, that his army should not be molested on its march through his country...[210]

"The Raja's brother, with two thousand horse was also sent to meet the army, and to deliver the following message:—'My brother is the subject and tributary of the King, but he begs permission to acquaint his Majesty, that Tahnesur is the principal place of worship of the inhabitants of the country: that if it is required by the religion of Mahmood to subvert the religion of others, he has already acquitted himself of that duty, in the destruction of the temple of Nagrakote. But if he should be pleased to alter his resolution regarding Tahnesur, Anundpal promises that the amount of the revenues of that country shall be annually paid to Mahmood; that a sum shall also be paid to reimburse him for the expense of his expedition, besides which, on his own part he will present him with fifty elephants, and jewels to a considerable amount.' Mahmood replied, 'The religion of the faithful inculcates the following tenet: That in proportion as the tenets of the prophet are diffused, and his followers exert themselves in the subversion of idolatry, so shall be their reward in heaven; that, therefore, it behoved him, with the assistance of God, to root out the worship of idols from the face of all India. How then should he spare Tahnesur?'

"This answer was communicated to the Raja of Dehly, who, resolving to oppose the invaders, sent messengers throughout Hindoostan to acquaint the other rajas that Mahmood, without provocation, was marching with a vast army to destroy Tahnesur, now under his immediate protection. He observed, that if a barrier was not expeditiously raised against this roaring torrent, the country of Hindoostan would be soon overwhelmed, and that it behoved them to unite their forces at Tahnesur, to avert the impending calamity.

"Mahmood having reached Tahnesur before the Hindoos had time to take measures for its defence, the city was plundered, the idols broken, and the idol Jugsom was sent to Ghizny to be trodden under foot..."[211]

Mathura (*Uttar Pradesh*)

"Mahmood having refreshed his troops, and understanding that at

---

[210]Ibid., p. 29.
[211]Ibid., p. 30.

some distance stood the rich city of Mutra, consecrated to Krishn-Vasdew, whom the Hindoos venerate as an emanation of God, directed his march thither and entering it with little opposition from the troops of the Raja of Delhy, to whom it belonged, gave it up to plunder. He broke down or burned all the idols, and amassed a vast quantity of gold and silver, of which the idols were mostly composed. He would have destroyed the temples also, but he found the labour would have been excessive; while some say that he was averted from his purpose by their admirable beauty. He certainly extravagantly extolled the magnificence of the buildings and city in a letter to the governor of Ghizny, in which the following passage occurs: 'There are here a thousand edifices as firm as the faith of the faithful; most of them of marble, besides innumerable temples; nor is it likely that this city has attained its present condition but at the expense of many millions of deenars, nor could such another be constructed under a period of two centuries.'[212]

"The King tarried in Mutra 20 days; in which time the city suffered greatly from fire, beside the damage it sustained by being pillaged. At length he continued his march along the course of a stream on whose banks were seven strong fortifications, all of which fell in succession: there were also discovered some very ancient temples, which, according to the Hindoos, had existed for 4000 years. Having sacked these temples and forts, the troops were led against the fort of Munj...[213]

"The King, on his return, ordered a magnificent mosque to be built of marble and granite, of such beauty as struck every beholder with astonishment, and furnished it with rich carpets, and with candelabras and other ornaments of silver and gold. This mosque was universally known by the name of the Celestial Bride. In its neighbourhood the King founded an university, supplied with a vast collection of curious books in various languages. It contained also a museum of natural curiosities. For the maintenance of this establishment he appropriated a large sum of money, besides a sufficient fund for the maintenance of the students, and proper persons to instruct youth in the arts and sciences...[214]

"The King, in the year AH 410 (AD 1019), caused an account of his exploits to be written and sent to the Caliph, who ordered it to be read

[212]Ibid., p. 34.

[213]Ibid., p. 35.

[214]Ibid., p. 36. Mahmūd was a pious Muslim who destroyed Hindu temples and idols in keeping with the tenets of Islam. Those who present him as a freebooter out to plunder temple treasures are either fools like Jawaharlal Nehru or knaves like Mohammad Habib, and Pandit Sunderlal. Mahmūd is too great an hero of Islam to be sacrificed in order to salvage the faith.

to the people of Bagdad, making a great festival upon the occasion, expressive of his joy at the propagation of the faith."[215]

East of the Jumna (*Uttar Pradesh*)

"In this year, that is AH 412, Sultān Mahmūd learnt that the people of Hindustān had turned against the Rājā of Qanauj...Nandā, the Rājā of Kālinjar attacked Qanauj because Rājā Kuwar (of Qanauj) had surrendered to Sultān Mahmūd. As a result of this attack Rājā Kuwar was killed. When Sultān Mahmūd learnt it, he collected a large army...and started towards Hindustān with a view to take revenge upon Rājā Nandā. As the army of Musalmāns reached the Jumnā, the son of Rājā Ānand Pāl...stood in the way of Mahmūd. The river of Jumnā was in spate at this time...and it became very difficult for the army to get across... But as chance would have it, eight royal guards of Mahmūd showed courage and crossed the river... they attacked the army of the Hindūs and dispersed it...the son of Ānand Pāl ran away with his chiefs. All the eight royal guards...entered a city nearby and they plundered it to their heart's content. They demolished the temples in that place..."[216]

Nardin (*Punjab*)

"About this time the King learned that the inhabitants of two hilly tracts, denominated Kuriat and Nardein, continued the worship of idols and had not embraced the faith of Islam...Mahmood resolved to carry the war against these infidels, and accordingly marched towards their country...The Ghiznevide general, Ameer Ally, the son of Arslan Jazib, was now sent with a division of the army to reduce Nardein, which he accomplished, pillaging the country, and carrying away many of the people captives. In Nardein was a temple, which Ameer Ally destroyed, bringing from thence a stone on which were curious inscriptions, and which according to the Hindoos, must have been 40,000 years old..."[217]

Somnath (*Gujarat*)

"The celebrated temple of Somnat, situated in the province of Guzerat, near the island of Dew, was in those times said to abound in riches, and was greatly frequented by devotees from all parts of Hindoostan...Mahmood marched from Ghizny in the month of Shaban

---

[215]Ibid., p. 37.

[216]Translated from the Urdu version of *Tārīkh-i-Firishta* by 'Abdul Haī Khwājah, Deoband, 1983, pt. I, p. 125.

[217]John Briggs, op. cit., pp. 38–39.

AH 415 (AD Sept. 1024), with his army, accompanied by 30,000 of the youths of Toorkistan and the neighbouring countries, who followed him without pay, for the purpose of attacking this temple...[218]

"Some historians affirm that the idol was brought from Mecca, where it stood before the time of the Prophet, but the Brahmins deny it, and say that it stood near the harbour of Dew since the time of Krishn, who was concealed in that place about 4000 years ago...Mahmood, taking the same precautions as before, by rapid marches reached Somnat without opposition. Here he saw a fortification on a narrow peninsula, washed on three sides by the sea, on the battlements of which appeared a vast host of people in arms...In the morning the Mahomedan troops advancing to the walls, began the assault...[219]

"The battle raged with great fury: victory was long doubtful, till two Indian princes, Brahman Dew and Dabishleem, with other reinforcements, joined their countrymen during the action, and inspired them with fresh courage. Mahmood at this moment perceiving his troops to waver, leaped from his horse, and, prostrating himself before God implored his assistance...At the same time he cheered his troops with such energy, that, ashamed to abandon their king, with whom they had so often fought and bled, they, with one accord, gave a loud shout and rushed forwards. In this charge the Moslems broke through the enemy's line, and laid 5,000[220] Hindus dead at their feet...On approaching the temple, he saw a superb edifice built of hewn stone. Its lofty roof was supported by fifty-six pillars curiously carved and set with precious stones. In the centre of the hall was Somnat, a stone idol five yards in height, two of which were sunk in the ground. The King, approaching the image, raised his mace and struck off its nose. He ordered two pieces of the idol to be broken off and sent to Ghizny, that one might be thrown at the threshold of the public mosque, and the other at the court door of his own palace. These identical fragments are to this day (now 600 years ago) to be seen at Ghizny. Two more fragments were reserved to be sent to Mecca and Medina. It is a well authenticated fact, that when Mahmood was thus employed in destroying this idol, a crowd of Brahmins petitioned his attendants and offered a quantity of gold if the King would desist from further mutilation. His officers endeavoured to persuade him to accept of the money; for they

[218]Ibid., pp. 40–41. Lure of plunder as well as religious merit made many Muslims join the army without pay. Islam like Christianity enables people to make the best of both the worlds.

[219]Ibid., pp. 41–42.

[220]Other accounts put the figure at 50,000.

said that breaking one idol would not do away with idolatry altogether; that, therefore, it could serve no purpose to destroy the image entirely; but that such a sum of money given in charity among true believers would be a meritorious act. The King acknowledged that there might be reason in what they said, but replied, that if he should consent to such a measure, his name would be handed down to posterity as 'Mahmood the idol-seller', whereas he was desirous of being known as 'Mahmood the destroyer': he therefore directed the troops to proceed in their work...[221]

"The Caliph of Bagdad, being informed of the expedition of the King of Ghizny, wrote him a congratulatory letter, in which he styled him 'The Guardian of the State, and of the Faith'; to his son, the Prince Ameer Musaood, he gave the title of 'The Lustre of Empire, and the Ornament of Religion'; and to his second son, the Ameer Yoosoof, the appellation of 'The Strength of the Arm of Fortune, and Establisher of Empires.' He at the same time assured Mahmood, that to whomsoever he should bequeath the throne at his death, he himself would confirm and support the same."[222]

Sultān Mas'ūd I of Ghazni (1030–1042)

Sonipat (Haryana)

"In the year AH 427 (AD 1036)...he himself marched with an army to India, to reduce the fort of Hansy...Herein he found immense treasure, and having put the fort under the charge of a trusty officer, he marched towards the fort of Sonput. Depal Hurry, the governor of Sonput, abandoned the place, and fled into the woods; but having no time to carry off his treasure, it fell into the conqueror's hands. Musaood having ordered all the temples to be razed to the ground, and the idols to be broken proceeded in pursuit of Depal Hurry..."[223]

Sultān Mas'ūd III of Ghazni (AD 1099–1151)

Uttar Pradesh

"In his reign Hajib Toghantugeen, an officer of his government, proceeded in command of an army towards Hindoostan, and being appointed governor of Lahore, crossed the Ganges, and carried his conquests farther than any Mussulman had hitherto done, except the Emperor Mahmood. Like him he plundered many rich cities and

---

[221]Ibid., pp. 43–44.
[222]Ibid., p. 49.
[223]Ibid., p. 63.

temples of their wealth, and returned in triumph to Lahore, which now became in some measure the capital of the empire, for the Suljooks having deprived the house of Ghizny of most of its territory both in Eeran and Tooran, the royal family went to reside in India."[224]

Sultān Muhammad Ghūrī (AD 1175–1206)

Varanasi (Uttar Pradesh)

"Mahomed Ghoory, in the mean time returning from Ghizny, marched towards Kunowj, and engaged Jye-chund Ray, the Prince of Kunowj and Benares...This prince led his forces into the field, between Chundwar and Etawa, where he sustained a signal defeat from the vanguard of the Ghiznevide army, led by Kootbood-Deen Eibuk, and lost the whole of his baggage and elephants...He marched from thence to Benares, where, having broken the idols in above 1000 temples, he purified and consecrated the latter to the worship of the true God..."[225]

Bihar

"Mahomed Ghoory, following with the body of the army into the city of Benares, took possession of the country as far as the boundaries of Bengal, without opposition, and having destroyed all the idols, loaded four thousand camels with spoils."[226]

Sultān Shamsu'd-Dīn Iltutmish (AD 1210–1236)

Ujjain (Madhya Pradesh)

"After the reduction of Gualiar, the King marched his army towards Malwa, reduced the fort of Bhilsa, and took the city of Oojein, where he destroyed a magnificent temple dedicated to Mahakaly, formed upon the same plan with that of Somnat. This temple is said to have occupied three hundred years in building, and was surrounded by a wall one hundred cubits in height. The image of Vikramaditya, who had been formerly prince of this country, and so renowned, that the Hindoos have taken an era from his death, as also the image of Mahakaly, both of stone, with many other figures of brass, were found in the temple. These images the King caused to be conveyed to Dehly, and broken at the door of the great mosque."[227]

---

[224]Ibid., p. 82.
[225]Ibid., pp. 100–01.
[226]Ibid., p. 108.
[227]Ibid., p. 119.

Sultān Jalālu'd-Dīn Khaljī (AD 1290–1296)

Malwa (Madhya Pradesh)

"The King, after the decease of his son, marched his army towards Runtunbhore, to quell an insurrection in those parts, leaving his son Arkully Khan in Dehly, to manage affairs in his absence. The enemy retired into the fort of Runtunbhore, and the King reconnoitred the place, but, despairing of reducing it, marched towards Oojein, which he sacked. At the same time also, he broke down many of the temples of Malwa, and after plundering them of much wealth, returned to Runtunbhore."[228]

Vidisha (Madhya Pradesh)

"In the year AH 692 (AD 1293), the King marched against the Hindoos in the neighbourhood of Mando, and having devastated the country in that vicinity, returned to Dehly. In the mean time, Mullik Allood-Deen, the King's nephew, governor of Kurra, requested permission to attack the Hindoos of Bhilsa, who infested his province. Having obtained leave, he marched in the same year to that place, which he subdued; and having pillaged the country, returned with much spoil, part of which was sent to the King. Among other things, there were two brazen idols which were thrown down before the Budaoon gate of Dehly, to be trodden under foot.

"Julal-ood-Deen Feroze was much pleased with the success and conduct of his nephew on this expedition, for which he rewarded him with princely presents, and annexed the province of Oude to his former government of Kurra."[229]

Sultān 'Alāu'd-Dīn Khaljī (AD 1296–1316)

Gujarat

"In the beginning of AH 697 'Alāu'd-Dīn sent Almās Beg and Nasrat Khān along with other chiefs of Dehlī and the army of Sindh, for the conquest of Gujarāt...Gujarāt had a very famous idol which was not only of the same name as Somnāt but was also equally prestigious. The Musalmans got hold of this idol and had it sent to Dehlī so that it could be trampled upon..."[230]

---

[228]Ibid., p. 170.

[229]Ibid., p. 171.

[230]'Abdul Haī Khwājah, op. cit., pt. I, p. 349. It appears to be the Śivaliṅga of the Rudramahālaya at Sidhpur.

Dwarasamudra (*Karnataka*)

In the year AH 710 (AD 1310), the King again sent Mullik Kafoor and Khwaja Hajy with a great army, to reduce Dwara Sumoodra and Maabir in the Deccan, where he heard there were temples very rich in gold and jewels...They found in the temple prodigious spoils, such as idols of gold, adorned with precious stones, and other rich effects, consecrated to Hindoo worship. On the sea-coast, the conqueror built a small mosque, and ordered prayers to be read according to the Mahomedan faith, and the Khootba to be pronounced in the name of Alla-ood-Deen Khiljy. This mosque remains entire in our days at Sett Bund Rameswur, for the infidels, esteeming it a house consecrated to God, would not destroy it."[231]

Sultān Fīrūz Shāh Tughlaq (AD 1351–1388)

Nagarkot Kangra (*Himachal Pradesh*)

"From thence the King marched towards the mountains of Nagrakote, where he was overtaken by a storm of hail and snow. The Raja of Nagrakote, after sustaining some loss, submitted, but was restored to his dominions. The name of Nagrakote was, on this occasion, changed to that of Mahomedabad, in honour of the late king...Some historians state, that Feroze, on this occasion, broke the idols of Nagrakote, and mixing the fragments with pieces of cow's flesh, filled bags with them, and caused them to be tied round the necks of Bramins, who were then paraded through the camp. It is said, also, that he sent the image of Nowshaba to Mecca, to be thrown on the road, that it might be trodden under foot by the pilgrims, and that he also remitted the sum of 100,000 tunkas, to be distributed among the devotees and servants of the temple."[232]

Sultān Sikandar Lodī (AD 1489–1517)

Mandrail (*Madhya Pradesh*)

"Sikundur Lody, having returned to Dholpoor, reinstated the Raja Vinaik Dew, and then marching to Agra, he resolved to make that city his capital. He stayed in Agra during the rains, but in the year AH 910 (AD 1504), marched towards Mundril. Having taken that place, he destroyed the Hindoo temples, and caused mosques to be built in their stead."[233]

---

[231]John Briggs, op. cit., pp. 213–14. Modern historians doubt if Malik Kāfūr reached Setubandha Rameśvaram.

[232]Ibid., p. 263. The word "temple" at the end of the passage stands for the Ka'ba.

[233]Ibid., p. 338.

Udit Nagar (*Madhya Pradesh*)

"Having returned to Agra, the King proceeded in the year AH 912 (AD 1506) towards the fort of Hunwuntgur, despairing of reducing Gualiar. Hunwuntgur fell in a short time, and the Rajpoot garrison was put to the sword, the temples were destroyed, and mosques ordered to be built in their stead..."[234]

Narwar (*Madhya Pradesh*)

"...In the following year (AH 913, AD 1506), the king marched against Nurwur, a strong fort in the district of Malwa, then in possession of the Hindoos. The Prince Julal Khan governor of Kalpy, was directed to advance and invest the place; and should the Hindoos resist, he was required to inform the King...The King remained for the space of six months at Nurwur, breaking down temples, and building mosques. He also established a college there, and placed therein many holy and learned men."[235]

Mathura (*Uttar Pradesh*)

"...He was firmly attached to the Mahomedan religion, and made a point of destroying all Hindoo temples. In the city of Mutra he caused musjids and bazars to be built opposite the bathing-stairs leading to the river and ordered that no Hindoos should be allowed to bathe there. He forbade the barbers to shave the beards and heads of the inhabitants, in order to prevent the Hindoos following their usual practices at such pilgrimages..."[236]

Sultān Ibrāhīm Lodī (AD 1517–1526)

Gwalior (*Madhya Pradesh*)

"...The Dehly army, arriving before Gualiar, invested the place...After the siege had been carried on for some months, the army of Ibrahim Lody at length got possession of an outwork at the foot of the hill, on which stood the fort of Badilgur. They found in that place a brazen bull, which had been for a long time an object of worship, and sent it to Agra, from whence it was afterwards conveyed to Dehly, and thrown down before the Bagdad gate (AH 924, AD 1518)."[237]

---

[234]I bid., p. 339.
[235]Ibid., pp. 339–40.
[236]Ibid., p. 343.
[237]Ibid., pp. 347–48.

Sultān Alāu'd-Dīn Mujāhid Shāh Bahmanī (AD 1375–1378)

Vijayanagar (Karnataka)

"Mujahid Shah, on this occasion, repaired mosques which had been built by the officers of Alla-ood-Deen Khiljy. He broke down many temples of the idolaters, and laid waste the country; after which he hastened to Beejanuggur...The King drove them before him, and gained the bank of a piece of water, which alone divided him from the citadel, where in the Ray resided. Near this spot was an eminence, on which stood a temple, covered with plates of gold and silver, set with jewels: it was much venerated by the Hindoos, and called, in the language of the country, Puttuk. The King, considering its destruction a religious obligation ascended the hill, and having razed the edifice, became possessed of the precious metals and jewels therein."[238]

Sultān Ahmad Shāh I Walī Bahmanī (AD 1422–1435)

Vijayanagar (Karnataka)

"Ahmud Shah, without waiting to besiege the Hindoo capital, overran the open country; and wherever he went put to death men, women, and children, without mercy, contrary to the compact made between his uncle and predecessor, Mahomed Shah, and the Rays of Beejanuggur. Whenever the number of slain amounted to twenty thousand, he halted three days, and made a festival celebration of the bloody event. He broke down, also, the idolatrous temples, and destroyed the colleges of the bramins. During these operations, a body of five thousand Hindoos, urged by desperation at the destruction of their religious buildings, and at the insults offered to their deities, united in taking an oath to sacrifice their lives in an attempt to kill the King, as the author of all their sufferings..."[239]

Kullum (Maharashtra)

"In the year AH 829 (AD 1425), Ahmud Shah marched to reduce a rebellious zemindar of Mahoor...During this campaign, the King obtained possession of a diamond mine at Kullum, a place dependent on Gondwana, in which territory he razed many idolatrous temples, and erecting mosques on their sites, appropriated to each some tracts of land to maintain holy men, and to supply lamps and oil for religious purposes..."[240]

---

[238]Ibid., Vol. II, p. 206–07.
[239]Ibid., p. 248.
[240]Ibid., p. 251.

Sultān 'Alāu'd-Dīn Ahmad Shāh II Bahmanī (AD 1436–1458)

"...He was averse from shedding human blood, though he destroyed many idolatrous temples, and erected mosques in their stead. He held conversation neither with Nazarenes nor with bramins; nor would he permit them to hold civil offices under his government."[241]

Sultān Muhammad Shāh II Bahmanī (AD 1463–1482)

Kondapalli (Andhra Pradesh)

"Mahomed Shah now sat down before Condapilly and Bhim Raj, after six months, being much distressed, sued for pardon; which being granted, at the intercession of some of the nobility, he surrendered the fort and town to the royal troops. The King having gone to view the fort, broke down an idolatrous temple, and killed some bramins, who officiated at it, with his own hands, as a point of religion. He then gave orders for a mosque to be erected on the foundation of the temple, and ascending a pulpit, repeated a few prayers, distributed alms, and commanded the Khootba to be read in his name. Khwaja Mahmood Gawan now represented, that as his Majesty had slain some infidels with his own hands, he might fairly assume the title of Ghazy, an appellation of which he was very proud. Mahmood Shah was the first of his race who had slain a bramin..."[242]

Kanchipuram (Tamil Nadu)

"...On his arrival at Condapilly, he was informed by the country people, that at the distance of ten days' journey was the temple of Kunchy the walls and roof of which were covered with plates of gold, and ornamented with precious stones; but that no Mahomedan monarch had as yet seen it, or even heard of its name. Mahomed Shah, accordingly, selected six thousand of his best cavalry, and leaving the rest of his army at Condapilly, proceeded by forced marches to Kunchy... Swarms of people, like bees, now issued from within, and ranged themselves under the walls to defend it. At length, the rest of the King's force coming up, the temple was attacked and carried by storm, with great slaughter. An immense booty fell to the share of the victors, who took away nothing but gold, jewels, and silver, which were abundant..."[243]

[241]Ibid., p. 269.
[242]Ibid., p. 306.
[243]Ibid., p. 308.

Sultān 'Alī 'Ādil Shāh I of Bijapur (AD 1557–1579)

Bankapur (*Karnataka*)

"...Ally Adil Shah, at the persuasions of his minister, carried his arms against Bunkapoor. This place was the principal residence of Velapa Ray, who had been originally a principal attendant of Ramraj; after whose death he assumed independence...[244]

"...Velapa Ray, despairing of relief, at length sent offers for surrendering the fort to the King, on condition of being allowed to march away with his family and effects, which Ally Adil Shah thought proper to grant, and the place was evacuated accordingly. The King ordered a superb temple within it to be destroyed, and he himself laid the first stone of a mosque, which was built on the foundation, offering up prayers for his victory. Moostufa Khan acquired great credit for his conduct, and was honoured with a royal dress, and had many towns and districts of the conquered country conferred upon him in jageer...[245]

Sultān Qulī Qutb Shāh of Golconda (AD 1507–1543)

Dewarconda (*Andhra Pradesh*)

"After his return the King proceeded to reduce the fortress of Dewurconda, strongly situated on the top of a hill, which after a long siege was taken, and the Hindoo palaces and temples, by the King's orders were consumed to ashes, and mosques built in their stead."[246]

Sultān Ibrāhīm Qutb Shāh of Golconda (AD 1550–1580)

Adoni (*Karnataka*)

"When the late king, Ibrahim Kootb Shah, had settled the countries of the Hindoos on his southern frontier, and despatched his commander, Ameer Shah Meer, to oppose the armies of his Mahomedan neighbours, he vested the management of the affairs of his government in the hands of one Moorhary Row, a Marratta bramin, to whom was attached a body of ten thousand infantry, under the command of Mahomedan officers of rank, with permission to beat the nobut. Moorhary Row was in every respect the second person in the state, not even excepting the princes of the blood-royal. In the latter end of the late king's reign, this unprincipled infidel proceeded with a force towards a famous temple near Adony, where he attacked the inhabitants, laid waste the country, and sacked it of its idols, made of gold and silver,

[244]Ibid., Vol. III, p. 82.
[245]Ibid., p. 84.
[246]Ibid., p. 212.

and studded with rubies. He levied also four lacks of hoons (160,000*l.*) from the inhabitants. At sight of the idols the King was taken seriously ill, and never recovered. He died on Thursday the 21st of Rubbeeoos-Sany, AH 988 (AD June 2, 1580) AD..."[247]

Sultān Muhammad Qulī Qutb Shāh of Golconda (AD 1580–1612)
Cuddapah (Andhra Pradesh)

"The sudden swelling of the rivers, and the absence of the King with his army, gave Venkutputty leisure to muster the whole of his forces, which amounted to one hundred thousand men. The leaders were Yeltumraj, Goolrung Setty, and Munoopraj, who marched to recover Gundicota from the hands of Sunjur Khan. Here the enemy were daily opposed by sallies from the garrison, but they perservered in the siege; when they heard that Moortuza Khan, with the main army of the Mahomedans, had penetrated as far as the city of Krupa, the most famous city of that country, wherein was a large temple. This edifice the Mahomedans destroyed as far as practicable, broke the idol, and sacked the city..."[248]

Kalahasti (Tamil Nadu)

"The King determined to spare neither men nor money to carry on the war against the Hindoos: he accordingly directed Etibar Khan Yezdy, the Hawaldar of Condbeer (henceforth called Moortuza Nuggur), to collect all the troops under his command, with orders to march towards Beejanuggur, and to lay in ashes all the enemy's towns in his route...Etibar Khan now proceeded to the town of Calistry, which he reached after a month's march from Golconda. Here he destroyed the Hindoo idols, and ordered prayers to be read in the temples. These edifices may well be compared in magnificence with the buildings and paintings of China, with which they vie in beauty and workmanship. Having given a signal example of the Mahomedan power in that distant country, the Hindoos did not dare to interrupt his return..."[249]

Sultān Muzaffar Shāh I of Gujarat (AD 1392–1410)
Somnath (Gujarat)

"...On the return of Moozuffur Khan to Guzerat, he learnt that in

[247]Ibid., p. 267. Murahari Rao was obviously a precursor of our present-day devotees of Secularism who are Hindus by accident of birth and who stop at nothing in order to please the Muslims.

[248]Ibid., p. 274.

[249]Ibid., pp. 276–77.

the western Puttun district the Ray of Jehrend, an idolater, refused allegiance to the Mahomedan authority. To this place Moozuffur Khan accordingly marched, and exacted tribute. He then proceeded to Somnat, where having destroyed all the Hindoo temples which he found standing, he built mosques in their stead; and leaving learned men for the propagation of the faith, and his own officers to govern the country, returned to Puttun in the year AH 798 (AD 1395)."[250]

Jhalawar (*Rajasthan*)

"...From Mundulgur Moozuffur Khan marched to Ajmeer, to pay his devotions at the shrine of Khwaja Moyin-ood-Deen Hussun Sunjury, from the whence he went towards Guzerat. On reaching Julwara, he destroyed the temples; and after exacting heavy contributions, and establishing his authority, he returned to Puttun..."[251]

Diu (*Gujarat*)

"...In the following year AH 804 (AD 1402), he marched to Somnat, and after a bloody action, in which the Mahomedans were victorious, the Ray fled to Diu. Moozuffur Shah having arrived before Diu laid siege to it, but it opened its gates without offering resistance. The garrison was, however, nearly all cut to pieces, while the Ray, with the rest of the members of his court, were trod to death by elephants. One large temple in the town was razed to the ground, and a mosque built on its site; after which, leaving his own troops in the place, Moozuffur Shah returned to Puttun."[252]

Sultān Ahmad Shāh I of Gujrat (AD 1411–1443)

Sompur (*Gujrat*)

"Ahmud Shah having a great curiosity to see the hill-fort of Girnal pursued the rebel in that direction...After a short time, the Raja, having consented to pay an annual tribute, made a large offering on the spot. Ahmud Shah left officers to collect the stipulated amount, and returned to Ahmudabad; on the road to which place he destroyed the temple of Somapoor, wherein were found many valuable jewels, and other property."[253]

---

[250]Ibid., Vol. IV, p. 3.
[251]Ibid., p. 4.
[252]Ibid., p. 5.
[253]Ibid., p. 10.

General order

"In the year AH 817 (AD 1414), Mullik Tohfa, one of the officers of the King's government, was ennobled by the title of Taj-ool-Moolk, and received a special commission to destroy all idolatrous temples, and establish the Mahomedan authority throughout Guzerat; a duty which he executed with such diligence, that the names of Mawass and Girass were hereafter unheard of in the whole kingdom."[254]

On way to Nagaur (Rajasthan)

"In the year AH 819 (AD 1416), Ahmud Shah marched against Nagoor, on the road to which place he plundered the country, and destroyed the temples..."[255]

Idar (Gujarat)

"...In the year 832 he marched again to Idur; and on the sixth of Suffur, AH 832 (AD Nov. 14, 1428) carried by storm one of the principal forts in that province, wherein he built a magnificent mosque..."[256]

Sultān Mahmūd Begḍhā of Gujarat (AD 1458–1511)

Girnar (Gujarat)

"The author of the history of Mahmood Shah relates, that in the year AH 872 (AD 1468), the King saw the holy Prophet (Mahomed) in a dream, who presented before him a magnificent banquet of the most delicate viands. This dream was interpreted by the wise men as a sign that he would soon accomplish a conquest by which he would obtain great treasures, which prediction was soon after verified in the capture of Girnal.

"In the year AH 873 (AD 1469), Mahmood Shah marched towards the country of Girnal, the capital of which bears the same name...[257]

"...The victorious army, without attacking the fort of Girnal, destroyed all the temples in the vicinity; and the King sending out foraging parties procured abundance of provisions for the camp...[258]

"The King, being desirous that the tenets of Islam should be propagated throughout the country of Girnal, caused a city to be built, which he called Moostufabad, for the purpose of establishing an honourable residence for the venerable personages of the Mahomedan religion,

[254]Ibid.

[255]Ibid., pp. 10–11.

[256]Ibid., p. 16. There is evidence that the mosque was raised on the site of a temple.

[257]Ibid., p. 31.

[258]Ibid., p. 32.

deputed to disseminate its principles; Mahmood Shah also took up his residence in that city..."[259]

Dwarka (Gujarat)

"Mahmood Shah's next effort was against the port of Jugut, with a view of making converts of the infidels, an object from which he had been hitherto deterred by the reports he received of the approaches to it...[260]

"The King, after an arduous march, at length arrived before the fort of Jugut, a place filled with infidels, misled by the infernal minded bramins...The army was employed in destroying the temple at Jugut, and in building a mosque in its stead; while measures, which occupied three or four months in completing, were in progress for equipping a fleet to attack the island of Bete..."[261]

Sultān Muzaffar Shāh II of Gujarat (AD 1511–1526)

Idar (Gujarat)

"The King, hearing of this disaster, instantly marched towards Idur. On reaching Mahrasa he caused the whole of the Idur district to be laid waste. Bheem Ray took refuge in the Beesulnuggur mountains; but the garrison of Idur, consisting of only ten Rajpoots, defended it against the whole of the King's army with obstinacy; they were, however, eventually put to death on the capture of the place; and the temples, palaces, and garden houses, were levelled with the dust..."[262]

Sultān Mahmūd Khaljī of Malwa (AD 1435–1469)

Kumbhalgadh (Rajasthan)

"...Sooltan Mahmood now attacked one of the forts in the Koombulmere district, defended by Beny Ray, the deputy of Rana Koombho of Chittor. In front of the gateway was a large temple which commanded the lower works. This building was strongly fortified, and employed by the enemy as a magazine. Sooltan Mahmood, aware of its importance, determined to take possession of it at all hazards; and having stormed it in person, carried it, but not without heavy loss; after which, the fort fell into his hands, and many Rajpoots were put to death. The temple was now filled with wood, and being set on fire, cold water was thrown on the stone images, which causing them to break,

---

[259]Ibid., p. 33.
[260]Ibid., p. 35.
[261]Ibid., p. 36.
[262]Ibid., p. 49.

the pieces were given to the butchers of the camp, in order to be used as weights in selling meat. One large figure in particular, representing a ram, and formed of solid marble, being consumed, the Rajpoots were compelled to eat the calcined parts with pan, in order that it might be said that they were made to eat their gods..."[263]

Mandalgadh (*Rajasthan*)

"On the 26th of Mohurrum, in the year AH 861 (AD Dec. 23, 1465), the King again proceeded to Mundulgur; and after a vigorous siege occupied the lower fort, wherein many Rajpoots were put to the sword, but the hill-fort still held out; to reduce which might have been a work of time but the reservoirs of water failing in consequence of the firing of the cannon, the garrison was obliged to capitulate, and Rana Koombho stipulated to pay ten lacks of tunkas. This event happened on the 20th of Zeehuj of the same year AH 861 (AD Nov. 8, 1457), exactly eleven months after the King's leaving Mando. On the following day the King caused all the temples to be destroyed, and musjids to be erected in their stead, appointing the necessary officers of religion to perform daily worship..."[264]

On Way to Kumbhalgadh (*Rajasthan*)

"Sooltan Mahmood, in the year AH 863 (AD 1485), again marched against the Rajpoots. On arriving at the town of Dhar, he detached Gheias-ood-Deen to lay waste the country of the Kolies and Bheels. In this excursion the Prince penetrated to the hills of Koombulmere, and on his return, having given the King some description of that fortress, Sooltan Mahmood resolved to march thither. On the next day he moved for that purpose, destroying all the temples on the road..."[265]

Sultān Mahmūd Shāh bin Ibrāhīm Sharqī of Jaunpur (AD 1440–1457)

Orissa

"...Mahmood Shah Shurky, having recruited his army, took the field again for the purpose of reducing some refractory zemindars in the district of Chunar, which place he sacked, and from thence proceeded into the province of Orissa, which he also reduced; and having destroyed the temples and collected large sums of money, returned to

[263]Ibid., pp. 125–26.
[264]Ibid., p. 135.
[265]Ibid., p. 136.

Joonpoor."[266]

Muhammad bin Qāsim (AD 712–715)

Debal (*Sindh*)

"On the receipt of this letter, Hijaj obtained the consent of Wuleed, the son of Abdool Mullik, to invade India, for the purpose of propagating the faith and at the same time deputed a chief of the name of Budmeen, with three hundred cavalry, to join Haroon in Mikran, who was directed to reinforce the party with one thousand good soldiers more to attack Deebul. Budmeen failed in his expedition, and lost his life in the first action. Hijaj, not deterred by this defeat, resolved to follow up the enterprise by another. In consequence, in the year AH 93 (AD 711) he deputed his cousin and son-in-law, Imad-ood-Deen Mahomed Kasim, the son of Akil Shukhfy, then only seventeen years of age, with six thousand soldiers, chiefly Assyrians, with the necessary implements for taking forts, to attack Deebul...[267]

"On reaching this place, he made preparations to besiege it, but the approach was covered by a fortified temple, surrounded by strong wall, built of hewn stone and mortar, one hundred and twenty feet in height. After some time a bramin, belonging to the temple, being taken, and brought before Kasim, stated, that four thousand Rajpoots defended the place, in which were from two to three thousand bramins, with shorn heads, and that all his efforts would be vain; for the standard of the temple was sacred; and while it remained entire no profane foot dared to step beyond the threshold of the holy edifice. Mahomed Kasim having caused the catapults to be directed against the magic flag-staff, succeeded, on the third discharge, in striking the standard, and broke it down.... Mahomed Kasim levelled the temple and its walls with the ground and circumcised the brahmins. The infidels highly resented this treatment, by invectives against him and the true faith. On which Mahomed Kasim caused every brahmin, from the age of seventeen and upwards, to be put to death; the young women and children of both sexes were retained in bondage and the old women being released, were permitted to go whithersoever they chose."[268]

Multan (*Punjab*)

"...On reaching Mooltan, Mahomed Kasim also subdued that prov-

[266]Ibid., p. 215.
[267]Ibid., p. 234.
[268]Ibid., p. 235.

ince; and himself occupying the city, he erected mosques on the site of the Hindoo temples."[269]

Sultān Jalālu'd-Dīn Mankbarnī of Khwarizm (AD 1222–1231)
Thatta (Sindh)

"...Julal-ood-Deen now occupied Tutta, destroyed all the temples, and built mosques in their stead; and on one occasion detached a force to Nehrwala (Puttun), on the border of Guzerat..."[270]

Sultān Sikandar Butshikan of Kashmir (AD 1389–1413)
Kashmir

"In these days he promoted a bramin, by name Seeva Dew Bhut, to the office of prime minister, who embracing the Mahomedan faith, became such a persecutor of Hindoos that he induced Sikundur to issue orders proscribing the residence of any other than Mahomedans in Kashmeer; and he required that no man should wear the mark on his forehead, or any woman be permitted to burn with her husband's corpse. Lastly, he insisted on all golden and silver images being broken and melted down, and the metal coined into money. Many of the bramins, rather than abandon their religion or their country, poisoned themselves; some emigrated from their native homes, while a few escaped the evil of banishment by becoming Mahomedans. After the emigration of the bramins, Sikundur ordered all the temples in Kashmeer to be thrown down; among which was one dedicated to Maha Dew, in the district of Punjhuzara, which they were unable to destroy, in consequence of its foundation being below the surface of the neighbouring water. But the temple dedicated to Jug Dew was levelled with the ground; and on digging into its foundation the earth emitted volumes of fire and smoke which the infidels declared to be the emblem of the wrath of the Deity; but Sikundur, who witnessed the phenomenon, did not desist till the building was entirely razed to the ground, and its foundations dug up.

"In another place in Kashmeer was a temple built by Raja Bulnat, the destruction of which was attended with a remarkable incident. After it had been levelled, and the people were employed in digging the found ation, a copper-plate was discovered, on which was the following inscription:- 'Raja Bulnat, having built this temple, was desirous of ascertaining from his astrologers how long it would last, and was informed

[269]Ibid., p. 238.
[270]Ibid., p. 244.

by them, that after eleven hundred years, a king named Sikundur would destroy it, as well as the other temples in Kashmeer'...Having broken all the images in Kashmeer, he acquired the title of the Iconoclast, 'Destroyer of Idols'..."[271]

Sultān Fath Shāh of Kashmir (AD 1485–1499 and 1505–1516)
Kashmir

"On the imprisonment of Mahomed, Futteh Khan, assuming the reigns of government, and being formally crowned, was acknowledged King of Kashmeer in the year 902; and appointed Suffy and Runga Ray, the two officers who had lately made their escape, his ministers. About this time one Meer Shumsood-Deen, disciple of Shah Kasim Anwur, the son of Syud Mahomed Noorbukhsh arrived in Kashmeer from Irak. Futteh Khan made over to this holy personage all the confiscated lands which had lately fallen to the crown; and his disciples went forth destroying the temples of the idolaters, in which they met with the support of the government, so that no one dared to oppose them. In a short time many of the Kashmeeries, particularly those of the tribe of Chuk, became converts to the Noorbukhsh tenets. The persuasion of this sect was connected with that of the Sheeas; but many proselytes, who had not tasted of the cup of grace, after the death of Meer Shumsood-Deen, reverted to their idols...."[272]

(47)
Tūzuk-i-Jahāngīrī

The author is the fourth Mughal emperor, Jahāngīr (AD 1605–1628). He wrote it himself as his memoirs upto the thirteenth year of his reign, that is, AD 1617. After that his ill-health forced him to give up writing and the work was entrusted to Mu'tamad Khān who continued writing it in the name of the emperor upto the beginning of the nineteenth year of the reign. Muhammad Hādī continued the memoirs upto Jahāngīr's death in 1628.

Ajmer (Rajasthan)

"...On the 7th Āzar I went to see and shoot on the tank of Pushkar, which is one of the established praying-places of the Hindus, with regard to the perfection of which they give (excellent) accounts that are incredible to any intelligence, and which is situated at a distance of

[271]Ibid., pp. 268–69. Another wishful reading of an ancient inscription.
[272]Ibid., pp. 279–80.

three kos from Ajmir. For two or three days I shot waterfowl on that tank, and returned to Ajmir. Old and new temples which, in the language of the infidels, they call Deohara are to be seen around this tank. Among them Rānā Shankar, who is the uncle of the rebel Amar, and in my kingdom is among the high nobles, had built a Deohara of great magnificence, on which 100,000 rupees had been spent. I went to see that temple. I found a form cut out of black stone, which from the neck above was in the shape of a pig's head, and the rest of the body was like that of a man. The worthless religion of the Hindus is this, that once on a time for some particular object the Supreme Ruler thought it necessary to show himself in this shape; on this account they hold it dear and worship it. I ordered them to break that hideous form and throw it into the tank. After looking at this building there appeared a white dome on the top of a hill, to which men were coming from all quarters. When I asked about this they said that a Jogī lived there, and when the simpletons come to see him he places in their hands a handful of flour, which they put into their mouths and imitate the cry of an animal which these fools have at some time injured, in order that by this act their sins may be blotted out. I ordered them to break down that place and turn the Jogī out of it, as well as to destroy the form of an idol there was in the dome..."[273]

Kangra (*Himachal Pradesh*)

"On the 24th of the same month I went to see the fort of Kāngra, and gave an order that the Qāzī, the Chief Justice (*Mir'Adl*), and other learned men of Islam should accompany me and carry out in the fort whatever was customary, according to the religion of Muhammad. Briefly, having traversed about one koss, I went up to the top of the fort, and by the grace of God, the call to prayer and the reading of the *Khutba* and the slaughter of a bullock which had not taken place from the commencement of the building of the fort till now, were carried out in my presence. I prostrated myself in thanksgiving for this great gift, which no king had hoped to receive, and ordered a lofty mosque to be built inside the fort...

"After going round the fort I went to see the temple of Durgā, which is known as Bhawan. A world has here wandered in the desert of error. Setting aside the infidels whose custom is the worship of idols, crowds of the people of Islam, traversing long distances, bring their

---

[273]*Tūzuk-i-Jahāngīrī*, translated into English by Alexander Rogers, first published 1909–1914, New Delhi Reprint, 1978, Vol. I, pp. 254–55.

offerings and pray to the black stone (image)...Some maintain that this stone, which is now a place of worship for the vile infidels, is not the stone which was there originally, but that a body of the people of Islam came and carried off the original stone, and threw it into the bottom of the river, with the intent that no one could get at it. For a long time the tumult of the infidels and idol-worshippers had died away in the world, till a lying brahman hid a stone for his own ends, and going to the Raja of the time said: 'I saw Durgā in a dream, and she said to me : They have thrown me into a certain place : quickly go and take me up.' The Raja, in the simplicity of his heart, and greedy for the offerings of gold that would come to him, accepted the tale of the brahman and sent a number of people with him, and brought that stone, and kept it in this place with honour, and started again the shop of error and misleading..."[274]

Varanasi (*Uttar Pradesh*)

"I am here led to relate that at the city of Banaras a temple had been erected by Rajah Maun Singh, which cost him the sum of nearly thirty-six laks of five methkally ashrefies. The principle idol in this temple had on its head a tiara or cap, enriched with jewels to the amount of three laks ashrefies. He had placed in this temple moreover, as the associates and ministering servants of the principal idol, four other images of solid gold, each crowned with a tiara, in the like manner enriched with precious stones. It was the belief of these Jehennemites that a dead Hindu, provided when alive he had been a worshipper, when laid before this idol would be restored to life. As I could not possibly give credit to such a pretence, I employed a confidential person to ascertain the truth; and, as I justly supposed, the whole was detected to be an impudent imposture. Of this discovery I availed myself, and I made it my plea for throwing down the temple which was the scene of this imposture and on the spot, with the very same materials, I erected the great mosque, because the very name of Islam was proscribed at Banaras, and with God's blessing it is my design, if I live, to fill it full with true believers."[275]

(48)
Tārīkh-i-Khān Jahān Lodī

The author, Ni'āmatu'llāh, was a historian in the court of the

[274]Ibid., Vol. II, pp. 223–25.

[275]Another manuscript of *Tūzuk-i-Jahāngīrī*, translated into English by Major David Price, Calcutta, 1906, pp. 24–25.

Mughal emperor Jahāngīr (AD 1605–1628). His *Tārīkh* is practically the same as his *Makhzan-i-Afghāni* except for the memoirs of Khān Jahān Lodī which have been added. Khān Jahān Lodī was one of the most illustrious generals of Jahāngīr. The history begins with Adam and comes down to AD 1612 when it was completed. Ni'āmatu'llāh refers to Hindus as "the most notorious vagabonds and rebels."

Sultān Mahmūd of Ghazni (AD 997–1030)

Somnath (Gujarat)

"After a long time, in AH 400, Allāh... conferred the honour of sultanate on Sultān Mahmūd Ghāzī, son of Subuktigīn... Nine men from among the Afghān chiefs...took to his court and joined his servants... The Sultān...gave to each one of them enamelled daggers and swords, horses of good breed and robes of special quality and, taking them with him, he set out with the intention of conquering Hindustān and Somnāt.

"Rāī Dāishalīm whom some historians have pronounced as Dābshalīm or Dābshalam was the great ruler of that country. The Sultān inflicted a smashing defeat on that Rājā, demolished and desecrated the idol temples there, and devastated that land of the infidels..."[276]

Sultān Sikandar Lodī (AD 1489–1517)

Dholpur (Madhya Pradesh)

"...Sikandar himself marched on Friday, the 6th Ramzān AH 906 (AD March, 1501), upon Dhūlpūr; but Rājā Mānikdeo, placing a garrison in the fort, retreated to Gwālior. This detachment, however, being unable to defend it, and abandoning the fort by night, it fell into the hands of the Muhammadan army. Sikandar on entering the fort, fell down on his knees, and returned thanks to God, and celebrated his victory. The whole army was employed in plundering and the groves which spread shade for seven *kos* around Bayāna were torn up from the roots...[277]

Mandrail (Madhya Pradesh)

"In Ramzān of the year 910 (AD 1504), after the rising of Canopus, he raised the standard of war for the reduction of the fort of Mandrāil;

---

[276]Translated from the Urdu version by Muhammad Bashīr Husain, second edition, Lahore, 1986, pp. 121–22.

[277]Elliot and Dowson, op. cit., Vol. V, p. 97. The Urdu version by Muhammad Bashir Husain adds that "all buildings were pulled down" (p. 166).

but the garrison capitulating, and delivering up the citadel, the Sultān ordered the temples and idols to be demolished, and mosques to be constructed. After leaving Mīān Makan and Mujāhid Khān to protect the fort, he himself moved out on a plundering expedition into the surrounding country, where he butchered many people, took many prisoners, and devoted to utter destruction all the groves and habitations; and after gratifying and honouring himself by this exhibition of holy zeal he returned to his capital Bayāna."[278]

Udit Nagar (*Madhya Pradesh*)

"In 912, after the rising of Canopus, the Sultān went towards the fort of Awantgar...

On the 23rd of the month, the Sultān invested the fort, and ordered the whole army to put forth their best energies to capture it... All of a sudden, by the favour of God, the gale of victory blew on the standards of the Sultān, and the gate was forced open by Malik 'Alāu-d dīn... The Rājpūts, retiring within their own houses, continued the contest, and slew their families after the custom of *jauhar*... After due thanks-giving for his victory, the Sultān gave over charge of the fort to Makan and Mujāhīd Khān, with directions that they should destroy the idol temples, and raise mosques in their places..."[279]

Narwar (*Madhya Pradesh*)

"...The Sultān set out for conquering the fort of Narwar. Those inside the fort asked for refuge when they became helpless because of the dearness of grains and scarcity of water; they sought security of their lives and left the fort together with their goods. The Sultān took over the fort, demolished the temples and idol-houses in it and built mosques, and fixed scholarships and stipends for the teachers and the taught. He resided for six months in the fort."[280]

Mathura (*Uttar Pradesh*)

"The Islamic sentiment (in him) was so strong that he demolished all temples in his kingdom and left no trace of them. He constructed *sarāis*, *bazārs*, *madrasas* and mosques in Mathurā which is a holy place of the Hindūs and where they go for bathing. He appointed government officials in order to see that no Hindū could bathe in Mathrā. No barber

---

[278]Ibid., p. 98.
[279]Ibid., pp. 100–01.
[280]Translated from the Urdu version, op. cit., p. 172.

was permitted to shave the head of any Hindū with his razor. That is how he completely curtailed the public celebration of infidel customs..."[281]

Thanesar (*Haryana*)

"Sultān Sikandar was yet a young boy when he heard about a tank in Thānesar which the Hindūs regarded as sacred and went for bathing in it. He asked the theologians about the prescription of the Shari'ah on this subject. They replied that it was permitted to demolish the ancient temples and idol-houses of the infidels, but it was not proper for him to stop them from going to an ancient tank. Hearing this reply, the prince drew out his sword and thought of beheading the theologian concerned, saying that he (the theologian) was siding with the infidels..."[282]

Sultān Ibrāhīm Lodī (AD 1517–1526)

Gwalior (*Madhya Pradesh*)

"...When the thought occurred to Sultān Ibrāhīm, he sent 'Āzam Humāyūn on this expedition...The Afghān army captured from the infidels the statue of a bull which was made of metals such as copper and brass, which was outside the gate of the fort and which the Hindūs used to worship. They brought it to the Sultān. The Sultān was highly pleased and ordered that it should be taken to Delhi and placed outside the 'Red Gate' which was known as the Baghdād Gate in those days. The statue was so fixed in front of the 'Red Gate' till the time of the Mughal emperor, Akbar the Great, who ordered in AH 999 that it be melted down and used for making cannon as well as some other equipment, which are still there in the government armoury. The author of this history...has seen it in both shapes."[283]

Sultān Sulaimān Karrānī of Bengal (AD 1563–1576)

Puri (*Orissa*)

"After Tāj Khān, his brother Sulaimān Karrāni took possession of the province of Gaur and proclaimed his independence...He also made up his mind to demolish all the temples and idol-houses of the infidels. As the biggest temple of the Hindūs was in Orissa and known as Jagannāth, he decided to destroy it and set out in that direction with a well-equipped force. Reaching there, he demolished the idol-house and laid

[281]Ibid., p. 178.
[282]Ibid., p. 179.
[283]Ibid., p. 199.

it waste. There was an idol in it known as that of Kishan... Sulaimān ordered that it be broken into pieces and thrown into the drain. In like manner, he took out seven hundred golden idols from idol-temples in the neighbouring areas...and broke them.[284]

"...When the armies of Islām entered that city, the women of the Brahmans, dressed in costly robes, wearing necklaces, covering their heads with colourful scarves and beautifying themselves in every way, took shelter at the back of the temple of Jagannāth. They were told again and again that a Muslim army that had entered the city would capture and take them away, and that those people would desecrate the temple after laying it waste. But the women did not believe it at all. They kept on saying. 'How could it happen? How could the soldiers of the Muslim army cause any injury to the idols?'

" When the army of Islām arrived near the temple, it made prisoners of those Hindū women. That is what surprised them most..."[285]

The *History of the Afghans in India AD 1545–1631* by M.A. Rahim (Karachi, 1961) quotes *Makhzan-i-Afghāna* while describing the exploits of Sulaimān Karrāni's general, Kālāpahār, in AD 1568. It says: "Every Afghān, who took part in the campaign, obtained as booty one or two gold images. Kāla Pahār destroyed the temple of Jagannāth in Puri which contained 700 idols made of gold, the biggest of which weighed 30 māns."[286]

(49)
Mir'āt-i-Sikandarī

The author, Sikandar bin Muhammad Manjhū bin Akbar, was in the employ of Azīz Kokā, the Mughal governor of Gujarat, and fought against Sultān Muzaffar Shāh III, the last independent sultān of Gujarat, who was dethroned in AD 1591.

He finished his history in 1611 or 1613. It relates the history of Gujarat from Muzaffar Shāh I to Muzaffar Shāh III.

Sultān Muzaffar Shāh I of Gujarat (AD 1392–1410)

Somnath (*Gujarat*)

"On his return (from Īdar) the Khān made up his mind to destroy Somnāt, that is, the temple of Paṭandev. But in the meanwhile he received a report that 'Ādil Khān, the ruler of Āsir and Burhānpur, had

---

[284]Ibid., p. 305.
[285]Ibid., pp. 305–06.
[286]Cited in *The Cult of Jagannath and the Regional Tradition of Orissa* by Anncharlotte Eschmann et al., New Delhi, second printing, 1981, p. 332, footnote 7.

crossed the border and stepped into the province of Sultānpur and Nadrabār which was under Gujarat...The Khān postponed his march to Paṭandev...

"In AH 799 (AD 1394–95) he invaded Jahdand (Jūnāgaḍh) which was in the Kindgdom of Rāi Bhārā and slaughtered the infidels there.

"From there he proceeded towards Somnāt, and destroyed the famous temple. He embellished that city with the laws of Islām."[287]

Sultān Ahmad Shāh I of Gujarat (AD 1411–1443)

Sidhpur (Gujarat)

His destruction of the Rudramahālaya and construction of a mosque on the same site, as described in *Mir'āt-i-Sikandarī*, has been related already in Chapter One. Strangely, the long verse cited from the Aligarh text has been omitted from the English translation by Fazlullah Lutfullah Faridi, originally published from Dharampur (Gujarat) and reprinted from Gurgaon in 1990.

General Order

"Thereafter in AH 823 (AD 1420–21) he proceeded to different parts of his kingdom for establishing order and good government...He got temples demolished and palaces and mosques constructed in their stead..."[288]

Sultān Mahmūd Begḍhā of Gujarat (AD 1458–1511)

Dwarka (*Gujarat*)

"On 17 Zilhijjā he started towards Jagat and reduced that place after marching continuously. The infidels of Jagat ran away to the island of Sānkhū. The Sultān destroyed Jagat and got its palaces dismantled. He got the idols broken..."[289]

Sankhodhar (*Gujarat*)

"...When the Sultān saw that the infidels had gone to that island, he ordered boats from the ports and proceeded to the island with his well-armed soldiers...The infidels did not stint in fighting with swords and guns. In the end the army of Islām achieved victory. A majority of the infidels were slaughtered. The Musalmāns started giving calls to prayers after mounting on top of the temples. They started destroying

---

[287]Translated from the Hindi version by S.A.A. Rizvi in *Uttara Taimūr Kālīna Bhārata*, Aligarh, 1959, Vol. II, p. 256.

[288]Ibid., p. 273.

[289]Ibid., p. 318.

the temples and desecrating the idols. The Sultān offered *namāz* out of gratefulness fo Allāh...He got a Jāmi' Masjid raised in that place..."[290]

Sultān Muzaffar Shāh II of Gujarat (AD 1511–1526)

Idar (*Gujarat*)

"...The Rājā of Īdar ran away to the mountains and on the fourth day the Sultān started from Morāsā and halted near Īdar. He ordered that the houses and temples of Īdar should be destroyed in such a way that no trace of them should remain."[291]

Sultān Bahādur Shāh of Gujarat (AD 1526–1537)

Vidisha (Madhya Pradesh)

"Afterwards he went towards Bhīlsā which country had been conquered for Islām by Sultān Shamsu'd-dīn (Altamsh), King of Delhī. Since eighteen years the estate of Bhīlsā had been subject to Silahdī, and the laws of Islām had been changed there for the customs of infidelity. When the Sultān reached the above place, he abrogated the ordinances of infidelity and introduced the laws of Islām, and slew the idolaters and threw down their temples..."[292]

(50)
Intikhāb-i-Jahāngīr Shāhī

The name of the author is not known. He was evidently a contemporary and a companion of Jahāngīr. The *Tabqāt-i-Shāh-Jahānī* mentions a work written by Shykh 'Abdul Wahāb and named *Akhlāq-i-Jahāngīrī*. This work may be the same as the *Intikhāb*. The Shykh died in 1622–23.

Nūru'd-Dīn Muhammad Jahāngīr PādShāh Ghāzī (AD 1605–1628)

Ahmadabad (*Gujarat*)

"One day at Ahmadabad it was reported that many of the infidel and superstitious sect of the *Seoras* (Jains) of Gujarāt had made several very great and splendid temples, and having placed in them their false gods, had managed to secure a large degree of respect for themselves and that the women who went for worship in those temples were polluted by them and other people...The Emperor Jahāngīr ordered them

[290]Ibid., p. 319.
[291]Ibid., p. 350.
[292]*Mir'āt-i-Sikandarī*, translated by Fazlullah Lutfallah Faridi, Dharampur (Gujarat), Gurgaon Reprint, 1990, p. 171.

banished from the country, and their temples to be demolished. Their idol was thrown down on the uppermost step of the mosque, that it might be trodden upon by those who came to say their daily prayers there. By this order of the Emperor, the infidels were exceedingly disgraced, and Islām exalted..."[293]

(51)
Tazkirātu'l-Mulūk

It is a history of sixteenth century Bijapur written in AD 1608–09 by Rafīu'd-Dīn Ibrāhīm Shīrāzī, an Iranian adventurer and diplomat.

Sultān 'Alī I 'Ādilshāh of Bijapur (AD 1557–1580)

Karnataka

"While campaigning in Karnataka following the fall of Vijayanagar 'Ali I's armies destroyed two or three hundred Hindu temples, and the monarch himself was said to have smashed four or five thousand Hindu images..."[294]

(52)
Tārīkh-i-Kashmīr

The author, Haidar Malik Chādurāh, was a Kashmirian nobleman in the service of Sultān Yūsuf Shāh (AD 1579–1586). He gives the history of Kashmir from the earliest times. Though mainly based on *Rājataraṅgiṇī*, there are some additions in the later period. It was begun in AD 1618 and finished sometime after 1620–21.

Sultān Sikandar Butshikan of Kashmir (AD 1389–1413)

Kashmir

"During the reign of Sultān Sikandar, Mīr Sayyīd Muhammad, son of Mīr Sayyīd Hamadanī,... came here, and removed the rust of ignorance and infidelity and the evils, by his preaching and guidance... He wrote an epistle for Sultān Sikandar on *tasawwuf*... Sultān Sikandar became his follower. He prohibited all types of frugal games. Nobody dared commit acts which were prohibited by the Sharīat... The Sultān was constantly busy in annihilating the infidels and destroyed most of the temples..."[295]

---

[293]Elliot and Dowson, op. cit., Vol. VI, p. 451. An additional excuse besides commandments of Allāh was invented in order to destroy the tempels.

[294]Summarised by Richard Maxwell Eaton in his *Sufis of Bijapur 1300–1700*, Princeton (U.S.A.), 1978, p. 68.

[295]*Tārīkh-Kashmīr*, edited and translated into English by Razia Bano, Delhi, 1991, p. 55.

Malik Mūsā of Kashmir

Kashmir

He was a powerful minister in the reign of Sultān Fath Shāh (AD 1489– 1516), but *Tārīkh-i-Kashmīr* presents him as the monarch. It says:

"Malik Mūsā ascended the throne in AH 907 (AD 1501). During his reign, he devoted himself to the obliteration of the infidels and busied himself with the spread of the religion of the prophet. He made desolate most of the temples where the infidels had practised idolatry. Wherever there was a temple, he destroyed it and built a mosque in its place... None of the Sultāns of Kashmīr after Sultān Sikandar... ever made such an effort for the spread of the Islamic faith as did Malik Mūsā Chādurāh, and for this auspicious reason he received the title of the 'Idol Breaker'."[296]

Sufi Mīr Shamsu'd-Dīn Irāqī

Kashmir

He was a sufi of the Kubrawiyya sect who came to Kashmir first in AD1481, next in AD 1501, and finally in 1505 in the reign of Sultān Fath Shāh. He found it convenient to work as a member of the Nūr Bakhsh Sufi sect. His doings are "anticipated" in the *Tārīkh-i-Kashmīr* in the following words:

"...Bābā Ūchah Ganāī went for circumambulation of the two *harms* (Mecca and Medina)...in search of the perfect guide (Pīr-i-Kāmil). He prayed to God (to help) him when he heard a voice from the unknown that the 'perfect guide' was in Kashmīr himself...Hazrat Shaikh, Bābā Ūchah Ganāī...returned to Kashmīr...All of a sudden his eyes fell upon a place of worship, the temples of the Hindus. He smiled; when the devotees asked the cause of (his smile) he replied that the destruction and demolition of these places of worship and the destruction of the idols will take place at the hand of the high horn Shaikh Shams-ud-Dīn Irrāqī. He will soon be coming from Irāq and shall turn the temples completely desolate, and most of the misled people will accept the path of guidance and Islām.... So as was ordained Shaikh Shams-ud-Dīn reached Kashmīr. He began destroying the places of worship and the temples of the Hindus and made an effort to achieve the objective."[297]

---

[296]Ibid., p. 61.
[297]Ibid., pp. 102–03.

(53)
Mir'āt-i-Mas'ūdī

It is a biography of Sayyid Sālār Mas'ūd Ghāzī whose tomb at Bahraich (Uttar Pradesh) occupies the site of a Sun Temple. It was written by Shykh 'Abdu'r-Rahmān Chishtī in the reign of Jahangir (1605–1628). He drew his main material from *Tawārīkh-i-Mahmūdī* by Mullā Muhammad Ghaznavī, a contemporary of Sultān Mahmūd of Ghazni (AD 997–1030). Sālār Mas'ud, according to this account, was the son of Sitr Mu'alla', a sister of Sultān Mahmūd, married to his general, Sālār Sāhū. Sālār Mas'ūd was born when the couple was staying in Ajmer. He is famous among the Muslims as *Ghāzi Miyān, Bālā Miyān* (revered boy) and *Hathīlā Pīr* (the obstinate saint). There are many stories current regarding how he led or sent many expeditions against the Hindu *Kāfirs* in all direction from his headquarters at Satrakh in the Barabanki District of Uttar Pradesh. He is supposed to have defeated many *Rājās*, plundered many towns, and destroyed many temples, particularly in Awadh. Many tombs all over Awadh and neighbouring areas are reputed to be the graves of his *Ghāzīs* (veterans) who became *Shahīds* (martyrs) in a prolonged *Jihād* (holy war) directed by him. He was finally caught and killed near Bahraich by a league of Hindu *Rājās*. The Sun Temple which was his target escaped this time, but was destroyed when another wave of Islamic invasion swept over the area at the end of the twelfth century.

Saiyyid Sālār Mas'ūd Ghāzī (AD 1013–1033)

Somnath (*Gujarat*)

"It happened that Mahmūd had long been planning an expedition into Bhardana, and Gujerat, to destroy the idol temple of Somnāt, a place of great sanctity to all Hindus. So as soon as he had returned to Ghaznī from his Khurasan business, he issued a *farmān* to the General of the army, ordering him to leave a confidential officer in charge of the fort of Kabuliz, and himself to join the court with his son Sālār Mas'ud...[298]

"It is related in the *Tārīkh-i Mahmūdī* that the Sultān shortly after reached Ghaznī, and laid down the image of Somnāt at the threshold of the Mosque of Ghaznī, so that the Musulmāns might tread upon the breast of the idol on their way to and from their devotions. As soon as the unbelievers heard of this, they sent an embassy to Khwāja Hasan Maimandī, stating that the idol was of stone and useless to the

[298]Elliot and Dowson, op. cit., Vol. II, p. 524.

Musulmāns, and offered to give twice its weight in gold as a ransom, if it might be returned to them. Khwāja Hasan Maimandī represented to the Sultān that the unbelievers had offered twice the weight of the idol in gold, and had agreed to be subject to him. He added, that the best policy would be to take the gold and restore the image, thereby attaching the people to his Government. The Sultān yielded to the advice of the Khwāja, and the unbelievers paid the gold into the treasury.

"One day, when the Sultān was seated on his throne, the ambassadors of the unbelievers came, and humbly petitioned thus: 'Oh, Lord of the world! we have paid the gold to your Government in ransom, but have not yet received our purchase, the idol Somnāt.' The Sultān was wroth at their words, and, falling into reflection, broke up the assembly and retired, with his dear Sālār Mas'ūd, into his private apartments. He then asked his opinion as to whether the image ought to be restored, or not? Sālār Mas'ūd, who was perfect in goodness, said quickly, 'In the day of the resurrection, when the Almighty shall call for Āzar, the idol-destroyer, and Mahmūd, the idol-seller, Sire! what will you say?' This speech deeply affected the Sultān, he was full of grief, and answered, 'I have given my word; it will be a breach of promise.' Sālār Mas'ūd begged him to make over the idol to him, and tell the unbelievers to get it from him. The Sultān agreed; and Sālār Mas'ūd took it to his house, and, breaking off its nose and ears, ground them to powder.

"When Khwāja Hasan introduced the unbelievers, and asked the Sultān to give orders to restore the image to them, his majesty replied that Sālār Mas'ūd had carried it off to his house, and that he might send them to get it from him. Khwāja Hasan, bowing his head, repeated these words in Arabic, 'No easy matter is it to recover anything which has fallen into the hands of a lion.' He then told the unbelievers that the idol was with Sālār Mas'ūd, and that they were at liberty to go and fetch it. So they went to Mas'ūd's door and demanded their god.

"That prince commanded Malik Nekbakht to treat them courteously, and make them be seated; then to mix the dust of the nose and ears of the idol with sandal and the lime eaten with betel-nut, and present it to them. The unbelievers were delighted, and smeared themselves with sandal, and ate the betel-leaf. After a while they asked for the idol, when Sālār Mas'ūd said he had given it to them. They inquired, with astonishment, what he meant by saying that they had received the idol? And Malik Nekbakht explained that it was mixed with the sandal and betel-lime. Some began to vomit, while others went weeping and lamenting to Khwāja Hasan Maimandī and told him what had occurred...[299]

"Afterwards the image of Somnāt was divided into four parts, as is described in the *Tawārīkh-i-Mahmūdī*. Mahmūd's first exploit is said to have been conquering the Hindū rebels, destroying the forts and the idol temples of the Rāi Ajipāl (Jaipāl), and subduing the country of India. His second, the expedition into Harradawa and Guzerāt, the carrying off the idol of Somnāt, and dividing it into four pieces, one of which he is reported to have placed on the threshold of the Imperial Palace, while he sent two others to Mecca and Medina respectively. Both these exploits were performed at the suggestion, and by the advice, of the General and Sālār Mas'ūd; but India was conquered by the efforts of Sālār Mas'ūd alone, and the idol of Somnāt was broken in pieces by his sold advice, as has been related. Sālār Sāhū was Sultān of the army and General of the forces in Iran...[300]

Awadh (*Uttar Pradesh*)

"...Mas'ūd hunted through the country around Bahraich, and whenever he passed by the idol temple of Sūraj-kund, he was wont to say that he wanted that piece of ground for a dwelling-place. This Sūraj-kund was a sacred shrine of all the unbelievers of India. They had carved an image of the sun in stone on the banks of the tank there. This image they called Bālārukh, and through its fame Bahraich had attained its flourishing condition. When there was an eclipse of the sun, the unbelievers would come from east and west to worship it, and every Sunday the heathen of Bahraich and its environs, male and female, used to assemble in thousands to rub their heads under that stone, and do it reverence as an object of peculiar sanctity. Mas'ūd was distressed at this idolatry, and often said that, with God's will and assistance, he would destroy that mine of unbelief, and set up a chamber for the worship of the Nourisher of the Universe in its place, rooting out unbelief from those parts...[301]

"Meanwhile, the Rāi Sahar Deo and Har Deo, with several other chiefs, who had kept their troops in reserve, seeing that the army of Islām was reduced to nothing, unitedly attacked the body-guard of the Prince. The few forces that remained to that loved one of the Lord of the Universe were ranged round him in the garden. The unbelievers, surrounding them in dense numbers, showered arrows upon them. It

[299]Ibid., pp. 525–27.
[300]Ibid., p. 527.
[301]Ibid., p. 538.

was then, on Sunday, the 14th of the month Rajab, in the aforesaid year 424 (14th June, 1033) as the time of evening prayer came on, that a chance arrow pierced the main artery in the arm of the Prince of the Faithful...[302]

(54)
Siyar al-Aqtāb

This work was completed in AD 1647 by Allāh Diyā Chishtī. It deals with many miracles performed by the Sufis, particularly of the Sābriyya branch of the Chishtiyya *silsilā*.

Shykh Mu'īn al-Dīn Chishtī of Ajmer (d. AD 1236)

Ajmer (Rajasthan)

"Although at that time there were very many temples of idols around the lake, when the Khwāja saw them, he said: 'If God and His Prophet so will, it will not be long before I raze to the ground these idol temples.'

"It is said that among those temples there was one temple to reverence which the Rājā and all the infidels used to come, and lands had been assigned to provide for its expenditure. When the Khwāja settled there, every day his servants bought a cow, brought it there and slaughtered it and ate it...

"So when the infidels grew weak and saw that they had no power to resist such a perfect companion of God, they... went into their idol temples which were their places of worship. In them there was a *dev*, in front of whom they cried out and asked for help...[303]

"...The *dev* who was their leader, when he saw the perfect beauty of the Khwāja, trembled from head to foot like a willow tree. However much he tried to say 'Ram, Ram', it was 'Rahīm, Rahīm' that came from his tongue... The Khwāja... with his own hand gave a cup of water to a servant to take to the *dev*... He had no sooner drunk it than his heart was purified of darkness of unbelief; he ran forward and fell at the Heaven-treading feet of the Khwāja, and professed his belief...

"The Khwāja said: 'I also bestow on you the name of Shādī Dev [Joyful Deva]'....[304]

"...Then Shādī Dev... suggested to the Khwāja, that he should now set up a place in the city, where the populace might benefit from his

---

[302]Ibid., pp. 546–47.
[303]Cited by P.M. Currie, op. cit., p. 74.
[304]Ibid., p. 75.

holy arrival. The Khwāja accepted this suggestion, and ordered one of his special servants called Muhammad Yādgīr to go into the city and set in good order a place for faqīrs. Muhammad Yādgīr carried out his orders, and when he had gone into the city, he liked well the place where the radiant tomb of the Khwāja now is, and which originally belonged to Shādī Dev, and he suggested that the Khwāja should favour it with his residence...[305]

"...Mu'īn al-dīn had a second wife for the following reason: one night he saw the Holy Prophet in the flesh. The prophet said: 'You are not truly of my religion if you depart in any way from my sunnat.' It happened that the ruler of the Patli fort, Malik Khitāb, attacked the unbelievers that night and captured the daughter of the Rājā of that land. He presented her to Mu'īn al-dīn who accepted her and named her Bībī Umiya."[306]

P.M. Currie comments:

"...The take-over of 'pagan' sites is a recurrent feature of the history of the expansion of Islam. The most obvious precedent is to be found in the Muslim annexation of the Hajar al-aswad at Mecca... Sir Thomas Arnol remarks that 'in many instances there is no doubt that the shrine of a Muslim saint marks the site of some local cult which was practised on the spot long before the introduction of Islam.'

"There is evidence, more reliable than the tradition recorded in the *Siyar al-Aqtāb*, to suggest that this was the case in Ajmer. Sculpted stones, apparently from a Hindu temple, are incorporated in the Buland Darwāza of Mu'īn al-dīn's shrine. Moreover, his tomb is built over a series of cellars which may have formed part of an earlier temple... A tradition, first recorded in the *'Anis al-Arwāh*, suggests that the Sandal Khāna is built on the site of Shādī Dev's temple."[307]

(55)
Bādshāh-Nāma

The author, 'Abdu'l Hamīd Lāhorī, was commissioned by Shāh Jahān himself to compile this history which is a voluminous work covering the first twenty years of Shāh Jahān's reign. Lāhorī died in 1654.

[305]Ibid., p. 80.

[306]Ibid., p. 83. The Sunnah of the Prophet prescribes that every true Muslim should force into his bed some captured women of the unbelievers.

[307]Ibid., pp. 86–87.

Nūru'd-Dīn Muhammad Jahāngīr Pādshāh Ghāzī (AD 1605–1628)

Many Places

"Perhaps these instances [Mewar, Kangra, and Ajmer] made a contemporary poet of his court sing his praises as the great Muslim emperor who converted temples into mosques."[308]

Shihābu'd-Dīn Muhammad Shāh Jahān Pādshāh Ghāzī (AD 1628–1658)

Varanasi (Uttar Pradesh)

"It had been brought to the notice of His Majesty that during the late reign many idol temples had been begun, but remained unfinished at Benares, the great stronghold of infidelity. The infidels were now desirous of completing them. His Majesty, the defender of the faith, gave orders that at Benares, and throughout all his dominions in every place, all temples that had been begun should be cast down. It was now reported from the province of Allahābād that seventy-six temples had been destroyed in the district of Benares."[309]

Orchha (Madhya Pradesh)

"At the Bundela capital the Islam-cherishing Emperor demolished the lofty and massive temple of Bir Singh Dev near his palace, and erected a mosque on its site."[310]

Kashmir

"Some temples in Kashmir were also sacrificed to the religious fury of the emperor. The Hindu temple at Ichchhabal was destroyed and converted into a mosque."[311]

(56)

Shāhjahān-Nāma

It was written by 'Ināyat Khān whose original name was Muhammad Tāhir Āshnā. It comes down to AH 1068 (AD 1657–58), the year when Aurangzeb seized power and imprisoned Shāh Jahān in the fort of Agra. It presents Shah Jahan as a pious Muslim vis-a-vis the Hindu Kāfirs.

---

[308]*Bādshāh Nāma* cited by Sri Ram Sharma, op. cit., p. 63.

[309]Elliot and Dowson, op. cit., Vol. VII, p. 36. Sri Ram Sharma op. cit. cites Lahorī to add that "three temples were destroyed in Gujarat" (p. 86).

[310]Quoted by Jadunath Sarkar, op. cit., Vol. I and II, p. 15. Sri Ram Sharma cites Lāhorī to add that "several other temples suffered the same fate and were converted into mosques" (p. 86).

[311]Cited by Sri Ram Sharma, op. cit., p. 86.

Shihābu'd-Din Muhammad Shāh Jahān Pādshāh Ghāzī (AD 1628–1658)

Orchha (Madhya Pradesh)

"When the environs of Orchha became the site of the royal standards, an ordinance was issued authorising the demolition of the idol temple, which Bir Singh Deo had erected at a great expense by the side of his private palace, and also the idols contained in it..."[312]

(57)
Mir'āt-i-'Ālam

The author, Bakhtāwar Khān, was a nobleman of Aurangzeb's court. He died in AD 1684. The history ascribed to him was really compiled by Muhammad Baqā of Saharanpur who gave the name of his friend as its author. Baqā was a prolific writer who was invited by Bakhtāwar Khān to Aurangzeb's court and given a respectable rank. He died in AD 1683.

Muhiyu'd-Dīn Muhammad Aurangzeb 'Ālamgīr Pādshāh Ghāzī (AD 1658–1707)

General Order

"Hindū writers have been entirely excluded from holding public offices, and all the worshipping places of the infidels and great temples of these infamous people have been thrown down and destroyed in a manner which excites astonishment at the successful completion of so difficult a task. His Majesty personally teaches the sacred *kalima* to many infidels with success...All the mosques in the empire are repaired at public expense. *Imāms*, criers to the daily prayers, and readers of the *khutba*, have been appointed to each of them, so that a large sum of money has been and is still laid out in these disbursements..."[313]

(58)
'Ālamgīr-Nāma

This work, written in AD 1688 by Mīrza Muhammad Kāzim, contains a history of the first ten years of Aurangzeb's reign.

---

[312]*The Shahjahan Nama* of 'Inayat Khan, translated by A.R. Fuller and edited and compiled by W.E. Beyley and Z.A. Desai, OUP, Delhi, 1990, p. 161.

[313]Elliot and Dowson, Vol. VII, p. 159.

Muhiyu'd-Dīn Muhammad Aurangzeb 'Ālamgīr Pādshāh Ghāzī (AD 1658–1707)

Palamau (Bihar)

"In 1661 Aurangzeb in his zeal to uphold the law of Islam sent orders to his Viceroy of Bihar, Dāud Khān, to conquer Palamau. In the military operations that followed many temples were destroyed..."[314]

Koch Bihar (Bengal)

"Towards the end of the same year when Mīr Jumla made a war on the Raja of Kuch Bihar, the Mughals destroyed many temples during the course of their operations. Idols were broken and some temples were converted into mosques."[315]

(59)
Mā'sīr-i-'Ālamgīrī

The author, Sāqī Must'ad Khān, completed this history in AD 1710 at the behest of 'Ināyatu'llāh Khān Kashmīrī, Aurangzeb's last secretary and favourite disciple in state policy and religiosity. The materials which Must'ad Khān used in this history of Aurangzeb's reign came mostly from the State archives which were thrown open to him.

Muhiyu'd-Dīn Muhammad Aurangzeb 'Ālamgīr Pādshāh Ghāzī (AD 1658–1707)

General Order

"The Lord Cherisher of the Faith learnt that in the provinces of Tatta, Multān, and especially at Benares, the Brahman misbelievers used to teach their false books in their established schools, and that admirers and students both Hindu and Muslim, used to come from great distances to these misguided men in order to acquire this vile learning. His Majesty, eager to establish Islām, issued orders to the governors of all the provinces to demolish the schools and temples of the infidels and with the utmost urgency put down the teaching and the public practice of the religion of these misbelievers."[316]

Varanasi (Uttar Pradesh)

"It was reported that, according to the Emperor's command, his officers had demolished the temple of Viswanāth at Kāshī."[317]

---

[314]Cited by Sri Ram Sharma, op. cit., p. 129.

[315]Ibid.

[316]*Maāsir-i-'Ālamgiri*, translated into English by Sir Jadu-Nath Sarkar, Calcutta, 1947, pp. 51–52.

[317]Ibid., p. 55.

Mathura (Uttar Pradesh)

"...During this month of Ramzan abounding in miracles, the Emperor as the promoter of justice and overthrower of mischief, as a knower of truth and destroyer of oppression, as the zephyr of the garden of victory and the reviver of the faith of the Prophet, issued orders for the demolition of the temple situated in Mathurā, famous as the Dehra of Kesho Rāi. In a short time by the great exertions of his officers the destruction of this strong foundation of infidelity was accomplished, and on its site a lofty mosque was built at the expenditure of a large sum...

"Praised be the august God of the faith of Islām, that in the auspicious reign of this destroyer of infidelity and turbulence, such a wonderful and seemingly impossible work was successfully accomplished. On seeing this instance of the strength of the Emperor's faith and the grandeur of his devotion to God, the proud Rajas were stifled and in amazement they stood like images facing the wall. The idols, large and small, set with costly jewels which had been set up in the temple were brought to Agra, and buried under the steps of the mosque of the Begam Sāhib, in order to be continually trodden upon. The name of Mathurā was changed to Islāmābād."[318]

Khandela (Rajasthan)

"...Dārāb Khān who had been sent with a strong force to punish the Rajputs of Khandela and to demolish the great temple of the place, attacked the place on the 8th March/5th Safar, and slew the three hundred and odd men who made a bold defence, not one of them escaping alive. The temples of Khandela and Sānula and all other temples in the neighbourhood were demolished..."[319]

Jodhpur (Rajasthan)

"On Sunday, the 25th May/24th Rabi. S., Khan Jahān Bahādur came from Jodhpur, after demolishing the temples and bringing with himself some cart-loads of idols, and had audience of the Emperor, who highly praised him and ordered that the idols, which were mostly jewelled, golden, silvery, bronze, copper or stone, should be cast in the yard (*jilaukhānah*) of the Court and under the steps of the Jām'a mosque, to be trodden on. They remained so for some time and at last their very names were lost..."[320]

---

[318]Ibid., p. 60.
[319]Ibid., p. 107.
[320]Ibid., pp. 108–09.

Udaipur (Rajasthan)

"...Ruhullah Khan and Ekkatāz Khan went to demolish the great temple in front of the Rānā's palace, which was one of the rarest buildings of the age and the chief cause of the destruction of life and property of the despised worshippers. Twenty *māchātoṛ* Rajputs who were sitting in the temple vowed to give up their lives; first one of them came out to fight, killed some and was then himself slain, then came out another and so on, until every one of the twenty perished, after killing a large number of the imperialists including the trusted slave, Ikhlās. The temple was found empty. The hewers broke the images.[321]

"On Saturday, the 24th January, 1680/2nd Muharram, the Emperor went to view lake Udaisāgar, constructed by the Rānā, and ordered all the three temples on its banks to be demolished.[322]

"...On the 29th January/7th Muharram, Hasan 'Ali Khan brought to the Emperor twenty camel-loads of tents and other things captured from the Rānā's palace and reported that one hundred and seventy-two other temples in the environs of Udaipur had been destroyed. The Khan received the title of Bahādur 'Alamgirshāhi...[323]

Amber (Rajasthan)

"Abū Turāb, who had been sent to demolish the temples of Amber, returned to Court on Tuesday, the 10th August/24th Rajab, and reported that he had pulled down sixty-six temples..."[324]

Bijapur (Karnataka)

"...Hamiduddin Khan Bahādur who had gone to demolish a temple and build a mosque (in its place) in Bijapur, having excellently carried out his orders, came to Court and gained praise and the post of dārogha of gusalkhānah, which brought him near the Emperor's person..."[325]

Iconoclasm was a part of Aurangezb's Islamic Piety

"...As his blessed nature dictated, he was characterized by perfect devotion to the rites of the Faith; he followed the teaching of the great Imām Abu Hanifā (God be pleased with him!), and established and enforced to the best of his power the five foundations of Islām...[326]

---

[321]Ibid., pp. 114–15.

[322]Ibid., p. 116.

[323]Ibid., pp. 116–17.

[324]Ibid., p. 120. Amber had been loyal to the Mughals since the days of Akbar, and, unlike Mewar and Marwar, given no offence to Aurangzeb.

[325]Ibid., p. 241.

[326]Ibid., p. 312.

"...Through the auspices of his hearty endeavour, the Hanafi creed (i.e., the Orthodox Sunni faith) has gained such strength and currency in the great country of Hindustan as was never seen in the times of any of the preceding sovereigns. By one stroke of the pen, the Hindu clerks (writers) were dismissed from the public employment. Large numbers of the places of worship of the infidels and great temples of these wicked people have been thrown down and desolated. Men who can see only the outside of things are filled with wonder at the successful accomplishment of such a seemingly difficult task. And on the sites of the temples lofty mosques have been built..."[327]

(60)
Akhbārāt

These were reports from different provinces compiled in the reign of Aurangzeb.

Muhiyu'd-Dīn Muhammad Aurangzeb 'Ālamgīr Pādshāh Ghāzī (AD 1658–1707)

Mathura (Uttar Pradesh)

"The Emperor learning that in the temple of Keshav Rai at Mathura there was a stone railing presented by Dara Shukoh, remarked, 'In the Muslim faith it is a sin even to look at a temple, and this Dara had restored a railing in a temple. This fact is not creditable to the Muhammadans. Remove the railing.' By his order Abdun Nabi Khan (the faujdar of Mathura) removed it."[328]

Ujjain (Madhya Pradesh)

"News came from Malwa that Wazir Khan had sent Gada Beg, a slave, with 400 troopers, to destroy all temples around Ujjain...A Rawat of the place resisted and slew Gada Beg with 121 of his men."[329]

Delhi

"The Emperor learnt from a secret news writer of Delhi that in Jaisinghpura Bairagis used to worship idols, and that the Censor on hearing of it had gone there, arrested Sri Krishna Bairagi and taken him with 15 idols away to his house; then the Rajputs had assembled, flocked to the Censor's house, wounded three footmen of the Censor

---

[327]Ibid., pp. 314–15.
[328]Quoted by Jadunath Sarkar, op. cit., Vol. III, p. 186.
[329]Quoted by Ibid., p. 187.

and tried to seize the Censor himself; so that the latter set the Bairagi free and sent the copper idols to the local subahdar."[330]

Pandharpur (Maharashtra)

"The Emperor, summoning Muhammad Khalil and Khidmat Rai, the *darogha* of hatchet-men...ordered them to demolish the temple of Pandharpur, and to take the butchers of the camp there and slaughter cows in the temple...It was done."[331]

On Way to the Deccan

"When the war with the Rajputs was over, Aurangzeb decided to leave for the Deccan. His march seems to have been marked with the destruction of many temples on the way. On 21 May 1681, the superintendent of the labourers was ordered to destroy all the temples on the route."[332]

Lakheri (?)

"On 27 September, 1681, the emperor issued orders for the destruction of the temples at Lakheri."[333]

Rasulpur (?)

"About this time, on 14 April, 1692, orders were issued to the provincial governor and the district fojdār to demolish the temples at Rasulpur."[334]

Sheogaon (?)

"Sankar, a messenger, was sent to demolish a temple near Sheogaon. He came back after pulling it down on 20 November, 1693."[335]

Ajmer (Rajasthan)

"Bijai Singh and several other Hindus were reported to be carrying on public worship of idols in a temple in the neighbourhood of Ajmer. On 23 June, 1694, the governor of Ajmer was ordered to destroy the temple and stop the public adoration of idol worship there."[336]

---

[330]Quoted by Ibid., p. 188.
[331]Quoted by Ibid. p. 189.
[332]Cited by Sri Ram Sharma, op. cit., p. 136.
[333]Ibid.
[334]Ibid., p. 137.
[335]Ibid.
[336]Ibid.

Wakenkhera (?)

"The temple of Wakenkhera in the fort was demolished on 2 March, 1705."[337]

Bhagwant Garh (Rajasthan)

"The newswriter of Ranthambore reported the destruction of a temple in Parganah Bhagwant Garh. Gaj Singh Gor had repaired the temple and made some additions thereto."[338]

Malpura (Rajasthan)

"Royal orders for the destruction of temples in Malpura Toda were received and the officers were assigned for this work."[339]

(61)
Fathiyya-i-'Ibriyya

This is a diary of Mīr Jumla's campaigns in Kuch Bihar and Assam. "By looting," writes Jadunath Sarkar, "the temples of the South and hunting out buried treasures, Mīr Jumla amassed a vast fortune. The huge Hindu idols of copper were brought away in large numbers to be melted and cast into cannon."[340]

Muhiyu'd-Dīn Muhammad Aurangzeb 'Ālamgīr Pādshāh Ghāzī (AD 1658–1707)

Koch Bihar (Bengal)

"Mir Jumla made his way into Kuch Bihar by an obscure and neglected highway...In six days the Mughal army reached the capital (19th December) which had been deserted by the Rajah and his people in terror. The name of the town was changed to Alamgirnagar; the Muslim call to prayer, so long forbidden in the city, was chanted from the lofty roof of the palace, and a mosque was built by demolishing the principal temple..."[341]

(62)
Kalimāt-i-Tayyibāt

This is a collection of letters and orders of Aurangzeb compiled by 'Inayatullāh in AD 1719 and covers the years 1699–1704 of Aurangzeb's reign.

---

[337]Ibid., p. 138.
[338]Ibid.
[339]Ibid., pp. 138–39.
[340]Jadunath Sarkar, op. cit., Vol.I and II, pp. 120–21.
[341]Summarised in Ibid., Vol. III, p. 103.

Muhiyu'd-Dīn Muhammad Aurangzeb 'Ālamgīr Pādshāh Ghāzī (AD 1658–1707)

Somnath (Gujarat)

"The temple of Somnath was demolished early in my reign and idol worship (there) put down. It is not known what the state of things there is at present. If the idolaters have again taken to the worship of images at the place, then destroy the temple in such a way that no trace of the building may be left, and also expel them (the worshippers) from the place."[342]

Satara (Maharashtra)

"The village of Sattara near Aurangabad was my hunting ground. Here on the top of a hill, stood a temple with an image of Khande Rai. By God's grace I demolished it, and forbade the temple dancers (*muralis*) to ply their shameful profession..."[343]

General Observation

"The demolition of a temple is possible at any time, as it cannot walk away from its place."[344]

Sirhind (Punjab)

"In a small village in the sarkār of Sirhind, a Sikh temple was demolished and converted into a mosque. An imām was appointed who was subsequently killed."[345]

(63)
Ganj-i-Arshadī

It is a contemporary account of the destruction of Hindu temples at Varanasi in the reign of Aurangzeb:

Muhiyu'd-Dīn Muhammad Aurangzeb 'Ālamgīr Pādshāh Ghāzī (AD 1658–1707)

Varanasi (Uttar Pradesh)

"The infidels demolished a mosque that was under construction and wounded the artisans. When the news reached Shāh Yasīn, he came to Banaras from Mandyawa and collecting the Muslim weavers, demol-

[342]Quoted in Ibid., Vol. III, pp. 185–86.
[343]Quoted in Ibid., Vol. I and II, p. 94.
[344]Quoted in Ibid., Vol. III, p. 188.
[345]Cited by Sri Ram Sharma, op. cit., p. 138.

ished the big temple. A Sayyid who was an artisan by profession agreed with one Abdul Rasūl to build a mosque at Banaras and accordingly the foundation was laid. Near the place there was a temple and many houses belonging to it were in the occupation of the Rajputs. The infidels decided that the construction of a mosque in the locality was not proper and that it should be razed to the ground. At night the walls of the mosque were found demolished. Next day the wall was rebuilt but it was again destroyed. This happened three or four times. At last the Sayyid hid himself in a corner. With the advent of night the infidels came to achieve their nefarious purpose. When Abdul Rasūl gave the alarm, the infidels began to fight and the Sayyid was wounded by Rajputs. In the meantime, the Musalman resident of the neighbourhood arrived at the spot and the infidels took to their heels. The wounded Muslims were taken to Shāh Yasīn who determined to vindicate the cause of Islam. When he came to the mosque, people collected from the neighbourhood. The civil officers were outwardly inclined to side with the saint, but in reality they were afraid of the royal displeasure on account of the Raja, who was a courtier of the Emperor and had built the temple (near which the mosque was under construction). Shāh Yasīn, however, took up the sword and started for Jihad. The civil officers sent him a message that such a grave step should not be taken without the Emperor's permission. Shāh Yasīn, paying no heed, sallied forth till he reached Bazar Chau Khamba through a fusillade of stones...The doors (of temples) were forced open and the idols thrown down. The weavers and other Musalmans demolished about 500 temples. They desired to destroy the temple of Beni Madho, but as lanes were barricaded, they desisted from going further."[346]

(64)
Kalimāt-i-Aurangzeb

This is another compilation of letters and orders by 'Ināyatu'llāh covering the years 1703–06 of Aurangzeb's reign.

Muhiyu'd-Dīn Muhammad Aurangzeb 'Ālamgīr Pādshāh Ghāzī (AD 1658–1707)

Maharashtra

"The houses of this country (Maharashtra) are exceedingly strong and built solely of stone and iron. The hatchet-men of the Government

[346]Ibid., pp. 144–45. The mosque demolished by Hindus had been built on the site of a temple recently destroyed.

in the course of my marching do not get sufficient strength and power (i.e., time) to destroy and raze the temples of the infidels that meet the eye on the way. You should appoint an orthodox inspector (*darogha*) who may afterwards destroy them at leisure and dig up their foundations."[347]

(65)
Muraq'āt-i-Abu'l Hasan

This is a collection of records and documents compiled by Maulāna Abu'l Hasan, one of Aurangzeb's officers in Bengal and Orissa during AD 1655–67.

Muhiyu'd-Dīn Muhammad Aurangzeb 'Ālamgīr Pādshāh Ghāzī (AD 1658–1707)

Bengal and Orissa

"Order issued on all *faujdars* of *thanas*, civil officers (*mutasaddis*), agents of jagirdars, *kroris*, and *amlas* from Katak to Medinipur on the frontier of Orissa:—The imperial paymaster Asad Khan has sent a letter written by order of the Emperor, to say, that the Emperor learning from the newsletters of the province of Orissa that at the village of Tilkuti in Medinipur a temple has been (newly) built, has issued his august mandate for its destruction, and the destruction of all temples built anywhere in this province by the worthless infidels. Therefore, you are commanded with extreme urgency that immediately on the receipt of this letter you should destroy the above-mentioned temples. Every idol-house built during the last 10 or 12 years, whether with brick or clay, should be demolished without delay. Also, do not allow the crushed Hindus and despicable infidels to repair their old temples. Reports of the destruction of temples should be sent to the Court under the seal of the *qazis* and attested by pious Shaikhs."[348]

(66)
Futūhāt-i-'Ālamgīrī

The author, Īshwardās Nāgar, was a Brahman from Gujarat, born around AD 1654. Till the age of thirty he was in the service of the Chief Qāzī of the empire under Aurangzeb. Later on, he took up a post under Shujā't Khān, the governor of Gujarat, who appointed him *amīn* in the *pargana* of Jodhpur. His history covers almost half a century of Au-

[347]Quoted in Jadunath Sarkar, op. cit., Vol. III, pp. 188–89.
[348]Quoted in Ibid., p. 187.

rangzeb's reign, from 1657 to 1700. There is nothing in his style which may mark him out as a Hindu. He sends to "hell" every Hindu who dies at the hands of Muslims or otherwise, while every Muslim who gets killed becomes a "martyr" and attains paradise.

Muhiyu'd-Dīn Muhammad Aurangzeb 'Ālamgīr Pādshāh Ghāzī (AD 1658–1707)

Mathura (Uttar Pradesh)

"When the imperial army was encamping at Mathura, a holy city of the Hindus, the state of affairs with regard to temples of Mathura was brought to the notice of His Majesty. Thus, he ordered the *faujdar* of the city, Abdul Nabi Khan, to raze to the ground every temple and to construct big mosques (over their demolished sites)."[349]

Udaipur (Rajasthan)

"The Emperor, wihtin a short time, reached Udaipur and destroyed the gate of Dehbari, the palaces of Rana and the temples of Udaipur. Apart from it, the trees of his gardens were also destroyed."[350]

(67)
Nau-Bahār-i-Murshid Qulī-Khānī

The author, Āzād al-Husainī, was a poor but learned immigrant from Persia, who presented this work in AD 1729 to Mīrza Lutfullāh surnamed Murshid Qulī II who had arrived in Dhaka in 1728 as the Deputy Governor of Shujāu'd-Dīn, the Mughal Governor of Bengal, Bihar and Orissa from 1727 to 1739.

Nasiru'd-Dīn Muhammad Shāh Bahādur Pādshāh Ghāzi (AD 1719–1748)

Udaipur (Tripura)

"Tipara is a country extremely strong...The Raja is proud of his strength and the practice of conch-blowing and idol-worship prevailed there...

"Murshid Quli II decided to conquer Tipara and put down idolatry there. He wrote to Sayyid Habibullah (the Commander-in-Chief), Md. Sadīq, Mir Hāshim, Shaikh Sirājuddin Md., and Mahdi Beg who were then engaged in the Chittogong expedition, that...they should set out

---

[349]*Futūhāt-i-'Ālamgirī*, translated into English by Tanseem Ahmad, Delhi, 1978, p. 82.

[350]Ibid., p. 130.

with their forces, observing every precaution, arrive close to the Kingdom of Tipara, and try to conquer it...[351]

"The Tipara soldiers did not fail to fight regardless of death. The Muslim troops invested the fort from four sides. A severe battle was fought. The zamindar's men lay dead in heaps. The victors entered the fort...The flag of Murshid Quli Khan was unfurled on the top of fort Udaipur. The Muslims raised the cry of *Allahu-ākbar* and the Muslim credo (There is no deity except Allah and Muhammad is His messenger), and demolished the temple of the zamindar which had long been the seat of idol-worship. Making a level courtyard on the side of the temple, they read the *Khutba* in the Emperor's name...The world-illuminating sun of the faith of Muhammad swept away the dark night of infidelity, and the bright day of Islam dawned."[351]

(68)
Kanzu'l-Mahfūz

The name and position of the author is not known. It deals with the history of the 'Ummayids, the Ghaznivids and the Muslim dynasties of India.

Muhiyu'd-Dīn Muhammad Aurangzeb 'Ālamgīr Pādshāh Ghāzī (AD 1658–1707)

Agra (Uttar Pradesh)

"In the city of Agra there was a large temple, in which there were numerous idols, adorned and embellished with precious jewels and valuable pearls. It was the custom of the infidels to resort to this temple from far and near several times in each year to worship the idols, and a certain fee to the Government was fixed upon each man, for which he obtained admittance. As there was a large congress of pilgrims, a very considerable amount was realized from them, and paid into the royal treasury. This practice had been observed to the end of the reign of the Emperor Shāh Jahān, and in the commencement of Aurangzeb's government; but when the latter was informed of it, he was exceedingly angry and abolished the custom. The greatest nobles of his court represented to him that a large sum was realized and paid into the public treasury, and that if it was abolished, a great reduction in the income of the state would take place. The Emperor observed, 'What you say is

---

[351]*Nau-Bahār-i-Murshid Quli-Khāni*, translated into English by Jadu Nath Sarkar and included in his *Bengal Nawābs*, Calcutta, Reprint, 1985, p. 4.

[352]Ibid., p. 7.

right, but I have considered well on the subject, and have reflected on it deeply; but if you wish to augment the revenue, there is a better plan for attaining the object by exacting the *jizya*. By this means idolatry will be suppressed, the Muhammadan religion and the true faith will be honoured, our proper duty will be performed, the finances of the state will be increased, and the infidels will be disgraced.'...This was highly approved by all the nobles; and the Emperor ordered all the golden and silver idols to be broken, and the temple destroyed..."[353]

(69)
Muntikhābu'l-Lubāb

The author, Hāshim 'Alī Khān, is better known by his designation of Khāfī Khān. His father was also a historian in the employ of Aurangzeb. He was brought up in the court of Aurangzeb, made a *dīwān*, but was ordered to stop writing history. He, however, continued writing in secret. Muhammad Shāh was pleased when he saw what had been written and named him Khāfi Khān. The work is also known as *Tārīkh-i-Khāfī Khān*. It starts with the invasion of Bābur in AD 1519 and comes upto the fourteenth year of Bahādur Shāh (AD 1719–1748). He refers to the Hindus as evil dogs, accursed wretches, etc.

Shihābu'd-Dīn Muhammad Shāh Jahān Pādshāh Ghāzī (1628–1658)

After describing the destruction of temples in Benares and Gujarat, this author stated that "The materials of some of the Hindu temples were used for building mosques."[354]

Hargaon (Uttar Pradesh)

"In AD 1630–31 (AH 1040) when Abdāl, the Hindu chief of Hargaon in the province of Allahabad, rebelled, most of the temples in the state were either demolished or converted into mosques. Idols were burnt."[355]

Muhiyu'd-Dīn Muhammad Aurangzeb 'Ālamgīr Pādshāh Ghāzī (1658–1707)

Golkonda (Andhra Pradesh)

"On the capture of Golkonda, the Emperor appointed Abdur Rahim

---

[353]Elliot and Dowson, op. cit., Vol. VIII, pp. 38–39.
[354]Cited by Sri Ram Sharma, op. cit., p. 86.
[355]Cited by Ibid., pp. 86–87.

Khan as Censor of the city of Haiderabad with orders to put down infidel practices and (heretical) innovations and destroy the temples and build mosques on their sites."[356]

Bijapur (Karnataka)

"The fall and capture of Bijapur was similarly solemnized though here the destruction of temples was delayed for several years, probably till 1698."[357]

Sikh Temples (Punjab)

"Aurangzeb ordered the temples of the Sikhs to be destroyed and the guru's agents (*masands*) for collecting the tithes and presents of the faithful to be expelled from the cities."[358]

Shāh 'Ālam Bahādur Shāh Pādshāh Ghāzī (AD 1707–1712)

Jodhpur (Rajasthan)

"Ajīt Singh...sent a message humbly asking that Khān Zamān and the *Kāzīu'I-Kuzāt* might come into Jodhpur, to rebuild the mosques, destroy idol-temples, enforce the provisions of the law about the summons to prayer and the killing of cows, to appoint magistrates and to commission officers to collect the *jizya*. His submission was graciously accepted, and his requests granted..."[359]

(70)
Mir'at-i-Ahmadī

This is the most important Persian history of Gujarat. It starts with the Hindu Rājās of Aṇhilwāḍ Pāṭan and ends with the establishment of Maratha rule in the eighteenth century. It was written after the Third Battle of Panipat in AD 1761. The author, 'Alī Muhammad Khān, came to Gujarat from Burhanpur in 1708–09 and, when grown up, had access to official records.

Sultān 'Alāu'd-Dīn Khaljī (AD 1296–1316)

Sidhpur (Gujarat)

"...When Raja Sidhraj Jaisingh Solanki became the king, he extended his conquest as far as Malwa and Burhanpur etc. and laid foun-

---

[356]Quoted in Jadunath Sarkar, op. cit., Vol. III, p. 188.
[357]Cited by Sri Ram Sharma, op. cit., p. 137.
[358]Quoted in Jadunath Sarkar, op. cit., Vol. III, p. 207, footnote.
[359]Elliot and Dowson, op. cit., Vol. VII, p. 405.

dation of lofty forts such as the forts of Broach and Dabhoi etc. He dug the tank of Sahastraling in Pattan, many others in Biramgam and at most places in Sorath. His reign is known as 'Sang Bast', the Age of Stone Buildings. He founded the city of Sidhpur and built the famous Rudramal Temple. It is related that when he intended to build Rudramal, he summoned astrologers to elect an auspicious hour for it. The astrologers said to him that some harm through heavenly revolution is presaged from Alauddin when his turn comes to the Saltanat of Dihli. The Raja relied on the statement of astrologers and entered into a pledge and pact with the said Sultan. The Sultan had said, 'If I do not destroy it under terms of the pact, yet I will leave some religious vestiges.' When, after some time, the turn of the Sultan came to the Saltanat of Delhi, he marched with his army to that side and left religious marks by constructing a masjid and a minar..."[360]

Somnath (Gujarat)

"In the year 696, six hundred and ninety-six, he sent an army for the conquest of Gujarat under the command of Ulugh Khan who became famous among the Gujaratis as Alp Khan and Nusrat Khan Jalesri. These Khans subjected Naharwala that is, Pattan and the whole of that dominion to plunder and pillage...They broke the idol of Somnat which was installed again after Sultan Mahmud Ghaznawi and sent riches, treasure, elephants, women and daughters of Raja Karan to the Sultan at Delhi..."[361]

Patan (Gujarat)

"After conquest of Naharwala and expulsion of Raja Karan, Ulugh Khan occupied himself with the government. From that day, governors were appointed on this side on behalf of the Sultans of Dilhi. It is said that a lofty masjid called Masjid-i-Adinah (Friday Masjid) of marble stone which exists even today is built by him. It is popular among common folk that error is mostly committed in counting its many pillars. They relate that it was a temple which was converted into a masjid... Most of the relics and vestiges of magnificence and extension of the ancient prosperity of Pattan city are found in the shape of bricks and dried clay, which inform us about the truth of this statement, scattered

[360]*Mirat-i-Ahmadi*, translated into English by M.F. Lokhandwala, Baroda, 1965, p. 27. This account is obviously a folktale because 'Alāu'd-Dīn Khaljī became a Sultān two hundred years after Siddharāja Jayasiṁha ascended the throne of Gujarat. Moreover, 'Alāu'd-Dīn never went to Gujarat; he sent his generals, Ulugh Khān and Nasrat Khān.

[361]Ibid., p. 28.

nearly to a distance of three kurohs (one kuroh=2 miles) from the present place of habitation. Remnants of towers of the ancient fortifications seen at some places are a proof of repeated changes and vicissitudes in population due to passage of times. Most of the ancient relics gradually became extinct. Marble stones, at the end of the rule of rajas, were brought from Ajmer for building temples in such a quantity that more than which is dug out from the earth even now. All the marble stones utilized in the city of Ahmedabad were (brought) from that place..."[362]

Sultān Muzaffar Shāh I of Gujarat (AD 1392–1410)

Somnath (Gujarat)

"He made efforts at the proclamation of the word of God (confession of the Muslim faith). He led an army for plundering the temple of Somnat, that is, Pattan Dev. He spread Islam at most of the places..."[363]

Sultān Ahmad Shāh I of Gujarat (AD 1411–1443)

Sidhpur (Gujarat)

"In the year 817, eight hundred and seventeen Hijri, he resolved to march with intent of jihad against the unbelievers of Girnar, a famous fort in Sorath. Raja Mandalik fought with him but was defeated and took refuge in the fort. It is narrated that even though that land (region) this time did not get complete brightness form the lamp of Islam, yet the Sultan subdued the fort of Junagadh situated near the foot of Girnar mountain. Most of the Zamindars of Sorath became submissive and obedient to him and agreed to pay tribute. After that, he demolished the temple of Sayyedpur in the month of Jamadi I of the year 818, eight hundred and eighteen Hijri...In the year 823, eight hundred and twenty-three Hijri, he attended to the establishment of administrative control over his dominion. He suppressed refractoriness wherever it was found. He demolished temples and constructed masjids in their places..."[364]

Sultān Mahmūd Begḍāh of Gujarat (AD 1458–1511)

Junagadh (Gujarat)

"Rao Mandalik saw that his fate was sealed. He fled at night to the fort and gave him a battle. When the warfare continued for some time provisions in the fort became scarce. He requested the Sultan in all humility to save his life. The Sultan agreed on condition of his accept-

[362]Ibid., p. 29.
[363]Ibid., p. 34.
[364]Ibid., pp. 37–38. Sayyedpur is Sidhpur.

ing Islam. Rao Mandalik came down from the fort, surrendered the fort's keys to the Sultan. The Sultan offered recitation of the word of Unity to him to repeat. He instantly recited it. The fort was conquered in the year 877, eight hundred and seventy-seven...In a few days, he populated a city which can be called Ahmedabad and named it Mustafabad. Rao Mandalik was given the title of Khan Jahan with a grant of jagir. He gave away as presents the gold idols brought from the temple of Rao Mandalik to all soldiers..."[365]

Sankhodhar (Gujarat)

"This victory took place in the year 878, eight hundred and seventy-eight; the island of Sankhodar was never conquered in any age by any king of the past. It is related that the Sultan performed two genuflexions of namaz out of thanksgiving at the time of demolishing the temple and breaking the idols of Jagat. He grew eloquent in recitation of praise out of gratitude to God. The Muslims raised calls to namaz (azan) by loud voice from top of temples...He built a masjid there."[366]

Idar (Gujarat)

"He marched towards Malwa, in the same month, from Muhammedabad for repulsion of unbelievers and defence of religious-minded Muslims. He halted at the town of Godhra for reinforcement of powerful forces when he received a report about insolence of the Raja of Idar. He, therefore, marched thither and ordered to demolish houses and temples of Idar. This event took place in the year 919, nine hundred and nineteen Hijri..."[367]

Muhiyu'd-Dīn Muhammad Aurangzeb 'Ālamgīr Pādshāh Ghāzī (AD 1658–1707)

Ahmadabad (Gujarat)

"During the Subedari of religious-minded, noble prince, vestiges of the Temple of Chintaman situated on the side of Saraspur built by Satidas jeweller, were removed under the Prince's order and a masjid was erected on its remains. It was named 'Quwwat-ul-Islam'..."[368]

Gujarat

"As it has come to His Majesty's knowledge that some inhabitants

[365]Ibid., pp. 47–48.
[366]Ibid., p. 48.
[367]Ibid., pp. 51–52.
[368]Ibid., p. 194. It was a Jain Temple built at great expense.

of the *mahals* appertaining to the province of Gujarat have (again) built the temples which had been demolished by imperial order before his accession,...therefore His Majesty orders that...the formerly demolished and recently restored temples should be pulled down."[369]

Vadnagar (Gujarat)

"The Emperor ordered the destruction of the Hateshwar temple at Vadnagar, the special guardian of the Nagar Brahmans."[370]

Malarina (Rajasthan)

"Salih Bahadur was sent to pull down the temple of Malarna."[371]

Sorath (Gujarat)

"In AD 1696–97 (AH 1108) orders were issued for the destruction of the major temples at Sorath in Gujarat."[372]

Dwarka (Gujarat)

"He stopped public worship at the Hindu temple of Dwarka."[373]

(71)
Tārīkh-i-Ibrāhīm Khān

It was composed by Nawāb Ibrāhīm Khān and written down by Mullā Baksh in the town of Benares. It was finished in the year AD 1786. It is mainly a history of the Marathas.

Ahmad Shāh Abdālī (AD 1747–1773)

Mathura (Uttar Pradesh)

"Ahmad Shāh Abdālī in the year AH 1171 (AD 1757–58), came from the country of Kandahār to Hindūstān, and on the 7th of Jumāda-l awwal of that year, had an interview with the Emperor 'Ālamgīr II, at the palace of Shāh-Jahānābād...After an interval of a month, he set out to coerce Rājā Sūraj Mal Jāt, who from a distant period, had extended his sway over the province of Āgra, as far as the environs of the city of Delhī. In three days he captured Balamgarh, situated at a distance of fifteen *kos* from Delhī...After causing a general massacre of the garrison he hastened towards Mathurā, and having razed that ancient sanctu-

---

[369]Quoted in Jadunath Sarkar, op. cit., Vol. III, p. 186.
[370]Quoted in Ibid., p. 188.
[371]Quoted in Ibid., p. 186.
[372]Cited by Sri Ram Sharma, op. cit., p. 137.
[373]Cited by Ibid., p. 138.

ary of the Hindūs to the ground, made all the idolaters fall a prey to his relentless sword..."[374]

(72)
Tārīkh-i-Husain Shāhī

It was written in AD 1797–98 by Sayyid Imāmu'd-Din al-Husain. We have not been able to obtain other particulars about it.

Ahmad Shāh Abdālī (AD 1747–1773)

Mathura (Uttar Pradesh)

"Idols were broken and kicked about like polo-balls by the Islamic heroes."[375]

(73)
Nishān-i-Haidarī

The author, Mīr Hussain 'Alī Kirmānī, describes his work as "the History of the Nawab Hyder Ali Khan Bahadur, and a commentary on the reign and actions of Tipu Sultan." He completed the work in AD 1802. We have been able to get an English translation of the second part only.

Tipu Sultan (AD 1782–1799)

Srirangapatnam (Karnataka)

"...At this time the Sultan determined to recommence the building of the Masjidi Ala, the erection of which had been suspended since the year 1198 Hijri, and the Daroghu Public buildings, according to the plan, which will be mentioned hereafter, completed it in two years, at the expense of three lakhs of rupees...

"...It is known that when the vile and rejected Brahman Khunda Rao...imprisoned the Nawab's Zanana and the Sultan (who was then a boy of six or seven years of age) in a house in the fort... there stood a Hindu temple, the area or space round which was large. The Sultan, therefore, in his infancy being like all children fond of play, and as in that space boys of Kinhiri Brahmin castes assembled to amuse themselves, was accustomed to quit the house to see them play, or play with them... It happened one day that a Fakir (a religious mendicant) a man of saint-like mind passed that way, and seeing the Sultan gave him a

---

[374]Elliot and Dowson, op. cit., Vol. VIII, pp. 264–65.

[375]Quoted by Jadunath Sarkar, *Fall of the Mughal Empire*, Vol. II, Fourth Edition, New Delhi, 1991, p. 70.

life bestowing benediction, saying to him, 'Fortunate child, at a future time thou will be the king of this country, and whey thy time comes, remember my words—take this temple and destroy it, and build a Masjid in its place, and for ages it will remain a memorial of thee.' The Sultan smiled, and in reply told him, 'that whenever, by his blessing, he should become a Padishah, or king, he would do as he (the Fakir) directed.' When, therefore, after a short time his father became a prince, the possessor of wealth and territory, he remembered his promise, and after his return from Nagar and Gorial Bundar, he purchased the temple from the adorers of the image in it (which after all was nothing but the figure of a bull, made of brick and mortar) with their goodwill, and the Brahmins, therefore, taking away their image, placed it in the Deorhi Peenth, and the temple was pulled down, and the foundations of a new Masjid raised on the site, agreeably to a plan of the Mosque built by Ali Adil Shah, at Bijapur, and brought thence."[376]

The nature of the purchase needs no comment.

(74)
Riyāzu's-Salātīn

This is a history of Bengal from the invasion of Bakhtiyār Khaljī to AD 1788 when the British were in complete control. The author, Ghulām Hussain Salīm of Zaidpur in Awadh, had migrated to Bengal and become a Postmaster in Malda. He died in AD 1817.

Ikhtiyāru'd-Dīn Muhammad Bakhtiyār Khaljī (AD 1202–1206)

Lakhnauti (Bengal)

"Muhammad Bakhtiyar sweeping the town with the broom of devastation, completely demolished it, and making anew the city of Lakhnauti...his metropolis, ruled over Bengal...and strove to put in practice the ordinances of the Muhammadan religion...and for a period ruling over Bengal he engaged in demolishing the temples and building mosques."[377]

Sulaimān Karrānī of Bengal (AD 1563–1576)

Orissa

"Kālāpahār, by successive and numerous fightings, vanquished the

---

[376]*History of Tipu Sultan Being a Continuation of The Neshan-i-Hyduri*, translated from Persian by Col. W. Miles, first published 1864, New Delhi Reprint, 1986, pp. 66–67.

[377]*Riyaz-us-Salatin*, translated into English by Abdus Salam, Delhi Reprint, 1976, pp. 63–64.

Rajah's forces, and brought to his subjection the entire dominion of Odīsah (Orissa), so much so that he carried off the Rani together with all household goods and chattels. Notwithstanding all this, from fear of being killed, no one was bold to wake up this drunkard of the sleep of negligence, so that Kālāpahār had his hands free. After completing the subjugation of the entire country, and investing the Fort of Bārahbāṭi, which was his (the Rajah's) place of sleep, Kālāpahār engaged in fighting...The firm Muhammadan religion and the enlightened laws of Islām were introduced into that country. Before this, the Musalman Sovereigns exercised no authority over this country. Of the miracles of Kālāpahār, one was this, that wherever in that country, the sound of his drum reached, the hands and the feet, the ears and the noses of the idols, worshipped by the Hindus, fell off their stone-figures, so that even now stone-idols, with hands and feet broken, and noses and ears cut off, are lying at several places in that country. And the Hindus pursuing the false, from blindness of their hearts, with full sense and knowledge, devote themselves to their worship!

It is known what grows out of stone:
From its worship what is gained, except shame?

"It is said at the time of return, Kālāpahār left a drum in the jungle of Kēonjhār, which is lying in an upset state. No one there from fear of life dares to set it up; so it is related."[378]

(75)
Bahār-i'Āzam

It is an account of a journey undertaken in 1823 by 'Āzam Jāh Bahādur "after he ascended the throne of the Carnatic as Nawwāb Wālājāh VI."[379] The author, Ghulām 'Abdul Qadir Nāzir, was his court scribe who accompanied the Nawwāb on this journey. Nāzir does not tell us that his patron was a Nawwāb only in name as he was living in Madras on British charity, his ancestral principality of Arcot having been ceded to the British in 1801. What he says instead is how the "Nawwāb" lost his temper when he learnt that the Muslims in his retinue were visiting the Hindu temples at Chidambaram and how he "gave strict orders" to British officers of the place "that no Muslim should be allowed to go over to the temple and enter it."[380] At a later stage, we are told that "the party marched forth...to the accompaniment of music

[378]Ibid., pp. 17–18.
[379]*Bahār-i-Āzam*, translated in English, Madras, 1960, p. 2.
[380]Ibid., pp. 18–19.

provided by dancing girls of the Hindu community."[381] The account names numerous Sufis etc., who came to the districts of Chingleput, North Arcot, South Arcot, Tiruchirapalli and Thanjavur and established Muslim places of worship. What these new monuments replaced becomes obvious from the following few instances.

Sufi Nātthar Walī

Tiruchirapalli (Tamil Nadu)

"It is said that in ancient days Trichila, an execrable monster with three heads, who was a brother of Rawan, with ten heads, had the sway over this country. No human being could oppose him. But as per the saying of the Prophet, 'Islam will be elevated and cannot be subdued', the Faith took root by the efforts of Hazarat Natthar Wali. The monster was slain and sent to the house of perdition. His image namely *but-ling* worshipped by the unbelievers was cut and the head was separated from the body. A portion of the body went into the ground. Over that spot is the tomb of the Wali, shedding rediance till this day."[382]

Sufi Shāh Bheka

"Shah Bheka...when he was at Trichinopoly during the days of Rani Minachi, the unbelievers who did not like his stay there harassed him. One day when he was very much vexed, he got upon the bull in front of the temple, which the Hindus worship calling it *swami*, and made it move on by the power and strength of the Supreme Life Giver...They abandoned the temple and gave the entire place on the *aruskalwa* as present to the Shah."[383]

Sufi Qāyim Shāh

"Qayim Shah...came here from Hindustan. He was the cause for the destruction of twelve temples. He lived to an old age and passed away on the 17th Safar AH 1193."[384]

---

[381]Ibid., p. 101.

[382]Ibid., p. 51. Hindu mythology from the Rāmāyaṇa has obviously been mixed up with the story of how Sayyid Nathar Shah (AD 969–1030) from Arabia destroyed a Śiva temple and converted it into his *khānqāh*. He died in AH 673, and the *khānqāh* became a *dargāh* which has since grown into an important place of Muslim pilgrimage.

[383]Ibid., p. 63. This is another garbled account of how a Hindu temple was converted into a Muslim *dargāh* during the time when Tiruchirapalli was occupied by Chandā Sāhib, the Dīwan of the Nawwāb of Arcot, and Rānī Mīnākshī committed suicide when thrown into prison through treachery.

[384]Ibid., p. 64.

Sufi Nūr Muhammad Qādirī
Vellore (Tamil Nadu)

"Hazarat Nur Muhammad Qadiri was the most unique man regarded as an invaluable person of his age. Very often he was the cause of the ruin of temples. Some of these were laid waste. He selected his own burial ground in the vicinity of the temple. Although he lived five hundred years ago, people at large still remember his greatness."[385]

(76)
Āsāru's-Sanādīd

It is a book on the antiquities of Delhi written by Sayyid Ahmad Khān, the famous founder of the Aligarh Muslim University. Its first edition was published in 1847, the second in 1854, and the third in 1904. A new edition with a long introduction, footnotes, comments, bibliography, and index has been published recently. We are reproducing relevant passages from this edition.

Qutbu'd-Dīn Aibak (AD 1192–1210)

Iron Pillar: "...In our opinion this pillar was made in the ninth century before (the birth of) Lord Jesus... When Rāi Pithorā built a fort and an idol-house near this pillar, it stood in the courtyard of the idol-house. And when Qutbu'd-Dīn Aibak constructed a mosque after demolishing the idol-house, this pillar stood in the courtyard of the mosque..."[386]

Idol-house of Rāi Pithorā: "There was an idol-house near the fort of Rāi Pithorā. It was very famous...It was built along with the fort in 1200 Bikarmī [Vikrama Saṁvat] corresponding to AD 1143 and AH 538. The building of this temple was very unusual, and the work done on it by stone-cutters is such that nothing better can be conceived. The beautiful carvings on every stone in it defy description...The eastern and northern portions of this idol-house have survived intact. The fact that the Iron Pillar, which belongs to the Vaishnava faith, was kept inside it, as also the fact that sculptures of Kirshan avatār and Mahādev and Ganesh and Hanumān were carved on its walls, leads us to believe that this temple belonged to the Vaishnava faith. Although all sculptures were mutilated in the times of Muslims, even so a close scrutiny can identify as to which sculpture was what. In our opinion there was a

[385]Ibid., p. 128.

[386]Translated from the Urdu of Āsāru's-Sanādid, edited by Khaleeq Anjum, New Delhi, 1990, Vol. I, p. 305.

red-stone building in this idol-house, and it was demolished. For, this sort of old stones with sculptures carved on them are still found."[387]

Quwwat al-Islām Masjid: "When Qutbu'd-Dīn, the commander-in-chief of Muizzu'd-Dīn Sām alias Shihābu'd-Dīn Ghūrī, conquered Delhi in AH 587 corresponding to AD 1191 corresponding to 1248 Bikarmī, this idol-house (of Rāi Pithorā) was converted into a mosque. The idol was taken out of the temple. Some of the images sculptured on walls or doors or pillars were effaced completely, some were defaced. But the structure of the idol-house kept standing as before. Materials from twenty-seven temples, which were worth five crores and forty lakhs of Dilwāls, were used in the mosque, and an inscription giving the date of conquest and his own name was installed on the eastern gate...[388]

"When Mālwāh and Ujjain were conquered by Sultān Shamsu'd-Dīn in AH 631 corresponding to AD 1233, then the idol-house of Mahākāl was demolished and its idols as well as the statue of Rājā Bikramājīt were brought to Delhi, they were strewn in front of the door of the mosque..."[389]

"In books of history, this mosque has been described as Masjid-i-Ādīnah and Jāma' Masjid Delhi, but Masjid Quwwat al-Islām is mentioned nowhere. It is not known as to when this name was adopted. Obviously, it seems that when this idol-house was captured, and the mosque constructed, it was named Quwwat al-Islām...."[390]

Sultān Shamsu'd-Dīn Iltutmish (AD 1210–1236)

Tomb of Sultān Ghārī: Sayyid Ahmad Khān notices this tomb and describes it as exquisite. He says that it was built in AH 626 corresponding to AD 1228 when the corpse of Sultān Nāsiru'd-Dīn Mahmūd, the eldest son of Sultān Shamsu'd-Dīn Iltutmish, who was Governor of Laknauti and who died while his father was still alive, was brought to Delhi and buried.[391] But the editor, Khaleeq Anjum, comments in his introduction that "the dome of the mosque which is of marble has been re-used and has probably been obtained from some temple", and that the domes on the four pavilions outside "are in Hindu style in their interior."[392] He

[387]Ibid., p. 310.
[388]Ibid., pp. 310–11.
[389]Ibid., p. 316.
[390]Ibid., p. 310.
[391]Ibid., p. 317.
[392]Ibid., p. 89.

provides greater details in his notes at the end of Sayyid Ahmad's work. He writes:

"...This is the first Muslim tomb in North India, if we overlook some others. And it is the third historical Muslim monument in India after Quwwat al-Islām Masjid and Aḍhāī Din Kā Jhoṅpṛā...Stones from Hindu temples have been used in this tomb also, as in the Quwwat al-Islām Masjid."[393]

"...In the middle of the corridor on the west there is a marble dome. A look at the dome leads to the conclusion that it has been brought from some temple. The pillars that have been raised in the western corridor are of marble and have been made in Greek style. It is clear that they belong to some other building..."[394]

Sultān Ghiyāsu'd-Dīn Tughlaq (AD 1320–1325)

Tomb of Ghiyāsu'd-Dīn Tughlaq: Similarly, Sayyid Ahmad notices this tomb in some detail but does not describe its Hindu features.[395] Khaleeq Anjum, however, says in his introduction that "corridors inside this tomb have been constructed in the style of Hindu architecture, and the pillars as well as the beams in the corridors are fully of Hindu fashion."[396] He repeats the same comments in his notes at the end."[397]

Nasīru'd-Dīn Muhammad Humāyūn Pādshāh Ghāzī (AD 1530–1540 and 1556)

Nīlī Chhatrī: "At the foot of Salīm Garh and on the bank of the Jamunā, there is a small Bārādarī near Nigambodh Ghāt... It is known as Nīlī Chhatrī because of the blue mosaic work on its dome. This Chhatrī was built by Humāyūn Bādshāh in AH 939 corresponding to AD 1533 in order to have a view of the river. Hindus ascribe this Chhatrī to the time of the Pāṇḍūs. Even if that is not true, this much is certain that the bricks with mosaic work which have been used in this Chhatrī have been taken from some Hindu place because the bricks bear broken and mutilated images. On account of a derangement of the carvings, some have only the head left, while some others show only the torso. This derangement of carvings also goes to prove that these bricks have been placed here after being taken out from somewhere else. According to the Hindus, Rājā Judhastar had performed a Jag [Yajña] at this Ghāt. It

---

393Ibid., Vol. III, p. 406.
394Ibid., p. 407.
395Ibid., Vol. I, p. 321.
396Ibid., p. 97.
397Ibid., Vol. III, p. 409.

is not inconceivable that in the Hindu era a Chhatrī had been built at some spot on this Ghāt in commemoration of the Jag, and that this Chhatrī was built in the reign of Humāyūn after demolition of that (older) Chhatrī...[398]

He repeats some of these comments while describing the Nigambodh Ghāt...[399]

(77)
Hadiqah-i-Shuhadā

This was written in the reign of Nawāb Wājid 'Alī Shāh of Awadh (AD 1847–1856) by Mīrza 'Alī Jān, an eyewitness of and active participant in the *jihād* led by Amīr 'Alī Amethawī in 1855 for recapturing the Hanumān Gaṛhī temple at Ayodhya. The temple had been converted into a mosque in the reign of Aurangzeb but restored when Muslim power suffered an eclipse. The work was written immediately after the failure of the *jihād* and published in 1856.

Zahīru'd-Dīn Muhammad Bābur Pādshāh Ghāzī (AD 1026–1030)
Ayodhya (Uttar Pradesh)

"Wherever they found magnificent temples of the Hindus ever since the establishment of Sayyid Salar Mas'ud Ghazi's rule, the Muslim rulers in India built mosques, monasteries and inns, appointed mu'azzins, teachers, and store-stewards, spread Islam vigorously and vanquished the Kafirs. Likewise, they cleared up Faizabad and Avadh, too, from the filth of reprobation (infidelity), because it was a great centre of worship and capital of Rama's father. Where there stood the great temple (of Ramjanmasthan), there they built a big mosque, and where there was a small *mandap* (pavilion), there they erected a camp mosque (*masjid-i-mukhtasar-i-qanati*). The Janmasthan temple is the principal place of Rama's incarnation, adjacent to which is the *Sita ki Rasoi*. Hence, what a lofty mosque was built there by king Babar in AH 923 (AD 1528) under the patronage of Musa Ashiqan ! The mosque is still known far and wide as the Sita ki Rasoi mosque. And that temple is extant by its side (*aur pahlu mein wah dair baqi hai*)."[400]

---

[398]Ibid., Vol. I, p. 334.
[399]Ibid., p. 361.
[400]Cited by Dr. Harsh Narain in his article, *Rama-Janmabhumi Temple: Muslim Testimony*, Indian Express, February 26, 1990.

(78)

Muraqqa'-i-Khusrawī

It was completed in 1869 by Shykh 'Azmat Alī Kākorwī Nāmī who was an eyewitness of much that happened in the reign of Wājid 'Alī Shāh. The work, known as *Tārīkh-i-Awadh* also, was published for the first time in 1986 by the Fakhruddin Ali Ahmad Committee, U.P., Lucknow, but the chapter dealing with the *jihād* led by Amīr 'Alī Amethawī was left out. This chapter was published separately by Dr. Zakī Kākorawī from Lucknow in 1987.

Zahīru'd-Dīn Muhammad Bābur Pādshāh Ghāzī (AD 1526–1530)

Ayodhya (Uttar Pradesh)

"According to old records, it has been a rule with the Muslim rulers from the first to build mosques, monasteries, and inns, spread Islam, and put (a stop to) non-Islamic practices, wherever they found prominence (of *kufr*). Accordingly, even as they cleared up Mathura, Bindraban etc., from the rubbish of non-Islamic practices, the Babari mosque was built up in AH 923 (?) under the patronage of Sayyid Musa Ashiqan in the Janmasthan temple (*butkhane Janmasthan mein*) in Faizabad Avadh, which was a great place of (worship) and capital of Rama's father...

"A great mosque was built on the spot where Sita ki Rasoi is situated. During the regime of Babar, the Hindus had no guts to be a match for the Muslims. The mosque was built in AH 923 (?) under the patronage of Sayyid Mir Ashiqan...Aurangzeb built a mosque on the Hanuman Garhi...The Bairagis effaced the mosque and erected a temple in its place. Then idols began to be worshipped openly in the Babari mosque where the Sita ki Rasoi is situated."[401]

(79)

Wāqi'āt-i-Mamalakat-i-Bījāpur

This is an Urdu work compiled in 3 volumes by Bashīr'ud-Dīn Ahmad in AD 1913–14 and published from Agra in 1915. The first two volumes are translations of *Basātīn al-Salātīn*, a general history of Bijapur written in 1811 by Muhammad Ibrāhīm Zubairī. The third volume contains details collected by Bashīru'd-Dīn Ahmad himself from the life-stories and sayings of Sufis.

[401]Cited by Ibid.

Sultān 'Alī 'Ādil Shāh I of Bijapur (AD 1558–1580)

Mudgal (Karnataka)

"And in Mudgal town located 75 miles south-east of Bijapur 'Ali I tore down two temples and replaced them with *ashurkhanas*, or houses used in the celebration of Shi'a festivals."[402]

(80)
Mosque Architecture of Pre-Mughal Bengal

This is a modern work published from Dacca (Bangladesh) in 1979. The author, Dr. Syed Mahmudul Hasan, had submitted it as his Ph.D. thesis to the University of London in 1965. He has been the Head of the Post-Graduate Department of Islamic History and Culture in Jagannath University College in Decca, a member of F.R.A.S. and F.S.A. (Scot), and has served on the staff of the Department of Eastern Art in the Ashmolean Museum, Oxford. The book is documented from impeccable sources, literary and archaeological. It carries 43 plates with 45 photographs of monuments, and of inscriptions etc. discovered in them. We have brought together, from different pages, the passages which relate to the same subject.

General and Persistent Practice

"The Muslim invaders were necessarily impressed by Indian architecture and sculpture, expressing as they do foreign religious emotions in terms of images and emblems. What they saw at Delhi, and the other cities of India, which they attacked, was absolutely foreign to them. Yet when they came to raise their own religious buildings, they were not averse to using the spoils of their temples...[403]

"The ruthless desecration and makeshift conversion of Indian temples into Mosques has led many scholars to regard Indo-Muslim architecture as nothing more than a local variety of hybrid nature. In point of fact, these early Indian mosques which were compiled from Brahamanical fragments, such as the Deval Masjid at Bodhan near Hyderabad, have no direct bearing on the general development of Mosque architecture in India.[404]

"On the other hand the use of the spoils of non-Muslim ruins was a widely recognised feature in early Muslim architecture...[405]

---

[402]Summarised from the *Wāqi'āt*, Vol. III, p. 575 by Richard Maxwell Eaton in his *Sufis of Bijapur 1300–1700*, Princeton (U.S.A.), 1978, p. 68.

[403]Syed Mahmudul Hasan, *Mosque Architecture of Pre-Mughal Bengal*, Dacca (Bangladesh), 1979, p. 33.

[404]Ibid.

[405]Ibid.

"Just as later Mughal painting is a harmonious blend of Persian and Indian artistic tradition, so the Indo-Muslim architecture of Delhi and Ajmer is a blend. In the Quwwat al-Islam at Delhi and the Arhai din-ka-Jhopra at Ajmer, existing remains bear unmistakable evidence that they were not merely compilations, but the distinctive, planned works of professional architects...[406]

"Although constructed of destroyed Hindu temples, the Mosques at Old Delhi and Ajmer once and for all set the fashion to be followed by later mosques in Muslim India...[407]

"The early formative phase of Indo-Muslim architecture, marked by the adaptation of Hindu, Buddhist or Jaina temples, is illustrated by the oldest Mosques at Delhi, Bengal, Jaunpur, Daulatabad, Patan, etc. In Malwa, also, spoils of Hindu temples were used...[408]

"Creighton says, 'It appears to have been the general practice of the Muhammadan conquerors of India, to destroy all the temples of the idolaters, and to raise Mosque out of their ruins.' The statement is of course a gross exaggeration, for innumerable contemporary Hindu and Buddhist temples still exist in the cities of India once conquered by the Muslims. 'Abid 'Ali seems to have carried the observation of Creighton further when he remarks, 'It seems to the writer that the builder of the Mosque [Chhoto Sona Masjid at Gaud] had collected the stones containing the figure of the Hindu gods from the citadel of Gaur where temples must have existed in the time of the earlier Hindu kings.' Incidentally, Ravenshaw gave illustrations of sculptured stones, representing stone capitals and *Makara* gargoyles, which have been discovered in Hazrat Pandua. Westmacott, however, thinks that the circular stone given in Ravenshaw's plate XXX 'formed a part of the high ornament or pinnacle with which both the Buddhist Stupas and later Hindu temples were usually crowned. I have seen similar pieces at Debkot, and elsewhere, often with a perforation through the centre, through which I conjecture that a rod of metal, or perhaps a column of molten lead may have been passed, to retain it in an upright position'. In the event of a prodigious abundance of Hindu temple building material scattered all over the province, it is difficult to pin-point the provenance of each stray sculptured piece used in the mosques of Gaud and Hazrat Pandua. The existence of any Hindu temple in the citadel or outside Gaud as 'Abid 'Ali tells us, is as difficult to prove as to obviate the fact

[406]Ibid., p. 34.
[407]Ibid., p. 38.
[408]Ibid., p. 43.

that no material was taken from Devikot or Bannagar in Dinajpur. Contradicting the views of 'Abid 'Ali, Stapleton says, 'On the other hand from Manrique's statement that, in 1641, he saw figures of idols standing in niches surrounded by carved grotesques and leaves in some stone reservoirs in Gaur, it is possible that except during periods of persecution the Muhammadan Kings of Gaur allowed idols and Hindu temples to remain unmolested in their capital.' Although examples of the use of Hindu material are not scarce, as proved by the discovery of three sculptured figures from Mahisantosh with Muslim ornament on the reverse side, now in the Varendra Research Society Museum, it would be wrong to say after Creighton that all the Hindu temples were desecrated by the Muslims to procure building material...[409]

"...The Indian Museum, Calcutta, as well as the *Bangiya Sahitya Parishad* Museum, Calcutta, acquired a large number of architectural objects from the ancient sites of Bengal, particularly, Gaud, Hazrat Pandua, Bagerhat, Hughli, Rajshahi, Dinajpur and elsewhere. Besides freshly quarried basalts, a large quantity of locally available building materials was employed by the architects of Gaud, Hazrat Pandua and elsewhere. Ravenshaw's unwarranted observation that 'Though it (Hazrat Pandua) cannot boast of such antiquity as Gaud, its remains afford stronger evidence than those of the latter city of its having been constructed mainly from the materials of Hindoo buildings', has been brushed aside by Westmacott, who thinks that Hazrat Pandua is older than Gaud. One of the strongest advocates of the Indianized form of Muslim structures is Havell, who is too intolerant to allow any credit to the Muslim builders for the use of radiating arches, domes, minarets, delicate relief works. He maintains that the central *mihrab* of the Adina Masjid (Pl. III) at Hazrat Pandua is so obviously Hindu in design as hardly to require comments. While Havell writes that 'The image of *Vishnu* or *Surya* has trefoil arched canopy, symbolizing the aura' of the god, of exactly the same type as the outer arch of the *mihrab*, Beglar says that the Muslims delighted in 'placing the sanctum of his orthodox cult (in this case the main prayer niche) on the spot, where hated infidel had his sanctum'. Saraswati is even more emphatic on this point when he contends, 'An examination of the stones used in the construction of the Adina Masjid (one of them bearing a Sanscrit inscription, recording merely a name of *Indranath*, in the character of the 9th century AD) and

---

[409]Ibid., pp. 163–64. His statement that "innumerable Hindu and Buddhist temples still exist in the cities of India once conquered by the Muslims", is a figment of his imagination. No city in North India can show a temple from pre-Islamic times.

those lying about in heaps all round, reveals the fact, which no careful observer can deny, that most of them came from temples that once stood in the vicinity.' Ilahi Bakhsh, Creighton, Ravenshaw, Buchanan-Hamilton, Westmacott, Beglar, Cunnigham, King, and a host of other historians and archaeologists bear glowing testimony to the utilization of non-muslim materials (Fig. 3b & Pl. V), but none of them ventured to say that existing temples were dismantled and materials provided for the construction of magnificent monuments in Gaud and Hazrat Pandua.[410]

"Creighton drew the sketches of a few Hindu sculptures which were evidently used in the Chhoto Sona Masjid at Gaud. These are the image of *Sivani*, the consort of *Siva*, *Varahaavatara* or *Vishnu* in the form of a Boar, *Brahmani*, consort of *Brahma*. In the British Museum there are a few images of Hindu and Buddhist character, such as the *Brahmani*, sketched by Creighton, and the seated Buddha figure (Pls. XLI-XLII). The Muslim builders out of sheer expediency felt no scruple to use these fragments in their mosques by concealing the carved sides into the wall and utilizing the flat reverse side of these black basalts for arabesque design in shallow carvings. Piecemeal utilization of Hindu sculptures were also to be seen in the earlier monuments, such as, the Mosque and Tomb of Zafar Khan at Tribeni, the Mosque at Chhoto Pandua, the Adina Masjid at Hazrat Pandua, etc. The British Museum and the Victoria and Albert Museum, both in London, the Indian Museum and the *Bangiya Sahitya Parishad* Museum, both at Calcutta, Varendra Research Society Museum, Rajshahi, provide large specimens of carved stones and architectural fragments used in the monuments of pre-Mughal Bengal. Ravenshaw photographed a circular stone pedestal and a gargoyle, which is now in the Indian Museum, Calcutta. Used obviously as the gargoyle in the Adina Masjid, it 'consists of a modification of an elephant's head with the eyes, horns and ears of a *sardula* (elephant).' Cunningham found in the pulpit of the Adina Masjid 'a line of Hindu sculpture of very fine bold execution.' Innumerable Hindu lintels, pillars, door-jambs, bases, capitals, friezes, fragments of stone carvings, dadoes, etc., have been utilized in such a makeshift style as to render 'improvisation' well-nigh impossible. In many cases as observed in the Quwwat al-Islam at Delhi and the Arhai-din-ka-Jhopra Mosque at Ajmer, pillars were inverted,

[410]Ibid., pp. 170–71. In subsequent passages he himself says that existing buildings were quarried for stones used in Mosques. Medieval Muslim historians say that all Hindu temples were destroyed and mosques raised at Lakhnauti, the site of Gaud, and Pandau.

joining the base with capitals, suiting neither pattern nor size. Still there is no denying the fact that Hindu materials were utilized, yet it would be far-fetched to say that existing Hindu temples were dismantled and converted by improvisation into mosques as observed in the early phase of Muslim architecture in Indo-Pak sub-continent. The ritual needs and structural properties of the Hindus and the Muslims are so diametrically opposite as to deter any compromise and, therefore, the early Muslim conquerors of Bengal said their prayer in mosques built out of the fragments of Hindu materials in the same way as their predecessors did at Delhi, Ajmer, Patan, Janupur, Dhar and Mandu, and elsewhere. In the event [absence?] of any complete picture of pre-Muslim Hindu art as practised in Gaud and Hazrat Pandua, it is an exaggeration to hold the view after Saraswati that 'indeed, every structure of this royal city (Hazrat Pandua) discloses Hindu materials in its composition, thus, disclosing that no earlier monument was spared.'[411]

"...During the Husain Shahi period the stone cutter's art was throughly practised and perfected, as walls of gates and mosques were adorned with stone, either quarried from Rajmahal hills or obtained from some existing buildings...[412]

"...The British Museum, London, has in its collection two sculptured pieces from Bengal, namely, the seated Buddha figure (Pl. XLIIa) and the image of Brahmani (Pl. XLIa). Both these images have on their obverse (Pls. XLIb, XLIIb) exquisitely carved diaper work of unmistakable Muslim workmanship. The Indian Museum, Calcutta, has a stone slab carved on the one side with the image of Durga, destroying *Mahisha* or Buffalow-demon, and on the reverse arabesque. The panel consisting of a scalloped arch with a lotus rosette on each of its sides, surrounded by richly foliated devices, is undoubtedly a Muslim work.[413]

"The Muslim calligraphers did not feel any scruple to utilize fragments of Hindu or Jaina sculpture in carving out beautiful inscriptions in elegant *Naskh*, *Thulth* and *Tughra*, keeping the images inside the wall..."[414]

Delhi

"...Delhi was the source of artistic inspiration for all the later provincial schools of Indo-Muslim architecture. Codrington remarks, 'At

[411]Ibid., pp. 171–72.
[412]Ibid., p. 183.
[413]Ibid.
[414]Ibid., p. 185.

Delhi, the Kutb-ul-Islam marks the beginning of Islamic architecture in India.' This formative phase of Mosque architecture in India began with the random utilization of temple spoils, Hindu architraves, corbelled ceilings, kumbha pillars with hanging bell-and-chain motifs, which were organised to fulfil the needs of congregational prayer. It is said that the columns of twenty-seven Hindu and Jaina temples were utilized in the great Mosque, at Delhi, rightly called the 'Might of Islam'. It was built by Qutb-al-Din Aybak in AH 587/AD 1191–92 on an ancient pre-Muslim plinth.[415]

"...Originally there were five domes in the *liwan* all compiled of Hindu fragments, as is evident from their corbelled interiors...[416]

"...Incidentally, it may be recalled that Beglar carried out excavations at the Quwat-al-Islam Mosque at Old Delhi under the supervision of Cunningham and noticed the foundation of pre-Muslim temples there..."[417]

Ajmer (Rajasthan)

"...To Iletmish we owe some of the finest Muslim works in India. The Arhai din ka-Jhopra, began by Qutab al-Din in AD 1198–99, was also completed by him. Tod had said of it that it was 'one of the most perfect as well as the most ancient monuments of Hindu architecture', on the evidence of certain four-armed figures to be seen on the pillars...[418]

"The Ajmer Mosque resembles the Delhi Mosque in its use of pre-Muslim materials as well as in its courtyard plan, arched screen, columnar *liwan* and *riwags* and use of reconstructed Hindu corbelled domes. All these features, except the fragments of Hindu and Jain carvings used in the work are essentially Islamic. The Ajmer Mosque indicates a further improvement in Mosque design... As Sardar puts it, 'These pillars have a greater height than those at the Kutub, and are more elegant in their sculpture and general appearance than the converted Mosques in Malwa and Ahmedabad.' "[419]

Badaun (Uttar Pradesh)

"The Jami Masjid of Badaun, also built by Iletmish is one of the largest mosques in India. Following the traditional courtyard plan, it

[415]Ibid., p. 37.
[416]Ibid.
[417]Ibid., p. 64.
[418]Ibid., p. 38.
[419]Ibid.

also utilizes Hindu temple pillars. The entrance arches of the gateways leading into the courtyard of the Mosque presumably recall those in the great Mosques at Delhi and Ajmer..."[420]

Bayana (Rajasthan)

"That the practice of utilizing the spoils of Hindu temples continued throughout the reign of Sultan Iletmish is proved by the Mosque of Ukha in Bayana (Uttar Pradesh), which is also on the site of a Hindu temple..."[421]

Dhar (Madhya Pradesh)

"The oldest of the Mosques in Malwa is the Kamal Maula Masjid which was built in Dhar in AH 803/AD 1400. Both this Mosque and the slightly later Jami or Lat Masjid are clearly adaptations of ruined Hindu temple material..."[422]

Mandu (Madhya Pradesh)

"The transfer of the capital from Dhar to Mandu by Dilwar Khan in AH 794/AD 1392, marks a new phase in the development of Mosque architecture in Malwa. The Mosque built by him in c. AH 808/AD 1405–06 is oblong in ground plan, the western side being formed by the *liwan*. Its roof is supported by Hindu pillars..."[423]

Gujarat

"It is true that Mosque architecture in Gujarat only began in the 14th century. When 'Ala-al-Din Khalji conquered and annexed the country to the Delhi Sultanate in the later part of the 13th century, there still flourished a singularly beautiful indigenous style of architecture. The early monuments of Gujarat, notably at Patan (Anhilvada) tell the same story of the demolition of local temples and the reconstruction of their fragments...[424]

"...In the beginning, at the Qutb, the Hindu element was confined architecturally to the trabeate constructive methods, and to part of the decoration, Islam contributing the plan and the embellishment of the Arabic lettering. In Gujarat, notably in the entrance porches of the Jami' Masjid at Cambay, much may fairly be described as literal recon-

[420]Ibid., p. 39.
[421]Ibid.
[422]Ibid., p. 43.
[423]Ibid., p. 44.
[424]Ibid., p. 45.

struction of Hindu work, as units in the established plan of a Muslim place of worship. These entrances have their parallels in the pavilions and *mandapas* of Hindu and Jaina temples still standing, for instance, at Modhera and Mount Abu..."[425]

Patan (Gujarat)

"The earliest recorded building in Gujarat is the Adina Masjid at Patan (Anhilvada), as stated above. This bears the same unusual name as that of the Mosque built by Sikandar Shah at Hazrat Pandua about fifty years later. The tomb of Sheikh Farid and the Adina Masjid at Patan, which are dated c. AH 700/AD 1300, correspond in their utilization of Hindu building material with the tomb and the Mosque of Zafar Khan Ghazi at Tribeni in Hooghly, Bengal, which are dated c. AH 705/AD 1305. The now demolished Adina Masjid at Patan, is said to have had one thousand and fifty pillars of marble and other stones taken from destroyed temples. Erected by Ulugh Khan, 'Ala'-al-Din Khalji's Governor, it measures 400 feet by 300 feet..."[426]

Bharuch (Gujarat)

"...Unlike the Patan Mosque, the Jami' Masjid of Bharoch, which is also dated c. AH 700/AD 1300 is a new creation. Although it does incorporate Hindu pillars, it is built on the usual Mosque plan with which we are familiar in earlier works. The brackets of the incorporated pillars and the carved interior of the corbelled domes are particularly fine. They, of course, necessarily recall the much earlier work of the Quwwat al-Islam at Delhi. It is important to realize that these primitive methods were still being used in the Indian provinces two hundred years after they were fully developed at Delhi..."[427]

Khambhat (Gujarat)

"...The Mosque of Cambay demonstrates the imposition of Khalji features, such as the arched screen of the *Jama'at Khana* Masjid at the *Dargah* of Nizam-al-Din Aulia in Delhi, upon the local trabeate forms of Gujarat Hindu architecture. Codrington writes, 'The Jami' Masjid at Cambay was finished in 1325, and is typical of these earlier buildings. It has all the appurtenances that Islam demands—cloisters, open courtyard, the covered place for prayer, *mimbar* and *mihrab*—but only the

[425]Ibid., p. 46.
[426]Ibid.
[427]Ibid.

west end is in any sense Islamic. As at Delhi and Ajmir, the pillars of the cloisters, and notably the entrance porches as a whole, are the relics of sacked Hindu shrines...' "[428]

Deccan

"Like all other provinces of India, the Deccan, also, witnessed the growth of a distinguished school of Muslim architecture. Its early phase is also, characterized by the adaptation of local temples, for the purpose of Muslin congregational prayer, as exemplified by the Deval Mosque of Bodhan in Nizamabad, near Hyderabad, dated AD 1318, which was formerly a Hindu shrine..."[429]

Bodhan (Maharashtra)

"...It is said that the star-shaped Jaina Temple built in the Chalukya style at Bodhan in the 9th or 10th century was, also, transformed into a Mosque during the reign of Muhammad Tughlaq (AH 726–52/AD 1325–51)."[430]

Daulatabad (Maharashtra)

"The Mosque of Qutb al-Din Mubarak Khalji at Daulatabad, dated AH 718/AD 1318, is probably the earliest surviving Muslim structure in the Deccan. It is a square, 260 feet each way, assembled into the usual orthodox plan out of destroyed Hindu pillars, brackets, and beams..."[431]

Pandua (Bengal)

"Beglar traces the origin of the Adina Masjid to pre-Muslim sources... He bases his arguments on the point that if the Adina Masjid occupies the site of a pre-Muslim Hindu temple, the name may be a reminiscent of Adisur, the so-called founder of the hitherto unidentified temple dating from the 7th century AD; however, he does not know that there is a mosque at Patan, called Adina, and that it is a Persian term for Friday. The use of fragments of Hindu or Buddhist architectural works in the Masjid do [does?] not prove that the site was pre-Muslim. They may have been brought there..."[432]

"...Beglar suggests that the *mihrab* of the Adina Masjid was transferred from a Hindu temple. He says, 'Of the Hindu sculpture, the most

---

[428]Ibid.
[429]Ibid., p. 49.
[430]Ibid., p. 50.
[431]Ibid.
[432]Ibid., 62 and 64 (Illustration on p. 63).

striking and superb is beyond question the trefoil arch and pillars of the main prayer niche.' But there are no grounds for his assertion. The Adina Masjid *mihrab*, forming a single work of art, must be accepted as contemporary with the fabric of the Masjid itself. But it must be admitted that the style is local...[433]

"Particular attention has been drawn to the curiously interesting designs of the archivolt of the niche. The conventional grotesque Lion's head at the crown and the *Kinnara* and *Kinnari* at the haunches, which appear in the lintel of the Vaishnava temple from Gaud, according to many scholars have been transformed into graceful foliage, palmette and sensuous tendrils...[434]

"The discovery of an odd fragment of Hindu sculpture found built into the steps of the staircase has led many scholars to ascribe a pre-Muslim origin to the Adina Masjid. As Cunningham puts it, 'The steps leading up to the pulpit have fallen down, and, on turning over one of the steps I found a line of Hindu sculpture of very fine and bold execution... The main ornament is a line of circular panels... formed by continuous intersecting lotus stalks. These are five complete panels, and two half-panels which have been cut through. These two contain portions of an elephant and a rhinoceros. In the complete panels are: (i) cow and a calf; (ii) human figures broken; (iii) a goose; (iv) a man and woman and a crocodile; (v) two elephants. The carving is deep and the whole has been polished.' This sculpture is still visible. It is, therefore, clear that the exigencies of the circumstances led to the utilization of some Hindu materials available on the site. Nevertheless, such mutilated fragments hardly testify to the fact that the Adina Masjid was built on the ruins of an ancient Indian temple.[435]

"The western wall of the northern prayer hall is pierced by two openings on either side of the zenana gallery, which reduce the number of niches (Fig. 3) between the pilaster of the back walls from the 16 found in the southern prayer hall to 14. These postern gateways (Figs. 3, 9, & Pls. IV, V), are built out of elements of Hindu door frames and, therefore, are unusual features, rarely found in Indian Mosques. It is hard to believe that they were provided for the use of the general worshippers. Probably they were for the use of the attendants, palanquin-bearers and entourage of the King and his ladies, who entered the Mosque through the adjoining Ladies' vestibule.[436]

---

[433]Ibid., p. 77.
[434]Ibid.
[435]Ibid., pp. 80–81.
[436]Ibid., pp. 81–82.

"...However, there is one exception shown in the northern hall, which differs from the other semi-circular niches. Here the trefoil arch corresponds generally with that of the central *mihrabs*. The arch itself has a superimposed ribbed roof, recalling Hindu architecture. The face of the trefoil is decorated with a lotus and diamond band, the pilasters on either side having *kumbha* bases and looped garlands on their shafts. All these details are different from the rest of the decorative motifs in the Adina Masjid. But there are no grounds for the suggestion that the work is Hindu or that it is built up of fragments of a destroyed Hindu temple. The space between the pilasters of this *mihrab* and the stone-face of the brick wall is filled with fragmentary remains of Hindu sculpture.[437]

"...The two postern gateways and the two doors are already mentioned. Beglar pointed out that the door frames of all these four door ways are built up of fragments from some other buildings. He identifies the work as being Hindu but admits that he does not know any local source from their fragments. The work is more or less of the same kind as that to be seen in the postern gate. In all these doorways various Indian motifs attracts undivided attention. These include pot and foliage, pilasters, door guardians and the intertwined *nagas* on the lintel. The utilization of non-Muslim materials in the Adina Masjid as well as in later Mosques in Gaud and Hazrat Pandua is supported by two fragments in the British Museum. They are cut in basalt and the first shows finely cut Muslim diaper work on one side and the figure of Buddha on the other (Pls. XLII, a-b). Another fragment has the image of probably the goddess Brahmani on the other side (Pls. XLI, a-b). The work indicates that these fragments came from Gaud or Hazrat Pandua.[438]

"...The entrance gateway to the Minar at Chhoto Pandua as well as that of the Eklakhi Mausoleum at Hazrat Pandua (Pl. XVI) provide parallels for zenana gatways. The floor of the zenana gallery with its worn basalt paving slabs is supported by the squat pillars of the prayer hall below. These support bays roofed by a corbelled construction of plain slabs placed across the corners of the bays. At earlier mosques, such as the Quwwat al-Islam, internal domes constructed in this way were removed from Hindu temples. Here the old Indian method is still utilized with fresh material...[439]

"A curiously interesting feature of the Adina Masjid is the square

---

[437]Ibid., p. 83.
[438]Ibid. pp. 85–86.
[439]Ibid., p. 86.

structure, adjoining the outer wall of the *qibla* on the northern side of the central *mihrab*. It communicates with the zenana gallery by lintelled doorways, formed by Hindu door jambs as stated earlier. According to Beglar it measures externally 54 feet by 48 feet, whereas 'Abid 'Ali notes that this roofless annexe is 42 feet square. It stands on a very high plinth, raising the floor to the level of the ladies' gallery. The plinth is built of random rubble work with conventionalised Buddhist railing ornament resembling those in the dadoes of the *qibla* wall of the mosque.[440]

"The real character as well as the distinguishing features of the Adina Masjid have yet to be determined. In the present crumbling state of this one-time 'wonder of the world', as Cunningham calls it, it is well nigh impossible to say whether this magnificent mosque occupies the site of any Hindu or Buddhist temple. A group of scholars failed to see in the impressive Adina Masjid anything more than a mere assemblage of Hindu or Buddhist fragments, arranged skilfully to adhere to a mosque plan. Ilahi Bakhsh started the controversy when he wrote, 'It is worth observing that in front of the *chaukath* (lintel) of the Adina Masjid, there was a broken and polished idol, and that there were other idols lying about. So it appears that, in fact, this mosque was originally an idol-temple.' Beglar steps up this controversy by saying, 'the Adina Masjid occupies the site, of a once famous, or at least a most important, and highly ornamented, pre-Muhammadan shrine'; he depends for his arguments on a Proto-Bengali inscription (Fig. 4b) discovered in the building which bears the name of Brahma. Saraswati seems to have carried the thesis too far when he writes, 'an examination of the stones used in the construction of the Adina Mosque (one of them bearing a Sanskrit inscription recording merely a name, Indranath, in character of the 9th century) and those lying about in heaps all around, reveals the fact, which no careful observer can deny, that most of them came from temples that once stood in the vicinity.' Beglar even went so far as to pin-point 'the sanctum of the temple, judging from the remnants of heavy pedestals of statues, now built into the pulpit, and the superb canopied trefoils, now doing duty as prayer niches, stood where the main prayer niche now stands; nothing would probably so tickle the fancy of a bigot, as the power of placing the sanctum of his orthodox cult (in this case the main prayer niche) on the spot, where hated infidel had his sanctum'. The existence of the foundation of a Hindu Temple in

[440]Ibid., pp. 90–91.

the Adina Masjid is as far-fetched as to consider the circular pedestal to the west of the *qibla* wall as remains of a Buddhist stupa (Fig. 3). It may be the base of a detached minar, as similar examples are to be seen in the mosques of Egypt, Persia and India..."[441]

Tribeni (Bengal)

"The existing tomb and mosque of Zafar Khan Ghazi at Tribeni is another example of contemporary Hindu fragments being utilized in Muslim structure...[442]

"The Mosque of Zafar Khan Ghazi is the earliest known example of Mosque architecture in Bengal, and 'is certainly the oldest in Bengal far anterior to any building at Gaud and Hazrat Pandua'. Marking the earliest phase of Muslim building activities, it incorporates fragments of non-Muslim monuments, like those of the Quwwat al-Islam Mosque in Delhi. R.D. Banerjee is of opinion that 'the Mosque of Tribeni was most probably a Vaishnava temple but relics of Buddhism and Jainism were found...' "[443]

"...Unmistakable Hindu workmanship is evident in the mutilated figures in some of the architectural fragments used—a phenomenon to be observed in the Adina Masjid at Hazrat Pandua, dated AH 776/AD 1374. There are five *mihrabs* in the *qibla* wall, the most striking being the central one. Tastefully carved multifoil brick arch of the central *mihrab* is supported by slender stone pillars of some Hindu temple...[444]

"...The utilization of non-Muslim building materials is to be taken as a matter of expediency for no mosque plan was ever superimposed on the traditional ground plan of temple architecture. In the light of this phenomena the mosques can hardly be regarded as mere improvisations of existing temples, as stated by R.D. Banerjee in the case of the Mosque of Zafar Khan. The Muslim architects did not feel any scruple to employ fragments of Hindu sculpture still bearing traces of iconographical art in their mosques, and furthermore Hindu workmanship is evident in the delicate stone carvings and sensuous tendrils, and corbelled domes."[445]

Gaud (Bengal)

"...Both Cunningham and Marshall accept Creighton's suggestion

[441]Ibid., p. 97.
[442]Ibid. p. 86.
[443]Ibid., p. 128.
[444]Ibid., p. 129.
[445]Ibid., p. 131.

that the Lattan Masjid was built in the year AH 880/AD 1475...[446]

"The *qibla* wall has three semi-circular niches, the central one being bigger than the side ones. These are all encrusted with glazed tiles. The *mihrab* to the north of the central niche has fragments of Hindu sculpture built into it...[447]

"...Although less ornate than those of the southern prayer chamber in the Adina Masjid, the Tantipara Masjid pillars have square bases, moulded bands and cubical abaci. Brown says that the pillars of this mosque are 'of the square and chamfered variety originally part of a Hindu temple', but this was not so. They are contemporary with the building. Certainly work of this character is known in Hindu building, and this seems to have misled Brown.[448]

"... Two rows of chamfered pillars, each carrying 5 pointed arches, divide the interior of the [Chhoto Sona] Mosque into 3 longitudinal aisles. In each row there are 4 pillars of black basalt which in their moulded string-courses, cubical pedestal, dog-tooth ornament and square abacus recall those of the supporting pillars of the zenana gallery in the Adina Masjid. Evidently they are much more attenuated in shape in the Chhoto Sona Masjid than those in the Adina Masjid. It is hard to ascertain their origins, but considering the enormous quantity of Hindu spoil used in the Chhoto Sona Masjid (Pls. XLI, XLII) and comparing its pillars with the carved stone pillars at the Bari Dargah which originally must have been brought from the Adina Masjid it may be said that they were taken from unidentifiable Hindu temples.[449]

"...Many of the stones used for casing the wall to give the illusion of a stone monument from distance are evidently Hindu. To quote Creighton, 'The stone used in these mosques had formerly belonged to Hindu temples destroyed by the zealous Muhammadans,' as will be evident from an inspection of Plates XLI and XLII, representing two slabs taken from this Building. Creighton's painting XVI represents a stone with the image of the Hindu deity, *Vishnu*, in the Boar incarnation, with shallow diaper carving on the reverse side. The figure of Sivani, the consort of Siva, one of the Hindu triad, appears on another stone sketched by Creighton (painting XVII). The mother figure evidently drawn from sculptured stones used in the Small Golden Mosque is that of Brahmani, given in Plate XLIa (Creighton's painting XVII). It

---

[446]Ibid., p. 123.
[447]Ibid. p. 122.
[448]Ibid., p. 131.
[449]Ibid., pp. 160–61.

is very interesting to point out in connection with the figure of Brahmani that it agrees in meticulous execution of details and perfection of style with that of the British Museum piece. Therefore, it is certain that Creighton drew his sketch from this black stone which curiously displays diaper work on the other side (Pl. XLIb) similar to that of Creighton's Plate XVI. Arabesque design in shallow stone carving, resembling delicate tapestry, appears also in another superb black basalt piece, shown in Plate XLIb, now in the British Museum. It has the image of a seated Buddha on one side thereby again indicating the utilization of non-Muslim material (Pl. XLIIa). This fascinating piece may well be attributed to the Chhoto Sona Masjid on the grounds of the close similarity of its diaper work with that of the stone sketched by Creighton in his Plate XVI, and of the existence of gilding in the shallow carvings of the diaper work."[450]

Rampal (Bengal)

"The famous Mosque of Baba Adam, (Fig. 17) the patron saint of the locality in the ancient Hindu site of Rampal where Raja Ballal Sena built his palace in the district of Dacca is an impressive architectural monument of pre-Mughal Bengal.[451]

"...Measuring 43 feet by 36 feet externally and 34 feet by 22 feet internally, the Mosque incorporated a number of beautifully carved stone pillars of unmistakable Hindu workmanship...[452]

"In the construction of this 6-domed mosque, measuring 36 feet by 24 feet, considerable amount of locally available materials from dilapidated Hindu monuments were employed as evident in the black carved basalts of the pillars, *mihrabs*, epigraphic slabs, etc..."[453]

Chhota Pandua (Bengal)

"'Next to Satgaon', writes D.G. Crawford, 'Pandua is the oldest place of Hughli District—once the capital of a Hindu Raja and is famous as the site of a great victory gained by the Musulmans under Shah Safi over the Hindus in about AD 1340.' Besides the Mosque and Tomb of Shah Safiuddin, the most outstanding architectural project of great magnitude is the Great Mosque at Chhoto Pandua... O'Malley and M.M. Chakravarti differ from Blockmann in ascribing Buddhist origin

[450]Ibid., p. 163.
[451]Ibid. p. 138.
[452]Ibid.
[453]Ibid., p. 141.

to these pillars and maintain that they were probably quarried from a Hindu temple. As put forward by Cunningham, 'The Mosque stands on a mound once the site of a Hindu temple, the pillars of which now support this mean-looking barn-like Masjid.' It would be far-fetched to maintain that the Great Mosque at Chhoto Pandua was built on the very foundation of a Hindu temple, like the improvised Tomb of Zafar Khan Ghazi at Tribeni, dated 14th century AD."[454]

Sadipur (Bengal)

"...A.K. Bhattacharya points out that an inscription in Arabic, carved in *Tughra* is found on the reverse of an image of Adinath, which is recovered from a ruined *Dargah* in the village Sadipur, P.S. Kaliachak, Malda."[455]

---

[454]Ibid., pp. 144–45.
[455]Ibid. p. 185.

CHAPTER EIGHT

SUMMING UP

Starting with Al-Bilādhurī who wrote in Arabic in the second half of the ninth century, and coming down to Syed Mahmudul Hasan who wrote in English in the fourth decade of the twentieth, we have cited from eighty histories spanning a period of more than twelve hundred years. Our citations mention sixty-one kings, sixty-three military commanders and fourteen sufis who destroyed Hindu temples in one hundred and fifty-four localities, big and small, spread from Khurasan in the West to Tripura in the East, and from Transoxiana in the North to Tamil Nadu in the South, over a period of eleven hundred years. In most cases the destruction of temples was followed by erection of mosques, *madrasas* and khānqāhs, etc., on the temple sites and, frequently, with temple materials. Allāh was thanked every time for enabling the iconoclast concerned to render service to the religion of Muhammad by means of this pious performance.

Some more kings or commanders or sufis who figure in these histories in a similar context may have remained unmentioned because we had access to the full texts only in a few cases; most of the time we had to remain content with excerpts or summaries made by modern historians in one context or the other. Many more localities have remained unspecified because quite often the histories under reference, instead of naming particular places, mention provinces and regions where large-scale destruction of temples took place as a result of general orders issued to this effect, or intensive campaigns undertaken for this purpose alone.

It is seldom that translations retain the full flavour of the language and meaning of the original works. In our case, some of the flavour must have been lost in citations which we had to translate into English from Urdu or Hindi renderings of the Persian texts. Even so, we feel that, taken together, the citations do bring out something of the religious zeal harboured by the historians concerned when they sat down to glorify Islam and highlight its heroes.

Coming to the heroes themeselves, some of them figure more prominently or frequently in our citations, such as Muhammad bin Qāsim, Mahmūd of Ghazni, Shamsu'd-Dīn Iltutmish, Alāu'd-Dīn Khaljī, Fīrūz Shāh Tughlaq, Ahmad Shāh I and Mahmūd Begḍha of Gujarat, Sikander Lodī, and Aurangzeb; they have earned permanent fame in the annals of Islam by doing what they did to Hindus in general and to Hindu temples in particular. But the others, too, do not come out discreditably if a state of mind or an expressed intention is any indication. Maybe, their achievements in this context have found a more detailed description in histories to which we have had no access.

It is highly doubtful if the Mughal period deserves the credit it has been given as a period of religious tolerance. Akbar is now known only for his policy of *sulh-i-kul*, at least among the learned Hindus. It is no more remembered that to start with he was also a pious Muslim who had viewed as *jihād* his sack of Chittor. Nor is it understood by the learned Hindus that his policy of *sulh-i-kul* was motivated mainly by his bid to free himself from the stranglehold of the orthodox *'Ulamā,* and that any benefit which Hindus derived from it was no more than a by-product. Akbar never failed to demand daughters of the Rajput kings for his harem. Moreover, as our citations show, he was not able to control the religious zeal of his functionaries at the lower levels so far as Hindu temples were concerned. Jahāngīr, like many other Muslim kings, was essentially a pleasure-seeking person. He, however, became a pious Muslim when it came to Hindu temples of which he destroyed quite a few. Shāh Jahān did not hide what he wanted to do to the Hindus and their places of worship. His Islamic record on this score was much better than that of Jahāngīr. The reversal of Akbar's policy thus started by his two immediate successors reached its apotheosis in the reign of Aurangzeb, the paragon of Islamic piety in the minds of India's Muslims. What is more significant, Akbar has never been forgiven by those who have regarded themselves as custodians of Islam, right upto our own times; Maulana Abul Kalam Azad is a typical example. In any case one swallow has never made a summer.

Certain localities also figure more prominently or more frequently in our citations, such as Multan, Thanesar, Kangra, Mathura, Somnath, Varanasi, Ujjain, Chidambaram, Puri, Dwarka, Girinar and Kanchipuram. The iconoclasts paid special attention to temples in these places or mounted repeated attacks on them. They knew that these were the holy cities of the Hindus, and entertained the fond hope that desecration of idols and destruction of temples in these sanctuaries was most likely to make the Hindus lose faith in their "false gods" and prepare them for receiving the "light of Islam". That, however, does not mean that destruction of temples at other places was in any sense less thorough. Our citations reveal more or less the same pattern everywhere, once the swordsmen of Islam got fired by their religious fervour.

It was not unoften that Hindu temples were admired by the iconoclasts for their strength or antiquity or exquisiteness or the expense incurred on their construction. We are told that they were "as firm as the faith of the faithful" and "a thousand years old". It was estimated that they must have cost so many "thousand thousand dirhams" or so many "lakhs of asharfies". But none of these plus points was reason enough for sparing them from the fate they deserved according to the Sunnah of the Prophet. They embodied an "age of darkness and error", they housed "false gods", and they enticed people away from the worship of the "one and only true God" — Allāh of the Qur'ān.

So the temples were attacked "all along the way" as the armies of Islam advanced; they were "robbed of their sculptural wealth", "pulled down", "laid waste", "burnt with naptha", "trodden under horse's hoofs", and "destroyed from their very foundations", till "not a trace of them remained". Mahmūd of Ghazni robbed and burnt down 1,000 temples at Mathura, and 10,000 in and around Kanauj. One of his successors, Ibrāhīm, demolished 1,000 temples each in Hindustan (Ganga–Yamuna Doab) and Malwa. Muhammad Ghūrī destroyed another 1,000 at Varanasi. Qutbu'd-Dīn Aibak employed elephants for pulling down 1,000 temples in Delhi. 'Ālī I 'īdil Shāh of Bijapur destroyed 200 to 300 temples in Karnataka. A sufi, Qāyim Shāh, destroyed 12 temples at Tiruchirapalli. Such exact or approximate counts, however, are available only in a few cases. Most of the time we are informed that "many strong temples which would have remained unshaken even by the trumpets blown on the Day of Judgment, were levelled with the ground when swept by the wind of Islām".

We find the Muslim historians going into raptures as they describe scenes of desecration and destruction. For Amīr Khusrū it was always an occasion to show off the power of his poetic imagination. When Jalālu'd-Dīn Khaljī wrought havoc at Jhain, "A cry rose from the temples as if a second Mahmūd had taken birth". The temples in the environs of Delhi were "bent in prayers" and "made to do prostration", by Alāu'd-Dīn Khaljī. When the temple of Somnath was destroyed and its debris thrown into the sea towards the west, the poet rose to his full height. "So the temple of Somnāth," he wrote, "was made to bow towards the Holy Mecca, and the temple lowered its head and jumped into the sea, so you may say that the building first said its prayers and then had a bath."

Our citations have a lot to tell about how the votaries of Islam viewed the idols of Gods and Goddesses enshrined in the temples.

Though the Arabic word used in the Qur'ān for idols is *ṣanam*, we find our historians using the word *but* which they had borrowed form the Persians. The Persian word was a corruption of the Sanskrit word "*Buddha*", with which the Persians had been famillar for a long time because there were many Buddhist temples in Seistan, Khurasan and Transoxiana. The word "*budd*" has actually been used in some of the histories when referring to idols which were burnt or which the infidels were prevented from worshipping. Small wonder that the temples which enshrined statues of the Buddha became special targets for the Islamic iconoclasts. We shall deal with this subject in greater detail at a later stage in this series; for now, it is sufficient to say that the death-blow to Buddhism, a religion centred round temples and monasteries and monks, was delivered by the armies of Islam and not by the much-maligned "Brahmanical reaction" as our Marxist "historians" are never tired of telling the world.

There was, however, one name which intrigued the iconoclasts for a long time, till the matter was cleared by some scholars of Islam in consultation with the Brahmans. It seems that the Arabs were familiar with the word "*Somanātha*" (which they pronounced as "Somnāt") even in the pre-Islamic period. Arab merchants who visited or lived in Gujarat must have told their countrymen about this faboulous Śiva temple. It is also possible that Somnath was a place of pilgrimage for the Arabs. The pre-Islamic Arabs were "idolaters" like the Hindus and could not but have felt reverence for "Somnāt". Something of this reverence seems to have survived even after Islam brought about a radical transformation in their religious values. We find reflection of it in the story that *Manāt*, a Goddess of the pagan Arabs, had escaped when the Prophet tried to get her, and taken refuge in the temple of "Somnāt"; the word "Somnāt" was split into "So" and "manāt" in order to support the story. We find references to this story in several histories. Once in a while another Arab Goddess, Lāt, was also suspected to be hiding at Somnath.

In any case, the Qur'ān had proclaimed that the idols were "deaf and dumb", could "neither help nor harm", and "did not know it when they were broken". Subsequent theologians extended the meaning of "broken" and explained that the idols did not know when they were robbed of their adornments or defiled or mutilated; their only function was to "deceive" those who had not been blessed by the "message of monotheism". So an iconoclast cut off the hands of a Hindu idol in Seistan and plucked out its eyes in order to demonstrate the "divine truth". Muhammad bin Qāsim took off the necklace of the idol at Multan and replaced it with a piece of cow's flesh. The idol did not "protest", nor did it do anything else in order to prove that it had any "power for good or evil". Other veterans of Islam tried other methods to show to the "infidels" that their "gods" were "helpless" and they themselves "misguided".

Again, we can depend upon the poetic powers of Amīr Khusrū. He quoted the Qur'ān before describing the iconoclasm at Somnath. "It seemed," he worte, "as if the tongue of the Imperial sword explained the meaning of the text: 'So he (Abraham) broke them (the idols) into pieces except the chief of them, that haply they may return to it.' Such a pagan country, the Mecca of the infidels, now became the Medina of Islam." The earliest historians relate that while Mahmūd broke the other idols, he carried the main "idol" unbroken to Ghazni. So the "big brother" did not know what had happened to the "little ones", as in the story of Abraham in the Qur'ān.[1] Khusrū's highest poetic performance, however, came when he described the scene at Chidambaram. "The stone idol called Ling Mahadeo," he sang, "which had been a long time established at that place and on which the women of the infidels rubbed their vaginas for (sexual) satisfaction, these upto this time the kick of the horse of Islam had not attempted to break...The Musalmans destroyed all the *lings* and Deo Narain fell down, and the other gods who had fixed their seats there raised their feet, and jumped so high, that at one leap they reached the fort of Lanka, and in that affright the *lings* themselves would have fled had they any legs to stand on."

To resume the story, some of the idols were made of precious metals and/or adorned with costly jewels; they had to be handled with care so that the faithful were not deprived of the booty promised by Allāh to those who removed his rivals out of the way. Such images were first divested of their jewellery, then they were broken or burnt, and finally melted down; the bullion and the jewels were forwarded to the caliph or the king, whoever happened to be the patron of the "holy expedition". Occasionally, the idols were simply collected and sent to the capital city and it was the despot there who decided what to do with them. They certainly provided "great fun" to the "chosen people" before being disposed off in whatever manner was found appropriate, depending upon the type of the idols. Those made of precious metals ended in the royal treasury. Those made of inferior metals were turned

[1]Qu'rān, 21.51-70.

into various instruments or vessels or used for decorative purposes such as door handles; later on, the bigger ones were recast to make cannon. Idols made of wood and stone etc., were broken and scattered on the doorsteps of mosques, particularly the Jāmi‘ Masjids, so that people on their way to prayers could trample or cleanse their soiled feet upon them, before entering the "sacred precincts".

Several instances are cited when the Hindus tried to ransom their idols, sometimes by expressing willingness to pay their weight in gold. All such offers were "rejected with contempt" because the hero concerned wanted to earn "merit in the eyes of Allāh" rather than "mere mammon". Those who want to explain away the destruction of Hindu temples in terms of economic motives, are called upon to explain these instances.

Mahmūd of Ghazni broke many idols with his own hand, including that of "Somnāt". He sent the pieces to Mecca, Medina and Baghdad, besides keeping some in his own capital at Ghazni. It was not for nothing that his coins struck at Lahore described him as "*butshikan*", idol-breaker. Subsequent sultāns followed his example. Unfortunately for them, the "accursed Mangol", Changiz Khān, overran a large part of Islamdom and blocked the way to the "holy cities" in the first quarter of the thirteenth century, just at the time when a vast field for breaking idols and collecting their pieces was opening before the heroes of Islam in Hind. In AD 1258, his grandson, Halākū, beat their own idol, the caliph, into pulp and got the "holy" city of Baghdad ploughed over. So the pieces had perforce to lie before mosques in lesser places—Lahore, Delhi, Lakhnauti, Daulatabad, Gulbarga, Madura, Burhanpur, Bidar, Mandu, Ahmadabad, Jaunpur, Agra, Ahmadnagar, Bijapur, Golkonda, Hyderabad, Aurangabad. They will be brought in by cart-loads in the time of Aurangzeb. One of our historians tells us that ‘Alī I ‘Ādil Shāh of Bijapur broke four to five thousand idols with his own hands while campaigning in Karnataka.

Meanwhile, other methods of telling the "truth" about the idols had been devised by the more imaginative among the swordsmen of Islam. Fīrūz Shāh Tughlaq had the idol at Purī perforated and dragged along the road to Delhi. The pieces of the idol at Kangra were given to the butchers for being used as weights while selling meat. The copper umberlla of the same idol he got recast into pots for heating water with which the faithful washed their "hands, feet and faces", before saying their prayers. Mahmūd Khaljī of Malwa had the idol at Kumbhalgadh reduced to lime which was put in *pans* (betel-leaves) and the Hindus were forced to "eat their god". He had taken literally a latter-day story of what Mahmūd of Ghazni had done to the idol of "Somnāt" when the Brahmans arrived in his capital to "ransom their God".

The Brahmans who were custodians of the idols and idol-houses, and "teachers of the infidels", also received their share of attention from the soldiers of Allāh. Our citations contain only stray references to the Brahmans because they have been compiled primarily with reference to the destruction of temples. Even so, they provide the broad contours of another chapter in the history of medieval India, a chapter which has yet to be brought out in full. The Brahmans are referred to as magicians by some Islamic invaders and massacred straight away. Elsewhere, the Hindus who are not totally defeated and want to surrender on some terms, are made to sign a treaty saying that the Brahmans will be expelled from the temples. The holy cities of the Hindus were "the nests of the Brahmans" who had to be slaughtered before or after the destruction of temples, so that these places were "cleansed" completely of "*kufr*" and made fit as "abodes of Islam".

Amīr Khusrū describes with great glee how the heads of Brahmans "danced from their necks and fell to the ground at their feet", along with those of the other "infidels" whom Malik Kāfūr had slaughtered during the sack of the temples at Chidambaram. Fīrūz Shāh Tughlaq got bags full of cow's flesh tied round the necks of Brahmans and had them paraded through his army camp at Kangra. Muhmūd Shāh II Bahmanī bestowed on himself the honour of being a *ghāzī*, simply because he had killed in cold blood the helpless Brāhmaṇa priests of the local temple after Hindu warriors had died fighting in defence of the fort at Kondapalli. The present-day progressives, leftists and *dalits* whose main plank is anti-Brahminism have no reason to feel innovative about their ideology. Anti-Brahminism in India is as old as the advent of Islam. Our present-day Brahmin-baiters are no more than ideological de-scendants of the Islamic invaders. Hindus will do well to remember Mahatma Gandhi's deep reflection—"if Brahmanism does not revive, Hinduism must perish."

The next step which the heroes of Islam took after a place had been "purged by the sword form the filth of impurity and the thorn of god-plurality" and the "foundations of infidelity destroyed", was to build mosques and *madrasas* etc., on the same sites where the temples stood, most often with the materials of those very temples. The operation was generally preceded by a pious ritual in which the victors prostrated themselves and praised Allāh "for the honour He bestows on Islām and the Musalmāns". Cows were slaughtered on the temple sites in order to render them unclean for the Hindus for all time to come; it had been noticed that the Hindus demolished the mosques and rebuilt their temples on the same sites whenever they recaptured a place. Now the mosques and *madrasas* could spread the "light of Islam" without interruption. Finally, the priests of Islam took over—the *khatībs*, the *mu'zzins*, the *muhtahsibs* and the *qāzīs*. The "uproar of the heathens gave way to shouts of *Allahū Akbar*" and the "strongholds of heathenism were made into abodes of Islām". Meanwhile, the endowments enjoyed by the temples had been transferred to the upcoming Islamic establishments, so that whatever temple priests had survived the slaughter had to starve while the Muslim clerics prospered.

The most significant feature of our histories, however, is the religious zeal felt or exhibited by the swordsmen of Islam before and after the "infidels" who resisted "were sent to hell", the Brahmans massacred or molested or expelled, idols desecrated, temples demolished, and mosques raised in their stead. The prophet of Islam appears in a dream and bids a sultān to start on the "holy expedition", leaving no doubt that the "victory of religion" was assured. Amīr Khusrū was very eloquent about the transformation that was taking place. When the hordes of Alāu'd-Dīn Khaljī sacked the temple of Somnath, he exulted, "The sword of Islām purified the land as the Sun purifies the earth." His enthusiasm broke all bounds when the same hordes swept over South India: "The tongue of the sword of the Khalifa of the time, which is the tongue of the flame of Islām, has imparted light to the entire darkness of Hindustān by the illumination of its guidance...and several capitals of the gods of the Hindus in which Satanism had prevailed since the time of Jinns, have been demolished. All these impurities of infidelity have been cleansed by the Sultān's destruction of idol-temples, beginning with his first expedition to Deogīr, so that the flames of the light of the law illumine all these unholy countries... God be praised !" One wonders whether the poet of Islam is being honoured or slandered when he is presented in our own times as the pioneer of Secularism. Or, perhaps, Secularism in India has a meaning deeper than that we find in the dictionaries or dissertations on political science. We may not be much mistaken if, seeing its studied exercise in blackening everything Hindu and whitewashing everything Islamic, we suspect that this Secularism is nothing more than the good old doctrine of Islam in disguise.

If our citations prove anything and prove it beyond a shadow of doubt, it is this that in doing what they did to Hindu temples the heroes of Islam were inspired by their religion and religion alone. They cannot be blamed if the plunder which occasionally preceded the destruction of temples was viewed by them as a well-deserved reward for doing service to Allah and his Last Prophet; they knew what the Qur'ān and the Sunnah had prescribed in very clear language and, therefore, had a clean conscience. It is a different matter altogether that their religion provided, more often than not, a cover, or an a *posteriori* justification as Professor Mohammed Habib would like to put it, for some of the basest motives in human nature and attracted to its standards some of the worst hoodlums and gangsters and blood-thristy bandits that the world has known. The fact that these despicable characters have been made to masquerade as *Mujāhids* and *Ghāzīs* and *Shahīds* and Sultāns and Sufis by Muslim historians can hoodwink no one except those who either do not know the facts or have the same moral standards as those of Islam.

Our Marxist professors and other pandits of Secularism are very much mistaken when they discover or invent economic and/or political motives for explaining away the crimes committed by Islam. Either they have remained totally ignorant of what the Theology of Islam prescribes vis-a-vis the unbelievers, their women and children, their properties, their homelands, their religious teachers, and their places of worship; or their deep-seated animus against everything Hindu has pushed them into the camp of those who are out to destroy everything for which this country has been held in high esteem down the ages. We shall, give them the benefit of doubt and assume that their ignorance of the Theology of Islam rather than their anti-Hindu animus is the culprit. We proceed to present that Theology in the chapter that follows.

SECTION IV

ISLAMIC THEOLOGY OF ICONOCLASM

CHAPTER NINE

THEOLOGY OF MONOTHEISM

The destruction of Hindu temples at the hands of Islamized invaders continued for more than eleven hundred years, from the middle of the seventh century to the end of the eighteenth.[1] It took place all over the cradle of Hindu culture, from Sinkiang in the North to Tamil Nadu in the South, and from Seistan in the West to Assam in the East.[2]

All along, the iconoclasts remained convinced that they were putting into practice the highest tenets of their religion. They also saw to it that a record was kept of what they prized as a pious performance. The language of the record speaks for itself. It leaves no doubt that they took immense pride in doing what they did.

It is inconceivable that a constant and consistent behaviour pattern, witnessed for a long time and over a vast area, can be explained except in terms of a settled system of belief which leaves no scope for second thoughts. Looking at the very large number of temples, big and small, destroyed or desecrated or converted into Muslim monuments, economic or political explanations can be only a futile, if not fraudulent, exercise. The explanations are not even plausible.

In fact, it is not at all difficult to locate the system of belief which inspired the behaviour pattern. We have only to turn to the scriptures of Islam—the Qur'ān and the Sunnah of the Prophet—and we run straight into what we are looking for. The principles and the pious precedents which were practised and followed by the subsequent swordsmen of Islam are, all of them, there.

The scriptures of Islam do not merely record what happened in the past; they also prescribe that what is recorded should be imitated by the faithful in the future, till the end of time. That is why the swordsmen of Islam who functioned in times much later than that of the Qur'ān and the Sunnah, did what they did. It is in the very nature of scriptures, as we shall see, that they make permanent what can otherwise be dated and dismissed as temporary aberrations.

Those scriptures are still being taught in hundreds of *maktabs* and *madrasas* spread over the length and breath of India, Pakistan and

[1]We are leaving for the time being the destruction that took place in Muslim princely states under British rule as also that which has continued since 1947 in Pakistan, Bangladesh and Kashmir.

[2]We are leaving for the time being the destruction which took place and is taking place in Indonesia and Malaysia.

Bangladesh. Missionaries of Islam that are turned out by these institutions, year after year, are never told by their teachers that the prescriptions regarding other people's places of worship stand abrogated or are out of date. At the same time, the swordsmen who destroyed innumerable temples and monasteries all over the vast cradle of Hindu culture, retain their halos as the heroes of Islam. That alone can explain why Hindu temples become the first targets of attack whenever Muslim mobs are incited against India by the mullas in Pakistan, Bangladesh and Kashmir.

It is, therefore, worthwhile to clarify what the word "scripture" stands for, before we take up the scriptues of Islam. The language of Christianity and Islam in the modern media has confused the language of religion, all along the line. Even scholars do not seem to know or care to clarify that scriptures as such are specific to the prophetic or revealed religions such as Judaism, Christianity and Islam, and that they remain unknown to the pagan[3] spiritual traditions such as that of the Hindus, the Chinese, the ancient Iranians, and the pre-Christian Greeks, Romans, Germans, Slavs, Scandinavians, Celts, etc.

The confusion has been further confounded by what passes for Secularism in this country. Most of our scribes in the mass media are either equally ignorant of all religions or equally indifferent to them. But they insist, with considerable vehemence, that all religions say the same things. Politicians in power are much worse. As they preside over the birthday functions or festivals related to Śrī Rāma, Śrī Krishṇa, Bhagavān Mahāvīra, Bhagavān Buddha and Guru Nānak on the one hand, and Jesus Christ and Prophet Muhammad on the other, they harangue the audience to follow the teachings in each case. It never occurs to them that Christianity and Islam have nothing in common with the Hindu spiritual traditions and that the followers of the former have tried and are trying their utmost to wipe out the latter.[4]

Meaning of Scripture

Etymologically, the word "scripture" is derived from the Latin "*scribere*", to write. In the lexicons of the revealed religions, however, the word does not refer to writing down of human speech or verbalizing

---

[3]The *Chambers 20th Century Dictionary* defines a pagan as "a heathen, one who is not a Christian, Jew, or Muslim..."

[4]The subject has been discussed in detail by Dr. Harsh Narain in his study, *Myths of Composite Culture and Equality of Religions*, published by Voice of India, New Delhi, 1991.

of human thought or recording of terrestrial events. Instead, it stands for the "Word of God" written in "the Book".

The word of God, in its turn, does not come to any and every one who seeks it, howsoever devoutly. Instead, it is "revealed" to some highly privileged persons known as "prophets". Everyone else has to learn it second-hand, and accept it as authentic even when it runs counter to one's experience, or reason, or moral sense, or all of them taken together. No one else can have direct knowledge of it or aspire to enter into the consciousness to which it was revealed, as in the case of pagan spiritual traditions which entitle every seeker to attain the consciousness of their greatest saints and sages, and know God directly and first-hand. Belief in the word of God as spoken by *the* Prophet and as written in *the* Book is, therefore, all that is needed for qualifying as one of the faithful. At the same time, mental belief and not moral behaviour is the criterion for judging a person's character.

Nor do the prophets take birth among any or every people. Etymylogically the word "prophet" is derived from the Greek "*phanai*", to speak, which is a cognate of the Sanskrit "*bhaṇa*". In the lexicons of the revealed religions, however, the prophet is no ordinary spokesman. Instead, he is the "spokesman of deity."[5] And he is "sent" only to the "Choosen People" with whom God intends to enter into a "Covenant".

So far there have been only three chosen people—the Jews, the Christians, and the Muslims. According to the covenants which God has entered into with them, each of them has been promised world-dominion and untold amounts of unearned wealth in exchange for making God known to all those who worship "other gods" and thus deny God's "Unity" and "Unique Majesty".

Rise of Theology

In due course, as the word of God is studied, systematized and interpreted, it gives birth to a supplementary discipline named Theology. Etymologically, the word "theology" is a compound of two Greeks words—"theos"[6] meaning "god", and "logos" meaning "word." But curiously enough, the ancient Greeks from whose language the compound has been constructed were unaware of the very notion of word of God. Theology was formulated and used for the first time by the Founding Fathers of the Christian Church for presenting their peculiar

[5]See the *Chambers 20th Century Dictionary* for the Meaning of Prophet.
[6]It is a cognate of the Sanskrit "*deva*".

creed to pagans in the Roman Empire. It had nothing whatsoever to do with any Greek religion or philosophy, of which there were quite a few before they were destroyed or subverted by Christianity. Islamic scholarship which flourished in the wake of the Prophet, fashioned another theology, more or less on the same pattern, a few hundred years later.

Theology is a large and complex subject. What concerns us here is some specific features which characterise it. One of those features is that the life-style of the Prophet and his companions/apostles is proclaimed as the "divine pattern of human conduct" which should be copied by everyone, everywhere, in order to qualify for salvation or paradise. According to another, the doings of the chosen people as they wage wars, conquer countries and convert or kill other people, are to be seen as the unfoldment of a "divine plan in human history".

What is most significant, however, is that theology notices and notifies three neat and sharp divisions. Firstly, it divides human history into two periods—an "age of ignorance" preceding the appearance of *the* Prophet, and an "age of illumination" following that event. Secondly, it bifurcates the human family into two factions—the "believers" who accept *the* Prophet as the one and only "mediator" between God and human beings, and the "unbelievers" who have either not heard of *the* Prophet at all or find him unacceptable for whatever reason. Thirdly, it breaks up the inhabited world into two camps—the lands ruled by the believers, and the lands where the unbelievers live.

Proceeding further, theology pronounces a permanent war, hailed as "holy", between the three sets of divisions. Religions and cultures which preceded the age of ignorance have to go and yield place to the religion and culture of the age of illumination. Next, the believers must strive, ceaselessly and by every means at their disposal, to covert the unbelievers to the new creed. Finally, the lands of the believers must be made into launching pads for missions as well as military expeditions to be sent to the lands of the unbelievers, so that the latter are conquerred and turned into lands of the believers.

Naturally, the places where the unbelievers worship and the institutions which sustain that worship, become the first and foremost targets of holy wars. The idols[7] of the unbelievers' Gods are at least mutilated, if they cannot be smashed to pieces. The temples where those Gods are worshipped are at least desecrated, if they cannot be destroyed. The schools and monasteries where the unbelievers learn their religion are

[7]The word "idol" is derived from the Greek "*idein*" to see, which is a cognate of the Sanskrit "*vid*", to perceive.

at least plunderd, if they cannot be razed to the ground. The saints, sages and scholars who guide the unbelievers are at least humiliated, driven out and deprived of livelihood, if they cannot be killed outright. The literature which enshrines the unbelievers' religion and culture is scattered to the winds, or burnt on the spot, or used as fuel in the homes of the believers. And so on, the war on the religion and culture of the unbelievers is total and unrelenting.

These operations are expected to help the unbelievers lose faith in their own Gods and acqire an awe for the God of the conqueror. The God of the conqueror stands glorified when new places of worship are raised on the sites of the old, preferably with the debris of those that have been deliberately demolished. And that God is fully vindicated when the believers tread under foot the idols of the unbelievers' Gods or their pieces, as they walk towards the new places of worship for offering prayers.

Finally, theology enjoins that the holy wars and all that they mean should be recorded meticulously and in lustrous language. These records testify to the unfoldment of the divine plan in human history in the past, and inspire future generations of believers to unfold it further. We have three extensive versions of this unfoldment or the triumph of the "true faith" over "false belief"—the Judaic, the Christian, and the Islamic. All of them glorify the "great heroes" who waged holy wars and heaped defeats and humiliations on the "infidels". The "rich rewards" which God bestowed on the believers for fulfilling their part of the covenant are also described at length. And succeeding generations of believers have, no doubt, felt inspired to follow in the footsteps of their "illustrious forefathers".

Role of Theology

Apart from providing the right perceptions, inspiring pious performances, and establishing illustrious precedents, theology serves another and, psychologically, a very useful purpose. It prepares the believers for feeling the "glow of faith" as they read or listen to the unfoldment of the divine plan in human history. The accounts are spiritually satisfying—how every trace of the religion and culture of the age of ignorance was wiped out, to start with, in the Prophet's own land of birth; how one land after another was invaded and laid waste without any provocation on the part of the victims of aggression; how innocent and defenceless people were massacred in cold blood and with a clean conscience; how large numbers of noncombatant men, women and children were captured and sold into slavery and concubinage; how native populations were reduced to the status of non-citizens, drawing water and hewing wood for the conqueror, and groaning under the weight of discriminatory levies and back-breaking disabilities; how great creations of graphic arts were mutilated or broken to pieces or trampled under foot; how edifices of exquisite beauty, embodying skills accumulated over ages, were pulled down and levelled with the ground; how whole libraries containing priceless works of science and literature, were burnt down; how saints and sages and scholars who had given no offence and meant no harm, were humiliated or manhandled or killed; how vast properties, moveable and immoveable, were misappropriated. And so on, the record is invariably crowded with the darkest crimes and fiendish cruelty. Only the believers find it fulfilling. For persons with normal moral sensibilities, it is a nightmare. The only point which goes in its favour is that it provides the best commentary on the doctrines of the creed concerned.

Looking at the character of the God of revealed religions, the quality of his words, the life-styles of his prophets, and the course of his divine plans in human history, one wonders whether the revealed religions do not reveal an Orwellian world abounding in marvels of doublethink and double-speak. Here one meets the Devil masquerading as God, and gangsters strutting around as prophets. Here one discovers that the scripture does not inspire spiritual seeking or moral discipline but, on the contrary, encourages the basest in human nature to run riot without any restraint. All in all, Theology stands out as another name for Demonology, and the revealed religions reveal themselves as no more than totalitarian ideologies of imperialism, of enslavement and genocide. They turn out to be older versions of what we have known as Communism and Nazism in our own times. A Secularism which puts them on par with the spiritual traditions of Hinduism is not only foolish but also mischievous. It misses the very meaning of religion, and shelters gangsterism.

Theology of Islam

Islam uses the Arabic language instead of Hebrew or Greek, but says the same things as the older revealed religions. Its only point of departure is that it abrogates the earlier revelations, and subordinates the earlier prophets to the "latest and the last".

Islam has hijacked Allāh from the pantheon of the pre-Islamic Arabs and turned him into a jealous God who tolerates no "other gods".

Allāh of Islam is no more than a reincarntion of Jehovah, the Judaic and the Christian God in the Bible.

The prophet of Islam, Muhammad, moulds himself, consciously and progressively, in the image of Moses. In fact, his very name, *Nabī,* has been taken from the Hebrew Iexicon.

Allāh now speaks only through the mouth of Muhammad. That is the Qur'ān, or the Book *(Kitāb).* Here also the word of God is borrowed, by and large, from the Bible. The only difference is that the Qur'ān lacks the literary merit and narrative coherence of the earlier scripture. It is a loose bundle of vehement utterances, without any chronological or thematic order, and has to be understood with the help of laborious, very often speculative, commentaries.

Again, Allāh acts in the life-style of Muhammad. That is the Sunnah of the Prophet. This divine pattern of human conduct knows all the answers. No pious Muslim has to use his own mental faculties or devise his own individual course of action. It is all laid down for him, from birth to death, and even beyond. As the theologians of Islam say, Muslims should not use their *aql* (reason); all they need is *naql* (imitation of the Prophet).

The covenant, *Miṣāq,* into which Allāh enters with the newly chosen people, the *Ummatu Muhammadī,* commands them to worship him alone and convert or kill or enslave those who worship other gods. Allāh's earlier covenants with the Jews or the *Ummatu Ibrāhīmī* and the Christians or the *Ummatu Īsā,* stand cancelled. Now onwards, Muslims alone are entitled to rule over the world and appropriate its wealth. There is a slight "improvement" also in the new covenant. Plunder of the infidels' properties, particularly their women and children, was not permitted to the earlier chosen people, while it has been prescribed as obligatory for the *Ummatu Muhammadī.*

The doings of the *Ummatu Muhammadī* in Arabia and many other lands manifest the divine plan in human history. The annals of Islam, the *Twārīkh,* which are an integral part of its theology, have been penned by some of its most pious scholars.

The theology of Islam, *Kalām,* deals with the same old divisions of human history, the human family, and the inhabited world. The period before Muhammad started receiving revelations and proclaimed his prophethood is denounced as *Jāhilīya,* the age of ignorance; the period succeeding that event is the age of *Ilm,* enlightenment. Those who recite the *Kalima* or confession of faith—*Lā Ilāha Illa'llāhū, Mahammadūn Rasūl'llāh* (there is no god but Allāh and Muhammad is *the*

Prophet)[8]—are *Mu'mins,* the believers; those who do not, are *Kāfirs*, the unbelievers. The lands ruled by the *Mu'mins* are *Dār al-Islām*, abodes of peace, while those where the *Kāfirs* live are *Dār al-Harb*, abodes of war, where the *Mu'mins* should ply their swords. It sounds logical that in popular Muslim parlance a *Kāfir* is often called a *Harbī*, that is, one who deserves treatment of the sword.

Finally, Islam enjoins a permanent war, *Jihād,* by the *Mu'mins* and against the *Kāfirs.* We need not give the details which we have already presented elsewhere, in principle as well as practice.[9] Suffice it to say that it is an extremely bloody affair, entailing continued wars of conquest, massacres, mass conversions by force, widespread plunder, enslavement of prisoner taken in war, collection of booty including non-combatant men and women and children, subjugation of native populations, and the rest. What concerns us here is that *Jihād* is centred round iconoclasm. In fact, the need for *Jihād* arises only because the *Kāfirs* worship their own Gods instead of Muhammad's Allāh. *Jihād,* therefore, remains incomplete till all places where those Gods are worshipped get levelled with the ground, and all saints and priests who spread and sustain *Kufr* are converted or killed.

Confining ourselves to India, "The Mohammedan conquest of India is probably the bloodiest story in history," according to Will Durant, the famous student of civilizations. He finds it "a discouraging tale, for its evident moral is that civilization is a precious thing whose delicate complex of order and liberty, culture and peace may at any time be overthrown by barbarians..."[10] But the pious Muslims read or listen to this story with immense satisfaction. They go into raptures as their heroes invade Sind and Hind, massacre the accursed *Kāfirs* without remorse, capture and sell into slavery large numbers of Hindu men and women and children, kill or heap humiliations on Hindu saints and scholars, desecrate or destroy idols of Hindu Gods and Goddesses, pull down Hindu temples or convert them into *masjids* and *madrasas,* reduce the Hindus to non-citizens in their own homeland, and misappropriate all properties, moveable and immoveable. And they get furious when they find the Hindus failing to admire Muhammad bin Qāsim, Mahmūd of Ghazni, Muhammad Ghūrī, Shamsu'd-Dīn Iltutmish,

[8]The first part of the *Kalima* is often translated as "there is no god but God," which is not only misconceived but positively mischievous. Allāh of the Qur'ān never claims to be the God of mankind; he prides in being the God of Muslims alone.

[9]*The Calcutta Quran Petition By Chandmal Chopra,* with two prefaces by Sita Ram Goel, second the enlarged edition, New Delhi, 1987, pp. 35–37.

[10]Will Durant, *The Story of Civilization,* Vol. I, *Our Oriental Heritage,* New York, 1972, p. 459.

Ghiyāsu'd-Dīn Balban, 'Alāu'd-Dīn Khaljī, Muhammad and Fīrūz Shāh Tughalaq, Sikandar Lodī, Bābur, Aurangzeb, and Ahmad Shāh Abdālī, to cite only the most notable among Muslim heroes in the history of India. The theology of Islam has thus performed to perfection the function it is intended to perform, even though the forefathers of an overwhelming majority of Muslims in India were victims of this theology.

In our specific context, namely, the destruction of Hindu temples, it should be more than sufficient if we merely cite what the Qur'ān says, in verse after verse and chapter after chapter, vis-a-vis the *mushriks* (polytheists) and the *aṣnām* (idols) they worship. Allāh of Islam leaves no one in doubt that he sanctions the destruction of "false gods" and the places where they receive homage. So is the case with the Sunnah of the Prophet. We have only to list the instances of iconoclasm which Muhammad undertook himself or ordered in his own lifetime, and we have more than suffcient pious precedents which the faithful are expected to follow. Anyone who says that the Qur'ān and the Sunnah do not enjoin the destruction of other people's places of worship has either not read the documents, or has failed to grasp the message, or is practising deliberate deception. No amount of apologetics can cover up or explain away the principle and the practice.

A mere narration of principle and practice, however, is likely to leave a mistaken impression. People who are not familiar with the rise and spread of Islam have been led away by the Big Lie that the people of Arabia rallied round a prophet and did, willingly and voluntarily, whatever he asked them to do, because they knew no better. This lie has succeeded to a great extent not only in the lands which are now occupied by the believers but also in India which has battled with Islam for more than thirteen hundred years. But nothing can be farther from the truth as told in the orthodox biographies of the Prophet. The people of Arabia resisted Muhammad and his message, and fought in defence of their ancient religion and culture, till they were forced to surrender in the face of a formidable military machine forged by him at Medina. The machine was financed by plunder obtained through widespread raids, and manned by desperados recruited from all over Arabia. Neither the Qur'ān nor the Sunnah of the Prophet can be understood or evaluated properly unless it is placed in its historical context, namely, the pre-Islamic Arab society and culture which had functioned for a long time to the satisfaction of the people concerned, till Muhammad appeared on the scene.

CHAPTER TEN

THE PRE-ISLAMIC ARABS

Muslim theologians and historians present a pretty dark picture of pre-Islamic Arabia. Its people, we are told, were unrepentant pagans and polytheists unaware of the Unity of God and the succession of his Prophets. They believed that Allāh, the one and only True God, stood in need of partners who could mediate between him and his creatures. Worse still, they gave daughters to Allāh while they preferred sons for themselves. They worshipped stones (*authān*) and statues (*aṣnām*) and offered sacrifices to satans. They had had no Prophet (*Rasūl*) and possessed no scripture (*Kitāb*) of their own. Consequently, they were ignorant of the Last Day (*Qiyāmat*), as also of Heaven (*Jannat*) and Hell (*Jahannam*). They revelled in blood feuds, and buried alive their female infants. Sons married their step-mothers, and the same man two or more uterine sisters. And so on, till the conviction grows on the readers or listeners that the pre-Islamic Arabs were despicable barbarians.

Christian theologians and historians follow suit. They do not endorse Muhammad as a prophet; in fact, they call him an impostor. All the same, they prefer him to the pagans and polytheists whom he fought and subdued. They do not concede that Muhammad's message was spiritually sound or morally adequate. Yet they hail his teachings as a marked improvement on the mode of worship and morals which prevailed earlier. Thus they stand solidly, though negatively, united with their Muslim counterparts in denouncing the state of affairs in pre-Islamic Arabia.

And there is no dearth of Hindu scholars, even Hindu saints, who join the chorus. Even those Hindus who are by no means enamoured of Islam and distrust or despise it as a religion, regard it none-the-less an immense improvement over what went in Arabia before its advent. They say that Islam united the "Arab rabble" into a "nation", and gave them at least the "rudiments of culture". It never occurs to these Hindus that Muslim scholars who denounce pre-Islamic Arabia view pre-Islamic India also as an "area of darkness" to which Islam brought "illumination" for the first time. Though Hindus have been victims of Islamic aggression for several centuries, few of them feel sympathy for victims of the same aggression elsewhere.

The pre-Islamic Arabs seem to have no case simply because no one and almost nothing has survived to tell their side of the story. Unlike the Hindus who have survived the onslaught of Islam and can compare what they had with what was brought in by Islam, the pre-Islamic Arabs have passed into what is more or less a total oblivion. The Prophet of Islam and his rightly-guided Caliphs saw to it that no trace was left of the pre-Islamic religion and culture of Arabia, not even in the consciousness of the converts. Franz Babinger writes vis-a-vis the pre-Islamic Sabaean civilization of Arabia: "The new creed had the greatest interest in obliterating all recollection of the pagan period, not only in stone monuments which still survived the natural weathering—these were destroyed to provide material for new buildings, or burned for lime or sometimes out of sheer vandalism—but also in literature, and even in consigning the ancient language to oblivion."[1] Whatever could not be wiped out was converted so completely as to look like a contribution of Islam. The Ka'ba and the Hajj ceremonies provide excellent examples. So does the Arabic language which, although it retains its old sounds and syntax, has been made to convey meanings and concepts which were foreign to it in its pristine state.

The greatest blow which pre-Islamic Arabia has suffered is the perversion of its history. An overwhelming majority of the Arabs had never heard of Abraham before Muhammad started mentioning him; those few who had, had no reason to like him in view of the contempt which his people, the Jews settled in Arabia, had continued to pour on the Arabs. Moreover, it was not long before the birth of Muhammad that the king of Yemen who had converted to the creed of Abraham had massacred thousands of Christianised Arabs. Therefore, the Arabs who were extremely tolerant in matters of belief could not but have looked askance at the very name of Abraham.[2] Yet the Prophet proclaimed that the Arabs were the progeny of Abraham through his elder son, Ismael ! He went much farther. He "discovered" that the foremost Arab temple, the Ka'ba at Mecca, had been built by Adam, renovated by his son, Seth, and rebuilt by Abraham! He accused the Arabs of having usurped, for polytheistic worship, a place which was orginally meant to be a mosque ! The theologians and historians who followed, abolished the real forefathers of the Arabs altogether and linked them to lineage of the Jews. Small wonder that every comprehensive history of Arabia written by pious Muslim chroniclers starts with Adam and Eve, and

---

[1]*First Encyclopaedia of Islam* 1913–1936, Leiden, 1987, Vol. VII, p. 15.

[2]See D.S. Margoliouth, *Mohammed and the Rise of Islam,* London, 1905, New Delhi Reprint, 1985, p. 73, "To the Meccans," he says, "he [Abraham] was not even a name."

fills its spaces with the progeny of Abraham.[3]

This Islamic version of Arab history would have continued to prevail if modern scholarship had not rescued the true version by means of painstaking research. "Our knowledge of the history," writes F. Hommel, "we owe partly to inscriptions found in the country, partly in contemporary literatures and monuments of other nations (Babylonians and Assyrians, Egyptians, Hebrews, Greeks and Romans) and partly also (for the centuries immediately preceding Muhammad) to early Islamic tradition... As early as the 3rd millennium BC the old Babylonian inscriptions mention a king Manium (also in the fuller form Mannudannu) or Magan of East Arabia; there is much to be said for the view that Magan was only a Sumerian rendering of an Arabic Ma'ān and that from this centre was founded (at a date unknown to us) the South Arabian kingdom of Ma'ān (later vocalisation Ma'īn) or the Minaean state which perhaps in the beginning embraced the whole of South Arabia... In addition a district named Melukh is mentioned as lying further off, probably covering Central and North West Arabia from which as well as from Magan the Sumerians e.g. Gudea of Sirgulla (about 2350 BC) imported a large quantity of products (wood, stone and metals) for their temples..."[4]

The same sources tell us about the Sabaeans who flourished in Arabia from 800 BC onwards, till they were "swept away by the wave of Muhammadan conquest." They practised "an ancient natural religion" in which "the sun, the moon and the planets" figured prominently. They "believed in the migration of the soul and in great world periods constantly renewed in an everlasting revolution," which remind us of the Hindu theories of rebirth and the yugas. They built "massive temples" and "handsome gold and silver statues of their chief gods."[5] The Greeks and the Romans knew "Saba and three other South Arabian kingdoms...as the areas which produce frankincense, myrrh, cassia and cinnamon"[6] and praised them "as brave soldiers, industrious tillers of the soil and traders and skilful sailors" who "sent out colonies or at least trading settlements into foreign lands, especially India."[7] Modern

---

[3]Converts to Islam in every other land follow the pattern. They disown their real forefathers and link themselves to this or that tribe of Jews or Arabs. Muslims of Afghanistan and Kashmir for instance regard themselves as descended from some lost tribes of Israel. Muslims of Bangladesh have produced learned treatises tracing their to Islamized invaders. But for the labours of Firdawsī, the Muslims of Iran would not have known that their infidel forefathers were great and glorious.

[4]*First Encyclopaedia of Islam*, op. cit., Vol. I, p. 377.

[5]*The Encyclopaedia Americana*, New York, 1952, Vol. XXIV, p. 77.

[6]*First Encyclopaedia of Islam*, op. cit., Vol. VII, p. 5.

[7]Ibid., p. 7.

archaeology has exposed "sculptures and remains of colonnades, palaces, temples, city walls, towers, public works, especially water-works etc., which confirm the brilliant picture of Sabaean culture..."[8]

Similar is the story of the Nabataeans who arose in North Arabia or Arabia Petraea about the same time as the Sabaeans in Arabia Flex or South Arabia, and extended their sway upto the frontiers of Hijaz. They were "never completely subjected either by the Assyrians, or the Medes, Persians or the Mecedonian kings." It was the Romans who conquered for the first time a part of the Nabataean kingdom in the north in AD 106 and named it *Provincia Arabia*. The Nabataeans too were great traders who "attained...the position of monopolists in Near Asia."[9] In their pantheon, which we know "mainly from tombs and votive inscriptions...the principal God was Dushara (Dhu'l-Sharā), the principal goddess Allāt."[10]

None of the Minaean or Sabaean or Nabataean inscriptions mentions Abraham or Ismael or any term indicative of the Judeo-Christian belief system which Muhammad will impose on the Arabs in the form of Islam. It is only towards the end of the pagan period that a South Arabian inscription dated AD 542–543 mentions for the first time "the power and grace and mercy of the Merciful (*Raḥmānān*) and his Messiah and the Holy Spirit."[11] The inscription was set up by Abraha, the Governor of South Arabia, on behalf of the Christian king of Abyssinia. How Abraha became what he became is an interesting story which explains the repugnance felt by the pagan Arabs for both Judaism and Christianity, as also for the names and terms associated with these creeds.

The Monophysite sect of Christianity had found refuge in Najran, a province of South Arabia, after it was expelled by the official Church from the Byzantine territory in the reign of Justinian I (AD 527–565). Some Arabs of Najran had also become converts to Christianity. Around the same time, Dhū Nūwas, king of Yemen which included Najran, had embraced Judaism. He declared war on the Christians of Najran when he found them unwilling to come into the fold of his own creed. "Dhū Nūwas," writes Ibn Ishāq, "came against them with his armies and invited them to accept Judaism, giving them the choice between that or death: they chose death. So he dug trenches for them;

[8]Ibid., p. 17.
[9]Ibid., Vol. VI, p. 801.
[10]Ibid., p. 802.
[11]Ibid., Vol. I, p. 377.

burnt some in fire, slew some with the sword, and mutilated them until he had killed nearly twenty thousand of them."[12]

The Christians of Najran appealed for help to the Negus, the Christian king of Abyssinia. An Abyssinian army under Aryāt descended on Yemen, defeated and killed Dhū Nūwas, and occupied the land. Under orders from the Negus, a third of the women and children of Yemen were captured, sent to Abyssinia, and sold into slavery.[13] The Arabs who had embraced Judaism were massacred. In due course, Abraha succeeded Aryāt as the Abyssinian Governor of Yemen. He set up the aforementioned Christian inscription. Later on, he swore that he would destroy the Ka'ba, the foremost temple of the pagan Arabs. He led an army to Mecca in AD 570, the same year in which Muhammad was born. The Ka'ba, however, escaped unhurt because of a miracle which turned away the Abyssinian horde and which the Arabs credited to Allāh, the presiding deity of their pantheon. Meanwhile, the pagan Arabs had had a first hand experience of what Judaism and Christianity stood for.

The religious strife which these alien creeds had brought to Arabia was unknown to the pre-Islamic Arabs who, like all pagans, were very liberal in matters of belief and modes of worship. They witnessed how the two exclusive creeds had combined to cause not only large-scale bloodshed but also a foreign invasion, entailing enslavement of Arab women and children and occupation of Arab territory by an alien army. The name of Abraham was associated with both the creeds, as also the word "*Raḥmān*". Naturally, the Arabs could not be expected to be fond of either the name or the word.

The historians of Islam mention Abraha's march on Mecca, as also his frustration and retreat in the face of a miracle. But they conceal the fact that the Ka'ba at that time was a place of pagan worship crowded with numerous idols of Gods and Goddesses. Instead, they lie and credit the miracle to the God of Abraham. That God, however, was nowhere near the Ka'ba during that period. Allāh who presided over the pagan pantheon had not yet been hijacked by Muhammad and converted into the exclusive God of Islam. In fact, it was the pagan character of the Ka'ba which had invited the attack by a Christian iconoclast. And it was the God of the pagans who had performed the miracle.

---

[12]Ibn, Ishāq, *Sīrat Rasūl Allāh*, translated into English by A. Gillaume, OUP, Karachi, Seventh Impression, p. 17. Ibn Ishāq (d. AD 767) was the first biographer of Muhammad.
[13]Ibid., p. 19.

Character of Pre-Islamic Arabs

Modern scholars have not only salvaged pre-Islamic Arab history; they have also pieced together a picture of the pagan Arabs among whom Muhammad was born. For the latter purpose they have had to depend solely on Islamic sources. They have done a creditable job in view of the fact that these sources were deliberately intended to black out or blacken whatever functioned in Arabia before the birth of Islam. They have succeeded in gleaning some good glimpses of people who stood up to Muhammad and challenged his claim of monopoly over truth. The material they have collected is meagre. Yet it does help us meet some men and women of sterling character and heroic bearing. The adversaries of Muhammad score over him and his companions hands down so far as qualities of head and heart are concerned.

This is not the occasion to go into greater detail about the shape of pre-Islamic society and culture in Arabia. In the present context, we have to confine ourselves to its pre-Islamic religion which Muhammad destroyed root and branch and replaced with alien prescriptions. So far as Muhammad's adversaries are concerned, let a professor from Pakistan speak, even though his views are coloured considerably by the historical lore of Islam:

"Although religion had little influence on the lives of pre-Islamic Arabs,[14] we must not suppose them to be an altogether lawless people. The pagan society of ancient Arabia was built on certain moral ideas, which may be briefly described here. They had no written code, religious or legal, except the compelling force of traditional custom which was enforced by public opinion; but their moral and social ideals have been faithfully preserved in their poetry, which is the only form of literature which has come down to us from those old days.

"The virtues most highly prized by the ancient Arabs were bravery in battle, patience in misfortune, loyalty to one's fellow tribesmen, generosity to the needy and the poor, hospitality to the guest and the wayfarer, and persistence in revenge. Courage in battle and fortitude in warfare were particularly required in a land where might was generally right and tribes were constantly engaged in attacking one another. It is, therefore, not a mere chance that in the famous anthology of Arabian verse, called the *Hamāsah*, poems relating to inter-tribal warfare occupy more than half of the book. These poems applaud the virtues most

[14]This statement has no basis, as well shall see. The pagan Arabs fought Muhammad in defence of a religion which they cherished. They had no other reason to quarrel with the Prophet.

highly prized by the Arabs—bravery in battle, patience in hardship, defiance of the strong, and persistence in revenge.

"The tribal organization of the Arabs was then, as now, based on the principle of kinship or common blood, which served as the bond of union and social solidarity. To defend the family and the tribe, individually and collectively, was, therefore, regarded as a sacred duty; and honour required that a man should stand by his people through thick and thin. If kinsmen sought help, it was to be given promptly, without considering the merits of the case. Chivalrous devotion and disinterested self-sacrifice on behalf of their kinsmen and friends were, therefore, held up as a high ideal of life."[15]

The king of Persia had said to one of the pre-Islamic Arab princes that the latter's people were inferior to every other people. The prince had replied, "What nation could be put before the Arabs for strength or beauty or piety, courage, munificence, wisdom, pride, or fidelity?...So liberal was he that he would slaughter the camel which was his sole wealth to give a meal to the stranger who came to him at night. No other nation had poetry so elaborate or a language so expressive as theirs. Theirs were the noblest horses, the chastest women, the finest raiment...For their camels no distance was too far, no desert too wild to traverse. So faithful were they to the ordinances of their religion that if a man met his father's murderer unarmed in one of the sacred months he would not harm him. A sign or look from one of them constituted an engagement which was absolutely inviolabe...If other nations obeyed a central government and a single ruler, the Arabs required no such institution, each of them being fit to be a king, and well able to protect himself, and unwilling to undergo the humitiation of paying tribute or hearing rebuke."[16] One is reminded of the republican clans in north Uttar Pradesh and Bihar among whom the Buddha was born, as also of those in Punjab and Sindh who robbed Alexander of his reputation of invincibility when they blunted his sword and turned him back. The Arabs who got regimented as Muhammad's *mujāhids* (holy warriors) lost this sense of honour and love of freedom. Treachery towards

---

[15]"Shaikh Inayatullah, former Professor of Arabic in the University of the Punjab, Lahore. 'Pre-Islamic Arabian Thought'. an article in *A History of Muslim Philosophy*, edited by M.M. Sharif, Lahore. 1961. Vol. I. pp. 133–34. The legend of Hātim Tayy, poet and knight. is still popular among Muslims. He represents the "ideal type of the Pre-Muhammadan Arab" because he "displayed in a high degree the virtues of *Murūwa*, particularly hospitality and liberality in the practice of which he paid no regard to his own needs". His "generosity has become proverbial" (*First Encyclopaedia of Islam*, op. cit., Vol. III, p. 290.

[16]D.S. Margoliouth, op. cit., pp. 2–3.

whomsoever the Prophet chose as his enemy, became their stock-in-trade. On the other hand, a mere frown from the Prophet made them cringe and crawl.

If a society and culture is to be judged by the status of its women, the pre-Islamic Arabs come out with flying colours. The very fact that they had many Goddesses in their pantheon, made them give a place of pride to their women. "Institutions of paganism," observes Margoliouth, "were not unfavourable to the prominence of those women who had the requisite gifts of courage or insight. And the ensuing narrative will show examples of women acting with originality and resolution, when there was room for the display of these qualities."[17] Muhammad's first wife, Khadījah, provides an excellent example of the independence which women enjoyed, and the enterprise they could display in the pre-Islamic Arab society. She was not only a wealthy merchant who managed her own business; she was also in a position to turn down proposals from powerful suitors and marry the man of her own choice. Hind, the wife of Muhammad's chief adversary, Abū Sufyān, was herself a firebrand who opposed Muhammad, tooth and nail. She followed her husband to the battlefield and sustained his morale in peace. When Abū Sufyān surrendered Mecca to Muhammad without a fight, she caught hold of him in the market-place and cried, "Kill this fat greasy bladder of lard ! What a rotten protector of the people!"[18] She was at her best when circumstances forced her to embrace Islam. The Prophet who baptised her asked her not to commit adultery. "Does a free woman commit adultery, O apostle of God ?" she asked. Next, the Prophet advised her not to "kill your childern." She said, "I brought them up when they were little and you killed them on the day of Badr when they were grown up, so you are the one to know about them."[19] It was Islam which robbed women of their high station in society and put them behind the veil or buried them in the harem. Ever since, the language of Islam has bracketed women (*zan*) with personal property (*zar* and *zamīn*) of the male. Chapters on marriage (*nikāh*) and divorce (*talāq*) in orthodox collections of *Hadīs*, and other standard works such as the *Hidāya* and the Fatwa-i-'*Ālamgīrī*, tell the true story of what Islam has done to women.

---

[17]Ibid., p. 30.

[18]Ibn Ishāq, op. cit., p. 548.

[19]Ibid., p. 533. It is a despicable lie that the pre-Islamic Arabs killed their children. Muhammad asked the Arabs not to commit this crime simply because the Jewish prophets had spoken against it, and not because he saw the Arabs committing it. Hind gave a fitting reply.

But the one great virtue for which the pre-Islamic Arabs put the Prophet and his companions to shame, was their catholicity in matters of religious belief and practice. The respect they showed towards other people's persuasions was fully in keeping with their pagan spiritual tradition. Ibn Ishāq testifies, "When the apostle openly displayed Islam as God ordered him, his people did not withdraw or turn against him, so far as I have heard, until he spoke disparagingly of their gods."[20] The Meccans made a very reasonable offer when Abū Tālib, Muhammad's uncle and protector, was on his death-bed. "You know," they said, "the trouble that exists between us and your nephew, so call him and let us make an agreement that he will leave us alone and we will leave him alone; let him have his religion and we will have ours." It was Muhammad who remained adamant. "You must say," he demanded, "There is no God but Allāh and you must repudiate what you worship beside him."[21] It cannot be held against the Meccans that they refused to be bullied. Abū Tālib himself stands out as an embodiment of the pagan virtue in this respect. He protected Muhammad to the end, without himself agreeing to renounce the religion of his forefathers. His only fault—and that has been the fault of all pagans—was his failure to understand that what his nephew was selling was not religion but something else.

It is, therefore, nothing short of slanderous to say that the pre-Islamic Arabs were barbarians devoid of religion and culture, unless we mean by religion and culture what the Muslim theologians mean. They were nothing of the sort. The fact that they failed to understand the ways of Muhammad and could not match his mailed fist in the final round, should not be held against them. It was neither for the first nor the last time that a democratic society succumbed in the face of determined gangsterism. We know how Lenin, Hitler and Mao Tse-tung succeeded in our own times. Nor should the image of what the Arabs became after they were forced into the fold of Islam be confused with what they were before. The crimes committed by the Islamized Arabs should not be blamed on the pagan Arabs. For it was Islam which brutalized the Arabs and turned them into bloodthirsty bandits who spread fire and sword, far and wide. In the majorty of mankind, the baser drives of human nature are never far from the threshhold. Islam brought them to the fore in case of the majority of Arabs.

---

[20]Ibid., op. cit., p. 118. Muslim apologists may say that abusing other people's Gods is not intolerance because that is what Islam means. But that is a different proposition.

[21]Ibid., p. 191–92.

CHAPTER ELEVEN

RELIGION OF PAGAN ARABIA

The Islamic sources do tell us that the pre-Islamic Arabs were *mushriks* (polytheists) "addicted" to worshipping numerous idols. But they do not inform us as to what those idols symbolized. The Qur'ān (2.257, 259; 4.52; 53.19;71.21) mentions some idols but only to denounce them. We reproduce below what Ibn Ishāq writes about them :

"They say that the beginning of stone worship among the sons of Ishmael was when Mecca became too small for them and they wanted more room in the country. Everyone who left the town took with him a stone from the sacred area to do honour to it. Wherever they settled they set it up and walked round it as they went round the Ka'ba. This led them to worship what stones they pleased and those which made an impression on them. Thus as generations passed they forgot their primitive faith and adopted another religion for that of Abraham and Ishmael. They worshipped idols and adopted the same errors as the peoples before them. Yet they retained and held fast practices going back to the time of Abraham, such as honouring the temple and going round it, the great and little pilgrimage, and the standing on 'Arafa and Muzdalifa, sacrificing the victims, and the pilgrim cry at the great and little pilgrimage, while introducing elements which had no place in the religion of Abraham. Thus, Kināna and Quraysh used the pilgrim cry: 'At Thy service, O God, at Thy service! At Thy service, Thou without an associate but the associate Thou hast. Thou ownest him and what he owns.' They used to acknowledge his unity in their cry and then include their idols with God, putting the ownership of them in His hand...[1]

"The people of Noah had images to which they were devoted. God told His apostle about them when He said: 'And they said, Forsake not your gods; forsake not Wudd and Suwā' and Yaghūth and Ya'ūq and Nasr. And they had led many astray.'

"Among those who had chosen those idols and used their names as compounds when they forsook the religion of Ishmael—both Ishmaelites and others—was Hudhayl b. Mudrika b. Ilyās b. Muḍar. They

---

[1]Ibid., op. cit., pp. 35–36. The word "*God*" in this passage and those that follow is a translation of the word "Allāh" The references to Abraham and Ishmael and their mode of worship at the Ka'ba may be ignored in the light of what we have stated above. The Ka'ba was a temple of the pagan Arabs who had never heard of Abraham or Ishmael or their religion.

adopted Suwā' and they had him in Ruhāṭ; and Kalb b. Wabra of Quḍā'a who adopted Wudd in Dūmatu'l-Jandal...

"An'um of Ṭayyi' and the people of Jurash of Madhḥij adopted Yaghūth in Jurash.

"Khaywān, a clan of Hamdān, adopted Ya'ūq in the land of Hamdān in the Yaman.

"Dhū'l-Kalā' of Ḥimyar adopted Nasr in the Himyar country.

"Khaulān had an idol called 'Ammanas in the Khaulān country...[2]

"The B. Milkān b. Kināna b. Khuzayma b. Mudrika b. Ilyās b. Muḍar had an image called Sa'd, a lofty rock in a desert plain in their country...

"Daus had an idol belonging to 'Amr b. Ḥumama al-Dausī.

"Quraysh had an idol by a well in the middle of the Ka'ba called Hubal. And they adopted Isāf (or Asāf) and Na'ila by the place of Zamzam, sacrificing beside them...[3]

"Every household had an idol in their house which they used to worship. When a man was about to set out on a journey he would rub himself against it as he was about to ride off: indeed that was the last thing he used to do before his journey; and when he returned from his journey the first thing he did was to rub himself against it before he went in to his family...

"Now along with the Ka'ba the Arabs had adopted Tawāghīt, which were temples which they venerated as they venerated the Ka'ba. They had their guardians and overseers and they used to make offerings to them as they did to the Ka'ba and to circumambulate them and sacrifice at them. Yet they recognized the superiority of the Ka'ba because it was the temple and mosque of Abraham the friend (of God).

"Quraysh and the B. Kināna had al-'Uzzā in Nakhla, its guardians and overseers were the B. Shaybān of Sulaym, allies of the B. Hāshim...

"Al-Lāt belonged to Thaqīf in Ṭā'if, her overseers and guardians being B. Mu'attib of Thaqīf.[4]

"Manāt was worshipped by al-Aus and al-Khazraj and such of the people of Yathrib[5] as followed their religion by the seashore in the direction of al-Mushallal in Qudayd.[6]

"Dhū'l-Khalaṣa belonged to Daus, Khaṭh'am, and Bajīla and the

---

[2]Ibid., p. 36.
[3]Ibid., p. 37.
[4]Ibid., p. 38.
[5]It was renamed Medina when Muhammad migrated to it.
[6]Ibid., pp. 38–39.

Arabs in their area in Tabāla...

"Fals belonged to Ṭayyi' and those hard by in the two mountains of Ṭayyi', Salmā and Aja'.

"Ḥimyar and the Yamanites had a temple in San'ā called Ri'ām.

"Ruḍā' was a temple of B. Rabī'a b. Ka'b b. Sa'd b. Zayd b. Manāt b. Tamīm...

"Dhū'l-Ka'abāt belonged to Bakr and Taghlib the two sons of Wā'il and Iyād in Sindād..."[7]

Hishām bin Muhammad al-Kalbī (d. AD 819) wrote a whole book, *Kitāb al-Aṣnām*,[8] describing what tribe worshipped what idol, at what place, and in what manner. But he did not know what those idols stood for. F. Krenkow comments: "From the description of the idols worshipped by the pre-Islamic Arabs, enumerated by Ibn al-Kalbī, the word Ṣanam appears to apply to objects of very varying character. Some were actual sculptures like Hubal, Isāf and Nāi'la; so were the other idols set up round the Ka'ba...Others were trees like al-'Uzzā and many were mere stones like al-Lāt. Stones are well-known as objects of worship by the Semites in general and the traditionist al-Dārimī states early in the first chapter of his *Musnad* that in the time of paganism the Arabs, whenever they found a stone remarkable for its shape, colour or size, set it up as an object of worship. Ibn al-Kalbī states that the Arabs were not content with setting up stones for idols, but even took such stones with them on their journeys..."[9]

This portrait of the pagan Arabs as primitive fetishists would have remained fixed for all time to come but for the non-Islamic sources which have been studied in recent times. The discovery of numerous inscriptions, particularly in South Arabia, has forced even Muslim scholars to revise their opinion to a certain extent. Shaikh Inayatullah writes:

"These Arabian deities, which were of diverse nature, fell into different categories. Some of them were personifications of abstract ideas, such as *jadd* (luck), *sa'd* (fortunate, auspicious), *riḍā'* (good-will, favour), *wadd* (friendship, affection), and *manāf* (height, highplace). Though originally abstract in character, they were conceived in a thoroughly concrete fashion. Some deities derived their names from the places where they were venerated. Dhu al-Khalaṣah and Dhu al-Shara may be cited as examples of this kind.

---

[7]Ibid. p. 39.

[8]Plural of *Ṣanam*, Dictionaries and commentaries on the Qur'ān define it as "an object which is worshipped besides God", being a thing made of wood, stone or metal.

[9]*First Encyclopaedia of Islam*, op. cit., Vol. VII, p. 147.

"The heavenly bodies and other powers of nature, venerated as deities, occupied an important place in the Arabian pantheon. The sun (*shams*, regarded as feminine) was worshipped by several Arab tribes and was honoured with a sanctuary and an idol. The name 'Abd Shams, 'Servant of the Sun,' was found in many parts of the country. The sun was referred to by descriptive titles also, such as *shāriq*, 'the brilliant one.' The constellation of the Pleiades (*al-Thurayya*), which was believed to bestow rain, also appears as a deity in the name 'Abd al-Thurayya. The planet Venus, which shines with remarkable brilliance in the clear skies of Arabia, was revered as a great goddess under the name of al-'Uzza, which may be translated as 'the Most Mighty.' It had a sanctuary at Nakhlah near Mecca. The name 'Abd al-'Uzza was very common among the pre-Islamic Arabs. The Arabian cult of the planet Venus has been mentioned by several classical and Syriac authors."[10]

The pre-Islamic Arab religion was, however, far more profound. As in the case of every pagan people, the pagan Arabs perceived divinity in everything in their environment, terrestrial as well as celestial. This will become clear as we take up the Arab Gods and Goddesses, one by one. Here we want to mention that the Minaeans, the Sabaeans and the Nabataeans worshipped more of less the same divinities, mostly under the same, though sometimes differing, names.

"First of all," writes H. Hommel, "as regards the religion of the South Arabians, as we find it in their inscriptions, it is a strongly marked star-worship, in which the cult of the moon-god, conceived as masculine, takes complete precedence of that of the sun, which is conceived as feminine. This is shown in the clearest fashion by the stereotyped series of gods (Minaean: 'Athar, Wadd, Nakruh, Shams; Haḍramawtic: 'Athar, Sīn, Hol, Shams; Qata-bānian: 'Athar, 'Amm, Anbai, Shams; Sabaean: 'Athar, Hawbas, Al-māku-hū, Shams); here we find throughout, a. 'Athar (the planet Venus conceived as masculine...as symbol of the sky) the god of the heavens mentioned first, b. Wadd or as the case may be, Sīn, 'Amm or Hawbas the real chief god i.e. the moon; c. Nakruh (the planet Saturn or Mars), or Hol, Anbai (messenger of the gods, Nebo) or Almāku-hū, his (the moon's) servant or messenger, and finally, d. Shams, the daughter of the moon-god to whom women may have appealed by preference and who therefore stands at the end of the whole enumeration. Besides these, a certain part was played by a great Mother-goddesses, the mother and con-

[10]Shaikh Inayatullah, op. cit., p. 128.

sort of the moon-god conceived as a personified lunar station, the Minaean Athirat, who was called Ḥarimtu among the Sabaeans and who was in all probability universally known as Ilāt (e.g. as a component part in names of persons, also in the shortened form Lāt). We may also mention various lesser 'Athar deities (confined later to the part played by Venus as morning or evening star), and among the West Sabaeans Ta'lab, a god of the bow who also bears merely the epithet Dhū Samawī 'lord of the heaveans', and to whom especially camels (*ibil*) are sacred (hence in Midian but probably in South Arabia Habul or Hubal etc.). It is a particularly favourite mode of thought to conceive the two chief aspects of the moon (waxing and waning moon) as twin deities, in which connection sometimes the one and sometimes the other phase is specially favoured according to the locality..."[11]

He continues: "In North West Arabia from Mekka onwards to Petra and further onwards to the Syrian desert (Palmyra) and the Ḥawrān, the same ideas prevailed, partly even appearing under the old names partly with new designations. Here we have especially to do with the cults of Mekka and of the whole Hidjāz shortly before Muhammad (al-Lāt and Hubal, in certain cases also al-Lāt, and Wudd, in addition al-'Uzzā, a feminine form of...Aziz-Lāt, the goddess of death Manāt, a god Ruḍā and others) and at an earlier period the still more important cult of the Nabataeans. Among the latter also we find the moon divided into twin deities: Dhū Sharā ('He of the mountain') and his Kharishā (the sun); the former especially in Petra and Habul (or Hubal) and his consort Manawāt; further also the Mother-goddess Ilāt and a god A'araā ('he with the white mark on his forehead,' originally perhaps only an epithet of Dusares)..."

He concludes: "But we may point out in conclusion that in all probability the Greeks borrowed[12] from Arabian incense merchants their Apollo and his mother Leto as also Dionysos and Hermes, in the same way as they took their additional letters Phi, Chi and Psi from the South Arabian alphabet...This would seem to prove definitively that South Arabian civilization with its gods, incense altars, inscriptions, forts and castles must have been in a flourishing condition as early as the beginning of the first millennium BC."[13]

[11]*First Encyclopaedia of Islam*, op. cit., Vol. 1, p. 379. References to similar Gods of other nations, mentioned in parentheses, have been left out.

[12]This theory of borrowing Gods in the case of pagan spiritual traditions does not mean much because the pagan psyche throws up spontaneously the same symbols everywhere.

[13]Ibid., p. 380.

Being at par with or even superior to the Greek pantheon, the Arab pantheon acquires a prestige which is seldom conceded to it except by scholars who have studied the subject. One reason is that the literature in which the Greek Gods and Goddesses figure has survived to a large extent, while the pre-Islamic Arab literature has disappeared more or less completely, so much so that even specialists find it difficult to believe that the pagan Arabs had any literature at all. Secondly, the Renaissance in Europe has restored the prestige of the Greek heritage, while people who feel the same pride in the pre-Islamic Arab heritage have yet to come foreward.

The Pagan Arab Pantheon

Now we can take up, in greater detail, individual Arab Gods and Goddesses, starting with the one who presided over the pantheon.

Al-Lāh

The name Allāh has become so much identified with Islam as to rule out any suspicion that he was the Great God of the pagan Arabs. "*Allāh*, in the Safā inscriptions, *Hallāh*, 'the god', enters into the composition of numerous personal names among the Nabataeans and other Northern Arabs of an early period e.g. *Zaid Allāhī*, 'increase of God' (that is increase of the family through the son given by God), *'Abd Allāhī*, and so forth. Among the heathen Arabs Allāh is extremely common, both by itself and in theophorous names. Wellhausen cites a large number of passages in which pre-Islamic Arabs mention Allāh as a great deity; and even if we strike out certain passages (for instance on the ground that the text has been altered by Muhammadan scribes) so many still remain over, and so many more which are above suspicion can without difficulty be found, that the fact is clearly established. Moreover, *Allāh* forms an integral part of various idiomatic phrases which were in constant use among the heathen Arabs. Of special importance is the terminology of the Qur'ān, which proves beyond all doubt that the heathen Arabs themselves regarded Allāh as the Supreme Being. The Nabataen inscriptions mention repeatedly the name of a deity accompanied by a title '*Alāhā*, 'the god'."[14]

The Qur'ān (13.17;29.61, 63;41.24;39.39; 43.87) itself provides ample evidence that the pre-Islamic Arabs regarded Allāh as "the creator and supreme provider" and "assigned to him a separate position

[14]*Encyclopaedia of Religion and Ethics*, Third Impression, Edinburgh, 1955, Vol. I, p. 664.

distinct from that of all other deities (6.137)." Here it becomes difficult "to distinguish between their views and the interpretation of their views adopted by Muhammad, especially their vocabulary and that of Muhammad. It will be seen, then, that whatever may have been the origin of the names applied, the religion of Mecca in Muhammad's time was far from simple idolatry." Both sides seem to say the same things about Allāh. "But though the name was the same for the Meccans and for Muhammad, their conception of the bearer of the name must have differed widely. The Meccans evidently had in general no fear of him; the fear of Allāh was an element in Muhammad's creed...The Meccans did not hesitate to disregard him and to cultivate the minor gods; Muhammad knew him as a jealous and vindictive sovereign who would assuredly judge and condemn in the end..."[15]

It is significant that while the sources, Islamic as well as others, mention idols of many Gods and Goddesses in the Ka'ba and elsewhere, they nowhere mention an idol of Allāh. The only explanation is that every God and Goddesses was seen by the pagan Arabs as representing Allāh who could be prayed to through any one of them. In fact, the Meccans pointed out to Muhammad (Qur'ān 6.149; 37.68) that "Allāh had never forbidden them to worship other gods with him."[16] Ibn Ishāq reports that 'Abdu'l-Muttalib "stood by Hubal praying to Allāh."[17] The Qur'ān is never tired of saying that those whom the idolaters associate with Allāh will not intercede for them on the last day. For the pagan Arabs, however, Allāh is no other than his associates; he is them and they are he. Of course, the pagans have no notion of the last day when alone Allāh will visit them; instead, they are aware of him every moment of their lives. He is present not in some high heaven but in and around them, in many names and forms. The character which the Qur'ān assigns to Allāh must have looked like a prison-house to the pagan Arabs; their Allāh could not be contained in concepts created by the external and shallow mind of man, nor was he helplessly dependent upon the services of a prophet.

The pagan poets "had already developed in Arabic a vivid power of wielding descriptive epithets vis-a-vis Allāh."[18] Many of the ninety-nine names (*Asmā'al-ḥūsnā*) which Muslim theologians mention, can

[15]*First Encyclopaedia of Islam*, op. cit., Vol. I, p. 302.

[16]Ibid.

[17]Ibn Ishāq, op. cit., p. 67. Allāh of the pagan Arabs reminds us of the *Devādhideva*, the God of Gods, in the Hindu spiritual tradition.

[18]*First Encyclopaedia of Islam*, op. cit., Vol. I, p. 303. Pagan epithets of Allāh remind us of the *Sahasrañama*-s in praise of many Hindu Gods and Goddesses.

be found in pagan poetry. Most probably, Allāh had many more names, may be a thousand, in the pagan parlance. It has been characteristic of pagan spirituality everywhere that it adorns with numerous names and forms whatever it adores. Muhammad retained only those names which did not offend his monotheism, and dropped the rest. He also added names which did not square with the pagan perception of Allāh but which went very well with the Allāh of his conception. *Al-Muṭakabbir*, the Haughty, looks like one such name. *Al-Muntaqīm*, the Avenger, is another. The most typical of Muhammad's contributions, however, is *al-Mughnī,* the Enricher, that is, by means of booty which includes, we may remember, the women and children of those who become victims of *Jihād*. Small wonder that one of the names of Muhammad's Allāh is *al-Zārr*, the Distresser. We find that the Qur'ān (58.11) uses the same name for Satan. As we shall see, that is exactly what Allāh came to mean in the doctrine as well as the history of Islam.

The two names, *ar-Raḥmān*, the Compassionate, and *al-Raḥīm*, the Merciful, are the most frequent in Muhammad's usage. They stand at the head of every Sūra of the Qur'ān except one. There is nothing intrinsically offensive in these names when applied to Allāh. In fact, they are more appropriate for the Allāh of the pagan Arabs than for the Allāh of Islam. Yet the Meccans found them the most objectionable. Muhammad had tacked them to Allāh while dictating to 'Ali the draft of the treaty at Hudaybiya. The Meccan representative protested and had them dropped. "Then the apostle," narrates Ibn Ishāq, "summoned 'Ali and told him to write 'In the name of Allah the Compassionate, the Merciful.' Suhayl said 'I do not recognize this; but write 'In thy name, O Allah.' The apostle told him to write the latter and he did so."[19] This was not the only occasion when the Meccans showed their repugnance for these names. They had all along accused Muhammad of importing alien names and imposing them upon Allāh. To them these names were Jewish and the Jews had been in league with Muhammad so far as Arabia's ancient religion and culture were concerned. They saw these names as symbols of the new-fangled creed which Muhammad was trying to foist on them. On the other hand, Muhammad insisted on using these names because, in his mind, they embodied all that he stood for.

Incidentally, "Traditions assign two hundred names to Muhammad."[20] It seems that the Prophet grew in size at the expense of Allāh

[19]Ibn Ishāq, op. cit., p. 504.
[20]Cyril Glasse, *The Concise Encyclopaedia of Islam*, London, 1989, p. 279.

who was made to look smaller and smaller. That was quite in keeping with the Prophet's own image of himself. He was out to block everyone else's access to Allāh while proclaiming himself as *Habīb Allāh, an-Nabī, ar-Rasūl* and *Khātim al-Anbiyā*. So it was no more sufficient that one believed in Allāh; one had also to believe in Muhammd as the only channel through which Allāh's will could be known. It was inevitable that, in due course, the Prophet became more important than the contrived god in whose name he spoke.

Al-Malik

There were other deities "whose titles themselves seem to designate them as occupying a position of supreme importance in the eyes of the worshippers." Al-Malik, 'the King,' was the name of such a deity. "In the days of Islām, *al-Malik* became one of the epithets of Allāh, and hence the name *'Abd al-Malik* survives among Muhammadans."[21]

Ba'l or Ba'al

"The divine title Ba'l or Ba'al, 'the lord,' which was very common among the Northern Semites, survived among the Arabs of the Sinai Peninsula in the form *al-Ba'lū* which occurs in their inscriptions together with the proper names *'Abd al-Ba'lī, Aus al-Ba'lī*, 'gift of the Lord,' and *Garm al-Ba'lī*, probably 'act of the Lord.' A trace of the worship of this god may be found in *Sharaf al-Ba'l*, the name of a place between Medina and Syria. The Arabs of later times were not aware that any such deity had existed, but certain phrases in their language clearly prove that he had once been known. Thus the term 'soil of *Ba'l'* or simply *'Ba'l'* is applied to land which does not require irrigation, but has an underground water supply, and therefore yields fruit of the best quality. In this case the god seems to be regarded as the lord of the cultivated land...Again, the verb *ba'la* and other derivatives of *Ba'l* mean 'to be bewildered,' properly 'to be seized by the god Ba'l'."[22]

El

"Among the Northern Arabs of early times, particularly in the region of Safā, the word El, 'God,' was still very commonly used as a separate name of the Deity. It is true that it does not actually occur except in compound proper names of persons, *Wahb El*, and many others. Some of these such as *Wahbīl*, 'gift of El,' *Abdīl*, 'Servant of El,'

[21]Encyclopaedia of Religion and Ethics, op. cit., p. 664.
[22]Ibid. See also the last para under Hubal in this section.

appear among the Arabs of a later age but at least in certain cases they must have been borrowed from the Sabaean language, while in other cases they are restricted to the extreme north of Arabia. It may be added that the divine name *Iayāl*, which occurs once in an ancient verse, is possibly a plural of majesty formed from El; *Uwāl* is a variation of the same name.[23]

"The names commonly used in dynasties, or distinguished families, who originally came from districts where Sabaean or some other peculiar dialect of southern Arabia was spoken, had naturally a tendency to spread among the Arabs in general."[24]

Al-Lāt

"The Sun-god who according to Strabo (784) was held in especial honour by the Nabataeans, is very probably to be identifited with *Allāt*...We have already seen that the sun is properly feminine in Arabic and in most other Semitic languages; hence the name *Allāt* which so far as we can judge means simply 'the Goddess,' is particularly suited in this case." The Greek historian, Herodotus, mentions an Arabian Goddess named Alilāt. "That Alilāt is identical with Allāt, a goddess frequently mentioned, has long been an acknowledged fact. References to Allāt were found in several Nabataean inscriptions; in one of them she is called the 'Mother of Gods.' Moreover, proper names compounded with Allāt appear both among the Nabataeans and the Palmyrenes... Among the later Arabs this goddess was no less venerated. In the Qur'ān (liii.50) she is one of the three daughters of Allāh. She is also mentioned occasionally in poetry. Thus one poet says: 'I swear to him, in the presence of the throng, by the salt, by the fire, and by Allāt who is the greatest of all.' Of the names compounded with Allāt, which were widely diffused, some at least must be of considerable antiquity ...The cult of the goddess flourished, in particular, at the sanctuary of Tā'if, a town to the east of Mecca; the tribe of Thaquīf, who dwelt in that district spoke of her as the 'mistress',"[25] that is, *al-Rabba*.[26] Among the Lihyan, a branch of the Hudhail, settled in the country north-east of Mecca, Allāt was worshipped "alongside typically Arab" dieties.[27]

---

[23]Ibid.

[24]Ibid., Footnote.

[25]*Encyclopaedia of Religion and Ethics*, op. cit., p. 661.

[26]*First Encyclopaedia of Islam*, Vol. VI, p. 1088.

[27]Ibid., Vol. V, p. 27. Allāt, reminds us of Aditi, the Mother of Gods in the Vedic pantheon.

Manāt

"Some Arabian dieties were originally personifications of abstract ideas...Time in the abstract was popularly imagined to be the cause of all earthly happiness and especially of all earthly misery. Muhammad in the Qur'ān (Sūra xlv. 23) blames the unbelievers for saying, 'It is Time that destroys us.' Her main sanctuary was a black stone among the Hudailīs in Qudaid, not far from Mecca on the road to Medina near a hill called Mushallal. She was however worshipped by many Arab tribes, primarily the Aws and Khazradj in Yathrib.[28] In Mecca she was very popular along with the goddesses al-Lāt and al-'Uzzā; the three (according to the Qur'ān) were regarded as Allāh's daughters, and in a weak moment Muhammad declared their worship permitted (cf. Sūra liii. 19 sqq.)...According to Ibn al-Kalbī, she was the oldest deity whose worship gave rise to that of the others, because names compounded with Manāt occur earlier than other theophoric names. Another view is found in Ibn Hishām, p.145, where 'the two daughters of 'Uzzā are Manāt and al-Lāt.' As an independent deity we find her in the Nabataen inscriptions of al-Hidjr...Manāt is connected in a peculiar way by some writers with the great *hadjdj*, for we are told that several tribes including the Aws and Khazradj assumed the *ihrām* at the sanctuary of Manāt and on conclusion of the rites cut their hair and dropped the *ihrām*..."[29]

The character of the Goddess can be inferred from her name. In Arabic *manīya* (plural, *manāya*) means "the alloted, fate, doom of death, destruction". Manāt, therefore, was primarily the Goddess of Time. "The poets are continually alluding to the action of Time (*dahr*, *zamān*) for which they often substitute 'the days,' or 'nights.' Time is represented as bringing misfortune, causing perpetual change, as biting, wearing down, shooting arrows that never miss the mark, hurling stones, and so forth...Occasionally we come across such passages as the following : 'Time has brought woe upon him, for the days and the (alloted) measure (*qadar*) have caused him to perish.' Various expressions are used by the poets in speaking of the 'portion' alloted to them or the goal that is set before them...Once we meet with the phrase 'till it be seen what the Apportioner shall apportion to thee' (*mā yamnī laka 'lamānī*), which apparently refers to a god...The word here translated 'apportion' originally means 'to count', hence to 'reckon' a thing to someone..."[30]

---

[28]This city became known as Medina after Muhammad migrated to it from Mecca in AD 622. It remained his seat till his death in AD 632. Later on, it was the capital of the Caliphate till 'Alī moved to Kufa.

[29]Ibid., op. cit., Vol. V, p. 231.

[30]*Encyclopaedia of Religion and Ethics*, op. cit., p. 661.

She is also the Goddess of Death. "*Manīya* appears in poetry as driving a man into the grave, piercing him with an arrow, handing to him the cup of death, lying in ambush for him, receiving him as a guest (when he is about to die), and so forth. Not unfrequently the possesive suffix is added, 'when my Manīya overtakes me,' 'his Manīya has come upon him,' and the like..."[31]

Al-'Uzzā

Her name means 'the Most Mighty.' She was a Goddess of the Sabaeans who, in due course, became popular all over Arabia. She embodied the cult of the planet Venus. "The Syrian poet Issac of Antioch, who lived in the first half of the 5th cent., bears witness to the worship of 'Uzzā by the Arabs of that period; in another passage he identifies 'Uzzā with the planet Venus...The Arabian cult of the Venus is mentioned like-wise by Ephrahim Syrus (who died in AD 373), by Jerome, Theodret, and later still by Evagrius...As early as the 2nd cent. or thereabout, references to a priest of this goddess occur in two Sinaitic inscriptions... Another Sinaitic inscription mentions the name *'Abd al-'Uzzā* which at a later time, just before the rise of Islam, was extremely common among the Arabs...'Uzzā figures in the Qur'ān (*Sūra* liii. 19) as one of the three great goddesses of Mecca, who were supposed to be daughters of Allāh. That Muhammad himself offered sacrifices to her in his younger days is expressely stated by tradition...

"Kuthrā which probably means 'the Most Rich,' the name of an idol destroyed by order of Muhammad, is perhaps only another title of 'Uzzā. We also read of a man call *'Abd Kuthrā*, belonging to the tribe of Tai, in the very centre of Arabia. Here the absence of the definite article proves that the name Kuthrā is ancient."[32]

Another poet is known to have sworn by the Sa'ida (Blessed) 'Uzzā. As as-Sa'ida is known to be the name of a Goddess worshipped at Medina, it is inferred that she was 'Uzzā. "She was especially associated with the Ghaṭafān but her principal sanctuary was in the valley of the Nakhla on the road from Tā'if to Mecca...It consisted of three samura (acacia) trees in one of which the goddess revealed herself...From these centres her cult spread among a number of Beduin tribes, the Khuzā'a, Ghanm, Kināna, Balī, Thakīf and especially the

---

[31]Ibid., One is reminded of the Hindu concept of *Kāla* which stands for both Time and Death, and parallel verses can be found in Hindu literature. We also know of Hindu temples dedicated to Mahākāla.

[32]*Encyclopaedia of Religion and Ethics*, op. cit., p. 660.

Quraish, among whom she gradually acquired a predominant position...Here she formed with al-Lāt and Manāt a trinity in which she was the youngest but came in time to overshadow the others...When in the year 3, Abū Sufyān set out to attack Muhammad he took the symbols of al-'Uzzā and al-Lāt with him. That of the two al-'Uzzā was the more important as the patron deity of Mecca is shown from Abū Sufyān's war cry: al-'Uzzā is for us and not for you...

"Her cult disappeared after this [destruction of her sanctuary], as did the numerous proper names, combinations of al-'Uzzā, while the masculine counterpart 'Abd al-'Azīz remained because 'Azīz was one of the names of Allāh..."[33]

Shams

"The Sun (*Shams*, construed as feminine) was honoured by several Arabian tribes with a sanctuary and an idol. The name *'Abd Shams*, 'servant of the Sun,' is found in many parts of the country. In the North we meet with the name *Amrishams*, 'man of the Sun'...

"For the worship of the rising Sun we have the evidence of the name *'Abd ash-Sharīq*, 'servant of the Rising One'...In the extreme South there was a God called *Dharīḥ* or *Dhirrīḥ*, which appears likewise to denote the rising Sun...Once we meet the name *'Abd Muharriq*; here *Muharriq*, 'the Burner,' may perhaps be another title of the Sun-god. The *Muharriq* who is mentioned as the ancestor of certain royal houses admits of a similar explanation."[34]

Sūra 91 of the Qur'ān is named *Ash-Shams*. The word "shams" survives in Muslim names also.

Dhu'sh-Sharā

He was an ancient Arab deity. "According to the Arab tradition he was a god who owned a reserved grazing ground (*ḥimā*) among the Dawsites with a hollow in which the water trickled down from the rocks, which is in agreement with the fact that the name 'Abd Dhu 'l-Sharā is found in this tribe. According to al-Kalbī also, this deity was worshipped among the related Banu 'l-Hārith...We meet with Dhu 'l-Sharā (Dusares) on more historical ground as a the chief god of the Nabataeans in whose inscriptions from Petra, the land east of Jordan and as far as al-Hidjr, he is often mentioned. His chief sanctuary was in Petra where a large black, quadrangular stone was dedicated to him in a

[33]*First Encyclopaedia of Islam*, op. cit., Vol. VIII, p. 1069.

[34]*Encyclopaedia of Religion and Ethics*, op. cit., p. 660.

splendid temple. He had another important sanctuary in Soada which was called Dionysias after him. His festival was celebrated here in August which is certainly connected with the fact that he was identified with Dionysos as the god of fertility, particularly of the vintage. In Petra and Elusa, on the other hand, his festival, according to Epiphanius, fell on the 25th day of December on which day 'the virgin called *Kkhbou* in Arabic and Dusares born of her were worshipped with Arabic hymns'...It naturally reminds one of the Arabic *ka'ab* 'a young maiden with breasts developed'; but it is also possible to connect it with ka'b 'cube' (cf, the Ka'ba at Mecca) according to which interpretation the god was thought to have been born from the stone."[35]

"...But there were several places called *ash-Sharā*, and the difficulty of determining with which of them the god was originally connected is increased by the fact that his cult goes back to very early times. The localities which bear this name appear to have been moist and rich in vegetation; such a spot, in the midst of a sterile country like Arabia, easily became a centre of worship." The fact that underneath his idol "stood a golden pedestal, and the whole sanctuary blazed with gold and votive offerings", as also the fact that his festival fell "about the time of the winter solstice", establish his "connexion with Sun-worship". He was the "patron of luxuriant vegetation", which further emphasizes his "character as a Sun-god."[36]

"Another god who appears to have been named after a place is Dhu 'l-Halasa or *Dhu 'l-Hulaṣa*. He was greatly venerated at a place in the north of Yemen, apparently the district now called 'Asir. Between his sanctuary and the sanctuary at Mecca there existed a certain amount of rivalry.

"From a grammatical point of view, the gods Dhu 'l-Kaffain, 'He who has two hands,' and Dhu'r-rijl, 'He who has a foot,' must be classed with the two forgoing ones. Perhaps these names may have been originaly applied to sacred stones, which by means of rude carving were made to bear a partial resemblance to the human form."[37]

Another God with a similar name was Dhu 'l-Khabṣa who was worshipped by al-Azd or al-Asd, "a widely ramified family of tribes" among which "the al-Aws and al-Khazradj of Medina and the Khuzā'a in and around Mecca were counted." They were worshippers of Manāt. The same tribe living in the mountains of Sarāt worshipped an idol

---

[35]*First Encyclopaedia of Islam*, op. cit., Vol. II, p. 965.

[36]*Encyclopaedia of Religion and Ethics*, op. cit., p. 663.

[37]Ibid.

named 'Ā'im.[38]

At-Thuraiyā

"The constellation of the Pleiades (ath-Thuraiyā) which was supposed to bestow rain, appears as a deity in the name *'Abd ath-Thuraiyā*; the name *'Abd Najm* refers also to the Pleiades, for the latter are often called simply *an-Najm*, 'constellation.'"[39]

"The word "*thuraiyā*" is a dimunitive of "*tharwā*" which means 'existing in plenty'...The constellation is so called because rain at its rising at the dawn brings *tharwā* i.e. great plenty. In any case, from early times the Pleiades have been credited with great influence on weather and the processes of nature dependent upon it...The constellation is also regarded as a diadem with jewels and it is mentioned in countless passages in the poets..."[40]

The word "*thuraiyā*" survives in the name Suraiya which is still common among Muslims everywhere. Sūra liii of the Qur'ān is named *An-Najm*. Najm and Najmā are also components of Muslim names.

Quzaḥ

He was an "ancient Arabian thundergod who shot hail from his bow and then hung the latter on the clouds." We meet him in the "combination *Qaus Quzaḥ*", the bow of Quzaḥ, meaning the rainbow.[41] Quzaḥ was also "the name of a certain spot, within the sacred territory of Mecca, where pilgrims were accustomed to kindle fire."[42] The Islamic lore is not quite logical about this God. He is described as a *shaiṭān* (devil) and also as an angel who looks after the clouds. The rainbow becomes Allāh's bow, bow of the prophet of Allāh, bow of the heavens, bow of the clouds, signs of heaven, etc., and the word loses its association with a God.

Wadd

"...also pronounced *Wudd* or *Udd* i.e. 'friendship,' 'affection,' was according to the Qur'ān (Sūra lxxi. 22) a god worshipped by the contempories of Noah. But it would be a mistake to conclude that his worship was obsolete in Muhammad's time, for we have sufficient

---

[38] *First Encyclopaedia of Islam*, op. cit., Vol. I, pp. 530–31.
[39] *Encyclopaedia of Religion and Ethics*, op. cit., p. 660.
[40] *First Encyclopaedia of Islam*, op. cit., Vol. VIII, p. 740.
[41] Ibid., op. cit., Vol. IV, p. 833.
[42] *Encyclopaedia of Religion and Ethics*, op. cit., p. 661. He reminds us of Indra of the Vedic pantheon in one of his roles.

evidence to the contrary. The poet Nābigha says once, 'Wadd greet thee!' There was a statue of this god at Dūma, a great oisis in the extreme North of Arabia. The name *'Abd Wadd* occurs in a number of wholly distinct tribes...As we are told that his statue had a bow and arrows attached to it we might be tempted to imagine that he was a kind of Eros, and this would imply a foreign origin. But though the root WDD means 'to love,' 'to feel affection' for an object, it is never used in a sexual sense. Moreover the statue in question bore not only a bow and arrows, but likwise a sword and lance from which hung a flag; the god was also fully clad and therefore does not look like a copy of the Greek Eros."[43]

Ch. Muhammad Ismail mentions an inscription which he saw in the Prince of Wales Museum of Western India, Bombay, in 1921. It was on one of the stones "brought from Aden by Colonel H.F. Jacob of the Indian Army, who was for a long time at Aden..."[44] The language of the inscription was "what may be called Himyaritic though Sabaean and South Arabic are also names given to it". Ch. Ismail read the inscription as saying, "The House No. 2 of Father Wadd", and commented: "Wadd was a god worshipped by the Arabs who often wore talismans bearing the name Wadd. The word itself is derived from *wudd* which means love. It was opposed to Nakruh, the god of hatred."[45]

The name of this God survives in *Al-Wadūd*, one of the ninety-nine names of Allāh meaning "the Loving One" (Qur'ān, xi. 92; lxxv. 14).

Ruḍā

She was a Goddess who symbolized 'goodwill' or 'favour'. "The commentary on a term in which the name is mentioned informs us that Ruḍā was worshipped in the shape of an idol by the great tribe of Tamīm. The proper name *'Abd Ruḍā* is found among several Arab tribes. To the nature of the deity in question the name supplies no clue...The remarkable fact that in the abovementioned verse Ruḍā is construed as feminine (whereas this grammatic form would normally be masculine), naturally suggests that at that period, about the time of Muhammad, people still realized that Ruḍā was merely an epithet applied to a goddess who properly bore some other name. But against this

[43]Ibid., p. 662.

[44]'A Himyaritic Inscription', article by Ch. Muhammad Ismail in *Indian Antiquary*, Vol. LVI (February, 1927), p. 21.

[45]Ibid., p. 22.

hypothesis, it may be urged that the name is of considerable antiquity, as is proved by the Palmyrene inscriptions, where it occurs separately in the form 'RSU, and in theophorous proper names as RSU... The RDU of the Safā inscriptions seems to denote the same deity."[46]

Jadd

It was the name of a deity venerated by various Semitic people. The word occurs in Nabataean inscriptions in the form *Gaddā*. "But since we meet the proper name *'Abd al-Jadd* in a few cases...and since the noun *judd*, 'luck,' remained in current use among the Arabs, it is more natural to regard the Nabataean *Gaddā* as an Aramaized form of the native Arabic *al-Gadd* (*al-Jadd*)."[47] The name is used in the Qur'ān (lxxii. 3) in the sense of 'greatness' and 'majesty'.

Sa'd

In Arab astronomy it is the common name for small groups of stars in the constellations Pegasus, Aquarius and Capricorn which augur good fortune. That is what the God Sa'd stood for. "According to a certain verse and statements of the commentator, Sa'd was the name given to a rock not far from Jidda, to which divine honours were paid. Moreover, we meet the name *'Abd Sa'd* in quite a different part of Arabia, to the north-east. At an earlier period a man's name which seems to be compounded with Sa'd occurs in the inscriptions of Safā"[48] Three of Muhammad's leading companions were named Sa'd—Sa'd ibn Abī Waqqās, Sa'd ibn Mu'az and Sa'd ibn 'Ubādah. The name seems to have survived, though in an abbreviated form, in the title of the thirty-eighth Sūra of the Qur'ān.

Manāf

The name means 'height', or 'high place'. "That Manāf was worshipped as a god is proved by the testimony of a verse, and is confirmed by the occurrence of a name *'Abd Manāf* which was especially common at Mecca and among the neighbouring tribe of Hudhail." The word *Mānaphis* is found in an ancient inscription from the Haurān and seems to be derived from *Manāphios*, the name of this God.[49]

"...It is said that one of Muhammad's ancestors—the pedigree being Muhammad b. 'Abd Allāh b. 'Abd al-Muṭṭalib b. Hāshim b. 'Abd

---

[46]Ibid.

[47]Ibid.

[48]Ibid.

[49]Ibid.

Manāf—received this name because his mother consecrated him to Manāf, who was then the chief deity of Makka.

"...Ibn Kalbī knows nothing of its whereabouts except that menstruating women were bound to keep themselves at a distance from it.

"The name does not occur either in the Qur'ān or in classical *hadith*. It derives from a root *n-w-f*, which in several Semitic languages conveys the meaning of 'being elevated'."[50]

Nasr

It was "One of the idols of ancient Arabs, mentioned in the Qur'ān, Sūrah lxxi. 23. It was an idol which, as its name implies, was worshipped under the form of *an eagle*."[51] Muhammad made this God a contemporary of Noah. "But it is to be noticed that the Sabaeans likewise had a god called Nasr..."[52]

'Auf

The name *'Abd 'Auf* was quite common among the Arabs. 'Auf means "the great bird of prey". The word is not found in this form in the Arab language at present. But "the verb *'afā*, which is derived from it, means 'to wheel in the air,' as birds of prey are wont to do." The word "has, in particular, the sense of *augurium*, and it may be that the name of the god did not refer to the bird but to the omen drawn from it; in this case 'Auf would be a synonymous of Sa'd."[53]

Yagūth

"The god Yagūth, whose name evidently means 'helper,' was according to the Qur'ān (*Sūra* lxxi. 23), another of the deities worshipped in the days of Noah...We find no trace of this god in early times...But at a later period we hear of a god Yagūth, whose idol was an object of contention among the tribes of Yemen, and the name *'Abd Yagūth* occurs in various part of Arabia, even in the tribe of Taghilib on the north-eastern frontier."[54]

"Yagūth had the shape of a lion."[55]

---

[50]*First Encyclopaedia of Islam*, op. cit., Vol. V, p. 227.

[51]Thomas Patrick Hughes, *Dictionary of Islam*, First Published 1885, New Delhi Reprint 1976, p. 431.

[52]*Encyclopaedia of Religion and Ethics,* op. cit., p. 663. He reminds us of Garuḍa in the Purāṇas.

[53]Ibid.

[54]Ibid.

[55]S.M. Zwemer, *The Influence of Animisn in Islam*, New York, 1920, p. 5.

Ya'uq and Suwā'

The idol of Ya'uq "was in the form of a horse, and was worshipped in Yemen. (Bronze images of this idol are found in ancient tombs and are still used as amulets)...

"Suwā', in the form of a woman, was said to be from antidiluvian times..."[56]

"The name of the god Ya'uq, who is mentioned in the Qur'ān together with Yagūth, probably means 'the Preserver'; his cult seems to have been confined to Yemen. Suwā', who is also included among gods worshipped by Noah's contemporaries (*Sūrā* lxxi. 20), was apparently of no great importance. He had a sanctuary at a place in the territory of the Hudhail, but none, so far as we know, elsewhere. The meaning of his name is altogether obscure. Neither Suwā' nor Ya'uq seems to occur in the theophorous proper names. It is hardly necessary to remark that the transferring of all these Arabian deities to the age of Noah was a fantastic anachronism due to Muhammad himself."[57]

Hubal

"Hubal was worshipped at Mecca; his idol stood in the Ka'ba, and appears to have been in reality, the god of that sanctuary...It would be unsafe to trust the descriptions of the idol in question which are given by writers of a later period; there is reason, however, to believe that the god had a human form. We may likewise accept as historical the statement that near him were kept divining arrows, used for the purpose of ascertaining his will or forecasting future events. It is related that the idol was brought by 'Amr b. Luḥai from Ma'āb (Moab), a tradition which may contain some elements of truth, for we have independent evidence indicating that the god was known in the North. He seems to be mentioned in a Nabataean inscription at Hejr; and the tribe of Kalb, who dwelt in the Syrian Desert, used the name of *Hubal* as the name of a person or clan; the same tribe...used in like manner the names of Īsāf and Nā'ila, two other deities peculiar to Mecca. Moreover, 'Amr b. Luḥai is the representative of the Huzā'a, a tribe who, according to tradition, occupied the sacred territory of Mecca before it passed into the hands of the Quraish. The assertion that'Amr introduced the worship of idols into Mecca for the first time is, of course, utterly incredible. But the hypothesis that Hubal was a late importation from a foreign country is further supported by the fact that we hear nothing of him in other

[56]Ibid.

[57]*Encyclopaedia of Religion and Ethics*, op. cit., p. 663.

parts of Arabia, and even at Mecca personal names compounded with *Hubal* were unknown. When the Meccans gained a victory over the Prophet in the immediate neighbourhood of Medina, their leader shouted, 'Hurrah for Hubal !' Thus they regarded him as the natural enemy of the God preached by Muhammad."[58]

"Another tradition indeed relates that Hubal was an idol of Banū Kināna, worshipped also by the Quraish, and had been placed in the Ka'ba by Khuzaima b. Mudrika wherefore it used to be called Hubal Khuzaima. It is further related that the idol was of red carnelian, in the form of a man; the Quraish replaced the right hand which was broken, by a golden one..."[59]

"Hubal was in the form of a man and came from Syria; he was the god of rain and had a high place of honour."[60]

"An idol, the God of the Moon..."[61]

"It is remarkable that there is no distinct allusion to the idol in the whole of the Qur'ān."[62]

"The learned Dr. Pocock... derives the name from the Hebrew *habba'l* or *habbe'l* and suggests... the appropriateness of *havel*, 'vanity!' Among the Arabs, Hubal seems to have had a double character, in which respect he resembled the Syrian idol Baal (properly, Ba'al), who was regarded both as the founder of the Babylonian empire, and as the sun personified as a deity. The opinion that Hubal was the same as the Babylonian or Syrian idol Ba'al or Bēl, or synonymous with it, is in fact supported by the testimony of the Arabian authorities, who relate that it was originally brought from Syria or Mesopotamia. Of course, the Arabian writers do not maintain that Hubal was identical with Ba'al: they admit, however, that it was an astronomical deity, which Ba'al also is believed to have been—whose designation, by the way, like that of 'the sun' among ourselves, always appears with the article—'Habba'al'. Further, Herodotus (and after him, Rawlison) held the opinion that Hubbal was 'the Jupiter of the Arabians'—presumably because he was believed to have the power of sending rain..."[63]

Isāf and Nā'ila

Muslim tradition says that "They were a man and woman of

[58]Ibid., pp. 663–64. Pagan spiritual traditions elsewhere are also known to have borrowed or exchanged idols. No idol is foreign to the pagan psyche.

[59]*First Encyclopaedia of Islam*, op. cit., Vol. III, p. 327.

[60]S.M. Zwemer, op. cit., p. 5.

[61]Cyril Glasse, op. cit., p. 160.

[62]Thomas Patrick Hughes, op. cit., p. 181.

[63]'The Oracle of Hubal', article in *Indian Antiquary*, Vol. XII, (January, 1883), p. 5.

Jurhum—Isāf b. Baghy and Nā'ila d. Dīk—who were guilty of sexual relations in the Ka'ba and so God transformed them into two stones."[64]

Obviously the tradition is a fabrication. As pointed out above, the tribe of Kalb in the Syrian Desert worshipped both of them as deities along with Hubal. The idols "stood near Mecca on the hills of Safa and Mirwa; the visitation of these popular shrines is now a part of the Muslim pilgrimage..."[65]They were no doubt "two sacred stones, but the origin of their names is so far unexplained."[66]

Al-Qais

He was an ancient God of the pagan Arabs. "He must have early disappeared as a deity, for al-Kalbī does not mention him in his *Kitāb al-Aṣnām* and he is not given in the various passages in Arab literature that give lists of the gods of the Djahilīya. But that he was at one time worshipped as a god may be deduced with considerable certainty from the tribal name 'Abd al-Qais and from the well-known personal and tribal name Imru' al-Qais." The name of a God mentioned in the Nabataean inscription from al-Ḥijr "can hardly be other than an Aramaic adaptation of al-Qais" who "had a sanctuary in al-Ḥijr in which copies of documents used to be deposited." The word "*qais*" carries several meanings in the dictionaries. De Goeje "has deduced the meaning 'Lord' from al-Hamdānī, Djazīrat al-'Arab."[67]

Al-Uqaiṣir

"...The name of a divinity of pre-Muhammadan Arabia, or better an epithet, the meaning of which (diminutive of *aqṣar*, 'he who has a stiff neck' or perhaps simply 'the short') seems to indicate an idol in a human shape. All that we know of the god (whose real name is unknown) goes back to the references to him by Ibn al-Kalbī, *Kitāb al-Aṣnām* followed by Yāqūt, *Mu'djam*...Al-Uqaiṣir was worshipped by the tribes of Quḍā'a, Lakhm, Djudhām, 'Amila and Ghaṭafān living on the plateau of the Syrian Desert. Verses in old poets quoted by Ibn al-Kalbī mention stones (*anṣāb*) put up around the sacred place, the 'garments' (*athwāb*), the ditch (*djafr*) into which were thrown the offerings, the cries and chants of the pilgrims...

---

[64]Ibn Ishāq, op. cit., p. 37.

[65]S.M. Zwemer, op. cit., p. 6.

[66]*First Encyclopaedia of Islam*, op. cit., Vol. III, p. 527. Hindu iconography is familiar with *Mithunas*, Gods and their Consorts, worshipped together.

[67]Ibid., Vol. IV, p. 651. There is considerable inscriptional evidence from South India about the Hindu practice of making various types of agreements in the temples, thus invoking the Gods and Goddesses as witnesses.

"As Wellhausen notes, the expressions used in the verses which Ibn al-Kalbī quotes in connection with al-Uqaiṣir must refer to a sanctuary as well as to an idol. We might then suppose that the epithet reflects the squat form of the building. It is worthwhile recalling that the name Uqaisir is also applied to a tribe, to individuals and even to a sword."[68]

Shai al-Qaum

We learn about this God from a Palmyrene and a Nabataean inscription. He is "the Companion of the people", "the kind god who rewards (or who is grateful), and who drinks no wine", that is, "to whom no libations of wine are offered."[69]

Duwar

"...was the virgins' idol and young women used to go around it in procession, hence its name."[70]

Conclusion

The deities listed in the foregoing few pages may sound too many to minds under the spell of monotheism. The fact, however, is that they are far too few and represent only what has been salvaged by modern scholarship form the extensive ruins caused by Islam. For the pagan Arabs, the whole of their homeland was honeycombed with temples and sanctuaries housing hundreds of divinities with as many Names and Forms. Every household had its ancestral deities which were joined by those brought in by the brides. Every locality, every oasis, every grove had its own presiding deity. So also every tribal territory. Finally, the national temple, the Ka'ba at Mecca, had as many as three hundred and sixty deities, the Names and Forms of which remain unknown except in the case of a few. "It seems that in course of time the various Arab tribes had brought in their gods and placed them in the Ka'ba, which had consequently acquired the character of the national pantheon for the whole of Arabia."[71]

The more pertitent point in the present context, however, is that the pagan Arabs were fully satisfied with their ancestral religion and felt no need for a replacement. Of course, they were not in the business of

---

[68]Ibid., Vol. VIII, p. 993.
[69]*Encyclopaedia of Religion and Ethics*, op. cit., p. 663.
[70]S.M. Zwemer, op. cit., p. 6.
[71]Shaikh Inayatullah, op. cit., p. 130.

saving souls and civilizing other people, which is what has come to count in the history of religion. But that is a "fault" inbuilt in the very genius of paganism. "Occupied with the reform of their own lives and the righting of actual wrongs, these persons made no noise and being earnest did not suppose that the replacement of one cult for another would make men virtuous; and Mohammed himself had occasion to draw a contrast between the conduct of his pagan and that of his believing son-in-law, greatly to the disadvantage of the latter. So far as the religious sentiment requires gratification, there is no evidence to show that paganism had failed to gratify it. We gather from the inscriptions of the pagan Arabs that a wealth of affection and gratitude was bestowed upon their gods and patrons."[72] In the pagan spiritual tradition people are expected to be "busy with themselves", that is, busy in improving their own morals by purifying their own consciousness. The prophetic tradition, on the other hand, harangues people to be "busy with the others", that is, saving other people from sin, infidelity, and the eternal hell-fire. That is why the prophetic tradition abounds in missions and *da'was*, crusades and *jihāds*.

It is often pointed out that no pagan Arab came foreward with a philosophical defence of his religion when it was assailed by Muhammad. The only defence which every pagan put up for his religion was that it was the religion of his forefathers and, as such, hallowed by time and tradition. A deeper reflection goes to show that this was indeed a very strong defence. What the monothesists dismiss as polytheism and idol-worship are natural to the normal human psyche. Moreover, honouring that which was honoured by one's ancestors keeps one rooted in one's history and culture. Cults which encourage one to denounce one's ancestors as barbarians or infidels, and one's past history as an age of ignorance, render one rootless and make one into a menace to one's neighbours. The Bible provides ample evidence of the normal people reverting to polytheism and idol-worship again and again, and the persistent and violent wars which the prophets had to wage for reimposing Jehovah on them. In any case, a religion stands in need of a philosophical defence only when it is already on a course of decline, and an inner dissatisfaction starts gnawing at the heart of its more perceptive adherents. There is no evidence that the pagan Arabs were suffering from such a psychosis on the eve of Islam. The confidence with which they spurned Muhammad's message and ridiculed his superior claims leaves

[72]D.S. Margoliouth, op. cit., p. 25.

little doubt that Arab Paganism was still in a state of good health. Though not so the environment in which this Paganism lived and breathed. The mental disorder glorified as monotheism was present in an epidemic form, not only all around it but also in its very midst. Arab Paganism was blissfully ignorant of what monotheism meant and the mischief it intended for a society which permitted it to spread.

CHAPTER TWELVE

MONOTHEISM SPREADS TO ARABIA

Monotheism had infected the Jews some two millenia before the birth of Muhammad. Moses had sold them into slavery to Jehovah, a demoniacal Spirit masquerading as the one and only God.[1] Many books of the Bible tell the blood-curdling story of what the Jews did to themselves and to the others when goaded by this Gangster. The end result was their own ruination, and their dispersal as slaves and refugees in all directions. Meanwhile, the disease had spread to West Asia, Europe and North Africa in the form of Christianity. It had destroyed the Greco-Roman civilization as well as Germanic paganism, and spread darkness wherever it went. Now it was getting ready to engulf Arabia which had survived so far as an island of sanity in the midst of a surging sea of madness.

The pagan Arabs, however, had remained unaware of the menace advancing on them from all sides. Abyssinia, their neighbour to the west, had been a Christian stronghold for long, and had even launched a crusade against them in recent times. The Byzantine Empire, their neighbour to the north, had gone Christian early in the fourth century, and was busy rooting out paganism within its own precincts. The Sassanian Empire of Persia, their neighbour to the east, was patronizing a Zoroastrianism which had lost its ancient Aryan genius and imbibed the spirit of Judaism and Christianity. It had become a monotheistic creed complete with *the* Prophet, *the* Book, the Last Day, and Heaven and Hell. The only point it missed and, therefore, lost the race to Judaism and Christianity, was missionary zeal; it was not yet out to force other people to its own way of worship.

Each of these neighbours was aspiring to invade and dominate Arabia. What kept them in check was their mutual rivalry. The peace which Arabia had enjoyed for long intervals was a byproduct of this balance of power. Even so, several Arab tribes in North and South Arabia had embraced Judaism or Christianity. Worse still, both Jews and

---

[1]This view of Jehovah was expressed by Marcion of the school of St. Paul, early in the second century AD. "The Old Testament he rejected *in toto* since it seemed to him, as it has seemed to many Christians since, to be talking of quite a different God: monstrous, evil-creating, bloody, the patron of ruffians like David" (*A Hislory of Christianity* by Paul Johnosn, Penguin Books, 1978, p. 46). This was also the view of the Gnostics, an early Christian sect. The "God" of the Bible and the Qur'ān was seen in this light by Thomas Jafferson, Thomas Paine, and Swami Dayananda as well.

Christians had settlements in the very heart of Arabia. The role which these preachy communities played in the rise of Islam has been highlighted by Muslims scholars themselves. Shaikh Inayatullah writes:

"In the century before Muhammad Arabia was not wholly abandoned to paganism. Both Judaism and Christianity claimed a considerable following among its inhabitants. Almost every calamity that befell the land of Palestine sent a fresh wave of Jewish refugees into Arabia, sometimes as far as Yemen. They had probably taken refuge there after the conquest of Palestine by Titus in AD 70. Jewish colonies flourished in Medina and several other towns of Ḥijāz. In the time of the Prophet, three large Jewish tribes, viz., the Naḍīr, Quraizah and Qainuqa', dwelt in the outskirts of Medīna, and the fact that the Prophet made an offensive and defensive alliance with them for the safety of the town shows that they were an important factor in the political life of those times. These colonies had their own teachers and centres of religious study. Judging by few extant specimens of their poetry, these refugees through contact with a people nearly akin to themselves, had become fully Arabicized both in language and sentiment. They, however, remained Jews in the most vital particular, religion, and it is probable that they exerted a strong influence over the Arabs in favour of monotheism.

"Another religious factor which was strongly opposed to Arabian paganism was the Christian faith. How early and from what direction Christianity entered Arabia is a question which it is difficult to answer with certainty but there is no doubt that Christianity was widely diffused in the southern and northern parts of Arabia at the time of the Prophet. Christianity is said to have been introduced in the valley of Najrān in northern Yemen from Syria, and it remained entrenched in spite of the terrible persecution it suffered at the hands of the Ḥimyarite king, Dhū Nawās, who had adopted the Jewish faith...Christianity in the south-west of Arabia received a fresh stimulus by the invasion of the Christian Abyssinians, who put an end to the rule of Dhū Nawās. There were Christians in Mecca itself; Waraqah ibn Naufal, a cousin of Khadījah, the first wife of the Prophet, was one of them. Christianity was also found among certain tribes of the Euphrates and the Ghassān who lived on the borders of Syria. Their conversion was due to their contact with the Christian population of the Byzantine Empire...The Christians were also found at Ḥīrah, a town in the north-east of Arabia, where Arab princes of the house of Lakhm ruled under the suzerainty of the Persian kings. These Christians who were called 'Ibād or the 'Servants of the Lord,' belonged to the Nestorian Church, and contributed to the diffusion of Christian ideas among the Arabs of the Peninsula.

"By the sixth century, Judaism and Christianity had made considerable headway in Arabia, and were extending their sphere of influence, leavening the pagan masses, and thus gradually preparing the way for Islam."[2]

Most of the Jews and Christians settled in Arabia were descendants of refugees who had fled at one time or the other from persecutions in the Byzantine and the Persian empires. Arab paganism had provided them not only protection but also freedom to practise and preach their creeds. They had, therefore, succeeded in making some converts among the Arabs. But the fact that they were refugees and that the pagan Arabs were their protectors, was soon forgotten. It was not long before the Jews and the Christians started using the security and the freedom for pouring contempt on Arab paganism. Medina in particular had become a Jewish stronghold. Gibbon tells us that this city with its wealthy and vociferous Jewish tribes had become famous all over Arabia as the City of the Book.[3] It was as sick with monotheism as a harlot with venereal desease. Small wonder that it became Muhammad's base of operations for imposing Islam on the rest of Arabia after he had to leave Mecca in utter despair. "The course of the following narrative will show," observes Margoliouth, "that Muhammad's mission at Meccah was a failure, and that it was only at Medinah...that he readily found a hearing, and that having turned Medinah into an armed camp, he was able partly by force and partly by bribes to subjugate Meccah, whence he proceeded quickly to subdue the rest of Arabia."[4]

It seems that the pagan Arabs, by and large, were not prone to catch the infection. They were happy with their healthy paganism but for a few persons, particulary among their educated elite, who equated religious superiority with superiority in material wealth, or military power, or both. Every society has individuals who get alienated from their own culture simply because that society happens to be poor or powerless. The pagan Arab society was no exception. Compared to the Abyssinian, Byzantine and the Persian empires, Arabia was poor in material wealth as well as military prowess. Some upper class Arabs

---

[2]Shaikh Inayatullah, op. cit., pp. 134–35. There is no evidence of leavening of the masses; only some members of the Arab elite were alienated from their society and culture.

[3]Edward Gibbon, *The Decline and Fall of the Roman Empire*, Modern Libary Edition, New York, Vol. III, p. 97.

[4]D.S. Margoliouth, op. cit., p. 31.

who travelled to the neighbouring lands or heard the gorgeous stories from others, were swept off their feet. They readily accepted the explanation, advanced by hawkers of monotheism, that the foreign lands were rich and powerful simply because each of them had a Prophet and a Book. Lenin, Mao Tse-tung, M.N. Roy, Jawaharlal Nehru and many others all over the world are excellent examples of the fascination which the power and wealth of foreign countries exercises over shallow but self-righteous minds; they start by despising themselves as members of a poor society, and end by despising their people and culture. Ibn Ishāq provides interesting evidence about the presence of such self-alienated Arabs in Mecca itself. He writes:

"One day when the Quraysh assembled on a feast day to venerate and circumambulate the idol to which they offered sacrifices, this being a feast which they held annually, four men drew apart secretly and agreed to keep their counsel in the bonds of friendship. They were (i) Waraqa bin Nufal; (ii) Ubaydullah b. Jahash; (iii) 'Uthmān b. al-Ḥuwayrith; and (iv) Zayd b. 'Amr. They were of the opinion that their people had corrupted the religion of their father Abraham, and that the stone they went round was of no account; it could neither hear, nor see, nor hurt, nor help.[5] 'Find for yourselves a religion,' they said; 'for by God you have none.' So they went their several ways in the lands, seeking the Ḥanīfiya, the religion of Abraham.

"Waraqa attached himself to Christianity and studied its scriptures until he had thoroughly mastered them. Ubaydullah went on searching until Islam came; then he migrated with the Muslims to Abyssinia taking with him his wife who was Muslim, Umm Habība d. Abū Sufyān. When he arrived there he adopted Christianity, parted from Islam, and died a Christian in Abyssinia.

"'Uthmān b. Ḥuwayrith went to the Byzantine emperor and became a Christian. He was given high office there.

"Zayd b. 'Amr stayed as he was. He accepted neither Judaism nor Christianity. He abandoned the religion of his forefathers and abstained from idols...saying that he worshipped the God of Abraham, and he publicly rebuked his people for their practices....

"Zayd b. 'Amr composed the following poem :

Am I to worship one lord or a thousand ?
If there are as many as you claim,
I renounce al-Lāt and al-'Uzzā both of them

[5]These words vis-a-vis idols are found very frequently in the Bible and will very soon appear in the Qur'ān.

As any strong-minded person would.
I will not worship al-'Uzzā and her two daughters,
Nor will I visit the two idols of Banū 'Amr.
I will not worship Hubal though he was our lord
In the days when I had little sense...
You will see the pious living in gardens,
While for the infidels hell fire is burning.
Shamed in life, when they die
Their breasts will contract in anguish...
Beware of putting another beside God
For the upright way has become clear.

"Then he went forth seeking the religion of Abraham questioning monks and Rabbis until he had traversed al-Mauṣil and the whole of Mesopotamia; then he went through the whole of Syria until he came to a monk in the high ground at Balaqā. This man, it is alleged, was well-versed in Christianity. He asked him about the Ḥanīfīya, the religion of Abraham and the monk replied. 'You are seeking a religion to which no one today can guide you, but the time of a prophet who will come forth from your own country which you have just left has drawn near. He will be sent with the Ḥanīfīya, the religion of Abraham, so stick to it, for he is about to be sent now and this is his time.' Now Zayd had sampled Judaism and Christianity and was not satisfied with either of them; so that at these words he went away at once making for Mecca; but when he was inside the country of Lakhm he was attacked and killed.

"Waraqa b. Naufal composed this elegy over him.

You were altogether in the right path Ibn 'Amr,
You have escaped hell's burning oven
By serving the one and only God
And abandoning vain idols."[6]

References to Ḥanīfīya, the religion of Abraham, in this story can be ignored as they obviously reflect wisdom by hindsight. It was not before Muhammad migrated to Medina and discovered that the Jews were not prepared to accept him as a prophet, that he invented a religion of Abraham distinct from both Judaism and Christianity. Till that time he had been seeking certificates from the People of the Book, the Jews and the Christians, to the effect that his teachings were in accordance with what was written in their scriptures. Equally anachronistic in this story is the prophecy about the advent of Muhammad. Orthodox

[6]Ibn Isḥāq, op. cit., pp. 98–101, 103.

biographers of the Prophet have put such prophecies in the mouths of several Jewish rabbis and Christian monks. They were only trying to be wise after the event. All that is true in the story of Waraqa etc., is that some Arabs were turning *away* from their ancestral religion and *towards* the alien cult of monotheism. At the same time, some prophets were also appearing in Arabia and claiming to be in direct communication with God.

Monotheism being a cult of prophets, its appearance in pagan Arabia was bound to produce some of this species. Prophethood is not at all a difficult profession if we go by their crop in the Bible. One has only to manage the requisite amount of self-deception and self-righteousness and go about shouting from the housetops that one's people have sunk into sin. One has also to be ready, if opportunity occurs, to use violence against one's own people. It was, therefore, only a copybook exercise for prophets who arose in pagan Arabia. They had only to ape their prototypes in the stories retailed to them by the Jews and the Christians. Muhammad was not the first of these novel Arab characters.

"Prophets indeed had arisen in Arabia before Mohammed: in Yemen among the Himyarites one Samaifa had imitated the exploits of old Zamolaxis: had hidden himself for a time and then reappeared, when a hundred thousand men prostrated themselves before their risen lord. Legends containing probably some germ of truth recorded how shortly before Mohammed one Khalid, son of Sinan, had been sent to preach to the tribe of 'Abs, and one Hanzalah, son of Safwan, to some other of the inhabitants of Arabia. In Yemamah, too, one Maslamah had given a sign that he was sent from God: through the neck of a bottle he introduced an egg unbroken to the bowl. Since Yemamah supplied Meccah with corn, the tradition that makes Muhammad a pupil of Maslamah has certainly some foundation."[7]

"According to Ibn Ishāq, Muhammad's enemies reproached him with having obtained his wisdom from a man of Yamāma named Raḥmān. Now we have ample evidence that Musailima, who preached in the name of Raḥmān was himself called Raḥmān. It is also worthy of note that the prophetic utterances attributed to Musailima recall the earliest Meccan sūras with their short rhyming sentences and curious oaths and have no resemblance to later Medinese sūras. In particular

[7]D.S. Margoliouth, op. cit., pp. 80–81. The phenomena of "prophets" arising in Arabia was comparable to the crop of "revolutionaries" arising all over the world in the wake of Lenin's *coup d'etat* in Russia in 1917.

the fact that all the Banū Ḥanīfa followed him into battle against the Medinese shortly after the death of Muhammad shows that he must have been active for a considerable time and was no imitator of Muhammad...According to Saif's account he must have been considerably influenced by Christianity for he speaks of the kingdom of heaven..."[8] Musailima had introduced *ṣalāt*, several times a day. He also maintained a *mu'azzin* and a *muqīm*.

It seems that these pretentious Arabs were not fully familiar with the institution of prophethood. The rise of a female prophet, Sajāh, shows their ignorance of the fact that prophethood in the Judaic and Christian traditions was strictly a male profession, and women supposed to be the source of sin, had no right to it. Sajāh was a woman of Banū Tamīm and one of the several prophets who sprang up shortly before Muhammad. "On the mother's side she was related to Taghilib, a tribe which comprised many Christians. She was a Christian herself, or at least had learnt much concerning Christianity from her relatives. Next to nothing is known concerning the import of her revelations and doctrines; she delivered her messages from a *minbar*, in rhymed prose, and was attended by a *mu'adhdhin* and a *hājib*. Her name, or one of her names for God, was 'the Lord of the clouds' (*rabb al-ṣahāb*)."[9] She joined forces with Musailima when the two of them were attacked by Muslim armies after the death of Muhammad. Muslim historians love to tell obscene stories about the marriage and the merry-making of the two "false prophets".

So there was nothing novel about Muhammad standing up one fine morning and proclaiming that he was the prophet sent by Allāh. The pagan Arabs were already used to such queer characters among their otherwise level-headed people. They pitied these prophets as victims possessed by evil spirits and offered the help of their medicine men. Obviously, they were impressed by no amount of prophetic talk.

It is, however, significant that the Arab prophets other than Muhammad are not known to have aroused the fierce opposition which Muhammad faced at Mecca and elsewhere. That was because they did not disparage the Arab Gods while preaching their monotheism. The pagans Arabs were not perturbed by prophets so long as the latter left their Gods alone. It was Muhammad who made them sit up when he spelled out the meaning of monotheism, namely, the dethronement of Arab Gods and the destruction of Arab temples. Muhammad will very

---

[8]*First Encyclopaedia of Islam*, op. cit., Vol. VI, p. 745.
[9]Ibid., Vol. VII, p. 44.

soon denounce the other Arab prophets also as impostors and liars because they either did not know the meaning of monotheism or were wilfully suppressing vital parts of the doctrine.

Chapter Thirteen

MEANING OF MONOTHEISM

As we shall see, the Allāh of the Qur'ān says again and again that he is not revealing anything new but only re-affirming what is already recorded in the earlier scripture, namely, the Bible. He is annoyed with the Jews in particular for their refusal to recognize Muhammad as a prophet when their own prophets were known to have spread the same message received from the same source. Muhammad, too, is pained that his people repudiate him without checking with the Jews and the Christians the truth of what he is proclaiming. Muslim theologians of later ages will deny that Muhammad learnt anything from the Bible. In their eagerness to invest Muhammad with an absolutely orignal inspiration, they will portray him as an illiterate (*ummī*) who could neither read nor write. But we will better believe Allāh and his prophet rather than the latter-day Muslim theologians, and proceed to examine what the Bible says vis-a-vis other people's gods and places of worship.

The Bible is, of course, a large and complex composition spanning several centuries and dealing with diverse subjects. We shall confine ourselves to the main theme which runs through all its book except most of the Psalms and Proverbs, namely, the struggle by a succession of prophets to make the Jews stick to a strict monotheism with all its implications. The prophets speak on behalf of a boastful being who introduces himself as Jehovah and thunders a thousand time that he alone is worthy of worship to the exclusion of all "other gods". Moses hails him as "a warrior" whose name "the nations heard and trembled."[1]

The story in the Bible starts a long time before Jehovah identifies himself to Moses. But that story is not relevant in the present context except at one point where Jacob asked his people to "rid yourselves of foreign gods you have among you" and "buried them under the terebinth tree."[2] For our purpose, the story acquires interest only after Moses leads his people out of Egypt and goes up to Mount Sinai where he has been summoned by Jehovah "in a peal of thunder."[3] That is when Moses receives the famous Ten Commandments.

The commandments that are relevant in the present context are the first two. Jehovah says, "I am the Lord your God who brought you out

---

[1]Exod. 15.3,14.
[2]Gen. 35.2.4.
[3]Exod. 19.19.

of Egypt, out of the land of slavery. You shall have no other gods set against me. You shall not have a carved image for yourself nor the likeness of anything in the heavens above, or on the earth below, or in the waters under the earth. You shall not bow down to them, for, I, the Lord your God am a jealous god. I punish the children for the sins of their forefathers to the third and fourth generations of those that hate me."[4] He does not make it clear how homage to other gods means hatred for him. He betrays the pathological state of mind in which a person feels slighted simply because some other person is praised. In any case, he goes ahead and lays down that "whoever sacrifices to any other god but the Lord shall be put to death under solemn ban."[5]

This was no empty threat as Moses proved soon after. While he went up to Mount Sinai for a second time his people down below melted their ornaments, made a golden calf, and started worshipping it with song and dance. Jehovah was furious. He threatened to destroy the whole lot of them, and Moses had a hard time pacifying him. Moses hurried down in order to handle the situation. "Then he took the calf they had made and burnt it; he ground it to powder, sprinkled it on water and made the Israelites drink it."[6] Next he took his place at the gate of the camp and said, "Who is on the Lord's side ? Come here to me; and the Levites all rallied to him. He said to them, 'These are the words of the Lord the God of Israel: Arm yourselves, each of you, with his sword. Go through the camp from gate to gate and back again. Each of you will kill his brother, his friend, his neighbour.' The Levites obeyed, and about three thousand of the people died. Moses then said, 'Today you have consecrated yourselves to the Lord, because you have each turned against his own son and his own brother and so have brought this blessing upon yourselves.' "[7] All ties of kinship which normal societies, particularly pagan societies, have prized stood dissolved in the new dispensation. A brotherhood of believers (or bandits) based on a commonly shared cult came into existence. Muhammad will also call upon the Muslims to do the same and acknowledge no relationship higher than obedience to the dictates of Islam.

Jehovah made it quite clear to the Jews that if they failed to punish

---

[4]Exod. 20.2-5; See also Exod. 20.23; 23.13,24; 34.17; Lev. 19.4; 26.1; Deut. 4.16, 23-24; 27.14-15; Jos. 24.14,23; 1sa. 42.8; Ezech. 20.6-8, 15-18, 23-24, 28-31, 39.

[5]Exod. 22.20; Lev. 20-1-5; Deut. 17.2-5.

[6]Exod. 32.20. Islamic invaders of India repeated the performance many times after burning Hindu idols. Mahmūd of Ghazni is the first to be credited with it in Muslim annals.

[7]Exod. 32.26-29. See also Deut. 13.6-11; 17.2-5

those among them who turned to other gods, he will take the matter in his own hands and inflict terrible calamities on the whole people. "If inspite of this you do not listen to me and still defy me, I will defy you in anger, and I myself will punish you seven times over for your sins. Instead of meat you shall eat your sons and your daughters. I will destroy your hill shrines and demolish your incense altars. I will pile your rotting carcases on the rotting logs that were your idols, and I will spurn you. I will make your cities desolate and destroy your sanctuaries... I will destroy your land and the enemies who occupy it shall be appalled. I will scatter you among the heathen and I will pursue you with the naked sword; your land shall be desolate and your cities heaps of rubble."[8] He left no one in doubt that he was a hardened gangster who would stop at no crime. We shall meet him again in the Qur'ān.

The "other gods" are not worth worshipping because they are "made by human hands out of wood and stone, gods that can neither see nor hear, neither eat nor smell."[9] Idols are not only dead matter but also "loathsome and abominable."[10] They cannot help, nor save you in an emergency.[11] We shall meet the same note in the Qur'ān. Allāh will also pity the people who bow before such "dead and dumb things".

The march towards the land, which Jehovah had long ago promised to deliver to his Chosen People, was resumed. Jehovah himself led the Jewish horde, assuming the form of a cloud. On the way he gave elaborate instructions about how he himself was to be worshipped. At last they were on the frontiers of the promised land. Jehovah briefed them how to proceed: "When the Lord your God brings you into the land which you are entering to occupy and drive out many nations before you—Hitites, Girgashites, Amorites, Cananites, Perrizites, Hivites and Jebusites, seven nations more numeous and powerful than you—when the Lord your God delivers them into your power and you defeat them, you must put them to death. You must not make a treaty with them or spare them. You must not intermarry with them, neither giving your daughters to their sons nor taking their daughters for your sons: if

---

[8]Lev. 26.27-33. See also Deut. 4.25-28; 6.14-15; 8.9-20; 30.17-18; 31.16-18; 32.16-17,21,23-25, 37-42; Jos. 23.16; 24.20, 1 Kings 11.1-13; 2 Chr. 7.19-20; 34, 24-25; Ps. 16.4; Isa. 19.1-4; Jer. 5.19; 7.16-20; 11.9-11; 16.18-21; 17.1-4; 18.21; 44.15-27; Ezech. 6.3-7, 13-14; 8.7-18; 16.35-43; Hos. 2.4-6; 10-13; 8.3-7; 10.1-8; 11.2-6; 13.1-3; Mich. 1.6-7; 5.13-14; Nah. 1.14; Zeph. 1.4-6; Zach. 11.17; Rev. 2.21-23.

[9]Deut. 4.28. See also Ps. 115.4-8; 134.15-18; Isa. 37.12,19,38; 41.22-24; 44.9-20, 46.6-7; Jer. 10.1-5, 8-9, 14-15; 16.20; Zach. 10.2; 1 Cor. 8.4.

[10]Deut. 7.26. See also Deut. 12.29-31; Jer. 4.1; 6.15; Acts 15.20; 1 Cor. 10.14; 2 Cor 6.15-18; Eph. 5.5; Col. 3.5; 1 Jn. 5.21.

[11]Deut. 32.37-38; Judges 10.13-14; Ps. 96.5; 97.7; Jer. 2.28.

you do, they will draw your sons away from the Lord and make them worship other gods. Then the Lord will be angry with you and quickly destroy you. But this is what you must do to them: pull down their altars, break their sacred pillars, hack down their sacred poles and destroy their idols by fire, for you are a people holy to the Lord your God; the Lord your God chose you out of all the nations on earth to be his special possession."[12]

Jehovah also warned the Jews against reformers who may appear among them. "When a prophet or dreamer appears among you and offers you a sign or a portent and calls on you to follow other gods whom you have not known and worshipped, then, even if the sign or portent should come true, do not listen to the words of that prophet or that dreamer...That prophet or that dreamer shall be put to death, for he has preached rebellion against the Lord who brought you out of Egypt and redeemed you from the path which the Lord your God commanded you to take. You must rid yourselves of this wickedness."[13] The gate was thus slammed for ever against any second thoughts on the subject. The Israelites were to remain in the prisonhouse of monotheism for all time to come.

The conquest of the promised land proceeded apace, accompanied by unmitigated slaughter and rapine.[14] Jehovah commanded his servants again and again not to leave alive anything that breathes. "So Joshua massacred the population of the whole region—the hill country, the Nageb, the Shephelah, the watersheds—and all their kings. He left no survivor, destroying everything that drew breath as the Lord God of Israel had commanded."[15] Jehovah took credit for all the victories and waxed eloquent in self-adulation.

But as the war of conquest drew to a close and the Jews settled down in the promised land they reverted more and more to the normal human habit of worshipping the Divine in many Names and Forms. They intermarried with the neighbouring non-Jewish tribes, defying the ban which Jehovah had imposed on them. The foreign brides brought their own Gods, and also priests who tended to those Gods. The defiance of Jehovah reached a new high in the reign of Solomon. He had seven hundred wives, most of them foreign princesses, and three hundred concubines who "turned his heart to follow other gods."[16] Je-

---

[12]Deut. 7.1-6. See also Exod. 23.23-24, 27.32-33; 34.10, 12-17; Num. 33.50-56; Deut. 7.16, 23-26; 8.19-20; 12.1-3; Jos. 6.17; 8.1-8, 28-29; 23.7.

[13]Deut. 13.1-5. See also Deut. 13.12-16; 18.20.

[14]See Jos. 6.21-24; 8.22-25, 28-29; 10.5-40.

[15]Jos. 10.40. See also Jos. 11.5-6, 8-9.

[16]I Kings 11.1-5.

hovah warned him twice but to no avail. Solomon simply ignored him, and he could not do a thing. He consoled himself that he was sparing Soloman for the sake of the latter's father, King David.

The Jewish kingdom split into two after the death of Solomon—Israel in the north with its seat at Samaria, and Judah in the south with its seat at Jerusalem. The scribes who wrote the story of Solomon credited Jehovah with a curse which broke the kingdom after Solomon's death. It was wisdom after the event. In any case, the worship of other gods continued unabated. Ahab, king of Israel, had married a foreign princess, Jezebel, who was a devotee of Baal. Temples were built for the new God where his priests presided. Ahab himself paid homage to him. Elijah, a self-appointed prophet, admonished the king but was dismissed with contempt. So Elijah took resort to trickery. He invited the priests of Baal to Mount Carmel in order to demonstrate to them the superiority of Jehovah over Baal. His swordsmen who lay in ambush seized four hundred and fifty priests. Elijah himself "took them down the Kishon and slaughtered them in the valley."[17] Then he ran away for dear life because queen Jezebel had summoned him.

The mantle of Elijah fell on Elisha. He earned his well-deserved reputation as a prophet by cursing some naughty children, forty-two of whom were torn to pieces by she-bears.[18] He egged on an adventurer, Jehu, who seized the throne of Israel after slaughtering the sons of Ahab, and getting Jezebel thrown out of a palace window so that "some of the blood splashed on the wall and the horses who trampled her under foot."[19] The worship of Baal, however, was far from finished in the kingdom, and many of his priests were still around. Guided by Elisha, Jehu announced that he, too, had become a devotee of Baal and was holding a great sacrifice in the big temple in the capital city. He invited all the priests of Baal and saw to it that all of them assembled. His armed guard fell on them suddenly and slaughtered them to the last man. The idols in the temple were brought out and burnt. The sacred poles were broken and the sacred pillars pulled down. The temple was turned into a lavatory. Jehovah blessed the enterprise and confirmed the kingdom in the family of Jehu for four generations.[20] Elisha lived thereafter a much satisfied man who had fulfilled his mission.

An so on, the story snowballs through the rest of the books in the

[17]1 Kings 18.17-40.
[18]2 Kings 2.23-24.
[19]2 Kings 9.33.
[20]2 Kings 10.18-30.

Bible. The common people in the two kingdoms relapse into polytheism and idol-worship, again and again. More prophets appear on the scene and do what Elijah and Elisha had done.[21] Each succeeding prophet turns out to be a gangster greater than the preceding one. They curse and torment their own people, and invoke calamities on them. But as the people remain indifferent to them, they feel utterly helpless and console themselves by praying for the "great day" when the Lord will destroy all other gods together with those who worshipped them.[22]

Jehovah himself had always been intemperate in his language vis-a-vis those who strayed away from the straight path. But as he feels more and more helpless in the face of his people's "obstinacy", his language becomes increasingly foul and ends by being downright obscene. He views the worship of other gods as adultery and fornication, and denounces both kingdoms as harlots given to wilful whoredom.

He addresses his prophet Ezekiel and says: "Son of man, cause Jerusalem to know her abominations[23]... And it came to pass after all thy wickedness, that thou hast also built unto thee an eminent place and made thee a high place in every street...and hast opened thy feet to every one that passed, and multiplied thy whoredoms.[24] Thou has also committed fornication with the Egyptians thy neighbours, great of flesh[25]... They give gifts to all whores: but thou givest thy gifts to all thy lovers, and hirest them, that they may come unto thee from every side for thy whoredom[26].. O harlot, hear the words of the Lord: Thus saith the Lord God: Because thy filthiness was poured out, and thy nakedness discovered through thy whoredoms with thy lovers, and with all the idols of thy abominations...I will gather all thy lovers with whom thou has taken pleasure...I will gather them round about against thee, and will discover thy nakedness unto them, that they may see all thy nakedness...And I will also give thee into their hands...and they shall stone thee with stones, and thrust thee through with their swords. And

[21]See 2 Kings 11.17-18; 23.4-6. 8,10-14; 15-16,19-20,24; 1 Chr.14.8-12; 2 Chr.14.2-5, 23.17; 33.1-15; 34.3-7 for some of the stories.

[22]See Isa. 2.18-21; 17.7-8; 31.7-8.

[23]Ezech. 16.2. "Abominations" means "idols".

[24]Ezech. 16.23-25. In plain language "eminent place" and "high place" mean a "brothel." The reference is to temples of other gods which came up in every street. "Opened thy feet to everyone that passed" means worshipping every other god.

[25]Ezech. 16.26. "Great of flesh" in plain language means "possessing a big male organ." The reference is to the size of gods from Egypt.

[26]Ezech. 16.33. What is meant by this passage is that people of Jerusalem worship gods who cannot reward them in exchange for their devotion. Jehovah cannot understand any worship which is spontaneous and without expectation of reward. He is fond of making convenants with his devotees, no matter whether he can fulfil them or not. He also threatens punishments, no matter whether he can carry them out or not.

they shall burn thy houses with fire...and I will cause thee to cease from playing the harlot, and thou also shall give no hire any more."[27]

In another message to the same prophet, Jehovah says, "Son of man, there were two women, the daughters of the same mother. And they committed whoredoms in Egypt; they committed whoredoms in their youth : there were their breasts pressed, and there they bruised the teats of their virginity."[28] Turning to Samaria, he pronounces: "Neither left she her whoredoms brought from Egypt : for in her youth they lay with her, and they bruised the breasts of her virginity, and poured their whoredoms upon her."[29] Coming back to Jerusalem, his language becomes filthier. "And when her sister saw this, she was more corrupt in her inordinate love than she, and in her whoredoms more than her sister in her whoredoms...For she doted upon their paramours whose flesh is as the flesh of asses and whose issue is like the issue of horses."[30]

Jehovah's character, as portrayed in the Bible, can now be summed up. He behaves like a bully and a coward par excellence, apart from his proclaiming, again and again, that he is a hardened gangster who has committed many crimes. He takes the whole credit every time the Jews are victorious and commit slaughter and rapine. But when the tables are turned on the Jews, he turns tail and blames the Jews for betraying him by worshipping other gods. The Jews on their part try to return to monotheism, and its concomitant, iconoclasm, again and again, on being admonished by their prophets. But their situation does not improve. They get defeated and enslaved successively by the Assyrians, the Babylonians, the Persians, the Mecedonians, the Seleucids, and the Romans. In the final round, the only country which they had occupied after making rivers of blood flow is lost to them for ever, and Jehovah's

---

[27]Ezech.16.35-41. Jehovah threatens to get Jerusalem destroyed by those very nations whose gods are worshipped in that kingdom. He will take credit when Jerusalem is attacked and destroyed by other nations, though he will have no hand in mobilizing the attacks. He is always wise after the event and his scribes pre-date his presence in the stories.

[28]Ezech.23.2-3. The passage means that the Jews used to worship others gods while they were in Egypt. Jehovah has a dirty mind and cannot help resorting to obscene language for stating simple facts which he finds unpleasant for his inflated ego. His language became the stock-in-trade of Christian and, later on, Muslim theologians.

[29]Ezech.23.8

[30]Ezech, 23.11-20. "Flesh" means the 'male organ" and "issue" the "semen" which pours out in orgasm. What is meant is that the people of Jerusalem loved to worship large-sized idols. See also Jer. 2.23-28; 3.1-2, 6-9, 13; 5.7-8; 11.13-15; 13.26-27; Ezech. 23.40-44;Hos. 1-2; 2.2; 3.1; 4.12-14; 5.3-4; 6.10; 9.1; Nah. 3.4-6. The same language is used for pagan Rome in Rev. 2.14,20-23; 14.8; 17.2; 18.3,9; 19.2. Early Christian missionaries in India used the same language for idol-worship by Hindus who felt puzzled because their morals were far better than those of the contemporary Christians. The language had to be deciphered before Hindus could grasp its import.

only temple at Jerusalem is destroyed from the foundations, never to be built again. Jehovah does not bat an eye. He remains unshaken in the hallucination that he is the Lord.

His final volte-face on the Jews is simply breath-taking. Another self-appointed prophet named Jesus follows in the footsteps of his predecessors and harangues the Jews to repent, for the Last Day is drawing near. He shows some miracles collects crowds, and gets picked up by the Roman police as a disturber of peace. Jehovah does not lift his little finger to save the his prophet from a cruel and shameful death; Jesus is crucified along with two common thieves. The prophets that follow beat their Lord's record in double-talk. On the one hand, they pin down the crime on the Jews, so that this already tormented people gets subjected to repeated pogroms for two thousand years. On the other hand, they spread the abominable superstition that Jesus was the Christ who mounted the cross willingly and voluntarily in order to wash with his own blood the sins of mankind![31] Knavery, thy name is prophethood.

Reading the Bible between the lines, however, one cannot resist the conclusion that Jehovah's blessing as well cursing is no more than wisdom by hindsight. Howsoever awsome he may sound, particularly because he has been for a long time the god of nations with bigger guns, he remains a contrived creation of a closed and cruel theology mounted mechanically on purely mundane happening. He does not exist and has never existed outside that theology, neither in history nor in any high heaven. The only dwelling place which can be assigned to him is in the dark drives of human nature. He has possessed successively or he has been appropriated by some bandit formations bent upon wanton aggression in order to carve out predatory empires. The fact that these formations advertise themselves as the Church or the *Ummah* should deceive no one.

Christianity which took over bodily the closed theology of Judaism committed the same crimes on a far more extensive scale. This is not the place to describe what the Christian theologians, missionaries and swordsmen did to the pagan people and their places of worship in Europe, Asia, Africa, the Americas and the Oceania; for the present we are dealing with the Islamic theology of iconoclasm, and the Bible has

---

[31]According to some Bible scholars Jesus himself staged his crucifiction in order to prove to his own advantage some Old Testament prophecies, and survived the ordeal to spread the story that he had risen from the dead. But here we are concerned with the version hawked by Christian tradition and theology.

come in because it is the source of that scourge. What we wish to point out is that in every case the Bible was their guidebook. "The introduction of Christianity, and more especially its establishment in the Roman Empire in the fourth century of our era, proved the destruction of pagan idols, however skilfully and elegantly formed. The crusade against the statues of gods commenced in the latter part of the reign of Constantine and continued gradually to advance, until under Theodosius the Younger it pervaded all parts of the Empire. Not that the Christians despised art or were incapable of appreciating aesthetic excellence, whether in painting or in sculpture, but their hostility to pagan idols was wholly of a religious nature."[32] Nearer home and as late as the sixteenth century, "At least from 1540 onwards, and in the island of Goa before that year, all the Hindu idols had been annihilated or had disappeared,[33] all the Hindu temples had been destroyed and their sites and building material were in most cases utilized to erect new Christian churches and chapels."[34] A complete history of Christian iconoclasm world-wide has yet to be compiled. But judging from what we find scattered in the histories of Christianity in different countries, there is enough evidence that for a long time the Bible left a trail of devastation wherever it went.

[32]Rev. James Gardner, *Faiths of the World*, London, 1860, New Delhi Reprint, 1986, Vol. I, p. 306. What Christian iconoclasm did in the Roman Empire has been partly documented in Pierre Chuvin, *A Chronicle of the Last Pagans*, Harvard University Press, U.S.A., 1990.

[33]Hindus took away quite a few of their idols and installed them in temples beyond the reach of the Christian missionaries who were protected by the Portuguese pirates.

[34]T.R. de Souza in M.D. David (ed.), *Western Colonialism in Asia and Christianity*, Bombay, 1988, p. 18. The destruction in Goa has been documented in A.K. Priolkar, *The Goa Inquisition*, Bombay, 1962 (reprinted by Voice of India, 1991), and that in Madras by Ishwar Sharan, *The Myth of St. Thomas and the Mylapore Shiva Temple*, Voice of India. 1991. What the Jesuits did in Pondicherry under the French has been summarized from the Diary of Anand Ranga Pillai in Sita Ram Goel, *History of Hindu-Christian Encounters*. Voice of India, 1989, pp. 377–86.

CHAPTER FOURTEEN

THE BIBLE APPEARS IN ARABIC

The Qur'ān can, without an exaggeration, be called the Bible in Arabic so far as its dominant theme is concerned. That dominant theme is monotheism with all its implications, of which the most important is iconoclasm. Our judgement is confirmed by the way the pagan Arabs responded to the Qur'ān.

The Allāh of the Qur'ān announced again and again that he was making his revelations available in the Arabic language so that the Arabs could have a scripture of their own.[1] The response from the Arabs, however, was far from positive. Biographers of the prophet inform us that the more the pagan Arabs came to know the Qur'ān the more hostile they became to it, till the man through whose mouth it was being conveyed left Mecca in total frustration. The only Arab audience which the Prophet could find was in Yathrib (Medina), the City of the Book.

Today the Qur'ān is regarded, not by the Muslims alone, as the greatest classic ever composed in the Arabic language. But the people to whom the language belonged before it was usurped by Islam, took no such pride in the composition. On the contrary, they felt extremely annoyed that their ancient language was being misused for a very profane purpose by a person whom, as we shall see, they thought demented and possessed by evil spirits.

We can very well understand their reaction to the Qur'ān if we consider its contents without being taken in by the hallow which has been built around it in centureis after the pagan Arabs were made to disappear from the scene. It is certainly a very strange document in Arabic which says precious little about Arabia, its geography, its history, its people, its society and its age-old culture, and pours unmitigated contempt on its religion and ways of worship. The pagan Arabs were not at all wrong if they concluded that Allāh of the Qur'ān was reducing their language to an empty shell in order to pack it with chronicles, characters and concepts that were not only alien but also wholly distasteful to them. We at this distance in time can see more clealy that Allāh was doing to Arabic what the Founding Fathers of the Christian Church had done to Greek and Latin, and what Lenin will do to Rus-

---

[1]Qur'ān, 12.2; 20.113; 26-195; 41.3; 43.3.

sian and Mao Tse-tung to Chinese, that is, using a language as a convenient cover for doctrines calculated to destory the culture which has produced it, and devastate the land in which it has flourished.

The Qur'ān does not contain a single worthwhile story from pre-Islamic Arabia, unless we accept as facts of history its concoctions about Abraham and the Ka'ba. For all its bulk, it is full of stories borrowed bodily from the Bible except for a few minor details where Allāh's memory falters or the latter-day Jewish tradition has offered embellishments. All its heroes are the biblical prophets. The list includes Ādam (Adam), Nūh (Noah), Idris (Enoch), Ibrāhīm (Abraham), Ismā'īl (Ishmael), Ishāq (Issac), Lūt (Lot), Yāqūb (Jacob), Yūsuf (Joseph), Mūsā (Moses), Hārūn (Aaron), Tālūt (Saul), Da'ūd (David), Sulaymān (Solomon), Ilyās (Elijah), Alyāsa' (Elisha), Ayyūb (Job), Hizqīl (Ezekiel), Yūnus (Jonah), Zakariya (Zacharias), Yāhya (John the Baptist), and Īsā Masīh (Jesus Christ). Maryam (Mary), the mother of Jesus, is also there. The only prophets who do not figure in the Bible are Hūd, Sālīh and Shua'ib. They, however, remain shadowy characters whose parentage and place of functioning cannot be determined with certainty. They look like figments of Allāh's imagination. In any case, they have been brought in only for playing the role in which their brothers from the Bible are cast, that is, cursing their own people and praying to Allāh to rain disasters on them.

The lion's share in the stories of the Qur'ān goes to Banū Isrā'īl (Children of Israel), that is, the biblical Jews. In these stories Allāh identifies himself with Jehovah and their tenor remains the same as in the Bible. Allāh reminiscences how he entered into a covenant with Abraham, and brought back his progeny from Egypt and into the promised land. Abraham is presented as the first Muslim which is the same as the first circumcised Jew. It is, however, Moses who looms larger than every other prophet. He is the subject of a large number of verses in the Qur'ān. He provides the perfect model which Allāh expects Muhammad to follow faithfully.

Muhammad himself is lifted clean out of his own people and pagan evironment, and placed squarely and firmly in the family of biblical prophets.[2] Allāh informs him that he is the Last Prophet[3] anticipated by the earlier prophets and in the older scriptures.[4] He is also assured that he is by no means alone in the midst of 'ignorant pagans" and that he

[2]Ibid., 4.163; 5.19; 7.157; 33.7; 36.3 among others
[3]Ibid., 33.40
[4]Ibid., 3.81; 7.157; 46.9; 61.6.

can always turn for help to those "who read the earlier Scripture (that was) before you."[5] For, what is being revealed to him was also revealed to Abraham, Ishmael, Issac, Jacob, Moses and Jesus.[6]

The main theme of the Qur'ān is also the same as that of the Bible, namely, a fierce war between monotheism (*tauhīd*) on the one hand, and idolatry (*shirk*) on the other. The only difference is that this time we miss most of Jehovah's thunder. Allāh too, condems, curses, and tries to frighten those who do not accept him as the only god, and refuse to accept Muhammad as the last prophet. He also tells stories of earlier people whom he had destroyed for their failure to follow his prophets. But the fury of the original gets diluted in the imitation. It must also be said to the credit of the Qur'ān that its Allāh does not employ obscene language. That may be due to the personl culture of the Prophet, or to the fact that, unlike Jehovah, Allāh did not have to face failure. He is certainly modest while introducing himself, which he does mostly in the third person. But the proposition remains unaltered. "He is Allāh," he says, "and there is no god save Him...Your God is only Allāh than whom there is no other god...He is Allāh the One...He is only One God...Your God is One God." Once in a while the proposition is put in the form of questions, "Is there any other god beside Allāh ?...Or have they other gods ?" The answer is always provided by Allāh himself and is invariably an emphatic "no". The refrain runs throughout the Qur'ān.

The only compromise which Allāh makes with his self-proclaimed status of absolute exclusiveness is in favour of prophets whom he needs from time to time in order to advertise his claims and extend his dominion. "Lo ! Your Lord is Allāh," he says, "Who created the heaven and the earth in six days, then established Himself on the Throne, directing all things. There is no intercessor with Him except after His permission."[7] That enables him to appoint the latest prophet and provide the second part of the Kalima, "Muhammad is the messenger of Allāh."

The principal task assigned to the Prophet is to see that Allāh alone is worshipped, obeyed and served, and to wage a relentless war against Allāh's rivals. Here, too, Allāh prefers to guide the Prophet at every stage of the compaign—how to launch an ideological blitzkrieg against the other gods and those who worship them; how to indoctrinate and marshal into a militant formation all those who opt for Allāh and break

---

[5]Ibid., 2.41; 3.199; 5.33; 10.94; 6.20, 114; 10.37; 17.107; 26.196; 28.52; 34.6; 46.10; 87.18.

[6]Ibid., 3.84; See also 5.44–46; 11.17; 45.16; 87.19.

[7]Ibid., 10.3. See also 34.23.

the kinship ties which bind them to their ancestral society; when and how to go on the offensive at selected fronts or all along the line; how to amass booty including the women and children of the idolaters, and apportion it among the faithful; how to force the defeated and the demoralised adversaries into the victorions fold; and how to annihilate pagan religion and culture till not a trace of them survives. Some protions of the Qur'an, particularly the Medinese Sūras, do sound like chapters in a treatise on war.[8]

Iconoclasm in the Qur'ān

The verses (*āyats*) which deal with idolatry and idolaters lie scattered in all chapters (*sūras*) of the Qur'ān; taken together they constitute the largest number, particularly in the Meccan Sūras, as compared to those devoted to other subjects. Many a time, the verses occur in the stories of prophets who came before Muhammad. But it is more than obvious that they are addressed to the pagan contempories of the Prophet. We have collected and collated them under several sections as the theme develops, stage by stage, till it reaches its climax, that is, Allāh's threat to destroy all peoples and human settlements where gods other than him are honoured.

The "other gods" mean idols, most of the time; this is clear by the word *ṣanam* (pl. *aṣnām*) which stands for carved statues, and *wathan* (pl. *awthān*) which stands for simple stones, trimmed or untrimmed. Sometimes the "other gods" are the Stars, the Sun and the Moon as well; we have seen that worship of these heavenly bodies was prevalent in pagan Arabia. But the description which we find most frequent in the Qur'ān is "partners ascribed to Allāh." The technical term used for this ascription is *shirk* which literally means "mixing" or "associating". The idolaters are consequently called *mushriks*, which term has acquired a stink in Islamic parlance. Witnessing the tantrums which Allāh throws constantly about "partners ascribed to him", we are left with a strong impression that the pagans had never neglected Allāh; they only preferred to worship him surrounded by his numerous companions who were his own Aspects, Names and Forms.[9]

---

[8]It is not an accident that Brigadier S.K. Malik of the Pakistan military establishment has quoted copiously from the Qur'ān in his *The Quranic Concept of War*, Lahore (n.d.), New Delhi Reprint, 1986. General Zia-ul-Haq, the late president of Pakistan, recommends the book which, in his own words, "brings out the Quranic philosophy on the application of military force within the context of the totality that is *Jehad*."

[9]Some scholars think that Muhammad used the term "partners" because, he was a businessmen. Allāh of the Qur'ān does sound like a racketeer out to consolidate a monopoly over worship which humans offer to the Divine.

Surveying the scene in pagan Arabia, Allāh of the Qur'ān notices with great anger as well as anguish that, though most of them worship Allāh, they always ascribe partners to him. What is worse, they worship females such as Al-Lāt, Al-Manāt and Al-'Uzzā, calling them daughters of Allāh.[10] They do not know that Allāh never had a consort and, therfore, no sons or daughters. They are also unfair to Allāh when they burden him with daughters, while they prefer sons for themselves.[11] Allāh informs the idolaters that these female deities are "mere names" invented by their forefathers and repeated by them, and that the worship of other gods, male or female, has received "no warrant", that is no scriptural authority. The "idolaters" are also accused of dividing their offerings between Allāh and the partners ascribed to him. But no offerings ever reach Allāh because the partners grab his portion as well as their own. And their worship in the Ka'ba is "naught but whistling and handclapping."[12] It seems that, like pagans everywhere and at all times, the pagans of Arabia also worshipped their Gods with song and dance.

Allāh also complains that the pagans pray to Allāh only when they are in trouble, but turn to other gods as soon as they are out of it. If asked why they do not worship Allāh alone and always, they say that they follow "the way of their forefathers"; they do not know that their forefathers were "unintelligent" and had received "no guidance". They also forget that it is Allāh who has created them and provides for them. On the contrary, they have invented lies in support of which they come out with no proof. And they persist in their error even when a Book has been sent to them. They have chosen mere "slaves" as their protectors instead of the "master", without realizing that slaves control nothing and can protect no one. Nor do they grasp the "simple truth" that if there were gods beside Allāh, both heaven and earth would have got disordered. The most unkindest cut of all, however, is that they invite Muhammad to disbelive in Allāh and turn to their gods. But Muhammad has not only no knowledge of their gods, he has also received proof to the contrary. It is the same proof which the earlier prophets

---

[10]A translator of the Qur'ān oberves in a footnote that these Arab Goddesses were like Lakshmī and Sarasvatī of the Hindus (*Qur'ān Majid* translated into Hindi by Muhammad Fārūq Khān, Rampur (U.P.), sixth reprint, 1976, p. 242). Hindus can accept the observation as a complement, though the translator frowns upon their Goddesses as "mere names without reference to any existence." In any case, it establishes kinship between Hindus and the Arab pagans. Hindu Gods and Godesses have invited the same invectives and physical onslaughts from the Islamic invaders and their remanants as the Arab Gods and Godesses did from the Prophet and his flock.

[11]Allāh of the Qur'ān, like Jehovah of the Bible, has great contempt for females. See Qur'ān, 16.57;37.149–53; 43.16-19; 52.39; 53.21-22,27; 65.1-7.

[12]Qur'ān, 12.106; 4.117; 6.101-102; 59.19-23; 6.137; 8.35.

had received. The idolaters thus compound their error by trying to drag Allāh's prophet down to their own degenerate level.[13]

Turning to Muhammad, Allāh issues a stern command: "Say: O mankind ! If you are in doubt about my religion then (know) that I worship not what you worship instead of Allāh, but I worship Allāh who causeth you to die, and I have been commanded to be of the believers...[14] There is no compulsion in religion. The right direction is henceforth distinct from error, and he who rejects false deities and believes in Allāh alone has grasped a firm handhold which will never break. Allāh is Hearer, Knower.'[15]

Coming to the "other gods", the cause of the whole quarrel, Allāh makes it quite clear that he himself has not appointed them, nor authorised their worship. The prophets and scriptures sent by him earlier can be consulted on the subject. He challenges the "idolaters" to produce proof to the contrary, if they have any. On the other hand, he has sent a scripture to Muhammad confirming the earlier prophets, and prohibiting the pagan practices in very clear words. The other gods "possess not an atom's weight either in heaven or on earth, nor have they any share in either". They do not "own so much as the white spot on a datestone".[16]

Allāh waxes eloquent about his own creation, which includes everything in the cosmos; the Qur'ān is crowded with verses in which its author revels in unbounded self-adultation. The exercise over, he challenges the "idolaters" to produce evidence that their gods have ever created anything. The truth, he says, is that they cannot create but are themselves created. They are dead, not living. If the "idolaters" want to know the worth of their gods, they should call them (the gods) and wait for an answer; they will wait in vain. For, the gods have no ears with which they may hear, and no eyes with which they may see. Also, they have no feet with which they may walk, and no hands with which they may hold anything. They are helpless, and dwell in darkness.[17]

Being deaf, dumb, blind and without limbs, the other gods can neither help anyone, nor hurt. If a fly snatches away something from

---

[13]Ibid., 3.98; 2.170; 30.40; 18.15; 4.153; 18.102, 21.22, 40.42; 40.66.

[14]Ibid., 10.40.

[15]Ibid., 2.256. The first line of this verse is often cited by apologists of Islam in support of their proposition that Islam stands for tolerance in matters of belief. The complete verse, however, says quite clearly that the unbelievers have no business to persist in error after the right guidance has come. All commentators on the Qur'ān proclaim, in unmistakable language, that this verse authorises Muslims to wipe out all other religions.

[16]Ibid., 48.47; 21.24-25; 34.22; 35.13.

[17]Ibid., 31.11; 25.3; 16.17; 16.21; 7.194-194; 13.16.

them, they do not have the strength to get it back. They are as frail and fragile as a spider's web. They cannot come to the rescue of those whom Allāh wants to hurt. Those who hope to be helped by the other gods on the Last Day, are in for great disappointment; they (the gods) have not been given any power of intercression on anyone's behalf. They can lead their devotees only to doom because they are "Satan's handiworks" like "strong drink and games of chance."[18]

The test will come on the Day of Judgment. Allāh is, however, in two minds about what will happen on that fateful day.

According to one version, his messengers will round up the "idolaters" and ask them about the whereabouts of their gods. The "idolaters" will say that the gods have "departed", that is, taken to their heels. At the same time, the "idolaters", will confess that they "have been disbelievers". They will be brought before Allāh who will ask the angels in his court whether they (angels) were the ones whom the "idolaters" worshipped. The angels will plead not-guilty and name the jinns. Allāh will then turn to the "idolaters" and ask them why they had come alone and not accompanied by their gods. The "idolaters" will deny that they were idolaters. Allāh's verdict after their denial is not recorded.[19] But it can be guessed that, because they were not believers, they will be consigned to eternal hell-fire, maybe of a lesser degree.

The second version is more consistent and in keeping with the spirit of the Qur'ān. It says that Allāh will command: "Assemble those who did wrong together with their wives and what they used to worship." All of them will be brought before Allāh. He will start by interrogating the gods. He will ask whether they misled the "idolaters", or the latter went astray on their own. The gods will declare that they did not choose their worshippers, but were chosen for worship without their consent; the forefathers of the "idolaters" had gone astray because Allāh had "made it easy" for them, and the succeeding generations had followed in their footsteps. Thus the gods will disassociate themselves from their devotees and plead their own innocence. They will, however, admit that they might have misled others because they themselves were in error. The "idolaters" will feel outraged and shout at the gods, "Didn't you come to us from the right and the left. Why are you blaming us alone?" The gods will remain unrepentant. They will hit back, "You were unbelievers on your own. We had no power to influence you."[20] What we find intriguing in this drama on the Day of Judgment

[18]Ibid., 25.55; 21.43; 29.40; 17.56; 36.23; 19.15; 43.86; 5.90.

[19]Ibid., 7.37; 34.40-41; 6.22-23. 95.

[20]Ibid., 37.22; 25.17-19; 28.63; 37.28-30.

is that the gods who were dead, blind, deaf, dumb and without any brains whatsoever, become alive all of a sudden, start seeing, hearing and speaking, and display wits like those of smart lawyers!

Allāh confides that he will set the devils to sow confusion in the camp of idolatry. The gods will turn against their worshippers, and vice versa. The doors of hell will be opened and the "idolaters" will be thrown into blazing fire. It is then that they will admit that they were wrong-doers and bewail that their gods had failed them. They will wish to have another life on earth, so that they may be among the believers. But it will be too late. Bound in chains, they will be dragged through boiling waters. No mediator will come forward to mediate for them.[21]

Next, Allāh recites the record of earlier prophets and wise men vis-a-vis the idols and idolaters. We will relate it chronologically.

Abraham chided his father Ezra and his people for being idolaters. He also rejected the worship of Stars, the Moon and the Sun, all of which he saw setting after rising. His people argued with him in favour of the ancestral way of worship. He asked them to produce scriptural proof in defence of their gods. At the same time, he sought forgiveness from Allāh for his father. He harangued his father not to worship those who neither hear, nor see, nor are helpful in any way. His father rejected the advice and threatened to stone him. Abraham now decided to demonstrate the worthlessness of the gods. He sneaked into a place of worship when his people were away and smashed all the idols to pieces except the biggest one among them. The people, when they came back and saw the scene, made enquiries. Some youngmen who had seen Abraham doing the deed reported the matter to them. So Abraham was questioned. He pointed an accusing finger at the big idol and said that the big one had smashed the smaller ones, and that the truth could be found out by questioning the pieces. His people said that idols were not known to speak. He shouted back, "Why then do you worship them? Fie on you and what you worship !" They got angry and tried to burn him alive. But Allāh cooled the fire and saved him. He told his people that it was not he but they and their gods who were fuel for hell-fire, where they will be tormented for ever. Then he separated himself from his people and proclaimed, "There has arisen between us and you hostility and hatred for ever until you believe in Allāh." Before he left, he informed his father, "I have sought forgiveness for you, though I know nothing for you from Allāh." His devotion was rewarded by Allāh with

[21]Ibid., 19.82-83; 16.86; 26.19-102; 40.74; 74.48.

a son, Issac, and a grandson, Jacob.[22]

Moses found his people adoring the golden calf soon after he brought them out of Egypt. He ordered them to slaughter with their own hands those among them who had gone astray. It was done. Moses also cursed Sāmirī, the man who had connived at the worship of the golden calf, so that Sāmirī became a leper in this life and fuel for hell-fire in the next. Moses burnt the golden calf and scattered the ashes on the sea.[23]

Solomon was informed by his pet hooper that the people of Saba' (Sheba of the Bible) were ruled by a woman and worshipped the Sun instead of Allāh. He wrote to the Queen of Saba' demanding that she and her people should come to the true faith. The Queen took fright and consulted her chieftains who went in a delegation to Solomon with rich presents. The king spurned the presents and demanded that the Queen be present in his court to settle the matter. The Queen had no choice. She went to Jerusalem, saw Solomon's power, and accepted that there was no god beside Allāh.[24]

Elijah warned his people not to worship Ba'al. They disregarded his advice and will face the doom on the Day of Judgment. Luqmān advised his son not to be an idolater and serve his parents. But if anyone's parents pressed their son to ascribe partners to Allāh, they were to be disobeyed. Ties of faith stood above ties of kinship. Coming down the road of time, seven young men in Palestine took refuge inside a cave and went to sleep when they saw their people degenerating into idolatry. They slept for three hundred years and thought it only a day when they were awakened by Allāh. One of them went out to find food and discovered that the Roman Empire was rid of idolatry and worshipped Allāh alone. The people in the town also learnt about the true believers in the cave and hailed them as followers of Jesus Christ. A mosque was erected over their graves when the seven faithful died after some time.[25]

Some of these stories are repeated several times and spread over several Sūras. Allāh tells them for the benefit of the "idolaters" of Arabia. He exhorts them to follow the path of Abraham, Moses, Solomon, Elijah, Luqmān and the seven young men; otherwise they were bound to become fuel for hell-fire. Had there been any other gods, they themselves would have tried to reach the throne and usurp Allāh's authority;

---

[22]Ibid., 6.75-82; 14.41; 19.42; 21.57-69, 98-100; 26.86; 60.4; 26.77.
[23]Ibid., 2.54; 29.96-97.
[24]Ibid., 27.22-24.
[25]Ibid., 37.123-128; 31.13-15; 18.9-21.

there would have been disorder in heaven as well as on earth.[26] If the "idolaters" fail to repent, Allāh threaterns to cast terror in their hearts; he tells them clear and loud that their abode will be hell-fire. He can never forgive idolatry which is the greatest crime. They will find no escape from the torments in hell, which is their journey's end. There will be an awning of fire above them, and a floor of fire underneath; they will not be able to drive it away from their faces, nor from their backs. We are leaving out the blood-curdling accounts, which abound in the Qur'ān, about what the fire will do to the victims, again and again, and for ever and ever.[27]

Finally, Allāh bares his fangs and comes out in his true colours. "And how many generations," he thunders, "We destroyed before them!...Had they any place of refuge? ...and they cried out when it was no longer time for escape... Not one of them but denied the messenger, therefore My doom was justified... We seized them unawares and lo ! they were dumb-founded. So of the people who did wrong the last remnant was cut off... And the heavens and the earth wept not for them, nor were they reprieved... How many townships have we destroyed! As a raid by night, or while they slept at noon, Our terror came upon them... Have they not travelled in the land and seen the nature of the consequences for those who were before them, and they were mightier than these in power? Say (unto them, O Muhammad): Travel in the land and see the nature of the sequel for the guilty! ...And when We would destroy a township, We send commandments to its folk who live at ease, and afterwards they commit abomination therein, and so the word (of doom) hath effect for it, and we annihilate it with complete annihilation...There is not a township but we shall destroy it ere the Day of Resurrection and punish it with dire punishment... And we verily have destroyed townships round about you... Allāh struck at the foundations of their buildings, and then the roof fell down upon them from above them, and the doom came upon them whence they knew not... Are they who plan ill-deeds then secure that Allāh will not cause the earth to swallow them? ...Or that He will not seize them in their going to and fro so that there be no escape for them? ...So think not that Allāh will fail to keep His promise to His messenger. Lo! Allāh is Mighty, Able to Requite."[28]

---

[26]Ibid.,3.95; 17.39; 42; 21.22; 3.151; 4.41; 14.30; 18.52; 39.16; 21.39.

[27]For detailed description of the torment see Ibid., 2.24; 4.56; 7.42; 10.4; 14.16-17; 17.97; 18.19;20.74; 22.19-22; 35.36-37; 44.44,50; 69.30-36.

[28]Ibid, 50.36; 38.3.14; 6.44-45; 44.29; 7.4; 35.44; 27.69; 17.16,58; 46.27; 16.26.45,46; 14.47. "Able to Requite' is a very mild translation of the Arabic "*Azīz al-lntiqām*", which means "Lover of Vengeance".

Lest the idolaters entertain the illusion that Allāh is bragging and does not mean business, he names the tribes and towns he destroyed in olden times. Nūh had warned his people repeatedly against idolatry. But they refused to renounce the gods of their forefathers. Allāh sent heavy rains, waters rose on all sides, and they were drowned.[29] Hūd taught his people in Ād not to worship any gods besides Allāh. They too were not prepared to give up the gods of their forefathers. Allāh sent violent storms which raged for seven nights and eight days, and they were swept away.[30] Sālih was sent as a prophet to his people in Thamūd. He invited them to worship Allāh alone and throw away their idols. They did not listen to him. Instead, they hamstrung his camel. Allāh caused an earthquake along with a great thunderclap in the sky, which turned their town upside down and they were buried in the debris.[31] Lūt lived in Sadūm when Allāh's angels arrived to punish the inhabitants for their sinfulness. The prophet advised them to repent and seek refuge in Allāh. They turned a deaf ear and threatened to throw him out. Allāh rained stones on them, and the town together with its people was totally destroyed.[32] Shua'ib invited the people of Madayan (Midian) to turn to Allāh. Their chiefs invited him to renounce Islam. Allāh's wrath caught up with them.[33] Mūsā and Hārūn were sent to Fir'ūn (Pharoah), and showed him many signs from Allāh. But Fir'ūn refused to become a believer, and threatened to imprison the prophets. He was drowned in the sea along with his army.[34] The "dwellers of Ar-Raas" and "folk of Tubba'" also denied the messengers whom Allāh had sent to them. They were wiped out.[35]

Allāh of the Qur'ān now throws away the mask he has worn in order to pass as Allāh of the pagan Arabs. He comes out in his true colours. He is no other than the old Jehovah of the Bible, the hardened gangster we have met in the earlier section. And like his earlier incarnation, he, too, is a denizen of the dark depths in human nature. Only the situation in which Jehovah alias Allāh intends to operate this time is totally different.

---

[29]Ibid., 71.21-28. The story is repeated in several other chapters.

[30]Ibid., 6.65; 7.70; 11.58; 26.136-140; 54.18-21. The story is repeated in several other charpters.

[31]Ibid., 7.73-74; 11.62-65; 26.158-159; 54.23-31. The story is repeated in several other chapters.

[32]Ibid., 7.80-84; 11.77-83; 26.54-58. The name of the town, Sadūm (Sodom of the Bible) is not mentioned in the Qur'ān but is given by commentators. The stroy is repeated in several other chapters.

[33]Ibid., 7.85.93. The story is found in several other chapters.

[34]Ibid., 10.148-53; 26.18-29; 28.40-42. The story is found in many other chapters.

[35]Ibid., 50.10-14. These places have not been identified with certainty.

The Jews living in Egypt after the collapse of their patrons, the Hyksos conquerors, belonged to a bedraggled community which had lost its moorings long ago. They hardly had a religion or culture of their own and, therefore, were prone to succumb to whosoever promised to be a saviour. Jehovah had not found it difficult to possess them through his mouthpiece, Moses, and terrorise them into more or less total submission. Moreover, he had indoctrinated them for forty long years before he led them into the promised land. The land was not their own, and they could slaughter and despoil its natives without inhibitions imposed by ties of kinship and a shared culture. The Jews could never stand up to Jehovah or question the doctrines he had taught them. Whenever they lapsed into natural religion normal to mankind, they suffered from a bad conscience. That is why prophets could always find a ready audience and flourish among them. Jehovah had a safe constituency even when he failed to fulfil his promises, or carry out his threats.

The pagans of Arabia whom Allāh of the Qur'ān had to face were, however, an altogether different cup of tea. The land in which they lived was the one in which their forefathers had lived and prospered for ages past. They had an ancient religion and culture of which they were mighty proud. They were not at all on the lookout for a new cult or a saviour who could rescue them from a miserable state, or lead them into a promised land. They did not cast covetous eyes on other people's patrimony, while they zealously guarded their own. They had a first-hand experience of monotheism during the short-lived Jewish regime in Yemen, and the Abyssinian invasion that followed. They felt amused by prophets foaming at the mouth, and dismissed them either as poets, or magicians, or plain lunatics. Thus they were ill-prepared to receive revelations from Allāh or warm up to a privileged messenger.

The Qur'ān has preserved portions of a debate which developed between the Meccans on the one hand and Muhammad on the other. "The history then of the first years of Mohammed's preaching at Mecca is not without events, but it is, in the main, the history of a debate, and a debate in which the speeches of the counsel of one side only are preserved. The Meccan Surahs of the Koran are rarely to be dated with precision : many are reports or notes of the same course of lectures repeated over and over again by the lecturer. Hence the order in which question after question was posed by the adversary is not known."[36] We are taking up that debate before we proceed to the other methods

[36]D.S. Margoliouth, op. cit., p. 125.

adopted by the Prophet for subduing the pagans of Arabia and destroying their places of worship. Even in its state of partial and partisan preservation, the debate provides deep insights into the working of the pagan mind, as also of the mechanics of monotheism.

Chapter Fifteen

MUHAMMAD AND THE MECCANS

The Prophet had kept his mission concealed for three years after he received the first revelations. The Muslim brotherhood had functioned as a secret society. Ibn Ishāq gives a list of persons who had joined.[1] "The advantage of the darkness for the first few years was great. The darkness saved it from being crushed at the outset. Ridicule and contempt could be more easily endured when some hundred persons were involved, than if the Prophet had been compelled to endure them by himself. It saved him, too, from the character of the eccentric sage (such as Waraqa and others had borne), investing him from his first public appearance with that of the leader of a party; it gave the Prophet time to secure over a reasonable number of people that influence which he could exercise to a reasonable degree."[2]

People in Mecca had, however, sensed that something was afoot. From the first, Muslims had been directed by Allāh to offer prayers in congregation. They could not do it inside the city so long as they were an underground organisation. "When the apostle's companions prayed," reports Ibn Ishāq, "they went to the glens so that people could not see them praying, and while Sa'd b. Abū Waqqās was with a number of the prophet's companions in one of the glens of Mecca, a band of polytheists came upon them while they were praying and rudely interrupted them. They blamed them for what they were doing until they came to blows, and it was on that occasion that Sa'd smote a polytheist with the jawbone of a camel and wounded him. That was the first blood to be shed in Islam."[3] No reprisals from the pagan side are reported.

Some more incidents of a similar kind happened and the offenders went unpunished. The pagans were not organised in an ideologically oriented group, secret or open, to be able to meet the challenge promptly and effectively. As it happens in every pluralistic society faced with an aggressive and determined minority, the Meccan majority showed only surprise and pain at what was happening. This state of helplessness displayed by the majority helped the Muslims to acquire contempt for it; some faint-hearted pagans chose to go over fast to what looked like the winning side. So the secret society felt sufficiently self-

---

[1]Ibn Ishāq, op. cit., pp. 116–17.
[2]D.S. Margoliouth, op. cit., p. 112.
[3]Ibn Ishāq, op. cit., p. 118.

confident to come out in the open. "People began to accept Islam, both men and women, in large numbers until the fame of it spread throughout Mecca, and it began to be talked about. Then God commanded His apostle to declare the truth of what he had received and make known His commandments to men and call them to Him. Three years elapsed from the time the apostle concealed his state until God commanded him to publish his religion, according to information which has reached me. Then God said, 'Proclaim what you have been ordered and turn aside from the polytheists.'"[4]

The "religion" proclaimed was very simple—the end of the world is near at hand; on the Last Day the dead will be raised and judged; those who had believed in Allāh as the only god and in Muhammad as the last Prophet will enter paradise for an everlasting life of the rarest pleasures; those who ascribed partners to Allāh or denied Muhammad's prophethood or did both will be thrown into blazing hell-fire and subjected to ever more terrible torments without end or relief. It was made quite clear at the very outset that belief in Allāh as the only God was not enough; it had to be accompanied by the belief that Muhammad was the only mediator through whom Allāh's mercy could be sought or obtained.

There were, of course, some novel ways of worshipping Allāh and leading a pious life. What startled the Meccans, however, was the polemics which accompanied the publicity of Islam. "To avow Islam meant to renounce publicly the national worship, to ridicule, and if possible to break down idols, and unabashedly to use the new salulation and to celebrate the new-fangled rites. For it must be remembered that Islam was in its nature polemical. Its Allah was not satisfied with worship, unless similar honour was paid to no other name; and his worship also was intolerant of idols, and of all rites not instituted by himself...Mohammed and Abu Bakr were planning an attack on the national religion, that cult which every Meccan proudly remembered had within their memory been defended by a miracle from the Abyssinian invaders and in their myths had often thus triumphed before. The gods they worshipped were, Mohammed and Abu Bakr asserted, no gods. For their worship these innovators would substitute that of the Jews whose power in South Arabia had recently been overthrown, and of the Christians with whose defeat the national spirit of Arabia had just awakened."[5]

---

[4]Ibid., p. 117. Allāh's command can be read in Qur'ān, 15.8-9, 94.
[5]D.S. Margoliouth, op. cit., p. 118–19.

The pagan response was slow in crystallizing. The first thing which the pagans did was to lead several delegations to Abū Tālib, Muhammad's uncle and guardian. They told him that his nephew had "cursed our gods, insulted our religion, mocked our way of life and accused our forefathers of error", and requested him to restrain the revolutionary. Abū Tālib was conciliatory and tried to persuade Muhammad to go slow. "Do not put on me a burden greater than I can bear", he said to his nephew. But the Prophet "continued on his way, publishing God's religion and calling men therein."[6] His uncle was in no position to stop him. "Perhaps Abu Talib and his numerous family could not afford to abandon their wealthy relative; and, indeed, had Mohammed not had some power over his uncle, it is unlikely that the latter would have submitted to the inconvenience which his nephew's mission brought on him."[7]

Meanwhile, Islam was having an impact on Meccan society which was even more painful for a people wedded to the solidarity of family and clan. Every family from which a member or members had converted to the new creed was under severe strain. Sons were not only becoming rude to their parents but also pouring contempt on the elders' way of life and worship. Brothers were becoming estranged. Marriages in which one of the partners had converted, were breaking up fast. As al-Walīd b. al-Mughīra, a man of standing in Mecca, observed, Muhammad looked like "a sorcerer who has brought a message by which he separates a man from his father, or from his brother, or from his wife, or from his family."[8]

"The view prevalent at Meccah concerning Mohammad appears to have been that he was mad—under the influence of a Jinn, one of the beings who were supposed to speak through poets and sorcerers. That this charge stung Mohammed to the quick may be inferred from the virulence with which he rejects it, and the invective with which he attacks the 'bastard' who had uttered it. He charges the author of the outrage with being unable to write and with being over head and ears in debt and threatens to brand him on his 'proboscis.'"[9] Allāh thundered on his prophet's behalf : "You are not a mad man...And you will see

[6]Ibn Ishāq, op. cit., p. 119.

[7]D.S. Margoliouth, op. cit., p. 123. It may be mentioned that Muhammad was married to a rich woman, Khadījah, and controlled her considerable wealth which he used for supporting his uncle's family as well as in the service of the mission to which his wife also subscribed.

[8]Ibn Ishāq, op. cit., p. 121.

[9]D.S. Margoliouth, op. cit., p. 121.

and they will see, which of you is the demented. Therefore obey not you the rejecters, who would have you compromise, that they may compromise : Neither obey you each feeble oath-monger, detractor, spreader abroad of slanders, hinderer, of the good, an aggressor, malefactor, greedy therewithal, intrusive. We shall brand him on the nose."[10]

This loss of temper on Allāh's part, however, served only to confirm the Meccans in their suspicion. Another incident gave strength to it. One day some Meccans were assembled in the precincts of the Ka'ba when Muhammad also happened to come by. The Meccans made some remarks within his hearing. Muhammad hit back, "By him who holds my life in His hand, I bring you slaughter."[11] The Meccans were stunned. They concluded that something had happened to Muhammad who had been known earlier as a man of even temper. Muhammad had claimed that an angel came to him often with Allāh's revelations. The Meccans became sure that he was being visited by some malevolent Spirit.

The Meccans sent 'Utba b. Rabī'a, one of their chiefs, to Muhammad. Among other offers made by 'Utba to Muhammad, one was that of providing medical relief. 'Utba said, "If this ghost which comes to you, which you see, is such that you cannot get rid of him, we will find a physician for you, and exhaust our means in getting you cured, for often a spirit gets possession of a man until he can be cured of it."[12] The Prophet remained calm, explained his mission to 'Utba, and recited some Qur'ān. 'Utba came back convinced that Muhammad was quite sane and advised the Meccans to leave him alone. "If (other) Arabs kill him, otheres will have rid you of him," he said.[13] The Meccans, however, did not agree with him. They decided to launch an offensive against the Prophet. Their patience had come to an end.

The questions which the Meccans posed and the observations they made are scattered over many chapters of Qur'ān. We have collected and sorted them out with reference to subject and logical sequence. "The objections recorded and ostensibly answered in the Koran appear to have been directed against every part and feature of the new system; against Mohammed personally, against his notion of prophecy, againt his style, his statements, his doctrines. It is impossible to suggest any chronological scheme for them."[14]

---

[10]Qur'ān, 68.2, 5-6, 8-13.
[11]Ibn Ishāq, op. cit., p. 131.
[12]Ibid., p. 132.
[13]Ibid., p. 133.
[14]D.S. Margoliouth, op., cit., p. 130.

The manner in which the debate is recorded in the Qur'ān is somewhat strange. The Meccans must have said what they said, to Muhammad and his Muslims directly, or among themselves. But the answers come invariably from Allāh in the form of revelations. It appears as if Allāh thought it hazardous to depend upon the credibility or the capacity of his prophet to meet the challenge. "The debate with which the earlier years were filled was conducted in a variety of ways. Occasionally the Prophet himself condescended to enter the arena, and confront his antagonists: he was indeed a powerful preacher and 'when he talked of the Day of Judgment his cheeks blazed, and his voice rose, and his manner was fiery'; apparently, however, he was not a ready debater, and was worsted when he tried the plan. Moreover, his temper in debate was not easily controlled, and he was apt to give violent and insulting answers to questioners. He therefore received divine instruction not to take part in open debate, to evade the question and and if questioned by the unbelievers, retire."[15]

Cynics may say that the Prophet was using Allāh as an alibi. Whatever be the truth, Allāh's interventon helped in preserving some very significant pagan statements, as we shall see. The biographers of the Prophet do indicate that a debate took place during his mission at Mecca. But their reports on the subject are one-sided, apart from being sketchy.

The style in which the pagan questions are posed and Allāh's answers stated in the Qur'ān is stereotyped. The points the Meccans made are preceded by the phrase, "They say", and Allāh's rejoinders by the phrase, "Say". Allāh looks like a prompter guiding from the wings an actor on the stage. Quite often, the debate is reported as having taken place between some earlier prophet and his people. It is obvious, however, that the participants meant are Muhammad and his pagan contemporaries. "More often then the controversy was conducted as it is...in election times, when different speakers address different meetings. The points are recorded and reported by members of the audience to the antagonists; who then proceed if they deem it worth while, in some manner to reply."[16]

To start with, the Meccans felt amused that a man like Muhammad, who was distinguished neither by birth nor breeding, should strut around proclaiming himself a prophet. Muhammad's followers also came from classes and occupations which were not very respectable ac-

---

[15]Ibid., p. 127. Allāhs' instruction to the Prophet can be read in Qur'ān 6.67.
[16]Ibid., pp. 127–28.

cording to Meccan standards. Allāh reports: "When they see you (O Muhammad) they treat you as a jest saying: Is he (the man) whom Allāh has sent as a messenger? He would have led us far away from our gods if we had not been staunch to them...Has he invented a lie concerning Allāh or is there some madness in him? ...Shall we forsake our gods for a mad poet ?...Or one of the gods has possessed you in an evil way...Shall we put faith in you when the lowest (people) follow you? ...We see you but mortal (man) like us, and we see not that any save the most abject among us follow you, without reflection. We behold in you no merit above us—nay, we deem you liars...We are surely better than this fellow who can hardly make (his meaning) clear...We do not understand much of what you say, and we see you weak among us...We are more (than you) in wealth, and in children...Why are not angels sent down unto us, and why do we not see our Lord?...If you cease not, you will soon be the outcast."[17]

Allāh keeps mum about his Prophet's birth and breeding. About the Prophet's followers he says that their past is not relevant after they have come to the true faith. He assures the Meccans that Muhammad is neither mad, nor a poet, nor possessed. He laments that the Meccans think too highly of themselves and are proud and scornful. He assures Muhammad that the time is fast approaching when it will be found out who is really mad, and that the disbelievers shall stand humbled.

Muhammad's and his followers' low birth and lack of breeding may sound a merit in our own times when an inverted snobbery, which prizes them above everything else, has been made fashionable by Marxism and allied ideologies; one has to hide one's high birth and breeding these days in order to pass muster. To the Meccans of the seventh century as to their contemporary societies, however, Muhammad's bio-data disqualified him, at least as a messenger from Allāh. Biographers of the prophet would not have taken the pains they took, and invented fables in order to invest Muhammad with a distinguished pedigree, had not his background been seen by them as a distinct disadvantage to his claims and career. Margoliouth has cited several early Muslim sources to conclude that Muhammad's grandfather, 'Abd al-Muṭṭalib, was a manumitted slave who made his living by means which were not considered honourable in Mecca at that time, namely, lending money and providing water and food to the pilgrims for a considera-

[17]Qur'ān, 25.41–42, 34.8; 37.36; 11.54; 26.111; 11.27; 43.52; 11.91; 34.35; 25.21; 26.167.

tion.[18] In any case, there is no escape from the evidence provided by the Qur'ān that Muhammad himself felt deeply hurt by the jibes hurled at him by the Meccans and sought consolation from Allāh. It appears that he himself shared the standards or prejudices of his age.

Another point which provided amusement to the Meccans was the Prophet's incapacity to perform miracles. He had himself invited the trouble by producing revelations in which the preceding prophets, particularly Moses and Jesus, had exhibited supernatural powers. Allāh reports: "They say: This is only a mortal like you who would make himself superior to you...He is only a man in whom there is a madness. So watch him for a while...This is only a mortal like you who eats whereof you eat, and drinks of what you drink...If you were to obey a mortal like yourselves, you surely will be losers...What ails the messenger of Allāh that he eats and walks in the markets? ...You are but mortals like us who would fain turn us away from what our fathers used to worship...shall mere mortals guide us? ...You are but a mortal man like us. Raḥmān has naught revealed to you but a lie... Is this other than a mortal man? Will you then succumb to magic when you see it? ...So bring some token if you are of the truthful...If only some portent were sent down upon him from his Lord...If only he would bring us a miracle from the Lord...Why are no portents sent down upon him? ...Why then have armlets of gold not been set upon him, or angles sent along with him? ...We shall not put faith in you till you cause a spring to gush forth from the earth for us, or you have a garden of date-palms and grapes and cause rivers to gush forth therein abundantly, or you cause the heavens to fall peacemeal as you have pretended, or bring Allāh and the angels as warrant, or you have a house of gold, or you ascend into heaven, and even then we will put no faith in your ascension till you bring down a book that w=e can read...Or why is not treasure thrown down unto him or why has he not a paradise from whence to eat?...You are following but a man bewitched..."[19]

Allāh assures the Meccans: "Your comrade errs not, nor is deceived... Surely he beheld him (the angel) on the horizon. Nor is he avid of the unseen..." He commands the Prophet: "Say: You are a warner only... Say: I am naught save a mortal messenger...Portents are with Allāh and I am a warner only... Allāh is able to send down a portent. But most of them know not..." He reminds Muhammed that the

[18]D.S. Margoliouth, op. cit., pp. 41–49.

[19]Qur'an. 23.24,25,33,34; 25.6; 14.10; 64.60; 36.15; 21.3; 26.154; 13.7; 20.133; 29.50; 43:53; 17.90-93; 25.8. The Meccans (36.15) have a fling at Raḥmān, the name which the Prophet gave to Allāh quite frequently. They hated this name.

Meccans are not likely to believe even if a miracle is shown to them. "The hour drew nigh and the moon was rent in twain. And if they behold a portent, they turn away and say: Prolonged illusion."[20] According to some commentators on the Qur'ān, this revelation refers to an actual miracle performed by the Prophet. One night the moon had split into two and Mount Hara was seen standing between the two parts. But the Meccans dismissed it as an illusion. Other commentators, however, say that this refers to a future event when the Last Day will be near at hand.

The Meccan stood firm by their gods; their faith in the gods was not at all shaken by Muhammad's attacks. Allāh reports: "When it was said unto them, There is no God save Allāh, they were scornful, and said : Shall we forsake our gods for a mad poet ?...And they marvel that a warner from among themselves has come. They say : This is a wizard, a charlatan. Makes he the gods One God ? This is an astounding thing...The chiefs among them go about exhorting: Go and be staunch by your gods. This is a thing designed (against) you. We have not heard this earlier in our religion. This is naught but an invention. Has a Reminder been revealed unto him alone among us? ...Why not Allāh speak to us, or some sign come to us? ...Had Allāh willed we would not have ascribed (unto him) partners, neither our forefathers... Had Allāh willed we would not have worshipped aught beside Him, we and our forefathers, nor forbidden aught commanded from Him...We worship them only that they may bring us near unto Allāh...He has invented a lie about Allāh..."[21]

Some of their observations were addressed to Muhammad, though reported by Allāh: "Enough for us is that wherein we found our forefathers. Have you come to us that we serve Allāh alone and foresake what our fathers worshipped ? Do you ask us not to worship what our forefathers worshipped ? We are in grave doubt concerning that to which you call us...Does your way of prayer command you that we should forsake that which our forefathers worshipped ?...We found our forefathers following a religion, and we are guided by their footprints. In what you bring we are disbelievers...O Wizard ! Entreat your Lord by the pact he has made with you, so that we may walk aright..."[22]

The Meccans were in no mood to accept the name which Muhammad wanted to foist on Allāh: "When they see you, they but choose you

---

[20]Ibid., 53.2; 81.23-24; 29.50; 13.7; 54.1-2.
[21]Ibid., 37.35-36; 38.4-8; 2.183; 6.149; 39.3; 42.24.
[22]Ibid., 5.104; 7.70; 11.62; 11.87; 43.22, 24, 49.

out of mockery: Is this (the man) who makes mockery of our gods ? And they would deny all mention of the Raḥmān...And when they are asked to adore Raḥmān, they say: What is Raḥmān? Are we to adore whatever you bid us? And it increases aversion in them...And when the son of Mary is quoted as an example, behold! the folk laugh out, and say: Are our gods better, or is he?...They call our revelations false with strong denial...And when the Qur'ān is recited unto them, they do not prostrate themselves."[23]

But, as Muhammad persisted in reviling their gods, the Meccans decided to hit back. They met him and said: "Muhammad, you will either stop cursing our gods, or we will curse your Allāh." They had understood finally that the Allāh whose will Muhammad was revealing was not the Allāh they worshipped. Allāh of the Qur'ān felt concerned at this new turn and revealed, "Had Allāh willed, they would not have been idolatrous. We have not set you as a keeper over them, nor are you responsible for them. Revile not those unto whom they pray beside Allāh lest they wrongfully revile Allāh through ignorance."[24] Ibn Ishāq observes: "I have been told that the apostle refrained from cursing their gods, and began to call them to Allāh."[25]

The Meccans, however, were not at all impressed by the revelations produced by the Prophet; they did not accept his claim that he received them from some higher source. They thought that he was inventing them himself. Allāh reports: "They say: This is naught else than the speech of a mortal man...This is naught else than an invented lie...Nay, say they, (these are but) muddled dreams, he has but invented it; nay, he is but a poet...And when our revelations are recited unto them, they say: We have heard. If we wish we can speak the like of this. This is naught but fables of the men of old..."[26]

Muhammad threw a challenge to the Meccans. Allāh prompted him: "Say: Then bring a sūrah like unto it, and call (for help) all you can besides Allāh if you are truthful."[27] The challenge was accepted by al-Naḍr b. Hārith, a Meccan chief, who said: "I can tell a better story than he...In what respect is Muhammad a better story-teller?"[28] He told several stories in verses which were like verses of the Qur'ān. Muhammad felt outraged and never forgave al Naḍr. "The effect of the criti

[23]Ibid., 21.36; 25.60; 43.57-58; 78.28; 84.En21.
[24]Ibid., 6.108-109.
[25]Ibn Ishāq, op. cit., p. 162.
[26]Qur'ān, 74.25; 34.43 (also 11.13, 35;32.3; 34.43; 46.8; 52.33); 21.5; 8.31.
[27]Ibid., 10.38.
[28]Ibn Ishāq, op. cit., p. 136. See also p. 163.

cism must have been very damaging; for when the Prophet at the battle of Badr got the man into his power, he executed him at once while he allowed the others to be ransomed."[29] Ibn Ishāq confirms that when the apostle was at al-Ṣafrā' on his way back from Badr. "al-Naḍr was killed by 'Alī..."[30] But while the Prophet was still in Mecca, Allāh thought it wise to pacify the pagans. He revealed: "It is not a poet's speech...nor diviner's speech. And if he had invented false sayings, we assuredly had taken him by the right hand, and severed his life-artery, and not one of you could have held us off from him."[31]

The more knowledgeable among the Meccans suspected that Muhammad was only repeating what he had learnt from the People of the Book, Jews and Christians. Allāh reports: "They say: And we know well that only a man teaches him...This is naught but a lie that he has invented and other folk have helped him so that they produced a slander and a lie...Fables of men of old which he has written down so that they are dictated to him morn and evening...One taught (by others), a mad man..."[32]

There were several stories current in Mecca regarding the particular person or persons who coached Muhammad in biblical lore which, they said, was all that came out in the Qur'ān. "One account says it was Jabar, a Greek servant to Amer Ebn al Hadrami, who could read and write well; another, that they were Jabar and Yesar, two slaves who followed the trade of sword cutlers at Mecca, and used to read the pentateuch and gospel and had often Mohammed as their auditor, when he passed that way. Another tells us it was Aīsh, or Yāsīh, a domestic of al Haweiteb Ebn Abd al 'Uzzā, who was a man of some learning, and had embraced Mohammedanism. Another supposes it was Kais, a Christian, whose house Muhammad frequented; another, that it was Addās, a servant of Otba Ebn Rabia..."[33]

Having seen the People of the Book from close quarters, the Meccans found it difficult to believe that divine knowledge had been sent to the Jews and the Christians long ago, and that they themselves were deprived of it till the advent of Muhammad. Allāh proceeds: "They say: The Scripture was revealed only to two sets of people before us, and we

[29]D.S. Margoliouth, op. cit., p. 135.

[30]Ibn Ishāq, op. cit., p. 308.

[31]Qur'ān, 69.41-42, 44-47.

[32]Ibid., 16.103; 25.4-5; 44.14. The Meccan allegation goes to show that Muhammad was not an illiterate as is asserted even in the Qur'ān (29.46,49).

[33]George Sale, *The Koran or Alcoran of Mohammed*, London (n.d), p. 233, footnote 1.

in sooth were not aware of what they read...If the Scripture had been revealed unto us, we surely would have been better guided than are they... Two magics which support each other...In both we are disbelievers... If it had been any good they would not have been before us in attaining it...This is an ancient lie."[34]

It had also been noticed that Muhammad produced revelations according to his convenience in the debate. Allāh complained: "And when we put a revelation in place of (another), they say: You are but inventing... Why is not the Qur'ān revealed unto him all at one."[35] Allāh had himself revealed that the Qur'ān was being read out from a "well guarded tablet" preserved in the highest heaven. Why was it then being doled out in bits and pieces? The Meccans suspected that the Prophet was inventing verses as occasion demanded.

The incident which confirmed their suspicion was that of the so-called Sanatic Verses. Tabarī has recorded: "When the apostle saw that his people turned their backs on him and he was pained by their estrangement from what he brought them from God he longed that there should come to him from God a message that would reconcile his people to him...Then God sent down, 'Have ye thought of Al-Lāt and al-'Uzzā and Manāt the third, the other, these are the exalted Gharānīq whose intercession is approved.'" The Meccans felt happy and thought that the strife was over, now that Muhammad had endorsed their Goddesses. But Muhammad had to face his own followers who felt betrayed. The verses were withdrawn soon after and replaced by another revelation. "So God annulled what Satan had suggested and God established His verses."[36]

So the Meccans turned down the Qur'ān totally and finally. Allāh reports: "Their chieftains said: We surely see you in foolishness and we deem you of the liars...It is all one to us whether you preach or are not of those who preach...Our hearts are protected from that unto which you (Muhammad) call us, and in our ears there is deafness, and between us and you there is a veil...They say (to their people): Heed not this Qur'ān, and drown the hearing of it."[37]

Having reaffirmed their Gods and rejeted Muhammad's prophethood as well as revelations, the Meccans made fun of the Last Day (*Yaumu'l Ākhir*) which is described by Allāh variously as Day of Res-

[34]Qur'ān, 6.157-58; 28.48; 46.11.
[35]Ibid., 16.101; 25.32;
[36]Insert in Ibn Ishāq, op. cit., pp. 165-66. Allah's replacement of the "Satanic Verses" can be read in Qur'ān, 53.19-27.
[37]Qur'ān, 7.66; 26.136; 41.5; 46.26.

urrection (*Yaumu'l Qiyamah*), Day of Separation (*Yaumu'l Faṣl*), Day of Reckoning (*Yaumu'l Hisāb*), Day of Awakening (*Yaumu'l Ba'l*), Day of Judgment (*Yaumu'l Dīn*), Day of Encompassing (*Yaumu'l Muḥit*) or simply as The Hour (*As-Sa'ah*).[38] "For Muhammad, a revivalist preacher seeking to strike terror in his hearers, the doctrines of resurrection and of the judgment were of the first importance, and the Qur'ān, in consequence, is full of references to them."[39] On this day, the dead are to be raised, judged, and sent to eternal heaven if they were believers, and to an eternal hell if they were unbelievers. The pagan Arabs, on the other hand, believed in survival of the human personality after death. In the absence of positive evidence it is difficult to give details of their doctrine. But if we go by what the Sabaeans believed, they stood for transmigration of souls.[40] So "the notion of the reconstruction of the decayed body seemed to them in the highest degree absurd, and Mohammed's promise of heavenly spouses occasioned mirth."[41]

Allāh reports: "They say: Shall we show you a man who will tell you (that) when you have become dispersed in death, with the most complete dispersal, still even then, you will be created anew. Has he invented a lie concerning Allāh or is there in him a madness?...This is a strange thing: When we are dead and have become dust like our forefathers, shall we verily be brought back? We were promised this forsooth, we and our forefathers. This is naught but fables of the men of old. Bring back our fathers if you speak the truth...When we are lost in the earth, how can we then be recreated?...Shall we really be restored to our first state: Even after we are crumbled bones? Then that will be a vain proceeding...There is naught but our life of this world; we die and we live, and naught destroys us save Time...We deem it but a conjecture, and are by no means convinced...And they swear by Allāh their most binding oaths (that) Allāh will not raise him who dies..."[42]

Allāh's rejoinder is also recorded in the Qur'ān: "We know what the earth takes, and with us is a recording Book...Thinks man we shall not assemble his bones. We are able to restore his very finger...Surely it will need but one Shout, and they will be awakened...Those of old and

[38]Ibid., 2.79; 77.14; 40.28; 30.56; 1.3; 11.85.
[39]*First Encyclopaedia of Islam*, op. cit., Vol. IV, p. 1018.
[40]*Encyclopaedia Americana*, New York, 19252, Vol. XXIV, p. 77.
[41]D.S. Margoliouth, op. cit., p. 138.
[42]Qur'ān, 34.7-8; 50.2-3; 27.67-68; 44.36; 45.32; 32.10; 79.10-12; 45.24, 32; 16.38. The reference to the earlier promise points to the Jews who had been proclaiming for a long time that the forefathers of the Arabs will be raised again and judged.

those of later times, will all be brought together to the tryst of an appointed day. Then you the deniers, you will eat of a tree called Zaqqum, and will fill your bellies therewith and thereon you will drink of boiling water, drinking as the camel drinks. This will be their welcome on the Day of Judgment..."[43]

The Meccans, however, were not cowed down by these threats. They challenged Muhammad to hurry up and bring down the doom upon them. Allāh reports: "They say: You have disputed with us and multiplied disputation with us. Now bring down upon us that wherewith you threaten us, if you are truthful... O Allāh! if this be indeed the truth from you, rain down stones on us or bring us some painful doom... Our Lord! Hasten us for our fate before the Day of Reckoning... They ask you of the Hour: When will it come to port?... When will the promise be fulfilled, if you are truthful? When is the Day of Judgment?... They say: The hour will never come to us..."[44] The Meccans threw this challenge again and again if the Qur'ān is to be believed.

Muhammad had to wriggle out of the situation. Allāh reports: "Say: Knowledge thereof is with my Lord. He alone will manifest it at the proper time... It comes not to you save unawares... But Allāh will not punish them while you (Muhammad) are with them... For every nation there is an appointed time... It is (only) then when it has befallen that you will believe...And it is in the Scriptures of the men of old. Is it not a portent for them that the doctors of the Children of Israel know it?...You are but a warner sent unto them...So withdraw from them and await (the event)..."[45]

"Thus then the years of the debate rolled on; in which parties increased in vehemence and antagonism, and in which the successful polemics of the Meccans on the new religion were met by ridicule and refutation of the religious notions current among the pagans. As has been said, the Meccan side is known only from the statements of the adversary, whose acquaintance with the Meccan religion may not have been very deep..."[46]

The poet Abū Qays b. al-Aslat whose pseudonym was Sayfī summed up the pagan position as follows:

Lord of mankind, serious things have happened.
The difficult and the simple are involved.

[43]Ibid., 50.4; 75.3-4; 79.13-14; 56.49-57.
[44]Ibid., 11.22; 8.32; 48.16; 7.187; 10.48; 32.28; 51.13; 34.3.
[45]Ibid., 7.187; 8.33; 10.49,51: 26.96-87; 79.45.
[46]D.S. Margoliouth, op. cit., p. 141.

Lord of mankind, if we have erred
Guide us to the good path.
Were it not for our Lord we should be Jews
And the religion of Jews is not convenient.
Were it not for our Lord we should be Christians
Along with the monks on Mount Jalīl.
But when we were created we were created
Ḥanīfs; our religion is from all generations.[47]

It may be noted that the Lord of the pagans is the Lord of mankind, and not the Lord of Muslims alone.

Muhammad's mission at Mecca had failed. Commenting on the last phase of the Meccan Sūras, F. Buhl says: "It is the weakest part of the Qur'ān, in which Muhammad's imagination became exhausted, and he was content with tiresome repetitions of his earlier ideas and especially with the tales of the prophets. The form becomes discursive, and more prosaic...The passages belonging to it show clearly that Muhammad would have become intellectually bankrupt if the migration to Medina had not aroused him to a new effort..."[48]

This is not the place to go into what the Prophet did after migration to Medina; the story has been documnented in detail by the biographers of the Prophet—surprise raids on trade caravans and tribal settlements; the use of plunder thus obtained for recruiting an ever-growing army of desperados; assassinations of opponents ordered, and blessed when successful; expropriation, expulsion and massacre of Jews who had lived for long in Medina; attack on and enslavement of Jews settled in Khybar; sale of women and children, captured in raids, for buying horses and arms; conquest of Mecca and the rest of Arabia by show as well as use of overwhelming force; and winning over to his fold, by means of bribes, the tricksters and the treacherous in every Arab tribe. He organised no less than eighty-six expeditions, twenty-six of which he led himself. He was getting ready to invade neighbouring lands when he died all of a sudden. What interests us in the present context are the revelations he produced vis-a-vis those who worship Gods other than his Allāh.

Believers were prohibited from contracting marriage relations with the idolaters;[49] they were forbidden to pray for the idolaters, even if the latter were their parents or kinsmen of the first degree.[50] Immediately

---

[47]Ibn Ishāq, op. cit., p. 201.
[48]*First Encyclopaedia of Islam*, op. cit., Volume IV, p. 1075.
[49]Qur'ān, 2.221.
[50]Ibid., 9.113-14.

after the conquest of Mecca, the Ka'ba which had been a pagan temple for ages past was placed out of bounds for the pagans; it was converted into a place of Muslim worship as we shall see. Allāh revised the history of Arabia in order to justify the usurpation. He revealed, "Say: Allāh speaks truth...The first sanctuary appointed for mankind was that at Becca...And (remember) when we prepared for Abraham the place of the (holy) House saying, Ascribe you nothing as partners unto Me, and purify my house for those who make the round (thereof) and those who stand and those who bow and make prostrations...It is not for the idolaters to tend Allāh's sanctuaries, bearing witness against themselves of disbelief...The idolaters only are unclean. So let them not near the Place of Inviolable worship after this year.."[51]

A permanent *jihād* (holy war) was pronounced on the idolaters: "Those who believe do battle for the cause of Allāh; and those who disbelieve do battle for the cause of idols. So fight the minions of the devil...Slay the idolaters wherever you find them, and take them (captive) and besiege them, and prepare for them each ambush..,"[52]

Going back to the debate at Mecca, it is obvious that in those days Allāh was keeping a diary of all that happened in the pagan metropolis between the Muslims on the one hand and the pagans on the other. It is difficult to believe that he recorded only that which the pagans said and igonored altogether that which they did to the Muslims. If this inference is correct, certain conclusions follow.

The bulk of the Qur'ān covers the Meccan period in the life of the Prophet. We do not find in any of the chapters even the hint of any physical method used by the Meccans towards Muhammad or his Muslims. The only violence we come across is in the language of Allāh who frets and fumes and threatens the Meccans with dire consequences, all too frequently and for no other reason than that the Meccans refuse to accept what is written in the scriptures of the Jews and the Christians, and stick to their own ancient religion. What credence, then, can be placed in the stories, sold by the biographers of Muhammad, that while the Prophet argued his case with patience and in a reasoned manner, his opponents did not know how to meet the challenge and resorted to physical methods? We find no evidence for these stories in the only contemporary source available to us, namely, the Qur'ān.

On the contrary, the biographers provide several broad hints of

[51]Ibid., 3.95-96; 22.26; 9.17,28. "Mecca" was also pronounced as "Becca" in olden times.

[52]Ibid., 4.76; 9.5.

violence threatened or committed by the zealots of Islam in the streets of Mecca. For instance, when 'Umar became a Muslim, he went to the Ka'ba and proclaimed to his fellow citizens, "There is no god but Allah, and Muhammad is the apostle of Allah! Whoever of you moves, I shall cut off his head with my bright scimitar, and shall send him to the Mansion of destruction."[53] Margoliouth observes: "The persons whose accession to Islam was most welcomed were men of physical strength, and much actual fighting must have taken place at Meccah before the Flight; else the readiness with which the Moslems after the Flight could produce from their number tried champions would be inexplicable. A tried champion must have been tried somewhere..."[54] We do not expect Allāh to find place for these Muslim doings in his diary. We also know his defence for slurring over the misdeeds of his minions. It is the same as that of every Marxist historian—"Comrade! I am a partisan. I have no use for bloody bourgois objectivity." All that we are saying is that we cannot help suspecting the stories which say that the Muslims were on the receiving end. They look very much like the products of Islamic martyrology.

Martyrs have been the stock-in-trade of prophetic creeds down the ages. Long before the prophet of Islam was born, the annalists of Judaism and Christianity had perfected the art of making the agressor look like the victim of aggression, and vice versa. The Bible was the masterpiece produced by this art. The biographers of the Prophet had only to borrow the art and practise it in the new context. The art continued to flourish in Christian and Muslim countries till the eighteenth century when it was rejected in the modern West and a new discipline of history-writing emerged. It was, however, revived in Soviet Russia under Stalin and had a fresh lease of life. Now Russia has also rejected it with repugnance. The only land in which it is being practised at present and on some scale is India. The Stalinist historians who were placed in positions of power in the regime of Jawaharlal Nehru and his Minister of "Education", Maulana Abul Kalam Azad, have been practising this art with considerable self-confidence. They are of course nowhere near the masters of yester years. It is seldom that apes acquire the looks of those they imitate. But they do create confusion till they are identified and exposed.

---

[53]*The Rauzat-us-Safa, or Garden of Purity* by Muhammad bin Khavendshah bin Mahmud translated into English by E. Rehatsek, first published 1893, Delhi Reprint 1982, Vol. I, pt. II, p. 183.

[54]D.S. Margoliouth, op. cit., p. 161.

Another conclusion follows from Allāh's silence over any mundane motives on the part of the Meccans when they stand up for their Gods. Allāh accused them of ignorance, obstinacy, temptations from Satan and the rest, but never of greed for the rich revenues brought in by pilgrims to the Ka'ba. It needs an investigation as to when and by whom this base motive was attributed to the Meccans for explaining their devotion to their religion. Allāh for sure had no part in spreading the canard. Whatever its origin, this much is certain that it must have acquired respectability with the spread of Marxism. By now it has become the most fashionable way of explaining the quarrel between Muhammad and his kinsmen. Marxists as well non-Marxists mouth it with equal conviction. Nearer home, the same mind has spread a similar canard about the Brahmins. We are told that the Brahmins proclaim and practise their "puerile priestcraft" not because they believe in any part of it but because it brings them mundane privileges and material profits. Those who have studied the history of Brahmins and are familiar with the depths of their spiritual traditions, and therefore dismiss the lies spread about them by Christian missionaries and Marxist mullahs, can very well judge the worth of the canard spread about the Meccans.

The motives of the converts to Islam were, however, not in doubt from the very first. "Of any moralising or demoralising effect which Mohammed's teaching had upon his followers, we cannot speak with precision. When he was at the head of the robber community it is probable that the demoralising influence began to be felt; it was then that men who had never broken an oath learnt that they might evade their obligations, and that men to whom the blood of their clansmen had been as their own began to shed it with impunity in the cause of God; and that lying and treachery in the cause of Islam received divine approval, hesitation to perjure oneself in that cause being reprehended as a weakness. It was then, too, that Moslems became distinguished by the obscenity of their language. It was then, too, that the coveting of goods and wives (possessed by Unbelievers) was avowed without discouragement from the Prophet...On the other hand, there is no evidence that the Moslems were either in personal or altruistic morality better than the pagans..."[55]

The war which Allāh of the Qur'ān had declared on pagan Gods was aimed at ensuring a moral holiday for his followers. The ancient religion of Arabia which centred round those Gods had established

[55]D.S Margoliouth, op. cit., p. 149.

certain moral standards and social conventions which kept the beast in man under restraint. The destruction of temples where the Gods were worshipped gave a clear signal that the beast had been unleashed.

Chapter Sixteen

THE PROPHET DESTROYS PAGAN TEMPLES

Judaism and Christianity had equipped the Prophet of Islam with an exclusive god and a sectarian scripture which declared war on pagan Gods and their places of worship. The Jews and Christians in Arabia, descended from immigrants or native converts, also provided practical demonstration of how to proceed vis-a-vis pagan temples, whenever and wherever these two sects acquired political power, howsoever shortlived.

We do not know what the Christianized Arabs on the borders of the Byzantine Empire did to pagan places of worship; the sources are silent on the subject. It is a safe bet that they must have followed in the footsteps of their mentors in the Empire. Some information, however, is available on what happened in Yemen, the southern province of Arabia. Some years before the birth of Muhammad, Tubba', the Himayrite king of Yemen, had converted to Judaism under the influence of two rabbis from Yathrib (Medina). He used state-power for converting his people to the new creed. "Now Ri'ām," reports Ibn Ishāq, "was one of the temples which they venerated and where they offered sacrifices and received oracles when they were polytheists. The two rabbis told Tubba' that it was merely a shayṭān which deceived them in this way and they asked to be allowed to deal with it. When the king agreed they commanded a black dog to come out of it and killed it—at least this is what the Yamanites say. Then they destroyed the temple and I am told that its ruins to this day show traces of the blood that was poured over it."[1] The blood must have been that of the pagans who courted death in defence of the temple.

Around the same time, some nobles of Najran, another principality in Yemen, were converted to Christianity by a missionary named Faymiyūn. "At this time," reports Ibn Ishāq, "the people of Najrān followed the religion of the Arabs worshipping a great palm-tree. Every year they had a festival when they hung on the tree any fine garment they could find and women's jewels. Then they sallied out and devoted

[1]Ibn Ishāq, op. cit., pp. 10–11. The pagan Gods are supposed to be dead matter in the lore of the prophetic creeds. But, as we have seen and shall see, these Gods not only speak but also produce live beings, animal as well as human, whenever they are threatened with destruction.

the day to it." Faymiyūn reported to the nobles that the palm-tree "could neither help nor hurt" and that "if he were to curse the tree in the name of God, He would destroy it, for He was God Alone without companion." The nobles agreed. Faymiyūn "invoked God against the tree and God sent a wind against it which tore it from its roots and cast it on the ground." The miracle helped the people of Najran to adopt the "law of Īsā b. Maryam" in which Faymiyūn "instructed them."[2] In plain language the story says that political power was used for forcing the people into the Christian fold and destroying their places of worship. Churches rose on the sites of sacred groves and pagan temples.

The Judaic regime in the neighbourhood of Najran, however, was militarily more powerful. As already related, the Himayrite king Dhū Nuwās marched on Najran, slaughtered thousands of Christians, and forced the rest into the fold of Judaism. It is not recorded what this hero of Judaism did to the Christian churches which had come up. But one can be sure that they were demolished or converted into synagogues.

In turn, the victory of Judaism was short-lived. The Christian king of Abyssinia sent an army which overthrew the Judaic regime in Yemen and imposed Christianity on the whole province. Abraha, the Abyssinian governor, demolished the synagogues and erected churches on their sites. He built a grand cathedral at San'ā', the seat of his government, and informed his king that "I have erected a house and built a church so as to put an end to the circumambulation of the Ka'bah by pilgrims and visitors."[3] He was looking forward to destroying the pagan temple in Mecca.

The excuse for Christian agression was provided by an Arab from Mecca who "went forth until he came to the cathedral and defiled it" during the night. Abraha made enquiries. He "learned that the outrage had been committed by an Arab who came from the temple in Mecca where the Arabs went on pilgrimage, and that he had done this in anger at his threat to divert the Arabs' pilgrimage to the cathedral, showing thereby that it was unworthy of reverence." He felt "enraged and swore that he would go to the temple and destroy it."[4] A Christian army equipped with elephants marched on Mecca and encamped in the outskirts of the city which the Arabs were in no position to defend against a formidable foe. But an epidemic or some other disaster forced the invaders to beat a retreat.

---

[2]Ibid., pp. 15–16.
[3]*The Rauzat-us-Safa*, op. cit., p. 33.
[4]Ibn Ishāq, op. cit., p. 22.

The Arabs in Yemen had meanwhile invited help from Persia. "The films of Judaism and Christianity," writes Margoliouth, "torn off the face of South Arabia, paganism it seems was restored: not indeed at Najran, where Christianity, remained, as in an island; but the rulers were pagans, and in league with the worst enemy of the Cross. Meanwhile the matters about which the sects were at variance were evoking interest in minds that had been alien from them."[5]

Muhammad was born in the year in which the Christian invasion of Mecca took place. The pagan Arabs celebrated for long what they regarded as a victory of their Gods over the Christian godling. Years later, after he had floated the myth of Abraham as the latest builder of the Ka'ba, Muhammad will pronounce that the defeat of the Christian army was brought about by the God of Abraham. But that was a big bluff prompted by the Jewish refusal to accept him as a prophet. "The connection of the Abraham-myth with the Ka'bah," observes Margoliouth, "appears to have been the result of later speculation, and to have been fully developed only when a political need for it arose."[6] It was a case of ideological usurpation of the place before physical misappropriation occured.

It is difficult to say at what stage of his life Muhammad became a convinced monotheist. The evidence available suggests that his evolution towards this creed was a slow process. Dealing with the years after his marriage to Khadījah and before he became a prophet, Margoliouth cites old Islamic sources and concludes that Muhammad was a polytheist for quite some time. "The names of some of the children show that their parents when they named them were idolaters. Nor is there anything to indicate that Mohammed was at this time of a monothestic or religious turn of mind. He with Khadijah performed some domestic rite in honour of one of the goddesses each night before retiring. At the wedding of his cousin, Abu Lahab's daughter, he is represented as clamouring for sport...He confessed to having at one time sacrified a grey sheep to Al-'Uzza—and probably did so more than once...A story which may be true shows us Mohammed with his stepson inviting the Meccan monotheist Zaid, son of 'Amr, to eat with them—of meat offered to idols: the old man refused..."[7]

Islamic hagiography, however, tells us that the Prophet was an uncompromising monotheist and a determined iconoclast from the

---

[5]D.S. Margoliouth, op. cit., p. 37.
[6]Ibid., p. 104.
[7]Ibid., pp. 69-70.

moment he was conceived in the womb of his mother. "It is related that on the morning of conception the idols in all the inhabited quarters of the earth were overturned..."[8] Mightier events took place on the night of his birth. A lake dried up, a river overflowed and the palace of the Persian monarch "so trembled that fourteen of its pinnacles fell to the ground." More significantly "news arrived from Estakhan that the fire of the chief temple of Persia, which had burned for a thousand years, had become extinguished."[9] Nearer home, the Pagans in Mecca witnessed a scene which left them distressed. "Another event of the night of the nativity took place when the Qoraish were holding a festival in honour of one of their idols, in whose temple they had at that time assembled, and were engaged in eating and drinking. They found, however, that their god had fallen to the ground, and set him up again; but as he was, a short time afterwards, again found prostrate on his face, the idolaters were much dismayed and erected him again. When they had done so the third time, a voice was heard from the cavity of the idol saying:

> All the regions of the earth, in the east and west,
> Respond to the nativity, whom its light strikes;
> And idolatry decreases, and the hearts of all
> The kings of the earth tremble with fear."[10]

As a baby, Muhammad was suckled by a desert woman, Ḥalīma. One day she came to Mecca to see the 'Ukāz fair, carrying Muhammad with her. An astrologer saw the baby and shouted, "Come here, O people of Hudayl, come here, O Arabs." People gathered round him, Ḥalīma among them. He pointed towards the baby and said, "He will slaughter people of your religion and smash your idols." Halīma took fright and ran away with the baby.[11]

Muhammad was more than three years old when Ḥalīma took him to Mecca with the intention of returning him to his family. But the child got lost when they arrived in the city. Ḥalīma was searching frantically for him when she met an old man who heard her story and wanted to help. "The foolish man," says the biographer, "went to Hobal, and after praising him as is the fashion of idolaters, he continued: 'This woman of the Bani Sa'ad says that she lost Muhammad the son of A'bd-ul-Muttalib; restore him to her if it so pleaseth thee'... As soon as that

---

[8]*The Rauzal-us-Safa*, op. cit., p 85.
[9]Ibid., pp. 89–90.
[10]Ibid., p. 92.
[11]Translated from 'Alāma Abdullāh al-Ahmadī's Urdu version of *Tabqāt-i-ibn Sa'd*, Part I: *Akhbār an-Nabī*, Karachi, (n.d.), p. 233.

misguided individual had pronounced these words Hobal fell prostrate on his face, and from the cavity of his statute the words were heard: 'What have I to do with Muhammad who will be the cause of our destruction? ...Tell the idolaters that he is the great sacrifice; that is to say, he will kill all, except those who will be so fortunate as to follow him.'"[12]

Muhammad was a young boy when he was invited by his uncles and aunts to join a celebration in honour of Buāna, a God to whom the Quraysh were much devoted. He was reluctant but yielded under pressure from the family. But when he came back, he was terribly frightened and looked depressed. His aunts asked what had happened to him. He said, "Whenever I went near an idol, I saw a man, white and tall, calling out to me, 'O Muhammad! get back, do not touch it.'"[13] He never joined a pagan celebration again.

Some time later, his people were sacrificing to Buāna. A voice came out of the idol's belly, "A strange thing has happened. We are being burnt in fire. Abeyance of *wahy* (revelation) has come to an end. A prophet has taken birth in Mecca. His name is Ahmad. He will migrate to Yathrib."[14]

His uncle, Abū Tālib, had taken Muhammad with a caravan going to Syria. The caravan halted near a monastery at Bostra where Bahira, a Christian monk, felt drawn towards Muhamad and made enquiries about him from the other Arabs. "When the people had finished eating," reports Ibn Ishāq, "and gone away Bahira got up and said to him, 'Boy, I ask you by al-Lāt and al-'Uzzā to answer my questions.' Now Bahira said this only because he had heard his people swearing by these gods. They allege that the apostle of God said to him, 'Do not ask me by al-Lāt and al-'Uzzā, for by Allah nothing is more hateful for me than these two gods.'"[15]

A similar event is reported to have happened in his youth when he was employed by Khadījah and travelled to Egypt with her merchandise. The caravan came across another Christian monk named Nasṭṭur who also fell for Muhammad. "Nasṭṭur...descended from the roof of his hermitage, and said to the apostle of Allah: 'I adjure thee by Lāt and U'zza to tell me what thy name is.' His holy and prophetic lordship replied: 'May thy mother be childless! Begone from me; for the Arabs

---

[12]*The Rauzat-us-Safa*, op. cit., Vol. I, pt. II, p. 115.
[13]*Tabqāt-i-Ibn Sa'd*, op. cit., pp. 245–46.
[14]Ibid., p. 250. Idols can speak when it concerns prophets.
[15]Ibn Ishāq, op. cit., p. 80.

have not uttered any words more disagreeable to me than thine.'"[16] At a latter stage in the same journey Muhammad had a dispute with a Jew on account of some business transaction. The Jew said; "I adjure you by Lāt and U'zza." Muhammad replied: "Whenever I pass by Lāt and U'zza, I turn away my face from them."[17]

Now, it is well-known that hagiography everywhere projects future events into the past. We have quoted from the hagiography of the Prophet not to decry it but to make the point that Islamic lore has always looked at Muhammad as a born iconoclast. This was not necessary because only his practices as a prophet provide the pious precedents. But hagiography hates to leave any loopholes, even if it has to invent events.

Hagiography yields place to history as we move into the period of Muhammad's prophethood. While initiating 'Alī b. Abū Tālib into Islam, Muhammad said: "I call you to God, the One without associate, to worship him and to disavow al-Lāt and al-'Uzzā." 'Alī was surprised as he had never heard such a thing before, and offered to consult his father, Abū Tālib. But Muhammad told him, "If you do not accept Islam, then conceal the matter." Next morning, 'Alī came and requested Muhammad to initiate him. He had made up his mind after a night's reflection. Muhammad said to him, "Bear witness that there is no god but Allah alone without associate, and disavow al-Lāt and al-'Uzzā." 'Alī became a Muslim but "concealed his Islam and did not let it be seen."[18] Islam at this time was a secret society.

Ibn Hanbal cites another tradition from 'Ali about what the Prophet attempted while Islam was being kept concealed. 'Alī said: "I and the Prophet walked till we came to the Ka'ba. Then the Prophet of Allāh said to me, 'Sit down.' Then he stood on my shoulders and I arose. But when he saw that I could not support him, he came down, sat down and said, 'Stand on my shoulders.' Then I climbed on his shoulders and he stood up and it seemed to me as if I could have touched the sky, had I wished. Then I climbed on the roof of the Ka'ba on which there was an image of copper and iron. Then I began to loosen it at its right and left side, in front and behind until it was in my power. Then the Prophet of Allāh called to me: 'Throw it down.' Then I threw it down so that it broke into pieces like a bottle. I then climbed down from the Ka'ba and hurried away with the Prophet, till we hid ourselves in the houses for

---

[16]*The Rauzat-us-Safa*, op. cit., p. 127.
[17]Ibid., p. 128.
[18]Insert from Ibn Khallikān in Ibn Ishāq, op. cit., p. 115.

fear some one might meet us."[19] Shi'ah theologians have transferred this adventure to the time when the Prophet reached Ka'ba after the conquest of Mecca.[20] But that is no more than a sectarian exercise. The language of the tradition connects the event to the time when Islam was still a secret society. Moreover, 'Alī is shown as a boy rather than a stalwart which he had become by the time Mecca was conquered.

Another incident relates to the time after Islam had come out into the open. It was reported to Hamzah, the Prophet's uncle, that Abū'l Ḥakam, a Meccan chief whom the Muslims called Abū Jāhl, had insulted Muhammad. Hamzah was still a pagan and, therfore, cared for kinship ties. He went to Muhammad who was sitting in the precincts of the Ka'ba, and said, "Thy uncle hast come to take vengeance on thy enemy." Muhammad asked him to leave alone the man "who has no uncle, neither father nor mother, no man of business, nor wazir," meaning himself. "But Hamzah swore by Lāt and U'zza saying, 'I have come only to aid and protect thee.'" The Prophet felt annoyed at his uncle's mention of the pagan Goddesses, and said, "I swear by that God who has sent me in truth, that if thou fightest long enough against infidels to be drowned in their blood, thou will only be removed further and further from the Lord of unity, until thou sayest, 'I bear witness that there is no god but Allah, and I testify that Muhammad is the apostle of Allah.'"[21]

On the whole, however, the situation in Mecca was unfavourable to the Prophet. The pagans were in a strong position and he could not touch their idols or places of worship, howsoever keen he might have been to desecrate or destroy them. His attempt to invite another Abyssinian invasion of Mecca for taking over the Ka'ba and turning it into a place of monotheistic worship, was also a failure. The Christian king was very kind to the Muslims whom Muhammad had sent to his court. His domestic situation, however, did not permit a foreign adventure. The Prophet's attempt to raise Tā'if against Mecca also ended in failure. He found himself utterly helpless against the pagan stronghold. He could only curse the idolaters and invoke Allāh's wrath against them.

It was in Medina that his followers started doing something concrete vis-a-vis the idols, after they had entered into a pact with him at al-'Aqaba for moving his headquarters to their city. Ibn Ishāq reports,

---

[19]*First Encyclopaedia of Islam*, op. cit., Vol. VII, p. 562.

[20]See *The Rauzat-us-Safa*, op. cit., Vol. II, pt. II, pp. 599–600. Also Saiyid Safdar Hosain, *The Early History of Islam*, Lucknow 1933, Delhi Reprint 1985, Vol. I, pp. 193–94.

[21]*The Rauzat-us-Safa*. op. cit., p. 179.

"When they came to Medina they openly professed Islam there. Now some of the shykhs still kept to their old idolatry, among whom was 'Amr b. al-Jamūh...whose son Mu'ādh had been present at al-'Aqaba and done homage to the apostle there. 'Amr was one of the tribal nobles and leaders and had set up in his house a wooden idol called Manāt as the nobles used to do, making it a god to reverence and keeping it clean. When the young men of B. Salama...and his own son Mu'ādh adopted Islam with the other men who had been at al-'Aqaba they used to creep in at night to this idol of 'Amr's and carry it away and throw it on its face into a cesspit. When the morning came 'Amr cried, 'Woe to you! Who has been at our gods this night?' Then he went in search of the idol and when he found it he washed it and cleaned it and perfumed it saying, 'By God, if I knew who had done this I would treat him shamefully.' When night came and he was fast asleep they did the same again and he restored the idol in the morning... This happened several times..."[22]

'Alī found a Muslim stealing idols in the night and getting them burnt, when he stayed for a few days in Qubā' after the Prophet had migrated from Mecca. Ibn Ishāq proceeds, "He used to say that in Qubā' there was an unmarried Muslim woman and he noticed that a man used to come to her in the middle of the night and knock on her door; she would come out and he would give her something. He felt very suspicious of him and asked her what was the meaning of this nightly performance as she was a Muslim woman without a husband. She told him that he was Sahl b. Hunayf b. Wāhib who knew that she was all alone and he used to break up the idols of his tribe at night and bring her the pieces to use as fuel..."[23]

The Prophet had also stayed at Qubā' in the course of his flight from Mecca. This was a place three miles outside Medina. A mosque was built here during the Prophet's stay. It was the first mosque in the history of Islam. The details of the site on which it was built are not available in the sources. But we are told something about the second and the major mosque built by the Prophet in Medina, soon after his arrival in that city. The site was a garden which he purchased. According to a tradition from Anas b. Mālik, "There were graves of the idolaters, dilapidated buildings and date trees [in the garden]. The Prophet gave the order and the graves of the idolaters were dug out, the dilapidated buildings levelled [with the ground], and the date trees cut

[22]Ibn Ishāq, op. cit., pp. 207.
[23]Ibid., pp. 227–28.

down."[24] Most probably the site was a sacred grove and the building that stood there were places of pagan worship, neglected or abandoned due to the rising tide of monotheism in Medina. This much at least is certain that the Prophet showed contempt for the graves of the idoalters. Cutting down of date trees was also a sacrilege according to pagan ethics. In days to come, Muslims will show veneration for graves in which their own brothers in faith are buried.

The available sources provide no evidence of the Prophet or his followers in Medina desecrating or destroying any pagan shrines or breaking idols, during the many expeditions they mounted on tribal settlements, far and near. It is unlikely that the biographers of the Prophet or other Muslim annalists suppressed the facts on this score, for acts of iconoclasm were a matter of pride for them and an essential element in their glorification of Islam. Most propbably the Muslims did not get proper opportunities for this, their favourite pastime, because most of the expeditions were surprise raids aimed at plunder. It is also probable that the Prophet did not want to show his hand before the right time and thus provoke more than normal resistance to his acts of aggression. Or, perhaps, it was the Prophet's strategy to break the morale of the pagans by slaughter and rapine before he moved on to their places of worship. Whatever the reason, all available evidence suggests that the Prophet was busy throughout this period in amassing booty and ransom for financing his military machine.

The Muslim army that finally moved on Mecca in the year AH 8 (AD 630) was a formidable force by Arabian standards of that time. Abbas b. Mirdās al-Sulamī, the Muslim poet, sang:

> With us on the day Muhammad entered Mecca
> Were a thousand marked men—the valley flowed with them.
> They had helped the aspostle and been present at his battles,
> Their marks on the day of battle being to the fore.
> In a strait place their feet were firm.
> They split the enemies' heads like colocynths.
> Their hooves had travelled Najd beforehand
> Till at last black Ḥijāz became subject to them.
> God gave him the mastery of it.
> The judgment of the sword and victorious fortune subdued it to us...[25]

---

[24]Translated from the Urdu version of *Saḥīh Bukhārī Sharīf*, New Delhi, 1984, Vol. I. p. 240. See also the Urdu version of *Sunn Nasāī Sharīf*, New Delhi, 1986, Vol. I, p. 240, and *Tārīkh-i-Ṭabarī*, Vol. I, *Sīrat an-Nabī*, Karachi (n.d.), p. 145.

[25]Ibn Hishām's notes in Ibn Ishāq, op. cit., p. 775. "Marked men" means men carrying military colours or standards signifying various formations.

Small wonder that Mecca surrendered without a fight. The pagan leader, Abū Sufyān, had developed cold feet as soon as he saw the marshalled ranks, and gone over to Islam. Very soon, he will be breaking the idols for which he had fought for long. "Abū Sufyān recited the following verses in which he excused himself for what had gone before:

By the life when I carried a banner
To give al-Lāt's cavalry the victory over Muhammad
I was like the one going astray in the darkness of the night,
But now I am led on the right track...[26]

The conquest of Mecca by Muhammad was the most significant event in the history of Islam. The success of the enterprise settled the character of Islam for all time to come. The lessons drawn from the success constitute the core of Islamic theology as taught ever since in the sprawling seminaries. The principal lessons are two. The first is that Muslims should continue resorting to violence on any and every pretext till they triumph; setbacks are temporary. The second lesson is that Islam should refuse to coexist or compromise with every other religion and culture, and use the first favourable opportunity to wipe out the others completely so that it alone may prevail. Our present context is concerned with the second lesson.

The Temple of Ka'ba

Soon after entering Mecca, the Prophet went to the Ka'ba, took its key from 'Uthmān B. Tālha, and entered it. Ibn Ishāq records, "There he found a dove made of wood. He broke it in his hands and threw it away." Next he turned to the idols which were housed in and around the temple. They were 360 in number. "The apostle was standing by them with a stick in his hand, saying, 'The truth has come and falsehood has passed away. Verily, falsehood is bound to pass away' (Sūra. 17.82).[27] Then he pointed at them with his stick and they collapsed on their backs one after the other. When the apostle prayed the noon prayer on the day of the conquest he ordered that all the idols which were round the Ka'ba should be collected and burned with fire and broken up. Faḍāla b. al-Mulāwwih al-Laythī said commemorating the day of the conquest:

Had you seen Muhammad and his troops
The day the idols were smashed when he entered,

---

[26]Ibn Ishāq, op. cit., p. 546.
[27]The verse was cited whenever Muslim invaders destroyed Hindu temples.

You would have seen God's light become manifest
And darkness covering the face of idolatry."[28]

"Biographical works are filled with the accounts of this proceeding, and that three hundred and sixty idols, the greatest whereof was Hobal, had been erected by the idolaters around the Ka'bah. In some copies we read that Eblis had fixed the bases of all these idols underground with lead, but that nevertheless when the apostle of Allah touched them with the lance or stick he had in his hands, and uttered the words: 'Truth had come, and falsehood has departed', the idols fell on their faces at the mere touch of the staff...There is a tradition ascribed to A'bdullah B. A'bbas that whenever his lordship pointed on that day to the face of an idol, the same immediately fell on its back, and whenever he pointed to the back it fell on its face."[29] The Islamic lore has thus turned into a miracle what was actually a show of brute physical force. "Muhammad when he entered Mekka as victor is stated to have struck them in the eyes with his bow before he had them dragged down and destroyed by fire."[30] The burning of the idols gave rise to another story in Islamic lore. "Upon the conquest of Mecca the Prophet cut open some of these idols with his sword and black smoke is said to have issued forth from them, a sign of the psychic influence which had made these idols their dwelling place."[31] One wonders what else except smoke could have come out when objects made of stone and wood were burnt. It is the privilege of Islamic lore to invest smoke with psychic power.

Hubal, the principal idol in the Ka'ba "was pulled down and used as a doorstep when the Prophet conquered Mecca and purified the Ka'bah."[32] This particular practice of the Prophet set up a pious precedent which was followed extensively when Islamic iconoclasm arrived in India. Many Hindu idols ended at the doorsteps of the principal mosques not only in Muslim capitals within India such as Ghazni, Kabul, Lahore, Multan, Nagore, Ajmer, Delhi, Jaunpur, Gaur, Daulatabad, Mandu, Ahmadabad, Gulbarga, Bidar, Bijapur, Ahmadnagar, Golkunda, Dhaka and Murshidabad, but also in far off places like Baghdad, Mecca and Medina, "The other stones which were worshipped as idols were actually used as corner-stones of the Ka'ba and as such we must consider also the Maqām Ibrāhīm."[33] This too was a

[28]Ibid., op. cit., p. 552.
[29]*The Rauzat-us-Safa*, op. cit., Vol. II, pt. II, p. 599.
[30]*First Encyclopaedia of Islam*, op. cit., Vol. VII, p. 147.
[31]Cyril Glasse op. cit., p. 179.
[32]Ibid., p. 160.
[33]*First Encyclopaedia of Islam*, op. cit., Vol. VII, pp. 147-48.

pious precedent which was followed extensively in India. A large number of mosques and other Muslim monuments in India have Hindu idols or their pieces embedded in their masonry.

There was only one idol which the Prophet not only spared but also consecrated with his kiss so that every Muslim who performs Hajj is expected to do the same. This was the black stone now described pompously as al-Ḥajar al-Aṣwad. The Muslims present on the occasion felt puzzled by the Prophet's partiality for this particular stone. They were informed that the black stone had descended directly from heaven. According to a well-known tradition (*hadīth*) from Ibn'Abbās, the Prophet told his people, "By Allāh, Allāh will lift it up on the Last Day. It will have two eyes with which it will see. It will have a tongue with which it will speak and stand witness for that man who had kissed it earnestly."[34] Other people's idols are stones, while one's own stone is God's spokesman! Many of his followers must have remained unimpressed by the mysterious pronouncement. A few years later, Caliph 'Umar (AD 632–44), while kissing the black stone, is reported to have said, "I know that you are a stone which can neither help nor hurt. I would not have kissed you, had I not witnessed the Prophet of Allāh kissing you."[35]

Idols were not the only "abominations" which the Prophet had to take care of in the Ka'ba. Ibn Ishāq and other biographers of the Prophet report that the "Quraysh had put pictures in the Ka'ba including two of Jesus son of Mary and Mary...The apostle ordered that the pictures would be erased except those of Jesus and Mary."[36] According to a tradition, as 'Umar began to wash out the pictures with the water of the well known as Zamzam, "Muhammad placed his hand on the pictures of Jesus and Mary and said, 'Wash out all except what is below my hands.' He then withdrew his hand."[37] There is no reason to doubt that the walls of the Ka'ba carried paintings. Pagans have always been as fond of presenting their pantheon and mythology through colour as through carving. But it is an invention that the paintings included those of Jesus and Mary. The pagans who had maintained the Ka'ba and decorated its walls with paintings were not only not enamoured of the Christian god and his mother, they actually entertained abhorrence for them. Allāh himself says in the Qur'ān that the disbelievers show disre-

---

[34]Translated from the Urdu version of *Mishkāt Sharif*, Delhi (n.d.), Vol. I, p. 572.
[35]Ibid., p. 574.
[36]Ibn Ishāq, op. cit., p. 552.
[37]*First Encyclopaedia of Islam*, op. cit., Vol. IV, p. 587.

spect for Īsā. Referring to 'Umar's act of effacing the paintings, Margoliouth observes, "Whom or what they represented we know only on Mohammed's authority, which we are not inclined to trust..."[38]

Scholars have made several speculations regarding the Prophet's attitude to the Ka'ba. Basing themselves on legends found in the biographies of the Prophet, some say that he had reverence for the national sanctuary but regretted its misuse by the pagans. Some others say that when he changed the Qibla from the Temple in Jerusalem to the Ka'ba in Mecca, he did so in order to conciliate Arab national sentiment. "We do not know the personal feelings of the youthful Muhammad towards the Ka'ba and the Meccan cult, but they were presumably of a conventional nature. What the biography of the Prophet tells us about his Meccan period in this respect can lay no claim to historical value. The Meccan revelations tell us nothing about these relations during the important period in the life of the Prophet. In any case, he felt no enthusiam for the Meccan sanctuary."[39]

In fact, there is a tradition that he wanted to destroy the Ka'ba. 'Ā'isha has reported him as saying to her that "if your people had not renounced ignorance promptly and become Musalmans, I would have demolished the Ka'ba and rebuilt it with two doors."[40] The tradition seems to be authentic because it inspired demolition and rebuilding of the Ka'ba on two subsequent occasions. "When A'bdullah Bin Zobeir heard this tradition he destroyed the building of the Qoraish whilst he held sway, and rebuilt the Ka'bah according to the intentions of his lordship the last of the prophets. When, however, Hajjāj Bin Yusuf undertook by order of A'bd-ul-Malik Merwān [AD 685–705] a compaign against A'bdullah Bin Zobeir and vanquished him, he destroyed the edifice built by the latter at the command of the same Khalifah and re-erected it as the Qoraish had built it during the lifetime of his holy and prophetic lordship. When Harūn-ur-Rashid became Khalifah he desired to annihilate the edifice of Merwān, and to rebuild the Ka'bah according to the model of A'bdullah Bin Zobeir. On this subject he consulted the Imām Mālek, but the latter replied: 'O commander of the faithful, let the Ka'bah alone, let it not become the sport of kings.' Accordingly Harūn renounced his intention."[41]

What was this "building of the Qoreish" which Ibn Zubayr demol-

---

[38]Margoliouth, op. cit., p. 387.
[39]*First Encyclopaedia of Islam*, Vol. IV, p. 587.
[40]Translated from the Urdu version of *Jāmi' Tirmizi*, New Delhi, 1983, Vol. I, p. 330.
[41]*The Rauzat-us-Safa*, op. cit., Vol. I, pt. II, p. 133.

ished and Hajjāj restored? This much is clear from Muslim accounts that it was a pagan temple housing the idols of many Gods. These acconts, however, insist that in the ancient past it was a place of monotheistic worship consecrated by Abraham. There is only one Muslim account which preserves a pagan tradition. "According to al-Mas'ūdī (Murūdj, iv, 47), certain people have regarded the Ka'ba as a temple devoted to the sun, the moon and the five planets. The 360 idols placed round the Ka'ba also point in the same direction. It can therefore hardly be denied that traces exist of an astral symbolism..."[42] That the Ka'ba was a centre of sun-worship is also confirmed by whatever memories of the pre-Islamic Hajj survive in Muslim accounts. "As soon as the sun was visible, the *ifāḍa* to Minā used to begin in pre-Islamic times. Muhammad therefore ordained that this should begin before sunrise; here again we have the attempt to destroy a solar rite. In ancient times they are said to have sung during the *ifāḍa, ashrīq thabīr kaimā nughīr*. The explanation of these words is uncertain; it is sometimes translated: 'Enter into light of morning, Thabir, so that we may hasten.'"[43]

It is pointed out by apologists of Islam that the Prophet did not convert the pagan temple into a mosque and that he only "restored" it to what it used to be in Abraham's time. We known that the Abraham story about the Ka'ba is a fabrication floated after the Prophet had left Mecca and quarrelled with the Jews of Medina. And there was no specific architectural design for a mosque developed during the lifetime of the Prophet; any structure, in any shape could serve the purpose. For the rest, everything that needs be done for depriving a place of its pagan character and converting it into a place of Islamic worship, was done by the Prophet. The conversion of the temple at Mecca into a mosque was complete when Bilāl stood on the roof of the Ka'ba and recited *azān*.

Idols in Mecca

In Mecca proper, Isāf and Nā'ila were the only other important idols outside the Ka'ba. They were the deities of as-Safa and al-Marwah. "On that occasion the lord of apostleship ordered A'li...to break to pieces Asāf and Nāylah...When these two idols were broken a rude black woman issued from one of them, when his holy and prophetic lordship said: 'This is Nāylah. But she will never any more be worshipped in your country.'"[44]

---

[42] *First Encyclopaedia of Islam,* op. cit., Volume IV, p. 591.

[43] Ibid., Vol. III, p. 200. We shall deal with this subject further in Appendix 2.

[44] *The Rauzat-us-Safa,* op. cit., Vol. II, pt. II, p. 599.

At the same time, "The proclaimer authorised by the apostle of Allāh went throughout Mecca calling upon all those who believe in Allāh and the Last Day to leave no idol unbroken in their homes."[45]

Having "purified" Mecca, the Prophet sent "expeditions to those idols which were in the neighbourhood and had them destroyed; these included al-'Uzzā, Manāt, Suwā', Buāna and Dhu'l-Kaffayn."[46]

The Temple of al-'Uzzā

"Then the apostle sent Khālid to al-'Uzzā which was in Nakhla. It was a temple which the tribe of Quraysh and Kināna and all Muḍar used to venerate. Its guardians were B. Shaybān of B. Sulaym, allies of B. Hāshim. When the Sulamī guardian heard of Khālid's coming he hung his sword on her, climbed the mountain on which she stood, and said:

O'Uzzā, make an annihilating attack on Khālid,
Throw aside your veil and gird up your train.
O 'Uzzā, if you do not kill this man Khālid
Then bear a swift punishment or become a Christian.

When Khālid arrived he destroyed her and returned to the apostle."[47] It is significant that the pagan priest saw no difference between becoming a Muslim and becoming a Christian.

The rest of the story is told in other sources. "He [the Prophet] asked him [Khālid], 'Did you see anything?' Khālid replied, 'Nothing.' He [the Prophet] said, 'Go again, and smash her to pieces.' Khālid went back, demolished the building in which the idol was housed, and started smashing the idol itself. The [pagan] priest raised a cry, 'O 'Uzzā, manifest your might.' All of a sudden a nude and dishevelled black woman came out of that idol. Khālid cut her down with his sword and took possession of the jewels and ornaments she wore. He reported the proceedings to the Prophet who observed. 'That was 'Uzzā. She will be worshipped no more.'"[48] There is a tradition that when the expedition was sent to Nakhla for the destruction of al-'Uzzā, the Prophet instructed Khālīd, "In whatever settlement you do not hear the *azān* or see no mosque, slaughter the people of that place."[49]

---

[45]*Tabqāt-i-Ibn Sa'd*, op. cit., p. 478. See also Martin Ling, *Muhammad*, Rochester, (Vermont, USA), 1983, p. 301.

[46]Ibid.

[47]Ibn Ishāq, op. cit., p. 565.

[48]*Tārīkh-i-Tabari*, op. cit., pp. 404–05.

[49]*Tabqāt-i-Ibn Sa'd*, op. cit., p. 488.

The Temple of Suwā‘

"The apostle of Allāh sent ‘Amr b. al-‘Ās towards [the temple of] Suwā‘, the idol of Huḍayl, in order to destroy it. When ‘Amr arrived there, the priest [of the temple] asked him, 'What do you want?' ‘Amr replied, 'The apostle of Allāh has commanded me to destroy this idol.' He [the priest] said, 'You cannot overpower him.' ‘Amr asked, 'Why?' He [the priest] said, 'He is well-protected.' ‘Amr said. 'You subscribe to falsehood even now? May you perish! Does he hear or see?' ‘Amr approached the idol and smashed it. Then he ordered his companions to demolish the house which contained [the temple's] treasure. That house yielded nothing."[50]

The Temple of Al-Manāt

"The expedition to Manāt was sent under Sa‘d b. Zayd al-Ashahlī in the Ramzān of AH 8.... It was the idol of Ghassān, Aws and Khazraj in al-Mushallal...Sa‘d started with twenty cavalrymen and reached there at a time when the priest was in attendance. The priest asked them, 'What do you want?' They said, 'Destruction of Manāt.' The priest exclaimed, 'You, and want to do this!' Sa‘d approached the idol. A black and nude and dishevelled woman came out and advanced towards him, cursing and beating her breast. The priest said, 'O Manāt, manifest your might.' Sa‘d started hitting her, and she was cut down. He had asked his companions to take care of the idol in the meanwhile. They smashed it. But the treasury yielded nothing,"[51] Other sources attribute the destruction of the sanctuary of Manāt in Qudayd to ‘Alī bin Abū Tālib, still others to Abū Sufyān.[52] One wonders whether more than one temple of Manāt was destroyed.

The Sacred Tree

Soon after the occupation of Mecca, the Prophet had to face a formidable alliance of pagan tribes that had assembled in the valley of Hunayn between Mecca and Tā'if. Ibn Ishāq records a tradition from Hārith b. Mālik: "We went forth with the apostle to the Hunayn fresh from paganism. The heathen Quraysh and other Arabs had a great green tree Dhātu Anwāt to which they used to come every year and hang their weapons on it and sacrifice beside it and devote themselves

[50]Ibid., p. 85.
[51]Ibid., pp. 485–86.
[52]*First Encyclopaedia of Islam*, op. cit., Vol. V, pp. 231-32.

to it for a day." As the newly converted pagans saw that tree, they said to the Prophet, "Make us a tree to hang things on such as they have." The Prophet chided them, comparing them to the people of Moses who wanted the latter to "make us a god even as they have gods."[53] It is not recorded whether the sacred tree was cut down at that time. Perhaps the Prophet was in a hurry. But it is a safe bet that it was marked for destruction.

The army of Islam suffered a severe setback in the first round of the Battle of Hunayn. The newly converted pagans were overjoyed. Abū Sufyān, when he saw the Muslims in headlong flight, observed, "They will not stop till they reach the seashore." A pagan who had been granted respite from conversion for a specified period asked, "Has not sorcery [Islam] come to an end today?"[54]

The Prophet himself was in great danger. The situation was saved by lack of tactical skill on the pagan side. They failed to pursue the demoralised Muslim army, and were defeated by the counter-attack which followed after the Muslims managed to regroup. The remnants of their defeated allies took refuge in the fortified town of Tā'if. A Muslim poetess sang:

> Allah's cavalry has beaten Al-Lāt's cavalry,
> And Allah best deserves to hold fast.[55]

Al-Lāt was the chief Goddess of the allied pagan tribes, and had a renowned sanctuary in Tā'if. So the army of Islam advanced towards this town.

Temple of Dhu'l Kaffayn

On the way the Prophet detached Tufayl b. 'Amr al-Dausī and sent him to destroy the temple of Dhu'l Kaffayn. It was maintained by his own tribe of Daus. He was to rejoin the main army after accomplishing the assignment. "He moved fast towards his people, and destroyed Dhu'l Kaffayn. As he set fire to the idol, starting from its face, he said:

> O Dhu'l Kaffayn! we are not of those that obey you,
> Our birth goes back much prior to your own.
> See, I have stuffed your heart with fire.

Four hundred men from his tribe followed him when he went back to the Prophet."[56]

---

[53]Ibn Ishāq, op. cit., pp. 568-69.
[54]*Tārīkh-i-Tabarī*, op. cit., p. 413.
[55]Ibn Ishāq, op. cit., p. 572.
[56]*Tabqāt-i-Ibn Sa'd*, op. cit., p. 496.

The army of Islam was full of confidence when it arrived outside Tā'if. The court poet of the Prophet, Ka'b b. Mālik sang:

Al-Lāt and Al-'Uzzā and Wudd are forgotten,
And we plunder them of their necklaces and earings.

And Shaddād b. 'Āriḍ al-Jushamī said:

Don't help Al-Lāt for God is about to destroy her
How can one who cannot help herself he helped?[57]

But the boast proved empty and al-Lāt survived on this occasion. Tā'if proved a hard nut to crack. "When he found the gates closed and determined resistance offered, he endeavoured to frighten the Thakafites by a wholesale destruction of their property. This was how he had dealt with the Banu Nadir. But the Thakafites were no Jews."[58] The siege had to be raised, though newly acquired heavy war-engines were employed for battering the city walls.

Temples Around Tā'if

The only satisfaction the Prophet could derive was from what he got done in the environs. He "ordered his glorious companions to fell the date-trees and to destroy the vineyards of the neighbourhood," which acts were considered serious crimes according to the ethics of pagan warfare. The Prophet had learnt the art of total war from the Judaic and Christian scriptures. He also indulged in his most favourite pastime. "It is related in some biographies that while the siege of Tāyf was being carried on, his holy and prophetic lordship appointed A'li Murtadza with a number of glorious companions to make excursions into the country, and to destroy every idol they could find...Thereon A'li, the Commander of the Faithful...destroyed all the idols of the Bani Hoāzān and Bani Thaqyf which were in that region. The apostle was waiting for his return near the gate of the fort of Tāyf, and as soon as the prince of saints had terminated his business, he joined the august camp, was received by the seal of prophets with the exclamation of the Takbyr..."[59] No count of temples destroyed is available in the sources. They must have been many. Islamic invaders of India followed the example whenever they besieged a town.

---

[57]Ibn Ishāq, op. cit., p. 588.
[58]D.S. Margoliouth, op. cit., p. 404.
[59]*The Rauzat-us-Safa*, op. cit., Vol. II, pt. II, pp. 630–31. *Takbīr* is the Muslim war-cry, *Allāhu Akbar*.

The Mosque of Opposition

"The apostle," reports Ibn Ishāq, "went on until he stopped in Dhū Awān a town an hour's light journey from Medina. The owners of the mosque of opposition had come to the apostle as he was preparing for Tabūk saying, 'We have built a mosque for the sick and needy and for nights of bad weather, and we should like you to come to us and pray for us there.' He said that he was on the point of travelling, and was preoccupied, or words to that effect, and that when he came back he would come to them and pray for them in it.

"When he stopped in Dhū Awān news of the mosque came to him, and he summoned Mālik b. al-Dukhshum...and Ma'n b. 'Adīy...and told them to go to the mosque of those evil men and destroy and burn it. They went quickly to B. Sālim b. 'Auf who were Mālik's clan, and Mālik said to Ma'n, 'Wait for me until I can bring fire from my people.' So he went in and took a palm-branch and lighted it, and then the two of them ran into the mosque where its people were and burned and destroyed it and the people ran away from it."[60]

The sources offer no evidence that this mosque was built on land acquired illegitimately, as some apologists of Islam like Ashgar Ali Engineer have been saying in the context of the Rāmajanmabhūmi controversy. The only point which emerges is that it was built by Muslims who did not see eye to eye with Muhammad. Margoliouth observes: "Of the rights and wrongs of this affair nothing decided will ever be known: the revelation in which it is mentioned,[61] and which contains a variety of oracles delivered in connection with the expedition to Tabuk, is in a tone of bitterness and vexation such as disappointment and opposition are likely to engender in a man of Mohammed's temperament. The people of Medinah and their new Bedouin allies are charged with harbouring Hypocrites: and it also appears that the Koran was beginning to give rise to criticism from which the Prophet had suffered at Meccah. When a new revelation comes down, people at Medinah ask each other sarcastically whether their faith had been increased. Knots of people are found talking and laughing: inspite of the most earnest denials, the Prophet is of the opinion that the Koran has provided the materials for their amusement...There is also one verse in the tirade suggesting that some of the malcontents disliked the plan of

---

[60]Ibn Ishāq, op. cit., p. 609.

[61]Qur'ān, Sūra 9. This is the last Sūra of Qur'ān, speaking chronologically. It shows the frustration of Muhammad at the failure of his mission. Allāh says that most people who had converted to Islam were hypocrites, that is, pagans at heart.

living on plunder which was now characteristic of Islam, and wished a more honest system inaugurated..."[62]

Obviously, the mosque of opposition was built by people who were monotheists like Muhammad but who did not believe that the doctrine enjoined bloodshed and rapine which had become the Muslims' daily practice. Small wonder that Allāh of the Qur'ān who sanctioned mass slaughter and endless accumulation of plunder by the faithful, did not approve of such "toothless" monotheism. So he moaned, "Is he who founded his building upon duty to Allāh and his good pleasure better; or he who founded his building on the brink of a crumbling, overhanging precipice so that it toppled with him into the fire of hell?"[63]

Invitations to Islam

The occupation of Mecca had sky-rocketted the prestige of the Prophet. "In deciding their attitude to Islam," writes Ibn Ishāq, "the Arabs were only waiting to see what happened to the clan of Quraysh and the apostle. For Quraysh were the leaders and guides of men, the people of the sacred temple, and the pure stock of Ishmael son of Abraham; and the leading Arabs did not contest this. It was Quraysh who had declared war on the apostle and opposed him; and when Mecca was occupied and Quraysh became subject to him and he subdued it to Islam, and the Arabs knew that they could not fight the apostle or display enmity towards him they entered into God's religion 'in batches' as God said,[64] coming to him from all directions."[65] Muhammad's war-machine was sending waves of terror towards all tribes, which was a very effective message. There was a debate afoot everywhere whether to fight for the ancient religion and tribal honour, or submit to Muhammad and become Muslim. The Prophet's intelligence network kept him informed of what was happening where. He was swift in exploiting the psychological crisis to his own advantage.

The groundwork had been done during the preceding two years. Ibn Sa'd provides a list of tribal chiefs to whom the Prophet had sent invitations to Islam, starting soon after the Treaty of Hudaybiya with the Meccans in the year AH 6.[66] The letters containing his messages

---

[62]D.S. Margoliouth, op. cit., pp. 424–45.
[63]Qur'ān, 9.109.
[64]Ibid., Sūra 110.
[65]Ibn Ishāq, op. cit., p. 628. Reference to Abraham and Ishmael may be ignored as concoctions.
[66]*Tabqāt-i-Ibn Sa'd*, op. cit., Part II, pp. 29–64.

were carried by special couriers selected from among his companions. The message varied according to the status and strength of the tribe concerned. Unfortunately, Ibn Sa'd has lumped together the invitations without regard for chronological sequence. This much, however, can be inferred that their tone became sharper as the author of the messages marched from one victory to another, the acme being reached in the conquest of Mecca and the Battle of Hunayn.

At first Muhammad wrote his letters beginning with *basmak al-Laham*, "I begin in the name of Allāh," after the custom of the Quraysh. A special revelation came and he was commanded to begin with *bismallāh*, "In the name of Allāh." Another revelation amended the formula to *bismallāh al-Raḥmān al-Raḥīm*, "In the name of Allāh, the Compassionate, the Merciful." Finally, it was revealed to him that he should begin with *bismallāh al-Raḥīm al-Waḥīd*, "In the name of Allāh, the Compassionate, the One."[67]

The general tenor of the messages sent was the same—dissociate from the idolaters which meant an order to destroy pagan temples and break idols; bear witness that Allāh is one without partners and Muhammad is his messenger; establish prayers which meant an order to build mosques; pay *zakāt* and other taxes to the central treasury at Medina; send to the Prophet one-fifth of the plunder obtained from raids on the polytheists; and keep the highways free from disturbance so that Muslim delegations can travel unmolested for converting people and collecting taxes. In exchange, the tribes were assured that they could keep their lands, their cattle, their wells, their gardens, their houses and such of their special customs as did not come in conflict with Islam. Defiance, they were warned, will entail slaughter of their men, capture of their women and children, and laying waste of their country. And punitive expeditions were sent to those tribal settlements which molested the Prophet's messengers or otherwise refused to abide by his dictates.[68] The fear was abroad that "the Prophet of Allāh may send a military force."[69] When Banī Tamīm refused to pay *zakāt*, they were attacked, and eleven of their women and thirty of their children were captured and dragged to Medina."[70]

The Year of Deputations

"When the apostle had gained possession of Mecca," reports Ibn

[67]Ibid., p. 35.
[68]Ibid., p. 53.
[69]Ibid., p. 62.
[70]Ibid., p. 67.

Ishāq, "and had finished with Tabūk, and Thaqīf had surrendered and paid homage, deputations from the Arabs came to him from all directions."[71] Ibn Sa'd lists as many as seventy-one deputations which waited on Muhammad in Medina, the last one being on behalf of the wolves.[72] It seems that the beasts also had taken fright and were prepared to become Muslims or the beasts felt that they, too, could confess the faith without suffering inconvenience.

Strangely enough, a deputation came to Muhammad from Tā'if soon after he had suffered a repulse outside that city. It seems that the morale of the people in this town has collapsed as they saw what was happening all around. The deputation met Muhammad even before he had reached Medina. It was led by 'Urwa b. Mas'ūd al-Thaqafī who was one of the leaders of resistance when Tā'if was besieged by the army of Islam. 'Urwa requested Muhammad to make him a Muslim so that he could go back and invite his people to the true faith. He was baptised and sent back. But "when he went up to an upper room and showed his religion to them they shot arrows at him from all directions, and one hit him and killed him."[73]

The debate in Tā'if, however, did not come to an end. One of their chiefs said, "We are in an impasse. You have seen how the affair of this man has progressed. All the Arabs have accepted Islam and you lack the power to fight them, so look to your ease...So after conferring together they dicided to send a man to the apostle as they had sent 'Urwa..."[74] The man approached for the job refused to go alone. Finally a deputation consisting of six chiefs reached Medina and met the Prophet.

The Temple of Al-Lāt

"Among the things they asked the apostle," reports Ibn Ishāq, "was that they should be allowed to retain their idol Al-Lāt undestroyed for three years. The apostle refused, and they continued to ask him for a year or two, and he refused; finally they asked for a month after their return home, but he refused to agree to any set time. All that they wanted as they were trying to show was to be safe from their fanatics and women and children by leaving her, and they did not want to frighten their people by destroying her until they had accepted Islam.

---

[71]Ibn Ishāq, op. cit., p. 627.
[72]*Tabqāt-i-Ibn Sa'd,* op. cit., Vol. II, pp. 64–136.
[73]Ibn Ishāq, op cit., p. 614.
[74]Ibid., p. 615.

The apostle refused this...They had also asked that he would excuse them from prayer and they should not have to break their idols with their own hands. The apostle said: 'We excuse you from breaking your idols with your own hands, but as for prayer there is no good in a religion which has no prayers.' They said that they would perform them though it was demeaning...

"When they had accomplished their task and had set out to return to their country the apostle sent with then Abū Sufyān and al-Mughīra to destroy their idol.They travelled with the deputation and when they neared al-Tā'if, al-Mughīra wanted to send on Abū Sufyān in advance. The latter refused and told him to go to his people while he stayed in the property of Dhū'l-Ḥaram.[75] When al-Mughīra entered he went up to the idol and struck it with a pick-axe. His people the B. Mu'attib stood in front of him fearing that he would be shot or killed as 'Urwa had been. The women of Thaqīf came out with their heads uncovered bewailing her and saying:

O weep for our protector
Poltroons would neglect her
Whose swords need a corrector.

Abū Sufyān, as al-Mughīra smote her with the axe, said, 'Alas for you, alas !' When al-Mughīra had destroyed her and taken what was on her and her jewels he sent for Abū Sufyān when her jewellery and gold and beads had been collected.

"Now Abū Mulayḥ b. 'Urwa and Qārib b. al-Aswad had come to the apostle before the Thaqīf deputation when 'Urwa was killed, desiring to separate themselves from Thaqīf and to have nothing to do with them...'Urwa asked the apostle to settle a debt his father had incurred from the property of the idol.The apostle agreed and Qārib b. al-Aswad asked for the same privilege for his father...The apostle said, 'But al-Aswad died a polytheist.' He answered, 'But you will be doing a favour to a Muslim a near relation,' meaning himself...The apostle ordered Abū Sufyān to satisfy the debts of 'Urwa and al-Aswad from the property of the idol..."[76]

'Urwa and al-Aswad show the stuff of which voluntary converts to Islam were made. Most of them were questionable characters.

Temples of B. Sa'd B. Bakr

They sent their chief, Ḍimām b. Tha'laba, to the Prophet. Ḍimām

[75]Al-Mughīra belonged to Tā'if and was an earlier convert.
[76]Ibn Ishāq, op. cit., pp. 615-17.

asked some questions and ended by becoming a Muslim. He went back to his people and said, "How evil are al-Lāt and al-'Uzzā!" His people rebuked him, "Heavens above, Ḍimām, beware of leprosy and elephantiasis and madness!" He replied, "Woe to you, they can neither hurt nor heal. God has sent an apostle and sent down to him a book, so seek deliverance thereby from your present state..."[77] He then destroyed the idols "It was not yet evening that day that all men and women became Musalmans. They built mosques and recited *azāns* so that people came to prayers."[78]

The Temple of B. Sulaym

Seven hundred people from B. Sulaym had waited on the Prophet while he was in Qudayd on his way to Mecca, which he occupied soon after. They went to him again after the conquest of Mecca, Battle of Hunayn and the siege of Tā'if. Their leader Ghādī b. 'Abd al-'Uzzā was the keeper of their temple. The Prophet bestowed upon him the estate of Rehātā which had a spring in it. He came back and composed the following couplets about the idol he had worshipped earlier:

How can that be God, on whom
The foxes came and staled?
He is abominable without a doubt,
He on whom the foxes staled.

He attacked the idol and smashed it to pieces. When he waited upon the Prophet with this report, he was asked, "What is your name?" He said, "Ghādī 'Abd al-'Uzzā." The Prophet said, "You are Rāshid b. 'Abd Raba."[79] People whose names referred to pagan Gods were always given new names by the Prophet—names which referred to the god of Islam.

The Christian Church of Yamāma

A deputation of nineteen men from B. Hanīfa came to Medina. They were given rich food and instructed in Islam by the Prophet. Each of them was given five ounces of silver as a gift. When they got ready to go back, the Prophet gave them a vessel of water with which he had performed his ablutions. He said, "When you return to your country, destroy the church, wash the site with water, and build a mosque on it." They did accordingly. The priest in charge of the church ran away. His

---

[77]Ibid., p. 635.
[78]*Tabqāt-i-Ibn Sa'd*, op. cit., Vol. II, p. 73.
[79]Ibid., p. 81.

days were over.[80]

The Temples of Fils and Ruḍā' in Tayy

"The Prophet sent 'Alī b. Abī Tālib towards the temple of Fils belonging to the tribe of Tayy, with an order to destroy it...He went with two hundred horsemen..."[81]

"'Alī inflicted atrocities on them and took prisoners from among them. He obtained two swords from the temple; one of them was named Rasūb, the other Makhzam. It was well-known that these swords had been brought as an offering to the temple by Hārith b. Abī Thamar. Among the prisoners was a sister of 'Adi b. Hātim..."[82] Hātim Tayy, the father of the girl, was a pagan chief renowned for his liberality. Islamic lore at present tells many stories about him without revealing that he was a pagan. The temple of Fils which was destroyed was on Mount Aja'. Another deity of Tayy was Ruḍā'.[83] His temple, too, met the same fate.

The Temple of 'Amm Anas

A deputation consisting of ten men came to Medina from Khaulan in the year AH 10. They informed the Prophet that they were Muslims. The Prophet asked, "What about your idol of 'Amm Anas?" They replied, "That is in a bad shape. We have exchanged him for Allāh whom you have brought. When we go back, we shall destroy him." They were instructed in Islam and entertained lavishly. After a few days, the Prophet ordered that each of them be given twelve and a half ounces of silver as reward. They went back and destroyed the idol of 'Amm Anas "even before they untied their luggage."[84]

The Temple of 'Uzra

A deputation of twelve men from B.'Uzra came to Medina and said to the Prophet, "We are worried about our people." The Prophet instructed them in Islam and gave them gifts. He was told that the idol of 'Uzra had spoken and confirmed his prophethood. He observed, "This seems to be a believing jinn."[85] Idols, too, it seems, could become believers. It is not recorded whether the idol was kept or removed.

---

[80]Ibid., p. 90-91.
[81]Ibid., p. 97.
[82]*Tarīkh-i-Tabarī*, op. cit., p. 445.
[83]*First Encyclopaedia of Islam*, op. cit., Vol. II, p. 624.
[84]*Tabqāt-i-Ibn Sa'd*, op. cit., Vol. II, p. 100.
[85]Ibid., p. 107.

The Temple of Al-Jahīna

'Amr b. Marrah al-Jahnī relates, "We had an idol which we used to honour. I was its keeper. When I heard of the Prophet, I destroyed it. Then I went to Medina and became a Muslim. I composed the following verse:

I bear witness that Allāh is true,
I am the first to renounce stone idols."[86]

The Temple of Farrāz

Ḍbab, a man from the tribe of Sa'd al-Ashīra attacked the idol named Farrāz and smashed it to pieces. He went with a deputation to the Prophet and said:

I became a follower of the Prophet
When he brought (good) intructions.
I consigned Farrāz to a status of dishonour,
I attacked him and left him in a state
As if he never existed; this is the time of revolution.[87]

The Temple of Dhu'l-Khalaṣa

Jarīr b. 'Abd-allāh al-Bahlī came to Medina with one hundred and fifty men. All of them professed Islam. The Prophet asked Jarīr about those whom he had left behind. Jarīr replied, "O apostle of Allāh! Allāh has made Islam dominant among them. *Azān* prevails from mosques and courtyards. They have destroyed the idols they used to worship." The Prophet asked, "What happened to the idol of Dhu'l Khalaṣa?" He was told, "He is as before. Allāh willing, we will be rid of him." The Prophet sent them back. Jarīr returned before long and reported, "I have destroyed the idol and taken whatever it wore. I set fire to it and reduced it to such a state that whoever had honoured him will now hate him. No one stopped us from doing this."[88]

"It is reported that after the burning and destruction of the idol-temple the inhabitants of Dhu'l-Khalasa attained the nobility of Islam. The treasury belonging to that temple contained much property and perfumes, all of which was brought to Medinah. When his holy and prophetic lordship heard what had taken place, and that the idol-temple had been demolished, he rejoiced greatly, inviting a benediction on Jaryr and his tribe..."[89]

---

[86]Ibid., p. 109.
[87]Ibid., p. 118.
[88]Ibid., pp. 123–24.
[89]*The Rauzat-us-Safa*, op. cit., Vol. II, pt. II, pp. 677–79.

"Some of the idols were made use of for other purposes, as for example the idol of Dhu'l-Khalaṣa, a white piece of marble in which a crown was carved and which was worshipped at Tabāla, a place on the road from Mekka to Yaman, was in the time of Ibn al-Kalbī (about AH 200) used as a stepping-stone under the mosque at Tabāla..."[90]

The Temple of Ruḍā'

It was the temple of B. Rabī'a, a branch of B. Tamīm. Al-Mustaughir b. Rabī'a, a man of the same tribe, destroyed it. He sang:

I smashed Ruḍā' so completely that
I left it a black ruin in a hollow.[91]

Surveying the scene in the year of deputations, Margoliouth sums up, "The iconoclasm which had raged at Medinah at the time of the Prophet's arrival spread far and wide, now it had been clearly proved that the old gods were incapable of defending themselves or of even taking revenge on those who broke them. Facts which had remained unheeded for generations suddenly began to suggest important inferences: one man observed that his god suffered himself to be desecrated by beasts, and declined henceforward to worship a deity on whom the foxes staled. The persons who hurry to place their incense on the altar of success are familiar figures in all ages: and many a comedy was enacted at these visits..."[92]

Conclusion

Thus the practices of the Prophet or his Sunnah vis-a-vis idols and idol-temples was added to prescriptions of the Qur'ān in this respect, and the Islamic theology of iconoclasm stood completed. Ever since, iconoclasm has been a prominent as well a permanent part of the theology of Islam.

Allāh had denounced the idols and their worship as abominable. His prophet got the idols broken or burnt, and their temples destroyed.

The Prophet added a few nuances on his own. He got the sites and materials of pagan temples used in the construction of mosques that replaced them. In many cases, idols were placed on the footsteps of the mosques so that the faithful could trample upon them while entering and coming out of Allāh's abodes. These acts, too, became pious precedents and were followed by Islamic invaders wherever they came across idols.

[90]*First Encyclopaedia Islam*, op. cit., Vol. VII, p. 147.
[91]Ibn Ishāq, op. cit., p. 39.
[92]D.S. Margoliouth, op. cit., pp. 431–32.

The Place of Sunnah in Islam

People who have not studied the theology of Islam as expounded in orthodox treatises, believe that Islam stands for obedience to the commandments of Allāh as revealed in the Qur'ān. They do not know that Allāh is no more than mere window-dressing and that for all practical purposes the Prophet rules the roost.

Muhammad had made Allāh into his private preserve when he proclaimed that no one except him knew the will of Allāh first-hand, and that he alone will intercede on the Day of Judgment for deciding who will enter paradise and who will sink into hell. Going further, he made Allāh helplessly dependent on the Muslim *millat* when he prayed on the eve of the battle of Badr, "O God, if this band perishes today, Thou will be worshipped no more."[93] This became a refrain in every Muslim prayer offered on the eve of every battle fought in the history of Islam against the infidels. Allāma Iqbal was not innovating when he addressed Allāh in his *Shikwah* and asked, "Did anyone before us bother about you?" *Shikwah* or complaint is a long poem written by the "great poet of Islam" in the first decade of this century, and expresses the anguish of Islam vis-a-vis the rise of Christians in the West and Hindus in India.

Muslims have a popular saying in Persian language, "*bā Khudā dīwānā bāsh wa bā Muhammad hoshiyār*," that is, one may become wild about Allāh but one should beware when it comes to Muhammad. *Khudā* is the Persian word for Allāh. Islam is, therefore, spelled out more correctly when it is called Muhammadanism. For, it is not Allāh but Muhammad who sits at the heart of Islam and controls its head as well.

The process of deifying the life-style of the Prophet had started in his own life-time. Margoliouth observes, "He inherited the devotion and adulation which had hitherto been bestowed on the idols; and though he never permitted the word worship to be used of the ceremonies of which he was the object, he ere long became hedged in with a state which differed little form that which surrounded a god..."[94] The concept of the Sunnah, that is, the practices of the Prophet, had also developed towards the end of his days.[95]

The rightly-guided Caliphs who followed the Prophet regarded the Sunnah as a sure key to success. Quirks of history, which gave many

---

[93]*Sīrat Rasūl Allāh,* op. cit., p. 300.
[94]D.S. Margoliouth, op. cit., p. 216.
[95]*Sīrat Rasūl Allāh*, op. cit., p. 645–46.

victories to the Muslim arms in the first century AH, convinced the theologians of Islam that the Sunnah was divine in its inspiration. They became busy in collecting and collating every detail of the Prophet's practices, from the act of coughing to that of waging holy wars and administrating what had become his exclusive kingdom. The Sunnah was soon placed on par with the Qur'ān. "In the Qur'ān," they propounded, "Allah speaks through Muhammad; in the *Sunnah*, He acts through him. Thus Muhammad's life is a visible expression of Allah's utterances in the Qur'ān. God provides the divine principle, Muhammad the living pattern."[96]

While the ulamā expounded the Sunnah to the sultāns, it was the sūfīs who practised it most meticulously. The very first sūfī illustrated what the Sunnah stood for. Farīdu'd-Dīn Attār gives the story of Uwaysh Qarnī who lived in the days of the Prophet but had never met or seen him. 'Umar and 'Alī were on a visit to Kufa when they learnt that Qarnī lived in the valley of 'Urfa, grazing cattle and eating dry bread. They went to see him. "The honourable Uwaysh said, 'You are Companions of the Prophet. Could you tell me which one of his sacred teeth was martyred in the battle of Uhud? Why have you not broken all your teeth out of reverence for the Prophet?' This said, he opened his mouth and showed that all his teeth were gone. He explained, 'When I learnt that a tooth of the Prophet had been martyred, I broke one of mine. Then I thought that perhaps some other tooth of his had been martyred. So I broke all my teeth, one after another. It is only after that that I felt at peace'. Having heard him the two Companions got awe-struck, and felt convinced that this was the correct conduct..."[97]

The Sunnah has been the prison-house in which the world of Islam has lived ever since. Every pious Muslim aspires to do things exactly as the Prophet did. Aping the Prophet in the matter of destroying other peoples places of worship, and building mosques with their materials is no exception. A Muslim who *can* do this pious deed but *does not* do it, disobeys the Prophet.

There are very few historical mosques, particularly Jāma' Masjids, in the world of Islam which do not stand on sites occupied earlier by other people's places of worship. Many Christian churches yielded place to mosques all over West Asia, North Africa, Spain and South-

---

[96]Ram Swarup, *Understanding Islam through Hadis: Religious Faith or Fanaticism?*, Voice of India, New Delhi, Second Reprint, 1987, p. vii.

[97]Shaykh Farīdu'd-Dīn Attār, *Tadhkirāt al-Awliyā'* translated into Urdu by Maulāna Zubayr Afzal Usmānī, Delhi n.d., p. 16.

eastern Europe, even though Christians were People of the Book whose places of worship were to be protected once they agreed to become *zimmīs*. Fire-temples of the Zoroastrians suffered the same fate all over what constituted the empire of Iran on the eve of the Muslim conquest. The greatest havoc, however, was wrought in the vast cradle of Hindu culture where hundreds of thousands of Buddhist, Brahmanical, Jain and other Hindu temples disappeared or yielded place to mosques and other Muslim monuments.

Today there are no Hindu temples in the Central Asian republics of Russia, Sinkiang province of China, Makran and Seistan provinces of Iran, and the whole of Afghanistan, all of which were honeycombed with them before the advent of Islam. Whatever Hindu temples had come up during the Sikh and British rule in what are now known as Pakistan and Bangladesh, are fast disappearing. The same has been happenning in the valley of Kashmir.

The Archaeological Survey of India, which included Pakistan and Bangladesh till 1947, has identified many mosques and other Muslim monuments which stand on the sites of Hindu temples and/or have temple materials embedded in their masonry. Many inscriptions in Arabic and Persian bear testimony that Hindu temples were destroyed for constructing mosques. Local traditions can point out many more mosques which have replaced Hindu temples. Cartloads of Hindu idols are known to have been brought and placed on the steps of the Jāmi' Masjids in several cities which were Muslim capitals at one time. Some of those idols may still be buried under the stairs of the same mosques. In short, the study of Islamic iconoclasm in this country, not to speak of the whole cradle of Hindu culture, has yet to make a meaningful start.

What we have proved beyond doubt is that destroying other people's places of worship and converting them into Muslim monuments is not only sanctioned but also prescribed by the tenents of Islam, the same way as reciting the *kalima*, doing *'namāz*, paying *zakāt*, keeping *rozah*, and going on *hajj*. Anyone who says that Islam does not permit this practice is either ignorant of the creed, or has been deceived by Islamic apologetics developed in recent time. If a Muslim scholar or politician makes this statement, he is talking tongue-in-cheek, and stands exposed as a knave.

SECTION V

APPENDICES

APPENDIX 1

MUSLIM DYNASTIES IN INDIA'S HISTORY

Muslim dynasties which figure in the history of India are divided, by modern historians of medieval India into two categories—Imperial and Provincial. Dynasties which ruled from Delhi/Agra are called Imperial Dynasties, whatever might have been the extent of their domain or power. On the other hand, dynasties which ruled independently of Delhi/Agra are labelled as Provincial Dynasties, even though some of them overshadowed the contemporary Imperial Dynasties in terms of territory controlled, or power wielded, or both.

Strangely enough, the Yamīnīs of Ghazni and the Shanshabānīs of Ghūr are not included in any of the two categories. They are supposed to be foreign dynasties having their seats outside India proper and being interested in expanding their domain in Islamic lands to their west and north as well. Medieval Muslim historians, however, do not look at the Yamīnīs and the Shanshabānīs in that way; they regard both of them as inextricably entwined with the history of India. We agree with the medieval Muslim historians. Firstly, Afghanistan was very much a part of India not only in the days of these dynasties but till as late as the disintegration of the Mughal empire in the eighteenth century. Secondly, the so-called Indian dynasties were prevented from intervening in the larger world of Islam not by any lack of willingness on their part but because, starting with the rise of the Mongols in the first quarter of the thirteenth century, the powers that arose in Persia and Transoxiana made it difficult for them to do so.

In any case, there is nothing Indian about any of the Muslim dynasties, no matter from where they functioned. All of them were equally foreign in terms of inspiration and behaviour, even if not always in terms of blood. A bandit who breaks into my house with sword in hand and occupies it by means of brute force, does not become a member of my family simply because he lives under my roof and fattens on my food; he remains a bandit, no matter how long the occupation lasts. He never acquires moral or legal legitimacy. Nor does that member of my family who takes to the ways of the bandit retain the ties which once bound us together; I am fully within my rights to look at him also as one of the bandit team. I am not impressed at all if the bandit believes in a right acquired by conquest or bestowed by a being named Allāh, and quotes from a book he deems as divine. Nor am I prepared, like Jawaharlal Nehru and his degenerate secularist clan, to consider the bandit a member of my family, simply because he drags into his bed my sister or daughter or some other female from my household. I am not called upon to recongnize his right to rule over me, and hesitate in throwing him out as soon as I can muster the strength to do so. I am, therefore, treating as foreign to India, more so to the intrinsic spirit of Indian culture, all Muslim dynasties which figure in the Islamic invasion of or rule over this country or any of its parts.

A brief descriptions of these dynasties together with the number of rulers which each of them had, is given below. Each king who figures in our citations, epigraphic or literary, is being given his number in the order of dynastic succession together with his reign-period.[1] That should suffice to place him and his doings in a proper historical perspective.

The dynasties have been listed in a chronological order, that is, with reference to the time at which they arose. There are several dynasties and many rulers who do not figure in our citations. That does not mean that none of them can be credited with the pious performance of destroying Hindu places of worship. For all we know, those dynasties and kings figure in histories which have remained inaccesible to us, particularly the provincial and local histories and the biographies of individual kings and commanders. The doings of sufis in this particular context are being taken up in subsequent volume of this series.

India had suffered the first attack from Islamic imperialism as early as 634, only two years after the death of the prophet of Islam at Medina; it was a naval expedition sent to the coast of Maharashtra in reign of Caliph 'Umar. This as well as many other expeditions mounted in subsequent years were repulsed from the coasts of Gujarat and Sindh, and the borders of Makran, Kabul and Zabul; in some of them the invaders suffered great slaughter and their military commanders were either killed or had to be ransomed out.

It was only in 712 that an Islamic invasion succeeded in occupying Sindh, Multan and some parts of the Punjab. Though the invaders led several raids into the interior, particularly towards Malwa and Gujarat, the episodes were shortlived and the invaders were soon locked up in two garrison towns—Multan and Mansurah—by the Indian counter-attacks mounted from Delhi, Kanauj, Rajasthan, Malwa and Gujarat. Meanwhile, another thrust into Balkh which took place at the same

[1]The dates given in the descriptions that follow are of the Christian Era.

time as that into Sindh resulted in the destruction of a renowned Buddhist Vihāra and the forcible conversion of the Pramukha family, the latter-day Barkamids of Baghdad.

Zabul (region around Ghazni) had defeated several Muslim invasions since 653 when Seistan became a base for Islamic armies. It, however, fell in 871 before an assault by the newly founded Saffārid Dynasty of Persia, and was lost for ever to India as a result of its population being converted *en masse* to Islam. The Saffārids were followed by the Sāmānids of Bukhara; one of their governors occupied Ghazni in 963. It was from this base that North India was overwhelmed in stages, and passed under Muslim occupation towards the close of the twelfth century.

In subsequent centuries, Islamic invasions surged forward into Central and South India and established several centres of Muslim power. More centres of Muslim power arose in North India as well whenever the Muslim dynasties at Delhi/Agra suffered a decline. The Indian people and princes fought the invaders at every step and rose in revolt, again and again, for more than five hundred years. Finally, the war of resistance was transformed into a war of liberation and Islamic dominance disappeared from most parts of India during the eighteenth century. If British imperialism had not intervened and saved some remnants of Islamic imperialism, the Muslim invasion of India would have become a story found only in books of history, and India would have been left with no "Muslim problem" as in the case of Spain which also had been invaded and occupied by Muslims for several centuries.

Muslim Dynasties

The Muslim dynasties which functioned from Sindh and Ghazni undertook destruction of Hindu temples *extensively* whenever and wherever they succeeded in raiding or occupying Indian territory. The same pattern was followed by the Muslim dynasties established at Delhi/Agra. Their hold, however, did not extend beyond major cities and towns. An *intensive* destruction of temples was undertaken by the Muslim dynasties which arose in the provinces—Sindh, Kashmir, Bengal, Avadh, Malwa, Gujarat, Maharashtra, Karnataka, Andhra Pradesh. There is no truth in the assumption that the provincial dynasties were lenient to Hindus and their places of worship because they had to depend upon Hindu support against the imperial dynasties. The truce, if it took place at all, was temporary in most cases.

I. The Caliphate (632–1258)

It was a republican institution created at Medina soon after the death of Prophet Muhammad. The first four caliphs were elected. The fifth caliph, however, inaugurated monarchical rule which was held successively by two families. The Caliphate, therefore, had three phases.

(A) The "Rightly-Guided" Caliphs (632–661)

There were four of them who ruled over an expanding empire from Medina and Kufa. Only one of them figures in our citations:

3. 'Usmān (646–656)

It was during his reign that one of his military commanders, Abd ar-Rahmān bin Samūrah, succeeded in occupying Seistan and parts of Zabul for a short time in 653.

(B) The Ummayads (661–749)

This dynasty, founded by the fifth caliph, had fourteen kings who ruled from Damascus. Only one of them figures in our citations:

6. Al-Walīd I (705–715)

It was during his reign that one of his generals, Muhammad bin Qāsim, succeeded in occupying Sindh and some parts of the Punjab between 712 and 715.

Another general, Qutaibah bin Muslim al-Bāhīlī, operated mostly in Khurasan and Transoxiana, which were cradles of Hindu culture at that time but not parts of India proper. He is also credited with the conquest of Balkh where he destroyed a famous Buddhist Vihāra.

(C) The Abbāsids (750–1258)

This dynasty succeeded the Umayyads and moved the seat of the Caliphate to Baghdad. Starting with the nineteenth caliph it had thirty-seven rulers, the last of whom was killed by Halākū, the Mongol conqueror, in 1258. After the reign of the eighth caliph, Mu'tāsim (833–842), of this dynasty, the rulers were non-entities and power passed into the hands of Turkish dynasties which rose one after another. Only two of them figure in our citations:

2. Al-Mansūr (754–775)

It was in his reign that his governor of Sindh, Hashām bin 'Amrū al-Taghlabī, led an expedition to Kandahar on the west coast of India in 756.

3. Al-Mahdī (775–785)
He sent, a naval expedition to the coast of Saurashtra in 776.

II. The Saffārid Dynasty of Seistan (871–900)

This Persian-Turkish dynasty arose when the Abbāsid Caliphate had weakened. It occupied Zabul and Sindh which included Multan at that time. It had only 2 rulers both of whom figure in our citations:

1. Yā'qūb bin Laith (871–875)
2. 'Amrū bin Laith (875–900)

III. The Qarāmitah Dynasty of Multan (980–1175)

After the Saffārids lost their hold on Sindh, Multan separated from the province and became an independent Muslim kingdom. By 980 it had become a stronghold of the Qarāmitah sect of the Isma'ilīs. Jalam bin Shaibān who figures in our citations cannot be placed in any dynastic successsion, nor assigned a reign-period. The only thing we know about him is that he destroyed the image of the famous Āditya Temple at Multan and killed its priests.

IV. The Yamīnī or Ghaznivid Dynasty (977–1186)

The Saffārid dominions in Khurasan, Seistan and Zabul had been taken over by the Sāmānids, a dynasty which had arisen more or less at the same time as the Saffārids and had its seat at Bukhara. Alptigīn, the Sāmānid governor of Khurasan, rebelled, occupied Ghazni in 963 and declared independence. The dynasty founded by him proved incompetent and the throne was seized in 977 by Subuktigīn, a manumitted slave of Alptigīn. Subuktigīn became the founder of the Ghaznivid Dynasty which came to be known as the Yamīnī Dynasty as well when the caliph at Baghdad was mighty pleased with the iconoclastic exploits of Subuktigīn's son, Mahmūd, and conferred on him the appellation of Yamīnu'd-Daulah.

The Yamīnī Dynasty had 18 rulers, the last two of whom functioned from Lahore after Ghazni was occupied by the Seljūks. Five of these rulers figure in our citations.

1. Amīr Subuktigīn (977–997)
2. Sultān Mahmūd (997–1030)
5. Sultān Mas'ūd I (1030–1042)
11. Sultān Ibrāhīm (1059–1099)
12. Sultān Mas'ūd III (1099–1151)

V. The Shanshabānī or Ghūrid Dynasty (1149–1206)

This dynasty arose in the Ghūr region of Afghanistan and had its seat at Firuz Koh. To start with, the rulers were tributaries of the Ghaznivids. They started becoming independent as the Ghaznivids got involved in a struggle with the Seljūks and suffered a decline. We have counted the Ghūrid rulers from Alāu'd-Dīn Jahānsūz who stormed and burnt down Ghazni in 1149. Ghazni was, however, occupied by the Seljūks soon after and, later on, by the Guzz Turks. It was only in 1175 that the Ghūrids succeeded in reoccupying it.

The Ghūrid king, Ghiyāsu'd-Dīn Muhammad bin Sām, who had succeeded his uncle Alāu'd-Dīn Jahānsūz at Firuz Koh, appointed his younger brother, Shihābu'd-Dīn Muhammad bin Sām, as the governor of Ghazni. Shihābu'd-Dīn (1175–1206) occupied Sindh and Multan, ousted the last Ghaznivid ruler from Lahore, defeated the Chauhāns of Ajmer and the Gāhaḍvāḍs of Kanauj, and extended his conquests upto the borders of Bengal. His conquests were consolidated mainly by his able general, Qutbu'd-Dīn Aibak. Another general of his, Ikhtiyāru'd-Dīn Bakhtiyār Khaljī, ousted the Senas of Bengal from Lakhnauti and led an unsuccessful expedition into Assam and Bhutan. Meanwhile, Shihābu'd-Dīn had become the king of Ghūr on the death of his brother in 1203 and styled himself as Muizzu'd-Dīn Muhammad bin Sām. He is popularly known as Muhammad Ghūrī, and regarded as the founder of Muslim rule in India. He was murdered in 1206 and the Shanshabānī dynasty came to an end.

Muhammad Ghūrī, Qutbu'd-Dīn Aibak, and Ikhtiyāru'd-Dīn Bakhtiyār Khaljī figure in our citations.

VI. The Khwārizmian Dynasty (1121–1231)

This powerful dynasty had its seat at Khwārizm (modern Khiva in the Turkmenian Republic of the erstwhile U.S.S.R). It had 6 rulers. It was overthrown by Chingiz Khān, the Mongol conqueror, in 1220 when its fifth ruler died in fight. The sixth and the last ruler, Jalālu'd-Dīn Mankbarnī, who figures in our citations, escaped to Sindh in 1222 and tried to establish a new kingdom. He had, however, to leave in 1223 via Makran and wandered to various places in Iran and Iraq till he was killed by the Kurds in 1231.

VII. The Mamlūk or Slave Dynasties of Delhi (1206–1290)

These were the three dynasties founded successively by Qutbu'd-Dīn Aibak, Shamsu'd-Dīn Iltutmish and Ghiyāsu'd-Dīn Balban, all of whom were manumitted slaves. With their seat at Delhi, the three dynasties had 10 rulers. The founder of the first dynasty, Qutbu'd-Dīn Aibak, figures in our citations mostly as a viceroy of Muhanmmad Ghūri, though he ruled as a sultān also from 1206 to 1210. The third ruler Shamsu'd-Dīn Iltutmish (1210–1236), the founder of the second Mamlūk Dynasty, also figures in our citations. He was a slave of Qutb'd-Dīn Aibak and became king after ousting Aibak's son. He extended his sway over the whole of North India by garrisoning a number of cities and towns and led expeditions against centres of Rājpūt power in Rajasthan, Bundelkhand and Malwa. He is regarded as the real builder of Muslim power in India, though Afghanistan, Sindh and a large part of the Punjab had, meanwhile, passed under Mongol occupation.

VIII. The Khaljī Dynasty of Delhi (1290–1320)

It succeeded the third and the last Mamlūk Dynasty and had only 3 rulers. All of them figure in our citations:

1. Jalālu'd-Dīn (1290–1296)
2. Alāu'd-Dīn (1296–1316)
3. Mubārak Shāh (1316–1320)

With his seat at Delhi, Alāu'd-Dīn extented Muslim hegemony or rule over Gujarat, Rajasthan, Malwa, Maharashtra, Telingana, Karnataka and Tamil Nadu by subduing or overthrowing one Rājpūt dynasty after another. The expedition to Gujarat was led by his brother and general, Ulugh Khān, while those to Maharashtra, Telingana, Karnataka and Tamil Nadu were commanded by his slave, Malik Kāfūr. He himself was in charge of expeditions to Rajasthan and Malwa.

IX. The Tughlaq Dynasty of Delhi (1320–1412)

This dynasty which took over at Delhi from the Khaljīs had 10 rulers, though its power declined steeply after the death of the third in 1381 and more or less disappeared after the invasion of Tīmūr in 1398. Five rulers of this dynasty figure in our citations:

1. Ghiyāsu'd-Dīn Tughlaq (1320–1325)
2. Muhammad bin Tughlaq (1325–1351)
3. Fīrūz Shāh (1351–1388)
4. Tughlaq Shāh bin Fīrūz Shāh (1388–1389)
5. Nasīru'd-Dīn Muhammad Shāh (1389–1394)

Muhammad bin Tughlaq had reconquered South India which had slipped out of the Muslim stranglehold after the eclipse of the Khaljīs.

But he lived to see the disintegration of his southern domain. Soon after, the Muslim Bahmanī Sultanate rose in the Deccan and the Hindu Vijayanagara Empire in the South.

X. The Shāh Mīr Dynasty of Kashmir (1339–1561)

Islamic power prevailed in Kashmir because the latter-day Hindu Rājās had employed a large number of Muslims in their army and administration. Most of these Muslims were refugees sent out by the Mongol invasion of Islamdom in the thirteenth century, even though some of them strutted around as Sayyids and Sufis. The founder of the Shāh Mīr Dynasty had only to stage a *coup d'etat*. The dynasty had 14 rulers of whom two figure in our citations:

6. Sikandar Butshikan (1389–1413)
12. Fath Shāh (1489–1499 and 1505–1516)

XI. The Bahmanī Dynasty of the Deccan (1347–1527)

The founder of this dynasty consolidated a widespread rebellion against Tughlaq rule in the Deccan, and proclaimed himself a sultān. It had its seat at Gulbarga before it moved to Bīdar in 1422. It had 15 rulers. The last five of them were kings only in name because power at Bidar passed into the hands of the Barīd Shāhī Dynasty and elsewhere into those of four other dynasties—the Nizām Shāhīs of Ahmadnagar, the 'Ādil Shāhīs of Bijapur, the Imād Shāhīs of Berar and the Qutb Shāhīs of Golconda—towards the close of the fifteenth century. Six Bahmanī rulers figure in our citations:

1. Alāu'd-Dīn Hasan (1347–1358)
2. Mujāhid Shāh (1375–1378)
5. Fīrūz Shāh (1379–1422)
6. Ahmad Shāh Walī (1422–1435)
7. Alāu'd-Dīn Ahmad Shāh II (1436–1458)
10. Muhammad Shāh II (1463–1480)

XII. The Muslim Dynasty of Gujarat (1392-1572)

The founder of this dynasty was a Rājpūt who was converted to Islam in the reign of Fīrūz Shāh Tughlaq. It had 10 rulers before Gujarat was conquered by the Mughals in 1527. Six of them figure in our citations:

1. Muzaffar Shāh I (1392–1410)
2. Ahmad Shāh I (1411–1443)
4. Qutbu'd-Dīn Ahmad Shāh II (1451–1458)

5. Mahmūd Begḍhā (1458–1511)
6. Muzaffar Shāh II (1511–1526)
7. Bahādur Shāh (1526–1537)

XIII. The Sharqī Dynasty of Jaunpur (1394–1479)

It was founded by a favourite eunuch of Fīrūz Shāh Tughlaq soon after the latter's death, and was overthrown by Bahlūl Lodī, the founder of the Lodī Dynasty of Delhi/Agra. One of its 6 rulers figures in our citations:

4. Mahmūd bin Ibrāhīm (1440–1457).

XIV. The Khaljī Dynasty of Malwa (1435–1531)

Malwa had become independent of Delhi under the Ghūrī Dynasty founded in 1390. It had 4 rulers when it was overthrown by the Khaljī Dynasty in 1435. The second dynasty also had 4 rulers. Two of them figure in our citations:

1. Mahmūd Shāh I (1435–1469)
2. Ghiyāsu'd-Dīn (1469–1500)

XV. Lodī Dynasty of Delhi/Agra (1451–1526)

The Tughlaq Dynasty had been succeeded at Delhi by the Sayyid Dynasty which ruled form 1412 to 1451. It was a weak dynasty and its last ruler invited Bahlūl Lodī, his governor of the Punjab, to take over. The second Lodī ruler shifted the capital from Delhi to Agra in order to be better able to dominate and expand into Central India. Of the 3 rulers of the Lodī Dynasty two figure in our citations:

2. Sikandar Lodī (1489–1517)
3. Ibrāhīm Lodī (1517–1526)

XVI. The Nizām Shāhī Dynasty of Ahmadnagar (1490–1630)

This dynasty was founded by one of the Bahmanī governors who was a Brahmin convert from Maharashtra. It had 11 rulers till its kingdom was annexed by the Mughals. One of them figures in our citations:

4. Murtazā Nizām Shāh (1565–1588)

XVII. The 'Ādil Shāhī Dynasty of Bijapur (1490–1686)

Founded by another of the Bahmanī governors, it had 9 rulers till the kingdom was conquered by the Mughals. One of them figures in our citations:

5. 'Alī I 'Ādil Shāh (1557–1580)

XVIII. The Qutb Shāhī Dynasty of Golconda (1507–1687)

Founded by a third Bahmanī governor, it had 7 rulers till it was overthrown by the Mughals. Four of them figure in our citations:

1. Qulī Qutb Shāh (1507–1543)
3. Ibrāhīm Qutb Shāh (1550–1580)
4. Muhammad Qulī Qutb Shāh (1580–1612)
6. Abdu'llāh Qutb Shāh (1626–1672)

XIX. The Mughal Dynasty of Agra/Delhi (1526-1857)

Founded by a new Islamic invader, Zahīru'd-Dīn Bābar, this dynasty had 21 rulers. But after 1712 when its seventh ruler died, the Mughal kings became playthings in the hands of powerful ministers and court factions. The Dynasty received a shattering blow from the invasion of Nādir Shāh in 1739. After the death of its fourteenth ruler, Muhammad Shāh, in 1748, its empire disintegrated very fast. In due course, Mughal rule became more or less confined to the Red Fort at Delhi where, too, the king lived at the mercy of the Marathas and, later on, the British. Nine Mughal rulers figure in our citations:

1. Bābur (1526–1530)
2. Humāyūn (1530–1538 and 1556)
3. Akbar (1556–1605)
4. Jahāngīr (1605–1628)
5. Shāh Jahān (1628–1658)
6. Aurangzeb (1658–1707)
7. Bahādur Shāh (1707–1712)
11. Farrukh Siyar (1713–1719)
14. Muhammad Shāh (1720–1748)

XX. The Sūr Dynasty of Agra/Delhi (1540-1556)

This dynasty rose to power by overthrowing the second Muhgal king, Humāyūn, and was in turn overthrown by him. It had four rulers, the last one of whom did not belong to the bloodline. Its first two rulers figure in our citations:

1. Sher Shāh (1540–1545)
2. Islām Shāh (1545–1554)

XXI. The Karrānī Dynasty of Bengal (1563–1576)

This dynasty arose when Sulaimān Karrānī, the governor of Bihar from the days of Sher Shāh Sūr, moved to Gaur in Bengal after the death of Islām Shāh Sūr and declared himself an independent king of

Bengal, Bihar and Orissa. Soon after, he moved his capital to Tandah. There were three rulers in this line, of whom the first, Sulaimān, (1563–1573), figures in our citations.

XXII. The Mughal Sūbāhdārs of Bengal (1717–1757)

The Mughal governors of Bengal (which included Bihar and Orissa also) became independent for all practical purposes after the passing away of Bahādur Shāh, the Mughal emperor, in 1712. Murshid Qulī Khān I who had become Sūbāhdār in 1717 nominated his son-in-law, Shujāu'd-Dīn, to succeed him. The capital of Bengal had meanwhile been moved from Dacca to Murshidabad. Murshid Qulī Khān II who figures in our citations was Shujāu'd-Dīn's son-in-law and was made the deputy governor in 1728 with his seat at Dacca. This first line of the independent Sūbāhdārs of Bengal was overthrown in 1739 by Alīvardī Khān whose grandson and successor, Sirāju'd-Daulah, was defeated by the British in 1757 in the Battle of Plassey.

XXIII. Abdālī or Durrānī Dynasty of Afghanistan (1747–1818)

The dynasty arose when, on the death of Nādir Shāh the Persian adventurer, one of his generals, Ahmad Khān Abdālī, styled himself as Ahmad Shāh Durr-i-Durrān (Pearl of the Age) and set up an independent principality in Afghanistan in 1747. With his seat at Qandhar he led seven invasions into the Punjab and farther afield. In one of his invasions (1762), he blew up the Harimandir at Amritsar, filled up the sacred tank with the debris, and desecrated the holy site by slaughtering cows on it. He died in 1773 and figures in our citations.

XXIV. Muslim Usurpers in Mysore (1761–1799)

There were only two of them, Hyder 'Alī (1761–1781) and his son, Tīpū Sultān (1782–1799). The second who died fighting the British in 1799, figures in our citations.

XXV. Sufis or Warrior Saints

Fourteen sufis or warrior saints figure in our citations. The list of this type of iconoclasts should have been much larger. But we could not get hold of the appropriate histories, most of which are in private collections. The histories that are printed these days are quite often edited in order to eschew "controversial materials".

APPENDIX 2

WAS THE KA'BA A ŚIVA TEMPLE?

Some years ago I read an article proposing that the Ka'ba was a Śiva temple before it was converted into a mosque by Prophet Muhammad. The article cited a long hymn in Arabic addressed to Mahādeva who, according to the article, was the presiding deity of the Ka'ba. The hymn, it was stated, had been composed in the reign of Vikramāditya of Ujjain in the first century BC.

A friend who got interested tried to get the hymn traced to the extant collection of pre-Islamic Arab poetry. He approached several libraries abroad but drew a blank. He as well as I then dismissed the proposition as the product of that school of Hindu historians according to whom every building everywhere in the world was a Hindu monument at one time.

But in the course of the present study I have run into some facts which force me to revise my judgment. I am not yet prepared to say that the Ka'ba was a Śiva temple. I, however, cannot resist the conclusion that it was a hallowed place of Hindu pilgrimage. The facts are being placed before the readers for whatever worth they possess.

Hindu Presence in Arabia

Plenty of archaeological and literary evidence has by now come to light to show that Indian ports on the coasts of Tamil Nadu, Malabar, Maharashtra, Gujarat, Sindh, Baluchistan and Makran had participated since pre-Harappan times in the rich and vigorous trade carried on between China, Malaysia, Indonesia, Sri Lanka and India on the one hand, and Iran, Arabia, Ethiopia, Egypt, West Asia and Europe on the other.[1] It is also known that agricultural, mineral and industrial products from India formed a major part of this trade. Colonies of Indian merchants existed all along the coasts of countries bordering on the Arabian Sea, the Persian Gulf, the Red Sea and the Mediterranean. At the same time, colonies of Arabian, Iranian, Ethiopian, Egyptian, Syrian and European merchants had come up all along the aforementioned

---

[1]Shaikha Haya Ali Al Khalifa and Michael Rice (ed.), *Bahrain through the ages, the Archaeology*, London, 1986, pp. 73–75, 94–107, 376–82; Andre Wink, *Al-Hind: The Making of the Indo-Islamic World*, Vol. I, OUP, 1990, Chapters II and III; Lokesh Chandra et. al. (ed.), *India's Contribution to World Thought and Culture: A Vivekananda Commemoration Volume*, Madras, 1970, pp. 579–88; Muhammad Abdul Nayeem, *Prehistory and Protohistory of the Arabian Peninsula*, Vol. I, *Saudi Arabia*, Hyderabad (India), 1990, pp. 160–69.

coasts of India. The Arabs and the Ethiopians had a larger presence as compared to the rest.

Ibn Ishāq provides evidence that Hindu presence in Arabia on the eve of Islam was pretty strong. When Yemen was invaded by the Abyssinians, Sayf b. Dhū Yazan, a chief of the dominant Himayrite clan of Arabs, went to Chosroes (Khusrū), the king of Iran, for help. "He said: 'O King, ravens have taken possession of our country.' Chosroes asked, 'What ravens, Abyssinians or Sindhians ?' 'Abyssianians,' he replied."[2] Ravens meant blacks, who were identified with Indians and Abyssianans in the minds of Arabs and Iranians at that time. Later on, a deputation from B. al-Hārith waited on the Prophet. "When they came to the apostle he asked who the people who looked like Indians were, and he was told that they were the B. al-Hārith b. Ka'b."[3] The Prophet, it seems, was quite familiar with Indians.

In an article, 'An Image of Wadd: A Pre-Islamic Arabian God', Ch. Muhammad Ismail observed:

"The image of Wadd has been described by an Arab commentator as 'the figure of a tall man wearing a loin-cloth with another cloth over it, with a sword hanging round his neck and also with a bow and quiver: in front of him a lance, with a flag attached to it.' It will be perceived that this does not at all describe the figure in the Plate attached, which shows a short man wearing a kilt with pleats, like that of a Scottish Highlander. On the head is a close fitting cap with a long tassel, which seems to represent a long strand of hair. It may be noted that Beduins, who come to Aden from the Hinterland, while even to this day shaving the lower parts of the head with a razor, keep a tuft on the crown, and sometimes a long strand of hair like the *badi* of the Hindus. From this I once thought that perhaps there existed a connection between the peoples of Arabia and those of the Indus Valley, and I sent a drawing of this image of Wadd to Sir John Marshall, who wrote in reply as follows: 'I do not think that there is any connection between the kilted figure (from Arabia) and the Indus people. Kilts were worn at all ages, and this figure I should take to be some 2,500 years later than those from Mohenjo-daro'; that is to say, he dated it at about 800 BC."[4]

Archaeological excavations since the days of Sir John Marshall have, however, proved beyond doubt that there were regular contacts

[2]*Sīrat Rasūl Allāh*, op. cit., p. 30.

[3]Ibid., p. 646. *Tārīkh-i-Tabarī*, op. cit., p. 46, reports the Prophet as saying, "*Yeh to Hindustāni ma'lūm hote hain.*"

[4]*Indian Antiquary*, Vol. LVIII (May, 1929), pp. 91–92.

between Arabia and Sindh, even in the days of the Indus valley civilization. As we have seen, Sindh, Baluchistan, Makran, Fars, Islands in the Persian Gulf, and South Arabia were parts of the same cultural spread.

The Pagan Arab Pantheon

Prolonged contacts through trade and travel led to rich cultural contacts, particularly because Hindus as well as Arabs were pagans, and neither of them harboured exclusivism characteristic of prophetic creeds. We have noted, while dealing with pre-Islamic Gods of Arabia, that some of them were like Hindu Gods. Students of comparative religion know that the pagan psyche, everywhere and always, has projected many similar forms and myths in respect of their divinities.

The Sabaeans of South of Arabia in particular were well-known for transacting the richest trade with India. They had established colonies all along the western coast of India. They were sun-worshippers and had a famous sun-temple in their area. As we have noted, they believed in transmigration and the cycles of *yugas*. But what is most significant, "The Arabs gave the name Būdasp to the mythical founder of the religion of the Sabaeans..."[5] Būdasp was no other than the Bodhisattva.

Coming to idols in Arabia, the worship most widely prevalent was that of Baal against whom the Bible and the Qur'ān hurl many invectives. Commenting on Qur'ān 37.123, Abdullah Yusuf Ali writes, "Both Ahab and Azariah were prone to lapse into the worship of Baal, the sun-god worshipped in Syria. That worship also included the worship of natural powers and procreative powers as in the Indian worship of the Lingam."[6] This is confirmed by W. Roberston Smith in his *Religion of the Ancient Semites*. He says that Baal was "symbolized in conical upright stones much like the *liṅga* of the Hindus" and represented "the male principle of reproduction."[7] Hindus present in Arabia could not but view Baal as the *Śivaliṅga*. Several such representations of Śiva must have been present among the idols in and around the Ka'ba, and many more in the Arabian sanctuaries elsewhere.

The Ka'ba

We have noted that the Ka'ba was a pagan temple crowded with idols and that the Islamic lore about its foundation by Abraham is pure

---

[5]*First Encyclopaedia of Islam*, op. cit., Vol. II, p. 770.

[6]*The Meaning of the Glorious Qur'ān*, Text, Translation and Commentary, Cairo, Third Edition, 1983, Vol. II, p. 1203, Footnote 4112.

[7]Summarised by Will Durant, op. cit., p. 309.

fiction. It should not, therefore, sound strange that Hindus present in Arabia took easily to worship in the Ka'ba. The pagan psyche responds with reverence to all idols, everywhere. The Muslim historian, Firishta, writes, "Before the advent of Islam, the Brahmans of India were always going on pilgrimage to the Ka'ba, for the worship of the idols there."[8] He cites earlier historians as his authorities on the subject.

It is also significant that Muslims continued to believe for a long time that Lāt and Manāt, two prominent pre-Islamic Arab Goddesses, had fled from Arabia when the Prophet tried to destroy them, and taken refuge in the temple of Somnath. The repeated expeditions which Muslim invaders led in the direction of this temple were partly inspired by this legend which originated in Arabia. Why a legend about Somnath? Simply because its famous temple on the coast of Saurashtra was a place of pilgrimage for pagan Arabs, in the same way as the Ka'ba was for the Hindus. This inference may not sound unwarranted when we view the fact that Prabhas Patan was one of the principal ports for the Indian trade with Arabia, and had a strong Arab presence in pre-Islamic times. We have already noted in chapter 3 that Arab presence in this port continued to be strong even in the post-Islamic period, down to the reign of the Vāghelās.

The Hindu Tradition

The Hindu tradition that the Ka'ba was a Śiva temple was very much alive in the days of Guru Nanak and is preserved in the *Janam Sākhīs*, particularly the *Makkē-Madīnē dī Goshatī*. It has to be investigated how far back in time the tradition goes. It cannot be said that it was invented by Guru Nanak.

In an article, *Guru Nanak's Travels in the Middle East*, Professor Surinder Singh Kohli writes: "In Arabia, the Guru clothed himself like Arabs. He had a staff in his hand, a prayer mat on his shoulder, the holy book under his arm and a long blue shirt reaching to his feet etc. He looked like a Sufi and everywhere people considered him to be a true *faqīr*. From Jedda, the Guru proceeded towards Mecca on foot. He reached Mecca late in the evening and fell asleep near Abraham's

---

[8]*Tārīkh-i-Firishta* translated into Urdu, Nawal Kishore Press, Lucknow, 1933, Vol. II, p. 498 corresponding to p. 311 of the Persian text. The sentence in Urdu reads, *"Aur Brahman Hindustān ke qibl zahūr Islām khāna-i-Ka'ba kī ziyārat aur wāhaṅ kē butoṅ kī prastish kē wāstē hameshah āmdo-shud kartē thē.*" See also *Tārīkh-i-Firishta*, translated into Urdu by Abd Illahi Khwaja, Deoband, 1983, Vol. II, p. 885; and John Briggs, op. cit., Vol. IV, p. 234. He observes in a footnote, "The subject is full of interest, opens an extensive field of investigation for the Oriental antiquary, as leading to the development of the history of a period at which India and Egypt were closely connected..."

Memorial behind the *Kābā*. When the sanitary inspector Jiwan Khān came in the morning, he admonished the Guru for sleeping with his feet towards the house of God...The Chief theologians of Islam who were present at Mecca at that time namely Maulvi Mohammad Hassan, Qāzī Rukn Dīn, Imām Jaffar and Pīr Abdul Bahav held discourses with the Guru regarding spiritual matters. The substance of these discourses was noted by Sayyad Mohammad Ghaus Salas Faquīr in his book in Persian, which was translated into Punjabi by bhāī Bhānā, according to Gyani Gyan Singh."[9]

Guru Nanak is reported to have said: "Mecca is an ancient place[10] of pilgrimage, and there is Liṅga of Mahādeva here. It was presided over by the Brāhmaṇas. One of the Brāhmaṇas, though born among them, became a Musalmān. He subverted the Atharvaveda and renamed it as Furqān. His own name was Muhammad which means the same as Mahādeva.[11] He, however, vitiated all other names, so that Hindu names stood cancelled and Muslim names came into vogue.[12] He swore by God, but got cows butchered. All Brāhmaṇas were forced to fall away from the proper path, though they continued raising cries to Allāh. The Kalima says that God is one, but Muhammad got his own name mixed up with that of God. He sent out an order to the wide world that all should become Musalmāns. Most of those who were men of substance did not obey the order; but those who were tormented by want rallied round him. He concocted some sort of a creed, and taught it to them. They joined him for plundering the people; no one joined him with any other motive."[13]

There is no evidence as yet that the pre-Islamic Arabs were Hindus, or bore Hindu names, or knew the Atharvaveda, or were guided by Brāhmaṇas.[14] The *Janam Sākhī* seems to have preserved the Hindu refugee version of what happened in Arabia after the advent of Islam. It

---

[9]Lokesh Chandra, et. al. (ed.), op. cit., p. 598.

[10]*Makkē-Madīnē dī Goshatī,* edited by Dr. Kulwant Singh, Panjabi University, Patiala, 1988, p. 49.

[11]By "Brahmaṇas" Guru Nanak means the priestly class, *al-Ḥums* among the pagan Quraysh. Furqān, of course, is the Qur'ān. The word "Muhammad" in Arabic means "he who is prayed to".

[12]It is on record that the Prophet changed all personal names which referred to ancient Gods and Goddesses of Arabia, and substituted them with Jewish names. The practice continues till today in all conversions to Islam.

[13]Translated from a Hindi version of *Makkē-Madīnē dī Goshatī*, op. cit., p. 188.

[14]Though the *al-Ḥums* who looked after the Ka'ba in the pre-Islamic period resembled the Brāhmaṇas in many respects (*First Encyclopaedia of Islam*, op. cit., Vol. III, p. 335).

is on record in Muslim histories that Hindus resident in lands invaded by Islam had to run for their lives. The same thing had happened in the Roman Empire after it was taken over by Christianity.

The common people everywhere are prone to interpret events in the language of their own culture. It may be that by the time the story reached Guru Nanak, or perhaps much earlier, the Ka'ba had become a Śiva temple in the eyes of Hindus, and the principal idol there a *Śivaliṅga*. The pagan priests who presided in the Ka'ba became Brāhmaṇas, and the Qur'ān a perversion of the Atharvaveda. What is quite obvious is that the Hindus, resident or present, in Arabia did not relish the revolution that had upturned Arabia's ancient religion, and imposed a new belief-system by means of brute force. The image of the Prophet and his followers formed by Hindus at that time was more than confirmed by their subsequent experience of Islam in their own homeland. They had no reason to revise the story which has persisted till today, in spite of the herculean efforts made by a whole state apparatus to proclaim the Prophet as "a great religious teacher", and to whitewhash Islam into "a noble faith". In any case, the subject needs serious investigation by scholars in the field.

APPENDIX 3

MEANING OF THE WORD "HINDU"

In the present study we have used the expression "Hindu temples" to cover Brahmanical as well as Buddhist, Jain, and Sikh temples. This sounds contrary to current usage in the world of scholarship as well as politics. But the history of the word "Hindu" supports our case. It was only in the nineteenth century that Western Indologists and Christian missionaries separated the Buddhists, the Jains, and the Sikhs from the Hindus who, in their turn, were defined as only those subscribing to Brahmanical sects. The missionaries invented another category, the Animists, which they employed in order to separate the tribals from the Hindus of their definition. It will, therefore, be worthwhile to survey the history of the word "Hindu", and see what it has meant, at what stage, and to whom.

A close study of literary and epigraphic sources shows that the word "Hindu" has appeared in our indigenous languages and popular parlance in a comparatively recent period, keeping in view the long span of our history. We do not find this word in any indigenous language prior to the establishment of Islamic rule in the thirteenth century. Even after that, the word was used rather sparsely in the local literature. Monier-Williams who compiled his famous dictionary from a large range of Sanskrit literature, could not find any indigenous root for this word. He says explicitly that the word is derived "from the Persian Hindū". Dictionaries of all indigenous languages say the same. So also the dictionaries of European languages.

The word "Hinduism" has been added to our vocabulary at a still more recent stage. It has been contributed by the discipline of Indology in the modern West. And the word gained wide currency in this country simply because the leaders of our national reawakening in the second half of the nineteenth century, espoused it as expressive of our national identity as well as our spiritual and cultural greatness. These leaders, down to Mahatma Gandhi, were not prepared to concede that Hinduism did not include Buddhism, or Jainism, or, for that matter, Sikhism.

Of course, some scholars of Hindutva have tried to trace the word "Hindu" to *Saptasindhu* which is mentioned in the Rigveda on several occasions. They want this word to have an indigenous as well as an ancient ring. The intention is understandable. But the excercise has remained forced, if nor far-fetched. Firstly, it does not notice that the expression used in the Rigveda is not *Saptasindhu* but *Saptasaindhvah*. Secondly, it ignores the fact that the Rigveda is not quite clear whether the expression stands for a country, or for a people, or simply for seven rivers in the Punjab. The expression seems to mean different things in different contexts. Thirdly, it does not explain why the change from "Sindhu" to "Hindu" took such a long time to surface in our indigenous languages. Lastly, and more singnificantly, it has not taken into account the fact that our countrymen were never known as Hindus in Southeast Asia in the pre-Islamic period, although they had a large presence there since centuries before the birth of Christ.

Going back to the pre-Islamic period in our own country, we find that our ancestors shared in common a name for their homeland. That was Bhāratavarṣa, which comprised at that time the present-day Seistan, Afghanistan, Pakistan, India, Nepal, and Bangladesh. They also shared in common a name for the spiritual-cultural complex to which they subscribed. That was *Sanātana Dharma*, which covered Brahmanism, Buddhism, Jainism, and also what is now known as Animism or tribal religion. But there is no evidence, literary or epigraphic, that they shared in common a name for themselves as a people. Some Purāṇas say that Bhāratavarṣa is the land of the *bhāratī santatiḥ*. The expression, however, is found nowhere else in the vast literature which has come to us from those times. In any case, this much is quite certain that our ancestors in those times did not use the word "Hindu" for describing themselves collectively. Hiuen Tsang who visited this country between AD 630 and 645 says that while the word "Shin-tu" (Chinese for "Hindu") could be heard outside our borders, it was unknown within the country.

Nor do we have a record of how our people identified themselves when they travelled abroad. It is not at all in doubt that they travelled a lot, and all the time. They were frequent visitors to far-off places in all directions, by land as well as sea. They went out individually as well as in groups. They adventured as sailors, as merchants, as princes, as monks, as priests, as scholars, as craftsmen, and in several other capacities. They had established many flourishing settlements in Southeast Asia, Australia, New Zealand, the Pacific Islands, and Central and South America towards the east, and in Iran, West Asia, East and North Africa, and Europe towards the west. Central Asia, China, Korea, and Japan were as familiar to them as their own homeland. But the literature which describes their voyages, or the epigraphs which testify to their presence abroad, do not yield any generic or national name by which they were known or made themselves known to the local people in foreign countries.

There is, therefore, no running away from the fact that the word "Hindu" occurs for the first time in the Avesta of the ancient Iranians who used this word for designating this country as well as as its people. They did not have to coin this word out of thin air. It was simply their way of pronouncing the word "Sindhu", the name of the mighty river which has always been a major landmark for travellers to this country from the north and the west. To start with, the word seems to have been used for provinces and the people in the vicinity of the Sindhu. But in due course, it was extended to cover all parts of this country and all its people. The word also spread to countries to the north and west of Iran. The ancient Greeks were quite familiar with the words "Indus" and "Indoi"—their way of pronouncing "Sindhu" and "Sindhīs". The ancient Arabs, Turks (Śakas, Kuṣāṇas, etc.), Mongolian (Hūṇas, Kirātas, etc.) and the Chinese were also familiar with the word, sometimes in their own variations on it such as "Shin-tu". It may thus be said that the word "Hindu" had acquired a national connotation, since the days of the Avesta, although in the eyes of only the foreigners. At the same time, it may be noted that the word was oblivious of the fact that "Hindus" were organized in numerous castes, and subscribed to many religious sects.

There is also evidence that at some stage in their history the ancient Iranians started using the word "Hindu" in more than a purely descriptive sense. The word seems to have acquired for them a derogatory meaning as well. Scholars are not quite certain, nor in complete agreement, about the nature of differences that developed between the Vedics of this country and the Avestans of Iran. The two people had had much in common, and for a long time, in the realm of language, religion, rituals, and ethical norms. It is surmised that the rift appeared with the rise of Zarathustra (Zoroaster) as a religious reformer in the region round Bāhlīka (Balkh), and became bitter by the time the Archaeminid Dynasty rose to power in Iran. Zorastrianism became the state religion of Iran, and the Iranians started looking down upon the Hindus as worshippers of "*dev*" (Skt. *deva*), their word for demon. They were using the word "*Ahura*" (Skt. Asura) for their own Deity.

The Iranians are known to have become more hostile to the Hindus as Buddhism spread in Khorasan and Central Asia, and the temples dedicated to *dev* were overshadowed by those dedicated to "*budd*" or "*but*"—their name for the Buddha statues. By the time the Islamized

Arabs appeared on the scene, the "black-faced Hindu" had become known to the Iranians as the *but-prast* (worshipper of the *budd* or *but*) par excellence. In fact, the word "Hindu" had become synonymous with the word "*but-prast*" in the Persian language which had developed out of ancient Pehlevi. Every Hindu place of worship was now being described as well despised as a *but-khāna*, house of *budd.* There were several other pejoratives which went with the word "Hindu" in Persian parlance. They have lived in Persian lexicons down to our own times. What is relevent in the present context is that the word "Hindu" had acquired a religious connotation also prior to the Islamic invasions, although in the language of only the Iranians. It may be noted again that the Iranians were oblivious of the fact that the worshippers of *dev* and *but* were divided in many religious denominations.

II

Of course, the Arab soldiers of Allāh and his Prophet did not have to depend on the Iranians for defining the Hindu as an idolater. They had their own patent word, "*mushrik*", which the Qur'ān had applied to the idolaters of Arabia. They also continued to use their own word in serious works on history and theology. But as the Islamized Arabs and Turks came to borrow heavily from Persian language and culture, they picked up the word "*but-prast*", and used it more and more frequently for the hated Hindu. In due course, this word came to predominate in the Islamic parlance vis-a-vis the people of this country. And what must have sounded painfully surprising as well as supremely profane to Iranian ears, the Muslims started using the word "*ātish-prast*" (fire-worshipper) also for the worshippers of the *dev* and the *but.* Thus the Hindu stood defined and despised as the "crow-faced *kāfir*, the "wicked *mushrik*", the "blind *but-prast*", and the "accursed *ātish-prast*", in the lexicons of Islam.

The story of how the armies of Islam advanced in different stages in different parts of this country, and what they did to the Hindus and their places of worship, has been documented in detail by many medieval Muslim chroniclers. They tell us that the soldiers of Allāh were rather fast in reaching for their swords and spears whenever and wherever they heard the word "*budd*" or "*but*". Buddhist temples, monasteries, and monks thus became their prime targets, as is witnessed by the Buddhist ruins and Muslim monuments built with Buddhist temple materials, all along the trail of Islamic invasions. The pertinent point in the present context, however, is that nowhere in the voluminous Muslim chronicles do we find the natives of this country known by a name other than Hindu. There were some Jews, and Christians, and Zoroastrians settled here and there, particularly along the West Coast. More people belonging to these communities continued to come from time to time throughout the period covered by the Muslim chronicles. We find that people belonging to these communities are always identified as such—*ahl-i-Yahūd* or *Banū Isrāīl*, *ahl-i-Naṣāra* or *Isāī*, and *ahl-i-Majūs* or *Ātish-prast*. The chronicles distinguish these communities from the Muslims on the one hand, and from the natives of this country on the other. It is only when they come to the natives that no more distinctions are noticed; all natives are identified as *ahl-i-Hunūd*—Hindu!

We know from numerous indigenous sources that at the time the Islamic invaders appeared on the scene, the natives of this country subscribed to numerous ways of worship. They knew and made themselves known as belonging to this or that religious sect or sub-sect. But the Muslim chronicles notice no Buddhists, no Jains, no Śaivites, no Śāktas, no Vaiṣṇavas, nor members of any other sect or sub-sect—neither at the beginning of Islamic conquests, nor during the period of Muslim rule, nor yet when Muslim domination draws towards its end. In all their narratives, all natives are attacked as Hindus, massacred as Hindus, plundered as Hindus, converted forcibly as Hindus, captured and sold in slave markets as Hindus, and subjected to all sorts of malice and molestation as Hindus.

The Muslims never came to know, nor cared to know, as to which temple housed what idol. For them all temples were Hindu *but-khānas*, to be desecrated or destroyed as such. They never bothered to distinguish the idol of one God or Goddess from that of another. All idols were broken or burnt by them as so many *buts*, or deposited in the royal treasury if made of precious metals, or strewn at the door-steps of the mosques if fashioned from inferior stuff. In like manner, all priests and monks, no matter to what school or order they belonged, were for the Muslims so many "wicked Brahmans" to be slaughtered or molested as such. In short, the word "Hindu" acquired a religious connotation for the first time within the frontiers of this country. The credit for this turn-out goes to the Muslim conquerors. With the coming of Islam to this country all schools and sects of Sanātana Dharma acquired a common denominator—Hindu!

We also know that at the time of Islamic invasions, the natives of this country stood organised in an hierarchy of many classes, castes, and sub-castes. But the invaders noticed no Kṣatriyas, no Vaiśyas, no Śūdras, nor any other class or caste distinctions. The only people they singled out for special mention were the Brahmans. But it was not because they knew or recognized them as a distinct caste; it was simply because the Brahmans were for them the "mine of *kufr* (infidelism) and *shirk* (idolatry)", the "misleaders of mankind", the "greatest enemies of Allāh and his Prophet", and the "magicians who ensured that Hindus burn for ever in the blazing fire of hell". Nor did the Muslims distinguish between high-caste and low-caste *kāfirs* while killing them, or converting them by force, or plundering their properties, or capturing them as well as their women and children for enslavement, or reducing them to the status of *zimmīs* for imposing harsh disablities and discriminatory taxes on them. In Muslim eyes, all natives constituted an undifferentiated society, a solid mass in which no constituent was distinct from another. Once again, it goes to the credit of the Muslim conquerors that the word "Hindu" acquired a national connonation within the borders of this country. The only natives who stood out of the ken were those who had converted to Islam, willingly or unwillingly.

The next thing that happened during the period of Muslim conquest and rule, was far more significant and fraught with far-reaching consequences. I am not in a position to determine more precisely the period during which the natives of this country espoused the word "Hindu" for themselves, and invested it with pride; that needs a study of contemporary Indian literature which I have not undertaken. All I can say at present is that by the time the Islamic sword swept over the South, and the Vijayanagara Empire took shape, the word "Hindu" was no more a hated word for the natives as it was for the foreign invaders.

A Kanarese inscription discovered in the Fort of Penugonda (now in Andhra Pradesh) and dated in Śaka saṁvat 1276 (AD 1354) describes Bukkā I of Vijayanagara as *hindurāya-suratrāṇa pūrva-paśchima-samudrādhipati*, that is, the Sultān among the Hindu kings, and lord of the eastern and western seas.[1] Next, we have the Satyamangalam (North Arcot District, Tamil Nadu) Copper Plate inscription of Devarāya II dated Śaka saṁvat 1346 (AD 1424) in which verse 8 says that "Through the wind (*which was produced*) by the flapping of the ears of the elephants on the field of battle, the Tulushka (ie Musalman) horsemen experienced the fate of cotton (ie were blown away)". Then follows the

[1]*Epigraphia Indica*, Vol. VI (1900–01), p. 327, footnote 2. A pun on the Muslim title "sultān" can also be detected. The word has been Sanskritized to "suratrāṇa" which may mean "defender of the Gods" as well as "defended by the Gods".

verse which applauds the king as "the Sultān among the Hindu kings as described by the bards".[2] Two more inscriptions of Devarāya, dated AD 1427 and 1428, award him the same honorific.[3] The fact that bards were using the word "Hindu" as a word of praise, leaves little doubt that the word was pulsating with great pride. A Jain inscription found at Sadri in Jodhpur District of Rajasthan, and dated Vikrama saṁvat 1496 (AD 1441) is still more specific. It says that Kumbhakarṇa of Mewar "received the title *Hiṁdu-suratrāṇa* by defeating the (Muslim) Sultāns of Dhillī and Gūrjaratrā".[4]

Some more inscriptions are worth citing in this context. They are being taken up in a chronological order. The Somalpuram Grant of Vijayanagara king Virūpākṣa is dated Śaka saṁvat 1389 (AD 1467). It describes the king ("in the glowing fire of whose valour, the Turushkas were scorched up") as "elevated by the titles such as *hindurāya-suratrāṇa*".[5] In the Hempe inscription of Krishnadevarāya, dated Śaka saṁvat 1430 (AD 1508), the *hindurāya-suratrāṇa* is described as "the destroyer of rogue tigers".[6] The hint is more than clear: rogue tigers are the Muslim invaders. The same description of him is found in his Udayambakam Grant dated Śaka saṁvat 1450 (AD 1528),[7] two years before he died. In an inscription found at the holy city of Gaya in Bihar, the Vijayanagara king Acyutadevarāya is eulogised as "*hindurāya-suratrāṇa*, the firm establisher of the Hindu kingdom".[8] His Unamanjeri Plate issued in Śaka saṁvat 1462 (AD 1540) calls him not only *hindurāya-suratrāṇa* but also *induvaṁśa-śikhāmaṇi* (the jewel in the crown of the lunar dynasty).[9] The same applause is reserved for Sadāśivarāya in his Kanuma Grant dated Śaka saṁvat 1470 (AD 1548), and the British Museum Plates dated Śaka saṁvat 1478 (AD 1556).[10]

Thus by the middle of the fourteenth century, the word "Hindu" had dropped the derogatory associations imposed on it by the ancient Iranians and the Islamic invaders, and acquired a lot of lustre in the eyes of our own countrymen. Native heroes such as Mahārāṇā Kumbhā, and Krishnadevarāya, who defeated the Islamic onslaught, were hailed as Hindu heroes in subsequent centuries. Padmanābha uses

---

[2]Ibid., Vol. III (1894–95), p. 40.
[3]Ibid., Vol. XIII (1915–16), p. 5, and Vol. XVII (1923-24), p. 111.
[4]Appendix volume to Vols. XIX-XXIII, pp. 109–10.
[5]Ibid., Vol. XVII (1920–21), p. 203.
[6]Ibid., Vol. I (1892), p. 365.
[7]Ibid., Vol. XIV (1917–18), p. 173.
[8]Ibid., Vol. XXXIII (1959–60), pp. 114–15.
[9]Ibid., Vol. III (1894–95), p. 148.
[10]Ibid., Vol. XIV (1917–18), p. 345, and Vol. IV (1896–97), p. 2.

the word "Hindu" for glorification of the Chauhān heroes of Jalor in his epic poem, *Kānhaḍade Prabandha*, which he composed in AD 1455. It will not be long before Mahārāṇā Pratāpa Siṁha of Mewar becomes renowned as *hindu-kula-kamala-divākara*, the Sun which brings bloom to the lotus that is the Hindu nation. Chhatrapati Shivāji, who turned back the tide of Islamic invasion and inaugurated the war of liberation from Islamic imperialism, will be hailed all over Bhāratavarśā as the saviour of *Hindu Dharma* and protector of its significant symbols—*gau-brāhmaṇa*, *śikhā-sūtra*, *devamūrti-devālaya*, and so on. So also Guru Gobind Singh, and Mahārājā Chhatrasāl.

And the word "Hindu" stood sanctified when Sanātana Dharma became known as Hindu Dharma. Numerous saint-poets arose in all parts of Bhāratavarṣa, sang hymns in praise of Hindu Dharma, and reminded their co-religionists that they were inheritors of a great and vast spiritual vision. The "law" of Islam threatened death to those who said that a religion other than Islam could also be true. But that did not deter Sant Kabir and Guru Nanak from proclaiming that Hindu Dharma was as good as any other. Guru Teg Bahadur defied the "law" of Islam at the very seat of its might, and offered his head in defence of his *tilaka* (religious mark on the forehead) and *janēū* (sacred thread).

III

Islamic imperialism had inflicted deep wounds on Hindu religion, culture, society, polity, economy, and environment. The wounds needed time to heel. All the same, Hindus had survived the Islamic onslaught, and come out of it with renewed pride in their spiritual and cultural traditions. The word "Hindu" had become an honoured word, and denoted, nationally as well as religiously, the natives of this country as a whole except those who had been forced or lured into the fold of Islam.

The gravest injury which Hindus had suffered at the hands of Islam was the destruction of their temples and monasteries, and the slaughter of Brāhmaṇas and Buddhist monks. Temples and monasteries were not mere places of worship and meditation; they were seats of higher learning as well. Brāhmaṇas and Buddhist monks were not only priests and spiritual practitioners; they were also leaders of larger Hindu thought. Thus Hindus had been hit in the solar plexus. They were still capable of marshalling plenty of heroism (*kṣātra*); but their capacity for a broader vision (*brāhmaṇya*) had suffered a steep decline. Even so, Islamic imperialism had failed to disarm the Hindus ideologically.

Islam has been, and remains till today, not much more than a system of glorified terrorism in spite of all its tom-tom about Allāh and the Book from high heaven. The only way it has ever known, either of breaking resistance to its onward march or of imposing its own cock-and-bull stories on a conquered people, has been that of brute force. It has never learnt the art of legitimizing itself in the eyes of the conquered people by selling to them some high-sounding scholarship. In fact, its own stock of ideas has remained less than limited, and its scholarship has been sterile and hide-bound. Nor has it ever tried to understand how other societies and cultures function and flourish. Forcible conversion is the only method it has known for pulling the conquered people out of their cultural moorings. In this country, it had remained incapable of searching for the sources of Hindu inspiration, or acquiring any worthwhile knowledge of how Hindu society and culture had functioned down the ages. It could never earn even a semblance of legitimacy in the eyes of Hindus at large, or shake any significant section of Hindus out of their ancestral moorings.

It is difficult to say how Hindus would have fared if a new imperialism from the West had not arrived on the scene at the very time when Islamic imperialism was on its last legs. The new imperialism had three faces—Christian, British, and Communist. It was far more competent than Islamic imperialism in terms of both means and methods. But the deadliest weapon it wielded was a new type of scholarship which it used in progressive stages for disarming the Hindus ideologically.

This scholarship was a many-splendoured mansion—Anthropology, Sociology, Historiography, Linguistics, Comparative Religion, Indology, German Idealism, French Positivism, British Utilitarianism, Soviet Marxism-Leninism, and the rest. It had some fascinating facets. Its essential theme, however, was only a variation on the Christian missionary lore in as much as it believed and had proved to its own satisfaction that the white man's world was the centre of the universe, that the white man's civilization was the highest achievement in human history, and that the white man had to shoulder the heavy burden of civilizing the rest of mankind which was seen as wallowing in varying stages of barbarism. But simply because this scholarship had surfaced in the same area and at the same time as Modern Science, it had come to pretend that it also shared the scientific spirit. Marxism-Leninism was the culmination of this masquerade.

This is not the occasion to go into details of how the latter-day imperialism mobilized this scholarship for mounting an unprecedented assault on the Hindu intellectual elite. What we are concerned with in the present context is the portrait of Hindus and Hinduism which this scholarship proceeded to paint. The salient features of the protrait which emerged at the end of the operation were as follows:

1. The oldest and the most sacred scripture of the Hindus, the Rigveda, provides impeccable evidence that a race of blood-thirsty barbarians, who worshipped equally blood-thirsty gods and who styled themselves as Aryans, invaded this country in the second millenium BC, slaughtered or enslaved all those natives who could not escape to the far South or forests and mountain fastnesses in the North, and settled down to live on the fat of this fertile land for all time to come.
2. With a view to perpetuate their stranglehold on the country and its native people, the Aryans created a caste system in which they themselves constituted the higher castes—Brāhmaṇas, Kṣatriyas, and Vaiśyas—while they reduced the conquered populace to the status of Śūdras and outcaste untouchables.
3. At the same time, the Aryans concoted a priestcraft, presided over by the wily Brahmins and couched in the complex Sanskrit literature, in order to legitimize and safeguard the caste system.
4. Whatever veneer of culture the Aryans managed to acquire, was borrowed by them from the native people whom the Sanskrit literature had shamelessly described as Dāsas, Dasyus, Asuras, Nāgas, Rākṣasas, and the rest.
5. That veneer of culture also took no time to come off when, at a subsequent stage, the custodians of Brahminism destroyed the shrines and slaughtered the saints of Buddhism and Jainism, simply because these rationalist and humanitarian religions questioned the iniquities and cruelties of the caste system and pleaded for a just and equalitarian social order.
6. But as the people's protest against the primitive superstitions, the puerile priestcraft, and the cruel caste system of Brahminism continued to grow, Brahminism diguised itself in a number of new-sounding cults—Śaivism, Śāktism, Vaiṣṇavism, etc.—and concocted a new series of Sanskrit literature—the Purāṇas and the Dharmaśāstras—in order to hoodwink the people and ensure the continuity of the caste system, with the crafty Brahmins sitting at its top and cornering unequal privilages as well as rich profits.
7. Thus the essence of Brahminism alias Hinduism has been, and

remains, the economically exploitative, socially oppressive, and culturally moribund caste system, no matter how many heaven-tearing philosophies it stocks in its shop in order to hide the fraud.

8. Hinduism alias Brahminism has continued, and will continue, to suppress, or sidetrack, or subvert by means of its sly syncretism, every single idea, religious or secular, which threatens the caste system and the domination of the deceitful Brahmins.
9. Speaking scientifically and in a historical perspective, *Hindus proper* are only the high castes in the present-day "Hindu society", and describing the rest of the people as Hindus is a dirty swindle.
10. Hindus alias the high caste descendants of the Aryan invaders have joined, and will continue to join, hands with any and every reactionary ideology and force—feudalism, capitalism, colonialism, American imperialism, etc.—in order to safeguared the caste system and its own stranglehold on the toiling masses of India.

We have presented in simple and straight language the lore which Christian, British and Communist imperialists came to sell with varying degrees of sophistication, in a large number of tomes, treatises, and articles in learned journals published by prestigious publishing houses such as the Oxford University Press. In any case, by now the so-called Dalit Movement is retailing this lore in the way we have summarized it, without being questioned by any of its highbrow hawkers.

The word "Hindu" was thus not only robbed of all the pride and prestige it had acquired over the past several centuries, but also made synonymous with foreign invaders who had committed no end to crimes against the native people. The word no more designated the vast majority of this country's population; on the contrary, it became the hallmark of a small minority which had conspired to masquerade as the majority. The Buddhists, the Jains, the Sikhs, and the Animists (new name for those subscribing to tribal religions) were taken out of the fold of Hinduism at one fell sweep. Finally, the "Dravidian South" was given a call to revolt against everything associated with the word "Hindu"—religion, culture, language, etc.

This was the lore which was taught in school and college textbooks of an educational system which had been designed and was being controlled by the British establishment and the Christian missions. This was the lore which was given the pride of place in Communist pamphlets and periodicals which started to proliferate from the 'twenties of this century onwards. And this was the lore by mouthing which a section in the Indian National Congress started strutting around as "progressive", "radical", "revolutionary", "socialist", and the rest. Pandit Jawaharlal Nehru became the leader of this section after a brief visit to the Soviet Union in 1927. And he started fancying himself as a great historian when his *Glimpses of World History* and *Discovery of India*, which revelled in this lore, were hailed as classics by the prestigious press in this country and abroad.

Meanwhile, Muslim historians of the Marxist schools had polished up a subsidiary thesis. Their main purpose was to salvage Islam from its blood-soaked history, and present the medieval Muslim rule in India as a native dispensation. Mohammad Habib of the Aligarh Muslim University came out with the thesis that the Islamic invaders had destroyed Hindu temples not in obedience to the tenets of Islam but out of their lust for loot. This thesis was lapped up immediately by Pandit Nehru and his progressive host in the Congress. Pandit Sunderlal picked up the hint and painted Islam and the medieval Muslim rule in glorious colours. The finishing touches were given by M.N. Roy who propounded that Islam had come to India for completing the social revolution which Buddhism had started but failed to accomplish because Brahminism had responded with fire and sword.

But the word "Hindu" had not yet become a dirty word. It still covered the Buddhists, the Jains, and the Sikhs except for some separatist fringes which had imbibed the monothestic theology of the Muslim-Christian combine or the Leftist lore. Stalwarts of Hindu re-awakening —Swami Dayananda, Bankim Chandra, Vivekananda, Sri Aurobindo —had seen through the Christian and the British game and given a strong lead which had not yet been exhausted. Mahatma Gandhi was still alive and was saying that "if Brahmanism does not revive, Hinduism must perish", that the caste system had provided strength to Hindu society during difficult times, and that "I will not like to live in an India which has ceased to be Hindu".

IV

The word "Hindu" started being brought into contempt on some scale in the truncated Hindu homeland with the rise of Pandit Nehru to supreme power in the post-independence period. He was a combined spokesman of all imperialist ideologies which had visited this country in the past—Islamic, Christian, British, and Communist. Small wonder that he placed the Ministry of Education in the hands of a Muslim-Marxist combine headed by Maulana Abul Kalam Azad. Christian missions were given full facilities to educate the Hindus, and convert as many of them as they could manage. The missionary apparatus started building itself anew, after a period of panic experienced by it when the British Raj was drawing to its end. Meanwhile, Mohammad Habib had come out with another thesis (1954), namely, that the so-called Muslim conquest of India was really a "turn of public opinion" or an "urban revolution" in which the Indian "working class" had preferred the *shariat* in place of the *smiriti*, and the Turks in place of the Thukuris. Nehru approved the thesis in a Preface. At the same time, he patronized the Communist Party of India, so that it very soon became a formidable force. All this was being done by him in the name of Secularism, which concept he had picked up from the modern West and perverted to mean the opposite of what it meant there.

Nehru's daughter, Mrs. Indira Gandhi, carried her father's game much farther. In her fight for a monopoly of power, she split the Congress Party, and made a common cause with the Communists. Well-known Communists and fellow-travellers were given positions of power in the ruling Congress Party, in the Government at the Centre as well in the States, and in prestigious institutions all over the country. The Muslim-Marxist combine of "historians" had already captured the Indian History Congress during the days of Pandit Nehru, and many honest historians had been hounded out of it. Now this combine was placed in control of the Indian Council of Historical Research and entrusted with extensive patronage. The combine took over the National Council of Educational Research and Training also, and laid down the guidelines for producing school textbooks on various subjects. The Jawaharlal Nehru University was created and financed on a fabulous scale in order to collect Communist professors from all over the country, and form them into a frontline brigade for launching all sorts of anti-Hindu campaigns.

The smokescreen for this Stalinist operation was provided by the slogan of Secularism which nobody was supposed to question, or examine as to what it had come to mean. Its meaning had to be accepted ex-cathedra, and as laid down by the Muslim-Marxist combine. In the new political parlance that emerged, Hinduism and the nationalism it inspired, became blackned as "Communalism". Small wonder that the word "Hindu" started becoming a dirty word in the academia as well as the media. The Sikhs had already opted out of the Hindu fold. The Jains started saying more and more loudly that they were not Hindus. The climax came when the Ramakrishna Mission and the Arya Samaj petitioned the High Courts for obtaining the status of non-Hindu religions. An article in the Constitution which gave certain concessions to non-Hindu educational institutions was being cited in defence of this volte-face. But that was only an excuse. The real reason was that nobody who thought he was somebody was prepared to be known as a Hindu any more.

The Bharatiya Jana Sangh had been launched by some Hindus who were already shying away from the word "Hindu", and opting for word "Bharatiya". It was taken over in due course by a pompous Nehruvian, and whoever objected to the coup was hounded out, or silenced. The party was now trying frantically to prove its Secular credentials. It was mortally afraid of being called a Hindu party, and frequently displayed its Muslim membership. Its tragedy was that the authentic Secularists were not prepared to accept its claims, although it had invited every stalwart of Secularism to use its platforms for delivering lectures on the sanctified subject. Again, the climax came when, under pressure from the newly-formed Janata Party of which the Bharatiya Jana Sangh had became a constitutent, the Rashtriya Swayamsevak Sangh (RSS) also got ready to consider dropping of the word "Hindu" from its constitution. One wonders how things would have turned out if the Janata Party government had not fallen before the critical session of the RSS could be held. In any case, leaders of the Bharatiya Janata Party, the reincarnation of the Bharatiya Jana Sangh, could be heard saying till recently that they could no more afford to be known as Hindus (*ab apnē āpko Hindū kahnē sē kām nahīṅ chalēgā*)!

That is the history of the word "Hindu", down to our own times. In the present work we have disregarded that part of its history which tells how imperialist ideologies have manipulated its meaning, and retained that part which tells how it came to signify everything that is native and natural to this country—the people, the social fabric, the cultural complex, and the vast spiritual vision. So far as honest historians are concerned, the word "Hindu" has covered, and continues to cover, all religions which took birth in this country, and the expression "Hindu temples" stands for temples where people subscribing to these indigenous religions worship.

Appendix 4
QUESTIONNAIRE FOR THE MARXIST PROFESSORS

We return to the Marxist professors with whom we started.

We have cited from eighty histories written by Muslims over a period of more than one thousand years. We have also cited several Islamic inscriptions which confirm what the historians say. The citations show how Hindu temples continued to be destroyed over a vast area and for a long time. We have added no "editorial comments" and given no "communal twist" to the events that took place. All along, we have kept to the actual language used by the Muslim historians.

We wonder if the professors will dismiss as "a mere listing of dates" the evidence we have presented. What we expect from the professors is that they will come forward with "historical analysis and interpretations" so that the destruction of Hindu temples mentioned in the Muslim narratives gets explained in terms of economic or political or any other non-religious motives.

We stick to our position, namely, that it is the theology of Islam which offers the only straight-forward and satisfactory explanation of why Muslim conquerors and rulers did what they did to Hindu places of worship. We have provided full facts about that theology, as also about the history of how it took its final shape. It would be most welcome if the professors come out with their comments on the character and meaning of this theology. In fact, we look forward to a Marxist explanation of it. What were the concrete material conditions and objective historical forces which gave rise to this theology in Arabia at that time?

Next, we refer to the second point which the professors had made in their letter to *The Times of India*. They had said that "acts of intolerance have been committed by followers of all religions". A subsequent sentence clarified what they meant; they had in mind the "Buddhist and Jain monuments" and "animist shrines destroyed by Hindus". As we have said, we do not share their philosophy of separating the Buddhists, the Jains and the Animists from the Hindus. But we agree to use their terms for the time being and request them to produce

1. A list of epigraphs which record the destruction of Buddhist and Jain monuments and Animist shrines by any Hindu, at any time;
2. Citations from Hindu literary sources describing destruction of

Buddhist and Jain monuments and Animist shrines by any Hindu, at any time;

3. The Hindu theology which says or even suggests that non-Hindu places of worship should be destroyed or desecrated or plundered, or which hails such acts as pious or meritorious;
4. A list of Hindu kings or commanders whom Hindus have hailed as heroes for desecrating or destroying or converting into Hindu places of worship any Buddhist or Jain monuments or Animist shrines;
5. A list of Buddhist and Jain monuments and Animist shrines which have been desecrated or destroyed or converted into Hindu places of worship in the remote or the recent past;
6. The names and places of Hindu monuments which stand on the sites occupied earlier by Buddhist or Jain monuments or Animist shrines, or which have materials from the latter embedded in their masonry;
7. Names of Buddhist, Jain and Animist leaders or organizations who have claimed that such and such Hindu monuments are usurpations, and demanded their restoration to the original occupants;
8. Names of Hindu leaders and organizations who have resisted any demand made by Buddhists or Jains or Animists for restoration of the latter's places of worship, or called for legislation which will maintain the status quo, or cried "Hinduism in danger", or staged street riots in support of their usurpations.

We think that this sort of concrete evidence alone can decide "the question of the limits to the logic of restoration of religious sites". There seems to be no other way. Sweeping generalizations based on slender or dubious evidence are no substitue for hard facts.

We hope that the professors will not resort to the hackneyed swear-words such as "Hindu communalism," "reactionary revivalism", and the rest. Swear-words offer no solutions. In any case, the time when swear-words carried weight has passed. It is no use inviting the other side to hit back in a similar manner.

If the professors fail to come out with answers to questions posed by us, and to present the evidence in support of their statements, we shall be forced to conclude that far from being serious academicians, they are cynical politicians hawking ad hoc or plausible explanations in the service of a party line. In fact, we shall be justified in saying that they are not Marxists but Stalinists. Marxism is a serious system of thought which offers consistent explanations. Stalinism, on the other hand, is an exercise in *suppressio veri suggestio falsi* in pursuit of a particular end.

Hindu scholars, leaders and organizations have so far ignored the loud and large-scale talk in the mass media, academia, and political circles about "Hindu intolerance" towards the Buddhists and the Jains and the Animists. Much damage has already been done to the image of Hinduism, and much more damage is likely to result if this talk is not challenged and stopped. How loose and irresponsible this talk can be is illustrated by the following instance.

I attended a seminar on the Mandal Commission Report held in the Gandhi Peace Foundation in October, 1990. One of the participants who spoke in support of the Report was Shri Hukam Dev Narain Singh Yadav, an MP of the Janata Dal at that time and a Minister in the Chandra Shekhar Government some time later. Speaking of Brahminical tyranny, he referred to the time "when rivers of the blood of Buddhist monks were made to flow in the Buddhist monasteries (*jab bauddha vihāroṅ mēṅ bauddha bhikṣuoṅ kē rakta kī nadiyāṅ bahāī gayī thīṅ*)." The following dialogue took place between myself and the speaker at the end of the latter's talk:

I : Could you kindly name the Buddhist monasteries where it happened, and also the time when it happened?

Speaker : I will not pretend that I know. I must have heard it from someone, or read it somewhere.

I : I give you six months for finding a single instance of Hindus murdering Buddhist monks. I am demanding only one instance, not two.

Speaker : I will try.

The speaker looked to me to be one of the finest men I had ever met. His voice had a ring of sincerity in whatever he said. His humility in presenting his point of view was more than examplary. I expected him to remember my question and provide an answer. But two and a half years have passed and there is no word from the eminent politician occupying a high position in the public life of this country.

I know that the evidence demanded by me does not exist. It is a Big Lie being spread by Hindu-baiters. Hindus have never done what they are being accused of. My only point in mentioning the incident is that even honest people can become victims of hostile propaganda which is not countered in good time.

II

When the first edition of this book came out, I sent a copy of it to Professor Romila Thapar of the Jawaharlal Nehru University in her capacity as the doyen of the Marxist historians. I also addressed to her the following letter on 27 June, 1991:

"I have posed a questionnaire for the school of historians which you lead. Please turn to pp. 408-410 of my recently published book (Hindu Temples: What Happened to Them, Volume II: The Islamic Evidence), a copy of which is being sent to you by registered post.

"You may also read pp. 47-68 and p.v which also discuss the position of your school.

"I am drawing your attention to these pages so that your school does not plead ignorance of them while maintaining silence. Of course, you are free to ignore the questionnaire as coming from a person who has had no standing in the academic world. I, however, feel that there are many people still left in this country who care for truth more than for position."

She was kind enough to reply by a letter dated 10 August 1991 which said:

" Your letter of 27 June was awaiting me on my recent return to Delhi.

"As regards the issues raised in the questionnaire included in your book, you are perhaps unaware of the scholarly work on the subject discussed by a variety of historians of various schools of thought. May I suggest that for a start, you might read my published lectures entitled, 'Cultural Transaction and Early India'."

I wrote back on 31 August 1991, and stated my position as follows:

"I acknowledge your letter of August 10.

"I wish you had refrained from striking the pose of superiority which has been for long the hallmark of your school of historians. It does not go well with academic discipline.

"For your information I have been primarily a student of ancient India's history and culture, and gone through a good deal of source material, literary as well as archaeological. One of the reasons I have wandered into India's medieval and modern history is that I want to know what happened to Hindu heritage at the hands of latter-day 'liberators'.

"May I request you not to suggest any further reading of your stuff? You threaten to do so when you use the words 'for a start' while recommending your present pamphlet. I am pretty familiar with the patent lore.

"I am sorry to say that your pamphlet has added nothing to my knowledge or perspective. The method of selecting facts and floating fictions is very well known to me. Christian missionaries have done far better with lesser fare.

"I am not commenting on the various propositions put forward in your pamphlet. The Questionnaire which I have addressed to you was framed in a particular context. In your letter published in *The Times of India* dated October 2, 1986, you had stated that handing over of Sri Rama's and Sri Krishna's birthplaces to the Hindus, and of disused mosques to the Muslims 'raises the question of the limits to the logic of restoration of religious sites. How far back do we go? Can we push this to the restoration of Buddhist and Jain monuments destroyed by Hindus? Or of the pre-Hindu animist shrines?' In my book I have welcomed the statement and said that 'the question can be answered satisfactorily only when we are prepared to face facts and a sense of proporition is restored'.

"I have gone ahead and compiled historical and theological data about Islamic iconoclasm from whatever Islamic sources I could lay my hands on during the last four years. More may follow as I get at more of this source material. In an earlier volume I have provided, in a preliminary survey, a list of around two thousands Muslim monuments which are known to stand on the sites of and/or have been built with the materials of Buddhist, Brahmanical and Jain temples. The list is likely to get enlarged as I continue to look into more archaeological reports.

"I have also compiled a list of Buddhist and Jain monuments supposed to have been destroyed or usurped by this or that Brahmanical sect, and Jain temples functioning at what were Brahmanical places of worship at earlier dates. I am seeking your help to enlarge the list of Buddhist and Jain monuments which were destroyed by those whom you call Hindus. Your writings and statements over the years go to show that you specilaize in this subject. What I am looking for in particular is the Hindu theology which inspires acts of intolerance. I expect you to guide me to it.

"My Questionnaire is not at all a challenge issued in a spirit of combat. It is only an appeal that sweeping statements should now yield place to hard facts so that we know precisely as to who did what, when, where, and under what inspiration. We should be in a position to compare the record of Islamic iconoclasm with that of Hindu iconoclasm, and draw fair conclusions regarding the character and role of the two religions. I for one am not interested in the restoration of religious sites, which I leave to the politicians.

"It is nobody's case that Hindu sects (in which I include Buddhists and Jains) did not use strong language vis-a-vis each other. Every Brahmanical sect has used strong language about other Brahmanical sects. So have the Buddhist, and the Jains, not only vis-a-vis Brahmanical sects but also about one another. The situation gets much worse when it comes to the sub-sects, whether Buddhist or Brahmanical or Jain. But strong language alone, whether in words or portrayals, is no evidence in the present context, unless it is followed by overt acts of destruction or usurpation.

"Secondly, I fail to understand the logic of placing Buddhists and Jains on one side of the fence, and Brahmanical sects on the other. What about Buddhists and Jains committing acts of intolerance vis-a-vis one another? For a start, I refer you to the *Mahavamsa* which says that the Buddhist king, Vattagamini (29–117 BC), destroyed a Jain *vihara* and built a Buddhist one on the same site. In the Sravana-Belgola Epitaph of Mallishena, the renowned Jain teacher, Akalanka, says that 'in the court of the glorious king Himasitala, I overcame all crowds of Bauddhas, most of whom had a shrewd mind (*vidagdha-atmano*), and I broke the (image of) Sugata with my foot (*padena visphotitah*) " (*EI.* III, 192 for Sanskrit text and 201 for English translation). The instances can be multiplied.

"Thirdly, I plead that presentation of evidence should not be an exercise in *suppressio veri suggestio falsi*. Your one line summary (p.18) of the Saiva inscription at Ablur is a case in point. The inscription says clearly (*El.* III, 255) that the dispute arose because the Jains in a body tried to prevent a Saiva from worshipping his own image, saying 'Jina is the (true) deity'. The Jains also undertook to 'pluck up our Jina and set up Siva' if the Saiva devotee performed a miracle. And the Jains went back on their plighted word when the miracle was shown. There was a quarrel and the Jina was broken by the Saivas. What is most significant, the Jain king, Bijjala, decided in favour of the Saivas when the dispute was referred to him. He dismissed the Jains, 'bidding them to go without saying further words'. The story ends with the Jain king showering favours on the Saivas.

"Dr. Fleet who has edited and translated this inscription along with four others found at the same place, gives summaries of two Lingayat puranas and the Jain *Bijjalacharitra*, and points out that the story in this inscription finds no support in the literary traditions of the two sects. Bijjal's inscription dated AD 1162 discovered at Managoli (*EI.* V,9-23) also does not support the story. The fact that the Saiva inscription at Ablur bears neither a date nor relates itself definitely to the reign of a king, makes it sound fishy. Authentic inscriptions do not usually deal in miracles. Obviously, the Saivas seem to have used the endowment of a Saiva temple in the Managoli inscription for mounting on it a story which was not related to any real events but satisfied sectarian spite.

"Dr. Fleet has cited from the Lingayat sources to show that there was nothing Brahmanical about the Lingayats. They harboured 'hostility to Brahmans' (p.239) and their doctrines 'included the persecution and extermination of all persons whose creed differed from that of the Lingayats' (p.240). Brahmanism in any shape or form should not be held responsible for the doings of this sect. There is evidence that this sect drew its inspiration directly from Muslim missionaries who abounded on the West Coast of India at the time it took shape.

"Incidentally, I have not been able to find anything relevant to the context in *EI.* XXVIII.1 which is mentioned in footnote 14 on page 18 of your pamphlet, along with *EI.*V.237. Is it a printing mistake? Kindly give me the correct reference so that I may examine the incident and credit it to your account if it is not already in my list. I hope it is not a case of strong language alone.

"Finally, I suggest that all cases of Brahmanical rulers building or endowing Buddhist and Jain temples, and Buddhist and Jain rulers doing the same for Brahmanical temples, should also be compiled for obtaining a total picture of the religious scene. You are very prompt in pointing out the few cases where Hindu temples were endowed or built under Muslim patronage, whenever the large-scale destruction of Hindu temples by Muslims is brought to your notice. Why do you always fail to point out the numerous cases of Brahmanical patronage of Buddhism and Jainism, while listing the few cases of Brahmanical persecution? If a few cases of Muslim patronage can atone for large-scale Islamic iconoclasm, the numerous cases of Brahmanical patronage should be able to do the same for a few cases of Brahmanical persecution. I hope I am not illogical."

I have not received even an acknowlegement of this letter from Professor Thapar, leave alone any comments on the points raised by me. Her silence has left me sad, for I was looking forward to a fruitful dialogue.

III

Lest Professor Thapar complains that in my letter to her I have not dealt with all instances of "Hindu intolerance" mentioned in her pamphlet, I reproduce below the entire evidence she has presented. She says:

"The persecution of Buddhists in Kashmir is referred to by Hsüan Tsang, but, lest it be thought that he being a Chinese Buddhist monk was prejudiced, the testimony of Kalhaṇa in the *Rājataraṅginī* should be more acceptable. Hsüan Tsang refers to the atrocities of Mihīrakula against the Buddhists both in Punjab and in Kashmir in the sixth century AD. Hsüan Tsang may well have been exaggerating when he lists the destruction of 1,600 Buddhist *stūpas* and *saṅghārāmas* and the killing of many thousands of Buddhist monks and lay-followers. Kalhaṇa gives an even fuller account of the king killing innocent people by the hundreds. This is often dismissed by attributing the anti-Buddhist actions of Mihīrakula to his being a Hūṇa. But it should not be forgotten that he was also an ardent Śaiva and gave grants of land in the form of *agrahāras* to the brahmans. In the words of Kalhaṇa: 'Brahmans from Gandhāra resembling himself in their habits and verily themselves the lowest of the twice-born accepted *agrahāras* from him.' It is possible that the recently discovered *stūpa* at Sanghol in Punjab, where sculpted railings were found in the vicinity of a *stūpa* dismantled and packed away, indicates this persecution of Buddhists in Kashmir and the wilful destruction of a *vihāra*, again by a Śaivite king. But on this occasion the king repented and built a new monastery for the Buddhist monks.

"Courtly literature, particularly plays written after the seventh century AD, is replete with invective against Buddhist and Jaina monks who are depicted as morally depraved, dishonest and altogether what one might call the scum of the earth. Mahendravarman's *Maṭṭavilāsa*, a farce, is amongst the earliest plays. In the *Mudrarākṣasa* of Viśākhadatta, a constant refrain states that it is inauspicious to see a Jaina monk. The *Prabodha-candrodaya* of Kṛṣṇa Miśra, a drama of the eleventh century, dwells on the theme of a Kapālika converting a Jaina and a Buddhist monk to Śaivism by offering them wine and women, both of which they are said to hanker after. In the Śaiva temples at Khajuraho, Jaina monks, especially of the *digambara* sect, are depicted in the worst possible erotic poses. Such references and depictions do not amount to persecution but reflect a contemptuous attitude towards Jaina and Buddhist monks which they would doubtless have found very galling, particularly as they occur in the literature and art of aristocratic groups.

The depiction of monks and ascetics as debauched may have been due to the court's contempt for a variety of ascetics, some of whom were associated with socially unacceptable practices. Such depictions in courtly literature may also have been an attempt to play down the authority associated with renouncers and ascetics in the popular mind. But it is significant that the Buddhists and Jainas are more commonly made the subject of attack.

'Evidence on the persecution of Jainas by Śaiva sects comes from a variety of sources. The earliest known cave temple originally dedicated by the Jainas in Tirunelveli district was, subsequently in the seventh century, converted into a Śaiva temple. This was not a case of appropriating the temple and gradually changing it. Quite clearly, the Jaina images were either destroyed or erased, sometimes only partially, and fresh Śaivite images carved in the same place. In the case of the partially erased sculpture it is possible to recognize traces of the original. Where the image is totally gouged out the desecration is visible.

"The Śaivite saint Jñāna Sambander is attributed with having converted the Pāṇḍya ruler from Jainism to Śaivism, whereupon it is said that eight thousand Jainas were impaled by the king. This episode is represented in painting and sculpture in medieval temples and is enacted to this day in some Śiva temples during their annual festival. In later times, attempts were made to appease the Jainas by royal patrons building Jaina, Śaiva and Vaiṣṇava temples in close proximity. But in these areas the Jaina temples soon fell into disrepair whilst the others flourished.

"Such activities were not restricted to a particular area. The Jaina temples of Karnataka went through a traumatic experience at the hands of the Lingāyatas or Vīraśaivas in the early second millennium AD. This would explain in part why some Jaina texts have pejorative references to Basava, who founded the Vīraśaiva sect. The Jaina temples at Lakkuṇḍi were located in the proximity of an affluent *agrahāra* and the Vaiṣṇava brahmans accepted Mahāvīra as an incarnation of Brahma. Later, however, one of the temples was converted into a Śaiva temple. At Huli, the temple of the five Jinas was converted into a *pañcaliṅgeśvara* Śaivite temple, the five *liṅgas* replacing the five Jina images in the *sancta*. Some other Jaina temples suffered the same fate. An inscription at Ablur in Dharwar eulogizes attacks on Jaina temples as retaliation for Jaina opposition to Śaivite worship. Sculpted panels at this site depict the smashing of Jaina images. In the fourteenth century the harassment of Jainas was so acute that they had to appeal for protection to the ruling power at Vijayanagara.

"Inscriptions of the sixteenth century from the Srisailam area of Andhra Pradesh record the pride taken by Vīraśaiva chiefs in beheading *svetāmbara* Jainas. The local records of this area refer to the frequent persecution of the Jainas. In Gujarat, Jainism flourished during the reign of Kumārapāla, but his successor persecuted the Jainas and destroyed their temples. However, Jainism was so well-established here that periodical persecution did not really shake it."[1]

She sums up: "It is historically important to know why this persecution of the Buddhists and Jainas occurred in particular by the Śaivas. I can only offer a few comments. At the religious level, it may have had to do with asceticism. Was Śiva seen as the ascetic *par excellence* and the patron deity of ascetics, and were Buddhist and Jaina monks seen as imposters? Did Buddhist and Jaina monks find the worship of the *lingam* offensive owing to the puritanism inherent in both these systems? Yet the Tantric versions of these systems conceded to practices and ideas which were opposed to puritanism. If the hostility related only to religious differences, then it should have surfaced earlier in time. It is interesting that it begins about the middle of the first millennium AD and gains force through the centuries until Buddhism eventually fled the country and Jainism was effectively limited to a few pockets. The persecution predates the coming of Islam to these areas, so that the convenient excuse that Islamic persecution caused the decline of these religions is not applicable."[2]

Interestingly, she has refrained from mentioning the persecution of Buddhists by Puśyamitra Śunga and Śaśāṅka of Gauḍa, and the melting of idols by king Harsha of Kashmir, which had so far figured most prominently in the writings of her school. I wonder whether she has realized that those allegations have no legs to stand upon, even though others of her school continue to harp on them. In any case, it may be assumed that her present list has exhausted the entire stock-in-trade in the Marxist shop on the subject of "Hindu intolerance". I will deal with these instances, one by one.

1. She has suppressed the fact, stated by Huen Tsang, that Mihīrakula had requested the Buddhist Sangha to teach him the tenets of Buddhism. The Sangha did not assign the task to a qualified teacher but sent a monk who had the rank of a servant.

---

[1]*Cultural Transaction and Early India: Tradition and Patronage*, Oxford University Press, Delhi, 1987, pp. 16–18.

[2]Ibid., p. 19.

Mihīrakula felt outraged at this insult and persecuted the Buddhists. It is highly doubtful if this Hūṇa tyrant had become a Śaiva. Kalhaṇa sees him only as a Hūṇa extending patronage to bad Brāhmaṇas. But even if he had, his fury had nothing to do with Śaivism. On the contrary, it was the fury of a tyrant whose ego had been hurt. Kashmir had known many Śaiva kings before Mihīrakula as well as after him. None of them is known to have persecuted the Buddhists. In fact, most of them are known to have been patrons of Buddhism. The only instance she cites is that of a king who repented and rebuilt the *vihāra* which he had pulled down in a fit of anger. We should welcome a similar instance of some Muslim ruler who repented and rebuilt the temple he had demolished. The difference arises because while it was a temporary lapse on the part of the Kashmiran king, Muslim rulers were inspired by a permanently prescribed theology.

2. Dragging in the unfinished *stūpa* at Sangol in this context is totally unwarranted. No archaeologist has said that the *stūpa* was "dismantled and packed away". All that is known is that many stones had been finished, and were meant to be parts of a *stūpa*. But no one knows for sure why they were left in pits and trenches. It is no more than a speculation that perhaps a Hūṇa invasion was feared. No other archaeologist or historian has surmised that Mihīrakula was leading this invasion, and that he inspired fear as a Śaiva. In any case, Professor Thapar is the first to say that this represents a case of persecution of the Buddhists by a Śaiva king. Her obssession has scored over her scruples.
3. The instances of Buddhist and Jain monks being made the subject of invectives in Sanskrit literature does not prove anything. Professor Thapar has herself stated in her present pamphlet that the Jain book *Paumacarya* denounces the Brāhmaṇas as "heretics and preachers of false doctrines who acquired their status through fraud."[3] Shall we say that the *Paumacarya* invites the Jains to persecute the Brāhmaṇas? I can cite many instances where the Brāhmaṇas have been abused in Buddhist and Jain literature in worse language. But I will not accuse the Buddhists and Jains of persecution of the Brāhmaṇas. And what about Buddhists and Jains hurling invectives on one another? Shall we say that Buddhists persecuted the Jains, and vice versa.

[3]Ibid., p. 15.

4. The persecution of Jains in the Pāṇḍya country by some Śaivas had nothing to do with Śaivism as such, but was an expression of a nationalist conflit which I will relate shortly. What I want to point out first is that most of the royal dynasteis which ruled in India, after the breakdown of the Gupta Empire and before the advent of Islamic invaders, were Śaiva—Maukharīs, Puṣyabhūtis, Gurjara-Pratihāras, and Gāhaḍavāḍs of Kānyakubja; Vākātakas of Nāndīvardhana and Vatsagulma; Pallavas of Kāñchipuram; Cholas of Tanjore; Chālukyas of Vātāpī, Kalyāṇa, and Veṅgī; Pāṇḍuvaṁśīs of Kosala and Mekala; Kalachurīs of Māhiṣmatī and Tripurī; Rāshtrakūṭas of Mānyakheṭa; Maitrakas of Valabhi; Guhilots of Mewar; Chāhmāṇas of Śākambharī, Naḍḍula and Jalor; Turkī and Hindū Shāhīs of Kabul, Zabul and Udbhāṇḍapura; Kārkoṭas and Utpalas of Kashmir; Tomaras of Haryana and Delhi; Parmāras of Malwa and Abu; Chaulukyas of Gujarat; Yādvas of Maharashtra; Kākatīyas of Andhra Pradesh; Hoyṣalas of Karnataka; Chandellas of Kalinjara—to recount only the most prominent of them. The Jains are known to have flourished everywhere; not a single instance of the Jains being persecuted under any of these dynasties is known. The instance she mentions from Gujarat was only the righting of a wrong which the Jains had committed under Kumārapala. Professor Thapar does not mention the Jain high-handedness which had preceded.

The conflict between the Jains and the Śaivas in the Pāṇḍya country has been dealt with in detail by M. Arunachalam in a monograph published eight years before Professor Thapar delivered the lectures which comprise her pamphlet.[4] He has proved conclusively, with the help of epigraphic and literary evidence, that the Kalabhara invaders from Karnataka had occupied Tamil Nadu for 300 years (between AD 250 and 550), and that they subscribed to the Digambara sect of Jainsim.[5] It so happened that some of the Kalabhara princes were guided by a few narrow-minded Jain ascetics, and inflicted injuries on some Śaiva and Vaiṣṇava saints and places of worship. They also took away the *agrahāras* which Brāhmaṇas had enjoyed in earlier times.[6] And

[4]*The Kalabharas in the Pandiya country and their Impact on the Life and Letters there,* University of Madras, 1979.

[5]Ibid., pp. 29–34.

[6]Ibid., pp. 95–100.

a reaction set in when the Kalabharas were overthrown. The new rulers who rose subcribed to Śavisim. It was then that the Jains were persecuted in some places, and some Jain places to worship were taken over by the Śaivas under the plea that these were Śaiva places in the earlier period.

But the reaction was confined to the Paṇḍya country. Jainism continued to flourish in northern Tamil Nadu which also had been invaded by the Kalabharas, where also the Śaivas and Vaiṣṇavas had been molested by the Jains, and where also the Śaivas had come to power once again. It is significant that though Buddhists also invite invectives in the same Śaiva literature, no instance of Buddhists being persecuted is recorded. That was because Buddhists had never harmed the Śaivas. It is also significant that the Vaiṣṇavas of Tamil Nadu show no bitterness against the Jains though they had also suffered under Kalabhara rule.

In any case, Professor Thapar should have mentioned the persecution of Śaivas practised earlier by the Paṇḍya king who was a Jain to start with, and who later on converted to Śaivism and persecuted the Jains. This is another instance of *suppressio vari suggestio falsi* practised very often by her school. Obviously, these persecutions had nothing to do with either Jainism or Śaivism, and were no more than the expressions of a king's personal predisposition.

Interestingly, the persecution of Jains in the Pāṇḍya country finds mention only in Śaiva literature, and is not corroborated by Jain literature of the same or subsequent period. Specialists of South India's history such as K.A.N. Sastri have dimissed the whole story as a Śaiva braggadocio without any basis in fact. The atrocities of the Islamic invaders, on the other hand, find mention not only in Muslim histories but also in contemporary Hindu literature. At any rate, these few instances cannot overshadow the fact that Jains and Śaivas have lived in perfect amity for a very long time, and over large areas. What is more important, neither Jains nor Śaivas have any theology sanctioning persecution of people belonging to other religious persuasions. Aberrations should be seen as aberrations, unless we are out to make mountains out of molehills.

5. As regards her statement that "Buddhism eventually fled the country and Jainsism was effectively confined to few pockets"

as a result of Hindu persecution in pre-Islamic days, one simply feels flabbergasted in the face of such colossal ignorance on the part of a professor of history. As regards Buddhism, we are quoting what Dr. B.R. Ambedkar has to say on the subject. After observing that the Persian word "*but*" meaning "*idol*" is derived from *Buddha*, he writes: "Thus the origin of the word indicates that in the Muslim mind idol worship had come to be identified with the religion of Buddha. To the Muslims they were one and the same thing. The mission to break idols thus became the mission to destroy Buddhism. Islam destroyed Buddhism not only in India but wherever it went. Bactria, Parthia, Afghanistan, Gandhara and Chinese Turkestan... in all these countries Islam destroyed Buddhism."[7] More precisely: "The Muslim invaders sacked the Buddhist universities of Nalanda [etc.]... They razed to the ground Buddhist monasteries with which the country was studded. The monks fled away in thousands... A very large number were killed outright by the Muslim commanders."[8] D.D. Kosambi, a historian of her own Marxist school, confirms that Nalanda was sacked "by a handful of Muslim raiders under Mohammed bin Bakhtyar Khalji... about AD 1200" and that "the tremendous complex at Sarnath which had grown up on the site of the first Buddhist sermon was wrecked beyond recovery, thus ending a continuous tradition of refuge and meeting-place for ascetics which went back to the centuries before Buddha."[9]

She would do well to read some histories of Buddhism and Jainism in this country to know that 1) Buddhism was flourishing all over the country when the Islamic invaders arrived on the scene; 2) both Buddhism and Jainism were being patronised by kings whom the Marxist lable as Hindus; 3) Buddhist monks fled to Nepal and Tibet only after thousands of them were massacred, and their monasteries destroyed by the Islamic marauders; 4) Buddhism continued to flourish all over Andhra Pradesh, Maharashtra, and Karnataka till attacked by the armies of Islam in the fourteenth century; 5) Buddhism did not survive the Islamic assault because, unlike Brahmanism and Jainism, it was centred round monasteries and monks; 6) Jainism has continued

---

[7]*Writings and Speeches,* published by the Government of Maharashtra, Volume 3, p. 229 (in the Chapter "The Decline and Fall of Buddhism.")

[8]Ibid., pp. 229–30.

[9]*The Culture and Civilization of Ancient India*, New Delhi, 1984, p. 18.

to flourish till today all over north India, Karnataka, Maharashtra and Gujarat as it did in the pre-Islamic period, in spite of prolonged Islamic persecution; and 7) there is evidence of a large number of Jain temples being destroyed in the Muslim invasions of southern Bihar and Jharkhand as well as of western and northern Bengal, during the thirteenth and subsequent centuries.

It is nobody's case that there was never any conflict among the sects and sub-sects of Sanātana Dharma. Some instances of persecution were indeed there. Our plea is that they should be seen in a proper perspective, and not exaggerated in order to whitewash or counter-balance the record of Islamic intolerance. Firstly, the instances are few and far between when compared to those listed in Islamic annals. Secondly, those instances are spread over several millennia while the fourteen centuries of Islam stand crowded with religious crimes of all sorts. Thirdly, none of those instances were inspired by a theology, while in the case of Islam a theology of intolerance has continued to question the character of Muslim kings who happened to be tolerant. Fourthly, Jains were not always the victims of persecution; they were persecutors as well once in a while. Lastly, no king or commander or saint who showed intolerance has been a Hindu hero, while Islam has hailed as heroes only those characters who excelled in intolerance.

It is not an accident that Professor Thapar's pamphlet consists of I.H. Qureishi Memorial Lecture, 1987, delivered in the St. Stephen's College, Delhi. Ishtiaq Husain Qureishi was a professor of medieval Indian history in this college when I was a student in another college of the same university. He was a well-known intellectual of the Muslim League and famous for floating the proposition that Hindus were far better off under Muslim rule than they were under that of their own princes in pre-Islamic India. He migrated to Pakistan after Partition, and was that country's Minister of Education for a term. He functioned, to the end of his life, as an apologist of Islamic imperialism as is evident from the numerous works of "research" he wrote or guided. One can hardly expect proper knowledge or perspective from "professors" who are patronized by such platforms.

Bibliography

Agrawala, V.S., *Masterpieces of Mathura Sculpture*, Varanasi, 1965.

Ahmad, Qeyamuddin (ed.), *Patna through the Ages*, New Delhi, 1988.

Alberuni's India, translated by E.C. Sachau, New Delhi Reprint, 1983

Annual Report of Indian Epigraphy, 1953–54, 1963–64, 1964–65, 1978–79 and 1980–81, New Delhi.

Archaeological Survey of India

Annual Report, 1906–07 and 1911–12, New Delhi Reprint, 1990.

Four Reports Made During the Years 1862–63–64–65 by Alexander Cunningham, Varanasi Reprint, 1972.

Arunachalam, M., *The Kalabharas in the Pantiya Country and their impact on the Life and Letters there*, Madras, 1979.

Attār, Shykh Farīdu'd-Dīn, *Tadhkirāt al-Awliyā*', translated into Urdu by Maulāna Zubayr Afzal Usmānī, Delhi, n.d.

Bābur-Nāma (*Memoirs of Bābur*), translated from the original Turki text of Zahiru'd-dīn Muḥammad Bābur Pādshāh *Ghāzī* by Annette Susannah Beveridge, Vols. I and II, New Delhi Reprint, 1979.

The Bible, translated into English, several editions.

Bloch, J. (ed.), *Indian Studies*, Volume in Honour of Edward James Rapson, London, 1931, Delhi Reprint, 1988.

Butterworth, Allen, and Chetty, Venugopaul V., *Copper-plate and Stone Inscriptions of South India*, Delhi Reprint, 1989.

The Calcutta Quran Petition By Chandmal Chopra, with two Prefaces by Sita Ram Goel, New Delhi, 1987.

The Chachnāmah, translated into English by Mirza Kalichbeg Fredunbeg, Delhi Reprint, 1979.

Chuvin, Pierre, *A Chronicle of the Last Pagans*, Harvard, 1990.

Currie, P.M., *The Shrine and Cult of Mu'in al-Dīn Chishtī of Ajmer*, OUP, 1989.

David, M.D. (ed.), *Western Colonialism in Asia and Christianity*, Bombay, 1988.

Day, See Nundo Lal Day.

Durrant., Will, *The Story of Civilization*, Vol. I, *Our Oriental Heritage*, New York, 1972.

Dwivedi, Girish Chandra, *The Jats: Their Role in the Mughal Empire*, New Delhi, 1979.

Eaton, Richard Maxwell, *Sufis of Bijapur 1300–1700*, Princeton, 1978.

Elliot and Dowson, *History of India as told by its own Historians*, 8 Volumes, Allahabad Reprint, 1964.

The Encyclopaedia Americana, Vol. XXIV, New York, 1952.

Encyclopaedia of Religion and Ethics, Vol. I, Third Impression, Edinburgh, 1955.

Epigraphia Indica

Vol. I (1892).

Vol. III (1894–95).

Vol. IV (1900–01).

Vol. XIII (1915–16).

Vol. XIV (1917–18).

Vol. XVII (1920–21).

Vol. XXIV (1937–38), New Delhi Reprint, 1982.

Vol. XXXII (1957–58).

Vol. XXXIII (1959–60).

Appendix Volume to Vols. XIX–XXIII.

Epigraphia Indica — Arabic and Persian Supplement

1959–61, 1962–63 and 1964–65, New Delhi Reprint, 1987.

1969, New Delhi, 1973.

1974, New Delhi, 1981.

Epigraphia Indo-Moslemica, 1907–12, 1913–20, 1921–30, 1931–36 and 1937–50, New Delhi Reprint, 1987.

Eschmann, Anncharllote et al., *The Cult of Jagannath and the Regional Traditions in Orrissa*, second printing, New Delhi, 1981.

First Encyclopaedia of Islam 1931–1936, 9 Volumes, Leiden Reprint, 1987.

Fourth Annual Report of the Minorities' Commission, New Delhi, 1983.

Futūhāt-i-Ālamgīrī of Ishwardas Nagar, translated into English by Tanseem Ahmad, Delhi, 1978.

Gardner, Rev. James, *Faiths of the World*, 2 Volumes, New Delhi Reprint, 1986.

Gibbon, Edward, *The Decline and Fall of the Roman Empire*, Vol. III, Modern Library Edition, New York, n.d.

Gillaume, A., *The Life of Muhammad*, A translation of Ibn Ishāq's *Sīrat Rasūl Allāh*, OUP, Eighth Impression, Karachi, 1987.

Glasse, Cyril, *The Concise Encyclopaedia of Islam*, London, 1987.

Goel, Sita Ram, *History of Hindu–Christian Encounters*, New Delhi, 1989.

Growse, F.S., *Mathura: A District Memoir*, third edition (1883) reprinted from Ahmedabad, 1978

Habib, Mohammad (ed.), *A Comprehensive History of India*, Vol. V, *The Delhi Sultanat*, First Reprint, New Delhi, 1982.

Harsh Naraian, *Myths of Composite Culture and Equality of Religions*, New Delhi, 1991.

Hasan, Syed Mahmudul, *Mosque Architecture of Pre-Mughal Bengal*, Decca, 1979.

Heyerdahl, Thor, *The Maladive Mystery*, Bethesda (Maryland, USA), 1986

History of the Rise and Fall of the Mahomedan Power in India, translated from the original Persian of Mahomed Kasim Ferishta, 4 Volumes, New Delhi Reprint, 1981.

Hosain, Saiyid Safdar, *The Early History of Islam*, Vol. I, Delhi Reprint, 1985.

Hughes, Thoman Patrick, *Dictionary of Islam*, New Delhi Reprint, 1976.

Ibn Ishaq, See Gillaume, A.

Imperial Gazetteer of India, Provincial Series, Madras, Vol. I, New Delhi Reprint, 1985.

Indian Antiquary, Vol. VIII, (June, 1879).

Indian Antiquary, Vol. LVIII, (May, 1929).

Indian Archaeology 1979–80 — A Review, New Delhi, 1983.

Indian Archaeology 1980–81 — A Review, New Delhi, 1983.

Ishwar Sharan, *The Myth of St. Thomas and the Mylapore Shiva Temple*, New Delhi, 1991.

Jāmi' Tirmizī, Arabic text with Urdu translation by Badī' al-Zamān, Vol. I, New Delhi, 1983.

Johnson, Paul, *A History of Christianity*, Penguin Books, 1978.

Kānhaḍade Prabandha of Padmanābha, text with translation into Gujarati by Kantilal Baldevram Vyas, 2 Volumes, Bombay, 1977.

(Al) Khalifa, Shaikha Haya Ali and Rice, Michael (ed.), *Bahrain through the Ages, the Archaeology*, London, 1986.

Khaljī Kālīna Bhārata, Persian texts translated into Hindi by S.A.A. Rizvi, Aligarh, 1955.

Kitāb Futūh Al-Buldān of al-Biladhuri, translated into English by F.C. Murgotte, New York, 1924.

Lal, K.S., *History of the Khaljis*, Revised edition, New Delhi, 1980.

Ling, Martin, *Muhammad*, Rochester (Vermont, USA), 1983.

Lokesh Chandra et. al. (ed.), *India's Contribution to World Thought and Culture: A Vivekananda Commemoration Volume*, Madras, 1970.

Luders, Heinrich, *Mathura Inscriptions*, Gottingen (Germany), 1961.

Maāsir-i-'Ālamgiri of Sāqi Must'ad Khan, translated into English and annotated by Sir Jadu-Nath Sarkar, Calcutta, 1947.

Majumdar, R.C. (ed.), *The History and Culture of the Indian People*

Volume IV : *The Age of Imperial Kanauj*, Third edition, Bombay, 1984.

Volume V : *The Struggle for Empire*, Third edition, Bombay, 1976.

Volume VI : *The Delhi Sultanate*, Bombay, 1960.

Volume VII : *The Mughal Empire*, Bombay, 1974.

Makkē Madīnē dī Goshatī, edited by Dr. Kulwant Singh, Patiala, 1988.

Malik, Brigadier S.K., *The Quranic Concept of War*, New Delhi Reprint, 1986.

Margoliouth, D.S., *Mohammed and the Rise of Islam*, New Delhi Reprint, 1985.

The Meaning of the Glorious Qur'ān, text, translation and commentary by Abdullah Yusuf Ali, 2 Volumes, third edition, Cairo, 1938.

Mirat-i-Ahmadi of Ali Muhammad Khan, translated into English by M.F. Lokhandwala, Baroda, 1965.

Mirati Sikandari or *The Mirror of Sikandar* by Sikandar, the son of Muhammad alias Manjhu Gujarati, translated by Fazlullah Lutfullah Faridi, Gurgaon Reprint, 1990.

Mirza, Mohammad Wahid, *The Life and Works of Amir Khusrau*, Delhi Reprint, 1974.

Mishkāt Sharīf, Arabic text with Urdu translation, Delhi, n.d.

Misra, Ram Gopal, *Indian Resistance to Early Muslim Invaders upto AD 1206*, Meerut City, 1983.

Mughal Kālīna Bhārata: Bābar, Persian text translated into Hindi by S.A.A. Rizvi, Aligarh, 1960.

Muṅhatā Naiṇasīrī Khyāta, edited by Badrīprasāda Sākariyā, Vol. 1, second edition, Jodhpur, 1984.

Muntakhābu-t-Tawārikh by 'Abdul-l-Qādir ibn-i-Mulūk Shāh known as Al-Badāonī, translated from the original Persian and edited by George S.A. Ranking, 3 Volumes, Patna Reprint, 1973.

Muraqqah-i-Khusrawi of Shykh Azmat Ali Kakorwi Nami, cited by Harsh Narain, 'Rama-Janmabhumi Temple: Muslim Testimony', *Indian Express*, February 26, 1990.

Nagarch, B.L., 'Recent Archaeological Discoveries from Rudramahālaya and Jāmi Masjid, Sidhpur', *Kusumāñjali: Shri Śivarāmamūrti Commemoration Volume*, Vol. II, Delhi, 1987.

Nau-Bahār-i-Murshid Quli Khāni by Āzād-al-Husaini, translated into English by Jadu-Nath Sarkar and included in his *Bengal Nawābs*, Calcutta Reprint, 1985.

Navalakhā, Gautama, 'Bhakti Sāhitya kā Durupayoga', *Haṁsa* Hindi monthly, New Delhi, June 1987.

Nayeem, Muhammad Abul, *Prehistory and Protohistory of the Arabian Peninsula*, Vol. 1, *Saudi Arabia*, Hyderabad (India), 1990.

Nāzim, Muhammad, *The Life and Times of Sultān Mahmūd of Ghazna*, second edition, New Delhi, 1971.

Nundo Lal Day, *The Geographical Dictionary of Ancient and Medieval India*, third edition, New Delhi, 1971.

Price, Major David, *Mahommedan History*, Vol. I, New Delhi Reprint, 1984.

Priolkar, A.K., *The Goa Inquisition*, New Delhi Reprint, 1991.

Qur'ān Majīd, Text with translations into English, Hindi and Urdu, Rampur (U.P.), sixth reprint, 1976.

Rahman, Abdur, *The Last Two Dynasties of the Shāhīs*, Delhi Reprint, 1988.

Ram Swarup: *Understanding Islam through Hadis: Religious Faith or Fanaticism?*, Second Reprint, New Delhi, 1987.

The Rauzat-us-Safa or, Garden of Purity, by Muhammad Khāvendshāh bin Mahmūd, translated into English by E. Rehatsek, 3 Volumes in 5 parts, Delhi Reprint, 1982.

The Rehalā of Ibn Battūta, translated into English by Mahdi Husain, Baroda, 1976.

Riyazu-s-Salatin of Ghulam Hussain Salim, translated into English by Abdus Salam, Delhi Reprint, 1976.

Rosen, Steven, *Archaeology and the Vaishnava Traditions: The Pre-Christian Roots of Krishna-Worship*, Calcutta, 1989.

Saḥih Bukhārī Sharīf, Arabic Text with Urdu Translation by Maulāna Abdu'l Hakim Khān Shāhjahānpurī, Vol. I, New Delhi, 1984.

Sale, George, *The Koran or Alcoran of Mohammed*, London, n.d.

Sarkar, Jadu Nath, *History of Aurangzeb*
Volume I and II, Calcutta, 1973 Impression
Volume III, Calcutta, 1972 Impression

Sarkar, Jadu Nath, *Bengal Nawabs*, Calcutta Reprint, 1985.

Sarkar, Jagdish Narayan, *The Art of War in Medieval India*, New Delhi, 1964.

Shahjahan Nama of 'Inayat Khan, translated by A.R. Fuller and edited and compiled by W.E. Beyley and Z.A. Desai, OUP, Delhi, 1990.

Sharif, M.M. (ed.), *A History of Muslim Philosophy*, Vol. I, Lahore, 1961.

Sharma, R.C., 'New Inscriptions from Mathurā' in *Mathurā: The Cultural Heritage*, edited by Doris Meth Sriniwasan, New Delhi, 1989.

Sharma, R.C., *Buddhist Art of Mathurā*, Delhi, 1984.

Sharma, Sri Ram, *Religious Policy of the Mughal Emperors*, Bombay, 1962.

Sunn Nasāī Sharīf, Arabic text with Urdu translation by 'Alāma Wahīd al-Zamān, Vol. I, New Delhi, 1986.

The Tabqāt-i-Akbarī of Khwājah Nizāmuddīn Ahmad, translated into English by Brajendranath De, Vol. I, Calcutta Reprint, 1973.

Tabqāt-i-Ibn Sa'd, translated into Urdu by 'Alāma Abdullāh al-Ahmadī, 2 Volumes, Karachi, n.d.

Tabqāt-i-Nāsirī of Maulānā Minhāj-ud-Dīn, Abū 'Umar-i-'Usmān, translated from original Persian manuscripts by Major H.G. Raverty, Vol. I, New Delhi Reprint, 1971.

Tārīkh-i-Firishta, translated into English by John Briggs under the title *History of the Rise of the Mahomedan Power in India*, 4 Volumes, New Delhi Reprint, 1981.

Tārīkh-i-Firishta, translated into Urdu by 'Abdul Haī Khwājah, 2 Volumes, Deoband, 1983.

Tārīkh-i-Firishta, translated into Urdu, Nawal Kishore Press, 2 Volumes, Lucknow, 1933.

Tārīkh-i-Firūz Shāhī of Zia al-Dīn Baranī, translated into Urdu by

Sayyid Mu'in al-Haqq, second edition, Lahore, 1983.

Tārīkh-i-Khān Jahānī wa Makhzan-i-Afghānī of Khwājah Ni'amatallāh Harwī, translated into Urdu by Muhammad Bashīr Husain, second edition, Lahore, 1986.

Tārīkh-i-Mubārak Shāhī of Yahya Sirhindī, translated into Urdu by Āftāb Ashghar, second edition, Lahore, 1982.

Tārīkh-i-Tabarī, translated into Urdu by Sayyid Muhammad Ibrāhīm, Vol. I: *Sīrat an-Nabī*, Karachi, n.d.

Thapar, Romila, 'The Early History of Mathurā, upto and including the Mauryan period' in *Mathurā: The Cultural Heritage*, edited by Doris Meth Sriniwasan, New Delhi, 1989.

Thapar, Romila, *Cultural Transaction and Early India: Tradition and Patronage*, OUP, Delhi, 1987.

Tughlaq Kālīna Bhārata, Persian texts translated into Hindi by S.A.A. Rizvi, 2 Volumes, Aligarh, 1956–57.

The Tūzuk-i-Jahāngīrī or Memoirs of Jahāngir, translated by Alexander Roger, edited by Henry Beveridge, third edition, New Delhi, 1978.

Tūzuk-i-Jahangīrī, translated into English by Major David Price, Calcutta, 1906.

Uttara Taimūra Kālīna Bhārata, Persian texts translated into Hindi by S.A.A. Rizvi, 2 Volumes, Aligarh, 1958–59.

Wink, Andre, *Al-Hind: The Making of the Indo-Islamic World*, Vol. I, OUP, 1990.

Zafar ul Wālih Bi Muzaffar Wa Ālihi, An Arabic history of Gujarat by Abdullāh Muhammad Al-Makki Al-Asafi Al-Ulughkhāni Hajji Ad-Dabir, translated by M.F. Lokhandwala, 2 Volumes, Baroda, 1970 and 1974.

Zimmer, Heinrich, *Art of Indian Asia*, 2 Volumes, Paperback edition, Princeton, 1983.

Zwemer, S.M., *The Influence of Animism in Islam*, New York, 1920.

INDEX